罗尔德·达尔短篇故事品读及汉译探索

第6卷

An Interpretation of Short Stories by Roald Dahl and an Exploration of Their Chinese Translations

Volume 6

陈 洁 王永胜 著

CHEN Jie, WANG Yong-sheng

哈爾濱工業大學出版社

内容提要

本书系对英国作家罗尔德·达尔"非儿童类"(个别篇章具有"儿童类"文学特点,但由于是罗尔德·达尔早期作品,也被收录进来,作为研究的对象)短篇故事(小说)进行研究所著系列图书中的第6卷,包括五部短篇小说。这些小说长短不一、难易各异,按照不同的主题分成三章加以编排,分别为"物极必反""结局难料"和"如堕雾中"。除第三章外,每章收录两篇作品,先做引导性的介绍,名为"原作导读";再给出小说的原文供读者阅读或作为翻译的参考,同时给出语言点及文化层面上的注释,以辅助理解,名为"原作释读";最后给出探索性的汉语译文,名为"翻译探索"。

本书适合英语专业大学本科生及研究生阅读、研究、翻译之用(不少小说也可供高中生阅读、学习),也适合广大的文学爱好者阅读,更适合从事英汉翻译或外国文学研究的学者、教师、学生等阅读、参考。

图书在版编目(CIP)数据

罗尔德·达尔短篇故事品读及汉译探索.第6卷/陈洁,王永胜著.—哈尔滨:哈尔滨工业大学出版社,2016.2

ISBN 978-7-5603-5804-8

Ⅰ.①罗… Ⅱ.①陈… ②王… Ⅲ.①短篇小说-小说研究-英国-现代②短篇小说-文学翻译-英国-现代 Ⅳ.①I561.074

中国版本图书馆CIP数据核字(2015)第308615号

策划编辑　田新华
责任编辑　田新华　丁桂焱
封面设计　思　华　高永利
出版发行　哈尔滨工业大学出版社
社　　址　哈尔滨市南岗区复华四道街10号　邮编150006
传　　真　0451-86414749
网　　址　http://hitpress.hit.edu.cn
印　　刷　哈尔滨市工大节能印刷厂
开　　本　880mm×1230mm　1/32　印张10.25　字数388千字
版　　次　2016年2月第1版　2016年2月第1次印刷
书　　号　ISBN 978-7-5603-5804-8
定　　价　38.00元

前　言

对于罗尔德·达尔(Roald Dahl, 1916—1990),中国读者耳熟能详的恐怕是他的一些儿童文学作品,而且国内外对他称呼最多的莫过于“儿童文学作家”。他的儿童文学作品的确十分畅销,已被翻译成多国文字出版发行,知名度颇高。可以说,在儿童文学作家中,罗尔德·达尔是最为成功、最为知名的作家之一。达尔的儿童文学作品得到很多国家小朋友的喜爱,例如《詹姆斯与大仙桃》(*James and the Giant Peach*)、《查利与巧克力工厂》(*Charlie and the Chocolate Factory*)、《魔法手指》(*The Magic Finger*)、《查利与大玻璃升降机》(*Charlie and the Great Glass Elevator*)、《了不起的狐狸爸爸》(*Fantastic Mr. Fox*)、《特威特夫妇》(*The Twits*)、《女巫》(*The Witches*)、《好心眼儿的巨人》(*The BFG*,这部小说1983年获“惠特布雷德奖”,即“Whitbread Award”)以及《玛蒂尔达》(*Matilda*)等。

然而,作为英国儿童文学作家的罗尔德·达尔还写过其他类型的文学作品,特别是那些“非儿童类”短篇小说(个别篇章具有“儿童类”文学特点,但由于是罗尔德·达尔的早期作品,也被收录进来,作为研究的对象,也可以说“成人类”短篇小说,也就是说,为成年人写的文学作品。当然,这些作品中有些具有“成人”色彩——含有色情内容,但达尔“成人”作品中的“成人”内容大多是比较“隐晦”的。这样的“成人”作品,基本收录在他的《迷情乱性》(*Switch Bitch*)一书中,也同样精彩。将这些作品称为“非儿童类”,主要针对达尔“儿童类”作品耀眼的光环而言。其实,这些“非儿童类”短篇故事(小说)绝大多数是达尔转笔写儿童文学作品之前完成的。“儿童类”作品的耀眼光环或多或少掩盖了一些“非儿童类”作品的光芒,而在中国,这些“非儿童类”作品的“光芒”几乎没有散发出来,很少为中国广大读者所熟知。这些作品受到西方19世纪现实主义文学的影响,多数采用现实主义的创作手法。同时,达尔也从美国短篇小说家欧·亨利(O. Henry)那里汲取了一定的营养。就达尔作品本身对人物和景物的描写来看,可以说,他是“20世纪英国变形精神世界的一位工笔画家”①。同他的儿童文学作品一样,他早期的这些“非儿童类”作品同样具有结尾出奇、结局令人意想不到等特点,更进一步说,达尔的此类短篇小说这方面的特点尤为突出。这类作品充满奇思妙想,人物刻画细腻入微,其中不乏道貌岸然者、悲观主义者、心理变态者。此类作品也不乏荒谬、贪婪、邪恶、虚伪的成分,其中的人物大都在“机关用尽”之时,一不小心就“栽了跟头”,或者在“聪明绝顶”之际,反而被自己的“聪明”所误。

罗尔德·达尔的父母是挪威人,但达尔本人1916年出生在英国格拉摩根郡的兰达夫(Llandaff, Glamorgan)②,并在雷普顿公学(Repton School)接受教育。第二次世界大战爆发,他应征入伍,加入英国皇家空军,驻扎在内罗毕。后来,他加入了驻利比亚的一个战斗机中队,受了重伤。之后,又作为一名战斗机飞行员到希腊和叙利亚参加战斗。1942年,达尔作为英国大使馆的空军助理专员去了华盛顿。华盛顿成为他人生的转折点,因为在那里他开始了自己的创作生涯。随后,他被调到情报部。战争结束的时候,他成为英国皇家空军中校。他的第一批短篇小说共有12篇,都是根据自己在战争期间的经历所写。这12篇作品首先发表在美国的一些主流杂志上,后来编撰成书出版,书名为《向你飞跃》(*Over to You*)。

罗尔德·达尔所有受到高度赞誉的作品都被译成多种文字,成为全世界的畅销书。安格利亚电视台(*Anglia Television*)将他的一些短篇小说改编成电视系列剧,冠以标题《出乎意料的故事集》(Tales of the Unexpected)。他的作品还包括两本自传——《男孩时代》

---

① 参见“陈钰,1985(4):66”,这里只不过将其中的“二十世纪”,规范性修改成“20世纪”。

② 格拉摩根原来是英国南威尔士的一个郡。

(*Boy*)和《独闯天下》(*Going Solo*),还有赢得很多赞誉的小说《我的叔叔奥斯瓦尔德》(*My Uncle Oswald*)以及《罗尔德·达尔倾心的鬼怪故事集》(*Roald Dahl's Book of Ghost Stories*)。最后一本是他自己编辑出版的。在生命的最后一年,他收集了一些奇闻轶事,并跟妻子弗利西蒂(*Felicity*)一起,整理了一些烹饪食谱,汇编成一本书。这本书于 1996 年由企鹅出版集团出版,书名为《罗尔德·达尔的烹饪书》(*Roald Dahl's Cookbook*)①。

罗尔德·达尔于 1990 年 11 月 23 日去世。英国《泰晤士报》(*The Times*)称其为"我们这一代人中最有影响力的作家之一,也是拥有极其广泛读者群的作家之一"(One of the most widely read and influential writers of our generation),并在写给他的讣告中写道:"孩子喜欢他写的故事,把他当成自己心目中最喜爱的人……他的作品将成为未来的经典之作"(Children loved his stories and made him their favourite... They will be classics of the future)。据报道,在 2000 年英国的"世界图书日"(World Book Day)投票中,罗尔德·达尔当选为"读者最喜爱的作家"(Favourite Author)②。

对于 20 世纪的英国作家罗尔德·达尔及其作品,《爱尔兰时报》(*Irish Times*)的一篇评论,可谓一语中的:"Roald Dahl is one of the few writers I know whose work can accurately be described as addictive. Through his tales runs a vein of macabre malevolence, the more effective because it springs from the slightest, almost inconsequential everyday things. The result is a black humour of the most sophisticated kind."(罗尔德·达尔是我所认识的为数不多的作家之一,可以准确无误地说,其作品令人沉醉、上瘾。他的作品始终贯穿着一条主线,这条主线令人毛骨悚然,充满恶意和凶险,但却更加行之有效,因为其来源是一

---

① 参见"Roald Dahl. *The Best of Roald Dahl* [M]. London: Penguin Books Ltd., 2006"。

② 参见"Roald Dahl. *The Collected Short Stories of Roald Dahl* [M]. London: Penguin Books Ltd., 1992"。

些不起眼的、几乎微不足道的日常事物。结果,最为错综复杂的黑色幽默便应运而生了)①。

抛开后来"儿童类"作品的耀眼光环不说,罗尔德·达尔在20世纪中叶之所以蜚声世界,就是因为他所创作的这些"非儿童类"的短篇小说(当然,个别篇章具有"儿童类"文学特点,预示性地展露出达尔后来作为儿童文学作家的一丝"光芒")。但是,当时中国翻译出版业不是很发达,对其作品的译介也不是很多。就算是有所译介,也处于零星的"散兵作战"状态,不成体系。在全球化浪潮滚滚而来的今天,研究罗尔德·达尔的这部分作品,并系统地进行翻译研究,如同打开尘封已久的大门,门内的景色依然会令当代中国读者惊喜不已。对于广大的英语学习者和文学爱好者来说,阅读达尔的这部分作品将会带来迥然不同的人生体验。

其实,罗尔德·达尔这部分短篇小说的实质和绝妙,可以从英美主流媒体的评价窥见一斑:

"Roald Dahl is the prince of storytellers." —— *Daily Mail*

"罗尔德·达尔是位讲故事的王子。" ——(英国)《每日邮报》

"The absolute master of the twist-in-the-tale" —— *The Observer*

"绝对的大师,其故事的结局出人意料。"

——(英国)《观察家报》

"These stories pack their punch." —— *The Observer*

"这些故事蓄满了惊人之力。" ——(英国)《观察家报》

"An unforgettable read, don't miss it." —— *Sunday Times*

---

① 著者译自 Roald Dahl (1916—1990)的"*The Best of Roald Dahl*"(《罗尔德·达尔小说精品集》)一书的封底(back cover)。此书由英国"Penguin Books Ltd."出版公司于2006年出版发行。

“一次难忘的阅读体验，不可错过。”

——(英国)《星期日泰晤士报》

“Dahl is too good a storyteller to become predictable, so you never know whether the tyrant or the tyrannized will win in the end.”

—— *Daily Telegraph*

“达尔的故事讲得太精彩了，结局简直令人无法预测。因此，你永远都无法得知，最后的赢家是残暴的人，还是受到残暴对待的人。”

——(英国)《每日电讯报》

“Dahl has the mastery of plot and characters possessed by great writers of the past, along with a wildness and wryness of his own. One of his trademarks is writing beautifully about the ugly, even the horrible.”

—— *The Los Angeles Times*

“达尔拥有以往伟大作家的资质——善于营造情节、精于刻画人物，但达尔也拥有自己荒诞不经的一面，以及自己的一套挖苦讥讽的手段。其中的一个标志就是他对丑陋之人的精妙刻画，更有甚者是对恐怖之人的精妙刻画。”

——(美国)《洛杉矶时报》

“An ingenious imagination, a fascination with odd and ordinary detail, and a lust for its thorough exploitation are the... strengths of Dahl's storytelling.”

—— *The New York Times Book Review*

“达尔写作的影响力在于其独特的想象力，在于其对稀奇古怪和平淡无奇的细节的着迷程度，在于其对细节完完全全加以利用的欲望。”

——(美国)《纽约时报·书评》

“The mind of Roald Dahl is quintessentially nasty and wicked.”

—— *The Washington Post*

“罗尔德·达尔的思维具有典型的特点，那就是肮脏和邪恶。”

——(美国)《华盛顿邮报》

在此前提下，研究并翻译罗尔德·达尔的“非儿童类”短篇小说，将具有一定的学术价值和社会价值，会为中国文学的百花园增添一个品种，会为文学爱好者和翻译者提供一个可供参考的文本。

在历时三年多对罗尔德·达尔“非儿童类”短篇小说进行研究和翻译的过程中，我们共收集到长短不一的此类作品60篇，并站在一定的角度，根据著者个人的理解，细加编排，精心安排，详加注释，最终通过翻译，引介给中国读者。

本书在对罗尔德·达尔短篇小说的翻译探索中，采取了严谨的翻译态度，形成了以下基本的翻译思路：

（1）人名、地名按照一定的标准进行“异化”式处理（极个别人名做了“归化”式处理），主要依据《世界人名翻译大辞典》（新华社译名室编，中国对外翻译出版公司1993年第一版或2007年第二版）以及《世界地名翻译大辞典》（周定国主编，中国出版集团、中国对外翻译出版公司2008年第一版）等，个别的人名、地名的翻译兼顾了流行的译法。

（2）绝大多数非国际化的度量衡单位，特别是英制的度量衡单位，采用“同化”或“归化”的处理方法，以便汉语思维者能形象化地加以理解。

（3）每一篇的题目都采用汉语四字格来处理，以求汉语的工整，发挥汉语四字格表达的优势，但同时最大限度地兼顾原文题目的字面含义。

（4）就汉语译文整体而言，尽量杜绝“翻译腔”，以保持汉语语言的纯洁性和规范性，但前提是确保对达尔小说原文的“忠实”。

（5）尽量完美地再现原文的风格，虽然做到这一点并不是轻而易举的事情。原文有些风格，在翻译中只能退其次而求之——基本上采用“归化”处理手法，照顾了汉语的通畅性。比如，原文中很多非标准的英语表达，汉译时就没有在“风格”上充分加以体现，这也是以后有待继续探索的一个翻译问题。

当然，“金无足赤，人无完人”，匆忙且蹒跚的步履必将会迈出“不和谐”的步伐。在对罗尔德·达尔的“非儿童类”短篇小说进行研究、翻译并成书的过程中，不当甚至错误之处在所难免，还望读者不吝赐教，多多批评，特别是多做文学翻译方面的批评。

需要特别声明的是，本系列书中所引用的罗尔德·达尔原著内容以及所做的翻译探索，旨在学术研究，不做商业用途。涉及相关版权的地方，已经做了引用和标注。

陈　洁　王永胜

2015 年 10 月 1 日于渤海大学

目　录

第一章　物极必反

汉语中,“物极必反”是一个成语,最初反映的是道家的哲学观点:“阴阳互动,欲触极则而反”,后指事物发展到极端,会向相反方向转化。

先秦道家著作《鹖冠子·环流》有这样的记载:“美恶相饰,命曰复周;物极则反,命曰环流”①。北宋理学家和教育家程颐(1033—1107)明确使用了“物极必反”一词,他认为每一事物发展到一定限度,即向反面转化,即所谓“物极必反,其理须如此”。

现今社会,“物极必反”同样适用。做什么事情都要有个“度”,关键是,这个“度”把握起来难度很大。把握好了,恰如其分;把握不好,则适得其反。

在英国作家罗尔德·达尔笔下,主人公对“度”的把握就有些糟糕了,甚至是糟糕透顶。一位妻子无意中发现一只猫具有音乐天赋,这本是好事,但这位妻子没有把握好与这只奇猫之间的“度”,惹得丈夫不满,结果是——物极必反;一对夫妻的初生婴儿不肯喝奶,结果身体状况越来越糟,愁坏了夫妻俩,但做丈夫的发现蜂王浆对婴儿厌食有奇效,就用来喂食婴儿,但没有把握好喂食的“度”,结果也是——物极必反。

① 参见商务印书馆辞书研究中心编《新华成语词典》2002 年 1 月第 1 版的相应条目。

走进罗尔德·达尔的世界,去体验《音乐奇猫》的奇妙,去品味《魔力王浆》的神奇,同时,去领略那物极必反、令人称奇的结局吧。

第一节　《音乐奇猫》*Edward the Conqueror*

罗尔德·达尔的《音乐奇猫》(*Edward the Conqueror*)首次发表于美国的一本文学性刊物《纽约客》(*The New Yorker*)杂志 1953 年 10 月号上。后来,这篇小说收录到《罗尔德·达尔短篇故事集锦》(*The Collected Short Stories of Roald Dahl*)、《罗尔德·达尔小说精品集》(*The Best of Roald Dahl*)、《五部畅销书集》(*5 Bestsellers*)、《吻了又吻》(*Kiss Kiss*)以及《罗尔德·达尔选集》(*The Roald Dahl Omnibus*)等书中。另外,这部小说还被改编成电视系列剧中的一集—— 1979 年 5 月 5 日播映的《出乎意料的故事集》(*Tales of the Unexpected*)第一部中的第 7 集(Episode 1.7),具有一定的影响力①。

达尔的这篇小说跟他的另一篇小说《音乐"大师"》(*Mr. Botibol*),可以说,具有"异曲同工"的创作主题,即"特异功能"式的创作主题。在《音乐"大师"》中,一个名叫博迪博尔的普通人时常出现"幻觉"——幻觉中的自己具有了音乐天赋,游刃有余地指挥着乐队演奏;《音乐奇猫》中,女主人公路易莎也有类似的幻觉——自己经常面对无数的观众弹奏钢琴,犹如大师一般,但是,一只流浪猫的出现,改变了她的幻觉世界,令她更加"奇幻"起来。

---

①　这部分信息以及本书以后此类部分中的资料都借鉴了克里斯廷·霍华德(Kristine Howard)创建并维护的网站"*Roald Dahl Fans. com*"(罗尔德·达尔粉丝网)中的部分信息,网址为:http://www. roalddahlfans. com/,由著者翻译整理。以后各章的此部分信息,若没特殊标明,其出处同此。

一、原作导读

女主人公路易莎喜欢弹钢琴，而且一弹起钢琴，就会想象自己面前坐着无数观众为自己欢呼。维瓦尔第、舒曼、李斯特、勃拉姆斯等大师都是她的偶像，而她的丈夫爱德华却不以为意。

十月里的一天，她跨出门，去喊在户外劳作的丈夫回家吃饭。她的丈夫当时在自家林地整理土地，焚烧荆棘，也就是那些多刺的灌木枝条。结果，他们遇上一只无家可归的猫，一直跟随他俩回到了家。尽管丈夫爱德华一再坚持不让猫进屋，但是路易莎还是收留了这只流浪猫。弹奏钢琴过程中，她发现这只猫很不一般——似乎能听懂音乐。经过几次试验，她坚信这只猫的确不一般，具有某种音乐方面的“特异功能”。事实上，她认为这只猫就是音乐大师李斯特“投胎转世”而来的。但是，她的丈夫爱德华却不以为然，认为妻子的行为过于荒谬，简直就是“痴心妄想”型的幻想狂。

在丈夫爱德华看来，那只猫就是一只流浪的野猫，没有什么了不起。因此，妻子对猫投入了大量的情感和精力，令他十分不满，甚至牢骚满腹。妻子路易莎却认为丈夫心胸不够开阔，竟然吃一只猫的醋。一番争论之后，路易莎发现猫和人都饿了，就进厨房准备吃的东西。

饭菜端上来后，她发现那只猫不见了，而丈夫却刚好从外面跨进屋子。

“我刚才出去，看看那堆火烧得怎么样。”他说。

她的双眼慢慢向上看去，停在他的两只手上。

“火很旺，还烧着呢，”他继续说，“我想，一整夜也不会熄灭的。”可是，她盯着他看的那个样子令他感到很不自在。

“怎么了？”他放低了打火机问道。随即，他低头一看，才猛然发现自己一只手背上有一道长长的、细细的抓痕——从指关节斜向延伸到手腕处，清晰可见。

“I just went out to see how the bonfire was going,” he said.

Her eyes travelled slowly upward and rested on his hands.

"It's still burning fine," he went on. "I think it'll keep going all night." But the way she was staring made him uncomfortable.

"What is it?" he said, lowering the lighter. Then he looked down and noticed for the first time the long thin scratch that ran diagonally clear across the back of one hand, from the knuckle to the wrist.

二、原作释读

本故事情节并不复杂,故事本身颇具奇幻色彩,读起来引人入胜。但是,有关音乐和投胎转世方面的表达,需要理解好。

Edward the Conqueror①

Louisa, holding a dishcloth in her hand, stepped out of the kitchen door at the back of the house into the cool October sunshine.

"Edward!" she called. "Ed—ward! Lunch is ready!"

She paused a moment, listening; then she strolled out on to the lawn and continued across it—a little shadow attending her—skirting② the rose bed and touching the sundial lightly with one finger as she went by. She moved rather gracefully for a woman who was small and plump, with a lilt in her walk and a gentle swinging of the shoulders and the arms. She

---

① 本部小说原文出自"DAHL, R. *The Best of Roald Dahl*[M]. London: Penguin Books Ltd., 2006"。

② skirt: *Verb* avoid or try to avoid fulfilling, answering, or performing (duties, questions, or issues) 沿……的边缘走;绕开;避开(e.g. He dodged the issue. 他绕开了这个问题。)

passed under the mulberry① tree on to the brick path, then went all the way along the path until she came to the place where she could look down into the dip② at the end of this large garden.

"Edward! Lunch!"

She could see him now, about eighty yards away, down in the dip on the edge of the wood the tallish narrow figure in khaki③ slacks④ and dark-green sweater, working beside a big bonfire⑤ with a fork in his hands, pitching brambles⑥ on to the top of the fire. It was blazing fiercely, with orange flames and clouds of milky smoke, and the smoke was drifting back over the garden with a wonderful scent of autumn and burning leaves.

Louisa went down the slope towards her husband. Had she wanted, she could easily have called again and made herself heard, but there was something about a first-class bonfire that impelled her towards it, right up close so she could feel the heat and listen to it burn.

"Lunch," she said, approaching.

"Oh, hello. All right—yes. I'm coming."

"What a good fire."

"I've decided to clear this place right out," her husband said.

---

① mulberry: *Noun* any of several trees of the genus Morus having edible fruit that resembles the blackberry 桑树

② dip: *Noun* a depression in an otherwise level surface 凹陷处(e.g. There was a dip in the road. 路上有一处塌陷下去了。)

③ khaki: *Noun* a sturdy twilled cloth of a yellowish brown color used especially for military uniforms (hypernym) fabric, cloth, material, textile 土黄色;黄卡其布

④ slack: *Noun* (often as "slacks") casual trousers 便裤;宽松裤

⑤ bonfire: *Noun* a large outdoor fire 营火;篝火

⑥ brambles: *Noun* any of various rough thorny shrubs or vines 荆棘

"I'm sick and tired of all these brambles." His long face was wet with perspiration. There were small beads of it clinging all over his moustache like dew, and two little rivers were running down his throat on to the turtleneck① of the sweater.

"You'd better be careful you don't overdo it, Edward."

"Louisa, I do wish you'd stop treating me as though I were eighty. A bit of exercise never did anyone any harm."

"Yes, dear, I know. Oh, Edward! Look! Look!"

The man turned and looked at Louisa, who was pointing now to the far side of the bonfire.

"Look, Edward! The cat!"

Sitting on the ground, so close to the fire that the flames sometimes seemed actually to be touching it, was a large cat of a most unusual colour. It stayed quite still, with its head on one side and its nose in the air, watching the man and woman with a cool yellow eye.

"It'll get burnt!" Louisa cried, and she dropped the dishcloth and darted swiftly in and grabbed it with both hands, whisking② it away and putting it on the grass well clear of the flames.

"You crazy cat," she said, dusting off her hands. "What's the matter with you?"

"Cats know what they're doing," the husband said. "You'll never find a cat doing something it doesn't want. Not cats."

"Whose is it? You ever seen it before?"

"No, I never have. Damn peculiar colour."

---

① turtleneck: *Noun* (Brit.) a high, round, close-fitting neck on a knitted garment(英国英语)编织衣的圆翻领;高翻领

② whisk: *Verb* [with obj. and adverbial of direction] take or move (someone or something) in a particular direction suddenly and quickly 迅速移动;飞快带走;急忙运送

The cat had seated itself on the grass and was regarding them with a sidewise look. There was a veiled inward expression about the eyes, something curiously omniscient① and pensive②, and around the nose a most delicate air of contempt, as though the sight of these two middle-aged persons—the one small, plump, and rosy, the other lean and extremely sweaty—were a matter of some surprise but very little importance. For a cat, it certainly had an unusual colour—a pure silvery grey with no blue in it at all—and the hair was very long and silky.

Louisa bent down and stroked its head. "You must go home," she said. "Be a good cat now and go on home to where you belong."

The man and wife started to stroll back up the hill towards the house. The cat got up and followed, at a distance first, but edging closer and closer as they went along. Soon it was alongside them, then it was ahead, leading the way across the lawn to the house, walking as though it owned the whole place, holding its tail straight up in the air, like a mast.

"Go home," the man said. "Go on home. We don't want you."

But when they reached the house, it came in with them, and Louisa gave it some milk in the kitchen. During lunch, it hopped up on to the spare chair between them and sat through the meal with its head just above the level of the table watching the proceedings with those dark-yellow eyes which kept moving slowly from the woman to the man and back again.

"I don't like this cat," Edward said.

"Oh, I think it's a beautiful cat. I do hope it stays a little while."

"Now, listen to me, Louisa. The creature can't possibly stay here. It belongs to someone else. It's lost. And if it's still trying to hang around this afternoon, you'd better take it to the police. They'll see it

---

① omniscient: *Adjective* infinitely wise 无所不知的

② pensive: *Adjective* persistently or morbidly thoughtful 沉思的;深思的

gets home."

After lunch, Edward returned to his gardening. Louisa, as usual, went to the piano. She was a competent pianist and a genuine music-lover, and almost every afternoon she spent an hour or so playing for herself. The cat was now lying on the sofa, and she paused to stroke it as she went by. It opened its eyes, looked at her a moment, then closed them again and went back to sleep.

"You're an awfully nice cat," she said. "And such a beautiful colour. I wish I could keep you." Then her fingers, moving over the fur on the cat's head, came into contact with a small lump, a little growth just above the right eye.

"Poor cat," she said. "You've got bumps on your beautiful face. You must be getting old."

She went over and sat down on the long piano stool but she didn't immediately start to play. One of her special little pleasures was to make every day a kind of concert day, with a carefully arranged programme which she worked out in detail before she began. She never liked to break her enjoyment by having to stop while she wondered what to play next. All she wanted was a brief pause after each piece while the audience clapped enthusiastically and called for more. It was so much nicer to imagine an audience, and now and again while she was playing—on the lucky days, that is—the room would begin to swim and fade and darken, and she would see nothing but row upon row of seats and a sea of white faces upturned towards her, listening with a rapt① and adoring concentration.

Sometimes she played from memory, sometimes from music. Today she would play from memory; that was the way she felt. And what should

① rapt: *Adjective* filled with an intense and pleasurable emotion: enraptured 着迷的;痴迷的;狂喜的(e.g. She shut her eyes and seemed rapt with desire. 她闭上双眼,一副如痴如醉的样子。)

the programme be? She sat before the piano with her small hands clasped on her lap, a plump rosy little person with a round and still quite pretty face, her hair done up in a neat bun at the back of her head. By looking slightly to the right, she could see the cat curled up asleep on the sofa, and its silvery-grey coat was beautiful against the purple of the cushion. How about some Bach① to begin with? Or, better still, Vivaldi②. The Bach adaptation for organ of the D minor Concerto Grosso③. Yes—that

---

① Bach: *Naun* Johann Sebastian Bach (1685—1750), German composer 约翰·塞巴斯蒂安·巴赫(1685—1750):德国作曲家。

② Vivaldi: *Noun* Antonio Lucio Vivaldi (1678—1741), Italian composer and violinist, one of the most important baroque composers. His feeling for texture and melody is evident in his numerous compositions such as *The Four Seasons* (concerto, 1725) 安东尼奥·卢西奥·维瓦尔第(1678—1741):意大利作曲家、小提琴家,最重要的巴洛克音乐风格作曲家之一,其音质感与旋律感体现在众多乐曲中,如协奏曲《四季》(1725)。

③ concerto grosso: *Noun* a musical composition for a group of solo instruments accompanied by an orchestra. The term is used mainly of baroque works. 大协奏曲(主要用于巴洛克风格的作品,巴洛克古时期相当盛行的一种乐曲形式,它是一种由一个独奏乐器小组与管弦乐联合演奏的音乐。)

first. Then perhaps a little Schumann①. Carnaval②? That would be fun. And after that—well, a touch of Liszt③ for a change. One of the *Petrarch*④ *Sonnets*⑤. The second one—that was the loveliest the F ma-

---

① Schumann: *Noun* Robert Alexander Schumann (1810—1856), German composer. He was a leading romantic composer, particularly noted for his songs (including settings of poems by Heinrich Heine and Robert Burns) and piano music. His other works include four symphonies and much chamber music. His wife Clara (1819—1896) was a noted pianist and composer. 罗伯特·亚历山大·舒曼(1810—1856):德国作曲家,最主要的浪漫主义作曲家,尤以创作的歌曲(包括为海涅和彭斯的诗谱的曲)和钢琴曲著名,其他作品包括四部交响乐和许多室内乐;妻子克拉拉(1819—1896)是著名钢琴家和作曲家。

② carnaval (often Carnival): *Noun* a period of public revelry at a regular time each year, typically during the week before Lent in Roman Catholic countries, involving processions, music, dancing, and the use of masquerade. 狂欢节;嘉年华会(尤指罗马天主教国家每年大斋节前一周内的公众狂欢,其中有游行、音乐、舞蹈及化装舞会。)

注:这部小说里,"Carnaval"则用作一首乐曲的名称,翻译成"狂欢节"。

③ Liszt: *Noun* Franz Liszt (1811—1886), Hungarian composer and pianist. He was a key figure in the romantic movement; many of his piano compositions combine lyricism with great technical complexity, while his twelve symphonic poems (1848 ~ 1858) created a new musical form. 弗朗兹·李斯特(1811—1886):匈牙利作曲家、钢琴家,浪漫主义运动重要人物,他的许多钢琴作品融合了抒情风格与复杂技巧,他的十二首交响诗(1848 ~ 1858)开创了新的音乐形式。

④ Petrarch (1304—1374): *Noun* Italian poet; Italian name Francesco Petrarca. His reputation is chiefly based on the *Canzoniere* (c. 1351 ~ 1353), a sonnet sequence in praise of a woman he calls Laura. 彼特拉克(1304—1374):意大利诗人,意大利语名弗朗切斯科·彼得拉克,主要以《抒情诗集》出名(约 1351 ~ 1353),这部十四行诗集赞美了一名被他称为劳拉的女子。

⑤ Petrarch Sonnets: *Noun* 这里指的是李斯特的作品《彼特拉克十四行诗》。

jor. Then another Schumann, another of his gay ones—Kinderscenen①. And lastly, for the encore②,

a Brahms③ waltz, or maybe two of them if she felt like it.

Vivaldi, Schumann, Liszt, Schumann, Brahms. A very nice programme, one that she could play easily without the music④. She moved herself a little closer to the piano and paused a moment while someone in the audience—already she could feel that this was one of the lucky days—while someone in the audience had his last cough; then, with the slow grace that accompanied nearly all her movements, she lifted her hands to the keyboard and began to play.

She wasn't, at that particular moment, watching the cat at all—as a matter of fact she had forgotten its presence—but as the first deep notes of the Vivaldi sounded softly in the room, she became aware, out of the corner of one eye, of a sudden flurry⑤, a flash of movement on the sofa to her right. She stopped playing at once. "What is it?" she said, turning to

---

① Kinderscenen: *Noun* 这里指的是舒曼的音乐作品，翻译成《儿时情景》。

② encore: *Int.* Exclamation called out by an audience at the end of a concert to request such a performance 再来一个！（听众要求重演一次的呼叫）

③ Brahms: *Noun* Johannes Brahms (1833—1897), German composer and pianist. He eschewed programme music and opera and concentrated on traditional forms. He wrote four symphonies, four concertos, chamber and piano music, choral works including the German Requiem (1857 ~ 1868), and nearly 200 songs. 约翰内斯·勃拉姆斯(1833—1897)：德国作曲家、钢琴家，作品多为非标题音乐，继承了古典传统；共创作了四部交响乐、四部协奏曲、室内和钢琴音乐、合唱曲以及近 200 首歌曲，包括《德意志安魂曲》(1857 ~ 1868)。

④ music: *Noun* the score or scores of a musical composition or compositions 乐谱；曲谱(e.g. The music was open on a stand. 乐谱打开着放在谱架上。)

⑤ flurry: *Noun* a brief period of commotion or excitement 一阵忙乱(或激动、兴奋等)

the cat. "What's the matter?"

The animal, who a few seconds before had been sleeping peacefully, was now sitting bolt upright[①] on the sofa, very tense, the whole body aquiver, ears up and eyes wide open, staring at the piano.

"Did I frighten you?" she asked gently. "Perhaps you've never heard music before."

No, she told herself. I don't think that's what is. On second thoughts, it seemed to her that the cat's attitude was not one of fear. There was no shrinking or backing away. If anything, there was a leaning forward, a kind of eagerness about the creature, and the face—well, there was rather an odd expression on the face, something of a mixture between surprise and shock. Of course, the face of a cat is a small and fairly expressionless thing, but if you watch carefully the eyes and ears working together, and particularly that little area of mobile skin below the ears and slightly to one side, you can occasionally see the reflection of very powerful emotions. Louisa was watching the face closely now, and because she was curious to see what would happen a second time, she reached out her hands to the keyboard and began again to play the Vivaldi.

This time the cat was ready for it, and all that happened to begin with was a small extra tensing of the body. But as the music swelled and quickened into that first exciting rhythm of the introduction to the fugue[②], a strange look that mounted almost to ecstasy began to settle upon the creature's face. The ears, which up to then had been pricked up

---

① bolt upright: with the back very straight 笔直(e. g. She sat bolt upright in bed. 她笔直地坐在床上。)

② fugue: *Noun* (Music) a contrapuntal composition in which a short melody or phrase (the subject) is introduced by one part and successively taken up by others and developed by interweaving the parts. (音乐)赋格曲

straight, were gradually drawn back, the eyelids drooped[1], the head went over to one side, and at that moment Louisa could have sworn that the animal was actually appreciating the work.

What she saw (or thought she saw) was something she had noticed many times on the faces of people listening very closely to a piece of music. When the sound takes complete hold of them and drowns them in itself, a peculiar, intensely ecstatic look comes over them that you can recognize as easily as a smile. So far as Louisa could see, the cat was now wearing almost exactly this kind of look.

Louisa finished the fugue, then played the siciliana[2], and all the way through she kept watching the cat on the sofa. The final proof for her that the animal was listening came at the end, when the music stopped. It blinked, stirred itself a little, stretched a leg, settled into a more comfortable position, took a quick glance round the room, then looked expectantly in her direction. It was precisely the way a concert-goer reacts when the music momentarily releases him in the pause between two movements of a symphony. The behaviour was so thoroughly human it gave her a queer agitated feeling in the chest.

"You like that?" she asked. "You like Vivaldi?"

The moment she'd spoken, she felt ridiculous, but not—and this to her was a trifle sinister—not quite so ridiculous as she knew she should have felt.

Well, there was nothing for it now except to go straight ahead with the next number on the Programme, which was *Carnaval*. As soon as she began to play, the cat again stiffened and sat up straighter; then, as it

① droop: *Verb* to sag, sink, bend, or hang down, as from weakness, exhaustion, or lack of support 弯曲或下垂;发蔫

② siciliana or siciliano: *Noun* a graceful folk dance of Sicily 西西里乡村舞蹈;西西里民间舞蹈

became slowly and blissfully saturated with the sound, it relapsed into the queer melting mood of ecstasy that seemed to have something to do with drowning and with dreaming. It was really an extravagant sight—quite a comical one, too—to see this silvery cat sitting on the sofa and being carried away like this. And what made it more screwy① than ever, Louisa thought, was the fact that this music, which the animal seemed to be enjoying so much, was manifestly too difficult, too classical, to be appreciated by the majority of humans in the world.

Maybe, she thought, the creature's not really enjoying it at all. Maybe it's a sort of hypnotic② reaction, like with snakes. After all, if you can charm a snake with music, then why not a cat? Except that millions of cats hear the stuff every day of their lives, on radio and gramophone and piano, and, as far as she knew, there'd never yet been a case of one behaving like this. This one was acting as though it were following every single note. It was certainly a fantastic thing.

But was it not also a wonderful thing? Indeed it was. In fact, unless she was much mistaken, it was a kind of miracle, one of those animal miracles that happen about once every hundred years.

"I could see you loved that one," she said when the piece was over. "Although I'm sorry I didn't play it any too well today. Which did you like best—the Vivaldi or the Schumann?"

The cat made no reply, so Louisa, fearing she might lose the attention of her listener, went straight into the next part of the programme—Liszt's *second Petrarch Sonnet*.

And now an extraordinary thing happened. She hadn't played more than three or four bars when the animal's whiskers began perceptibly to

---

① screwy: *Adjective* (informal, chiefly N. Amer.) rather odd or eccentric (主要为北美的非正式用法)古怪的;怪异的

② hypnotic: *Adjective* inducing sleep 催眠的

twitch. Slowly it drew itself up to an extra height, laid its head on one side, then on the other, and stared into space with a kind of frowning concentrated look that seemed to say, "What's this? Don't tell me. I know it so well, but just for the moment I don't seem to be able to place it." Louisa was fascinated, and with her little mouth half open and half smiling, she continued to play, waiting to see what on earth was going to happen next.

The cat stood up, walked to one end of the sofa, sat down again, listened some more; then all at once it bounded to the floor and leaped up on to the piano stool beside her. There it sat, listening intently to the lovely sonnet, not dreamily this time, but very erect, the large yellow eyes fixed upon Louisa's fingers.

"Well!" she said as she struck the last chord. "So you came up to sit beside me, did you? You like this better than the sofa? All right, I'll let you stay, but you must keep still and not jump about." She put out a hand and stroked the cat softly along the back, from head to tail. "That was Liszt," she went on. "Mind you, he can sometimes be quite horribly vulgar, but in things like this he's really charming."

She was beginning to enjoy this odd animal pantomime①, so she went straight on into the next item on the programme, Schumann's *Kinderscenen*.

She hadn't been playing for more than a minute or two when she realizedthat the cat had again moved, and was now back in its old place on the sofa. She'd been watching her hands at the time, and presumably that was why she hadn't even noticed its going; all the same, it must have been an extremely swift and silent move. The cat was still staring at

① pantomime: *Noun* a dramatic entertainment, originating in Roman mime, in which performers express meaning through gestures accompanied by music(源于古罗马的)哑剧

her, still apparently attending closely to the music, and yet it seemed to Louisa that there was not now the same rapturous enthusiasm there'd been during the previous piece, the Liszt. In addition, the act of leaving the stool and returning to the sofa appeared in itself to be a mild but positive gesture of disappointment.

"What's the matter?" she asked when it was over. "What's wrong with Schumann? What's so marvellous about Liszt?" The cat looked straight back at her with those yellow eyes that had small jet-black bars lying vertically in their centres.

This, she told herself, is really beginning to get interesting—a trifle spooky①, too, when she came to think of it. But one look at the cat sitting there on the sofa, so bright and attentive, so obviously waiting for more music, quickly reassured her.

"All right," she said. "I'll tell you what I'm going to do. I'm going to alter my programme specially for you. You seem to like Liszt so much, I'll give you another."

She hesitated, searching her memory for a good Liszt; then softly she began to play one of the twelve little pieces from *Der Wethnachtsbaum*②. She was now watching the cat very closely, and the first thing she noticed was that the whiskers again began to twitch. It jumped down to the carpet, stood still a moment, inclining its head, quivering with excitement, and then, with a slow, silky stride, it walked around the piano, hopped up on the stool, and sat down beside her.

They were in the middle of all this when Edward came in from the

---

① spooky: *Adjective* like or befitting a spook or ghost; suggestive of spooks 使人想到鬼的;吓人的

② *Der Weihnachtsbaum*: *Noun Christmas Tree* (in English), a suite of 12 pieces written by Franz Liszt in 1873 ~ 1876, with revisions in 1881.《圣诞树》(李斯特的组曲,由12首曲子构成,1873 ~ 1876年间写成,修改于1881年。)

garden.

"Edward!" Louisa cried, jumping up. "Oh, Edward, darling! Listen to this! Listen what's happened!"

"What is it now?" he said. "I'd like some tea." He had one of those narrow, sharp-nosed, faintly magenta faces, and the sweat was making it shine as though it were a long wet grape.

"It's the cat!" Louisa cried, pointing to it sitting quietly on the piano stool. "Just wait till you hear what's happened!"

"I thought I told you to take it to the police."

"But, Edward, listen to me. This is terribly exciting. This is a musical cat."

"Oh, yes?"

"This cat can appreciate music, and it can understand it, too."

"Now stop this nonsense, Louisa, and for God's sake let's have some tea. I'm hot and tired from cutting brambles and building bonfires." He sat down in an armchair, took a cigarette from a box beside him, and lit it with an immense patent① lighter that stood near the box.

"What you don't understand," Louisa said, "is that something extremely exciting has been happening here in our house while you were out, something that may even be... well... almost momentous."

"I'm quite sure of that."

"Edward, please!"

Louisa was standing by the piano, her little pink face pinker than ever, a scarlet rose high up on each cheek. "If you want to know," she said, "I'll tell you what I think."

"I'm listening, dear."

"I think it might be possible that we are at this moment sitting in the

---

① patent: *Adjective* of high quality 精巧的;别致的;上等的

presence of—" She stopped, as though suddenly sensing the absurdity of the thought.

"Yes?"

"You may think it silly, Edward, but it's honestly what I think."

"In the presence of whom, for heaven's sake?"

"Of Franz Liszt himself!"

Her husband took a long slow pull at his cigarette and blew the smoke up at the ceiling. He had the tight-skinned, concave① cheeks of a man who has worn a full set of dentures② for many years, and every time he sucked at a cigarette, the cheeks went in even more, and the bones of his face stood out like a skeleton's. "I don't get you," he said.

"Edward, listen to me. From what I've seen this afternoon with my own eyes, it really looks as though this might be some sort of a reincarnation③."

"You mean this lousy cat?"

"Don't talk like that, dear, please."

"You're not ill, are you, Louisa?"

"I'm perfectly all right, thank you very much. I'm a bit confused I don't mind admitting it, but who wouldn't be after what's just happened? Edward, I swear to you."

"What did happen, if I may ask?"

Louisa told him, and all the while she was speaking, her husband

---

① concave: *Adjective* curved like a segment of the interior of a circle or hollow sphere; hollow and curved 凹的

② denture: *Noun* an artificial replacement of one or several of the teeth (partial denture), or all of the teeth (full denture) of either or both jaws; dental prosthesis(一副)假牙

③ reincarnation: *Noun* the belief that on the death of the body the soul transmigrates to or is born again in another body 再投胎;再生;转世

lay sprawled in the chair with his legs stretched out in front of him, sucking at his cigarette and blowing the smoke up at the ceiling. There was a thin cynical smile on his mouth.

"I don't see anything very unusual about that," he said when it was over. "All it is—it's a trick cat. It's been taught tricks, that's all."

"Don't be so silly, Edward. Every time I play Liszt, he gets all excited and comes running over to sit on the stool beside me. But only for Liszt, and nobody can teach a cat the difference between Liszt and Schumann. You don't even know it yourself. But this one can do it every single time. Quite obscure Liszt, too."

"Twice," the husband said. "He's only done it twice."

"Twice is enough."

"Let's see him do it again. Come on."

"No," Louisa said. "Definitely not. Because if this is Liszt, as I believe it is, or anyway the soul of Liszt or whatever it is that comes back, then it's certainly not right or even very kind to put him through a lot of silly undignified tests."

"My dear woman! This is a cat—a rather stupid grey cat that nearly got its coat singed① by the bonfire this morning in the garden. And anyway, what do you know about reincarnation?"

"If the soul is there, that's enough for me," Louisa said firmly. "That's all that counts."

"Come on, then. Let's see him perform. Let's see him tell the difference between his own stuff and someone else's."

"No, Edward. I've told you before, I refuse to put him through any more silly circus tests. He's had quite enough of that for one day. But I'll tell you what I will do. I'll play him a little more of his own music."

---

① singe: *Verb* to burn superficially or slightly; scorch 浅表烧焦

"A fat lot that'll prove."

"You watch. And one thing is certain—as soon as he recognizes it, he'll refuse to budge① off that stool where he's sitting now."

Louisa went to the music shelf, took down a book of Liszt, thumbed through it quickly, and chose another of his finer compositions—the B minor Sonata②. She had meant to play only the first part of the work, but once she got started and saw how the cat was sitting there literally quivering with pleasure and watching her hands with that rapturous concentrated look, she didn't have the heart to stop. She played it all the way through. When it was finished, she glanced up at her husband and smiled. "There you are," she said. "You can't tell me he wasn't absolutely loving it."

"He just likes the noise, that's all."

"He was loving it. Weren't you, darling?" she said, lifting the cat in her arms. "Oh, my goodness, if only he could talk. Just think of it,

---

① budge: *Verb* [usu. with negative] make or cause to make the slightest movement(使)微微移动

② sonata: *Noun* a classical composition for an instrumental soloist, often with a piano accompaniment. It is typically in several movements with one (especially the first) or more in sonata form 奏鸣曲

dear—he met Beethoven① in his youth! He knew Schubert② and Mendelssohn③ and Schumann and Berlioz④ and Grieg⑤

---

① Beethoven: *Noun* Ludwig van Beethoven (1770—1827), German composer 路德维希·范·贝多芬(1770—1827):德国作曲家。

② Schubert: *Noun* Franz Schubert (1797—1828), Austrian composer. His music is associated with the Romantic Movement for its lyricism and emotional intensity, but belongs in formal terms to the classical age. His works include more than 600 songs, the *Trout* piano quintet (1819), and nine symphonies. 弗朗茨·舒伯特(1797—1828):奥地利作曲家,他的音乐充满抒情的诗意和奔放的感情,与浪漫主义风格紧密相连,但正式归类的话,他属于古典主义时代;作品包括600多首歌曲,钢琴五重奏《鳟鱼》(1819)和九部交响曲。

③ Mendelssohn: *Noun* Felix Mendelssohn (1809—1847), German composer and pianist; full name Jakob Ludwig Felix Mendelssohn-Bartholdy. His romantic music is elegant, light, and melodically inventive. Notable works include the oratorios *Fingal's Cave* (1830 ~ 1832) and *Elijah* (1846) and eight volumes of Lieder ohne Worte (*Songs Without Words*) for piano. 费利克斯·门德尔松(1809—1847):德国作曲家、钢琴家,全名雅各布·路德维格·费利克斯·门德尔松-巴托尔迪。他的浪漫主义音乐高雅、轻快,旋律具有创新风格;代表作品包括清唱剧《芬戈尔洞》(1830 ~ 1832)、《以利亚》(1846)和八集钢琴曲《无词歌》。

④ Berlioz: *Noun* Hector Berlioz (1803—1869), French composer; full name Louis-Hector Berlioz. Notable works: *Les Troyens* (opera, 1856 ~ 1859), *Symphonie fantastique* (1830), and *La Damnation de Faust* (cantata, 1846). 埃克托尔·柏辽兹(1803—1869):法国作曲家,全名路易-埃克托尔·柏辽兹;代表作品:歌剧《特洛伊人》(1856 ~ 1859)、《幻想交响曲》(1830)及大合唱曲《浮士德的沉沦》(1846)。

⑤ Grieg: *Noun* Edvard Grieg (1843—1907), Norwegian composer, conductor, and violinist. Famous works include the *Piano Concerto in A minor* (1869) and the incidental music to Ibsen's play *Peer Gynt* (1876). 爱德华·格列格(1843—1907):挪威作曲家、指挥家、小提琴家,著名作品有《A小调钢琴协奏曲》(1869)和易卜生的戏剧《彼尔·金特》的配乐(1876)。

and Delacroix[①] and Ingres[②] and Heine[③] and Balzac[④]. And let me

---

① Delacroix: *Noun* Ferdinand Victor Eugène Delacroix (1798—1863), French painter, the chief painter of the French romantic school. He is known for his use of vivid colour, free drawing, and exotic, violent, or macabre subject matter. Notable works: *The Massacre at Chios* (1824). 费迪南·维克托·尤金·德拉克鲁瓦(1798—1863):法国画家,法国浪漫主义画派的主要代表人物,以运用鲜明的颜色、自由的绘画风格和奇异、激烈或恐怖的主题著称;代表作品:《希俄斯大屠杀》(1824)。

② Ingres: *Noun* Jean Auguste Dominique Ingres (1780—1867), French painter. A pupil of Jacques-Louis David, he vigorously upheld neoclassicism in opposition to Delacroix's romanticism. Notable works: *Ambassadors of Agamemnon* (1801) and *The Bather* (1808). 让·奥古斯特·多米尼克·安格尔(1780—1867):法国画家,雅克路易·达维德的学生。他大力支持新古典主义,反对德拉克鲁瓦的浪漫主义;代表作品:《亚加米农的使者》(1801)和《浴女》(1808)。

③ Heine: *Noun* Christian Johann Heinrich Heine (1797—1856), German poet; born Harry Heine. Much of his early lyric poetry was set to music by Schumann and Schubert. In 1830 Heine emigrated to Paris, where his works became more political. 克里斯蒂安·约翰·海因里希·海涅(1797—1856):德国诗人;出生名哈里·海涅,早期的许多抒情诗被舒曼和舒伯特配乐,1830 年移居巴黎后,作品更具政治色彩。

④ Balzac: *Noun* Honoré de Balzac (1799—1850), French novelist. He is chiefly remembered for his series of ninety-one interconnected novels and stories known collectively as *La Comédie humaine*, which includes *Eugénie Grandet* (1833) and *Le Père Goriot* (1835). 奥诺雷·德·巴尔扎克(1799—1850):法国小说家,以包括 91 部系列小说的巨著《人间喜剧》闻名,包括《欧也妮·葛朗台》(1833)和《高老头》(1835)等。

see... My heavens, he was Wagner's① father-in-law! I'm holding Wagner's father-in-law in my arms!"

"Louisa!" her husband said sharply, sitting up straight. "Pull yourself together." There was a new edge to his voice now, and he spoke louder.

Louisa glanced up quickly. "Edward, I do believe you're jealous!"

"Of a miserable grey cat!"

"Then don't be so grumpy② and cynical about it all. If you're going to behave like this, the best thing you can do is to go back to your gardening and leave the two of us together in peace. That will be best for all of us, won't it, darling?" she said, addressing the cat, stroking its head. "And later on this evening, we shall have some more music together, you and I, some more of your own work. Oh, yes," she said, kissing the creature several times on the neck, "and we might have a lit-

---

① Wagner: *Noun* Wilhelm Richard Wagner (1813—1883), German composer. He developed an operatic genre which he called music drama, synthesizing music, drama, verse, legend, and spectacle. Notable works: *The Flying Dutchman* (opera, 1841), *Der Ring des Nibelungen* (a cycle of four operas, 1847 ~ 1874), *Tristan and Isolde* (music drama, 1859), *and the Siegfried Idyll* (1870). 威廉·理查德·瓦格纳(1813—1883):德国作曲家,创造了他称为音乐剧的歌剧形式,集音乐、戏剧、诗歌、传奇和表演于一体;代表作品:歌剧《漂泊的荷兰人》(1841)、四部曲《尼贝龙根的指环》(1847 ~ 1874)、音乐剧《特里斯丹与绮瑟》(1859)和《齐格菲的牧歌》(1870)。

② grumpy: *Adjective* surly or ill-tempered; discontentedly or sullenly irritable; grouchy 脾气坏的;性情暴躁的;生气的

tle Chopin[①], too. You needn't tell me—I happen to know you adore Chopin. You used to be great friends with him, didn't you, darling? As a matter of fact if I remember rightly—it was in Chopin's apartment that you met the great love of your life, Madame Something-or-Other. Had three illegitimate children by her, too, didn't you? Yes, you did, you naughty thing, and don't go trying to deny it. So you shall have some Chopin," she said, kissing the cat again, "and that'll probably bring back all sorts of lovely memories to you, won't it?"

"Louisa, stop this at once!"

"Oh, don't be so stuffy, Edward."

"You're behaving like a perfect idiot, woman. And anyway, you forget we're going out this evening, to Bill and Betty's for canasta[②]."

"Oh, but I couldn't possibly go out now. There's no question of that."

Edward got up slowly from his chair, then bent down and stubbed[③] his cigarette hard into the ashtray. "Tell me something," he said quietly.

---

① Chopin: *Noun* Frédéric Franc ois Chopin (1810—1849), Polish-born French composer and pianist; Polish name Fryderyk Franciszek Szopen. Writing almost exclusively for the piano, he composed numerous mazurkas and polonaises inspired by Polish folk music, as well as nocturnes, preludes, and two piano concertos (1829; 1830). 弗雷德里克·弗朗索瓦·肖邦(1810—1849):波兰出生的法国作曲家、钢琴家;波兰语名,弗里德里克·弗朗齐歇克·索彭。作品大多为钢琴曲,受波兰民间音乐启发,写就众多玛祖卡舞曲和波洛涅兹舞曲,作品还包括夜曲、序曲和两部钢琴协奏曲(1829;1830)。

② canasta: *Noun* [mass noun] a card game resembling rummy, using two packs. It is usually played by two pairs of partners, and the aim is to collect sets (or melds) of cards 凯纳斯特纸牌游戏

③ stub: *Verb* extinguish (a lighted cigarette) by pressing the lighted end against something 掐灭;捻熄(e. g. She stubbed out her cigarette in the overflowing ashtray. 她在已经满溢的烟灰缸里掐灭了香烟。)

"You don't really believe this—this twaddle① you're talking, do you?"

"But of course I do. I don't think there's any question about it now. And, what's more, I consider that it puts a tremendous responsibility upon us, Edward—upon both of us. You as well."

"You know what I think," he said. "I think you ought to see a doctor. And damn quick, too."

With that, he turned and stalked out of the room, through the French windows②, back into the garden.

Louisa watched him striding across the lawn towards his bonfire and his brambles, and she waited until he was out of sight before she turned and ran to the front door, still carrying the cat.

Soon she was in the car, driving to town.

She parked in front of the library, locked the cat in the car, hurried up the steps into the building, and headed straight for the reference room. There she began searching the cards for books on two subjects—REINCARNATION and LISZT.

Under REINCARNATION she found something called *Recurring Earth-Lives—How and Why*, by a man called F. Milton Willis, published in 1921. Under LISZT she found two biographical volumes. She took out all three books, returned to the car, and drove home.

Back in the house, she placed the cat on the sofa, sat herself down beside it with her books, and prepared to do some serious reading. She would begin, she decided, with Mr. F. Milton Willis's work. The

---

① twaddle: *Noun* trivial, feeble, silly, or tedious talk or writing 废话;蠢话;无聊话

② French window: *Noun* (usu. as "French windows") each of a pair of glazed doors in an outside wall, serving as a window and door, typically opening on to a garden or balcony 落地长窗

volume was thin and a trifle soiled①, but it had a good heavy feel to it, and the author's name had an authoritative ring.

The doctrine of reincarnation, she read, states that spiritual souls pass from higher to higher forms of animals. "*A man can, for instance, no more be reborn as an animal than an adult can re-become a child.*"

She read this again. But how did he know? How could he be so sure? He couldn't. No one could possibly be certain about a thing like that. At the same time, the statement took a good deal of the wind out of her sails②.

"*Around the centre of consciousness of each of us, there are, besides the dense outer body, four other bodies, invisible to the eye of flesh, but perfectly visible to people whose faculties of perception of superphysical things have undergone the requisite development...*"

She didn't understand that one at all, but she read on, and soon she came to an interesting passage that told how long a soul usually stayed away from the earth before returning in someone else's body. The time varied according to type, and Mr. Willis gave the following breakdown③:

Drunkards and the unemployable 40 ~ 50*YEARS*
Unskilled labourers 60 ~ 100*YEARS*
Skilled workers 100 ~ 200*YEARS*

---

① soiled: *Adjective* dirty, stained, or tarnished 脏的;污染的

② take the wind out of someone's sails: frustrate someone by unexpectedly anticipating an action or remark 先发制人;冷不防挫败某人

③ breakdown: *Noun* an explanatory analysis, especially of statistics(尤指统计学中的)分析(e.g. a detailed cost breakdown 一个详细的成本分析)

*The bourgeoisie*① 200 ~ 300 *YEARS*

The upper-middle classes 500 *YEARS*

The highest class of gentleman farmers 600 ~ 1 000 *YEARS*

Those in the Path of Initiation 1 500 ~ 2 000 *YEARS*

Quickly she referred to one of the other books, to find out how long Liszt had been dead. It said he died in Bayreuth② in 1886. That was sixty-seven years ago. Therefore, according to Mr. Willis, he'd have to have been an unskilled labourer to come back so soon. That didn't seem to fit at all. On the other hand, she didn't think much of the author's methods of grading. According to him, "the highest class of gentleman farmer" was just about the most superior being on the earth. Red jackets and stirrup cups③ and the bloody, sadistic murder of the fox. No, she thought, that isn't right. It was a pleasure to find herself beginning to doubt Mr. Willis.

Later in the book, she came upon a list of some of the more famous reincarnations. Epictetus④, she was told, returned to earth as Ralph

① bourgeoisie: *Noun* [treated as sing. or pl.] the middle class, typically with reference to its perceived materialistic values or conventional attitudes 中产阶级

② Bayreuth: *Noun* a town in Bavaria where Wagneris buried and where festivals of his operas are held regularly 拜罗伊特(巴伐利亚的城市,瓦格纳的墓葬地,当地定期为瓦格纳举办歌剧节。)

③ stirrup cup: *Noun* a cup of wine or other alcoholic drink offered to a person on horseback who is about to depart on a journey(献给上马欲行者的)饯行酒

④ Epictetus: *Noun* (c. 55—135), Greek philosopher, who preached the common brotherhood of man and advocated a Stoic philosophy 爱比克泰德(约 55—135 年):希腊哲学家,宣扬人类友爱和斯多葛哲学。

Waldo Emerson①. Cicero② came back as Gladstone③, Alfred④ the

---

① Emerson: *Noun* Ralph Waldo Emerson (1803—1882), American philosopher and poet. He evolved the concept of Transcendentalism, which found expression in his essay *Nature* (1836). 拉尔夫·沃尔多·爱默生(1803—1882):美国哲学家、诗人,发展了超验论思想,该思想在其1836年的散文《论自然》中得以表现。

② Cicero: *Noun* Marcus Tullius Cicero (106—143 bc), Roman statesman, orator, and writer. As an orator and writer Cicero established a model for Latin prose; his surviving works include speeches, treatises on rhetoric, philosophical works, and letters. A supporter of Pompey against Julius Caesar, in the *Philippics* (143 bc) he attacked Mark Antony, who had him put to death. 马库斯·图利乌斯·西塞罗(公元前106—前143):罗马政治家、雄辩家、作家;作为雄辩家和作家,西塞罗为拉丁语散文确立了典范,存世作品包括演说、辩术论文、哲学著作和信件;他支持庞培反对尤利乌斯·恺撒,在《反腓力辞》(公元前143年)中抨击马克·安东尼,为后者处死。

③ Gladstone: *Noun* William Ewart Gladstone (1809—1898), British Liberal statesman, Prime Minister 1868 ~ 1874, 1880 ~ 1885, 1886, and 1892 ~ 1894. At first a Conservative minister, he later joined the Liberal Party, becoming its leader in 1867. His ministries saw the introduction of elementary education, the passing of the Irish Land Acts and the third Reform Act, and his campaign in favour of Home Rule for Ireland. 威廉·尤尔特·格莱斯顿(1809—1898):英国自由党政治家,1868 ~ 1874年、1880 ~ 1885年、1886年和1892 ~ 1894年任首相,起初他是保守党大臣,后加入自由党,并于1867年成为自由党领袖;在他任职期间,引进了初等教育,通过了爱尔兰土地法案和第三个选举法修正法案,并发起了支持爱尔兰自治的运动。

④ Alfred: *Noun* Alfred (849—899), king of Wessex 871 ~ 899; known as Alfred the Great. Alfred's military resistance saved SW England from Viking occupation. A great reformer, he is credited with the foundation of the English navy and with a revival of learning. 阿尔弗烈德(849—899):西撒克斯国王(871 ~ 899),通称"阿尔弗烈德大王";阿尔弗烈德的武装反抗使英格兰西南部免于遭受北欧海盗侵占;作为伟大的改革家,他被认为奠定了英格兰海军和学术复兴基础。

Great as Queen Victoria①, William② the Conqueror as Lord Kitchener③. Ashoka Vardhana④, King of India in 272 B. C. , came back as Colonel

---

① Victoria: *Noun* Victoria (1819—1901), queen of Great Britain and Ireland 1837 ~ 1901 and empress of India 1876 ~ 1901. She took an active interest in the policies of her ministers, but largely retired from public life after Prince Albert's death in 1861. 维多利亚女王(1819—1901):大不列颠及爱尔兰女王(1837 ~ 1901)及印度女皇(1876 ~ 1901);她积极关注政务,但 1861 年阿尔伯特亲王去世之后,几乎退出公众生活。

② William: *Noun* William I (c. 1027—1087), reigned 1066 ~ 1087, the first Norman king of England; known as William the Conqueror. He invaded England and defeated Harold II at the Battle of Hastings (1066). He introduced Norman institutions and customs (including feudalism) and instigated the *Domesday Book*. 威廉一世(约 1027—1087):1066 ~ 1087 年在位,英格兰的第一位诺尔曼国王;通称"征服者威廉";他入侵英国,并在黑斯廷斯战役(1066)中打败哈罗德二世;引进包括封建主义在内的诺尔曼人制度和习俗,并编制了《末日审判书》。

③ Kitchener: *Noun* Horatio Herbert Kitchener, 1st Earl Kitchener of Khartoum (1850—1916), British soldier and statesman. At the outbreak of the First World War he was made Secretary of State for War. He had previously defeated the Mahdist forces at Omdurman in 1898, served as Chief of Staff in the Second Boer War, and been Commander-in-Chief (1902 ~ 1909) in India. 霍拉肖·赫伯特·基奇纳,第一任喀土穆基奇纳伯爵(1850—1916):英国军人、政治家,第一次世界大战爆发时被任命为陆军大臣,此前曾于 1898 年在乌姆杜尔曼击败马赫迪起义军,在第二次布尔战争中任参谋长,1902 ~ 1909 年任印度总司令。

④ Ashoka Vardhana: *Noun* King of Maurya Empire 阿育王(印度孔雀王朝的国王)

Henry Steel Olcott, an esteemed American lawyer. Pythagoras① returned as Master Koot Hoomi, the gentleman who founded the Theosophical Society② with Mme Blacatsky③ and Colonel H. S. Olcott (the esteemed American lawyer, alias Ashoka Vardhana, King of India). It didn't say

---

① Pythagoras: *Noun* Pythagoras (c. 580—500 bc), Greek philosopher; known as Pythagoras of Samos. Pythagoras sought to interpret the entire physical world in terms of numbers, and founded their systematic and mystical study; he is best known for the theorem of the right-angled triangle. His analysis of the courses of the sun, moon, and stars into circular motions was not set aside until the 17th century. 毕达哥拉斯(约公元前580—前500年):希腊哲学家,通称"萨摩斯的毕达哥拉斯";毕达哥拉斯寻求用数解释整个物质世界,对数进行了系统的、神秘的研究,以直角三角形定理最为著名;他有关太阳、月亮和恒星循环运动的分析一直流行至17世纪。

② Theosophical Society: *Noun* The Theosophical Society is an organization formed in 1875 to advance theosophy. 这个表达通常译作"神智学社"(创建于1875年),是一个研究、分析并发表从古至今任何宗教及神秘传统资讯的组织。

③ Blavatsky: *Noun* Helena Petrovna Blavatsky (1831—1891), Russian spiritualist, born in Ukraine; born Helena Petrovna Hahn; known as Madame Blavatsky. In 1875 she co-founded the Theosophical Society in New York. 海伦娜·彼得罗夫娜·布拉瓦茨基(1831—1891):俄国女唯灵论学者,生于乌克兰,原名海伦娜·彼得罗夫娜·哈恩,世称"布拉瓦茨基夫人";1875年在纽约与他人共同创立神智学社。

who Mme Blavatsky had been. But "Theodore Roosevelt[①]," it said,

"*has for numbers of incarnations played great pans as a leader of men... From him descended the royal line of ancient Chaldea, he having been, about* 30 000 *B. C., appointed Governor of Chaldea by the Ego we know as Caesar*[②] *who was then ruler of Persia*[③]... *Roosevelt and Caesar have been together time after time as military and administrative leaders; at one time, many thousands of years ago, they were husband and wife...*"

That was enough for Louisa. Mr. F. Milton Willis was clearly nothing but a guesser. She was not impressed by his dogmatic assertions. The fellow was probably on the right track, but his pronouncements were extravagant, especially the first one of all, about animals. Soon she hoped to be able to confound[④] the whole Theosophical Society with her proof that man could indeed reappear as a lower animal. Also that he did not

---

① Roosevelt: *Noun* Theodore Roosevelt (1858—1919), American Republican statesman, 26th President of the US 1901 ~ 1909; known as Teddy Roosevelt. He was noted for his antitrust laws and successfully engineered the American bid to build the Panama Canal (1904 ~ 1914). He won the Nobel Peace Prize in 1906 for negotiating the end of the Russo-Japanese War. 西奥多·罗斯福(1858—1919):美国共和党政治家,美国第26任总统(1901 ~ 1909),人称"泰迪·罗斯福";他以其反托拉斯法著称,并成功策划了美国开凿巴拿马运河的投标(1904 ~ 1914);因调停俄日战争获1906年诺贝尔和平奖。

② Caesar: *Noun* a title of Roman emperors, especially those from Augustus to Hadrian 凯撒(罗马皇帝称号,尤指罗马帝国从奥古斯都至哈德良期间的皇帝称号。)

③ Persia: *Noun* a former country of SW Asia, now called Iran 波斯(亚洲西南部的一个古国,现称伊朗。)

④ confound: *Verb* to contradict or refute (an argument, etc) 证明……有错

have to be an unskilled labourer to come back within a hundred years.

She now turned to one of the Liszt biographies, and she was glancing through it casually when her husband came in again from the garden.

What are you doing now?" he asked.

"Oh—just checking up a little here and there. Listen, my dear, did you know that Theodore Roosevelt once was Caesar's wife?"

"Louisa," he said, "look—why don't we stop this nonsense? I don't like to see you making a fool of yourself like this. Just give me that goddamn cat and I'll take it to the police station myself."

Louisa didn't seem to hear him. She was staring open-mouthed at a picture of Liszt in the book that lay on her lap. "My God!" she cried. "Edward, look!"

"What?"

"Look! The warts① on his face! I forgot all about them! He had these great warts on his face and it was a famous thing. Even his students used to cultivate little tufts of hair on their own faces in the same spots, just to be like him."

"What's that got to do with it?"

"Nothing. I mean not the students. But the warts have."

"Oh, Christ," the man said. "Oh, Christ God Almighty."

"The cat has them, too! Look, I'll show you."

She took the animal on to her lap and began examining his face. "There! There's one! And there's another! Wait a minute! I do believe they're in the same places! Where's that picture?"

It was a famous portrait of the musician in his old age, showing the fine powerful face framed in a mass of long grey hair that covered his ears

① wart: *Noun* a small, often hard, abnormal elevation on the skin, usually caused by a papomavirus 肉赘

and came half-way down his neck. On the face itself, each large wart had been faithfully reproduced, and there were five of them in all.

"Now, in the picture there's one above the right eyebrow." She looked above the right eyebrow of the cat. "Yes! It's there! In exactly the same place! And another on the left, at the top of the nose. That one's there, too! And one just below it on the cheek. And two fairly close together under the chin on the right side. Edward! Edward! Come and look! They're exactly the same."

"It doesn't prove a thing."

She looked up at her husband who was standing in the centre of the room in his green sweater and khaki slacks, still perspiring freely. "You're scared, aren't you, Edward? Scared of losing your precious dignity and having people think you might be making a fool of yourself just for once."

"I refuse to get hysterical about it, that's all."

Louisa turned back to the book and began reading some more. "This is interesting," she said. "It says here that Liszt loved all of Chopin's work except one—the Scherzo① in B flat, minor. Apparently he hated that. He called it the 'Governess Scherzo', and said that it ought to be reserved solely for people in that profession."

"Edward, listen. As you insist on being so horrid② about all this, I'll tell you what I'm going to do. I'm going to play this scherzo right now and you can stay here and see what happens."

---

① scherzo: *Noun* (Music) a vigorous, light, or playful composition, typically comprising a movement in a symphony or sonata(音乐)谐谑曲(通常构成交响乐或奏鸣曲的一个乐章)

② horrid: *Adjective* (informal) very unpleasant or disagreeable(非正式)令人讨厌的;不合意的(e. g. The teachers at school were horrid. 学校里的老师令人讨厌。)

"And then maybe you will deign[①] to get us some supper."

Louisa got up and took from the shelf a large green volume containing all of Chopin's works. "Here it is. Oh yes, I remember it. It is rather awful. Now, listen—or, rather, watch. Watch to see what he does."

She placed the music on the piano and sat down. Her husband remained standing. He had his hands in his pockets and a cigarette in his mouth, and in spite of himself he was watching the cat, which was now dozing on the sofa. When Louisa began to play, the first effect was as dramatic as ever. The animal jumped up as though it had been stung, and it stood motionless for at least a minute, the ears pricked up, the whole body quivering. Then it became restless and began to walk back and forth along the length of the sofa. Finally, it hopped down on to the floor, and with its nose and tail held high in the air, it marched slowly, majestically, from the room.

"There!" Louisa cried, jumping up and running after it. "That does it! That really proves it!" She came back carrying the cat which she put down again on the sofa. Her whole face was shining with excitement now, her fists were clenched white, and the little bun on top of her head was loosening and going over to one side. "What about it, Edward? What do you think?" She was laughing nervously as she spoke.

"I must say it was quite amusing."

"Amusing! My dear Edward, it's the most wonderful thing that's ever happened! Oh, goodness me!" she cried, picking up the cat again and hugging it to her bosom. "Isn't it marvellous to think we've got Franz Liszt staying in the house?"

---

① deign: *Verb* [no obj., with infinitive] do something that one considers to be beneath one's dignity 屈尊(e.g. She did not deign to answer the maid's question. 她不屑于回答女仆的问题。)

"Now, Louisa. Don't let's get hysterical."

"I can't help it, I simply can't. And to imagine that he's actually going to live with us for always!"

"I beg your pardon?"

"Oh, Edward! I can hardly talk from excitement. And do you know what I'm going to do next? Every musician in the whole world is going to want to meet him, that's a fact, and ask him about the people he knew—about Beethoven and Chopin and Schubert—"

"He can't talk," her husband said.

"Well—all right. But they're going to want to meet him anyway, just to see him and touch him and to play their own music to him, modern music he's never heard before."

"He wasn't that great. Now, if it had been Bach or Beethoven..."

"Don't interrupt, Edward, please. So what I'm going to do is to notify all the important living composers everywhere. It's my duty. I'll tell them Liszt is here, and invite them to visit him. And you know what? They'll come flying in from every corner of the earth!"

"To see a grey cat?"

"Darling, it's the same thing. It's him. No one cares what he looks like. Oh, Edward, it'll be the most exciting thing there ever was!"

"They'll think you're mad."

"You wait and see." She was holding the cat in her arms and petting[①] it tenderly but looking across at her husband, who now walked over to the French windows and stood there staring out into the garden. The evening was beginning, and the lawn was turning slowly from green to

① pet: *Verb* [with obj.] stroke or pat (an animal) affectionately 抚摸(动物);爱抚(e. g. The cats came to be petted. 那些猫跑来想得到抚摸。)

black, and in the distance he could see the smoke from his bonfire rising up in a white column.

"No," he said, without turning round, "I'm not having it. Not in this house. It'll make us both look perfect fools."

"Edward, what do you mean?"

"Just what I say. I absolutely refuse to have you stirring up a lot of publicity about a foolish thing like this. You happen to have found a trick cat. O. K.—that's fine. Keep it, if it pleases you. I don't mind. But I don't wish you to go any further than that. Do you understand me, Louisa?"

"Further than what?"

"I don't want to hear any more of this crazy talk. You're acting like a lunatic."

Louisa put the cat slowly down on the sofa. Then slowly she raised herself to her full small height and took one pace forward. "Damn you, Edward!" she shouted, stamping her foot. "For the first time in our lives something really exciting comes along and you're scared to death of having anything to do with it because someone may laugh at you! That's right, isn't it? You can't deny it, can you?"

"Louisa," her husband said. "That's quite enough of that. Pull yourself together now and stop this at once." He walked over and took a cigarette from the box on the table, then lit it with the enormous patent lighter. His wife stood watching him, and now the tears were beginning to trickle① out of the inside corners of her eyes, making two little shiny rivers where they ran through the powder on her cheeks.

"We've been having too many of these scenes just lately, Louisa,"

---

① trickle: *Verb* [no obj., with adverbial of direction] (of a liquid) flow in a small stream(液体)滴;淌(e.g. A solitary tear trickled down her cheek. 一颗泪珠滑下她的脸颊。)

he was saying. "No no, don't interrupt. Listen to me. I make full allowance for the fact that this may be an awkward time of life for you, and that—"

"Oh, my God! You idiot! You pompous idiot! Can't you see that this is different, this is—this is something miraculous? Can't you see that?"

At that point, he came across the room and took her firmly by the shoulders. He had the freshly lit cigarette between his lips, and she could see faint contours① on his skin where the heavy perspiration had dried up in patches. "Listen," he said. "I'm hungry. I've given up my golf and I've been working all day in the garden, and I'm tired and hungry and I want some supper. So do you. Off you go now to the kitchen and get us both something good to eat."

Louisa stepped back and put both hands to her mouth. "My heavens!" she cried. "I forgot all about it. He must be absolutely famished②. Except for some milk, I haven't given him a thing to eat since he arrived."

"Who?"

"Why, him, of course. I must go at once and cook something really special. I wish I knew what his favourite dishes used to be. What do you think he would like best, Edward?"

"Goddamn it, Louisa!"

"Now, Edward, please. I'm going to handle this my way just for once. You stay here," she said, bending down and touching the cat gently with her fingers. "I won't be long."

Louisa went into the kitchen and stood for a moment, wondering

---

① contour: *Noun* the outline of a figure or body; the edge or line that defines or bounds a shape or object 外形;轮廓

② famish: *Verb* [no obj.] be extremely hungry 极度饥饿

what special dish she might prepare. How about a soufflé? A nice cheese soufflé? Yes, that would be rather special. Of course, Edward didn't much care for them, but that couldn't be helped.

She was only a fair cook, and she couldn't be sure of always having a soufflé come out well, but she took extra trouble this time and waited a long while to make certain the oven had heated fully to the correct temperature. While the soufflé was baking and she was searching around for something to go with it, it occurred to her that Liszt had probably never in his life tasted either avocado① pears or grapefruit②, so she decided to give him both of them at once in a salad. It would be fun to watch his reaction. It really would.

When it was all ready, she put it on a tray and carried it into the living-room. At the exact moment she entered, she saw her husband coming in through the French windows from the garden.

"Here's his supper," she said, putting it on the table and turning towards the sofa. "Where is he?"

Her husband closed the garden door behind him and walked across the room to get himself a cigarette.

"Edward, where is he?"

"Who?"

"You know who."

"Ah, yes. Yes, that's right. Well—I'll tell you." He was bending forward to light the cigarette, and his hands were cupped around the enormous patent lighter. He glanced up and saw Louisa looking at him—at his shoes and the bottoms of his khaki slacks, which were damp from

---

① avocado: *Noun* (Also as "avocado pear") a pear-shaped fruit with a rough leathery skin, smooth oily edible flesh, and a large stone 鳄梨

② grapefruit: *Noun* a large round yellow citrus fruit with an acid juicy pulp 葡萄柚(大而圆的黄色柑橘类水果,果肉酸且多汁)

walking in long grass.

"I just went out to see how the bonfire was going," he said.

Her eyes travelled slowly upward and rested on his hands.

"It's still burning fine," he went on. "I think it'll keep going all night."

But the way she was staring made him uncomfortable.

"What is it?" he said, lowering the lighter. Then he looked down and noticed for the first time the long thin scratch that ran diagonally① clear across the back of one hand, from the knuckle② to the wrist.

"Edward!"

"Yes," he said, "I know. Those brambles are terrible. They tear you to pieces. Now, just a minute, Louisa. What's the matter?"

"Edward!"

"Oh, for God's sake, woman, sit down and keep calm. There's nothing to get worked up about, Louisa! Louisa, sit down!"

三、翻译探索

在这篇小说中,达尔"卖弄"了不少音乐方面的知识,包括音乐家及其音乐作品。这就构成了翻译的难点,需要仔细查询,认真处理。另外,还有一些"投胎转世"方面的文字表达也要处理好。

---

① diagonal: *Adjective* (of a line) straight and at an angle; slanting 斜线的;斜的(e.g. a tie with diagonal stripes 一个有斜纹的领结)

② knuckle: *Noun* a part of a finger at a joint where the bone is near the surface, especially where the finger joins the hand 指关节;指节(e.g. Charlotte rapped on the window with her knuckles. 夏洛特用指节轻敲着窗户。)

音乐奇猫

路易莎手里拿着一块洗碗布，跨出厨房的门，门设在房子的后面。外面，十月艳阳高照，有些凉爽。

“爱德华！”她喊道，“爱——德——华！午饭好了！”

她停了停，听听有没有动静。接着，向草坪溜达，继而穿过草坪，走过一小块阴影区域，绕过玫瑰花坛。绕过花坛的时候，她用手指轻轻碰了碰那个日晷。对于一个身体丰满、个头矮小的女性来说，她走起路来，姿态十分优雅，步履轻松愉快，双肩和双臂轻柔地摇摆。她从那棵桑树下走过，走上一条砖铺的小路。沿着小路走下去，一直走到一个地方停下，从那里她可以俯瞰这个大花园尽头那个凹陷的地方。

“爱德华！吃午饭啦！”

现在，她看得见爱德华了，离她有七十多米远，就在下方林子边的凹陷处。他细细的身材，个子有点偏高，下身穿土黄色卡其布做的宽松裤，上身穿一件深绿色毛线衫。他生起一堆火，双手举着叉子，叉起枝条往火堆上扔。火烧得旺旺的、烈烈的。火焰是橘黄色的，冒出一团团奶白色的烟雾，烟雾向身后飘去，飘浮在花园上空，散发出秋天特有的甜美气味，那气味伴随着燃烧的叶子飞来舞去。

路易莎沿着斜坡向她丈夫走去。要是她愿意喊，是可以轻易地再次喊出声来，让他听见的。但是，这堆火简直太棒了，有某种魔力迫使她径直走了过去。一走近，她就感受到那股热浪，听到“呼呼、啦啦”燃烧的声音。

“吃午饭啦。”她边说边靠近。

“噢，嗨，好的——好，我就来。”

“多旺的一堆火啊！”

“我已经决定把这个地方清理干净，”她丈夫说，“这些枝条令我厌烦透顶。”由于出汗，他那张脸湿乎乎的，上唇胡须上沾满了一粒一粒的像露珠一样的汗滴。两条小溪沿着他的喉部流淌，淌到毛线衫的圆领上。

“你最好当心一点，爱德华，别劳累过度。”

“路易莎啊，我真的希望你不要把我当成七老八十的。活动活动对谁都不会造成什么伤害的。”

“没错，亲爱的，这我知道。哇，爱德华！ 看啊！ 看啊！”

丈夫转身看着路易莎，路易莎正用手指指向火堆对面稍远的地方。

“看呐，爱德华！ 是一只猫！”

隔着火堆看去，一只大块头的猫端坐在地上，毛色极其与众不同。那只猫离火堆很近，有时候看起来火焰似乎真的烧到它身上了。它一动不动地待着，头歪向一侧，伸出鼻子嗅着什么，黄色的眼睛盯着这对男女，显得从容不迫、镇定自若。

“会烧着它的！”路易莎喊道，随后扔掉手里的洗碗布，飞奔过去，双手抓起猫，快速走开，把它放到草地上一个远离火焰的安全地带。

“你这只猫，简直是疯了，”她一边拍掉手上的灰尘，一边责怪道，“你这是怎么啦？”

“猫很清楚自己在做什么，”丈夫说，“你永远也看不到有哪只猫做了自己不喜欢的事。否则，就不叫猫啦。”

“谁家的猫啊？ 你以前见到过吗？”

这只猫坐到草地上，斜视着他俩。它的两只眼睛里隐藏着内心没有表达出来的某种东西，露出一种无所不知、深思熟虑的眼神，令人感到很是好奇。它那只鼻子极其微妙地显露出一副蔑视的神态，仿佛在说：看看你俩，都人到中年，一个个子矮小、身体丰满、肤色红润，另一个细细瘦瘦、大汗淋漓；看到你俩，我意想不到，却不足挂齿。对于一只猫而言，它身体的颜色无疑与众不同——纯银灰色，中间无半点蓝色杂毛，而且，身上的毛长长的，如丝般柔滑。

路易莎弯下腰，拍了拍猫的头部。“你必须回家，”她说，“现在，做只乖猫，回家去，回到属于你的地方。”

夫妻俩沿着小山上去，向自家房子溜达过去。那只猫站了起来，跟着他俩。刚开始，它只是远远地跟着，但接下来却越跟越近，越跟越紧，很快就和他俩并肩而行，随后就超过了他俩，走到了前面。它领着他俩穿越草坪,来到房前,就好像这地方是属于它的。然后,举起尾巴,笔直地竖起,就像一根旗杆。

"回家去,"男的说道,"赶快回去,我们可不想要你。"

可是,他们进屋后,那只猫也跟了进去。路易莎就在厨房给了它一些牛奶喝。午饭期间,它就跳上他俩之间的空椅子上蹲坐着,伸出头刚好超过餐桌表面,那双黑黄相间的眼睛缓缓地移动,一会看看女的,一会又看看男的,整个午饭的时间,就一直这样看着。

"我不喜欢这只猫。"爱德华说。

"噢,我认为它很漂亮的。我真的希望它多待一会儿。"

"现在,路易莎,听我说啊。这只动物是不可能待在这里的,它走失了,是别人家的。要是今天下午它还是游荡不回家,你最好叫警察。警察会妥善处理,送它回家的。"

午饭后,爱德华继续摆弄他的花园去了。像往常一样,路易莎坐到了钢琴旁。她钢琴弹得很拿手,真的酷爱音乐,每天下午都要花一个小时左右的时间弹琴。那只猫现在躺在沙发上,她走过沙发时还停下来拍了拍它。拍的时候,它眼睛睁了一下,然后又闭上,接着睡觉了。

"你真是一只好猫啊,"她说,"颜色还这么漂亮,真希望能够养你这只猫。"说完,她用手指摸了摸猫头部的软毛,无意中触摸到一个小小的肿块,这个肿块长在它右眼上方。

"可怜的猫咪,"她说,"你漂亮的脸上起块块了,你一定是年纪不小啦。"

她走了过去,坐到钢琴前的长凳上,却并没有马上开始弹奏。她每天弹琴前的一个特殊的小乐趣就是把日常的弹琴练习当作音乐会来安排:演奏前,精心挑选曲目,详细安排曲目顺序。要是因为不知道下一曲要弹什么而停止下来、破坏了雅兴,她是非常讨厌的。她要做的就是在一首曲子弹完后,暂停一下,等待热情的观众鼓掌,喊着要她再来一曲。弹奏时,不时地想象台下观众一片,那感觉要好得多了。特别是,要是哪一天幸运的话,就感觉屋子仿佛在摇晃、旋转,接着暗淡下来。此时,她只能看到一排一排的座位,还有海水般涌动的白色的脸孔——那一张张面孔抬起来，看向她，听得如醉如痴，崇拜得五体投地。

有的时候，她凭记忆演奏；有的时候，她看乐谱弹奏。今天，她要凭记忆演奏了。演奏什么曲目好呢？她坐在钢琴前，两只纤细的手紧紧扣在膝盖上。她身体丰满、肤色红润，圆圆的脸依然相当的俊俏，头发盘了起来，挽到脑后，利索地打了一个圆圆的发髻。她眼睛余光向右一看，看到那只猫在沙发上蜷缩成一团，“呼呼”睡着了。在紫色坐垫的映衬下，它那一身银灰色的软毛十分漂亮。开场来首巴赫的，怎么样呢？或者，更好的，来首维瓦尔第的，也就是巴赫作品改编的那首管风琴曲：D 小调大协奏曲，如何？是的，就先弹这首。接着，或许弹一点舒曼的，《狂欢节》怎么样？嗯，不错。然后嘛——嗯，换换样，弹弹李斯特的《彼特拉克十四行诗》中的一曲：第二曲 E 大调——最优美的一首，怎么样？然后，再来一首舒曼的——他的另一首欢快的曲子：《儿时情景》。最后嘛，应观众“再来一个”的呼喊，就演奏一首勃拉姆斯的华尔兹圆舞曲——要是她来了兴致，也可以弹两首的。

维瓦尔第、舒曼、李斯特、舒曼、勃拉姆斯，这是一个很不错的曲目演奏顺序，可以凭记忆，不用看乐谱，轻松地弹下去。她稍微向前靠近钢琴一点儿，暂停一会儿，因为观众中有人最后咳嗽了一下。她已经感觉到，今天是一个幸运的日子。接着，她举起双手，放到琴键上，开始演奏起来，她刚才的每一个动作都是缓缓的，还带着那么几分优雅。

就在开始演奏的那一刻，她根本就没有去看那只猫——确切地说，她忘记了它的存在。可是，当维瓦尔第的第一组低沉的音符轻柔地在屋子里响起的时候，她眼角的余光觉察到有什么东西突然一阵乱动。定睛一看，发现是沙发上有东西猛然间动了起来。她立即停下来。“什么东西啊？”她边说边转向那只猫，“怎么回事啊？”

几秒钟之前，这只动物还一直在安安稳稳地睡大觉，可现在却腾地笔直坐在沙发上，一副紧张的神态：整个身体抖动起来，两只耳朵竖立，一双眼睛圆睁，盯着钢琴。

“我吓着你了吗?”她轻轻地问,“或许,你以前从来没有听过音乐吧。”

“不会的啊,”她对自己说,“我想,不会是这样的。”再一寻思,在她看来,这只猫的样子似乎不是害怕,因为它既没有收缩身体,也没有向后退步。要是说这只动物有什么反应的话,倒是身体前倾,显示出要急切弄明白什么东西的样子。她看到猫脸上有一种相当古怪的表情——既有吃惊之情,又有愕然之态。当然啦,猫的脸很小,也没有什么表情可言。但是,要是仔细看看它的眼睛和耳朵,特别是耳朵下方那一小块皮肤一动一动的,稍微向一侧移动,就会感觉它在表达某些很强烈的情感。路易莎仔细地观察它那张脸,因为她很好奇,想看看再来一次的话,会怎么样。她双手伸向琴键,又开始弹奏维瓦尔第的曲子。

这次,那只猫显然有所准备,所以一开始只是身体一激灵,又紧张了一下。但是,随着音乐渐渐增强、渐渐加快,曲子过渡到了赋格曲的令人兴奋的节奏上。此时,这只动物的脸上开始出现一种奇怪的表情——几乎是如醉如痴:两只笔直竖起的耳朵慢慢地向后收,眼皮下垂,头歪向一边。至此,路易莎可以发誓地说,这只动物实际上是在欣赏音乐作品。

她所看到的——或者说,她认为她所看到的——是她多次注意到的现象:人在专心听一首乐曲时,脸上会露出类似的表情。当音乐完全控制人的身心、使人沉浸其中的时候,一种独特的、痴迷的表情就会呈现出来。这种表情很容易辨别出来,那就是微笑。就目前路易莎所能看到的,这只猫面部的表情跟人的几乎一模一样。

路易莎弹完赋格曲部分,就接着弹奏西西里舞曲,而且在整个弹奏过程中,她眼睛一直没有离开过沙发上的那只猫。对她来说,最能证明这只动物在听她弹奏的证据来自于乐曲的结尾部分,就是在她停下来不弹的时候:那只猫眨眨眼,身体轻微动弹一下,一条腿伸展开来,换成一种更加舒服的姿势,快速在屋子四周扫视一眼,然后满怀期待地看着她。这恰恰是音乐会观众在两首交响曲间隙短暂放松时所表现出来的样子。它的行为完完全全就是人的行为,这令她胸口产生一种怪异的、激动的感觉。

“你喜欢刚才的?”她问道。“你喜欢维瓦尔第的?”

话刚一出口,她就感觉有些荒诞不经。但是,对她而言,此时却产生了那么一点点的预感:这件事起码不像她了解和感觉的那样荒诞不经。

噢,现在也没什么啦,只是要继续弹奏曲目单上的下一首,也就是《狂欢节》。她刚开始弹,那只猫就又挺直身体,更加笔直地端坐着。紧接着,它慢慢地、不无喜悦地沉浸于音乐之声,再度陷入方才那种怪异的、如醉如痴的状态,那种融合的情绪如同跃入水中,如同进入梦乡。那场景看起来真的是有点虚幻,也相当的滑稽:一只银光闪闪的猫坐在沙发上,如此忘乎所以、得意忘形。路易莎认为,这事比先前更加不着边际的是,这首曲子太古典,世界上大多数人欣赏起来难度都太大。这是明摆着的事实,可是,这只猫似乎陶醉其中,喜欢得不得了。

她想,或许这个小家伙并不是真的喜欢音乐。或许它的行为有点催眠反应,就像蛇听到音乐那样。可不是嘛,音乐能魔法般地控制蛇,为什么就不能控制猫呢?除非数以百万计的猫在一生中每一天都听音乐这种东西,或者通过收音机听,或者通过留声机听,或者通过钢琴演奏来听,才不会有催眠反应。可是,就她所知,从来没有这样的情况发生,没有一只总听音乐的猫出现过。看这只猫的行为,它似乎能跟得上每一个音节。当然,这件事情太难以置信了。

可是,再一想,难道这不也是一件美妙的事情吗?的确如此。事实上,要是她没有搞错的话,这就是一个奇迹,一个动物创造的奇迹,那可是好几百年才能遇到一次的奇迹啊。

“我看得出,你很是喜欢刚才那首,”弹完后,她说,“尽管今天我哪一首也没有弹得太好。我很抱歉。哪一首你最喜欢呢?维瓦尔第的,还是舒曼的?”

这只猫并没有回答。因此,路易莎唯恐失去这位知音观众,就径直弹奏曲目单上的下一首——李斯特的《彼特拉克十四行诗》中的第二曲。

现在,一件异乎寻常的事情发生了。刚弹到三四小节的地方,就可以觉察到那只猫的长须开始抽动。只见它身体慢慢抬起,抬到一个特别高的位置,头歪向一边,再歪向另一边,眼睛盯着空中,有点聚精会神又眉头紧锁的样子,似乎在说:"这是什么?别告诉我答案啊。我太熟悉了,但这会儿似乎又对不上号。"路易莎兴奋不已,她那小嘴半张半笑,继续往下弹,等着看看下一步究竟会有什么情况发生。

这只猫站起来,走到沙发的一头,又端坐下来,多听了一些,然后"腾"地跳到地板上,随后"嗖"地跃上钢琴前的长登上,靠到她身边。它坐在路易莎身旁,神情专注地听着这首动听的十四行诗曲子。这一次,不是如同进入梦乡一般,而是挺直了身体,两只大大的、黄色的眼睛紧紧地盯着路易莎的手指。

"噢,"她敲完最后一个和弦说道,"那么,你是主动上来坐到我的旁边,是吧?这里比沙发更好吗?好吧,我不撵你走,可你必须静静地坐着,不要蹦来跳去啊。"她伸出一只手,轻轻抚摸这只猫的后背,从头部抚摸到尾巴。"刚才弹的是李斯特的,"她继续说,"告诉你啊,他这个人有时候相当的低俗不堪,但是在音乐这方面,他魅力非凡。"

她开始喜欢上这种与动物间奇特的、哑剧式的交流方式。因此,她就直接弹奏曲目单上的下一首,也就是舒曼的《儿时情景》。

刚弹一两分钟的功夫,她就意识到,这只猫又动了。现在,它回到沙发上原先的位置。她当时弹奏时,一直看着自己的手,就想当然地推测,那就是她没有注意到它离开的原因。尽管如此,它离开的速度一定相当快,而且悄无声息。那只猫仍然盯着她,很明显,仍然仔细听着音乐。但是,在路易莎看来,那种狂喜劲儿和热情劲儿跟听前一曲——李斯特的——就不一样了。不仅如此,它离开凳子、返回沙发的动作本身看起来不温不火,但那姿态明摆着有点失望之情。

"你怎么啦?"弹完后她问,"舒曼怎么啦?李斯特有什么绝妙之处吗?"那只猫径直回头看着她,可以看到它那两只黄色眼睛的中心部位垂直地立着两道乌黑发亮的小杠杠。

她自言自语,这事真的很有意思啊。稍加思考,她觉得这事却也有点吓人。可是,看一眼那只猫端坐在沙发上,两眼发亮、聚精会神,等待继续听下去,她就很快心安理得、倍感安慰了。

"好吧,"她说,"对你说啊,我要开始了。我要把曲目为你特别更改一下。你似乎对李斯特喜欢有加,我就为你再来一首吧。"

她再三思考着,从记忆里搜索李斯特的精彩曲目。随后,就轻柔地弹奏出十二首组曲《圣诞树》中的一曲。现在,她仔细观察这只猫。首先映入眼帘的是,它的长须又开始抽动,紧接着跳到地毯上,静静站立一会,头倾斜着,因为兴奋而颤动。然后,它缓慢地迈着丝般柔滑的步子,绕着钢琴走着,随即"嗖"地跃上凳子,坐到她身旁。

就在这一节骨眼上,爱德华从花园回来,走进屋子。

"爱德华!"路易莎边喊边跳了起来,"哇,爱德华啊,亲爱的!听我说!听听发生什么大事了!"

"现在吗,什么事?"他问,"我想喝点茶。"他那张脸窄窄的,稍微带点紫红色,鼻子尖尖的。由于出汗,他那张脸亮光光的,就像一粒长长的、湿漉漉的葡萄。

"就是那只猫啦!"路易莎指着安安静静坐在长凳上的猫大声说,"听我把话说完,你就知道发生什么大事啦!"

"我想,我告诉过你把它送到警察局的。"

"可是,爱德华,听我说。这简直太令人兴奋了。这是一只音乐奇猫。"

"哦,是吗?"

"这只猫能欣赏音乐,也懂得音乐。"

"路易莎,不要胡扯啦。看在老天的面子上,我们喝点茶吧。砍枝条续火,弄得我又热又累。"他一屁股坐到扶手椅子里,从旁边烟盒里取出一根香烟,拿起烟盒旁边那个款式超棒、样子别致的打火机,"啪"的一声,点着了香烟。

"你不明白的是,"路易莎说,"你出去干活的时候,就在我们家里发生了一件事情,相当地令人兴奋,这件事情甚至是……怎么说呢……意义非凡的。"

"对此,我确信无疑。"

“爱德华,拜托！听着。”

路易莎站在钢琴旁,她那张粉红色的小脸比方才更加粉嘟嘟了,每一只脸颊高起的部分还带有鲜红的玫瑰色。“要是你愿意听,”她说,“我就把我的想法告诉你。”

“我听着呢,亲爱的。”

“我想,或许可能的是,我们俩此时此刻坐在——”她停了下来,就好像突然间感觉到自己的想法有些荒唐可笑。

“是吗?”

“爱德华,你可以认为我的想法愚蠢可笑,但实话实说,我就是这么想的。”

“看在老天的面子上,坐在谁的面前?”

“坐在弗朗兹·李斯特的面前!”

她丈夫慢慢地、长长地吸了一口香烟,抬头把烟雾喷向天花板。他算是一个男子汉了,身上皮肤紧巴巴的;由于多年佩戴一整套假牙,两只面颊凹陷下去,而且每次往里吸烟,面颊凹陷得就更厉害,面颊骨也就更突出了,像骷髅一般。“我没明白你说的意思。”他说。

“爱德华,听我说。从今天下午我的亲眼所见,看起来那情形实质上或许就是某种投胎转世,真的。”

“你是说这只讨厌的猫?”

“亲爱的,请不要那样说。”

“路易莎,你没有得什么病,对吗?”

“我安然无恙,十分感谢。我只是有点迷茫,这点我承认。但是,发生刚才的事情之后,有谁不会迷茫呢?爱德华,我向你发誓——”

“要是我可以问的话,到底发生什么事了?”

路易莎跟他讲了。这边,她滔滔不绝地讲,那边,她丈夫的身体伸展开来坐在椅子上,双腿伸到了前面,吸着香烟,再把烟雾喷向天花板。他的嘴上露出一丝微笑,一副不是十分相信的神态。

“我看不出这有什么奇特之处,”听完后,他说道,“只不过,这只猫会点小把戏,有人教过它此类把戏,仅此而已。”

“爱德华,别犯傻了。每次我一弹李斯特的曲子,他就兴奋不已,跑过来跳上凳子,坐到我旁边。只是弹李斯特的时候,他才这样。要是有人教的话,也教不出李斯特和舒曼的区别来呀,就连你也不知道有什么区别的。但是,这只猫每次都能区别开来。李斯特的,也是相当晦涩难懂的。"

"两次,"丈夫说,"他这样做,也就两次。"

"两次足矣。"

"我们看看他再做一次试试,快啊。"

"不,"路易莎说,"肯定不做了。原因就是,如果这只猫是李斯特的话——我相信是的,或者不管怎么说,是李斯特的魂魄也好,或者李斯特的什么再生的话也好,那么,让他经受这么多愚蠢可笑的、有失体面的测试,就很不合适、很不友好了。"

"我亲爱的老婆啊!那只是一只猫啊。一只相当愚蠢的灰颜色的猫啊。今天早晨在花园里,那堆火不是差点把它的毛烧焦了吗?话说回来了,对于投胎转世,你了解多少呢?"

"要是这只猫是他的魂魄投胎的话,对我来说,了解得就足矣,"路易莎肯定地说,"那就是至关重要的了解。"

"你可得了吧。要是李斯特的话,我们看看他的表现吧。我们看看他能否辨别出他自己的东西跟他人的东西的区别吧。"

"不,爱德华。前面我已经说过'不'了。我拒绝让他再经受什么愚蠢的、马戏团表演式的测试。这一天,他经受的测试已经相当多了,可我要告诉你我会怎么做的。我要再为他弹奏一点他自己的作品。"

"那样也好,也完全可以证明。"

"你看着吧。有一件事情是肯定的——只要他辨认出自己的作品,他就会坐在那条长凳上,就坐在现在他坐的位置上,死活不会挪窝的。"

路易莎走到放音乐书的架子那儿,取下一本李斯特的书,用大拇指快速地捻过一页又一页,选中了他的另一首指法弹奏曲,即 B 小调奏鸣曲。她本来打算只演奏这部作品的第一乐章,但是一旦演奏起来,看到那只猫端坐在那儿愉悦地浑身颤动,神情专注、欣喜若狂地看着她的双手弹奏,她就不想半道停下来了,而是一直弹奏下去。弹完后,她抬起头看看她的丈夫,微微一笑。“看到了吧,”她说,“这下你不会对我说,他绝对不喜爱李斯特吧。”

“他就是喜欢这样的响动,仅此而已。”

“他那是喜爱李斯特的曲子。难道不是吗,亲爱的?”她问道,把猫抱了起来。“啊,我的天呐,他要是会说话可就好了。亲爱的,你就想一想吧——他青年时代可见过贝多芬啊!他还认识舒伯特、门德尔松、舒曼、柏辽兹、德拉克罗瓦、安格尔、海涅,还有巴尔扎克。哇,让我想想还有谁……我的天啊,他是瓦格纳的老丈人!我现在胳膊里抱的,是瓦格纳的老丈人啊!”

“路易莎!”她的丈夫坐直身体,尖声喊道,“正常点吧。”现在,他说话的声音不同于刚才,音量更高了。

路易莎抬头,快速看了一眼。“爱德华,我敢相信,你那是在吃醋!”

“啊,当然,当然啦。我吃醋了——和一只讨厌的、灰颜色的猫的争风吃醋!”

“那么,对这事不要再气急败坏、百般怀疑了。要是你的表现还像这样不改的话,你最好回去忙你的园艺,让我们两个在一起安安静静地待着。那样对我们大家都是再好不过的了,对不对啊,亲爱的?”她轻轻抚摸着猫的头,对着猫说道。“今晚再晚一些时间,我们一起再来些音乐,就我和你,再演奏一些你自己的作品。哇,就这样定啦,”她边说边在这个小家伙脖子上吻了几下,“或许,我们也演奏一点肖邦的曲子。不用你告诉我,我凑巧知道你崇拜肖邦的。你们曾经是最要好的朋友,对不对啊,亲爱的?事实上,要是我没有记错的话,就是在肖邦住的公寓里,你遇到了你人生中伟大的爱情,跟那个什么……什么夫人的伟大爱情。你们也有了三个私生子,对吧?是的,你做过这事,你这个坏坏的小东西,你可不要试图抵赖啊。所以嘛,再来点肖邦的,”她又亲吻一下这只猫,说道,“或许,那会把你各种美好的记忆带回来,是吧?”

“路易莎,立刻打住!”

“哦，爱德华，不要这样陈腐、无趣。”

“老婆啊，你完完全全就是一个白痴。再者说，今晚我们要出去的，去比尔和贝蒂的家玩凯纳斯特纸牌游戏，你不要忘了。”

“噢，可是现在看来我不大可能出去了。这一点毫无疑问了。”

爱德华慢慢从椅子上站起身来，然后一弯腰，香烟往烟灰缸里使劲一戳，弄灭了。“告诉我吧，”他平静地说，“你不是真的相信这事儿，就是你刚才说的荒唐事儿，对不对？”

“可问题是，我当然相信的。我想，现在这事是毋容置疑的。况且，爱德华，我认为，这事让我们承担起巨大的责任，我们俩承担的，包括你。”

“你知道我是怎么想的吗？”他说，“我想，你应该去看医生，而且，该死的，要赶紧去。”

说完这话，他转过身，大步走出房间，穿过落地窗，回花园去了。

路易莎看着他大踏步穿过草坪，向着他生起的那堆火，还有那些枝条奔了过去。她一直等到她丈夫从视线中消失，才转回身，跑向前门，仍然抱着那只猫。

很快，她钻进小汽车，驱车到城里去了。

她把车停在图书馆门前，把那只猫锁到车子里，就匆匆忙忙上了台阶，走了进去，直奔查阅室。在那里，她从卡片上检索两个主题——“投胎转世”和“李斯特”——来找要看的书。

在“投胎转世”主题下，她发现了一本名为《地球生命再生：如何再生？为何再生？》的书，作者是 F·米尔顿·威利斯，出版时间是 1921 年。在“李斯特”主题下，她找到了两本传记方面的书。她把三本书都借出来，回到车里，驱车回家。

回到家中，她把猫放到沙发上，自己拿着那三本书坐到猫旁边，准备认认真真地阅读一番。她决定先看 F·米尔顿·威利斯先生的作品。这本书有些脏，但并无大碍；书很薄，但摸起来有一种厚重感——不错的感觉；看作者的名字，感觉很权威。

通过阅读，她得知，投胎转世学说认为，精神之魂从高级生命体向更高级生命体转移。“比如说，一个人不能再生为一个动物，就像一个成年人不能投胎成一个孩子,两者是一样的。”

她把上面那段话又读了一遍。可是,他是怎么知道的?他怎么如此肯定?他不可能未卜先知的。不可能有谁对这样的事情十拿九稳的。同时,这段话对她十分不利。

“在我们每个人意识中心的周围区域,除了密度极大的外部躯体外,还有其他四个主体部分,肉眼是看不到的。但是,对于超物质世界里的具有感知能力的人来说,这四个部分是可见的,因为这些人经历了必要的发展阶段……”

上面这一段她根本就读不懂,但还是继续往下读。很快,她看到了很有意思的一段,说的是一个人的灵魂离开尘世多长时间,才能返回,最终转世,附到他人躯体上。人的类型不同,投胎转世的时间长短也不一样。书的作者威利斯先生给出了如下统计分析结果:

醉汉和无工作能力者　40~50年

无技能的体力劳动者　60~100年

有技能的工作者　100~200年

中产阶层人士　200~300年

中上阶层人士　500年

最上阶层的男性农场主　600~1 000年

创业初始阶段人士　1 500~2 000年

她赶忙翻开另外两本书中的一本,要查查李斯特死去多长时间。那本书说,他1886年死于拜罗伊特,也就是六十七年前的事情。因此,根据威利斯先生的分析,这么短时间内就投胎转世的人,生前一定是无技能的体力劳动者,那似乎一点也不符合李斯特的实际情况。再者说,她对那本书的作者的划分方法根本没有多加考虑,没有当回事。依作者看,“最上阶层的男性农场主”还是地球上最上等群体类型呢。看看这群人:身穿红色夹克衫,脚踏马镫,手拎着喝完临行酒的杯子,然后就去血腥地、惨无人性地猎杀狐狸。她寻思着:不,他分析得不对。她发现自己竟开始怀疑大名鼎鼎的作家威利斯先生,不禁有点得意起来。

过了一些时候,她在这本书里看到作者列举了一些有名的投胎转世先例。书中说,爱比克泰德作为拉尔夫·沃尔多·爱默生返回尘世;西塞罗转世为格拉德斯通;阿尔弗雷德大帝投胎成维多利亚女王;征服王威廉转成基奇纳勋爵;生于公元前272年的印度阿育王投胎为亨利·斯蒂尔·奥尔科特上校——深受尊敬的美国律师;毕达哥拉斯转世为库特·胡米大师,也就是创立神智学社的那位绅士,这个学社是他跟布拉瓦茨基夫人以及亨利·斯蒂尔·奥尔科特上校联合创立的,这位上校就是那个深受尊敬的美国律师,也就是印度阿育王投胎转世而来的那位。书中没有说拉瓦茨基夫人是谁,但是却对西奥多·罗斯福详加描述如下:

在很多次投胎转世过程中,西奥多·罗斯福作为人类的领袖,屡次扮演着重要角色……从他那里传下来了古代卡尔迪亚王国的王室血脉。约公元前30 000年,他被任命为卡尔迪亚王国的国君。任命他的人叫埃戈,也就是我们熟知的凯撒,当时是波斯的统治者……作为军事和行政领导人,罗斯福和凯撒曾多次共同谋事;数千年前,他们一度做过夫妻……

对于路易莎来说,读到这里,已经足矣。很显然,F·米尔顿·威利斯先生只是猜测而已。对于他武断的说法,路易莎并没有放在心上。这个家伙说的或许在理,但是,他所宣扬的很不切实际,特别是第一点,就是不能投胎为动物那一点。随即,她就希望用自己的证据驳倒神智学社整套的观点。她的证据就是,人的确可以投胎转世,成为低等动物。同时,她也要证明,投胎为低等动物的人也未必是无技能的体力劳动者,转世的时间也未必局限在一百年之内。

现在,她翻开了另一本有关李斯特的传记书,随意翻阅着、扫视着。就在这时,她的丈夫又从花园回来,走进房间。

“你在干什么呢?”他问。

“啊——只是这翻翻,那看看,找点证据确定一下。听我说啊,亲爱的,你知道西奥多·罗斯福一度是凯撒的妻子吗?”

“路易莎啊,”他说,“你看看你——我们为什么不能干点别的,不这样无聊呢?我不喜欢看到你这样子,简直就是傻子。把那只该死的猫给我,我亲自送到警察局。”

路易莎似乎没有听到他说的话。她盯着膝盖上那本书里的一幅李斯特的肖像,边看边张大了嘴巴。“我的天啊!”她叫道,“爱德华,看呐!”

“什么?”

“看呐!他脸上的那几个肉赘!我怎么竟没有想起来肉赘的事啊!他脸上那几个肉赘太伟大、太有名了,他的几个学生那时候甚至在自己脸上相同的位置上蓄几撮毛,就是为了看起来像他啊。”

“那样做,与这只猫有什么关系?”

“没什么关系。我是说与学生没有什么关系,但与肉赘大有关系。”

“噢,天啊,”丈夫说,“噢,天啊!我万能的青天大老爷啊!”

“这只猫也有肉赘!看,我找给你看啊。”

她把猫抱到膝盖上,在猫脸上寻找起来。“这儿呢!这儿有一个!这儿还有一个!等一下!我敢保证,肉赘长的位置也一样!那幅肖像哪去了?”

音乐家的这幅肖像知名度是很高的,是他老年时的样子:面部细腻,活力十足,衬托在一团长长的、灰颜色的毛发里,毛发盖住了耳朵,一直垂下来,把半个脖颈也遮住了。就在那张脸上,每一块大的肉赘都得到了逼真无误的再现,总共有五块。

“现在看呐,肖像上有一块肉赘位于右眼眉的上方。”她看了看那只猫右眼眉的上方。“是的!就是那个位置,一模一样的位置!另一块在左边,就在鼻子的顶端。肖像上也是那个位置!往下,就在面颊上,有一块。还有两块彼此靠得很近,在右边,就在下巴底下。爱德华!爱德华!过来,看看呐!两者简直是一模一样。”

“什么也证明不了的。”

她抬头看了丈夫一眼，发现他站在屋子中间，上身穿着他那件绿色的毛线衫，下身还是那条黄卡其布做的宽松裤，汗水仍然恣意地流淌。“爱德华，你害怕了，对吗？害怕失去你那宝贵的尊严，害怕平生第一次别人看你的笑话，认为你或许是傻子一个。”

“这事我就是不想大肆渲染，仅此而已。”

路易莎转回身去，继续往下读。“这真有意思啊，”她说，“书里说，李斯特喜欢肖邦所有作品，就有一首除外——降B小调谐谑曲。很明显，他不喜欢那首的，称之为‘家庭女教师式谐谑曲’，而且还说，那首曲子应该是单独为那个行当里的人量身定做的。”

“那又怎么样？”

“爱德华，听着啊。鉴于你对整个事情的反感程度，我就告诉你我打算怎么做吧。我打算马上弹奏这首谐谑曲。你就待在原地别动，看看结果会怎样。”

“然后，或许劳烦你屈尊一下，晚饭弄点什么吃的吧。”

路易莎站起身，从书架上拿下一大本绿色封皮的书，那里包含肖邦所有作品。“就是这本书。噢，是的，我想起来了。这首曲子十分糟糕。现在，你就听听——或者说，看看。观察一下，看看猫会有什么举动。”

她把乐谱放到钢琴上，坐了下来，而她丈夫还是站着不动。他双手插到衣兜里，嘴里叼着一支烟，只顾看着那只正在沙发上打盹的猫。路易莎刚开始弹的时候，这只猫的反应跟前面的一样，令人激动：小家伙一下子跳了起来，好似被什么蛰了一下，至少有一分钟的时间，站着一动不动；双耳竖立，整个身体颤动起来。接下来，它就坐立不安，开始在沙发上来回走动，从一头走向另一头。最后，干脆跳到地板上，鼻子仰起，尾巴高高地竖向空中，开始慢慢地、雄赳赳地走出房间。

“看呐，”路易莎边喊边跳起来追了上去，“这就是证明！这就是真正的证据！”她抱着猫回来，又放到了沙发上。现在，她满脸都是无比兴奋的表情。两手攥紧拳头，把手都攥白了。她头顶那个小小的、圆圆的发髻开始松动，偏向了一边。“怎么样啊，爱德华？你认为呢？”说话的时候，她笑了起来，笑得有点紧张兮兮的。

“我不得不说，这相当有趣儿。”

“怎么是‘有趣儿’啊！我亲爱的爱德华，这是亘古未有的、极其美妙的事！啊，天呐！”她喊完，又抱起猫，拥抱到胸前，“想象一下啊，弗朗兹·李斯特到我们家了。想到这一点，难道不就是美妙之至的吗？”

“现在，路易莎，你我最好都要淡定。”

“我情不自禁，简直无法控制。特别是想象到，他实际上要永远跟我们生活在一起啊！”

“我怎么没有听清楚呢？”

“哦，爱德华！我激动过头，几乎说不出话来。你知道，我下一步要做什么吗？全世界的音乐家，没有一个不想见到他的，这是事实。见到他，打听一下他认识的人——贝多芬啦，肖邦啦，舒伯特啦——”

“他不能说话的。”她丈夫说。

“啊——那好吧。可是，那些人还是想见见他的，仅仅是看看、摸摸也行，为他演奏他们自己的音乐。要知道，他从未听过现代音乐的。”

“他有那么伟大吗？现在，假设这只猫是巴赫，或者贝多芬……”

“爱德华，拜托你别插嘴。那么，我要通知世界各地活着的、重量级的作曲家，这是我的职责。我对他们说，李斯特在我家，邀请他们前来拜访。你知道会怎么样吗？他们会从世界各个角落纷纷飞来！”

“来看这只灰猫？“

“亲爱的，有什么区别吗？猫就是他，他就是猫，谁也不会在意他的长相。噢，爱德华，这将是破天荒的、最激动人心的事情！“

“大家会认为，你疯了。”

“你等着瞧吧。”她胳膊抱着那只猫，用手轻柔地抚摸着，但眼睛却看向她丈夫。只见他走到落地窗前，站在那儿，向外看着花园。天就要黑下来，草坪由绿色慢慢地变成了黑色。再往远处观瞧，他看到他生起的那堆火冒出一根白色的烟柱，笔直地升腾到空中。

“不，”他头也不回地说道，“我谁都不允许来，不要到这个家来。大家一来，就只能是看笑话，笑我俩是呆头呆脑的傻子。”

“爱德华，你什么意思啊？”

“就我说的这个意思。我绝对不允许你像这样做傻事，闹得沸沸扬扬的。你只是‘瞎猫碰到一个死耗子’——但你碰到的是一只会点把戏的猫。好吧，既然碰到，你愿意养就养起来，我不介意的。但是，希望你别做得太过火。你明白我的意思吗，路易莎？”

“什么太过火的事情？”

“我不想再听你疯言疯语了。你的行为简直就是精神错乱。”

路易莎慢慢地把猫放到沙发上，然后慢慢挺起她那矮小的身体站了起来，并向前迈出一步。“去你的，爱德华！”她使劲跺着脚骂道，“我们俩这一辈子，第一次出现这么激动人心的事情，而你却吓得要死，一副事不关己的样子，就是因为有人会笑话你啊！我说你说对了，是不是？你无法否认，对吧？”

“路易莎，”她丈夫说，“这事就到此为止。现在，正常点，立刻打住。”他走过去，从桌上的盒里里拿出一根香烟，用那个款式超棒、样子别致的打火机点着了香烟。他妻子站在那儿看着他。现在，她眼窝里开始“啪嗒啪嗒”地淌眼泪，像两条闪闪发光的小河冲开她面颊上的胭脂香粉往下流淌。

“路易莎，最近一段时间以来，我们家出现太多类似的场景，”他说，“不，不，不要打断我的话。听我说。我充分理解、完全承认，这或许是你人生中难以应对的时刻，可是——”

“噢，天呐！你这个蠢货！你这个妄自尊大的蠢货！难道你看不出，这次的事情不一样吗？难道你看不出，这次发生的是一件超自然的神奇之事吗？难道你看不出来吗？”

就在她激动反问的当儿，他穿过房间走到她面前，紧紧抓住她的两只肩膀。他的两片嘴唇之间夹着刚刚点着的香烟。她看到丈夫皮肤上有一道道不甚明显的轮廓线，那是刚才大汗淋漓的地方蒸干后留下的斑痕。“听着，”他说，“我饿了。我高尔夫球都顾不上打，一整天待在花园里劳作。现在又累又饿，只想吃点晚饭。你也要吃的。

所以啊,现在就去厨房,赶快张罗点好吃的吧。"

路易莎倒退一步,双手捂着嘴。"我的老天啊!"她喊道,"我怎么一点也没有想到,他一定是饿极了。自打他来这儿时算起,除了牛奶,我还没有给过他一丁点东西吃呢。"

"谁?"

"还有谁,当然是他啦。我必须去做点真正特殊口味的东西。但愿我知道他以前最喜欢吃的是什么饭菜。爱德华,你知道他最喜欢吃什么吗?"

"去你的,路易莎!"

"现在,爱德华,拜托别这样。不问你了,就这次,交给我自己处理好了,一会就好。你待着别动,"她说完,弯下腰,用手指轻轻地触摸那只猫,"我去去就来。"

路易莎走进厨房,站了一会,想着该准备什么特殊口味的饭菜。鸡蛋饼怎么样?煎一盘奶油鸡蛋饼?对,那就相当不一般了。当然,爱德华不太喜欢吃这口,但也只能这样了。

她做饭也就一般般,也没有把握每次都能把奶油鸡蛋饼煎得很成功。但是,这次她格外用心,等了很长时间以确保炉子完全加热到正确的温度。她一边煎鸡蛋,一边找配料。找着找着,她一下子心血来潮,想到李斯特一生中或许从没有尝过鳄梨或者葡萄柚是什么滋味,所以她决定在同一种沙拉中同时放进这两种水果。看着他吃完后做出的反应,一定很有意思,真的会很有意思的。

她把做好的食物盛到一只盘子里,端进起居室。就在进屋的瞬间,她看到她丈夫从花园回来,穿过落地窗,也走进屋子。

"他的晚饭好了,"她边说,边把盘子放到桌子上,随后身体转向沙发,"他哪去了?"

她丈夫随手关上花园门,走过屋子,取出一只香烟。

"爱德华,他哪里去了?"

"谁?"

"你知道是谁。"

"哦,是的,是的,我知道。噢,对你说吧。"他向前倾斜身体,点着了烟，双手还是呈杯子形状，捧住那个款式超棒、样子别致的打火机。他抬起头，看到路易莎正看着他，看着他脚上那双鞋，还有那条黄卡其布做的宽松裤的裤腿。因为刚趟过草坪，草长得很高，裤腿都弄湿了。

"我刚才出去，看看那堆火烧得怎么样。"他说。

她的双眼慢慢向上看去，停在他的两只手上。

"火很旺，还烧着呢，"他继续说，"我想，一整夜也不会熄灭的。"

可是，她盯着他看的那个样子令他感到很不自在。

"怎么了？"他放低了打火机问道。随即，他低头一看，才猛然发现自己一只手背上有一道长长的、细细的抓痕——从指关节斜向延伸到手腕处，清晰可见。

"爱德华！"

"噢，"他应道，"我知道了。那些枝条真难摆弄，能把你刮成碎片的。现在，路易莎，稍等等。怎么回事啊？"

"爱德华！"

"噢，看在老天的分上，老婆，坐下来，要冷静。什么事儿让你如此激动不已啊。路易莎！路易莎，坐下来啊！"

第二节 《魔力王浆》*Royal Jelly*

罗尔德·达尔的《魔力王浆》(*Royal Jelly*)首次发表于《暮光地带杂志》①(*The Twilight Zone Magazine*)1983年2月号上。后来，这

① 此杂志名为著者所译。根据英文版"维基百科"的介绍，这本杂志创刊于1981年，克莱因(Klein)当时任主编，以刊登恐怖小说为主，同时也刊登一些奇幻类小说以及一些近乎科幻类型的小说(Beginning in 1981 and with T. E. D. Klein as editor, "*The Twilight Zone Magazine*" featured horror fiction and to some extent other forms of fantasy and some borderline science fiction)。

篇小说收录到《罗尔德·达尔短篇故事集锦》(*The Collected Short Stories of Roald Dahl*)、《最佳恐怖故事集》(*Best Tales of Terror*)、《罗尔德·达尔小说精品集》(*The Best of Roald Dahl*)、《五部畅销书集》(*5 Bestsellers*)、《吻了又吻》(*Kiss Kiss*)、《罗尔德·达尔选集》(*The Roald Dahl Omnibus*)等书中。另外,这部小说还被改编成电视系列剧中的一集——1980 年 3 月 1 日播映的《出乎意料的故事集》(*Tales of the Unexpected*)第二部中的第 1 集(Episode 2.1)。另外,由爱德华·皮瑟布里奇(Edward Petherbridge)朗读的有声读物《吻了又吻》(*Kiss Kiss*)中,也收录了这篇小说,可见其影响力之大。

值得一提的是,除了上述《最佳恐怖故事集》(*Best Tales of Terror*)之外,很多恐怖故事集也将这篇小说收入囊中,由此可见这篇小说具有一定的恐怖性,甚至有人认为是"自己读过的最恐怖的小说之一"①。其恐怖之处恐怕在于故事的结局吧,可能就恐怖在达尔最后对婴儿的那番描述上面。

一、原作导读

这篇小说情节简单,主要围绕泰勒一家展开,人物主要有三个:丈夫艾伯特、妻子梅布尔以及他们的初生婴儿——厌食的小女儿。

刚出生的小女儿不肯喝奶,这可愁坏了母亲梅布尔。女儿从生下来起,就不肯进食,体重不断下降,这吓坏了做母亲的梅布尔。梅布尔感到绝望,甚至疯狂,但却无能为力,就连医生也无计可施。

丈夫艾伯特也不知所措,就开始阅读养蜂方面的书籍。他对养蜂很有一套,目前的生计也主要靠养蜂和卖蜂蜜来维持。这天晚上,他读到了一段关于蜂王浆的描述,顿时有点茅塞顿开的感觉:

---

① 这是克里斯廷·霍华德(Kristine Howard)所持的观点(Personally, I think [sic] this is one of Dahl's scariest stories)。参见她创建并维护的网站"*Roald Dahl Fans. com*"(罗尔德·达尔粉丝网),网址为:http://www.roalddahl-fans.com/。

所有幼虫从卵里孵化出来之后，在起初的三天时间里，就会被大量喂食蜂王浆。但是，三天过后，对于所有那些命中注定要成为雄蜂或者工蜂的幼虫来说，就用蜂蜜和花粉把这种宝贵的食物稀释后，再喂养它们。另一方面，对于命中注定要成为蜂王的幼虫，在它们整个幼虫生长期，就用纯王浆大量喂养它们。蜂王浆由此得名。

Royal jelly is fed in concentrated form to all bee larvae for the first three days after hatching from the egg; but beyond that point, for all those who are destined to become drones or workers, this precious food is greatly diluted with honey and pollen. On the other hand, the larvae which are destined to become queens are fed throughout the whole of their larval period on a concentrated diet of pure royal jelly. Hence the name.

艾伯特深受启发，他想这东西对蜜蜂起作用，也会对自己的女儿起作用吧。于是，他决定试一试，让妻子休息，自己担当起整个晚上照看婴儿的任务。第二天早晨醒来走下楼梯后，梅布尔吃惊地得知，女儿一个晚上喝下了大量的牛奶。她还当场目睹丈夫给婴儿喂奶时婴儿急不可耐将整瓶牛奶喝光的情景。于是，她变得好奇起来：丈夫是怎么治好女儿的厌食症呢？令梅布尔大为震惊和不快的是，艾伯特最终承认自己往孩子的奶粉配方中加入了大量的蜂王浆。他用大量的事实和数据说话，说服她相信：蜂王浆这东西对女儿有奇效。但是，她就是不买账，并且还说，就算这种东西对孩子起作用，但是去年蜂蜜歉收，没挣到多少钱，也不想让丈夫用那么多蜜蜂来生产蜂王浆了。因此，她不赞成他再用蜂王浆来喂食婴儿。

再一次给孩子喂奶时，孩子喝下两瓶，身体看起来胖多了。夫妻俩给婴儿称量了一下，发现女儿体重增加了许多，但是，她有些害怕，因为女儿尽管肚子变大令体重有所增加，但胳膊和腿还是细细的，而且肚子上还长出了绒毛——棕色之中略带一点黄色调。于是，梅布尔指责丈夫给婴儿服用了过量的蜂王浆。对此，丈夫艾伯特没有否认,仍然想用事实让妻子彻底信服这东西的神奇功效。他向妻子承认,去年他将一半的蜜蜂用来生产蜂王浆,供自己服用,以期望能使自己更加具备生育能力,而且的确有效果——女儿降生就是很好的例证。此时,梅布尔突然发现:

丈夫脖子那儿根本看不到皮肤,就连两只耳朵下方的周边部分也看不见皮肤了。整个看不见皮肤的这一区域,一直延伸到衬衫的领口处,全部由一层稍短的、如丝般光滑的绒毛覆盖着,黑色之中略微带点黄色调。

There was no skin showing at all on the neck, not even at the sides below the ears. The whole of it, to a point where it disappeared into the collar of the shirt, was covered all the way around with those shortish silky hairs, yellowy black.

再看看自己的初生婴儿,她也突然发现:

婴儿一丝不挂地躺在桌子上,看起来胖胖的、白白的,睡得沉沉的。这个婴儿看起来就像某种大块头的、幼虫阶段的生活行将结束的蛆,而且上下颚和翅膀已经发育齐全,很快就会破茧而出,融入这个世界之中。

The baby was lying naked on the table, fat and white and comatose, like some gigantic grub that was approaching the end of its larval life and would soon emerge into the world complete with mandibles and wings.

故事的最后,妻子梅布尔听到丈夫艾伯特说:

"梅布尔,你为什么不把孩子盖好呢?"他问,"我们可不愿意让我们的小女王感冒的。"

"Why don't you cover her up, Mabel?" he said. "We don't want our little queen to catch a cold."

二、原作释读

这部作品的恐怖之处恐怕在于故事的结尾，阅读时也仔细体会结尾处达尔用词的精妙，这也是理解全篇的关键。

Royal Jelly①

"It worries me to death, Albert, it really does," Mrs. Taylor said.

She kept her eyes fixed on the baby who was now lying absolutely motionless in the crook② of her left arm.

"I just know there's something wrong."

The skin on the baby's face had a pearly translucent③ quality and was stretched very tightly over the bones.

"Try again," Albert Taylor said.

"It won't do any good."

"You have to keep trying, Mabel," he said.

She lifted the bottle out of the saucepan of hot water and shook a few drops of milk on to the inside of her wrist, testing for temperature.

---

① 本部小说原文出自"DAHL, R. *The Best of Roald Dahl*[M]. London: Penguin Books Ltd., 2006"。

royal jelly: *Noun* [mass noun] a substance secreted by honeybee workers and fed by them to larvae which are being raised as potential queen bees(蜜蜂的)蜂王浆

② crook: *Noun* a bend in something, especially at the elbow in a person's arm 弯曲部分(尤指胳膊肘的弯曲处)(e.g. Her head was cradled in the crook of Luke's left arm. 她的头枕在卢克的左胳膊肘内。)

③ translucent: *Adjective* (of a substance) allowing light, but not detailed shapes, to pass through; semi-transparent(物质)半透明的(e.g. her beautiful translucent skin 她那半透明的美丽肌肤)

"Come on," she whispered. "Come on, my baby. Wake up and take a bit more of this."

There was a small lamp on the table close by that made a soft yellow glow all around her.

"Please," she said. "Take just a weeny① bit more."

The husband watched her over the top of his magazine. She was half dead with exhaustion, he could see that, and the pale oval face, usually so grave and serene, had taken on a kind of pinched② and desperate look. But even so, the drop of her head as she gazed down at the child was curiously beautiful.

"You see," she murmured. "It's no good. She won't have it."

She held the bottle up to the light, squinting③ at the calibrations④. "One ounce again. That's all she's taken. No—it isn't even that. It's only three-quarters. It's not enough to keep body and soul together, Albert, it really isn't. It worries me to death."

"I know," he said.

"If only they could find out what was wrong."

"There's nothing wrong, Mabel. It's just a matter of time."

"Of course there's something wrong."

"Dr. Robinson says no."

---

① weeny: *Adjective* (informal) tiny(非正式)微小的;细小的

② pinched: *Adjective* tense and pale from with cold, worry, or hunger(因寒冷、忧虑或饥饿而)紧张的和脸色苍白的

③ squint: *Verb* [no obj.] look at someone or something with one or both eyes partly closed in an attempt to see more clearly or as a reaction to strong light(为了能看清楚或由于强光而)眯着眼看(e. g. The bright sun made them squint. 明亮的阳光使他们眯起眼来。)

④ calibration: *Noun* [count noun] each of a set of graduations on an instrument 刻度

"Look," she said, standing up. "You can't tell me it's natural for a six-week-old child to weigh less, less by more than two whole pounds than she did when she was born! Just look at those legs! They're nothing but skin and bone!"

The tiny baby lay limply on her arm, not moving.

"Dr. Robinson said you was to stop worrying, Mabel. So did that other one."

"Ha!" she said. "Isn't that wonderful! I'm to stop worrying!"

"Now, Mabel."

"What does he want me to do? Treat it as some sort of a joke?"

"He didn't say that."

"I hate doctors! I hate them all!" she cried, and she swung away from him and walked quickly out of the room towards the stairs, carrying the baby with her.

Albert Taylor stayed where he was and let her go.

In a little while he heard her moving about in the bedroom directly over his head, quick nervous footsteps going tap tap tap on the linoleum① above. Soon the footsteps would stop, and then he would have to get up and follow her, and when he went into the bedroom he would find her sitting beside the cot as usual, staring at the child and crying softly to herself and refusing to move.

"She's starving, Albert," she would say.

"Of course she's not starving."

"She is starving. I know she is. And Albert?"

"Yes?"

"I believe you know it too, but you won't admit it. Isn't that

---

① linoleum: *Noun* [mass noun] a material consisting of a canvas backing thickly coated with a preparation of linseed oil and powdered cork, used especially as a floor covering(亚麻)油地毡;漆布

right?"

Every night now it was like this.

Last week they had taken the child back to the hospital, and the doctor had examined it carefully and told them that there was nothing the matter.

"It took us nine years to get this baby, Doctor," Mabel had said. "I think it would kill me if anything should happen to her."

That was six days ago and since then it had lost another five ounces.

But worrying about it wasn't going to help anybody, Albert Taylor told himself. One simply had to trust the doctor on a thing like this. He picked up the magazine that was still lying on his lap and glanced idly down the list of contents to see what it had to offer this week:

AMONG THE BEES IN MAY
HONEY COOKERY
THE BEE FARMER AND THE B. PHARM
*EXPERIENCES IN THE CONTROL OF NOSEMA*①
THE LATEST ON ROYAL JELLY
*THIS WEEK IN THE APIARY*②
*THE HEALING POWER OF PROPOLIS*③

---

① nosema: *Noun* a spore-forming parasitic protozoan that chiefly affects insects 微粒子虫

② apiary: *Noun* a place where bees are kept; a collection of beehives 养蜂场;蜂窝群

③ propolis: *Noun* [mass noun] a red or brown resinous substance collected by honeybees from tree buds, used by them to fill crevices and to fix and varnish honeycombs 蜂胶

*REGURGITATIONS*①
BRITISH BEEKEEPERS ANNUAL DINNER
ASSOCIATION NEWS

All his life Albert Taylor had been fascinated by anything that had to do with bees. As a small boy he often used to catch them in his bare hands and go running with them into the house to show to his mother, and sometimes he would put them on his face and let them crawl about over his cheeks and neck, and the astonishing thing about it all was that he never got stung. On the contrary, the bees seemed to enjoy being with him. They never tried to fly away, and to get rid of them he would have to brush them off gently with his fingers. Even then they would frequently return and settle again on his arm or hand or knee, any place where the skin was bare.

His father, who was a bricklayer②, said there must be some witch's stench③ about the boy, something noxious④ that came oozing⑤

---

① regurgitate: *Verb* [with obj.] bring (swallowed food) up again to the mouth 将(咽下的食物)回流(到口中);反胃(e. g. Gulls regurgitate food for the chicks. 鸥回返食物来哺育雏鸟。)

② bricklayer: *Noun* a person whose job is to build walls, houses, and other structures with bricks 泥瓦匠;砌砖工人

③ stench: *Noun* a strong and very unpleasant smell 恶臭(e. g. the stench of rotting fish 烂鱼的恶臭)

④ noxious: *Adjective* harmful, poisonous, or very unpleasant 有害的;有毒的;让人厌恶的(e. g. They were overcome by the noxious fumes. 他们被有毒烟气熏倒了。)

⑤ ooze: *Verb* [no obj. , with adverbial of direction] (of a fluid) slowly trickle or seep out of something; move in a slow, creeping way(液体)渗出;慢慢流出(e. g. Blood was oozing from a wound in his scalp. 鲜血从他头上的伤口处慢慢渗出。)

out through the pores of the skin, and that no good would ever come of it, hypnotizing① insects like that. But the mother said it was a gift given him by God, and even went so far as to compare him with St. Francis and the birds.

As he grew older, Albert Taylor's fascination with bees developed into an obsession, and by the time he was twelve he had built his first hive. The following summer he had captured his first swarm. Two years later, at the age of fourteen, he had no less than five hives standing neatly in a row against the fence in his father's small back yard, and already—apart from the normal task of producing honey—he was practising the delicate and complicated business of rearing his own queens, grafting larvae② into artificial cell cups, and all the rest of it.

He never had to use smoke when there was work to do inside a hive, and he never wore gloves on his hands or a net over his head. Clearly there was some strange sympathy between this boy and the bees, and down in the village, in the shops and pubs, they began to speak about him with a certain kind of respect, and people started coming up to the house to buy his honey.

When he was eighteen, he had rented one acre of rough pasture alongside a cherry orchard down the valley about a mile from the village, and there he had set out to establish his own business. Now, eleven years later, he was still in the same spot, but he had six acres of ground instead of one, two hundred and forty well-stocked hives, and a small

---

① hypnotize or hypnotise: *Verb* capture the whole attention of (someone); fascinate 深深吸引(某人);使着迷(e. g. The barman seemed hypnotized by the pub's female singer. 酒吧男招待似乎被这位酒吧歌女深深吸引了。)

② larva: *Noun* the active immature form of an insect, especially one that differs greatly from the adult and forms the stage between egg and pupa, e. g. a caterpillar or grub(昆虫的)幼虫

house he'd built mainly with his own hands. He had married at the age of twenty and that, apart from the fact that it had taken them over nine years to get a child, had also been a success. In fact, everything had gone pretty well for Albert until this strange little baby girl came along and started frightening them out of their wits① by refusing to eat properly and losing weight every day.

He looked up from the magazine and began thinking about his daughter.

That evening, for instance, when she had opened her eyes at the beginning of the feed, he had gazed into them and seen something that frightened him to death—a kind of misty vacant stare, as though the eyes themselves were not connected to the brain at all but were just lying loose in their sockets like a couple of small grey marbles.

Did those doctors really know what they were talking about②?

He reached for an ash-tray and started slowly picking the ashes out from the bowl of his pipe with a matchstick.

One could always take her along to another hospital, somewhere in Oxford perhaps. He might suggest that to Mabel when he went upstairs.

He could still hear her moving around in the bedroom, but she must have taken off her shoes now and put on slippers because the noise was very faint.

He switched his attention back to the magazine and went on with his reading. He finished the article called "*Experiences in the Control of Nosema*", then turned over the page and began reading the next one, "*The Latest on Royal Jelly*". He doubted very much whether there would

---

① be frightened (scared) out of one's wits: be extremely frightened; be immobilized by fear 吓得魂不附体

② know what one is talking about: be expert or authoritative on a specified subject 对某个主题很在行

be anything in this that he didn't know already:

"*What is this wonderful substance called royal jelly?*"

He reached for the tin of tobacco on the table beside him and began filling his pipe, still reading.

*Royal jelly is a glandular*① *secretion produced by the nurse bees to feed the larvae immediately they have hatched from the egg. The pharyngeal*② *glands of bees produce this substance in much the same way as the mammary glands*③ *of vertebrates produce milk. The fact is of great biological interest because no other insects in the world are known to have evolved such a process.*

All old stuff, he told himself, but for want of anything better to do, he continued to read.

*Royal jelly is fed in concentrated form to all bee larvae for the first three days after hatching from the egg; but beyond that point, for all those who are destined to become drones*④ *or workers, this precious food is*

---

① glandular: *Adjective* of, relating to, or affecting a gland or glands(与)腺(有关)的;对腺产生影响的

② pharyngeal: *Adjective* of or relating to the pharynx(与)咽(有关)的

③ mammary gland: *Noun* the milk-producing gland of women or other female mammals 乳腺

④ drone: *Noun* a male bee in a colony of social bees, which does no work but can fertilize a queen 雄蜂;公蜂

*greatly diluted*① *with honey and pollen. On the other hand, the larvae which are destined to become queens are fed throughout the whole of their larval period on a concentrated diet of pure royal jelly. Hence the name.*

Above him, up in the bedroom, the noise of the footsteps had stopped altogether. The house was quiet. He struck a match and put it to his pipe.

Royal jelly must be a substance of tremendous nourishing power, for on this diet alone, the honey-bee larva increases in weight fifteen hundred times in five days.

That was probably about right, he thought, although for some reason it had never occurred to him to consider larval growth in terms of weight before.

This is as if a seven-and-a-half-pound baby should increase in that time to five tons.

Albert Taylor stopped and read that sentence again. He read it a third time.

This is as if a seven-and-a-half-pound baby...

"Mabel!" he cried, jumping up from his chair. "Mabel! Come here!"

He went out into the hall and stood at the foot of the stairs calling for her to come down.

---

① dilute: *Verb* [with obj.] (Usu. as "be diluted") make (a liquid) thinner or weaker by adding water or another solvent to it(加水或其他溶剂以)冲淡;稀释(e.g. Bleach can be diluted with cold water. 漂白剂可用冷水稀释。)

There was no answer.

He ran up the stairs and switched on the light on the landing. The bedroom door was closed. He crossed the landing and opened it and stood in the doorway looking into the dark room. "Mabel," he said. "Come downstairs a moment, will you please? I've just had a bit of an idea. It's about the baby."

The light from the landing behind him cast a faint glow over the bed and he could see her dimly now, lying on her stomach with her face buried in the pillow and her arms up over her head. She was crying again.

"Mabel," he said, going over to her, touching her shoulder. "Please come down a moment. This may be important."

"Go away," she said. "Leave me alone."

"Don't you want to hear about my idea?"

"Oh, Albert, I'm tired," she sobbed. "I'm so tired I don't know what I'm doing any more. I don't think I can go on. I don't think I can stand it."

There was a pause. Albert Taylor turned away from her and walked slowly over to the cradle where the baby was lying, and peered in. It was too dark for him to see the child's face, but when he bent down close he could hear the sound of breathing, very faint and quick. "What time is the next feed?" he asked.

"Two o'clock, I suppose."

"And the one after that?"

"Six in the morning."

"I'll do them both," he said. "You go to sleep."

She didn't answer.

"You get properly into bed, Mabel, and go straight to sleep, you understand? And stop worrying. I'm taking over completely for the next twelve hours. You'll give yourself a nervous breakdown going on like this."

"Yes," she said. "I know."

"I'm taking the nipper and myself and the alarm clock into the spare room this very moment, so you just lie down and relax and forget all about us. Right?" Already he was pushing the cradle out through the door.

"Oh, Albert." she sobbed.

"Don't you worry about a thing. Leave it to me."

"Albert..."

"Yes?"

"I love you, Albert."

"I love you too, Mabel. Now go to sleep."

Albert Taylor didn't see his wife again until nearly eleven o'clock the next morning.

"Good gracious me!" she cried, rushing down the stairs in dressing-gown① and slippers. "Albert! Just look at the time! I must have slept twelve hours at least! Is everything all right? What happened?"

He was sitting quietly in his armchair, smoking a pipe and reading the morning paper. The baby was in a sort of carry-cot② on the floor at his feet, sleeping.

"Hullo, dear," he said, smiling.

She ran over to the cot and looked in. "Did she take anything, Albert? How many times have you fed her? She was due for another one at ten o'clock, did you know that?"

---

① dressing gown or dressing-gown: *Noun* a long loose robe, typically worn after getting out of bed or bathing(起床或洗澡后穿)晨衣;浴袍

② carrycot or carry-cot: *Noun* (Brit.) a small portable bed for a baby(英国英语)手提式婴儿床

Albert Taylor folded the newspaper neatly into a square and put it away on the side table. "I fed her at two in the morning," he said, "and she took about half an ounce, no more. I fed her again at six and she did a bit better that time, two ounces..."

"Two ounces! Oh, Albert, that's marvellous!"

"And we just finished the last feed ten minutes ago. There's the bottle on the mantelpiece. Only one ounce left. She drank three. How's that?" He was grinning proudly, delighted with his achievement.

The woman quickly got down on her knees and peered at the baby.

"Don't she look better?" he asked eagerly. "Don't she look fatter in the face?"

"It may sound silly," the wife said, "but I actually think she does. Oh, Albert, you're a marvel! How did you do it?"

"She's turning the corner," he said. "That's all it is. Just like the doctor prophesied①, she's turning the corner."

"I pray to God you're right, Albert."

"Of course I'm right. From now on, you watch her go."

The woman was gazing lovingly at the baby.

"You look a lot better yourself too, Mabel."

"I feel wonderful. I'm sorry about last night."

"Let's keep it this way," he said. "I'll do all the night feeds in future. You do the day ones."

She looked up at him across the cot, frowning. "No," she said. "Oh no, I wouldn't allow you to do that."

"I don't want you to have a breakdown, Mabel."

"I won't, not now I've had some sleep."

---

① prophesy: *Verb* [with obj.] say that (a specified thing) will happen in the future 预言;预告;预知(e.g. Jacques was prophesying a bumper harvest. 雅克预言有一场大丰收。)

"Much better we share it."

"No, Albert. This is my job and I intend to do it. Last night won't happen again."

There was a pause. Albert Taylor took the pipe out of his mouth and examined the grain on the bowl. "All right," he said. "In that case I'll just relieve you of the donkey work①, I'll do all the sterilizing② and the mixing of the food and getting everything ready. That'll help you a bit, anyway."

She looked at him carefully, wondering what could have come over him all of a sudden.

"You see, Mabel, I've been thinking..."

"Yes, dear."

"I've been thinking that up until last night I've never even raised a finger to help you with this baby."

"That isn't true."

"Oh yes it is. So I've decided that from now on I'm going to do my share of the work. I'm going to be the feed-mixer and the bottle-sterilizer. Right?"

"It's very sweet of you, dear, but I really don't think it's necessary..."

"Come on!" he cried. "Don't change the luck! I done it the last three times and just look what happened! When's the next one? Two o'clock, isn't it?"

---

① donkey work: *Noun* [mass noun] (informal) the boring or laborious part of a job; drudgery(非正式)累活;苦工(e. g. supervisors who get a research student to do the donkey work 找研究生干杂活的导师)

② sterilize or sterilise: *Verb* [with obj.] make (something) free from bacteria or other living micro-organisms 消毒;使无菌(e. g. Babies' feeding equipment can be cleaned and sterilized. 婴儿的喂养工具可以洗净和消毒。)

"Yes."

"It's all mixed," he said. "Everything's all mixed and ready and all you've got to do when the time comes is to go out there to the larder① and take it off the shelf and warm it up. That's some help, isn't it?"

The woman got up off her knees and went over to him and kissed him on the cheek. "You're such a nice man," she said. "I love you more and more every day I know you."

Later, in the middle of the afternoon, when Albert was outside in the sunshine working among the hives, he heard her calling to him from the house.

"Albert!" she shouted. "Albert, come here!" She was running through the buttercups② towards him.

He started forward to meet her, wondering what was wrong.

"Oh, Albert! Guess what!"

"What?"

"I've just finished giving her the two-o'clock feed and she's taken the whole lot!"

"No!"

"Every drop of it! Oh, Albert, I'm so happy! She's going to be all right! She's turned the corner just like you said!" She came up to him and threw her arms around his neck and hugged him, and he clapped her on the back and laughed and said what a marvellous little mother she was.

---

① larder: *Noun* a room or large cupboard for storing food(家中的)食物贮藏室;食物橱;大食品柜

② buttercup: *Noun* a herbaceous plant with bright yellow cup-shaped flowers, which is common in grassland and as a garden weed. All kinds are poisonous and generally avoided by livestock 毛茛;金凤花(e.g. The fields were golden with buttercups. 田里是一片金黄色的金凤花。)

"Will you come in and watch the next one and see if she does it again, Albert?"

He told her he wouldn't miss it for anything, and she hugged him again, then turned and ran back to the house, skipping over the grass and singing all the way.

Naturally, there was a certain amount of suspense in the air as the time approached for the six o'clock feed. By five thirty both parents were already seated in the living-room waiting for the moment to arrive. The bottle with the milk formula in it was standing in a saucepan of warm water on the mantelpiece. The baby was asleep in its carry-cot on the sofa.

At twenty minutes to six it woke up and started screaming its head off.

"There you are!" Mrs. Taylor cried. "She's asking for the bottle. Pick her up quick, Albert, and hand her to me here. Give me the bottle first."

He gave her the bottle, then placed the baby on the woman's lap. Cautiously, she touched the baby's lips with the end of the nipple. The baby seized the nipple between its gums and began to suck ravenously① with a rapid powerful action.

"Oh, Albert, isn't it wonderful?" she said, laughing.

"It's terrific, Mabel."

In seven or eight minutes, the entire contents of the bottle had disappeared down the baby's throat.

"You clever girl," Mrs. Taylor said. "Four ounces again."

Albert Taylor was leaning forward in his chair, peering intently into the baby's face. "You know what?" he said. "She even seems as though she's put on a touch of weight already. What do you think?"

---

① ravenous: *Adjective* extremely hungry 饿极的

The mother looked down at the child.

"Don't she seem bigger and fatter to you, Mabel, than she was yesterday?"

"Maybe she does, Albert. I'm not sure. Although actually there couldn't be any real gain in such a short time as this. The important thing is that she's eating normally."

"She's turned the corner," Albert said. "I don't think you need worry about her any more."

"I certainly won't."

"You want me to go up and fetch the cradle back into our own bedroom, Mabel?"

"Yes, please," she said.

Albert went upstairs and moved the cradle. The woman followed with the baby, and after changing its nappy, she laid it gently down on its bed. Then she covered it with sheet and blanket.

"Doesn't she look lovely, Albert?" she whispered. "Isn't that the most beautiful baby you've ever seen in your entire life?"

"Leave her be now, Mabel," he said. "Come on downstairs and cook us a bit of supper. We both deserve it."

After they had finished eating, the parents settled themselves in armchairs in the living-room, Albert with his magazine and his pipe, Mrs. Taylor with her knitting. But this was a very different scene from the one of the night before. Suddenly, all tensions had vanished. Mrs. Taylor's handsome oval face was glowing with pleasure, her cheeks were pink, her eyes were sparkling bright, and her mouth was fixed in a little dreamy smile of pure content. Every now and again she would glance up from her knitting and gaze affectionately at her husband. Occasionally, she would stop the clicking of her needles altogether for a few seconds and sit quite still, looking at the ceiling, listening for a cry or a whimper① from upstairs. But all was quiet.

"Albert," she said after a while.

"Yes, dear?"

"What was it you were going to tell me last night when you came rushing up to the bedroom? You said you had an idea for the baby."

Albert Taylor lowered the magazine on to his lap and gave her a long sly look.

"Did I?" he said.

"Yes." She waited for him to go on, but he didn't.

"What's the big joke?" she asked. "Why are you grinning like that?"

"It's a joke all right," he said.

"Tell it to me, dear."

"I'm not sure I ought to," he said. "You might call me a liar."

She had seldom seen him looking so pleased with himself as he was now, and she smiled back at him, egging him on.

"I'd just like to see your face when you hear it, Mabel, that's all."

"Albert, what is all this?"

He paused, refusing to be hurried.

"You do think the baby's better, don't you?" he asked.

"Of course I do."

"You agree with me that all of a sudden she's feeding marvellously and looking one hundred percent different?"

"I do, Albert, yes."

---

① whimper: *Noun* a low, feeble sound expressive of such emotions 抽泣声；呜咽声(e.g. She gave a little whimper of protest. 她发出小声的抗议。)

"That's good," he said, the grin widening. "You see, it's me that did it."

"Did what?"

"I cured the baby."

"Yes, dear, I'm sure you did." Mrs. Taylor went right on with her knitting.

"You don't believe me, do you?"

"Of course I believe you, Albert. I give you all the credit, every bit of it."

"Then how did I do it?"

"Well," she said, pausing a moment to think. "I suppose it's simply that you're a brilliant feed-mixer. Ever since you started mixing the feeds she's got better and better."

"You mean there's some sort of an art in mixing the feeds?"

"Apparently there is." She was knitting away and smiling quietly to herself, thinking how funny men were.

"I'll tell you a secret," he said. "You're absolutely right. Although, mind you, it isn't so much how you mix it that counts. It's what you put in. You realize that, don't you, Mabel?"

Mrs. Taylor stopped knitting and looked up sharply at her husband. "Albert," she said, "don't tell me you've been putting things into that child's milk?"

He sat there grinning.

"Well, have you or haven't you?"

"It's possible," he said.

"I don't believe it."

He had a strange fierce way of grinning that showed his teeth.

"Albert," she said. "Stop playing with me like this."

"Yes, dear, all right."

"You haven't really put anything into her milk, have you? Answer me properly, Albert. This could be serious with such a tiny baby."

"The answer is yes, Mabel."

"Albert Taylor! How could you?"

"Now don't get excited," he said. "I'll tell you all about it if you really want me to, but for heaven's sake keep your hair on①."

"It was beer!" she cried. "I just know it was beer!"

"Don't be so daft, Mabel, please."

"Then what was it?"

Albert laid his pipe down carefully on the table beside him and leaned back in his chair. "Tell me," he said, "did you ever by any chance happen to hear me mentioning something called royal jelly?"

"I did not."

"It's magic," he said. "Pure magic. And last night I suddenly got the idea that if I was to put some of this into the baby's milk..."

"How dare you!"

"Now, Mabel, you don't even know what it is yet."

"I don't care what it is," she said. "You can't go putting foreign bodies like that into a tiny baby's milk. You must be mad."

"It's perfectly harmless, Mabel, otherwise I wouldn't have done it. It comes from bees."

"I might have guessed that."

"And it's so precious that practically no one can afford to take it. When they do, it's only one little drop at a time."

"And how much did you give to our baby, might I ask?"

"Ah," he said, "that's the whole point. That's where the difference lies. I reckon that our baby, just in the last four feeds, has already

---

① keep your hair on: (Brit. informal) used to urge someone not to panic or lose their temper(非正式英国英语用法)(用于劝告)保持镇静！别发脾气！别激动！

swallowed about fifty times as much royal jelly as anyone else in the world has ever swallowed before. How about that?"

"Albert, stop pulling my leg."

"I swear it," he said proudly.

She sat there staring at him, her brow wrinkled, her mouth slightly open.

"You know what this stuff actually costs, Mabel, if you want to buy it? There's a place in America advertising it for sale at this very moment for something like five hundred dollars a pound jar! Five hundred dollars! That's more than gold, you know!"

She hadn't the faintest idea what he was talking about.

"I'll prove it," he said, and he jumped up and went across to the large bookcase where he kept all his literature about bees. On the top shelf, the back numbers① of the *American Bee Journal* were neatly stacked alongside those of the *British Bee Journal*, *Beecraft*, and other magazines. He took down the last issue of the *American Bee Journal* and turned to a page of small classified advertisements at the back.

"Here you are," he said. "Exactly as I told you. '*We sell royal jelly— $480 per lb.* ② *jar wholesale.*' "

He handed her the magazine so she could read it herself.

"Now do you believe me? This is an actual shop in New York, Mabel. It says so."

"It doesn't say you can go stirring it into the milk of a practically new-born baby," she said. "I don't know what's come over you, Albert, I really don't."

---

① back number: *Noun* an issue of a periodical earlier than the current one 过期期刊

② lb.: *Abbreviation* (Latin) pound(s) (in weight)(拉丁语)(重量单位)同"pound"或"pounds"

"It's curing her, isn't it?"

"I'm not so sure about that, now."

"Don't be so damn silly, Mabel. You know it is."

"Then why haven't other people done it with their babies?"

"I keep telling you," he said. "It's too expensive. Practically nobody in the world can afford to buy royal jelly just for eating except maybe one or two multimillionaires. The people who buy it are the big companies that make women's face creams① and things like that. They're using it as a stunt②. They mix a tiny pinch③ of it into a big jar of face cream and it's selling like hot cakes④ for absolutely enormous prices. They claim it takes out the wrinkles."

"And does it?"

"Now how on earth would I know that, Mabel? Anyway," he said, returning to his chair, "that's not the point. The point is this. It's done so much good to our little baby just in the last few hours that I think we ought to go right on giving it to her. Now don't interrupt, Mabel. Let me finish. I've got two hundred and forty hives out there and if I turn over maybe a hundred of them to making royal jelly, we ought to be able to supply her with all she wants."

"Albert Taylor," the woman said, stretching her eyes wide and

---

① face cream: *Noun* [mass noun] cosmetic cream applied to the face to improve the complexion 面霜

② stunt: *Noun* something unusual done to attract attention 引人注目的花招；吸引人的举动；噱头(e. g. The story was spread as a publicity stunt to help sell books. 这个故事是为了帮助卖书而散布的噱头。)

③ pinch: *Noun* an amount of an ingredient that can be held between fingers and thumb 一小撮；少量(e. g. Add a pinch of salt. 加上一小撮盐。)

④ sell like hot cakes: (informal) be sold quickly and in large quantities(非正式)销路很好；卖得快又多

staring at him. "Have you gone out of your mind?"

"Just hear me through, will you please?"

"I forbid it," she said, "absolutely. You're not to give my baby another drop of that horrid jelly, you understand?"

"Now, Mabel..."

"And quite apart from that, we had a shocking honey crop last year, and if you go fooling around with those hives now, there's no telling what might not happen."

"There's nothing wrong with my hives, Mabel."

"You know very well we had only half the normal crop last year."

"Do me a favour, will you?" he said. "Let me explain some of the marvellous things this stuff does."

"You haven't even told me what it is yet."

"All right, Mabel. I'll do that too. Will you listen? Will you give me a chance to explain it?"

She sighed and picked up her knitting once more. "I suppose you might as well get it off your chest, Albert. Go on and tell me."

He paused, a bit uncertain now how to begin. It wasn't going to be easy to explain something like this to a person with no detailed knowledge of apiculture① at all.

"You know, don't you," he said, "that each colony has only one queen?"

"Yes."

"And that this queen lays all the eggs?"

"Yes, dear. That much I know."

"All right. Now the queen can actually lay two different kinds of

---

① apiculture: *Noun* technical term for bee-keeping 同"bee-keeping",养蜂;养蜂业

eggs. You didn't know that, but she can. It's what we call one of the miracles of the hive. She can lay eggs that produce drones, and she can lay eggs that produce workers. Now if that isn't a miracle, Mabel, I don't know what is."

"Yes, Albert, all right."

"The drones are the males. We don't have to worry about them. The workers are all females. So is the queen, of course. But the workers are unsexed females, if you see what I mean. Their organs are completely undeveloped, whereas the queen is tremendously sexy. She can actually lay her own weight in eggs in a single day."

He hesitated, marshalling his thoughts.

"Now what happens is this. The queen crawls around on the comb and lays her eggs in what we call cells. You know all those hundreds of little holes you see in a honeycomb? Well, a brood comb is just about the same except the cells don't have honey in them, they have eggs. She lays one egg to each cell, and in three days each of these eggs hatches out into a tiny grub①. We call it a larva."

"Now, as soon as this larva appears, the nurse bees—they're young workers all crowd round and start feeding it like mad. And you know what they feed it on?"

"Royal jelly," Mabel answered patiently.

"Right!" he cried. "That's exactly what they do feed it on. They get this stuff out of a gland in their heads and they start pumping it into the cell to feed the larva. And what happens then?"

He paused dramatically, blinking at her with his small watery-grey eyes. Then he turned slowly in his chair and reached for the magazine that he had been reading the night before.

---

① grub: *Noun* the larva of an insect, especially a beetle 蛴螬;昆虫的幼虫

"You want to know what happens then?" he asked, wetting his lips.

"I can hardly wait."

"'*Royal jelly*,'" he read aloud, "'*must be a substance of tremendous nourishing power, for on this diet alone, the honeybee larva increases in weight fifteen hundred times in five days*!'"

"How much?"

"Fifteen hundred times, Mabel. And you know what that means if you put it in terms of a human being? It means," he said, lowering his voice, leaning forward, fixing her with those small pale eyes, "it means that in five days a baby weighing seven and a half pounds to start off with would increase in weight to five tons!"

For the second time, Mrs. Taylor stopped knitting.

"Now you mustn't take that too literally, Mabel."

"Who says I mustn't?"

"It's just a scientific way of putting it, that's all."

"Very well, Albert. Go on."

"But that's only half the story," he said. "There's more to come. The really amazing thing about royal jelly, I haven't told you yet. I'm going to show you now how it can transform a plain dull-looking little worker bee with practically no sex organs at all into a great big beautiful fertile queen."

"Are you saying our baby is dull-looking and plain?" she asked sharply.

"Now don't go putting words into my mouth, Mabel, please. Just listen to this. Did you know that the queen bee and the worker bee, although they are completely different when they grow up, are both hatched out of exactly the same kind of egg?"

"I don't believe that," she said.

"It's as true as I'm sitting here, Mabel, honest it is. Any time the bees want a queen to hatch out of the egg instead of a worker, they can do it."

"How?"

"Ah," he said, shaking a thick forefinger in her direction. "That's just what I'm coming to. That's the secret of the whole thing. Now what do you think it is, Mabel, that makes this miracle happen?"

"Royal jelly," she answered. "You already told me."

"Royal jelly it is!" he cried, clapping his hands and bouncing up on his seat. His big round face was glowing with excitement now, and two vivid① patches of scarlet had appeared high up on each cheek.

"Here's how it works. I'll put it very simply for you. The bees want a new queen. So they build an extra-large cell, a queen cell we call it, and they get the old queen to lay one of her eggs in there, The other one thousand nine hundred and ninety-nine eggs she lays in ordinary worker cells. Now. As soon as these eggs hatch into larvae, the nurse bees rally② round and start pumping in the royal jelly. All of them get it, workers as well as queen. But here's the vital thing, Mabel, so listen carefully. Here's where the difference comes. The worker larvae only receive this special marvellous food for the first three days of their larval life, after that they have a complete change of diet. What really happens is they get weaned③, except that it's not like an ordinary weaning because it's so sudden. After the third day they're put straight away on to more or less routine bees' food—a mixture of honey and pollen and

---

① vivid: *Adjective* (of a colour) intensely deep or bright(色彩)浓重的;鲜艳的

② rally: *Verb* assemble in a mass meeting 集合(e. g. Up to 50 000 people rallied in the city centre. 多达 50 000 人聚集在市中心。)

③ wean: *Verb* [with obj.] accustom (an infant or other young mammal) to food other than its mother's milk 使(婴儿、哺乳动物幼崽)断奶

then about two weeks later they emerge from the cells as workers."

"But not so the larva in the queen cell! This one gets royal jelly all the way through its larval life. The nurse bees simply pour it into the cell, so much so in fact that the little larva is literally floating in it. And that's what makes it into a queen!"

"You can't prove it," she said.

"Don't talk so damn silly, Mabel, please. Thousands of people have proved it time and time again, famous scientists in every country in the world. All you have to do is take a larva out of a worker cell and put it in a queen cell that's what we call grafting—and just so long as the nurse bees keep it well supplied with royal jelly, then presto! —it'll grow up into a queen! And what makes it more marvellous still is the absolutely enormous difference between a queen and a worker when they grow up. The abdomen is a different shape. The sting is different. The legs are different. The..."

"In what way are the legs different?" she asked, testing him.

"The legs? Well, the workers have little pollen baskets① on their legs for carrying the pollen. The queen has none. Now here's another thing. The queen has fully developed sex organs. The workers don't. And most amazing of all, Mabel, the queen lives for an average of four to six years. The worker hardly lives that many months. And all this difference simply because one of them got royal jelly and the other didn't!"

"It's pretty hard to believe," she said, "that a food can do all that."

"Of course it's hard to believe. It's another of the miracles of the

---

① pollen basket: *Noun* (Entomology) a flattened area fringed with hairs on the hind leg of a social bee, used for carrying pollen(昆虫学)(工蜂后腿上的)花粉筐

hive. In fact it's the biggest ruddy① miracle of them all. It's such a hell of a big miracle that it's baffled the greatest men of science for hundreds of years. Wait a moment. Stay here. Don't move."

Again he jumped up and went over to the bookcase and started rummaging among the books and magazines.

"I'm going to find you a few of the reports. Here we are. Here's one of them. Listen to this." He started reading aloud from a copy of the *American Bee Journal*:

"*Living in Toronto② at the head of a fine research laboratory given to him by the people of Canada in recognition of his truly great contribution to humanity in the discovery of insulin③, Dr. Frederick A. Banting④ became curious about royal jelly. He requested his staff to do a basic fractional analysis...*"

---

① ruddy: *Adjective* (Brit. informal, dated) used as a euphemism for "bloody"(非正式英国英语的古旧用法)非常的;极度的;十足的;该死的(用作"bloody"的委婉语)

② Toronto: *Noun* the capital of Ontario and the largest city in Canada, situated on the north shore of Lake Ontario; pop. 612 300 (1991); metropolitan area pop. 3 550 000 (1991) 多伦多(安大略省省会,加拿大最大城市,位于安大略湖北岸;1991年市区人口612 300,城市人口3 550 000。)

③ insulin: *Noun* [mass noun] (Biochemistry) a hormone produced in the pancreas by the islets of Langerhans, which regulates the amount of glucose in the blood. The lack of insulin causes a form of diabetes(生物化学)胰岛素

④ Banting: *Noun* Sir Frederick Grant Banting (1891—1941), Canadian physiologist and surgeon. With the assistance of C. H. Best, Banting discovered insulin in 1921 ~ 1922, using it to treat the previously incurable and fatal disease diabetes. Nobel Prize for Physiology or Medicine (1923, shared with J. J. R. Macleod) 弗雷德里克·格兰特·班廷爵士(1891—1941):加拿大生理学家、外科医生,1921 ~ 1922年在C·H·贝斯特的协助下发现了胰岛素,并运用于治疗当时为不治之症的糖尿病,1923年与麦克劳德同获诺贝尔生理医学奖。

He paused.

"Well, there's no need to read it all, but here's what happened. Dr. Banting and his people took some royal jelly from queen cells that contained two-day-old larvae, and then they started analysing it. And what do you think they found?"

"They found," he said, "that royal jelly contained phenols①, sterols②, glycerils③, dextrose④, and—now here it comes—and eighty to eighty-five percent unidentified acids!"

He stood beside the bookcase with the magazine in his hand, smiling a funny little furtive⑤ smile of triumph, and his wife watched him, bewildered.

He was not a tall man; he had a thick plump⑥ pulpy-looking body that was built close to the ground on abbreviated legs. The legs were

---

① phenol: *Noun* [mass noun] (Chemistry) a mildly acidic toxic white crystalline solid obtained from coal tar and used in chemical manufacture, and in dilute form (under the name carbolic) as a disinfectant(化学)苯酚;石炭酸

② sterol: *Noun* (Biochemistry) any of a group of naturally occurring unsaturated steroid alcohols, typically waxy solids(生物化学)甾醇;固醇

③ glyceril: 这里的"glyceril"疑为"glycerol"之误。

glycerol: *Noun* a colourless, sweet, viscous liquid formed as a by-product in soap manufacture. It is used as an emollient and laxative, and for making explosives and antifreeze 甘油;丙三醇(被用作缓和剂和轻泻剂,并用于制造炸药和防冻剂)

④ dextrose: *Noun* [mass noun] (Chemistry) the dextrorotatory form of glucose (and the predominant naturally occurring form)(化学)右旋糖;葡萄糖

⑤ furtive: *Adjective* attempting to avoid notice or attention, typically because of guilt or a belief that discovery would lead to trouble; secretive 偷偷摸摸的;鬼鬼祟祟的;秘密的;遮遮掩掩的(e.g. They spent a furtive day together. 他们在一起偷偷摸摸地过了一天。)

⑥ plump: *Adjective* having a full rounded shape 饱满的;丰满的;圆润的(e.g. The berries were plump and sweet. 这些浆果饱满而甘甜。)

slightly bowed. The head was huge and round, covered with bristly① short-cut hair, and the greater part of the face—now that he had given up shaving altogether—was hidden by a brownish yellow fuzz② about an inch long. In one way and another, he was rather grotesque to look at, there was no denying that.

"Eighty to eighty-five percent," he said, "unidentified acids. Isn't that fantastic?" He turned back to the bookshelf and began hunting through the other magazines.

"What does it mean, unidentified acids?"

"That's the whole point! No one knows! Not even Banting could find out. You've heard of Banting?"

"No."

"He just happens to be about the most famous living doctor in the world today, that's all."

Looking at him now as he buzzed around in front of the bookcase with his bristly head and his hairy face and his plump pulpy body, she couldn't help thinking that somehow, in some curious way, there was a touch of the bee about this man. She had often seen women grow to look like the horses that they rode, and she had noticed that people who bred birds or bull terriers③ or pomeranians④ frequently resembled in some small but startling manner the creature of their choice. But up until now

---

① bristly: *Adjective* (of hair or foliage) having a stiff and prickly texture(毛发或树叶)坚硬扎人的

② fuzz: *Noun* a fluffy or frizzy mass of hair or fibre 蓬松(或卷曲)的毛发(或纤维、绒毛、卷毛)

③ bull terrier: *Noun* a short-haired dog of a breed that is a cross between a bulldog and a terrier 一种短毛猛犬;短毛杂种犬

④ Pomeranian: *Noun* a small dog of a breed with long silky hair, a pointed muzzle, and pricked ears 波美拉尼亚狗;波美拉尼亚犬

it had never occurred to her that her husband might look like a bee. It shocked her a bit.

"And did Banting ever try to eat it," she asked, "this royal jelly?"

"Of course he didn't eat it, Mabel. He didn't have enough for that. It's too precious."

"You know something?" she said, staring at him but smiling a little all the same. "You're getting to look just a teeny bit like a bee yourself, did you know that?"

He turned and looked at her.

"I suppose it's the beard mostly," she said. "I do wish you'd stop wearing it. Even the colour is sort of bee-ish, don't you think?"

"What the hell are you talking about, Mabel?"

"Albert," she said. "Your language."

"Do you want to hear any more of this or don't you?"

"Yes, dear, I'm sorry. I was only joking. Do go on."

He turned away again and pulled another magazine out of the bookcase and began leafing through the pages. "Now just listen to this, Mabel. '*In 1939, Heyl experimented with twenty-one-day-old rats, injecting them with royal jelly in varying amounts. As a result, he found a precocious*① *follicular*② *development of the ovaries*③ *directly in proportion to the quantity of royal jelly injected.*'"

"There!" she cried. "I knew it!"

---

① precocious: *Adjective* (of a child) having developed certain abilities or inclinations at an earlier age than usual(儿童)过早发育的;早熟的(e.g. He was a precocious, solitary boy. 他是个早熟的孤独男孩。)

② follicular: *Adjective* relating to, having, or resembling a follicle or follicles 小囊的;滤泡的;卵泡的

③ ovary: *Noun* a female reproductive organ in which ova or eggs are produced, present in humans and other vertebrates as a pair 卵巢

"Knew what?"

"I knew something terrible would happen."

"Nonsense. There's nothing wrong with that. Now here's another, Mabel. '*Still and Burdett found that a male rat which hitherto*① *had been unable to breed, upon receiving a minute daily dose of royal jelly, became a father many times over.*'"

"Albert," she cried, "this stuff is much too strong to give to a baby! I don't like it at all."

"Nonsense, Mabel."

"Then why do they only try it out on rats, tell me that? Why don't some of these famous scientists take it themselves? They're too clever, that's why. Do you think Dr. Banting is going to risk finishing up with precious ovaries? Not him."

"But they have given it to people, Mabel. Here's a whole article about it. Listen." He turned the page and again began reading from the magazine. "'*In Mexico, in 1953, a group of enlightened physicians began prescribing minute doses of royal jelly for such things as cerebral*②

---

① hitherto: *Adverb* until now or until the point in time under discussion 迄今为止;到某时为止

② cerebral: *Adjective* of the cerebrum of the brain 脑的;大脑的(e. g. a cerebral haemorrhage 脑溢血)

*neuritis*①, *arthritis*②, *diabetes*③, *autointoxication*④ *from tobacco, impotence*⑤ *in men, asthma*⑥, *croup*⑦, *and gout*⑧... *There are stacks of signed testimonials... A celebrated stock-broker in Mexico City contracted a particularly stubborn case of psoriasis*⑨. *He became physically unattractive.*

---

① neuritis: *Noun* [mass noun] (Medicine) inflammation of a peripheral nerve or nerves, usually causing pain and loss of function(医学)神经炎

② arthritis: *Noun* [mass noun] a disease causing painful inflammation and stiffness of the joints 关节炎

③ diabetes: *Noun* [mass noun] a disorder of the metabolism causing excessive thirst and the production of large amounts of urine 糖尿病;多尿症

④ autointoxication: *Noun* [mass noun] (Medicine) poisoning by a toxin formed within the body itself(医学)自身中毒;自体中毒

⑤ impotent: *Adjective* (of a man) abnormally unable to achieve an erection or orgasm(男人)阳痿的

⑥ asthma: *Noun* [mass noun] a respiratory condition marked by attacks of spasm in the bronchi of the lungs, causing difficulty in breathing. It is usually connected to allergic reaction or other forms of hypersensitivity 哮喘;气喘(常与过敏有关)

⑦ croup: *Noun* [mass noun] inflammation of the larynx and trachea in children, associated with infection and causing breathing difficulties 格鲁布;哮吼(因变态反应、异物、感染或新生物引起之急性喉阻塞,主要发生于婴儿和儿童,表现为共鸣性犬吠样咳、声嘶和持续喘鸣。)

⑧ gout: *Noun* [mass noun] a disease in which defective metabolism of uric acid causes arthritis, especially in the smaller bones of the feet, deposition of chalk-stones, and episodes of acute pain 痛风

⑨ psoriasis: *Noun* [mass noun] (Medicine) a skin disease marked by red, itchy, scaly patches(医学)牛皮癣;银屑病

*His clients began to forsake*① *him. His business began to suffer. In desperation he turned to royal jelly—one drop with every meal—and presto! —he was cured in a fortnight. A waiter in the Cafe Jena, also in Mexico City, reported that his father, after taking minute doses of this wonder substance in capsule form, sired*② *a healthy boy child at the age of ninety. A bullfight promoter in Acapulco*③, *finding himself landed with a rather lethargic*④*-looking bull, injected it with one gramme of royal jelly (an excessive dose) just before it entered the arena. Thereupon, the beast became so swift and savage that it promptly dispatched two picadors*⑤, *three horses, and a matador*⑥, *and finally...'"*

"Listen!" Mrs. Taylor said, interrupting him. "I think the baby's crying."

Albert glanced up from his reading. Sure enough, a lusty⑦ yelling noise was coming from the bedroom above.

"She must be hungry," he said.

His wife looked at the clock. "Good gracious me!" she cried,

---

① forsake: *Verb* [with obj.] (chiefly poetic/literary) abandon (someone or something)(主要用在诗歌/文学上)抛弃;遗弃(人或物)(e. g. He would never forsake Tara. 他永远不会抛弃塔拉。)

② sire: *Verb* [with obj.] be the male parent of (an animal)(雄性种兽)繁殖(幼兽)

③ Acapulco: *Noun* a port and resort in southern Mexico, on the Pacific coast; pop. 592 290 (1990) 阿卡普尔科(墨西哥南部港市及旅游胜地,在太平洋沿岸,1990年人口592 290。)

④ lethargic: *Adjective* affected by lethargy; sluggish and apathetic 懒散的;无力的;冷淡的(e. g. I felt tired and a little lethargic. 我觉得累,有点儿懒洋洋的。)

⑤ picador: *Noun* (in bullfighting) a person on horseback who goads the bull with a lance(斗牛用语)(骑马用长矛刺牛使之发怒的)斗牛士助手

⑥ matador: *Noun* a bullfighter whose task is to kill the bull 斗牛士

⑦ lusty: *Adjective* healthy and strong; full of vigour 强健的;精力充沛的

jumping up. "It's past her time again already! You mix the feed, Albert, quickly, while I bring her down! But hurry! I don't want to keep her waiting."

In half a minute, Mrs. Taylor was back, carrying the screaming infant in her arms. She was flustered① now, still quite unaccustomed to the ghastly nonstop racket② that a healthy baby makes when it wants its food. "Do be quick, Albert!" she called, settling herself in the armchair and arranging the child on her lap. "Please hurry!"

Albert entered from the kitchen and handed her the bottle of warm milk. "It's just right," he said. "You don't have to test it."

She hitched the baby's head a little higher in the crook of her arm, then pushed the rubber teat③ straight into the wide-open yelling mouth. The baby grabbed the teat and began to suck. The yelling stopped. Mrs. Taylor relaxed.

"Oh, Albert, isn't she lovely?"

"She's terrific, Mabel—thanks to royal jelly."

"Now, dear, I don't want to hear another word about that nasty stuff. It frightens me to death."

"You're making a big mistake," he said.

"We'll see about that."

The baby went on sucking the bottle.

---

① fluster: *Verb* [with obj.] [Often as adj. flustered] make (someone) agitated or confused 使慌张;使激动;使慌乱(e. g. Rosamund seemed rather flustered this morning. 罗莎蒙德今天早上似乎有些心神不宁。)

② racket: *Noun* [in sing.] a loud unpleasant noise; a din 喧嚷(声);吵闹(声);骚闹;纷乱(e. g. The kids were making a racket. 孩子们在大声喧哗。)

③ teat: *Noun* (Brit.) a thing resembling this, especially a perforated plastic bulb by which an infant or young animal can suck milk from a bottle(英国英语)橡皮奶头

"I do believe she's going to finish the whole lot again, Albert."

"I'm sure she is," he said.

And a few minutes later, the milk was all gone.

"Oh, what a good girl you are!" Mrs. Taylor cried, as very gently she started to withdraw the nipple. The baby sensed what she was doing and sucked harder, trying to hold on. The woman gave a quick little tug, and plop, out it came.

"Waa! Waa! Waa! Waa! Waa!" the baby yelled.

"Nasty old wind①," Mrs. Taylor said, hoisting the child on to her shoulder and patting its back.

It belched twice in quick succession.

"There you are, my darling, you'll be all right now."

For a few seconds, the yelling stopped. Then it started again.

"Keep belching her," Albert said. "She's drunk it too quick."

His wife lifted the baby back on to her shoulder. She rubbed its spine. She changed it from one shoulder to the other. She laid it on its stomach on her lap. She sat it up on her knee. But it didn't belch again, and the yelling became louder and more insistent every minute.

"Good for the lungs," Albert Taylor said, grinning. "That's the way they exercise their lungs, Mabel, did you know that?"

"There, there, there," the wife said, kissing it all over the face. "There, there, there."

They waited another five minutes, but not for one moment did the screaming stop.

"Change the nappy," Albert said. "It's got a wet nappy, that's all it is." He fetched a clean one from the kitchen, and Mrs. Taylor took

---

① wind: *Noun* [mass noun] (Brit.) air swallowed while eating or gas generated in the stomach and intestines by digestion(英国用法)肠气;胃气

the old one off and put the new one on.

This made no difference at all.

"Waa! Waa! Waa! Waa! Waa!" the baby yelled.

"You didn't stick the safety pin through the skin, did you, Mabel?"

"Of course I didn't," she said, feeling under the nappy with her fingers to make sure.

The parents sat opposite one another in their armchairs, smiling nervously, watching the baby on the mother's lap, waiting for it to tire and stop screaming.

"You know what?" Albert Taylor said at last.

"I'll bet she's still hungry. I'll bet all she wants is another swig① at that bottle. How about me fetching her an extra lot?"

"I don't think we ought to do that, Albert."

"It'll do her good," he said, getting up from his chair. "I'm going to warm her up a second helping②."

He went into the kitchen, and was away several minutes. When he returned he was holding a bottle brimful of milk.

"I made her a double," he announced. "Eight ounces. Just in case."

"Albert! Are you mad? Don't you know it's just as bad to overfeed as it is to underfeed?"

"You don't have to give her the lot, Mabel. You can stop any time you like. Go on," he said, standing over her. "Give her a drink."

Mrs. Taylor began to tease the baby's upper lip with the end of the nipple. The tiny mouth closed like a trap over the rubber teat and sud-

---

① swig: *Noun* [with obj.] a drink in large draughts 大口喝;痛饮

② helping: *Noun* a portion of food served to one person at one time(食物的)一份;一客

denly there was silence in the room. The baby's whole body relaxed and a look of absolute bliss came over its face as it started to drink.

"There you are, Mabel! What did I tell you?"

The woman didn't answer.

"She's ravenous, that's what she is. Just look at her suck."

Mrs. Taylor was watching the level of the milk in the bottle. It was dropping fast, and before long three or four ounces out of the eight had disappeared.

"There," she said. "That'll do."

"You can't pull it away now, Mabel."

"Yes, dear. I must."

"Go on, woman. Give her the rest and stop fussing."

"But Albert..."

"She's famished, can't you see that? Go on, my beauty," he said. "You finish that bottle."

"I don't like it, Albert," the wife said, but she didn't pull the bottle away.

"She's making up for lost time, Mabel, that's all she's doing."

Five minutes later the bottle was empty. Slowly, Mrs. Taylor withdrew the nipple, and this time there was no protest from the baby, no sound at all. It lay peacefully on the mother's lap, the eyes glazed with contentment, the mouth half-open, the lips smeared① with milk.

"Twelve whole ounces, Mabel!" Albert Taylor said. "Three times the normal amount! Isn't that amazing!"

The woman was staring down at the baby. And now the old anxious tight-lipped look of the frightened mother was slowly returning to her

---

① smear: *Verb* [with obj.] coat or mark (something) messily or carelessly with a greasy or sticky substance(用油或黏性物质随便胡乱)涂抹(某物)(e.g. His face was smeared with dirt. 他的脸上涂满了泥。)

face.

"What's the matter with you?" Albert asked. "You're not worried by that, are you? You can't expect her to get back to normal on a lousy four ounces, don't be ridiculous."

"Come here, Albert," she said.

"What?"

"I said come here."

He went over and stood beside her.

"Take a good look and tell me if you see anything different."

He peered closely at the baby. "She seems bigger, Mabel, if that's what you mean. Bigger and fatter."

"Hold her," she ordered. "Go on, pick her up."

He reached out and lifted the baby up off the mother's lap. "Good God!" he cried. "She weighs a ton!"

"Exactly."

"Now isn't that marvellous!" he cried, beaming. "I'll bet she must be back to normal already!"

"It frightens me, Albert. It's too quick."

"Nonsense, woman."

"It's that disgusting jelly that's done it," she said. "I hate the stuff."

"There's nothing disgusting about royal jelly," he answered, indignant.

"Don't be a fool, Albert! You think it's normal for a child to start putting on weight at this speed?"

"You're never satisfied!" he cried. "You're scared stiff when she's losing and now you're absolutely terrified because she's gaining! What's the matter with you, Mabel?"

The woman got up from her chair with the baby in her arms and started towards the door. "All I can say is," she said, "it's lucky I'm here to see you don't give her any more of it, that's all I can say." She went out, and Albert watched her through the open door as she crossed the hall to the foot of the stairs and started to ascend, and when she reached the third or fourth step she suddenly stopped and stood quite still for several seconds as though remembering something. Then she turned and came down again rather quickly and re-entered the room.

"Albert," she said.

"Yes?"

"I assume there wasn't any royal jelly in this last feed we've just given her?"

"I don't see why you should assume that, Mabel."

"Albert!"

"What's wrong?" he asked, soft and innocent.

"How dare you!" she cried.

Albert Taylor's great bearded face took on a pained and puzzled look. "I think you ought to be very glad she's got another big dose of it inside her," he said. "Honest I do. And this is a very big dose, Mabel, believe you me."

The woman was standing just inside the doorway clasping the sleeping baby in her arms and staring at her husband with huge eyes. She stood very erect, her body absolutely still with fury, her face paler, more tight-lipped than ever.

"You mark my words," Albert was saying, "you're going to have a nipper① there soon that'll win first prize in any baby show in the entire country. Hey, why don't you weigh her now and see what she is? You want me to get the scales, Mabel, so you can weigh her?"

---

① nipper: *Noun* (informal) a child, especially a small boy（非正式）小孩（尤指小男孩）

The woman walked straight over to the large table in the centre of the room and laid the baby down and quickly started taking off its clothes. "Yes!" she snapped. "Get the scales!" Off came the little nightgown, then the undervest.

Then she unpinned the nappy and she drew it away and the baby lay naked on the table.

"But Mabel!" Albert cried. "It's a miracle! She's fat as a puppy!"

Indeed, the amount of flesh the child had put on since the day before was astounding. The small sunken chest with the rib bones showing all over it was now plump and round as a barrel, and the belly was bulging high in the air. Curiously, though, the arms and legs did not seem to have grown in proportion. Still short and skinny, they looked like little sticks protruding from a ball of fat.

"Look!" Albert said. "She's even beginning to get a bit of fuzz on the tummy① to keep her warm!" He put out a hand and was about to run the tips of his fingers over the powdering of silky yellowy-brown hairs that had suddenly appeared on the baby's stomach.

"Don't you touch her!" the woman cried. She turned and faced him, her eyes blazing, and she looked suddenly like some kind of little fighting bird with her neck arched over towards him as though she were about to fly at his face and peck his eyes out.

"Now wait a minute," he said, retreating.

"You must be mad!" she cried.

"Now wait just one minute, Mabel, will you please, because if you're still thinking this stuff is dangerous... That is what you're

---

① tummy: *Noun* (informal) a person's stomach or abdomen(非正式)(人的)胃;肚子

thinking, isn't it? All right, then. Listen carefully. I shall now proceed to prove to you once and for all, Mabel, that royal jelly is absolutely harmless to human beings, even in enormous doses. For example—why do you think we had only half the usual honey crop last summer? Tell me that."

His retreat, walking backwards, had taken him three or four yards away from her, where he seemed to feel more comfortable.

"The reason we had only half the usual crop last summer," he said slowly, lowering his voice, "was because I turned one hundred of my hives over to the production of royal jelly."

"You what?"

"Ah," he whispered. "I thought that might surprise you a bit. And I've been making it ever since right under your very nose." His small eyes were glinting① at her, and a slow sly smile was creeping around the corners of his mouth.

"You'll never guess the reason, either," he said. "I've been afraid to mention it up to now because I thought it might... well... sort of embarrass you."

There was a slight pause. He had his hands clasped high in front of him, level with his chest, and he was rubbing one palm against the other, making a soft scraping noise.

"You remember that bit I read you out of the magazine? That bit about the rat? Let me see now, how does it go? '*Still and Burden found that a male rat which hitherto had been unable to breed...*'" He hesitated, the grin widening, showing his teeth.

"You get the message, Mabel?"

---

① glint: *Verb* (of a person's eyes) shine with a particular emotion(眼睛表达某种情感时)闪光(e.g. His eyes glinted angrily. 他的眼睛闪着愤怒的光芒。)

She stood quite still, facing him.

"The very first time I ever read that sentence, Mabel, I jumped straight out of my chair and I said to myself if it'll work with a lousy rat, I said, then there's no reason on earth why it shouldn't work with Albert Taylor."

He paused again, craning his head forward and turning one ear slightly in his wife's direction, waiting for her to say something. But she didn't.

"And here's another thing," he went on. "It made me feel so absolutely marvellous, Mabel, and so sort of completely different to what I was before that I went right on taking it even after you'd announced the joyful tidings①. Buckets of it I must have swallowed during the last twelve months."

The big heavy haunted-looking eyes of the woman were moving intently over the man's face and neck. There was no skin showing at all on the neck, not even at the sides below the ears. The whole of it, to a point where it disappeared into the collar of the shirt, was covered all the way around with those shortish silky hairs, yellowy black.

"Mind you," he said, turning away from her, gazing lovingly now at the baby, "it's going to work far better on a tiny infant than on a fully developed man like me. You've only got to look at her to see that, don't you agree?"

The woman's eyes travelled slowly downward and settled on the

① tidings: *Plural Noun* (poetic/literary) news; information(诗歌/文学)消息;音讯

baby. The baby was lying naked on the table, fat and white and comatose①, like some gigantic grub that was approaching the end of its larval life and would soon emerge into the world complete with mandibles② and wings.

"Why don't you cover her up, Mabel?" he said. "We don't want our little queen to catch a cold."

三、翻译探索

这篇故事中,达尔"卖弄"的是养蜂方面的知识,又将之跟故事情节完美结合到一起。翻译的难点,当然是在于跟蜜蜂有关的表达,要兼顾这方面的专业知识的理解和汉语表达的通畅。

魔力王浆

"艾伯特,这个小宝贝,我担心得要死。真的担心啊。"泰勒太太说。

她的眼睛始终没有离开这个婴儿。现在,婴儿正躺在她左胳膊的臂弯里,一动也不动。

"我就知道,有什么地方不对劲儿。"

婴儿脸部的皮肤如珍珠般颜色,呈半透明状,紧巴巴地沿骨骼表面铺展开来。

"再试一次。"艾伯特·泰勒说。

"一点儿用也没有。"

---

① comatose: *Adjective* (humorous) (of a person or thing) extremely exhausted, lethargic, or sleepy, typically as a result of overdrinking or taking drugs(幽默)(尤指饮酒过量或吸毒引起的)(人或事物)耗尽的;精疲力竭的;无精打采的;昏昏欲睡的

② mandible: *Noun* either half of the crushing organ in an arthropod's mouthparts(节肢动物的)口器上部(或下部)

“梅布尔,你必须不间断地尝试。”他说。

她把奶瓶从装有热水的深平底锅里取出来,晃了晃,然后把几滴牛奶滴到手腕内侧,试试温度是否合适。

“求求你,”她小声说,“求求你,我的小宝贝。醒醒啊,再喝点儿吧。”

她旁边的桌子上有一盏小灯,发出柔柔的黄色光,萦绕在她的周围。

“拜托了,”她说,“就再喝那么一小点儿吧。”

丈夫透过杂志上方看着她。他看得出,她整个人已经累得快支撑不住了。她那张椭圆形的脸,往常是那么的严肃和宁静,现在已经带有一点紧张和绝望的神色。说来奇怪的是,即便如此,她低头看着孩子时的样子还是那么可爱、漂亮。

“你看到了,”她嘟囔着,“没有用的,她就是不肯喝。”

她对着灯举起了奶瓶,眯起眼睛看着瓶子上的刻度。

“又喝下半两多一点儿,就喝下这么多。不——甚至没有这么多。只喝下了半两的四分之三,还不足以维持生命。艾伯特,这孩子维持生命都困难,我担心死了。”

“我知道。”他说。

“要是能查出问题所在,就好了。”

“什么问题都没有,梅布尔,只是时间的问题。”

“肯定有什么地方不对劲儿。”

“鲁宾逊医生说,什么问题都没有。”

“看看啊,”她边说边站了起来,“六周大的孩子体重越来越轻,比她出生时的体重下降了将近一公斤啊。你不能对我说,这事很自然吧。就看看她那两只瘦腿吧!不亚于皮包骨啊!”

这只微小的婴儿躺在她的臂弯里,无精打采、一动不动。

“鲁宾逊医生叫你不要担心,梅布尔,换了其他人也会要你这么做的。”

“哈!”她惊讶地叫道,“说的比唱的还好听!我怎么能不担心啊!”

“现在，梅布尔。”

“他要我怎么做呢？把这事当成某种玩笑吗？”

“他没有那么说。”

“我恨这些医生！我恨所有的医生！”她叫道。然后，抱着婴儿，晃动着身体，快步离开房间，向楼梯走去。

艾伯特·泰勒待在原地，任凭她走开。

没过多大一会儿，他听到她在头顶正上方的卧室里走来走去的声音。上方亚麻布油地毡上传来急促的“嗒嗒嗒”的脚步声，声音里充满了紧张、不安的情绪。紧接着，脚步声就听不见了，每当这时，他就会站起身来，跟上去。等他走进卧室，就一定会看到她跟往常一样坐在婴儿床的旁边，盯着婴儿轻声地哭着，任凭他如何劝说也不肯动地方。

“她饿坏了，艾伯特。”她一定会这样说。

“她肯定不饿。”

“她饿坏了。我就知道，她饿了，艾伯特，你知道吗？”

“知道什么？”

“我相信你也是知道的，但你不肯承认。我说的对吗？”

现在这段时间，每晚就是像这样度过的。

上周，他们又带孩子去医院了。医生仔细做了检查后说，这孩子根本没有什么大不了的问题。

“医生，我们花了九年时间才有这么一个孩子，”梅布尔当时这样说，“我想，她要是有什么三长两短的话，我就会活不下去的。”

从那时起，六天时间过去了。婴儿体重又减少近三两。

艾伯特·泰勒对自己说，担心是不管什么用的。这样的事，就得听医生的。他拿起仍然放在膝盖上的那本杂志，漫无目的地浏览着目录，看看这周有什么事情发生：

五月蜜蜂记事

蜂蜜烹调法

蜂农与蜂蜜药剂师

微粒子虫控制经验谈

蜂王浆的最新动态

本周蜂场信息

蜂胶的治愈力

反刍现象

英国养蜂人年度聚餐

协会新闻

在艾伯特·泰勒的一生中,只要是与蜜蜂有关的东西,他都会为之着迷。还是小孩子的时候,他就经常徒手捉蜜蜂,然后拿着蜜蜂往家跑,展示给母亲看。有时候,他会把蜜蜂放到脸部,任其在脸颊和脖子上乱爬。最令人称奇的是,他从来没有被蜜蜂蛰过。恰恰相反,蜜蜂似乎很喜欢跟他在一起。跟他在一起时,那些蜜蜂从来都没有要飞走的意思,所以嘛,为了驱走它们,他就不得不用手指轻轻地将它们一一弹掉。即便是这样,它们还是会屡屡飞回,再次落到他的胳膊上、手上,或者膝盖上。反正就是说,只要有皮肤裸露出来的地方,它们都会落到上面去。

他的做泥瓦匠的父亲说,这孩子身上一定具有巫婆的某种恶臭气息。这种令人生厌的气息从他皮肤的毛孔里渗出来,什么好处都没有,只能招引来像蜜蜂那样的昆虫。可是,他母亲却说,那是上帝赐予他的天赋,她甚至更进一步,把儿子跟圣弗朗西斯及其小鸟相提并论。

随着艾伯特·泰勒渐渐长大,他对蜜蜂的着迷程度已经演变成一种痴迷的状态。十二岁时,他就做了自己的第一只蜂箱。就在那年的夏天,他捉到了自己的第一窝蜜蜂。两年后,也就是他十四岁那年,他的蜂箱数量就不下五只了。在他父亲那个小小的后院里,这些蜂箱紧靠着栅栏,整整齐齐地一字排开。除了让蜜蜂正常地产蜜之外,他已经开始做些微妙而复杂的活计,就是自己饲养蜂王,自己把幼虫移嫁到人工蜂窝中,还有一些诸如此类的活计。

在蜂箱内部操作时,他从不使用烟熏的方法,手上从来不戴手套，头上从来不蒙网罩。很明显，这个男孩跟蜜蜂之间有着某种奇怪的、情感上的和谐关系。村子上下、店铺里、酒馆里，人们开始用一种尊敬的口吻谈论他，也开始纷纷登门买他的蜂蜜。

十八岁时，他租下六亩多的一块高低不平的牧场。这块牧场位于山谷的下方，沿着一片樱桃园伸展开来，离村子有三里多地。于是，他就着手在那儿建立起自己的生意场。到现在为止，十一年过去了，他仍然留在原地未动，但是，拥有的却不是六亩多地，而是三十六亩多，还拥有两百四十只贮备情况良好的蜂箱，以及一座小房子。那房子的大部分是他亲手建的。二十岁时，他结了婚，婚姻很成功，但有一个不争的事实就是，夫妻俩花了九年的时间才有了这么一个孩子。实际上，对于艾伯特而言，一切都是相当的顺利。但是，这个奇怪的小女儿一降生，情况就不一样了。她拒绝适量进食，体重一天天下降。这可把夫妻俩吓着了，吓得不知所措。

他杂志也看不下去了，抬起头，开始考虑女儿的问题。

就拿今天晚上来说吧。开始喂奶时，女儿睁开了眼睛。他凝视着她那双眼睛，从中他看出了某种令他吓得要死的东西：一种迷蒙的、傻傻的目光，那目光有点发空的感觉。那双眼睛好像根本没有与大脑连在一起，而是松松垮垮地放在眼窝里，就像弹子球游戏中用的一对弹子。

那些医生真的很在行吗？

他伸手够来一只烟灰缸，开始用一根火柴杆慢慢地把烟灰从烟斗锅里抠出来。

如果有必要，总是可以把她送到另一家医院，或许可以送到牛津某地的医院。这一点，上楼的时候他或许可以跟梅布尔建议一下。

他仍然可以听到她在楼上的卧室里走来走去的声音，但是现在，她可能已经脱下鞋子，换上了拖鞋，因为脚步声很是微弱。

他又把注意力转移到杂志上，接着阅读起来。看完一篇名为《微粒子虫控制经验谈》的文章后，就翻过一页，开始读下一篇《蜂王浆的最新动态》。在这一方面，是否还有什么他不知道的事情呢？可以说，对此他是了如指掌的。

“这种很美妙的、被称作蜂王浆的东西是什么呢?”

他伸手拿来身旁桌子上的那个烟草盒,一边阅读,一边往烟斗里装填烟草。

蜂王浆是一种腺分泌物。这种东西是由保育蜂分泌出来的,用来喂养刚刚从卵里孵化出来的幼虫。蜜蜂用咽腺分泌出这种物质,这跟脊椎动物用乳腺分泌出乳汁几乎相差无几。这个事实本身具有生物学上的伟大意义,因为这个世界上没有任何其他种类的昆虫进化出这样一套分泌程序。

他对自己说,这都是老生常谈,但是,反正没有其他更好的事情能做,他就继续往下读。

所有幼虫从卵里孵化出来之后,在起初的三天时间里,就会被大量喂食蜂王浆。但是,三天过后,对于所有那些命中注定要成为雄蜂或者工蜂的幼虫来说,就用蜂蜜和花粉把这种宝贵的食物稀释后,再喂养它们。另一方面,对于命中注定要成为蜂王的幼虫,在它们整个幼虫生长期,就用纯王浆大量喂养它们。蜂王浆由此得名。

在他的头顶,就在楼上的卧室里,脚步声已经完全听不见了。整座房子也随之安静下来。他擦着一根火柴,放到烟斗上。

蜂王浆一定是一种营养无比丰富的物质,因为单单靠吃这一种食物,蜜蜂幼虫的体重就会在五天之内增加一千五百倍。

他想,那样说还真是八九不离十。但是,出于某种原因,他以前从来没有想到要把幼虫的生长期跟体重联系起来。

这就好比一个体重不到三公斤半的婴儿，在同一时期内，体重增加到五吨。

艾伯特·泰勒停了下来，又读了一遍上面那句话。

接着，他又读了一遍，已经是第三遍了。

这就好比一个体重不到三公斤半的婴儿……

"梅布尔！"他从椅子上跳了起来喊道，"梅布尔！快来啊！"

他走进门厅，站在楼梯底端，喊她下来。

但是，没有回应。

他跑上楼梯，打开了楼梯顶部平台上的电灯开关，发现卧室的门紧闭着。于是，他穿过平台，打开卧室的门，站到门里，往黑暗的房间里看去。"梅布尔！"他喊道，"来楼下一会儿，好吗？我有一点儿想法，是关于咱婴儿的想法。"

他身后平台上的灯光微弱地投射到床上。现在，他也能借此模糊看见她，她正俯卧在床，头埋进枕头里，两只胳膊搭在头上。她又哭了。

"梅布尔，"他说完，朝她走去，摸了摸她的一只肩膀，"拜托，下楼一会儿吧。我要说的或许很重要。"

"走开，"她说，"我想一个人待着。"

"我的想法，难道你不想听吗？"

"哦，艾伯特，我很累啊，"她抽泣着说道，"我累得很，连自己要做什么都不知道了。我想，我无法支撑下去；我想，我无法忍耐下去。"

一阵沉默之后，艾伯特·泰勒转身离开她，慢慢地走向摇篮，朝里面看去，婴儿正躺在那里。房间里太黑了，他看不清孩子的脸，但当他弯腰凑近的时候，能听见呼吸声——很微弱，却很急促。"下一次什么时间喂奶呢？"他问。

"我想，是两点吧。"

"再下一次呢？"

"早上六点。"

“那么，两次都我来吧，”他说，“你就睡觉吧。”

她没有吱声。

“梅布尔，你就上床好好睡吧，脱下外衣、倒头就睡，明白吗？什么都不要牵挂。接下来的十二小时，你就完完全全交给我好了。再像这样下去，你非得把自己的神经弄垮了不可。”

“好吧，”她说，“我知道了。”

“目前，我把孩子，还有闹钟都挪到空房间去。这样，你就能躺下，放松身心，忘掉一切。可以吗？”说着说着，他就已经推着摇篮，穿过了房门。

“噢，艾伯特。”她抽泣着说。

“什么都不要担心，交给我好了。”

“艾伯特……”

“什么事？”

“我爱你，艾伯特。”

“梅布尔，我也爱你。现在，睡觉吧。”

艾伯特·泰勒再一次看到妻子时，已经是第二天上午将近十一点了。

“我的老天啊！”她一边沿着楼梯往下跑，一边叫道。她身穿睡袍、脚踩拖鞋就下来了。“艾伯特！看看几点了啊！我睡了至少十二小时啊！一切都好吗？怎么样？”

他正安静地坐在扶手椅上，抽着烟斗、读着晨报。他脚边的地板上放了一个手提式的婴儿床，孩子正躺在那里睡觉呢。

“嗨，亲爱的。”他微笑着打了招呼。

她跑向婴儿床，向里看去。“艾伯特，她喝点没有呢？你给她喂几次了？按照预计，十点的时候，应该再喂一次的，你知道吗？”

艾伯特·泰勒把报纸整整齐齐地折成一个长条，然后在靠墙的桌子上放好。“早晨两点喂的时候，”他说，“她喝下半两都不到，仅此而已。六点喂的时候，情况就更好一点了，喝下一两多……”

“一两多！噢，艾伯特，那真是奇妙啊！”

“还有呢，最后一次喂的时间是十分钟前。你看看壁炉台上的那只奶瓶吧。里面只剩下半两多一点儿，她喝下将近二两了。怎么样？”他很有成就感，张嘴一笑，笑中带有愉悦和自豪。

这位妻子立即在婴儿床边跪了下来，看着孩子。

“她看起来气色是否好多了？”他急切地问道，“小脸儿看起来是否胖了一点？”

“听起来也许愚蠢可笑，”妻子说，“但我真地认为，你说的没错。噢，艾伯特，你真了不起啊！你怎么做到的？”

“她正在好转，”他说，“仅此而已。就像医生预言的那样，她正在好转。”

“艾伯特，我向老天祈祷，保佑你说的正确无误。”

“我说的，当然正确无误。从现在起，你就瞧着她好起来吧。”

这位妇女看着孩子，眼中充满了爱意。

“梅布尔，你自己看起来也好多了。”

“我感觉好极了。昨晚的事儿，我很抱歉。”

“我们这样办吧，”他说，“以后，晚上喂奶的事我全包了，你只负责白天的。”

她从小床的另一端抬起头，皱起眉头，看了他一眼。“不，”她说，“噢，不。我不愿意你那样做。”

“梅布尔，我不想让你的身体垮掉。”

“我不愿意，不愿意你那样做，何况我已经睡得差不多了。”

“我们共同承担，情况会好得多。”

“不，艾伯特。这是我的工作，我也打算完全承担。昨晚的事儿，不会再发生的。”

暂停了一会儿。艾伯特·泰勒从嘴上移开烟斗，看了看烟斗锅里的烟草燃烧后的纹理。“好吧，”他说，“就依你吧。但是，我就做点单调乏味的工作，以减轻点儿你的负担。我就干点消毒、搅拌的事儿，把喂奶前的一切工作都帮你做好。不管怎么说，那样做，也能多少帮上你一点儿。”

她抬起头仔仔细细地看着他，心里感到纳闷儿：有什么东西促使他突然间来了个一百八十度的大转弯儿呢？

“你知道的,梅布尔,我一直在想……”

“亲爱的,想什么呢?”

“我一直在想,直到到昨天晚上,在帮你拉扯孩子这方面,我甚至连一根手指头也没抬一下。”

“你说的不是事实。”

“噢,我说的是实话。所以,从现在起,我要尽我一份力。我就搅拌孩子喝的东西,给奶瓶消消毒,可以吗?”

“你真是可爱、体贴啊,亲爱的。但是我认为,没有那个必要……”

“得啦!”他喊道,“别把好运转走了!我已经喂过三次,你只需看看结果啊!下一次什么时间?两点,对吗?”

“对。”

“都搅拌好了,”他说,“所有要喂的都已经搅拌好了。到喂奶的时候,你所要做的就是到食品柜去取一下,然后再热一下。那就算是我帮上忙了,是不是呢?”

这位妻子站了起来,走到他身边,亲了下他的脸颊。“你真是太好了,”她说,“我越来越爱你,一天比一天更了解你了。”

后来,在下午过去一半的时候,他听到她从房子里喊他,当时他正在外面的阳光下侍弄蜂箱呢。

“艾伯特!”她叫道,“艾伯特,过来呀!”她正穿过一片金凤花向他跑来。

他迎上前,想知道有什么不妥的事情发生。

“噢,艾伯特!猜猜发生什么啦!”

“什么?”

“两点钟那顿我刚刚喂完,她全都喝光了啊!”

“不会吧!”

“一滴也不剩啊!噢,艾伯特,我太高兴了!她就要好起来啦!就像你说的,她正在好转啊!”她走近他,双臂缠着他的脖子,拥抱起来。他拍了拍她的后背,开心地笑了,说着她是一位多么不可思议的、可爱的母亲之类的话语。

“艾伯特,下一次喂奶的时候,你能进来看看她是如何又一次喝下去的吗?”

他告诉她说,不管怎么忙他也不会错过的,她听后又拥抱了他一下,然后转过身,往家跑,边跑边在草地上跳跃,还一路唱着歌。

六点钟那次喂奶时间快要到来的时候,某种悬念就开始飘荡开来,这是自然而然的。到五点三十分的时候,父母俩就已经安稳地坐在起居室里,等待这一时刻的到来。壁炉台上放了一个装有热水的深平底锅,里面放了一只奶瓶,里面装的是按照配方搅拌好的牛奶。沙发上那个手提式的婴儿床里,孩子正在睡觉。

五点四十分时,孩子醒了。一醒来,就开始拼命“哇哇”地哭闹个不停。

“瞧瞧啊!”泰勒太太叫道,“她要奶瓶呢。艾伯特,快把她抱起来,抱到我这里来。不过,先把奶瓶给我。”

他把奶瓶递了过去,然后把孩子放到她的大腿上。她小心翼翼地刚让奶嘴接触到婴儿的嘴唇,婴儿就一下子用牙龈部分叼住奶嘴,开始快速地、强有力地吸吮起来,一副如饥似渴、急不可耐的样子。

“噢,艾伯特,难道这不是奇迹吗?”她说完,开心地笑了。

“太棒了,梅布尔。”

七八分钟的功夫,整个一瓶奶顺着婴儿的喉咙流下,消失不见啦。

“真是聪明的乖乖女,”泰勒太太说,“又将近二两半。”

艾伯特·泰勒身体在椅子上向前一倾,专注地看了看婴儿的脸。“你知道吗?”他说,“看起来,她甚至好像增加了一点儿体重。你认为呢?”

母亲低头看了孩子一眼。

“梅布尔,对你来说,难道她看起来不比昨天壮一点、胖一点了吗?”

“或许是吧,艾伯特,但我不敢肯定。尽管在像这样短的时间内,实际上不可能有什么真正意义上的增加,但重要的是,她正常进食了。”

"她已经好转，"艾伯特说，"我想，你再也不用为她担心了。"

"我当然不会担心了。"

"梅布尔，你希望我上楼，把摇篮送回卧室吗？"

"好的，受累了。"她说。

艾伯特上楼去挪动摇篮。妻子抱着孩子，随后上了楼。换了尿布之后，轻轻地把孩子放到床上，然后用被单和毯子把孩子盖好。

"艾伯特，孩子看起来难道不可爱吗？"她低声说道，"难道她不是你整个生命中看到的最漂亮的孩子吗？"

"梅布尔，现在让她自己睡吧，"他说，"到楼下，做点晚饭吃吧。我们俩都该吃晚饭了。"

父母两人吃完饭后，分别在起居室的椅子上坐下。艾伯特抽着烟斗，看起了杂志，泰勒太太则开始织东西。跟前一个晚上任何一个场景比较起来，这个场面迥然不同。突然之间，所有的紧张感都烟消云散。泰勒太太那张秀美的、椭圆形的脸上闪耀着喜悦之情，脸颊变得粉红，双眼明亮地闪烁着，就连嘴上也凝结了一丝柔美的微笑，显露出一副十足满意的样子。她不时地会从编织活计中抬起头来，情意绵绵地凝视着丈夫。在某个时候，她也会偶尔完全停下来几秒钟，也不让织针发出"咔嗒"的声音，自己则静悄悄地坐在那儿，眼睛瞅着天花板，听着楼上发出的哭叫声，或者呜咽声。但是，什么声音也没有。

"艾伯特。"过了一会她说道。

"听着呢，亲爱的，什么事？"

"昨晚，你匆忙进入卧室，要对我说什么事呢？当时你说关于这个婴儿，你有一个想法。"

艾伯特·泰勒放低杂志，放到大腿上，眼睛看着她，看了好一会，露出诡异的神色。

"我说过吗？"他问。

"是的。"她等着他继续说下去，但他却没有开口。

"是什么那么好笑呢？"她问，"为什么你咧着嘴，笑成那样？"

"没事儿，就是一个玩笑。"他说。

“亲爱的,告诉我吧。”

“我不敢肯定,是否应该对你讲,”他说,“你或许会说我谎话连篇的。”

她很少看到他像目前这样洋洋自得。她回应以微笑,催促他继续讲下去。

“梅布尔,你一听我讲话,就会抬起头,我就喜欢这时候看看你的脸。就是这样的。”

“艾伯特,快说说,这一切都是什么?”

他暂停下来,不愿意有人催促自己。

“你的确认为,孩子好多了,是不是呢?”他问。

“当然啦。”

“突然一下子,她进食状态极佳,看起来与以前有着天壤之别。我这样说,你同意吗?”

“是的,艾伯特。我同意。”

“那就好,”他说。说完后,嘴咧得更宽了。“要知道,这都是我的功劳。”

“什么功劳?”

“我治好了婴儿。”

“是的,亲爱的,我肯定这是你的功劳。”泰勒太太干脆继续低头织东西了。

“我说的,你不相信。对吗?”

“艾伯特,我当然相信你说的。功劳都归你,每一份都归你。”

“那么,我是怎么做到的呢?”

“这个啊,”她说,随后停下来,想了一会儿,“我想嘛,你只不过是一个出色的搅拌师。自从你开始做搅拌的活计以来,她就越来越好转了。”

“你的意思是说,在搅拌方面,还有某种技巧吗?”

“很明显,是的。”她只顾编织,暗自发笑,心想:男人真够有意思的。

“我要告诉你一个秘密,”他说,“你说的绝对正确无误,但要提醒你一点就是,如何搅拌还不是至关重要的。关键是,搅拌前,你往里面放进什么东西。梅布尔,你意识到我说的是什么了吧,是不是呢?”

泰勒太太停下不织了,抬起头,严厉地看着丈夫。“艾伯特,”她说,“你一直往孩子的牛奶里放东西,你要对我说的,是这样的吗?”

他坐在那儿,只顾咧着嘴笑。

“那么,你是放了,还是没放?”

“这是可能的。”他说。

“我不相信。”

他咧嘴笑的样子很奇怪,也很夸张,好多牙齿都露了出来。

“艾伯特,”她说,“可不要这样跟我开玩笑啊。”

“好的,亲爱的。好吧。”

“说真的,孩子的牛奶里,你什么也没有放,对吗?如实回答我,艾伯特。对于这样一个微小的婴儿,弄不好,事情会很严重的。”

“梅布尔,答案就是——放了。”

“艾伯特·泰勒!你怎么能这样?”

“现在,不要激动,”他说,“要是你真想让我讲,我就把一切告诉你。但是,你可要保持镇定,头脑要冷静。”

“是啤酒!”她喊道,“我就知道,你放的是啤酒!”

“拜托,不要这样傻里傻气,梅布尔。”

“那么,会是什么?”

艾伯特小心地将烟斗放到身旁的桌子上,随之身体在椅子上向后一靠。“告诉我,”他说,“你曾经不管是偶然也好,是凑巧也好,是否听我提起过一种叫蜂王浆的东西?”

“没有。”

“这东西很具魔力,”他说,“魔力十足。昨晚,我突然间有了一个想法:要是我把这东西放一些,放进婴儿的牛奶里……”

“你怎么竟敢这样做啊!”

“现在,梅布尔,你甚至不知道这东西为何物呢。”

“我才不管它为何物呢,”她说,“往一个微小婴儿的奶中放异物，你竟然做得出。你一定是疯了。”

“梅布尔，它绝对没有任何害处。否则的话，我就不会往里放的。这东西来自于蜜蜂。”

“我早就应该猜到的。”

“这东西太宝贵了，几乎没有人能付得起钱买来服用的。要是买得起的话，一次也只能用那么一小滴。”

“我可以问问吗，你一次给我们的孩子用多少？”

“啊，”他说，“你可问到点子上了，也是与其他人不同之处。在喂过的四次中，我估计，我们的孩子所吞下的王浆数量，约是世界上任何一个人以前吞下数量的五十倍。怎么样？”

“艾伯特，别耍我了。”

“我发誓来保证，这是真的。”他自豪地说道。

她坐在那儿盯着他，她的额头皱起，嘴巴轻微张开着。

“梅布尔，你要是去买的话，你知道这东西的实际价格吗？就现在，美国有一个地方做广告推销它，一罐的价格约五百美元啊！每罐还不到一斤重呢，就五百美元！你知道的，那比金子还贵啊！”

他说的是什么意思，她一点点也不明白。

“我证明给你看。”他说。然后，跳了起来，走到一个大大的书橱跟前，那里存放的全是有关蜜蜂方面的文献。顶层架子上放的是一摞过期期刊，刊名是《美国蜜蜂杂志》，并排摆放的还有《英国蜜蜂杂志》和《蜜蜂技艺》等杂志。他取下最后一期《美国蜜蜂杂志》，翻到后部的一页，上面刊登的是一小块、一小块的分类广告。

“你看呐，”他说，“正如我所言，‘我们出售蜂王浆，批发价是一罐＄480（“＄”是“美元”的意思——译者注），每罐重量约一斤。’”

他把杂志递给她，让她亲自看看。

“现在，你相信我的话了吧？梅布尔，这是美国一家实体店的广告，说的就是这个价。”

“但是，广告并没有说，可以把它掺进几乎是刚出生的婴儿喝的奶里啊，”她说，“我不知道你脑子里进什么东西了，艾伯特，我真的不知道。”

"我就是要把她治好,难道不是吗?"

"现在,对于你说的,我不是那么肯定。"

"梅布尔,你真是傻得不可救药。你清楚,实际情况就是这样的。"

"就算这样,为什么其他人没有对他们自己的婴儿也这样做呢?"

"我要跟你说多少遍呢,"他说,"这东西太昂贵了。这个世界上几乎没有谁能付得起钱把蜂王浆买来,仅仅是为了吃。当然,一两个大款除外,那也得是财富达到数百万的大款。买这东西的都是一些大公司,买来制造女性面霜之类的产品。这些公司在产品中使用这东西,也只是作为一种噱头,一大罐子面霜中就微微地掺入那么一点点的王浆,但是产品却十分畅销,价格是绝对的高。产品宣传得也好:蜂王浆能去皱。"

"真能去皱吗?"

"听我说,梅布尔,我上哪儿能知道答案呢?可不管怎么说,"他说,随后回到椅子上,"那不是关键所在,关键点在这儿:就在刚刚过去的几个小时的时间里,这东西给我们的小女儿带来好处多多。因而我想,我们应该继续给她服用。现在,不要插嘴,梅布尔,让我把话说完。就在外面,我拥有二百四十只蜂箱。如果我把其中的一百只蜂箱用来生产蜂王浆的话,我们就能为她提供她所需要的所有的蜂王浆。"

"艾伯特·泰勒。"这位妻子说道。只见她眼睛瞪得大大的,盯着他。"你是不是精神失常了?"

"就听我说到底儿,好吗?"

"我严厉禁止使用它,"她说,"绝对不许用。那个令人讨厌的蜂王浆,一滴也不要给我女儿用了。你听明白了吗?"

"现在,梅布尔……"

"撇开那个不谈,我们去年的蜂蜜产量已经够糟糕透顶的啦。要是现在你还瞎鼓弄那些蜂箱的话,或许还会发生什么事情,很难说的。"

"梅布尔,我的那些蜂箱没有任何问题。"

“你清楚得很,去年的产量只是正常产量的一半。”

“行行好,好吗?”他恳求道,“就让我解释一下这东西带来的一些奇妙之处吧。”

“你甚至还没有告诉我,这东西为何物呢。”

“好吧,梅布尔,我也顺便告诉你一下。你会听吗?你会给我一个解释的机会吗?”

她叹了口气,随后再次织了起来。“艾伯特,我想啊,你也不妨一吐为快,接着给我讲吧。”

他暂停一会儿。现在,他反而不知道从何讲起了。向一个根本没有详细了解过养蜂知识的人解释类似这样的事情,还真不是件容易的事情。

“你知道的,”他说,“每个蜂群只有一个蜂王,不是吗?”

“这个我知道。”

“所有的卵都是这个蜂王产下的,这个你知道吗?”

“是的,亲爱的。我也就知道这么多了。”

“好的,现在听着。事实上,这个蜂王能够产下两种不同类型的卵。这个你就不知道了,但是,的确如此。这就是我们所说的蜂群里的奇迹。蜂王产下的卵能够孕育出雄蜂,也能孕育出工蜂。梅布尔,现在看来,那要不算是奇迹的话,我真不知道还有什么能称得上是奇迹。”

“是的,艾伯特,是奇迹。”

“雄蜂就是那些性别为公的蜜蜂。对它们,我们没有什么好担心的。工蜂都是母的,当然,蜂王也是母的。但问题是,工蜂都是些没有繁殖能力的母蜂,你明白我的意思吧。工蜂的性器官完全没有发育出来,而蜂王特别具有性能力。一天之内,她的实际产卵量相当于自己的体重。”

他迟疑一下,开始组织安排自己的思绪。

“现在嘛,情况是这样发生的。蜂王在蜂巢里爬来爬去,把卵产下来,产到一个个小室里,我们称之为蜂窝。你知道,就是蜂巢里那些成千上百的小洞,看过吗?孵化蜂巢跟其他类型的蜂巢几乎是一样的,区别就在于,在孵化蜂巢里,蜂窝里装的不是蜂蜜,而是蜂卵。一个蜂窝里,蜂王只产下一枚卵。三天之内,每一枚卵就会孵化出来,成为一个个微小的蛆,我们称之为幼虫。”

“现在,幼虫一孵化出来,保育蜂就挤在幼虫周围,疯一般给幼虫喂食。保育蜂其实就是一些年轻的工蜂。你知道保育蜂用什么喂幼虫吗?”

“蜂王浆。”梅布尔耐着性子回答。

“对,没错!”他喊道,“喂的正是这种东西。这些保育蜂从其头部的腺体里分泌出这种东西,然后注入蜂窝,用以喂养幼虫。接下来,又会怎样呢?”

他戛然而止、暂停下来,冲着她眨眨他那双浅灰色的小眼睛。然后,他在椅子上慢慢地转了一下身体,伸手拿起前一天晚上一直阅读的那本杂志。

“你想知道接下来发生的事情吗?”他舔了舔嘴唇问道。

“我几乎等不及啦。”

“‘蜂王浆,’”他朗读起来,“‘一定是一种营养无比丰富的物质,因为单单靠吃这一种食物,蜜蜂幼虫的体重就会在五天之内增加一千五百倍!’”

“多少倍?”

“梅布尔,一千五百倍啊!要是拿人来衡量的话,你知道那意味着什么吗?那意味着,”他边说边放低了声音,身体前倾,用那双小小的、灰色的眼睛死死地盯着她,“那意味着,在五天之内,一个出生时体重不到三公斤半的婴儿,体重增加到五吨!”

泰勒太太又停下来,不织了,这已经是第二次了。

“梅布尔,现在,你千万不能按字面教条地理解。”

“谁说我要教条理解了?”

“这只是一种科学的说法,仅此而已。”

“很好,艾伯特。继续。”

“但是,那只是说完了一半,”他说。“还有更多要说的。我还没有告诉你蜂王浆真正令人称奇的地方呢。下面,我就要跟你说说蜂王浆的奇特之处，说说它是如何把一只普普通通的、样子不出奇的、几乎没有性器官的工蜂转变成一只伟大非凡的、体型硕大的、好看漂亮的、生育能力极强的蜂王的。"

"你是说我们的女儿样子不出奇，人也普普通通吗？"她尖锐地问道。

"噢，梅布尔，拜托你不要把你的意思强加到我身上。就好好听着吧。尽管蜂王和工蜂长成之后具有天壤之别，但是它们几乎都由完全相同类型的卵孵化出来的。这个你知道吗？"

"我不信。"她回应。

"这是真的，就像我坐在这儿一样的真实。梅布尔，这是千真万确的。不管什么时候，只要蜜蜂想从卵中孵化出蜂王，而不是工蜂，它们就能够做到。"

"如何做到？"

"啊，"他边说，边冲着她这边晃动着他的一根食指，"那就是我要谈到的，是整个这件事情的秘密所在。现在，梅布尔，你认为是什么东西促使奇迹发生呢？"

"蜂王浆，"她回答，"你已经告诉过我的。"

"正是蜂王浆啊！"他大声说道。然后，他两手一拍，从座位上弹跳起来。现在，他那张圆圆的大脸洋溢着兴奋的神情，每边脸颊较上方的位置上都出现一个鲜明的猩红色斑块。

"这个过程是这样的。我会简单明了地跟你说的。蜜蜂想要一个新的蜂王，它们就要建造一个超大型的巢室，我们称之为蜂王窝。然后，它们就让老蜂王在那里把其中一枚卵产下。另外的一千九百九十九枚卵就产到普通的工蜂蜂窝里。现在，卵一孵化出来成为幼虫，保育蜂就集结而来，开始注入蜂王浆。不管是工蜂幼虫，还是蜂王幼虫，都会吃到蜂王浆。但是，梅布尔，这里就有一个至关重要的事情存在了，也就是区别所在，所以你要仔仔细细听好了。在幼虫生长期内，这种特殊的、创造奇迹的食物，工蜂幼虫只是在头三天里才能吃到。那之后，它们的食谱就完全变了。实际发生的情况是，它们给断奶了，只不过跟普通意义上的断奶有所不同，因为普通的断奶是突然间一下子断掉的。第三天过后，就直接用多少带点常规意义上的蜜蜂食物喂养它们，也就是蜂蜜和花粉的混合物。这样，约两周过后，它们就飞出蜂窝，成为工蜂。”

“但是，躺在蜂王窝里的那只幼虫就不是这样的啦！在整个幼虫生长期里，这只幼虫始终能吃到蜂王浆。保育蜂只管一个劲儿往里注入蜂王浆，数量之大，可以说，这只小小的幼虫简直就是漂浮在蜂王浆之中。因此，这只幼虫就被造就成一只蜂王了！”

“你无法证明的。”她说。

“拜托，梅布尔，不要那样傻乎乎的。成千上万的人已经反反复复证明了，包括世界上所有国家的著名科学家。你需要做的就是，把幼虫从工蜂窝里拿出，放入蜂王窝里，我们称之为移嫁。这样，只要保育蜂提供充足的王浆，那么，这只幼虫就如同变戏法一般，说变就变！它就会长成一只蜂王啦！更为奇妙的是，长成后，蜂王跟工蜂绝对是具有天壤之别的。腹部形状不同，螯针不同，后足不同，还有……”

“后足哪方面不同？”她问道，想测试他一下。

“后足？哦，工蜂的后足长有小小的花粉筐，用以搬运花粉，但蜂王就没有。现在，还有另一件事情。蜂王有发育完全的性器官，但工蜂就没有。梅布尔，最令人称奇的是，蜂王的平均寿命为四到六年，而工蜂几乎没有活那么长的。所有这些不同，都是因为蜂王浆的缘故：一个总能吃到王浆，而其他那些就不能了！”

“一种食物能有这么大功效，”她说，“太匪夷所思了。”

“当然啦，难以相信。这是蜂群的另一个奇迹。事实上，这是蜂群所有奇迹中最大的、最耀眼的奇迹。这个奇迹大得不得了，甚至数百年以来，就连最伟大的科学家都迷惑不解。等一下，待在那儿别动。”

“我给你找几篇报道吧。找到了，这是其中的一篇。听着啊。”他开始朗读某期《美国蜜蜂杂志》上的一篇文章：

“‘弗雷德里克·A·班廷医生现在住在多伦多市。为表彰他对人类做出的、真正伟大的贡献——胰岛素的发现，加拿大人民赠送给他一个精良的研究实验室，实验室由他领导。他对蜂王浆颇感兴趣，并要求他的手下人员对其进行分馏分析……'"

他暂停下来。

"看来，没有必要全部读出来，但情况是这样的。班廷医生跟他的手下从蜂王窝里取出一些蜂王浆，然后开始分析。窝里的幼虫孵化出来有两天了。你想想，他们发现了什么？"

"他们发现，"他说，"蜂王浆里含有苯酚、固醇、丙三醇、葡萄糖，而且，现在还发现，它里面的百分之八十至八十五为各种无法识别的酸类物质。"

他手里拿着那本杂志，站在书柜的旁边，脸上稍微露出一丝滑稽的、神秘的、沾沾自喜的微笑。而他的妻子则看着他，显示出一副疑惑不解的样子。

他个子不高，身体又粗又圆，敦实地架在他那两条短短的、稍微有点弯曲的腿上，而两只腿则稳稳地戳在地面上，整个人看起来肉呼呼的。他的头又大又圆，上面的头发剪得又短又硬。由于完完全全不想再刮胡子，他脸上大部分地方覆盖在一层蓬松的毛发之下，那毛发约有二十五毫米长，黄色之中稍微带有一点棕色。不管从哪一方面来看，他看上去都相当的古怪、荒诞，这一点不容否认。

"百分之八十至八十五，"他说，"为各种无法识别的酸类物质。这难道不异乎寻常吗？"他又转向书架，开始搜寻其他杂志。

"各种无法识别的酸类物质，这是什么意思？"

"你问到点子上了。没人知道什么意思啊！甚至连班廷本人也得不出什么结论。你听说过班廷吗？"

"没有。"

"他也就是很偶然地成为世界上最为知名的医生，而且是当今还活着的医生，仅此而已。"

现在，她看着他，看着他那头发剪得又短又硬的头部，看着他那毛茸茸的脸，看着他那粗圆而肉呼呼的身体，再加上她听到的、他站在书柜前说话时发出的"嗡嗡嗡"的声音，无论如何，她都情不自禁地想,丈夫带有那么一点儿蜜蜂的样子。真是奇怪啊。她经常看到有些骑马的女性,越长越像她们所骑的马。她也注意到,那些养鸟、养短毛杂种犬,或者养波美拉尼亚犬的人,经常长得像他们所养之物。当然,这种像的程度不是很大,但是相似的样子着实令人吃惊不已。可是,直到目前为止,她才想到,他的丈夫看起来或许像一只蜜蜂。这个想法让她不寒而栗。

"那么,班廷以前吃过这东西没有?"她问,"我指的是王浆。"

"梅布尔,他当然没有吃过。他买不起那东西,太昂贵了。"

"你知道吗?"她始终轻轻微笑着,一边盯着他,一边问。"你本人看起来,开始有那么一点点像一只蜜蜂了。你知道吗?"

他转过来看着她。

"我想,主要是由于那些胡须吧,"她说,"我真的希望你别再留胡须。就连胡须的颜色也有点像蜜蜂的颜色。难道你不认为是这样的吗?"

"梅布尔,你说的是些什么该死的话呢?"

"艾伯特,"她说,"注意你的用词。"

"你到底想不想听我继续说下去?"

"想听,亲爱的。对不起,我只是说笑一下。请继续吧。"

他又转过身,从书柜里抽出另一本杂志,"哗哗"翻起来。"梅布尔,现在听我读这段:'1939年,海尔用一些二十一天大的老鼠做实验,给它们注射剂量不等的蜂王浆。结果他发现,老鼠的卵巢出现过早发育的现象,发育的大小与所注射的蜂王浆剂量成正比。'"

"哇!"她叫道,"我知道了啊!"

"知道什么?"

"我知道某种可怕的事情就要发生了。"

"胡说。什么事都不会发生的。梅布尔,听听另一段。'无独有偶,伯德特发现,尚无繁殖能力的公老鼠,要是每天注射少量的蜂王浆,就会做很多次父亲了。'"

"艾伯特,"她叫道,"这东西给婴儿用,太过于强烈啊!我一点也不喜欢。"

“瞎说,梅布尔。”

“那么,你告诉我,为什么他们只是在老鼠身上用呢?这些有名的科学家,为什么不自己服用呢?他们聪明过头了,这就是原因。最终会长出弥足珍贵的卵巢,你认为班廷医生会冒那个险吗?他才不会呢。”

“可是,梅布尔,他们也在人身上用啊。这里有一整篇文章都是关于这个的,听着。”他翻到这本杂志的那一页,又开始读了起来。“‘1953年在墨西哥,一组颇有见地的内科医生开始开含有小剂量蜂王浆的处方。开这样的处方,主要是针对大脑神经炎、关节炎、糖尿病、吸烟导致的自体中毒、阳痿、哮喘、哮吼、痛风……这里有一大堆有名有姓的例证……墨西哥城的一位著名的证券经纪人患上一种特别顽固的牛皮癣,整个人也打不起精神来,他的客户纷纷离他而去,他的生意一落千丈。绝望之中,他求助于蜂王浆,每顿饭用上一滴——如同变戏法似的,说变就变!两周的时间,他就痊愈了。也是在墨西哥城,耶那咖啡馆的一名服务生说,他父亲服用了少剂量的含有这种奇妙之物的胶囊后,竟然当上了一个健康男婴的爸爸,尽管他父亲已经是九十岁的高龄。阿卡普尔科市的一个斗牛赛承办人,发现自己弄到的那头公牛看起来特别无精打采。于是,就在这头牛进入竞技场之前,给它注射了一克的蜂王浆——这个剂量超标了。因此,这头公牛在竞技场上动作迅猛、粗野无比,当时就顶死了两名斗牛士助手、三匹马、一个斗牛士,最后……’”

“听听,”泰勒太太打断了他的话,说道,“我想,孩子在哭呢。”

艾伯特抬眼瞧了瞧。的的确确,楼上的卧室里传来了嚎啕的声音,显得强健、有力。

“她一定是饿了。”他说。

他妻子看了眼时钟。“我的老天啊!”她叫道,随即跳了起来,“又过喂奶的时间了!艾伯特,你搅拌,快点儿,我去把她抱下来!但是,要快啊!我可不想让孩子干着急。”

半分钟后,泰勒太太就下来了。她抱着婴儿,婴儿“哇哇”哭叫着。孩子一下子健康起来,要起吃的来,就片刻不停歇地哇哇哭闹,这真有点吓人。她现在有些手忙脚乱,仍然不太习惯。“艾伯特,快点!”她喊道。然后,自己在扶手椅上坐好,把孩子放到大腿上。“拜托,快!”

艾伯特从厨房赶过来,把一瓶热好的牛奶递给她。“刚刚好,”他说,“你不用尝啦。”

她在臂弯里把孩子的头稍微向上抬了抬,然后把橡皮奶头径直塞进孩子嚎啕大哭时张得大大的嘴巴。婴儿攫住奶头就猛地吸吮起来。此时,哭闹声停了,泰勒夫人也松了一口气。

“哦,艾伯特,她难道不可爱吗?”

“可爱极了,梅布尔。蜂王浆的功劳啊。”

“亲爱的,现在,我一点都不想听到那个讨厌的东西。它让我怕得要死。”

“你大错特错了。”他说。

“我们走着瞧吧。”

婴儿吸吮着。

“艾伯特,我还是相信,她会喝得精光。”

“我确信,会的。”他回应。

几分钟过后,牛奶全没了。

“哇,真是一个乖女孩!”泰勒太太大声说,同时开始轻轻往外拉奶嘴。婴儿感觉到她要做什么,于是吸得更紧,并尽量挺住,不让拔出来。泰勒太太稍微一用力,动作迅速地往外一拔,只听得“砰”的一声,奶嘴就被拔了出来。

“哇啊! 哇啊! 哇啊! 哇啊! 哇啊!”婴儿顿时哭闹起来。

“胃里总是有气儿,真讨厌。”泰勒夫人说完,举起孩子竖到肩上,拍着孩子的后背。

孩子不间歇地快速打了两个嗝。

“这就好了,我的宝贝,现在起一切都好了。”

哭叫声停了几秒钟。接着,又开始了。

“让她继续打嗝,”艾伯特说,“她喝得太快了。”

他妻子又把孩子举起来,竖到肩上。她揉搓着孩子的脊柱,并把孩子从一只肩膀换到另一只肩膀上。然后，让孩子俯卧在她的腿部，接着又扶孩子坐到她的膝盖上。可是，孩子却没有再打嗝，哭叫声反而越来越大，一分钟比一分钟更不稳定。

“对肺部有好处，”艾伯特·泰勒咧嘴一笑，说道，“肺部就是这样训练出来的。梅布尔，你知道吗？”

“喔，喔，喔，”妻子一边说，一边把婴儿的脸亲了一遍，“喔，喔，喔。”

“换换尿布，”艾伯特说，“是尿布湿了，没错。”他从厨房拿来一条干净的。泰勒太太抽出原来那条，换上了新的。

但是，根本没有什么改观。

“哇啊！哇啊！哇啊！哇啊！哇啊！”婴儿再次哭闹起来。

“梅布尔，那枚安全别针，你没有扎到孩子的皮肤吗？”

“当然没有，”她回答。随后，她就用手指往尿布底下摸，以防万一。

父母两个人各自坐在扶手椅上，你看着我，我看着你，面带微笑，紧张兮兮。婴儿坐在母亲的膝盖上。他俩都看着婴儿，等着婴儿疲劳。到那时，也就不再嚎叫了。

“你知道吗？”艾伯特最终开口了。

“什么？”

“我敢肯定，她还没有喝好。我敢打赌，她只是想大口地吸一下奶瓶。我再给她额外添点，怎么样？”

“艾伯特，我想，我们不应该那么做。”

“对她有好处，”他说，然后从椅子上站了起来，“我再去给她热一瓶吧。”

他进了厨房，但是好几分钟过去了，人还没有回来。回来时，手里举起满满一瓶牛奶。

“这次是两倍的量，”他说，“半斤，以防不够喝。”

“艾伯特！你疯啦！饮食过量的坏处不亚于饮食不足，难道你不知道吗？”

“梅布尔，你也用不着全都给她喝下去。什么时候不想让她喝，你停下便是。开始吧，”他站立着，俯身在她的上方，说道，“给她喝喝看。”

泰勒太太开始用奶嘴头拨弄婴儿的嘴唇，婴儿的那张小嘴紧紧地叼住奶嘴，如同贝壳一般紧紧地闭着，屋子里刹那间鸦雀无声。一旦开始喝起来，婴儿整个身体都松弛下来，脸上露出一副欣喜若狂的表情。

“看啊，梅布尔！我说什么来着？”

妻子没有吭声。

“她那是饿极了，事实如此。只要看看她喝的样子就知道了。”

泰勒太太观察着瓶子里牛奶的水平面，发现下降得很快。不一会儿的功夫，半斤牛奶中约有一半左右消失了。

“好了，”她说，“可以啦。”

“梅布尔，现在可不能拿开。”

“不，亲爱的，必须拿掉。”

“老婆，继续啊。给她喝完，别再说这说那了。”

“可是，艾伯特……”

“她饿得不行了，难道你看不出吗？接着来，我漂亮的老婆，”他说，“把那瓶喝光。”

“艾伯特，我不喜欢这样，”妻子说道。但说归说，却并没有把奶瓶拿开。

“她要把没有喝到的补回来呢，梅布尔，就是这个样子的。”

五分钟后，瓶子空空如也。泰勒太太慢慢地往回抽奶嘴。这次，婴儿没有抵制，也没有发出任何声音，只是安安静静地躺在母亲的大腿部位，两只眼睛心满意足地凝视着，小嘴半张着，双唇沾满了牛奶。

“梅布尔，将近八两啊！”艾伯特·泰勒说道，“是正常量的三倍啊！真让人吃惊！”

妻子低头看着孩子。现在，她的脸上又露出以往那种表情——忧心忡忡的母亲脸上所带有的那种表情：焦虑不安、嘴巴紧闭、抑郁寡欢。

“你怎么啦？”艾伯特问，“不是为那个担心，对吗？要是一次喝那可怜的一两半还不到的话,你怎么能期望孩子恢复正常呢。别再傻了。"

"过来,艾伯特。"她说。

"什么?"

"我说,过来。"

他走了过去,站在她旁边。

"看一眼啊,看看有什么不一样的地方。"

他靠到近前,看着婴儿。"她似乎变大了一些。梅布尔,你指的是这个吗? 大多了,也胖多了。"

"抱抱看,"她吩咐道,"快啊,把孩子抱起来。"

他伸出手把孩子从母亲的大腿部位抱了起来。"老天啊!"他喊道,"重如铅块啊!"

"正是。"

"那么,这难道不是奇迹啊!"他喜形于色地大声说道,"我敢说,她一定已经恢复得差不多啦!"

"那才让我担惊受怕呢,艾伯特,来得也太快了。"

"老婆,瞎说。"

"都是那讨厌的蜂王浆惹的祸,"她说,"我恨那东西。"

"蜂王浆没有错,不令人讨厌的。"他回答,显得有些愤慨。

"别像傻子一样啊,艾伯特! 一个孩子以这个速度增加体重,你认为是正常的吗?"

"你就是没有满足的时候!"他大喊,"孩子体重一天天下降时,你吓得要死、两眼发直。现在,孩子体重在增加,而你却又惊恐不安、不以为然。梅布尔,你到底怎么啦?"

妻子抱着孩子从椅子上站起身来,向门口走去。"我能说的就是,"她说道,"看到你不再给她喝这东西,我就感到幸运无比。那就是我要说的。"门开着,她走了出去。艾伯特看着她穿过门厅,走到楼梯底部,然后开始上楼。但上到三四级楼梯的时候,她停住了,一动不动地停了好几秒钟,好像是想起了什么事情。随后,她一转身,又走下来,速度很快,再次进屋。

“艾伯特。”她说。

“什么事儿？”

“我猜测，最后这次喂奶的时候，里面一点儿也没有掺蜂王浆，对吗？”

“梅布尔，我不明白你为什么会那样猜测。”

“艾伯特！”

“有什么不妥吗？”他轻轻地问，显得很无辜。

“你胆子真够大啊！”她叫道。

艾伯特·泰勒那张大大的、满是胡须的脸上露一副痛苦而迷惑的表情。“我想，她肚子里又喝下一大瓶，你应该很高兴才对啊，”他说，“实话实说，我掺了，而且掺得剂量很大。梅布尔，你要相信我。”

妻子刚好跨进门，紧紧抱着睡着的孩子，瞪大了眼睛看着丈夫。她笔挺地站立，身体由于极度愤怒而变得僵直，脸比以前更灰白，嘴唇闭得也更紧了。

“你记下我的话，”艾伯特说，“不出多久，你的孩子就会在全国婴儿秀大赛上赢得头奖。哎，我说，你为什么现在不称称她的体重，看看是多少呢？梅布尔，要我把秤拿来，让你给她称一下吗？”

妻子径直走到屋子中间一张大桌子前，放下孩子，开始麻利地给孩子脱衣服。“好啊！”她猛地说道，“拿秤来吧！”孩子睡袍脱下了，紧接着贴身内衣也脱下了。

然后，她取下尿布上的安全别针，把尿布抽走。这样，婴儿就一丝不挂地躺在桌子上了。

“但，梅布尔！”艾伯特大声说，“这就是奇迹啊！她跟小狗狗一样胖乎乎的啊！”

的确如此。自打前一天起，这孩子的发胖程度很是出乎意料。以前胸部瘪瘪的，一根根肋骨清晰可见，可现在却丰满、鼓胀起来，就像圆桶一样，而且腹部也向外鼓起。尽管如此，胳膊和腿似乎并没有成比例生长起来，依然那么短、那么皮包骨，看起来就像从肥肉球上支起来一根根的小棍棍儿，真是既奇怪又有意思。

“看看！”艾伯特说，“孩子的小肚子上甚至长出一根根小绒毛，这有助于保暖啊！”他伸出一只手，意欲用手指尖触摸一遍孩子胃部那层毛茸茸的外表，不知道从什么时候起，那里突然出现一层如丝一般光滑的绒毛，棕色之中略带一点黄色调。

“千万别碰啊！”妻子叫道。她转身面向他，眼里冒起了火。突然之间，她看起来像某种就要开始打斗的小鸟，冲着他把脖子弯成拱形，就好像要奔着他的脸飞去，然后啄出他的双眼。

“现在，稍等啊。”他边说，边向后撤去。

“你一定是疯了！”她叫道。

“现在，梅布尔，就等一会儿，好吗？如果你还认为这东西很危险的话……那正是你的想法，难道我说错了吗？那么，好吧，你听仔细了。梅布尔，我现在继续向你证明一次，而且是一劳永逸地证明一次，那就是，即使大剂量地服用，蜂王浆对人也绝对是没有任何伤害的。例如，去年夏天我们的蜂蜜产量只是正常的一半，你认为是为什么呢？告诉我答案啊。”

他这么一后撤，退出了几步，就站到离她三四米远的地方了，站在那儿他感觉似乎更舒服一些。

“去年夏天我们的产量只有一半的原因就是，”他放低声音，慢悠悠地说，“我把一百只蜂箱做了调整，转而生产蜂王浆了。”

“你什么了？”

“哦，”他小声说，“我想，我说的或许令你感到一点点意外。从转型的那一刻起，我就在你的眼皮子底下生产蜂王浆。”他的那双小眼睛一闪一闪地看着她，一丝缓缓的、诡异的微笑渐渐爬上他的嘴角。

“你也永远猜不出我为什么要这样做的，”他说，“直到现在，我还不敢向你提起这事儿，因为我想，这事儿或许……怎么说呢……会让你难堪的。”

稍微停顿一下。他把双手高高举起，紧扣在身前，与胸部齐平。一只手掌跟另一只手掌揉搓着，发出刮擦的声音。

“杂志里我给你读的那小段，你记得吗？就是关于老鼠的那一部分。现在让我想想啊，那段怎么说来着？‘无独有偶，伯德特发现，尚无繁殖能力的公老鼠……'"他不知道该不该继续往下读,仍然笑着,嘴咧得更宽,一些牙齿露了出来。

"梅布尔,你体会到其中的意思了吗?"

她面对着他,一动不动地站立着。

"梅布尔,当初乍一读到那句话的时候,我一下子就从椅子上跳了起来,对自己说,这东西要是对令人生厌的老鼠起作用的话,就没有理由不对艾伯特·泰勒起作用的,也不应该不起作用啊。"

他又停了一下,向前伸长了脖子,一只耳朵稍微转向他妻子的方向,等待听她说点什么。但是,她什么也没说。

"还有一件事儿,"他继续说,"这事儿我感到绝对是奇妙无比,梅布尔。这事儿也使我跟从前简直是判若两人。自从你告诉我那个快乐无比的好消息后,这事我就继续做下去,就是服用这东西。在过去的一年里,这东西,我无法说清楚到底吞下多少了。"

妻子那双大大的、沉重的眼睛仔仔细细地在丈夫的脸上、脖子上移动着,显得有些焦虑不安。丈夫脖子那儿根本看不到皮肤,就连两只耳朵下方的周边部分也看不见皮肤了。整个看不见皮肤的这一区域,一直延伸到衬衫的领口处,全部由一层稍短的、如丝般光滑的绒毛覆盖着,黑色之中略微带点黄色调。

"提醒你一下,"他说完就转过身去,充满爱意地看着孩子,"这东西用在微小的婴儿身上,比用在像我这样完全长成的人身上,效果会更好一些。你只要看看孩子一眼,就明白了。难道你不同意我说的吗?"

妻子的目光慢慢地向下移动,落在孩子身上。婴儿一丝不挂地躺在桌子上,看起来胖胖的、白白的,睡得沉沉的。这个婴儿看起来就像某种大块头的、幼虫阶段的生活行将结束的蛆,而且上下颚和翅膀已经发育齐全,很快就会破茧而出,融入这个世界之中。

"梅布尔,你为什么不把孩子盖好呢?"他问,"我们可不愿意让我们的小女王感冒的。"

第二章　结局难料

如果历史能倒退的话，有些事件的结局恐怕就难以预料了。宋代词人李清照的一首五言绝句《夏日绝句》这样写道："生当做人杰，死亦为鬼雄。至今思项羽，不肯过江东。"李清照的这首诗道出了一个历史事实，那就是："无颜见江东父老"的项羽选择在乌江边举剑自刎结束了自己的生命而成就了一段慷慨悲壮的历史，李清照对此举是大加赞赏的。而唐代诗人杜牧的一首七绝则是这样写的：

胜败兵家事不期，包羞忍耻是男儿。
江东子弟多才俊，卷土重来未可知。①

这就提出了一个历史的假设：回到历史的原点，要是项羽当初"过江东"会怎样？那就会有一个难以预料的结局了。就连晚唐诗人杜牧在上一首诗的结句不也写下"卷土重来未可知"这样不确定的话语吗？只可惜，这种历史假设说并不成立。

从英国作家罗尔德·达尔的作品中，也可以寻找到这样难料的结局。拥有豪宅的家族企业继承人巴兹尔·特顿爵士娶了一位精明强干的外国女子，她在六年的时间里将"特顿报业"经营得井井有条。但问题是，特顿夫人与杰克·哈多克少校打得火热，这一点巴兹尔士

① 杜牧《题乌江亭》，转引自《全唐诗》第523卷第027首。

也看出个端倪了,但他不动声色,并没有表露出来。有一次,特顿家举办聚会,哈多克少校为特顿夫人在特顿家的花园为其拍照,结果她的脖子卡到了一尊著名雕塑的圆孔里,丈夫巴兹尔爵士赶到,开始解救。结局会向什么方向转变,颇为难料——这就是《贵妇之颈》里的故事。年迈的德廖利后背上的文身竟是一名闻名遐迩的画家的作品,很是值钱,很多买家都愿意出高价购买。可问题是,这幅画是刺在德廖利的皮肤上的,如何出售?结局颇为难料——这就是《人皮刺青》里的情景。

"贵妇之颈"是否能得以保全?"人皮刺青"是否还能与人共存?在罗尔德·达尔的笔下,这些故事恐怕都是结局难料的。

第一节 《贵妇之颈》*Neck*

罗尔德·达尔的《贵妇之颈》(*Neck*)被收录在《罗尔德·达尔短篇故事集锦》(*The Collected Short Stories of Roald Dahl*)、《如你之人》(*Someone like You*)、《出人意料故事集》(*Tales of the Unexpected*)、《完全出人意料故事集》(*Completely Unexpected Tales*)、《五部畅销书集》(5 *Bestsellers*)、《〈伟大写手〉及其他故事集》(*The Great Automatic Grammatizator and Other Stories*)、《〈卖伞男子〉及其他故事集》(*The Umbrella Man and Other Stories*)、《罗尔德·达尔选集》(*The Roald Dahl Omnibus*)以及《罗尔德·达尔二十九篇成人故事集》(*Twenty Nine Kisses from Roald Dahl*)等书中。此外,这部小说也被改编成电视系列剧——1979年4月28日播映的《出乎意料的故事集》(*Tales of the Unexpected*)第一部中的第6集(*Episode* 1.6),可见其影响力之大。

一、原作导读

这篇小说是以第一人称"我"(姓名未交代)的视角展开的,但叙述者"我"是"隐身"的——地位无足轻重,属于"看热闹""围观"的类型,起到了"纽带"或者"桥梁"的作用,可以看成作家罗尔德·达尔本人的化身。

故事开篇,"我"向读者交代了巴兹尔·特顿爵士的历史——从父亲那儿继承了一个报业帝国,最终娶了一个名叫纳塔利娅的外国女子为妻。作为一家晚报的社会版专栏作家,"我"参加了一次宴会。宴会上,"我"认识了特顿夫人,闲聊之中约好了下一个周末要到特顿爵士的宅邸拜访。

约定时间到了。"我"驱车按时到达,陶醉于伍顿私邸(特顿家的房产)的豪华:庭院里到处都是修剪成各种形状的花木,还有喷水池和一尊尊名家雕塑。一进门,"我"立刻"嗅"出这座舒适的豪宅里有一股不对劲儿的味道。"我"换衣服的时候,特顿家的管家杰尔克斯走了进来,跟"我"谈论起小费的事情。奇怪的是,他提出不要小费,但"我"要是在牌局中赢钱了,就给他三分之一作为小费,"我"最终同意了他的提议。但是离开前,杰尔克斯透露了一些特顿夫人打牌的"软肋",这令我很不快,感觉这位管家不太喜欢特顿夫人以及某些在座的客人,包括经常跟特顿夫人打牌做搭档的杰克·哈多克少校。很显然,这位少校跟特顿夫人打得火热。第二天,特顿爵士陪"我"在他的房宅周围溜达,边溜达边向"我"介绍他的家史。

"现在,我们在这儿稍微休息一会儿好吗?"溜达半个多小时后,巴兹尔爵士这样问道。于是,我们在一张白色的长凳上坐了下来,长凳设在一座睡莲池的边上,池里游的尽是鲤鱼和金鱼。我们各自点燃了香烟。我们所在的地方比周围的地面要高些,离那座私邸有一些距离。从我们坐的位置看,各个花园在我们下方铺展开来,就像庭院建筑老书里的素描图样一般,有树篱、草坪、台地、喷泉,这些共同构成了一个个漂亮的、或方或圆的图案。

"Shall we rest here now a little while?" Sir Basil said after we had walked for more than half an hour. So we sat down on a white bench beside a water-lily pond full of carp and goldfish, and lit cigarettes. We were some way from the house, on a piece of ground that was raised above its surroundings, and from where we sat the gardens were spread out below us like a drawing in one of those old books on garden architecture, with the hedges and lawns and terraces and fountains making a pretty pattern of squares and rings.

远处的草坪上,一名男子和一名女子在追逐嬉戏,女子在各种雕塑前做出各种姿势,然后男子为女子拍照。女子开玩笑似地将头伸进一座雕塑的圆孔内,男子从圆孔的另一头亲吻那个女子,但不幸的是,那个女子的头似乎卡住、拔不出来了。特顿爵士和"我"聊天的时候都看到了这一幕,但那对男女却浑然不知。于是,特顿爵士和"我"前去查看,结果发现那男子是哈多克少校,女子是特顿夫人。被卡住的特顿夫人大喊大叫,态度蛮横,甚至对丈夫破口大骂,毫不在意。见此情景,做丈夫的特顿爵士吩咐管家杰尔克斯去取工具,以便劈开雕塑的圆孔,解救妻子纳塔利娅。

杰尔克斯取来一把斧子和一个锯,同时伸到巴兹尔跟前,让他挑选。但是,他拿斧子的手稍微多向前伸出一点点:

我看到巴兹尔爵士有点恍恍惚惚地伸出手,从杰尔克斯手中接过斧子。就在紧紧握住斧柄的一瞬间,他似乎意识到要求他做的是什么事,整个人一下子活跃起来了。

I saw him reach out in a dreamy sort of way, accepting it from Jelks, and then, the instant he felt the handle in his grasp he seemed to realize what was required of him and he sprang to life.

二、原作释读

这篇小说阅读起来,具有一定的难度。首先,单词障碍较多,有些词还比较生僻。其次,涉及园艺方面的内容,恐怕不太好理解。同时,达尔对于某些专业知识的"显摆",极大程度上构成了阅读理解的障碍。

Neck[①]

When, about eight years ago, old Sir William Turton died and his son Basil inherited The Turton Press (as well as the title), I can remember how they started laying bets around Fleet Street[②] as to how long it would be before some nice young woman managed to persuade the little fellow that she must look after him. That is to say, him and his money.

The new Sir Basil Turton was maybe forty years old at the time, a bachelor, a man of mild and simple character who up to then had shown no interest in anything at all except his collection of modern paintings and sculpture. No woman had disturbed him; no scandal or gossip had ever touched his name. But now that he had become the proprietor of quite a large newspaper and magazine empire, it was necessary for him to emerge from the calm of his father's country house and come up to London.

---

① 本部小说原文出自"DAHL, R. *The Collected Short Stories of Roald Dahl* [M]. London: Penguin Books Ltd., 1992"。

② Fleet Street: *Noun* a street in central London in which the offices of national newspapers were located until the mid 1980s (often used to refer to the British Press) 舰队街(位于伦敦中心,20 世纪 80 年代中期以前许多报馆集中于此,因此常被用来指英国报业。)

Naturally, the vultures① started gathering at once, and I believe that not only Fleet Street but very nearly the whole of the city was looking on eagerly as they scrambled for the body. It was slow motion, of course, deliberate and deadly slow motion, and therefore not so much like vultures as a bunch of agile② crabs clawing for a piece of horsemeat under water.

But to everyone's surprise the little chap proved to be remarkably elusive③, and the chase dragged on right through the spring and early summer of that year. I did not know Sir Basil personally, nor did I have any reason to feel friendly towards him, but I couldn't help taking the side of my own sex and found myself cheering loudly every time he managed to get himself off the hook④.

Then, round about the beginning of August, apparently at some secret female signal, the girls declared a sort of truce⑤ among themselves

---

① vulture: *Noun* a large bird of prey with the head and neck more or less bare of feathers, feeding chiefly on carrion and reputed to gather with others in anticipation of the death of a sick or injured animal or person 兀鹰;秃鹫

vulture: *Noun* a contemptible person who preys on or exploits others 贪婪的人;劫掠成性者

② agile: *Adjective* able to move quickly and easily 敏捷的(e.g. His vague manner concealed an agile mind. 他含糊的风格掩盖了他敏捷的头脑。)

③ elusive: *Adjective* difficult to find, catch, or achieve 难以发现(或捉住、得到)的;易逃脱的(e.g. Success will become ever more elusive. 成功将变得愈发难以获得。)

④ off the hook: (informal) no longer in difficulty or trouble(非正式)摆脱困境(或麻烦)(e.g. I lied to get him off the hook. 为了让他摆脱麻烦我撒了谎。)

⑤ truce: *Noun* an agreement between enemies or opponents to stop fighting or arguing for a certain time 休战;停战(e.g. The guerrillas called a three-day truce. 游击队宣布休战三天。)

while they went abroad, and rested, and regrouped, and made fresh plans for the winter kill. This was a mistake because precisely at that moment a dazzling creature called Natalia something or other, whom nobody had heard of before, swept in from the Continent, took Sir Basil firmly by the wrist and led him off in a kind of swoon① to the Registry Office② at Caxton Hall where she married him before anyone else, least of all the bridegroom, realized what was happening.

You can imagine that the London ladies were indignant, and naturally they started disseminating③ a vast amount of fruity gossip about the new Lady Turton ("That dirty poacher④," they called her). But we don't have to go into that. In fact, for the purposes of this story we can skip the next six years, which brings us right up to the present, to an occasion exactly one week ago today when I myself had the pleasure of meeting her ladyship for the first time. By now, as you must have guessed, she was not only running the whole of The Turton Press, but as a result had become a considerable political force in the country. I realize that other women have done this sort of thing before, but what made her

---

① swoon: *Noun* an occurrence of fainting 昏厥(e. g. Her strength ebbed away and she fell into a swoon. 她的力气越来越小,然后就昏倒了。)

② registry office: *Noun* another term for register office (used in informal and non-official use)(非正式、非官方用语)意义同"register office"

register office: *Noun* (in the UK) a local government building where civil marriages are conducted and births, marriages, and deaths are recorded with the issue of certificates(英国)民事登记处(办理结婚手续或出生、死亡登记。)

③ disseminate: *Verb* [with obj.] spread or disperse (something, especially information) widely 散布;传播(某物,尤指信息)(e. g. Health authorities should foster good practice by disseminating information. 卫生部门应该通过散布信息的方法鼓励好的做法。)

④ poacher: *Noun* a person who hunts or catches game or fish illegally 偷猎者

particular case unusual was the fact that she was a foreigner and that nobody seemed to know precisely what country she came from—Yugoslavia①, Bulgaria②, or Russia.

So last Thursday I went to this small dinner party at a friend's in London, and while we were standing around in the drawing-room before the meal, sipping good Martinis and talking about the atom bomb and Mr. Bevan, the maid popped her head in to announce the last guest.

"Lady Turton," she said.

Nobody stopped talking; we were too well mannered for that. No heads were turned. Only our eyes swung round to the door, waiting for the entrance.

She came in fast—tall and slim in a red-gold dress with sparkles on it—the mouth smiling, the hand outstretched towards her hostess, and my heavens, I must say she was a beauty.

"Mildred, good evening!"

"My dear Lady Turton! How nice!"

I believe we did stop talking then, and we turned and stared and stood waiting quite meekly to be introduced, just like she might have

---

① Yugoslavia: *Noun* a federation of states in SE Europe, in the Balkans 南斯拉夫(欧洲东南部巴尔干半岛的联邦国家)

② Bulgaria: *Noun* a country in SE Europe on the western shores of the Black Sea; pop. 8 798 000 (est. 1991); official language, Bulgarian; capital, Sofia. Part of the Ottoman Empire from the 14th century, Bulgaria remained under Turkish rule until the late 19th century, becoming independent in 1908. A communist state was set up by the Soviets after the Second World War, and a multiparty democratic system was introduced in 1989. 保加利亚(欧洲东南部的一个国家,在黑海的西海岸,1991年估计人口8 798 000;官方语言为保加利亚语,首都索非亚;14世纪起是奥斯曼帝国的一部分,此后直到19世纪末一直受土耳其统治,1908年独立,第二次世界大战后被苏联人建成共产主义国家,1989年实行多党民主制。)

been the Queen or a famous film star. But she was better looking than either of those. The hair was black, and to go with it she had one of those pale, oval, innocent fifteenth-century Flemish① faces, almost exactly a Madonna② by Memling③ or Van Eyck④. At least that was the first impression. Later, when my turn came to shake hands, I got a closer look and saw that except for the outline and colouring it wasn't really a Madonna at all—far, far from it.

The nostrils for example were very odd, somehow more open, more flaring than any I had seen before, and excessively arched. This gave the whole nose a kind of open, snorting look that had something of the wild

---

① Flemish: *Adjective* of or relating to Flanders, its people, or their language (与)佛兰德斯(有关)的;(与)佛兰德斯人(有关)的;(与)佛兰德斯语(有关)的

② Madonna: *Noun* (usu. as "madonna") a picture, statue, or medallion of the Madonna, typically depicted seated and holding the infant Jesus 圣母画像(或雕像)

③ Hans Memling (also spelled Memlinc; c. 1430—1494) was a German-born painter who moved to Flanders and worked in the tradition of Early Netherlandish painting. From the 1460s until the end of his life he became one of the leading artists, painting both portraits and several large religious works, continuing the style he learned in his youth from his masters such as Rogier van der Weyden. 汉斯·梅姆灵(约1430—1494):生于德国的画家,后来移居到佛兰德斯,并在那儿以早期荷兰主义的手法进行绘画创作。从15世纪60年代起直到生命最后一刻,他始终是肖像和宗教题材绘画的领军人物之一,继承了他从罗吉耶·范·德·韦登等大师那里学到的画风。

④ Van Eyck: *Noun* Jan Van Eyck (c. 1370—1441), Flemish painter. He made innovative use of oils, bringing greater flexibility, richer and denser colour, and a wider range from light to dark. Notable works: *The Adoration of the Lamb* (known as the Ghent Altarpiece, 1432) in the church of St. Bavon in Ghent and *The Arnolfini Marriage* (1434). 简·凡·爱克(约1370—1441):佛兰德斯画家,他改革油画技术,使之更为灵活、色彩更鲜艳浓厚、色泽变化更丰富;著名作品有:《羔羊受崇敬》(1432年,以"根特祭坛画"而为人所知)和《阿诺弗尼夫妇肖像》(1434)。

animal about it the mustang①.

And the eyes when I saw them close, were not wide and round the way the Madonna painters used to make them, but long and half-closed, half smiling, half sullen, and slightly vulgar, so that in one way and another they gave her a most delicately dissipated② air. What's more they didn't look at you directly. They came to you slowly from over on one side with a curious sliding motion that made me nervous. I tried to see their colour, thought it was pale grey, but couldn't be sure.

Then she was led away across the room to meet other people. I stood watching her. She was clearly conscious of her success and of the way these Londoners were deferring③ to her. "Here am I," she seemed to be saying, "and I only came over a few years ago, but already I am richer and more powerful than any of you." There was a little prance④ of triumph in her walk.

A few minutes later we went in to dinner, and to my surprise I found myself seated at her ladyship's right. I presumed that our hostess had done this as a kindness to me, thinking I might pick up some material for the social column I write each day in the evening paper. I settled myself down ready for an interesting meal. But the famous lady took no notice of me at all; she spent her time talking to the man on her left; the host.

---

① mustang: *Noun* an American feral horse which is typically small and lightly built 野马

② dissipated: *Adjective* (of a person or way of life) overindulging in sensual pleasures(人或生活方式)浪荡的;沉迷于酒色的(e. g. dissipated behaviour 放荡之举)

③ defer: *Verb* [no obj.] (defer to) submit humbly to (a person or their wishes or qualities) 尊崇(人或其意愿、素质)(e. g. He deferred to Tim's superior knowledge. 他折服于蒂姆渊博的知识。)

④ prance: *Noun* an act or instance of prancing 腾跳;昂首阔步

Until at last, just as I was finishing my ice-cream, she suddenly turned, reached over, picked up my place card and read the name. Then, with that queer sliding motion of the eyes she looked into my face. I smiled and made a little bow. She didn't smile back, but started shooting questions at me, rather personal questions—job, age, family, things like that in a peculiar lapping voice, and I found myself answering as best I could.

During this inquisition it came out among other things that I was a lover of painting and sculpture.

"Then you should come down to the country some time and see my husband's collection." She said it casually, merely as a form of conversation, but you must realize that in my job I cannot afford to lose an opportunity like this.

"How kind of you, Lady Turton. But I'd simply love to. When shall I come?"

Her head went up and she hesitated, frowned, shrugged her shoulders and then said, "Oh I don't care. Any time."

"How about this next weekend? Would that be all right?"

The slow narrow eyes rested a moment on mine, then travelled away. "I suppose so, if you wish. I don't care."

And that was how the following Saturday afternoon I came to be driving down to Wooton① with my suitcase in the back of the car. You may think that perhaps I forced the invitation a bit, but I couldn't have got it any other way. And apart from the professional aspect, I personally wanted very much to see the house. As you know, Wooton is one of the

---

① 这里的"Wooton"以及本段中提到的"Longleat""Wollaton""Montacute"等都是英国早期遗留下来的著名的私人宅邸。

truly great stone houses of the early English Renaissance①. Like its sisters, Longleat, Wollaton, and Montacute, it was built in the latter half of the sixteenth century when for the first time a great man's house could be designed as a comfortable dwelling, not as a castle, and when a new group of architects such as John Thorpe and the Smithsons were starting to do marvellous things all over the country.

It lies south of Oxford, near a small town called Princes Risborough② not a long trip from London—and as I swung in through the main gates the sky was closing overhead and the early winter evening was beginning.

I went slowly up the long drive, trying to see as much of the grounds as possible, especially the famous topiary③ which I had heard such a lot about. And I must say it was an impressive sight. On all sides there were massive yew trees④, trimmed and clipped into many different comical shapes—hens, pigeons, bottles, boots, armchairs, castles, egg-cups, lanterns, old women with flaring petticoats⑤, tall pillars, some crowned

---

① Renaissance: *Noun* the revival of art and literature under the influence of classical models in the 14th ~ 16th centuries 文艺复兴

② Princes Risborough: *Noun* It is a small town in Buckinghamshire, England. 里斯伯勒王子(位于英格兰白金汉郡的一个小镇)

③ topiary: *Noun* shrubs or trees clipped into ornamental shapes in such a way (被修剪的)林木;整形树(e.g. a cottage surrounded by topiary and flowers 一处被整形树和花卉包围的农舍)

④ yew tree or yew: *Noun* a coniferous tree which has red berry-like fruits, and most parts of which are highly poisonous. Yews are linked with folklore and superstition and can live to a great age; the timber is used in cabinetmaking and (formerly) to make longbows 紫杉;红豆杉

⑤ petticoat: *Noun* a woman's light, loose undergarment hanging from the shoulders or the waist, worn under a skirt or dress(女裙或女装里面轻且宽松的)衬裙

with a ball, others with big rounded roofs and stemless mushroom finials①—and in the half darkness the greens had turned to black so that each figure, each tree, took on a dark, smooth sculptural quality. At one point I saw a lawn covered with gigantic chessmen, each a live yew tree, marvellously fashioned. I stopped the car, got out and walked among them, and they were twice as tall as me. What's more the set was complete, kings, queens, bishops②, knights③, rooks④ and pawns⑤ standing in position as for the start of a game.

Around the next bend I saw the great grey house itself, and in front of it the large entrance forecourt enclosed by a high balustraded wall with

---

① finial: *Noun* a distinctive section or ornament at the apex of a roof, pinnacle, canopy, or similar structure in a building(建筑物的)叶尖饰;尖顶饰

② bishop: *Noun* a chess piece, typically with its top shaped like a mitre, that can move in any direction along a diagonal on which it stands. Each player starts the game with two bishops, one moving on white squares and the other on black(国际象棋中的)象

③ knight: *Noun* a chess piece, typically with its top shaped like a horse's head, that moves by jumping to the opposite corner of a rectangle two squares by three. Each player starts the game with two knights(棋子)马

④ rook: *Noun* a chess piece, typically with its top in the shape of a battlement, that can move in any direction along a rank or file on which it stands. Each player starts the game with two rooks at opposite ends of the first rank(国际象棋中的)车

⑤ pawn: *Noun* a chess piece of the smallest size and value, that moves one square forwards along its file if unobstructed (or two on the first move), or one square diagonally forwards when making a capture. Each player begins with eight pawns on the second rank, and can promote a pawn to become any other piece (typically a queen) if it reaches the opponent's end of the board(国际象棋中的)卒

small pillared pavilions① at its outer angles. The piers② of the balustrades③ were surmounted④ by stone obelisks⑤—the Italian influence on the Tudor⑥ mind—and a flight of steps at least a hundred feet wide led up to the house.

As I drove into the forecourt I noticed with rather a shock that the fountain basin in the middle supported a large statue by Epstein⑦. A lovely thing, mind you, but surely not in sympathy with its surroundings. Then, looking back as I climbed the stairway to the front door, I saw that on all the little lawns and terraces round about there were other modern

---

① pavilion: *Noun* a summer house or other decorative building used as a shelter in a park or large garden(公园或大花园中的)凉亭;亭子;阁

② pier: *Noun* a solid support designed to sustain vertical pressure, in particular(尤指用以承受垂直压力的)固体支架

③ balustrade: *Noun* a railing supported by balusters, especially one forming an ornamental parapet to a balcony, bridge, or terrace(尤指形成阳台、桥梁或平台的装饰性矮墙的)护栏;扶手

④ surmount: *Verb* [usu. be surmounted] stand or be placed on top of 站在上面;被放置在……上(e. g. The tomb was surmounted by a sculptured angel. 坟墓上立着一座天使雕塑。)

⑤ obelisk: *Noun* stone pillar, typically having a square or rectangular cross section, set up as a monument or landmark 方尖碑;(用作里程碑的)方尖塔

⑥ Tudor: *Adjective* of or relating to the English royal dynasty which held the throne from the accession of Henry VII in 1485 until the death of Elizabeth I in 1603. (与)都铎王朝(有关)的(该王朝始自1485年亨利七世登基,终至1603年伊丽莎白一世驾崩。)

⑦ Epstein: *Noun* Sir Jacob Epstein (1880—1959), American-born British sculptor. A founder member of the vorticist group, he later had great success in his modelled portraits of the famous, in particular his *Einstein* (1933). 雅各布·爱泼斯坦爵士(1880—1959):美国出生的英国雕刻家,漩涡画派创始人之一,后在名人肖像雕刻方面获得巨大成功,代表作为《爱因斯坦》(1933)。

statues and many kinds of curious sculpture. In the distance I thought I recognized Gaudier Brzeska①, Brancusi②, Saint - Gaudens③, Henry Moore④, and Epstein again.

The door was opened by a young footman⑤ who led me up to a bedroom on the first floor. Her ladyship, he explained, was resting, so were the other guests, but they would all be down in the main drawing-room in an hour or so, dressed for dinner.

Now in my job it is necessary to do a lot of weekending. I suppose I spend around fifty Saturdays and Sundays a year in other people's houses, and as a result I have become fairly sensitive to unfamiliar atmosphere. I can tell good or bad almost by sniffing with my nose the mo-

---

① Gaudier Brzeska: *Noun* Henri Gaudier - Brzeska (1891—1915) was a French sculptor who developed a rough hewn, primitive style of direct carving. 亨利·高迪-布热斯卡(1891—1915):法国雕塑家,创造了粗削式直接雕塑的原始风格。

② Brancusi: *Noun* Constantin Brancusi (1876—1957), Romanian sculptor, who spent much of his working life in France. His sculpture represents an attempt to move away from a representational art and to capture the essence of forms by reducing them to their ultimate, almost abstract, simplicity. 康斯坦丁·布兰库兹(1876—1957):罗马尼亚雕塑家,在法国度过其大部分职业生涯;他的雕塑代表这样一种尝试,即脱离具象派艺术,通过将形式极度简化为抽象单纯的状态,来抓住形式的实质。

③ Saint-Gaudens (1848—1907): *Noun* U.S. sculptor; born in Ireland. 圣高登斯(1848—1907):生于爱尔兰的美国雕塑家。

④ Henry Moore (1898—1986) was an English sculptor and artist. He was best known for his semi - abstract monumental bronze sculptures. 亨利·摩尔(1898—1986):英国雕塑家和艺术家,以他带有半抽象性质的大型铸铜雕塑闻名。

⑤ footman: *Noun* a liveried servant whose duties include admitting visitors and waiting at table(穿制服的)侍者;男仆

ment I get in the front door; and this one I was in now I did not like. The place smelled wrong. There was the faint, desiccated① whiff of something troublesome in the air; I was conscious of it even as I lay steaming luxuriously in my great marble bath; and I couldn't help hoping that no unpleasant things were going to happen before Monday came.

The first of them—though more of a surprise than an unpleasantness—occurred ten minutes later. I was sitting on the bed putting on my socks when softly the door opened, and an ancient lopsided② gnome③ in black tails slid into the room. He was the butler, he explained, and his name was Jelks, and he did so hope I was comfortable and had everything I wanted.

I told him I was and had.

He said he would do all he could to make my weekend agreeable. I thanked him and waited for him to go. He hesitated, and then, in a voice dripping with unction④, he begged permission to mention a rather delicate matter. I told him to go ahead.

To be quite frank, he said, it was about tipping. The whole business of tipping made him acutely miserable.

Oh? And why was that?

Well, if I really wanted to know, he didn't like the idea that his

---

① desiccated: *Adjective* (figurative) lacking interest, passion, or energy(喻)枯燥乏味的;苍白无力的(e.g. a desiccated history of ideas 枯燥乏味的思想史)

② lopsided: *Adjective* with one side lower or smaller than the other 向一侧倾斜的;歪的(e.g. a lopsided grin 歪着嘴笑)

③ gnome: *Noun* (informal) a small ugly person(非正式)矮小丑陋的人

④ unction: *Noun* a manner of expression arising or apparently arising from deep emotion, especially as intended to flatter 甜言蜜语;虚情假意(e.g. The headlines gloated with the kind of effusive unction only the English press can muster. 那些标题采用只有英国报界敢用的过度谄媚表达洋洋自得之情。)

guests felt under an obligation to tip him when they left the house—as indeed they did. It was an undignified proceeding for the tipping and the tipped. Moreover, he was well aware of the anguish① that was often created in the minds of guests such as myself, if I would pardon the liberty, who might feel compelled by convention to give more than they could really afford.

He paused, and two small crafty② eyes watched my face for a sign. I murmured that he needn't worry himself about such things as far as I was concerned.

On the contrary, he said, he hoped sincerely that I would agree from the beginning to give him no tip at all.

"Well," I said. "Let's not fuss about it now, and when the time comes we'll see how we feel."

"No, sir!" he cried. "Please, I really must insist."

So I agreed.

He thanked me, and shuffled③ a step or two closer. Then, laying his head on one side and clasping his hands before him like a priest, he gave a tiny apologetic shrug of the shoulders. The small sharp eyes were still watching me, and I waited, one sock on, the other in my hands,

---

① anguish: *Noun* [mass noun] severe mental or physical pain or suffering (精神或肉体上的)极度痛苦;剧痛(e. g. She shut her eyes in anguish. 她极为痛苦地闭上了眼睛。)

② crafty: *Adjective* clever at achieving one's aims by indirect or deceitful methods 狡诈的;诡计多端的(e. g. A crafty crook faked an injury to escape from prison. 狡猾的骗子假装受伤逃出了监狱。)

③ shuffle: *Verb* [no obj., with adverbial] walk by dragging one's feet along or without lifting them fully from the ground 拖着脚走(e. g. I stepped into my skis and shuffled to the edge of the steep slope. 我穿上滑雪板,拖着脚走到陡峭的山坡边。)

trying to guess what was coming next.

All that he would ask, he said softly, so softly now that his voice was like music heard faintly in the street outside a great concert hail, all that he would ask was that instead of a tip I should give him thirty-three and a third percent of my winnings at cards over the weekend. If I lost there would be nothing to pay. It was all so soft and smooth and sudden that I was not even surprised.

"Do they play a lot of cards, Jelks?"

"Yes, sir, a great deal."

"Isn't thirty-three and a third a bit steep①?"

"I don't think so, sir."

"I'll give you ten percent."

"No, sir, I couldn't do that." He was now examining the finger-nails of his left hand, and patiently frowning.

"Then we'll make it fifteen. All right?"

"Thirty-three and a third, sir. It's very reasonable. After all, sir, seeing that I don't even know if you are a good player, what I'm actually doing, not meaning to be personal, is backing a horse and I've never even seen it run."

No doubt you think I should never have started bargaining with the butler in the first place, and perhaps you are right. But being a liberal-minded person, I always try my best to be affable② with the lower classes. Apart from that, the more I thought about it, the more I had to

---

① steep: *Adjective* (informal) (of a price or demand) not reasonable; excessive(非正式)(价格或需求)难以接受的;过高的(e.g. a steep membership fee 过高的会员费)

② affable: *Adjective* friendly, good-natured, or easy to talk to 友好的;性情温和的;和蔼可亲的(e.g. an affable and agreeable companion 和蔼可亲、讨人喜欢的同伴)

admit to myself that it was an offer no sportsman had the right to reject.

"All right then, Jelks. As you wish."

"Thank you, sir." He moved towards the door, walking slowly sideways like a crab; but once more he hesitated, a hand on the knob. "If I may give a little advice, sir—may I?"

"Yes?"

"It's simply that her ladyship tends to overbid her hand."

Now this was going too far. I was so startled I dropped my sock. After all, it's one thing to have a harmless little sporting arrangement with the butler about tipping, but when he begins conniving① with you to take money away from the hostess then it's time to call a halt.

"All right Jelks. Now that'll do."

"No offence, sir, I hope. All I mean is you're bound to be playing against her ladyship. She always partners Major Haddock."

"Major Haddock? You mean Major Jack Haddock?"

"Yes, sir."

I noticed there was a trace of a sneer around the corner of Jelks's nose when he spoke about this man. And it was worse with Lady Turton. Each time he said "her ladyship" he spoke the words with the outsides of his lips as though he were nibbling a lemon, and there was a subtle, mocking inflection② in his voice.

"You'll excuse me now, sir. Her ladyship will be down at seven o'clock. So will Major Haddock and the others." He slipped out of the door leaving behind him a certain dampness in the room and a faint smell

---

① connive: *Verb* conspire to do something considered immoral, illegal, or harmful 共谋;阴谋(e. g. The government had connived with security forces in permitting murder. 政府已和安全部队暗中勾结默许谋杀。)

② inflection: *Noun* the variation of the pitch of a musical note 变音;转调

of embrocation①.

Shortly after seven, I found my way to the main drawing-room, and Lady Turton, as beautiful as ever, got up to greet me.

"I wasn't even sure you were coming," she said in that peculiar lilting voice. "What's your name again?"

"I'm afraid I took you at your word, Lady Turton. I hope it's all right."

"Why not?" she said. "There's forty-seven bedrooms in the house. This is my husband." A small man came around the back of her and said, "You know, I'm so glad you were able to come." He had a lovely warm smile and when he took my hand I felt instantly a touch of friendship in his fingers.

"And Carmen La Rosa," Lady Turton said.

This was a powerfully built woman who looked as though she might have something to do with horses. She nodded at me, and although my hand was already half-way out she didn't give me hers, thus forcing me to convert the movement into a noseblow.

"You have a cold?" she said. "I'm sorry."

I did not like this Miss Carmen La Rosa.

"And this is Jack Haddock."

I knew this man slightly. He was a director of companies (whatever that may mean), and a well-known member of society. I had used his name a few times in my column, but I had never liked him, and this I think was mainly because I have a deep suspicion of all people who carry their military titles back with them into private life—especially majors

① embrocation: *Noun* [mass noun] a liquid used for rubbing on the body to relieve pain from sprains and strains(治疗扭伤的)涂擦剂

and colonels. Standing there in his dinner-jacket① with his full-blooded② animal face and black eyebrows and large white teeth, he looked so handsome there was almost something indecent③ about it. He had a way of raising his upper lip when he smiled, baring his teeth, and he was smiling now as he gave me a hairy brown hand.

"I hope you're going to say some nice things about us in your column."

"He better had," Lady Turton said, "or I'll say some nasty ones about him on my front page."

I laughed, but all three of them, Lady Turton, Major Haddock, and Carmen La Rosa had already turned away and were settling themselves back on the sofa. Jelks gave me a drink, and Sir Basil drew me gently aside for a quiet chat at the other end of the room. Every now and then Lady Turton would call her husband to fetch her something—another Martini, a cigarette, an ashtray, a handkerchief—and he, half rising from his chair, would be forestalled④ by the watchful Jelks who fetched it for him.

---

① dinner jacket or dinner-jacket: *Noun* a man's short jacket without tails, typically a black one, worn with a bow tie for formal occasions in the evening(多指黑色配蝴蝶结领结用于晚间正式场合的男士)无尾礼服

② full-blooded: *Adjective* [attrib.] of unmixed race 纯血统的;纯种的(e.g. a full-blooded Cherokee 纯血统的彻罗基人)

③ indecent: *Adjective* not conforming with generally accepted standards of behaviour or propriety; obscene 下流的;猥亵的(e.g. The film was grossly indecent. 这部电影下流不堪。)

④ forestall: *Verb* act in advance of (someone) in order to prevent them from doing something 抢在(某人)之前采取行动(以防止其做某事)(e.g. She made to rise but Erika forestalled her and got the telephone pad. 她准备起身,但埃里卡抢先拿起了电话记事本。)

Clearly, Jelks loved his master; and just as clearly he hated the wife. Each time he did something for her he made a little sneer with his nose and drew his lips together so they puckered① like a turkey's bottom.

At dinner, our hostess sat her two friends, Haddock and La Rosa, on either side of her. This unconventional arrangement left Sir Basil and me at the other end of the table where we were able to continue our pleasant talk about painting and sculpture. Of course it was obvious to me by now that the Major was infatuated② with her ladyship. And again, although I hate to say it, it seemed as though the La Rosa woman was hunting the same bird.

All this foolishness appeared to delight the hostess. But it did not delight her husband. I could see that he was conscious of the little scene all the time we were talking; and often his mind would wander from our subject and he would stop short in mid-sentence, his eyes travelling down to the other end of the table to settle pathetically for a moment on that lovely head with the black hair and the curiously flaring nostrils. He must have noticed then how exhilarated she was, how the hand that gestured as she spoke rested every now and again on the Major's arm, and how the other woman, the one who perhaps had something to do with horses, kept saying, "Nata – li – a? Now Nata – li – a, listen to me!"

"Tomorrow," I said, "you must take me round and show me the sculptures you've put up in the garden."

---

① pucker: *Verb* [no obj.] (especially of a person's face or a facial feature) tightly gather or contract into wrinkles or small folds(尤指某人脸部或面貌)起皱;起褶(e. g. The child's face puckered, ready to cry. 孩子皱起脸,就要哭了。)

② infatuate: *Verb* (be infatuated with) be inspired with an intense but short-lived passion or admiration for 被(一时强烈的激情或爱慕)冲昏头脑;迷恋(e. g. She is infatuated with a handsome police chief. 她迷恋着一位英俊的警长。)

"Of course," he said, "with pleasure." He glanced again at the wife, and his eyes had a sort of supplicating① look that was piteous beyond words. He was so mild and passive a man in every way that even now I could see there was no anger in him, no danger, no chance of an explosion.

After dinner I was ordered straight to the card table to partner Miss Carmen La Rosa against Major Haddock and Lady Turton. Sir Basil sat quietly on the sofa with a book.

There was nothing unusual about the game itself; it was routine and rather dull. But Jelks was a nuisance②. All evening he prowled around us, emptying ashtrays and asking about drinks and peering at our hands. He was obviously short-sighted and I doubt whether he saw much of what was going on because as you may or may not know, here in England no butler has ever been permitted to wear spectacles nor for that matter, a moustache. This is the golden, unbreakable rule and a very sensible one it is too, although I'm not quite sure what lies behind it. I presume that a moustache would make him look too much like a gentleman, and spectacles too much like an American, and where would we be then I should like to know? In any event Jelks was a nuisance all evening; and so was Lady Turton who was constantly called to the phone on newspaper business.

At eleven o'clock she looked up from her cards and said, "Basil, it's time you went to bed."

"Yes, my dear, perhaps it is." He closed the book, got up, and

---

① supplicate: *Verb* [no obj.] ask or beg for something earnestly or humbly 恳求;哀求;祈求

② nuisance: *Noun* a person, thing, or circumstance causing inconvenience or annoyance 讨厌的人(或东西、情况)(e.g. An unreasonable landlord could become a nuisance. 一个不讲道理的房东会讨人厌。)

stood for a minute watching the play. "Are you having a good game?" he asked.

The others didn't answer him so I said, "It's a nice game."

"I'm so glad. And Jelks will look after you and get anything you want."

"Jelks can go to bed too," the wife said.

I could hear Major Haddock breathing through his nose beside me, and the soft drop of the cards one by one on to the table, and then the sound of Jelks's feet shuffling over the carpet towards us.

"You wouldn't prefer me to stay, m'lady①?"

"No. Go to bed. You too, Basil."

"Yes, my dear. Good night. Good night all."

Jelks opened the door for him, and he went slowly out followed by the butler.

As soon as the next rubber② was over, I said that I too wanted to go to bed.

"All right," Lady Turton said. "Good night."

I went up to my room, locked the door, took a pill, and went to sleep.

The next morning, Sunday, I got up and dressed around ten o'clock and went down to the breakfast-room. Sir Basil was there before me, and Jelks was serving him with grilled kidneys and bacon and fried tomatoes. He was delighted to see me and suggested that as soon as we had finished eating we should take a long walk around the grounds. I told him nothing would give me more pleasure.

Half an hour later we started out, and you've no idea what a relief

---

① m'lady = my lady

② rubber: *Noun* (Bridge) a unit of play in which one side scores bonus points for winning the best of three games(桥牌)一盘胜局

it was to get away from that house and into the open air. It was one of those warm shining days that come occasionally in mid-winter after a night of heavy rain, with a bright surprising sun and not a breath of wind. Bare trees seemed beautiful in the sunlight, water still dripping from the branches, and wet places all around were sparkling with diamonds. The sky had small faint clouds.

"What a lovely day!"

"Yes—isn't it a lovely day!"

We spoke hardly another word during the walk; it wasn't necessary. But he took me everywhere and I saw it all—the huge chessmen and all the rest of the topiary. The elaborate garden houses, the pools, the fountains, the children's maze whose hedges were hornbeam and lime① so that it was only good in summer when the leaves were out, and the parterres②, the rockeries, the greenhouses with their vines and nectarine③ trees. And of course, the sculpture. Most of the contemporary European sculptors were there, in bronze, granite, limestone, and wood; and although it was a pleasure to see them warming and glowing in the sun, to me they still looked a trifle out of place in these vast formal surroundings.

"Shall we rest here now a little while?" Sir Basil said after we had walked for more than half an hour. So we sat down on a white bench be-

---

① lime or lime tree: *Noun* the evergreen citrus tree which produces this fruit, widely cultivated in warm climates 酸橙树(广泛栽培与温暖气候区)

② parterre: *Noun* a level space in a garden occupied by an ornamental arrangement of flower beds 花坛;花圃

③ nectarine: *Noun* a peach of a variety with smooth, thin, brightly coloured skin and rich firm flesh 油桃;蜜桃

side a water-lily pond full of carp① and goldfish, and lit cigarettes. We were some way from the house, on a piece of ground that was raised above its surroundings, and from where we sat the gardens were spread out below us like a drawing in one of those old books on garden architecture, with the hedges and lawns and terraces and fountains making a pretty pattern of squares and rings.

"My father bought this place just before I was born," Sir Basil said. "I've lived here ever since, and I know every inch of it. Each day I grow to love it more."

"It must be wonderful in summer."

"Oh, but it is. You should come down and see it in May and June. Will you promise to do that?"

"Of course," I said. "I'd love to come," and as I spoke I was watching the figure of a woman dressed in red moving among the flower-beds in the far distance. I saw her cross over a wide expanse of lawn, and there was a lilt in her walk, a little shadow attending her, and when she was over the lawn, she turned left and went along one side of a high wall of clipped yew until she came to another smaller lawn that was circular and had in its centre a piece of sculpture.

"This garden is younger than the house," Sir Basil said. "It was laid out early in the eighteenth century by a Frenchman called Beaumont, the same fellow who did Levens, in Westmorland②. For at least a year

---

① carp: *Noun* a deep-bodied freshwater fish, typically with barbels around the mouth. Carp are farmed for food in some parts of the world and are often kept in large ponds 鲤鱼

② Westmorland: *Noun* a former county of NW England. In 1974 it was united with Cumberland and northern parts of Lancashire to form the county of Cumbria. 威斯特摩兰郡(原英格兰西北部的一个郡,1974年与坎伯兰郡以及兰开夏郡的北部地区一起组成坎布里亚郡。)

he had two hundred and fifty men working on it."

The woman in the red dress had been joined now by a man, and they were standing face to face, about a yard apart, in the very centre of the whole garden panorama, on this little circular patch of lawn, apparently conversing. The man had some small black object in his hand.

"If you're interested I'll show you the bills that Beaumont put in to the Duke while he was making it."

"I'd like very much to see them. They must be fascinating."

"He paid his labourers a shilling a day and they worked ten hours."

In the clear sunlight it was not difficult to follow the movements and gestures of the two figures on the lawn. They had turned now towards the piece of sculpture, and were pointing at it in a sort of mocking way, apparently laughing and making jokes about its shape. I recognized it as being one of the Henry Moores, done in wood, a thin smooth object of singular① beauty that had two or three holes in it and a number of strange limbs protruding.

"When Beaumont planted the yew trees for the chess-men and the other things, he knew they wouldn't amount to much for at least a hundred years. We don't seem to possess that sort of patience in our planning these days, do we? What do you think?"

"No," I said. "We don't."

The black object in the man's hand turned out to be a camera, and now he had stepped back and was taking pictures of the woman beside the Henry Moore. She was striking a number of different poses, all of

① singular: *Adjective* exceptionally good or great; remarkable 非凡的;卓越的;杰出的(e.g. He had the singular good fortune not to die in the trenches. 他运气特别好,没有死在战壕中。)

them, so far as I could see, ludicrous① and meant to be amusing. Once she put her arms around one of the protruding wooden limbs and hugged it, and another time she climbed up and sat side-saddle on the thing, holding imaginary reins in her hands. A great wall of yew hid these two people from the house, and indeed from all the rest of the garden except the little hill on which we sat. They had every right to believe they were not overlooked, and even if they had happened to glance our way—which was into the sun—I doubt whether they would have noticed the two small motionless figures sitting on the bench beside the pond.

"You know, I love these yews." Sir Basil said. "The colour of them is so wonderful in a garden because it rests the eye. And in the summer it breaks up the areas of brilliance into little patches and makes them more comfortable to admire. Have you noticed the different shades of greens on the planes and facets of each clipped tree?"

"It's lovely, isn't it."

The man now seemed to be explaining something to the woman, and pointing at the Henry Moore, and I could tell by the way they threw back their heads that they were laughing again. The man continued to point, and then the woman walked around the back of the wood carving, bent down and poked her head through one of its holes. The thing was about the size, shall I say, of a small horse, but thinner than that, and from where I sat I could see both sides of it—to the left, the woman's body, to the right, her head protruding through. It was very much like one of those jokes at the seaside where you put your head through a hole in a board and get photographed as a fat lady. The man was photographing her now.

---

① ludicrous: *Adjective* so foolish, unreasonable, or out of place as to be amusing滑稽有趣的;荒唐可笑的(e.g. It's ludicrous that I have been fined. 我被罚了款,这太荒唐了。)

"There's another thing about yews," Sir Basil said. "In the early summer when the young shoots come out..." At that moment he paused and sat up straighter and leaned slightly forward, and I could sense his whole body suddenly stiffening.

"Yes," I said, "when the young shoots come out?"

The man had taken the photograph, but the woman still had her head through the hole, and now I saw him put both hands (as well as the camera) behind his back and advance towards her. Then he bent forward so his face was close to hers, touching it, and he held it there while he gave her, I suppose, a few kisses or something like that. In the stillness that followed, I fancied I heard a faint faraway tinkle of female laughter coming to us through the sunlight across the garden.

"Shall we go back to the house?" I asked.

"Back to the house?"

"Yes, shall we go back and have a drink before lunch?"

"A drink? Yes, we'll have a drink." But he didn't move. He sat very still, gone far away from me now, staring intently at the two figures. I also was staring at them. I couldn't take my eyes away; I had to look. It was like seeing a dangerous little ballet in miniature from a great distance, and you knew the dancers and the music but not the end of the story, not the choreography①, nor what they were going to do next, and you were fascinated, and you had to look.

"Gaudier Brzeska," I said. "How great do you think he might've become if he hadn't died so young?"

"Who?"

---

① choreography: *Noun* [mass noun] the sequence of steps and movements in dance or figure skating, especially in a ballet or other staged dance 舞蹈动作编排; 花样滑冰动作编排(e.g. The rumbustious choreography reflects the themes of the original play. 欢腾的舞蹈动作编排反映了原剧的主题。)

"Gaudier Brzeska."

"Yes," he said. "Of course."

I noticed now that something queer was happening. The woman still had her head through the hole, but she was beginning to wriggle her body from side to side in a slow unusual manner, and the man was standing motionless, a pace or so away watching her. He seemed suddenly uneasy the way he stood there, and I could tell by the drop of the head and by the stiff intent set of the body that there was no laughter in him any more. For a while he remained still, then I saw him place his camera on the ground and go forward to the woman, taking her head in his hands; and all at once it was more like a puppet show than a ballet, with tiny wooden figures performing tiny, jerky movements, crazy and unreal, on a faraway sunlit stage. We sat quietly together on the white bench, and we watched while the tiny puppet man began to manipulate the woman's head with his hands. He was doing it gently, there was no doubt about that, slowly and gently, stepping back every now and then to think about it some more, and several times crouching down to survey the situation from another angle. Whenever he left her alone the woman would start to wriggle her body, and the peculiar way she did it reminded me of a dog that feels a collar round its neck for the first time.

"She's stuck," Sir Basil said.

And now the man was walking to the other side of the carving, the side where the woman's body was, and he put out his hands and began trying to do something with her neck. Then, as though suddenly exasperated①, he gave the neck two or three jerky pulls, and this time the sound of a woman's voice, raised high in anger, or pain, or both,

---

① exasperate: *Verb* [with obj.] irritate intensely; infuriate 激怒;使气恼(e.g. She grew exasperated with his inability to notice anything. 他什么都没觉察到使她很是生气。)

came back to us small and clear through the sunlight.

Out of the corner of one eye I could see Sir Basil nodding his head quietly up and down. "I got my fist caught in a jar of boiled sweets once," he said, "and I couldn't get it out."

The man retreated a few yards, and was standing with hands on hips, head up, looking furious and sullen. The woman, from her uncomfortable position, appeared to be talking to him, or rather shouting at him, and although the body itself was pretty firmly fixed and could only wriggle, the legs were free and did a good deal of moving and stamping. "I broke the jar with a hammer and told my mother I'd knocked it off the shelf by mistake." He seemed calmer now, not tense at all, although his voice was curiously flat. "I suppose we'd better go down and see if we can help."

"Perhaps we should."

But still he didn't move. He took out a cigarette and lit it, putting the used match carefully back in the box.

"I'm sorry," he said. "Will you have one?"

"Thanks, I think I will." He made a little ceremony of giving me the cigarette and lighting it for me, and again he put the used match back in the box. Then we got up and walked slowly down the grass slope.

We came upon them silently, through an archway① in the yew hedge, and it was naturally quite a surprise.

"What's the matter here?" Sir Basil asked. He spoke softly, with a dangerous softness that I'm sure his wife had never heard before.

"She's gone and put her head through the hole and now she can't

---

① archway: *Noun* a curved structure forming a passage or entrance 拱道;拱门

get it out," Major Haddock said. "Just for a lark①, you know."

"For a what?"

"Basil!" Lady Turton shouted, "Don't be such a damn fool! Do something, can't you!" She may not have been able to move much, but she could still talk.

"Pretty obvious we're going to have to break up this lump of wood," the Major said. There was a small smudge② of red on his grey moustache, and this, like the single extra touch of colour that ruins a perfect painting, managed somehow to destroy all his manly looks. It made him comic.

"You mean break the Henry Moore?"

"My dear sir, there is no other way of setting the lady free. God knows how she managed to squeeze it in, but I know for a fact that she can't pull it out. It's the ears get in the way."

"Oh dear," Sir Basil said. "What a terrible pity. My beautiful Henry Moore."

At this stage Lady Turton began abusing her husband in a most unpleasant manner, and there's no knowing how long it would have gone on had not Jelks suddenly appeared out of the shadows. He came sidling silently on to the lawn and stationed himself at a respectful distance from Sir Basil, as though awaiting instructions. His black clothes looked perfectly ridiculous in the morning sunlight, and with his ancient pink-white face and white hands he was like some small crabby③ animal that has

---

① lark: *Noun* something done for fun, especially something mischievous or daring; an amusing adventure or escapade 嬉耍;玩笑;顽皮举动(e.g. I only went along for a lark. 我跟着去只是找点乐。)

② smudge: *Noun* a blurred or smeared mark on the surface of something 污迹(e.g. a smudge of blood on the floor 地板上的一块血迹)

③ crabby: *Adjective* irritable 易怒的;暴躁的;脾气坏的

lived all its life in a hole under the ground.

"Is there anything I can do, Sir Basil?" He kept his voice level, but I didn't think his face was quite straight[1]. When he looked at Lady Turton there was a little exulting glimmer in his eyes.

"Yes Jelks, there is. Go back and get me a saw or something so I can cut out this section of wood."

"Shall I call one of the men, Sir Basil? William is a good carpenter."

"No, I'll do it myself. Just get the tools and hurry."

While they were waiting for Jelks, I strolled away because I didn't want to hear any more of the things that Lady Turton was saying to her husband. But I was back in time to see the butler returning, followed now by the other woman, Carmen La Rosa, who made a rush for the hostess.

"Nata-li-a! My dear Nata-li-a! What have they done to you?"

"Oh shut up," the hostess said. "And get out of the way, will you."

Sir Basil took up a position close to his lady's head, waiting for Jelks. Jelks advanced slowly, carrying a saw in one hand, an axe in the other, and he stopped maybe a yard away. Then he held out both implements in front of him so his master could choose, and there was a brief moment—no more than two or three seconds—of silence, and of waiting, and it just happened that I was watching Jelks at this time. I saw the hand that was carrying the axe come forward an extra fraction of an inch towards Sir Basil. It was so slight a movement it was barely noticeable—a tiny pushing forward of the hand, slow and secret, a little offer, a little

① straight: *Adjective* (of a look) bold and steady(神态)大胆沉着的;从容的(e.g. He gave her a straight, no-nonsense look. 他从容认真地看了她一眼。)

coaxing offer that was accompanied perhaps by an infinitesimal① lift of the eyebrow.

I'm not sure whether Sir Basil saw it, but be hesitated, and again the hand that held the axe came edging forward, and it was almost exactly like that card trick where the man says "Take one, whichever one you want," and you always get the one he means you to have. Sir Basil got the axe. I saw him reach out in a dreamy sort of way, accepting it from Jelks, and then, the instant he felt the handle in his grasp he seemed to realize what was required of him and he sprang to life.

For me, after that, it was like the awful moment when you see a child running out into the road and a car is coming and all you can do is shut your eyes tight and wait until the noise tells you it has happened. The moment of waiting becomes a long lucid② period of time with yellow and red spots dancing on a black field, and even if you open your eyes again and find that nobody has been killed or hurt, it makes no difference because so far as you and your stomach were concerned you saw it all.

I saw this one all right, every detail of it, and I didn't open my eyes again until I heard Sir Basil's voice, even softer than usual, calling in gentle protest to the butler.

"Jelks," he was saying, and I looked and saw him standing there as

---

① infinitesimal: *Adjective* extremely small 极微小的;无穷小的;无限小的(e.g. an infinitesimal pause 瞬间的停顿)

② lucid: *Adjective* showing ability to think clearly, especially in the intervals between periods of confusion or insanity 清醒的;神志清明的;头脑清楚的(e.g. He has a few lucid moments every now and then. 他不时会清醒一会儿。)

calm as you please[①], still holding the axe. Lady Turton's head was there too, still sticking through the hole, but her face had turned a terrible ashy grey, and the mouth was opening and shutting making a kind of gurgling[②] sound.

"Look here, Jelks," Sir Basil was saying. "What on earth are you thinking about. This thing's much too dangerous. Give me the saw." And as he exchanged implements I noticed for the first time two little warm roses of colour appearing on his cheeks, and above them, all around the corners of his eyes, the twinkling tiny wrinkles of a smile.

三、翻译探索

本篇小说的翻译,有不少专有名词方面的障碍,特别是某些名不见经传的地名和大名鼎鼎的艺术家的名字,要仔细查找,准确翻译。无从查找的,只有根据读音规则来创造性地翻译了。另外,这篇小说中,达尔还"炫耀"了不少园艺方面的知识,这些方面的知识要理解好,才能忠实地传达原作。这一方面的翻译,还有待进一步探索。

贵妇之颈

大约八年前,就在老威廉·特顿爵士离世之际,他的儿子巴兹尔继承了"特顿报业"(也继承了他的头衔)。我能够记得的是,舰队街上上下下的那些人是如何开始下注的,赌的是某位令人满意的年轻女子会花费多长时间来说服这个小伙子,让他信服:她一定会照看好

---

① as... as you please: (informal) used to emphasize the manner in which someone does something, especially when this is seen as surprising(非正式)(用于强调某人做事的方式,尤指被认为是令人诧异的方式)非常……(e. g. She walked forward as calm as you please. 她非常冷静地朝前走去。)

② gurgle: *Verb* [no obj.] make a hollow bubbling sound like that made by water running out of a bottle 发出汩汩声(如同水从瓶中流出的声音)

他,也就是说,照看好他,还有他的钱。

当时,这位新继承人——巴兹尔·特顿爵士——约有四十岁,是一个单身汉,性格温和,天真直率。继承财产之际,他感兴趣的,除了他自己收藏的现代绘画和雕塑之外,没有别的——没有女人令他心烦意乱,没有流言蜚语缠身,也没有人说长道短。可是眼下,他已经拥有一个庞大的报刊杂志帝国,他就有必要从他父亲幽静的乡村宅第走出来,来到伦敦这座大城市。

自然而然的是,贪婪的秃鹫立刻开始集结而来。我相信,不仅是整条舰队街,几乎就连整个伦敦城,都急不可耐地将目光投射过来,急匆匆地直奔尸体而来。当然,这是一个慢速移动的过程,极其缓慢却从容不迫。因此呢,这些缓慢移动着的倒不像是秃鹫,而更像是一大群螃蟹,从水下爬向一块马肉。

但是,出乎大家意料的是,这位小伙子可没有那么轻易就范。那一年,这场追逐战拖过了春天,一直拖到初夏。我并不认识巴兹尔本人,也没有任何理由向他表示友好,但是,作为同性别之人,我情不自禁地站在他的一边,而且,他每一次成功脱逃,我都大声喝彩。

接下来,大概在八月份刚开始的时候,这些追逐不休的女子很明显接收到某种神秘的女性信号,纷纷宣布进入某种休战状态,奔赴海外进行休整,重整旗鼓,重新筹划,意欲展开冬季猎杀行动。这可是一个错误之举,因为就在那时,一种光彩夺目的生物从欧洲大陆横扫而来。这个人名不见经传,叫纳塔利娅什么的,或者别的什么名字。她紧紧攥住巴兹尔的手腕,拽着他来到卡克斯顿厅的婚姻登记处,几乎要把他拽晕了。大家——尤其是新郎——还没有弄明白是怎么回事呢,她就在那里注册登记,嫁给了他。

你可以想象,伦敦的那些女子是多么愤慨,于是,自然而然地,她们就开始大量散布一些关于这位新来的特顿夫人的富有挑逗性的流言蜚语(她们称她为"那个下贱的偷猎者")。但是,我们没有必要去深究细节了。事实上,出于本故事的需要,我们可以跳过接下来的六年时间,直接跳到六年后的现在,回到正好一周前的今天。当时,我本人有幸第一次见到了这位夫人。你一定能猜得出,到现在为止,她不仅经营起整个“特顿报业”，而且最终成为这个国家一股相当大的政治力量。我意识到，别的女性以前也做过类似的事情，但是，她的不同寻常之处在于，她是个外国人，也没有人确切地了解她来自哪一个国家——或者是南斯拉夫，或者是保加利亚，或者是俄罗斯。

最终，在上周四，我去了伦敦的一个朋友在家里举办的这个小型晚宴。吃饭前，我们大家站在客厅的四处，小口品尝着上等的马提尼酒，谈论着原子弹和贝文先生。这时，女仆突然探进头来，宣布说，最后一名客人到了。

“特顿夫人。”她说。

没有一个人停止交谈。对于客人到来这件事儿，我们大家的举止都十分得体。没有一个人转过头去。大家只是把眼睛转向门口，等待着有人进来。

她快速走进来——个子高挑，身材苗条，身穿金铜色连衣裙，上面闪闪发亮。她的嘴在微笑，一只手伸向女主人。我的天呐，我必须说的是，她就是美人一个。

“晚上好，米尔德里德！”

“我亲爱的特顿夫人！太棒了！”

我想，当时我们确确实实停止了交谈，纷纷转头，眼睛盯了过去。大家都站在那儿，相当温顺地等待着被引见引见，就好像她或许能成为女王或者电影明星似的。但是，她比那些人当中任何一位都要漂亮。她一头黑发，黑发衬托的是一副天真的椭圆脸孔——脸色灰白，具有15世纪佛兰德斯人的脸部特征。她简直就是梅姆灵画笔下的圣母玛利亚，或者是凡·爱克画笔下的圣母玛利亚。最起码，第一印象是这样的。后来，轮到跟我握手的时候，我近距离地看了看，发现除了轮廓和着色之外，她并不是什么圣母玛利亚，离圣母玛利亚还差很远、很远的距离呢。

比方说，那两只鼻孔就很怪异，不怎么样，比我以前所见过的任何的鼻孔都更张开一些、更像喇叭的形状，而且过度地拱起。这样，她的整个鼻子看起来就有点开阔，有点喷鼻息的感觉，类似于某种野生动物——野马——的鼻子。

还有那双眼睛。闭合的时候,我看到,那双眼睛并不像圣母玛利亚画家画得那样宽、那样圆,而是带有长长的、半睁半闭的、半笑不笑的、半怒不怒的样子,还轻微有点粗俗的神态。这样,不管怎么说,那双眼睛令她具有一种极其微妙的浪荡气质。更有甚者,那双眼睛根本不正视你,而是从一侧的上方慢慢向你移动——是一种很古怪的滑移,令我紧张不安。我还是尽量要弄清楚那双眼睛是什么颜色的——尽管是浅灰色的,但我不能肯定。

接着,有人带着她穿过房间,去见其他客人。我站在那儿,看着她。很显然,她意识到自己是位成功人士,也意识到这些伦敦人对她的仰慕之情。"我来了,"她似乎这样说道,"我来到这里只有几年的光景,可是,我现在比你们任何人都有钱有势。"她走起路来,稍微带有一种昂首阔步的胜利姿态。

几分钟过后,我们大家进去吃晚饭。令我吃惊的是,我竟坐到了这位夫人的右侧。我猜想,这肯定是女主人安排的,算是对我的一种善意的表示。女主人认为,这样安排,我或许能为我每天都撰稿的晚报的社会版栏目寻到些素材呢。于是,我坐定,安顿下来,准备吃这顿很有意思的饭菜了。可问题是,这位有名的女士根本没有注意到我的存在。她将时间都用来跟左边的男子聊天了,那位男子就是我们今天晚宴的男主人。到了最后,就在我要吃完冰淇淋的时候,她突然间转过头来,向前倾斜着身体,拿起我的座位牌,看了看上面的名字。然后,用她那种怪异的滑移眼神,盯着我的脸。我微笑一下,微微欠了欠身。她没有以微笑回应我,却发出一连串的问题来,尽是些私人的问题,像工作、年龄、家庭什么的。她说话的声音很奇特,声音有点重叠的感觉。我竟然尽力予以回答了。

从这一系列的盘问中,有两点凸显出来:我很喜欢绘画,也很喜欢雕塑。

"那么,你真应该找时间到乡下,看看我丈夫的藏品。"她说者无意——仅仅作为谈话的方式,但我听者有心——你必须意识到,在我的工作中,像这样的机会我是万万不可错过的。

"太谢谢您啦,特顿夫人。我乐意之至。我何时能来呢?"

她抬起头，迟疑了一下，皱起眉头，耸了耸双肩，然后说道："噢，什么时候都可以，我无所谓的。"

"接下来的这个周末如何？周末可以吗？"

她窄窄的眼睛慢慢滑移过来，看了我一会儿，然后又移开。"要是你愿意的话，我想是可以的。我无所谓的。"

就这样，随后而来的这个星期六的下午，我就开车直奔伍顿私邸，车后装的是我的手提箱。你或许会认为，我得到这个邀请有点强加于人的意思，但是，如果不这样，我是不可能得到这样的机会的。排除职业方面的因素，我个人也很想看看那座私邸。要知道，伍顿私邸是英国文艺复兴早期真正伟大的石头私邸之一。跟其姊妹篇一样——包括朗利特私邸、沃拉顿私邸和蒙塔丘特私邸，伍顿私邸始建于16世纪后半叶。当时，一位伟人的房子被设计成舒适的住所，而不是一座城堡，这实属首开先河。当时，一批新兴起的建筑师，像约翰·索普、史密森夫妇等，开始在全英国做出一些不可思议的事情。

伍顿私邸位于牛津市以南，靠近一座名叫里斯伯勒王子的小镇。从伦敦驱车前往，路途不是很远。开车从大门拐进这座私邸时，夜幕就要降临，初冬的傍晚开始了。

我将车慢慢驶上私家车道，尽可能多看看庭园，特别是庭院里修剪整形的花木，这些花木名气很大，如雷贯耳。我必须说的是，看完之后，令人难忘。四周都是大片的紫杉树，这些树被人修剪成各种令人忍俊不禁的形状——有母鸡、鸽子、瓶子、靴子、扶手椅、城堡、蛋杯、灯笼，有穿着花哨衬裙的年迈妇女，还有高高的柱子，一些柱子上面顶着一个球，另一些柱子上面顶着一个大大的圆顶，顶端再饰以无茎的蘑菇形状。半明半暗之中，所有的绿色都变成了黑色，以至于每一个造型、每一棵树都呈现出一种黝黑的、光滑的质感，犹如雕塑一般。在其中一个地方，我看到一个草坪，上面分布着巨大的棋子，每一个棋子都是一颗活着的紫杉树，造型极其巧妙。我停车、下车，在棋子中间行走起来，发现每个棋子都有我两倍高。更有甚者，棋的布局很完整——王、后、象、马、车、卒俱全，都站立到位，等待棋局开始。

转过一个弯后，我看到了这座伟大的私邸。房前是大大的、做入口用的前庭,前庭四周是高高的、安装了护栏的墙壁,墙壁的外角处修建了小小的、由柱子支撑的凉亭。护栏支撑在石质方尖碑上——意大利风格对英国都铎王朝建筑思想影响的结果。一段台阶向上,通往私邸,台阶至少有三十米宽。

将车驶入前庭时,我注意到喷水池中央撑起一尊巨大的、由爱泼斯坦创作的雕塑,这令我吃惊不小。这尊雕塑可爱至极,但是,要知道,它与周围环境很不协调。我沿着台阶爬上正门,然后向后一看,发现所有的小草坪和周围的台地上,都竖起了另外一些现代雕像,还有各种各样奇妙的雕塑。在远处,我想,我可以辨认出一些大师的作品,像高迪·布热斯卡、布兰库兹、圣高登斯、亨利·穆尔,而且,我又看到了爱泼斯坦的作品。

一位年轻的、穿着制服的男仆开了门,引导我上到二楼的一间卧室。他解释说,夫人正在休息,其他客人也在休息,但是,大约一个小时后,大家都会穿戴整齐,到楼下的主会客厅共进晚餐。

现在,干我这一行的,周末不休息是常有的事。一年之中,大约有五十个周六和周日是在别人家里度过的。因此,我对完全陌生的环境相当敏感。刚一跨进正门,几乎只需用鼻子一嗅,我就能辨别出情况的好与坏。现在进入的这家,我不喜欢,因为这地方闻起来不对劲儿,空气中有一种微弱的、干燥的难闻气息——似乎有某种东西令人心烦。这一点,即便是躺在热气腾腾的、舒适豪华的、体积大大的大理石浴缸里,我也能感觉出来。于是,我禁不住希望:周一到来之前,不要发生任何令人不快的事情。

十分钟后,事与愿违,第一件这样的事情就来了——这件事尽管不那么令人不快,却着实令人意想不到。当时,我正坐在床上穿袜子,门就轻轻地被人推开了。开门溜进来的,是一个苍老的、面相丑陋的小矮人,身体向一侧歪斜,穿着黑色的燕尾服。他解释说,他是这里的管家,名字叫杰尔克斯。他还说,他衷心希望我在这里能舒心安逸,我需要的东西都不缺。

我告诉他说,我很舒心,什么都不缺。

他说,他会尽其所能,让我的周末过得惬意。对此,我表示感谢,等着他离开。他迟疑了一会儿，然后，用一种充满虚情假意的声音，请求我允许他说出一件相当难以启齿的事情。我告诉他，请便。

他说，十分坦诚地讲，这事儿是关于小费的，整个付小费的行当令他极其痛苦不堪。

哦？为什么会那样呢？

如果我真的想知道答案的话，好吧，他说，客人离开这里的时候，迫于无奈才给他小费，他不喜欢这样，但客人的确也是这样做的。这对于给小费的和收小费的来说，都是一种难堪的过程。况且，他已经充分意识到，这个过程经常对我这样的客人所造成的身心上的巨大痛苦。如果我能宽恕他的鲁莽直言，他觉得客人是根据惯例迫不得已才给的小费，而且给的小费已经超出了客人们真正的承担能力。

他暂停一下，两只狡诈的小眼睛观察着我的脸，看看我有没有什么反应。我嘟嘟囔囔地说，对我而言，他没有必要担心此类给小费的事情。

他说，正相反，他衷心希望我从一开始就同意：一点小费都不给他。

“这个嘛，”我说，“现在，我们不要在这件小事儿上纠缠不休啦。到时候，我们都会知道我们彼此的感受如何了。”

“不，先生！”他大声说。“拜托，我真心坚持不要的。”

于是，我就同意了。

他表示感谢，拖着双脚向我走近了一两步，头歪向一边，双手在身前抱紧，像牧师做出的动作，然后，他轻轻地耸了耸肩，表示歉意。他那两只尖锐的小眼睛仍然观察着我，我等着——两只手捏住一只袜子，另一只袜子则套到了脚上——看他下一步要干什么。

现在，他说话的声音很轻微，轻微得就像从音乐大厅外面的大街上微弱地听到里面传出的音乐声。他轻声细语地说，他要问的，没有别的，就是我不给他小费，而是将这个周末我赌牌所赢的钱的百分之三十三点三三给他。要是我赌输了，就一分钱不用给他了。

他说得如此轻描淡写、如此平静，尽管如此突如其来，但我甚至并不感到吃惊。

"杰尔克斯,他们总是玩牌吗?"

"是的,先生,经常玩儿。"

"百分之三十三点三三,难道不是太高了一点儿吗?"

"我不这样认为,先生。"

"我给你百分之十。"

"不,先生,我不能接受。"现在,他仔细地检查起自己左手的手指甲来,皱起了眉头,但并没有不耐烦的意思。

"那么,就百分之十五,可以了吗?"

"百分之三十三点三三,先生,很合情合理的。说到底,先生,要知道,我甚至不知道你水平如何。我不是针对你个人而言的,我现在的所作所为,不亚于把注押在一匹我从来没有看见奔跑过的马的身上。"

毫无疑问,你会想,我从一开始就不要跟这位管家讨价还价。你这样想,或许是对的,但是,作为一名开明大度之人,我总是尽量做到对低阶层的人友善和蔼。此外,这件事我越想,越不得不承认,他开出的条件,换上哪个赌家,都无法拒绝的。

"那么,好吧,杰尔克斯,就按你说的来。"

"谢谢您,先生。"他向门口移动,侧着身体移得很慢,就像是一只螃蟹。但是,一只手把在门把手上的时候,他又迟疑一下。"先生,如果我可以给你一点意见——可以吗?"

"什么意见?"

"很简单,那就是,对于手里的牌,夫人经常叫得过高。"

现在,这事儿做得有些太过了。我吃惊得不得了,袜子也从手中掉落。毕竟,关于付小费的事儿,跟管家商定好赌钱所得,对谁都没有害处。那是一回事儿,但是,他开始跟你密谋要从女主人那里非法赢钱,那就是另一回事儿了——该叫停、予以制止了。

"好啦,杰尔克斯,现在,到此为止。"

"我希望,先生,请勿见怪。我要表达的意思只是,你一定会跟夫人对阵的,因为她总是跟哈多克少校搭档。"

"哈多克少校?你是指杰克·哈多克少校吗?"

“正是，先生。”

杰尔克斯提到这个人的时候，我注意到，他的鼻角露出一丝嘲讽的样子。一提到特顿夫人，情况更糟一些。每一次说到“夫人”的时候，他是用双唇的外侧发出这个词的，就好像在一点点啃柠檬似的，而且，他的声音里有一种语调的变化，这种变化很微妙，带有嘲弄的意味。

“现在，很抱歉，先生。夫人七点下来，哈多克少校和其他客人也会在七点下来。”他溜出门，屋子里留下一种潮湿的感觉，还有一丝治疗扭伤的涂擦剂的味道。

七点刚过不久，我就走向主会客厅。特顿夫人起身迎接我，她还像从前那么漂亮。

“我甚至不敢肯定你会来，”她说道，声音还是那样奇特，轻柔地上下起伏，“再说说，你叫什么名字来着？”

“我想，我是照着你的话去做的，特顿夫人。我希望，这样做不会有冒失之处。”

“为什么不照做呢？”她说，“这座房子有四十七间卧室呢。这位是我的丈夫。”

一位矮个子男子从她背后绕上前来，说道：“要知道，你能来，我很高兴。”他的笑容令人愉快、令人温暖。他握住我的手的时候，我立刻感觉到他的手指传达出来的一丝友谊的气息。

“这位是卡门·拉罗莎。”特顿夫人介绍道。

这是一名体格魁梧的女子，看起来好像跟马有点关联。她冲我点了点头，但并没有向我伸出手来——尽管我的手已经伸出去一半了，但不得不缩回去，抹了把鼻子。

“你感冒了？”她问，“我很抱歉。”

我不喜欢这位卡门·拉罗莎女士。

“这位是杰克·哈多克。”

我对这名男子多少了解一点。他是一些公司的头头（管他是什么样的头头呢），也是社会上的一位知名人士。我的栏目里好几次登过他的名字，但是我从来都没有喜欢过这个人。我想，这其中的原因主要是,对于所有把军衔带回到个人生活中的人,我是心存深深疑虑的,特别是对于少校、上校这样的军衔。他站在那儿,身着无尾礼服,长了一张正宗的动物般的脸孔,眉毛黑黑的,牙齿又大又白,看起来帅气得有点下流的感觉。他一微笑就会抬起上嘴唇,牙齿也就裸露出来。现在,他伸出一只棕色的、毛茸茸的手,正冲我微笑呢。

"我希望,在你的栏目里,你能帮我们说些好听的。"

"他最好是说些好听的,"特顿夫人接道,"否则的话,我就在我的头版说他一些坏话。"

我大笑起来,可是,他们三个——特顿夫人、哈多克少校和卡门·拉罗莎——已经转过身去,各自坐回到沙发上了。杰尔克斯递给我一杯酒,巴兹尔爵士轻轻地将我拉到一旁,拉到屋子的另一头,跟我悄声交谈。不一定什么时候,特顿夫人就会喊她丈夫为她拿这个、拿那个的——马提尼、香烟、烟灰缸、手绢等,而这位做丈夫的一听到喊声就从椅子上半站起来——每每此时,时刻留意的杰尔克斯就会抢先一步,替他取来东西。

显而易见,杰尔克斯爱他的主人,而同样显而易见的是,他不喜欢这位做妻子的。每次为她做事的时候,他的鼻子就显示出一点儿嘲讽的样子,双唇闭得紧紧的,皱得像火鸡的屁股似的。

用餐时,我们的女主人让她的两位客人——哈多克和拉罗莎——坐在她的旁边,一边一个。这种打破常规的安排令我和巴兹尔爵士坐到了桌子的另一端,正好我们俩可以继续我们刚才愉快的交谈,谈论绘画和雕塑。当然,在我看来,现在这位少校是迷恋上这位夫人了。尽管我不愿意说,但我还要说的是,名叫拉罗莎的女子看起来似乎也在追猎少校这只鸟。

这一切愚蠢之举似乎令这位女主人很愉悦,但并不令她的丈夫愉悦。我看得出,我跟他交谈的时候,他始终注意着现场的一些微小的举动。他还经常跑题,话说到一半就戛然而止,眼睛移向桌子的另一端,可怜巴巴地落在那个可爱的脑袋上——上面有黑黑的头发和喇叭形的鼻孔——停留了一会儿。当时,他一定注意到,她是多么神采飞扬,还有她那只手:一边说话,一边做着手势,还不时地放到少校的胳膊上。他还注意到，另一个女人——那个或许跟马有点关联的女人，一个劲儿地说："纳塔——利——娅？纳塔——利——娅，现在，听我说！"

"明天，"我说，"你一定得带我四处转悠一下，给我看看你在花园里竖起的雕塑。"

"当然啦，"他说，"乐意之至。"他再一次将目光瞥向妻子，双眼中带有一种哀求的眼神，那眼神无以言表，令人心生怜悯。他这个人无论哪方面都温和友善、消极被动，即使现在我也能看得出，他这个人没有发怒的表情，没有危险的举动，没有爆发的冲动。

晚饭后，我被直接叫到牌桌前跟拉罗莎搭档，对阵哈多克少校和特顿夫人。巴兹尔爵士拿起一本书，安静地坐在沙发上。

牌局本身没有什么稀奇之处，都是老套路，令人颇感枯燥、乏味，但是，杰尔克斯令人生厌。整个晚上，他都在我们周围晃来晃去，一会儿倒倒烟灰缸，一会儿问问喝什么，还一个劲儿瞥我们手里的牌。很显然，他是个近视眼。对于他能够看到多少这一点，我表示怀疑，因为不管你了解与否，在英国这个地方，从不允许管家戴眼镜。同样的道理，也从不允许管家留胡子。这是一条黄金法则，牢不可破，也是一条切合实际的法则，尽管我不敢肯定其背后的动机是什么。我猜测呢，胡子会令管家看起来更像是一位绅士，而眼镜会令他看起来更像是一个美国人。那样的话，我想知道的是，我们的主人往哪摆呢？不管怎么说，整个晚上，杰尔克斯令人生厌。同样地，特顿夫人也令人生厌，总是有人喊她去接电话，电话里谈的是报社生意方面的问题。

十一点钟的时候，她的眼神离开了手中的牌，抬起头说道："巴兹尔，你上床睡觉的时间到了。"

"是的，我亲爱的，或许到了。"他将书合上，立起身，站了一小会儿，看着牌局的进展情况。"你们玩得很好吧？"他问道。

其他几个人没有应声，于是，我说道："玩得不错。"

"我很高兴。杰尔克斯会照料你们，想要什么就找他。"

"杰尔克斯也可以去睡了。"这位妻子说道。

我能够听见我旁边哈多克少校通过鼻子呼吸的声音，还能听到一张张牌落下来发出的轻微的声音。紧接着，我听见杰尔克斯在地毯上拖着脚步向我们走来发出的声音。

“你不愿意我待在这儿吗，夫——夫人？”

“是的，去睡吧。巴兹尔，你也一样。”

“好的，我亲爱的，晚安。大家晚安。”

杰尔克斯为他开了门，他慢慢走了出去，管家跟在后面。

下一轮胜负分出后，我就说，我也想去睡了。

“那好吧，”特顿夫人说，“晚安。”

我上楼进了自己的房间，锁上门，服下一片药，进入了梦乡。

第二天早晨，也就是星期天的早晨，我起床，穿好衣服，已经是十点左右了。下楼来到吃早餐的房间，发现巴兹尔爵士在我之前来到，杰尔克斯给他端上了烤腰子、咸肉和炒西红柿。看到我，爵士很高兴，提议说，一吃完就到庭院四周多转转。我对他说，那样的话，我求之不得、乐意之至。

半小时过后，我们出去了。你想象不出，从那座房子里走出来，来到户外，多么令人感到轻松愉快。又是阳光明媚的天气，暖洋洋的。冬季过半的时节，一夜大雨过后，偶尔会出现这样的天气：阳光照耀，令人意想不到，而且，没有一丝风。阳光下，光秃秃的树木看起来很美，雨水依然沿着枝条滴落，周围潮湿的地方闪耀着钻石般光芒。天空隐隐浮现出小小的云朵。

“天气多好啊！”

“是啊——多好的天啊！”

散步转悠过程中，我们几乎再没有说过别的话，也没有那个必要。但是，他带我到处逛了一遍，我也把整个庭院看了个遍——有大大的棋子；还有修剪整形的花木；有精心设计的园亭、水池、喷泉；有孩子玩的迷宫，迷宫的树篱由角树和酸橙树组成，因而只有在夏天，叶子都长出来的时候才算得上是好迷宫；有花坛、假山；有温室，里面生长着藤本植物和油桃树；当然了，还有雕塑，多数是当代欧洲雕塑家的作品，有青铜材质的、花岗岩材质的、石灰岩材质的，还有木头材质的。尽管看到这些雕塑沐浴着阳光、闪耀着光芒，但是，依我来看，在这片偌大的古典私邸四周，它们看起来有点格格不入。

“现在，我们在这儿稍微休息一会儿好吗？”溜达半个多小时后，巴兹尔爵士这样问道。于是，我们在一张白色的长凳上坐了下来，长凳设在一座睡莲池的边上，池里游的尽是鲤鱼和金鱼。我们各自点燃了香烟。我们所在的地方比周围的地面要高些，离那座私邸有一些距离。从我们坐的位置看，各个花园在我们下方铺展开来，就像庭院建筑老书里的素描图样一般，有树篱、草坪、台地、喷泉，这些共同构成了一个个漂亮的、或方或圆的图案。

“就在我出生前，我父亲买下了这个地方，”巴兹尔爵士说，“我一直住在这儿，熟悉这里的一分一毫。一天天过去，我对这里的爱也一天天增加。”

“这里夏天一定美妙无比。”

“噢，的确如此。五六月份的时候，你应该过来看一看。你会答应吗？”

“当然啦，”我回答，“我很愿意来的。”我说话的时候，看到了一个女子的身影。那个女子穿着红色的衣服，在远处的花坛间移动。我看见她横穿过一大片宽宽的草坪，步履轻松而欢快，一个小小的影子伴随着她。越过草坪的时候，她转向一侧，沿着修剪过的、高高的紫杉树墙的边缘走，一直走到另一片小一些的草坪上，那是一块圆形的草坪，草坪中间立着一尊雕塑。

“这个花园要比这座私邸年轻，”巴兹尔爵士说道，“一个法国人，名叫博蒙，在18世纪早期设计了这个花园，跟设计威斯特摩兰郡利文斯庄园的是同一个人。这家伙雇用了二百五十名工人干了至少一年的时间，才完工。”

现在，一名男子跟那个红衣女子站在了一起，他们面对面站立着，中间隔着不到一米的距离。他俩就站在整座花园所构成的一幅全景画的正中心，站在那块小小的圆形草坪上面。很显然，他们站在那儿说着话。那个男子的一只手里拿着某种小小的、黑色的东西。

“要是你感兴趣的话，我可以拿给你看看那位博蒙当时开给这块地盘主人的那些账单。”

“我倒是很想看看,一定很引人入胜。”

“他一天给劳工一个先令,他们一天劳作十个小时。”

清澈透明的天空下,阳光明媚。我的目光跟着草坪上的两个身影移动,看清他们的一举一动,不是什么困难的事情。现在,他俩转向了那尊雕塑,一副嘲弄的样子指着那尊雕塑。很显然,他俩对其形状发笑,开着玩笑。我认出来了,那是一尊亨利·穆尔的木质雕塑作品,是个薄薄的、光滑的物件,具有非凡的美感,其上有两三个圆孔,还有很多奇形怪状的肢体伸展出来。

“博蒙种植那些紫衫棋子树以及其他植物的时候,他清楚,它们至少在一百年的时间里不会有什么惊人之处。现如今,我们搞规划的时候,似乎没有那种耐性了,对吧?你怎么看呢?”

“是的,”我说,“我们没有那种耐心。”

我最终看明白了,那个男子手里拿着的黑色的东西是一个照相机。现在,他向后退去,为站在亨利·穆尔旁边的那个女子拍照。她摆出了多种不同的姿势。就我所见到的来说,所有的姿势都很滑稽荒唐,意在逗乐耍笑。有一次,她伸出双臂搂住其中一个凸出的肢体,拥抱起来;还有一次,她竟然爬了上去,两腿搭在一侧,整个人骑到了雕塑上,双手还紧握着假想中的缰绳。一堵紫杉树大墙将这两个人跟整个私邸隔开、遮掩起来,也的的确确跟整个花园隔开、遮掩起来——我们坐下休息的小山丘除外。他俩也有充分的理由相信,没有谁会俯视他们。即便是他俩偶尔会向我们这儿瞥一眼,那也是逆着太阳光瞥一眼。至于能否注意到池塘边的长凳上坐着的两个一动不动的小小身影,我持怀疑的态度。

“要知道,我爱这些紫杉树,”巴兹尔爵士说道,“在一座花园中,它们的颜色漂亮极了,很养眼。夏季,紫杉的颜色将绚烂的景色分割成一小块、一小块的区域,令这个地方赏心悦目、舒服惬意。每棵树修剪出来的平面和斜面都呈现出不同的绿色色调,你注意到没有?”

“很可爱,的确。”

现在,那个男的手指向亨利·穆尔,似乎在向那个女的解释着什么。根据他俩头部后仰的样子，我可以看出，他们又在大声发笑。男子的手继续指着，女子接下来绕到了木制雕塑的后面，弯下腰，将头从其中一个圆孔里伸了出来。要我说，这件东西的大小相当于一匹小马，但比小马要单薄。从我坐着的地方，它的两侧都能够看得见：左侧是女子的身体，右侧是女子伸出来的脑袋。那场景很像是海滩上的一种玩笑之举：将头从一块板子的圆孔伸出，看起来成了一个胖女人，然后让人给你拍照。现在，男子正给她照相呢。

“关于紫杉树，还有另一件事情，”巴兹尔爵士说，“初夏，嫩枝长出来的时候……”就在那一刻，他停了一下，更加笔直地坐起，身体稍稍前倾。我感觉到，他的整个身体突然间变得僵硬起来。

“嗯，”我说，“嫩枝长出来的时候，怎么了？”

男子拍完照，但是女子仍然将头伸出圆孔。现在，我看到他将双手连同相机放到身后向她走去。接着，俯身向前，脸贴近她的脸，接触到一起，并保持不动的姿势。我想，他当时吻了她几下，或者做了某种类似吻的动作吧。随后，一阵沉静。想象之中，我隐隐听到远处传来女子嘎嘎的笑声，那笑声穿越花园的光线，传到我们这边来。

“我们回到房中好吗？”我问。

“回到房中？”

“是啊，我们走回去，趁还没吃午饭，喝一杯好吗？”

“喝一杯？噢，我们得喝一杯。”但是，他没有动地方，而是静静地坐着，思绪现在离我很远，眼睛专注地盯着那两个身影。我也盯着他们看了起来，一看不要紧，目光就无法移开了。我必须得看一看，就像从很远的地方观看一出险象环生的微型芭蕾舞剧——你了解音乐和舞者，但是，不了解故事的结局，不了解舞技如何，也不了解下一步会发生什么。你为之着迷，必须得看一看。

“高迪·布热斯卡，”我说，“要不是那么年纪轻轻就死去的话，你认为他或许会伟大到什么程度？”

“谁？”

“高迪·布热斯卡。”

“是的，”他说，“当然啦。”

现在,我注意到,某种古怪的事情就要发生。那个女子仍然将脑袋伸出圆孔,但是,身体却开始慢慢地左右扭动起来,那样子很是不同寻常。那名男子一动不动地站立着,离她大约一步之遥,观察着她。从他站立的样子看来,他似乎在突然之间变得不安起来。从他低头的方式和身体僵直、专注的状态来看,我可以说,他再也没有发出任何笑声。有那么一会儿,他一动不动地站立着。接下来,我看见他将相机放到地上,走近那女子,双手把住她的脑袋。转瞬之间,场面变换,变得更像是木偶表演,而不是芭蕾展示:远方洒满阳光的舞台上,两个微小的木偶人物造型,做着细微的表演动作,那动作忽动忽停、疯狂失控、虚幻不实。

我们坐在白色的长凳上,默不作声,观看着,只见微小的木偶男开始用双手摆弄女子的脑袋,动作很轻微,这一点毫无疑问——轻微而缓慢。木偶男还不时地向后退去,思考一番,有好几次还蹲伏下来,从另一个角度审视一下现场的情形。他只要一放手,女子便开始扭动身体。她这种奇特的行为让我想起一个情景:第一次戴上项圈的狗,对项圈做出情绪化的反应。

"她给卡住了。"巴兹尔爵士说。

现在,男子走向雕塑的另一边——女子身体所在的那一边,伸出双手,要开始尝试做点什么,以解她脖子的燃眉之急。接着,就好像突然间变得怒不可遏似的,他猛地将她的颈项拉了两三下。这一次,女子的声音穿越太阳光线,又传到我们的耳朵。那声音抬得很高,听起来也许是生气,也许是痛苦,也许是既生气又痛苦。

用眼角的余光,我能够看到,巴兹尔爵士的头暗自上下点了点。"有一次,我的拳头卡进了一个装着硬糖果的罐子,"他说,"拿不出来了。"

那男子后退了几米,双手放到屁股上站立着,将头抬起,看起来满腔怒火、闷闷不乐。从摆出的不舒适的姿势来看,那女子似乎正在跟他说着什么,或者更准确地说,冲着他大喊大叫。尽管她的身体被固定得紧紧的,只能扭来扭去,但是,双腿还是灵活自如地来回动弹,又踩又踏的。

"我用一把锤子将罐子打碎，然后对母亲说，我不小心将罐子从架子上碰掉打碎了。"现在，他似乎镇定了一点，不再那样绷紧了神经，尽管他的声音平淡得有些出奇。"我想，我们最好下去看看能否帮得上什么忙。"

"或许，我们应该帮忙的。"

但是，他依然没有动地方，而是拿出一支香烟，点燃后将烧过的火柴放回盒中。

"不好意思，"他说，"你抽吗？"

"谢谢，我想来一支。"他稍显拘谨地将烟递给我，并为我点上，然后又将烧过的火柴放回盒子中。随后，我们俩站起身，缓缓地走下草坡。

我们没有出声，穿过紫杉树墙上的一道拱门，走近他们。当然，我们的到来是一件令他们大吃一惊的事情。

"这儿发生什么事情了？"巴兹尔爵士问道。他说话声音很轻微，轻微的声音里含有危险的成分。我敢肯定，他的妻子以前从未听到过他的这种声音。

"她去那儿，将头伸出圆孔，可现在却拔不出来了，"哈多克少校解释道，"就是为了好玩儿，你知道的。"

"为了什么？"

"巴兹尔！"特顿夫人喊道，"不要该死的犯傻了！行动起来，你赶快！"或许她不能够自如移动，但是，她仍然能够讲话。

"特别明显的是，我们要把这块木头破开，"哈多克少校说。他灰色的胡须上有一小块红色的污迹。就像是一幅画作上一抹多余的颜色，毁掉了画作的完美一样，不知怎么的，这个污迹破坏了他身上所有的男子汉形象，令他看起来如跳梁小丑一般。

"你是说，把亨利·穆尔破开？"

"我亲爱的先生啊，让这位女士脱身，没有别的法子啦。天知道她是怎么将脑袋挤进去的，但是，我了解的一个事实就是，她无法将脑袋拔出来，碍事的是两只耳朵。"

"噢，亲爱的，"巴兹尔爵士说，"太可惜啦。我漂亮的亨利·穆尔啊。”

到了这个阶段，特顿夫人开始极其不痛快地对她的丈夫大骂出口了。要不是杰尔克斯突然间从阴影里闪了出来，这种情形会持续多久还不得而知呢。他在草坪上悄悄地滑动脚步，然后站稳身体，离巴兹尔爵士有一定的距离，好像是在等候命令似的。在早晨明媚的阳光下，他穿的那件黑色的衣服十分滑稽可笑，再加上他那苍老的、白色中透出粉色的脸，还有那双白色的手，令他看起来就像是某种脾气乖戾的小动物——整个一生都生活在地下洞穴里的小动物。

“我能帮上什么忙吗，巴兹尔爵士？”他的声音很是平静，但是我想，他的表情不是十分从容。看着特顿夫人的时候，他的眼睛里轻微闪耀着点点狂喜的光芒。

“嗯，杰尔克斯，有你做的。回去给我拿一个锯，或者其他什么东西，我好将木头的这一部分切掉。”

“巴兹尔爵士，我叫其中一个男雇员来行吗？威廉干得一手好木匠活。”

“不用，我自己就能干。只要把工具拿来就行——快啊。”

他们等杰尔克斯的当儿，我溜达着走开了，因为我不想再听到特顿夫人数落她丈夫的那些话语。但是，我及时地赶了回来，正好看到管家返回，后面跟着另外那名女子——卡门·拉罗莎。她一来，就急匆匆奔向女主人。

“纳塔——利——娅！纳塔——利——娅！他们对你都做了些什么呀？”

“喔，闭嘴，”女主人说，“走开，别碍事，好吗？”

巴兹尔爵士站在靠近夫人头部的一个位置上，等待着杰尔克斯。杰尔克斯一只手拿着一个锯，另一只手拿着一把斧子，慢悠悠地走上前，停在不到一米的距离上。然后，他将两件工具都举到身前，让主人挑选。这时，出现了短暂的沉默和片刻的等待——至多两三秒时间，碰巧在这一时刻，我看了眼杰尔克斯，看见杰尔克斯拿斧子的那只手多向巴兹尔那儿伸出一点点，也就是多伸出那么几厘米。这一举动轻微得很，几乎注意不到。那只手不过就是微微地向前那么一推，推得极其缓慢，不为人知，如同一个小小的主动提议——一个带有哄骗性质的小小的提议，其间或许还伴随着眉毛的瞬间扬起。

这一情景，我不敢肯定巴兹尔爵士是否看到了，但是，他迟疑起来。此时，拿斧子的那只手又一次悄悄向前伸出，那动作跟纸牌中的把戏几乎如出一辙——握住一叠牌，男子说："抽出一张，想抽哪张就抽哪张。"结果，你总是会抽到他打算让你抽出的那张。巴兹尔爵士接过斧子。我看到巴兹尔爵士有点恍恍惚惚地伸出手，从杰尔克斯手中接过斧子。就在紧紧握住斧柄的一瞬间，他似乎意识到要求他做的是什么事，整个人一下子活跃起来了。

自那之后，对我而言，那事情就像是这样糟糕的一幕：你看到一个孩子跑上马路，而一辆车却驶了过来。你所能做的就是：紧闭双眼，等待着噪声传来——表明事故发生了。等待的时刻变得漫长，但是你却头脑清醒，感觉到黑色的田野上跳跃着黄色的斑点，还跳跃着红色的斑点。即便是你再次睁开双眼，发现既没有人丢命，也没有人受伤，情况也没有什么不同，因为不管是你本人，还是你的胃，都经历了这一切。

眼前这一幕我无疑都看到了，而且一览无遗。听到巴兹尔的声音，我再次睁开了眼睛。他的声音比平常温柔多了，那声音是对管家提出温和的抗议而发出的。

"杰尔克斯，"他当时说，我循声看了过去，看见他站在那儿，非常镇静，仍然握着那把斧子。特顿夫人的脑袋如故，还是从圆孔伸出来，依然卡在那儿，但是，她的脸却变得灰白，嘴张张合合，发出某种汩汩的声音。

"听着，杰尔克斯，"巴兹尔爵士当时说，"你到底在想什么嘛。这东西太过于危险了，把锯给我吧。"就在他换工具的时候，我第一次注意到他的脸颊上泛起两小块热乎乎的玫瑰一样颜色的斑点。两块色斑之上，就在两只眼角周围区域，闪现出一些由微笑而生出的细小皱纹。

第二节 《人皮刺青》*Skin*

罗尔德·达尔的《人皮刺青》(*Skin*)首次发表在《纽约客》(*The New Yorker*,也有人译作《纽约人》)杂志1952年5月17日出版的那一期上。后来,这篇小说又收录到《罗尔德·达尔短篇故事集锦》(*The Collected Short Stories of Roald Dahl*)、《如你之人》(*Someone like You*)、《出人意料故事集》(*Tales of the Unexpected*)、《完全出人意料故事集》(*Completely Unexpected Tales*)、《五部畅销书集》(*5 Bestsellers*)、《罗尔德·达尔小说精品集》(*The Best of Roald Dahl*)、《〈卖伞男子〉及其他故事集》(*The Umbrella Man and Other Stories*)、《〈人皮刺青〉及其他故事集》(*Skin and Other Stories*)、《罗尔德·达尔选集》(*The Roald Dahl Omnibus*)以及《罗尔德·达尔二十九篇成人故事集》(*Twenty Nine Kisses from Roald Dahl*)等书中。此外,这部小说也被改编成电视系列剧——1980年3月8日播映的《出乎意料的故事集》(*Tales of the Unexpected*)第二部中的第2集(Episode 2.2),可见其影响力之大。

一、原作导读

达尔的这篇故事中嵌套着另一个故事,算是"故事中的故事",也算是采用了英文写作中的"闪回法"(flashback)的作品,而汉语写作中则称其为"倒叙"。

1946年冬日里的一天,寒风刺骨,一位名叫德廖利的老人拖着沉重的脚步沿着丽弗里大街漫无目的地走着。在一家画馆的橱窗前,老人停住了脚步,看着橱窗内陈列的那幅画以及那幅画的作者名字"哈伊姆·苏蒂纳(1894—1943)"。此时,老人思绪翻腾,在自己模糊的记忆力搜寻,终于回忆起来:

德廖利呆呆地盯着那幅画,凭着记忆,模糊地感觉到这幅画里似乎有什么地方自己很熟悉。他想,这画古里古怪的。虽说古里古怪,却奇特异常,但是,我喜欢……哈伊姆·苏蒂纳……苏蒂纳……"我的天啊,"他突然大叫起来,"我可爱的小卡尔梅克,就是他啊。我可爱的小卡尔梅克竟然有画陈列在巴黎顶级画馆里!真是难以想象!"

Drioli stared at the picture, wondering vaguely what there was about it that seemed familiar. Crazy painting, he thought. Very strange and crazy—but I like it... Chaim Soutine... Soutine... "By God!" he cried suddenly. "My little Kalmuck, that's who it is! My little Kalmuck with a picture in the finest shop in Paris! Just imagine that!"

顿时,往事涌上了心头。三十年前的一个夜晚,德廖利怀揣着当天挣的钞票,手里拎着几瓶酒,从自己开的文身馆回到了家。家中,他的小卡尔梅克,也就是上面提到的已故画家苏蒂纳,正为德廖利的妻子乔西画像。他们三个喝得酩酊大醉之际,德廖利突发奇想,道出了一个想法:他想要小卡尔梅克在他的背上画一幅画,然后照着这幅画文身——当然,德廖利答应现场教他如何文身。小卡尔梅克提出条件说,只要德廖利的妻子同意做模特,他就同意在他的背上作画,然后再刺青。几乎一夜的时间过去了,一幅美妙之至的刺青画最终完成,小卡尔梅克还在德廖利肾的上部刺上自己的签名。第一次世界大战爆发,小卡尔梅克从此杳无音讯。第二次世界大战爆发,德廖利的妻子乔西死于这场战争,他自己的生意也一落千丈。穷困潦倒的德廖利年事已高,但不愿沿街乞讨,所以就回到了家乡巴黎,想找点事儿做,以便糊口。在大街游荡之际,偶然瞥见了他的小卡尔梅克的画作。

突然,德廖利一闪念,转过身,推开画馆的门,走了进去。

On a sudden impulse, Drioli turned, pushed open the door of the gallery and went in.

但是,画馆的工作人员不让他进去,这令他非常生气。

“我,也有!”德廖利喊道,“我,也有,有一幅这位画家的作品!他是我的朋友。我有一幅画,是他给我的。”

“I, too!” Drioli was shouting. “I, too, have a picture by this painter! He was my friend and I have a picture which he gave me!”

德廖利脱掉衣服,将后背展露给众人。在场的人都惊呆了,纷纷出价要购买他后背上带有署名的人皮刺青画,这令德廖利哭笑不得:即使自己同意卖的话,又怎么能让买家将画带走呢?最终,德廖利决定跟其中一个自称为戛纳一家叫布里斯托尔旅馆经理的人走,他提出的条件很诱人:住豪华宾馆,吃山珍海味,偶尔到海滩上走走,让客人欣赏一下他后背上苏蒂纳的那幅迷人的刺青画作。

一两个星期之后,苏蒂纳的一幅画,是一位女子的头部肖像画,开始在布宜诺斯艾利斯销售。这幅画的绘画方式很是奇特,画框装帧精美,表面光亮夺目。那幅画——还有戛纳没有一家叫作布里斯托尔的旅馆那件事,着实让人有一点点浮想联翩……

It wasn't more than a few weeks later that a picture by Soutine, of a woman's head, painted in an unusual manner, nicely framed and heavily varnished, turned up for sale in Buenos Aires. That —and the fact that there is no hotel in Cannes called Bristol—causes one to wonder a little...

二、原作释读

阅读本篇小说要注意叙事角度的切换,阅读思路要跟得上作家罗尔德·达尔角度的切换。另外,还要体会好作家在揭露人性方面的一些细腻的刻画。

Skin[①]

That year—1946—winter was a long time going. Although it was April, a freezing wind blew through the streets of the city, and overhead the snow clouds moved across the sky.

The old man who was called Drioli shuffled painfully along the sidewalk of the rue de Rivoli. He was cold and miserable, huddled[②] up like a hedgehog[③] in a filthy black coat, only his eyes and the top of his head visible above the turned-up collar.

The door of a cafe opened and the faint whiff[④] of roasting chicken brought a pain of yearning to the top of his stomach. He moved on glancing without any interest at the things in the shop windows—perfume, silk ties and shirts, diamonds, porcelain, antique furniture, finely bound books. Then a picture gallery. He had always liked picture galleries. This one had a single canvas on display in the window. He stopped to look at it. He turned to go on. He checked[⑤], looked back; and now, suddenly, there came to him a slight uneasiness, a movement of the memory, a distant recollection of something, somewhere, he had seen before. He looked again. It was a landscape, a clump of trees leaning

---

① 本部小说原文出自“DAHL, R. *The Best of Roald Dahl* [M]. London: Penguin Books Ltd., 2006”。

② huddle: *Verb* curl one's body into a small space（身子）缩成一团（e. g. She huddled up close to him. 她紧紧偎依着他。）

③ hedgehog: *Noun* relatively large rodents with sharp erectile bristles mingled with the fur 刺猬

④ whiff: *Noun* a smell that is only smelt briefly or faintly 一阵（微弱的）气味（e. g. I caught a whiff of peachy perfume. 我闻到一阵桃子似的香味。）

⑤ check: *Verb* stop for a moment, as if out of uncertainty or caution 停止；停顿

madly over to one side as if blown by a tremendous wind, the sky swirling and twisting all around. Attached to the frame there was a little plaque①, and on this it said: CHAIM SOUTINE (1894—1943).

Drioli stared at the picture, wondering vaguely what there was about it that seemed familiar. Crazy painting, he thought. Very strange and crazy—but I like it... Chaim Soutine... Soutine... "By God!" he cried suddenly. "My little Kalmuck, that's who it is! My little Kalmuck with a picture in the finest shop in Paris! Just imagine that!"

The old man pressed his face closer to the window. He could remember the boy—yes, quite clearly he could remember him. But when? The rest of it was not so easy to recollect. It was so long ago. How long? Twenty—no, more like thirty years, wasn't it? Wait a minute. Yes—it was the year before the war, the first war, 1913. That was it. And this Soutine, this ugly little Kalmuck, a sullen② brooding boy whom he had liked—almost loved—for no reason at all that he could think of except that he could paint.

And how he could paint! It was coming back more clearly now—the street, the line of refuse③ cans along the length of it, the rotten smell, the brown cats walking delicately over the refuse, and then the women, moist fat women sitting on the doorsteps with their feet upon the cobblestones of the street. Which Street? Where was it the boy had lived?

---

① plaque: *Noun* an ornamental tablet, typically of metal, porcelain, or wood, that is fixed to a wall or other surface in commemoration of a person or event (尤指金属、陶瓷或木质的固定在墙上或其他平面上以纪念某人或某事件的)饰板;匾

② sullen: *Adjective* bad-tempered and sulky 脾气坏的;愠怒的;郁郁寡欢的;阴郁的(e.g. a sullen pout 一副愠怒撅嘴的样子)

③ refuse: *Noun* [mass noun] matter thrown away or rejected as worthless; rubbish 废料;废物;垃圾

The Cité Falguiére, that was it! The old man nodded his head several times, pleased to have remembered the name. Then there was the studio with the single chair in it, and the filthy red couch that the boy had used for sleeping; the drunken parties, the cheap white wine, the furious quarrels, and always, always the bitter sullen face of the boy brooding over his work.

It was odd, Drioli thought, how easily it all came back to him now, how each single small remembered fact seemed instantly to remind him of another.

There was that nonsense with the tattoo, for instance. Now, that was a mad thing if ever there was one. How had it started? Ah, yes—he had got rich one day, that was it, and he had bought lots of wine. He could see himself now as he entered the studio with the parcel of bottles under his arm the boy sitting before the easel①, and his (Drioli's) own wife standing in the centre of the room, posing for her picture.

"Tonight we shall celebrate," he said. "We shall have a little celebration, us three."

"What is it that we celebrate?" the boy asked, without looking up. "Is it that you have decided to divorce your wife so she can marry me?"

"No," Drioli said. "We celebrate because today I have made a great sum of money with my work."

"And I have made nothing. We can celebrate that also."

"If you like." Drioli was standing by the table unwrapping the parcel. He felt tired and he wanted to get at the wine. Nine clients in one day was all very nice, but it could play hell with② a man's eyes. He had

① easel: *Noun* an upright tripod for displaying something (usually an artist's canvas) 画架;黑板架

② play hell (or merry hell) with: cause damage to 造成损失;损坏(e. g. The rough road played hell with the tyres. 凹凸不平的路损坏了轮胎。)

never done as many as nine before. Nine boozy① soldiers and the remarkable thing was that no fewer than seven of them had been able to pay in cash. This had made him extremely rich. But the work was terrible on the eyes. Drioli's eyes were half closed from fatigue, the whites streaked with little connecting lines of red; and about an inch behind each eyeball there was a small concentration of pain. But it was evening now and he was wealthy as a pig, and in the parcel there were three bottles—one for his wife, one for his friend, and one for him. He had found the corkscrew② and was drawing the corks from the bottles, each making a small plop③ as it came out.

The boy put down his brush. "Oh, Christ," he said. "How can one work with all this going on?"

The girl came across the room to look at the painting. Drioli came over also, holding a bottle in one hand, a glass in the other.

"No," the boy shouted, blazing up④ suddenly. "Please—no!" He snatched the canvas from the easel and stood it against the wall. But Drioli had seen it.

"I like it."

"It's terrible."

"It's marvellous. Like all the others that you do, it's marvellous.

---

① boozy: *Adjective* (informal) characterized by drinking large quantities of alcohol(非正式)大醉的;嗜酒的(e.g. a boozy lunch 一顿豪饮的午餐)

② corkscrew: *Noun* a device for pulling corks from bottles, consisting of a spiral metal rod that is inserted into the cork and a handle that extracts it(拔软木塞的)螺丝起子;瓶塞钻

③ plop: *Noun* a short sound as of a small, solid object dropping into water without a splash(固态物体无水花掉到水里发出的)扑通声

④ blaze up: (figurative) suddenly become angry(比喻用法)勃然大怒(e.g. He blazed up without warning. 他突如其来地大发雷霆,叫人猝不及防。)

I love them all."

"The trouble is," the boy said, scowling, "that in themselves they are not nourishing. I cannot eat them."

"But still they are marvellous." Drioli handed him a tumblerful① of the pale-yellow wine. "Drink it," he said. "It will make you happy."

Never, he thought, had he known a more unhappy person, or one with a gloomier face. He had spotted him in a cafe some seven months before, drinking alone, and because he had looked like a Russian or some sort of an Asiatic②, Drioli had sat down at his table and talked.

"You are a Russian?"

"Yes."

"Where from?"

"Minsk③."

Drioli had jumped up and embraced him, crying that he too had been born in that city.

"It wasn't actually Minsk," the boy had said. "But quite near."

"Where?"

"Smilovichi, about twelve miles away."

"Smilovichi!" Drioli had shouted, embracing him again. "I walked there several times when I was a boy." Then he had sat down again,

---

① tumbler: *Noun* a drinking glass with straight sides and no handle or stem 平底酒杯(边面平直,无柄无脚)

tumblerful: *Noun* as much as a tumbler will hold; enough to fill a tumbler 一平底酒杯的量

② Asiatic: *Adjective* relating to or deriving from Asia(与)亚洲(有关)的;源于亚洲的(e. g. Asiatic coastal regions 亚洲沿海国家)

③ Minsk: *Noun* the capital of Belarus, an industrial city in the central region of the country; pop. 1 613 000 (1990) 明斯克(白俄罗斯首府,该国中部工业城市,1990 年人口 1 613 000。)

staring affectionately at the other's face. "You know," he had said, "you don't look like a western Russian. You're like a Tartar①, or a Kalmuck②. You look exactly like a Kalmuck."

Now, standing in the studio, Drioli looked again at the boy as he took the glass of wine and tipped it down his throat in one swallow. Yes, he did have a face like a Kalmuck—very broad and high-cheeked, with a wide coarse nose. This broadness of the cheeks was accentuated by the ears which stood out sharply from the head. And then he had the narrow eyes, the black hair, the thick sullen mouth of a Kalmuck, but the hands—the hands were always a surprise, so small and white like a lady's, with tiny thin fingers.

"Give me some more," the boy said. "If we are to celebrate, then let us do it properly."

Drioli distributed the wine and sat himself on a chair. The boy sat on the old couch with Drioli's wife. The three bottles were placed on the floor between them.

"Tonight we shall drink as much as we possibly can," Drioli said. "I am exceptionally rich. I think perhaps I should go out now and buy some more bottles. How many shall I get?"

---

① Tartar: *Noun* (historical) a member of the combined forces of central Asian peoples, including Mongols and Turks, who under the leadership of Genghis Khan conquered much of Asia and eastern Europe in the early 13th century, and under Tamerlane (14th century) established an empire with its capital at Samarkand. (历史上的用法)鞑靼人(包括蒙古人和土耳其人在内的中亚人联合部队的成员之一,13世纪早期在成吉思汗的率领下征服了亚洲大部分地区和东欧,14世纪在帖木儿的统治下建立了帝国,定都撒马尔罕。)

② Kalmuck or Kalmyk: *Noun* a member of a Mongoloid people of Buddhist tradition, who migrated from W China in the 17th century 卡尔梅克人(在17世纪从中国西部迁移出的有佛教传统的蒙古族人)

"Six more," the boy said. "Two for each."

"Good. I shall go now and fetch them."

"And I will help you."

In the nearest cafe Drioli bought six bottles of white wine, and then carried them back to the studio. They placed them on the floor in two rows, and Drioli fetched the corkscrew and pulled the corks, all six of them; then they sat down again and continued to drink.

"It is only the very wealthy," Drioli said, "who can afford to celebrate in this manner."

"That is true," the boy said. "Isn't that true, Josie?"

"Of course."

"How do you feel, Josie?"

"Fine."

"Will you leave Drioli and marry me?"

"No."

"Beautiful wine," Drioli said. "It is a privilege to drink it."

Slowly, methodically, they set about getting themselves drunk. The process was routine, but all the same there was a certain ceremony to be observed, and a gravity to be maintained, and a great number of things to be said, then said again—and the wine must be praised, and the slowness was important too, so that there would be time to savour the three delicious stages of transition, especially (for Drioli) the one when he began to float and his feet did not really belong to him. That was the best period of them all—when he could look down at his feet and they were so far away that he would wonder what crazy person they might belong to and why they were lying around on the floor like that, in the distance.

After a while, he got up to switch on the light. He was surprised to see that the feet came with him when he did this, especially because he couldn't feel them touching the ground. It gave him a pleasant sensation of walking on air. Then he began wandering around the room, peeking slyly at the canvases stacked against the walls.

"Listen," he said at length. "I have an idea." He came across and stood before the couch, swaying gently. "Listen, my little Kalmuck."

"What?"

"I have a tremendous① idea. Are you listening?"

"I'm listening to Josie."

"Listen to me, please. You are my friend my ugly little Kalmuck from Minsk and to me you are such an artist that I would like to have a picture, a lovely picture—"

"Have them all. Take all you can find, but do not interrupt me when I am talking with your wife."

"No, no. Now listen. I mean a picture that I can have with me always... forever... wherever I go... whatever happens... but always with me... a picture by you." He reached forward and shook the boy's knee. "Now listen to me, please."

"Listen to him," the girl said.

"It is this. I want you to paint a picture on my skin, on my back. Then I want you to tattoo over what you have painted so that it will be there always."

"You have crazy ideas."

"I will teach you how to use the tattoo. It is easy. A child could do it."

"I am not a child."

"Please..."

"You are quite mad. What is it you want?" The painter looked up into the slow, dark, wine-bright eyes of the other man. "What in heaven's name is it you want?"

---

① tremendous: *Adjective* (informal) extremely good or impressive; excellent (非正式)极好的;给人以极深刻印象的;出色的(e. g. The crew did a tremendous job. 全体人员工作出色。)

"You could do it easily! You could! You could!"

"You mean with the tattoo?"

"Yes, with the tattoo! I will teach you in two minutes!"

"Impossible!"

"Are you saying I do not know what I am talking about?"

No, the boy could not possibly be saying that because if anyone knew about the tattoo it was he Drioli. Had he not, only last month, covered a man's whole belly with the most wonderful and delicate design composed entirely of flowers? What about the client who had had so much hair upon his chest that he had done him a picture of a grizzly bear① so designed that the hair on the chest became the furry coat of the bear? Could he not draw the likeness② of a lady and position it with such subtlety③ upon a man's arm that when the muscle of the arm was flexed the lady came to life and performed some astonishing contortions④?

"All I am saying," the boy told him, "is that you are drunk and this is a drunken idea."

"We could have Josie for a model. A study⑤ of Josie upon my back. Am I not entitled to a picture of my wife upon my back?"

---

① grizzly bear: powerful brownish-yellow bear of the uplands of western North America 大灰熊;棕熊

② likenesses: *Noun* [count noun] a portrait or representation 肖像;画像;照片(e.g. the only known likeness of Dorothy as a young woman 已知唯一的多萝西年轻时的画像)

③ subtlety: *Noun* [mass noun] the quality or state of being subtle 微妙;细致;精巧;敏锐(e.g. the textural subtlety of Degas 德加作品的巧妙)

④ contortion: *Noun* the act of twisting or deforming the shape of something 扭曲;弄歪;歪曲

⑤ study: *Noun* a piece of work, especially a drawing, done for practice or as an experiment(尤指绘画的)习作;试作;试画

"Of Josie?"

"Yes." Drioli knew he only had to mention his wife and the boy's thick brown lips would loosen and begin to quiver.

"No," the girl said.

"Darling Josie, please. Take this bottle and finish it, then you will feel more generous. It is an enormous idea. Never in my life have I had such an idea before."

"What idea?"

"That he should make a picture of you upon my back. Am I not entitled to that?"

"A picture of me?"

"A nude study," the boy said. "It is an agreeable idea."

"Not nude," the girl said.

"It is an enormous idea," Drioli said.

"It's a damn crazy idea," the girl said.

"It is in any event an idea," the boy said. "It is an idea that calls for a celebration."

They emptied another bottle among them. Then the boy said, "It is no good. I could not possibly manage the tattoo. Instead, I will paint this picture on your back and you will have it with you so long as you do not take a bath and wash it off. If you never take a bath again in your life then you will have it always, as long as you live."

"No," Drioli said.

"Yes—and on the day that you decide to take a bath I will know that you do not any longer value my picture. It will be a test of your admiration for my art."

"I do not like the idea," the girl said. "His admiration for your art is so great that he would be unclean for many years. Let us have the tattoo. But not nude."

"Then just the head," Drioli said.

"I could not manage it."

"It is immensely simple. I will undertake to teach you in two minutes. You will see. I shall go now and fetch the instruments. The needles and the inks. I have inks of many different colours—as many different colours as you have paints, and far more beautiful..."

"It is impossible."

"I have many inks. Have I not many different colours of inks, Josie?"

"Yes."

"You will see," Drioli said. "I will go now and fetch them." He got up from his chair and walked unsteadily, but with determination, out of the room.

In half an hour Drioli was back. "I have brought everything," he cried, waving a brown suitcase. "All the necessities of the tattooist are here in this bag."

He placed the bag on the table, opened it, and laid out the electric needles and the small bottles of coloured inks. He plugged in the electric needle, then he took the instrument in his hand and pressed a switch. It made a buzzing sound and the quarter inch of needle that projected from the end of it began to vibrate swiftly up and down. He threw off his jacket and rolled up his sleeve. "Now look. Watch me and I will show you how easy it is. I will make a design on my arm, here."

His forearm was already covered with blue markings, but he selected a small clear patch of skin upon which to demonstrate.

"First, I choose my ink—let us use ordinary blue—and I dip the point of the needle in the ink... so... and I hold the needle up straight and I run it lightly over the surface of the skin like this... and with the little motor and the electricity, the needle jumps up and down and punctures the skin and the ink goes in and there you are. See how easy it is... see how I draw a picture of a greyhound here upon my arm..."

The boy was intrigued. "Now let me practise a little—on your arm."

With the buzzing needle he began to draw blue lines upon Drioli's arm. "It is simple," he said. "It is like drawing with pen and ink. There is no difference except that it is slower."

"There is nothing to it. Are you ready? Shall we begin?"

"At once."

"The model!" cried Drioli. "Come on, Josie!" He was in a bustle① of enthusiasm now, tottering② around the room arranging everything, like a child preparing for some exciting game. "Where will you have her? Where shall she stand?"

"Let her be standing there, by my dressing table. Let her be brushing her hair. I will paint her with her hair down over her shoulders and her brushing it."

"Tremendous. You are a genius."

Reluctantly, the girl walked over and stood by the dressing table, carrying her glass of wine with her.

Drioli pulled off his shirt and stepped out of his trousers. He retained only his underpants and his socks and shoes, and he stood there swaying gently from side to side, his small body firm, white-skinned, almost hairless. "Now," he said, "I am the canvas. Where will you place your canvas?"

"As always, upon the easel."

"Don't be crazy. I am the canvas."

"Then place yourself upon the easel. That is where you belong."

---

① bustle: *Noun* a rapid bustling commotion 闹哄哄地忙乱;奔忙

② totter: *Verb* [no obj., with adverbial] move in a feeble or unsteady way 蹒跚;跌跌撞撞;踉跄(e.g. a hunched figure tottering down the path 一个一路踉跄的驼背身影)

"How can I?"

"Are you the canvas or are you not the canvas?"

"I am the canvas. Already I begin to feel like a canvas."

"Then place yourself upon the easel. There should be no difficulty."

"Truly, it is not possible."

"Then sit on the chair. Sit back to front, then you can lean your drunken head against the back of it. Hurry now, for I am about to commence."

"I am ready. I am waiting."

"First," the boy said, "I shall make an ordinary painting. Then, if it pleases me, I shall tattoo over it." With a wide brush he began to paint upon the naked skin of the man's back.

"Ayee! Ayee!" Drioli screamed. "A monstrous centipede① is marching down my spine!"

"Be still now! Be still!" The boy worked rapidly, applying the paint only in a thin blue wash so that it would not afterwards interfere with the process of tattooing. His concentration, as soon as he began to paint, was so great that it appeared somehow to supersede② his drunkenness. He applied the brush strokes with quick jabs③ of the arm, holding the wrist stiff, and in less than half an hour it was finished.

"All right. That's all," he said to the girl, who immediately

---

① centipede: *Noun* chiefly nocturnal predacious arthropod having a flattened body of 15 to 173 segments each with a pair of legs the foremost being modified into poison fangs 蜈蚣

② supersede: *Verb* [with obj.] take the place of (a person or thing previously in authority or use); supplant 取代(先前掌权的人或正在使用的事物)(e. g. The older models have now been superseded. 较旧的样式现在已经被取代了。)

③ jab: *Noun* a sharp hand gesture (resembling a blow) 猛击;戳

returned to the couch, lay down, and fell asleep.

Drioli remained awake. He watched the boy take up the needle and dip it in the ink; then he felt the sharp tickling sting as it touched the skin of his back. The pain, which was unpleasant but never extreme, kept him from going to sleep. By following the track of the needle and by watching the different colours of ink that the boy was using, Drioli amused himself trying to visualize what was going on behind him. The boy worked with an astonishing intensity. He appeared to have become completely absorbed in the little machine and in the unusual effects it was able to produce.

Far into the small hours① of the morning the machine buzzed and the boy worked. Drioli could remember that when the artist finally stepped back and said, "It is finished," there was daylight outside and the sound of people walking in the street.

"I want to see it," Drioli said. The boy held up a mirror, at an angle, and Drioli craned his neck to look.

"Good God!" he cried. It was a startling sight. The whole of his back, from the top of the shoulders to the base of the spine, was a blaze of colour—gold and green and blue and black and scarlet. The tattoo was applied so heavily it looked almost like an impasto②. The boy had followed as closely as possible the original brush strokes, filling them in solid, and it was marvellous the way he had made use of the spine and

---

① small hours: the hours just after midnight 午夜以后;下半夜;凌晨

② impasto: *Noun* [mass noun] (Art) the process or technique of laying on paint or pigment thickly so that it stands out from a surface(艺术)厚涂(法)

the protrusion① of the shoulder blades② so that they became part of the composition. What is more, he had somehow managed to achieve—even with this slow process—a certain spontaneity③. The portrait was quite alive; it contained much of that twisted, tortured quality so characteristic of Soutine's other work. It was not a good likeness. It was a mood rather than a likeness, the model's face vague and tipsy, the background swirling around her head in a mass of dark-green curling strokes.

"It's tremendous!"

"I rather like it myself." The boy stood back, examining it critically. "You know," he added, "I think it's good enough for me to sign." And taking up the buzzer again, he inscribed his name in red ink on the right-hand side, over the place where Drioli's kidney was.

The old man who was called Drioli was standing in a sort of trance, staring at the painting in the window of the picture-dealer's shop. It had been so long ago, all that—almost as though it had happened in another life.

And the boy? What had become of him? He could remember now that after returning from the war—the first war—he had missed him and had questioned Josie.

"Where is my little Kalmuck?"

"He is gone," she had answered. "I do not know where, but I heard it said that a dealer had taken him up and sent him away to Céret to make more paintings."

---

① protrusion: *Noun* something that bulges out or is protuberant or projects from a form 伸出;突出

② shoulder blade: *Noun* either of two flat triangular bones one on each side of the shoulder in human beings 肩胛

③ spontaneity: *Noun* the quality of being spontaneous and coming from natural feelings without constraint 自发性;自动

"Perhaps he will return."

"Perhaps he will. Who knows?"

That was the last time they had mentioned him. Shortly afterwards they had moved to Le Havre① where there were more sailors and business was better. The old man smiled as he remembered Le Havre. Those were the pleasant years, the years between the wars, with the small shop near the docks and the comfortable rooms and always enough work, with every day three, four, five sailors coming and wanting pictures on their arms. Those were truly the pleasant years.

Then had come the second war, and Josie being killed, and the Germans arriving, and that was the finish of his business. No one had wanted pictures on their arms any more after that. And by that time he was too old for any other kind of work. In desperation he had made his way back to Paris, hoping vaguely that things would be easier in the big city. But they were not.

And now, after the war was over, he possessed neither the means nor the energy to start up his small business again. It wasn't very easy for an old man to know what to do, especially when one did not like to beg. Yet how else could he keep alive?

Well, he thought, still staring at the picture. So that is my little Kalmuck. And how quickly the sight of one small object such as this can stir the memory. Up to a few moments ago he had even forgotten that he had a tattoo on his back. It had been ages since he had thought about it. He put his face closer to the window and looked into the gallery. On the walls he could see many other pictures and all seemed to be the work of the same artist. There were a great number of people strolling around.

---

① Le Havre: a port in northern France, on the English Channel at the mouth of the Seine; pop. 197 220 (1990) 勒阿弗尔(法国北部港口,位于英吉利海峡的塞纳河河口附近,1990 年人口 197 220。)

Obviously it was a special exhibition.

On a sudden impulse, Drioli turned, pushed open the door of the gallery and went in.

It was a long room with thick wine-coloured carpet, and by God how beautiful and warm it was! There were all these people strolling about looking at the pictures, well-washed dignified people, each of whom held a catalogue in the hand. Drioli stood just inside the door, nervously glancing around, wondering whether he dared go forward and mingle with this crowd. But before he had had time to gather his courage, he heard a voice beside him saying, "What is it you want?"

The speaker wore a black morning coat. He was plump and short and had a very white face. It was a flabby① face with so much flesh upon it that the cheeks hung down on either side of the mouth in two fleshy collops②, spanielwise③. He came up close to Drioli and said again, "What is it you want?"

Drioli stood still.

"If you please," the man was saying, "take yourself out of my gallery."

"Am I not permitted to look at the pictures?"

"I have asked you to leave."

Drioli stood his ground. He felt suddenly overwhelmingly outraged.

"Let us not have trouble," the man was saying. "Come on now,

---

① flabby: Adjective lacking firmness or stiffness 肌肉松垂的;肥胖的

② collop: *Noun* a slice of meat 肉片

③ spaniel: *Noun* any of several breeds of small to medium-sized gun dogs with a long silky coat and long frilled ears 长毛垂耳狗

-wise: Suffix forming adjectives and adverbs of manner or respect such as "clockwise" "otherwise" (构成形容词和副词的后缀,如"clockwise" "otherwise"等)表示"样子""位置"或"方向"。

this way." He put a fat white paw on Drioli's arm and began to push him firmly to the door.

That did it. "Take your goddam hands off me!" Drioli shouted. His voice rang clear down the long gallery and all the heads jerked around as one—all the startled faces stared down the length of the room at the person who had made this noise. A flunkey① came running over to help, and the two men tried to hustle② Drioli through the door. The people stood still, watching the struggle. Their faces expressed only a mild interest, and seemed to be saying, "It's all right. There's no danger to us. It's being taken care of."

"I, too!" Drioli was shouting. "I, too, have a picture by this painter! He was my friend and I have a picture which he gave me!"

"He's mad."

"A lunatic③. A raving④ lunatic."

"Someone should call the police."

With a rapid twist of the body Drioli suddenly jumped clear of the two men, and before anyone could stop him he was running down the gallery shouting, "I'll show you! I'll show you! I'll show you!" He flung off his overcoat, then his jacket and shirt, and he turned so that his

---

① flunkey or flunky: *Noun* (chiefly derogatory) a liveried manservant or footman(主要用于贬义)穿特殊制服的男仆

② hustle: *Verb* [with obj. and adverbial of direction] force (someone) to move hurriedly or unceremoniously in a specified direction 强迫(某人往特定方向)匆忙前往(e. g. I was hustled away to a cold cell. 我被强迫带至寒冷的单人牢房。)

③ lunatic: *Noun* a person who is mentally ill (not in technical use) 精神病患者;疯子(非技术用语)

④ raving: *Adjective* (informal) used to emphasize the bad or extreme quality of someone or something(非正式)非常的;极端的

naked back was towards the people.

"There!" he cried, breathing quickly. "You see? There it is!"

There was a sudden absolute silence in the room, each person arrested in what he was doing, standing motionless in a kind of shocked, uneasy bewilderment. They were staring at the tattooed picture. It was still there, the colours as bright as ever, but the old man's back was thinner now, the shoulder blades protruded more sharply, and the effect, though not great, was to give the picture a curiously wrinkled, squashed① appearance.

Somebody said, "My God, but it is!"

Then came the excitement and the noise of voices as the people surged forward to crowd around the old man.

"It is unmistakable!"

"His early manner, yes?"

"It is fantastic, fantastic!"

"And look, it is signed!"

"Bend your shoulders forward, my friend, so that the picture stretches out flat."

"Old one, when was this done?"

"In 1913," Drioli said, without turning around. "In the autumn of 1913."

"Who taught Soutine to tattoo?"

"I taught him."

"And the woman?"

"She was my wife."

The gallery owner was pushing through the crowd towards Drioli. He

① squashed: *Adjective* that has been violently compressed 压碎的;压扁的

was calm now, deadly serious, making a smile with his mouth. "Monsieur[1]," he said, "I will buy it." Drioli could see the loose fat upon the face vibrating as he moved his jaw. "I said I will buy it, Monsieur."

"How can you buy it?" Drioli asked softly.

"I will give two hundred thousand francs for it." The dealer's eyes were small and dark, the wings of his broad nose-base were beginning to quiver.

"Don't do it!" someone murmured in the crowd. "It is worth twenty times as much."

Drioli opened his mouth to speak. No words came, so he shut it; then he opened it again and said slowly. "But how can I sell it?" He lifted his hands, let them drop loosely to his sides. "Monsieur, how can I possibly sell it?" All the sadness in the world was in his voice.

"Yes!" they were saying in the crowd. "How can he sell it? It is part of himself!"

"Listen," the dealer said, coming up close. "I will help you, I will make you rich. Together we shall make some private arrangement over this picture, no?"

Drioli watched him with slow, apprehensive eyes. "But how can you buy it, Monsieur? What will you do with it when you have bought it? Where will you keep it? Where will you keep it tonight? And where tomorrow?"

"Ah, where will I keep it? Yes, where will I keep it? Now, where will I keep it? Well, now..." The dealer stroked the bridge of his nose with a fat white finger. "It would seem," he said, "that if I take the picture, I take you also. That is a disadvantage." He paused and stroked

---

① Monsieur: *Noun* used as a French courtesy title; equivalent to English "Mr." 先生(法语中对男性的尊称)

his nose again. "The picture itself is of no value until you are dead. How old are you, my friend?"

"Sixty-one."

"But you are perhaps not very robust①, no?" The dealer lowered the hand from his nose and looked Drioli up and down, slowly, like a farmer appraising an old horse.

"I do not like this," Drioli said, edging away. "Quite honestly, Monsieur, I do not like it." He edged straight into the arms of a tall man who put out his hands and caught him gently by the shoulders. Drioli glanced around and apologized. The man smiled down at him, patting one of the old fellow's naked shoulders reassuringly with a hand encased in a canary②-coloured glove.

"Listen, my friend," the stranger said, still smiling. "Do you like to swim and to bask③ yourself in the sun?"

Drioli looked up at him, rather startled.

"Do you like fine food and red wine from the great châteaux of Bordeaux?" The man was still smiling, showing strong white teeth with a flash of gold among them. He spoke in a soft coaxing manner, one gloved hand still resting on Drioli's shoulder. "Do you like such things?"

"Well yes," Drioli answered, still greatly perplexed. "Of course."

"And the company of beautiful women?"

"Why not?"

---

① robust: *Adjective* (of a person, animal, or plant) strong and healthy; vigorous(人)强壮的;(动、植物)强健的;粗壮的;茁壮的

② canary: *Adjective* (also as "canary yellow") [mass noun] a bright yellow colour resembling the plumage of a canary 鲜黄色

③ bask: *Verb* [no obj.] lie exposed to warmth and light, typically from the sun, for relaxation and pleasure(舒适地)取暖;晒太阳(e. g. sprawled figures basking in the afternoon sun 躺着享受午后阳光的人)

"And a cupboard full of suits and shirts made to your own personal measurements? It would seem that you are a little lacking for clothes."

Drioli watched this suave① man, waiting for the rest of the proposition.

"Have you ever had a shoe constructed especially for your own foot?"

"No."

"You would like that?"

"Well..."

"And a man who will shave you in the mornings and trim your hair?"

Drioli simply stood and gaped②.

"And a plump attractive girl to manicure③ the nails of your fingers?"

Someone in the crowd giggled.

"And a bell beside your bed to summon your maid to bring your breakfast in the morning? Would you like these things, my friend? Do they appeal to you?"

Drioli stood still and looked at him.

---

① suave: *Adjective* (especially of a man) charming, confident, and elegant (尤指男性)有吸引力的;自信的;温文尔雅的(e.g. All the waiters were suave and deferential. 所有侍者都温文尔雅、毕恭毕敬。)

② gape: *Verb* [no obj.] stare with one's mouth open wide, typically in amazement or wonder 目瞪口呆地凝视(e.g. They gaped at her as if she was an alien. 他们目瞪口呆地看着她,好像她是个外星人。)

③ manicure: *Noun* a cosmetic treatment of the hands involving cutting, shaping, and often painting of the nails, removal of the cuticles, and softening of the skin 修指甲

"You see, I am the owner of the Hotel Bristol in Cannes①. I now invite you to come down there and live as my guest for the rest of your life in luxury and comfort." The man paused, allowing his listener time to savour this cheerful prospect. "Your only duty—shall I call it your pleasure—will be to spend your time on my beach in bathing trunks②, walking among my guests, sunning yourself, swimming, drinking cocktails. You would like that?"

There was no answer.

"Don't you see all the guests will thus be able to observe this fascinating picture by Soutine. You will become famous, and men will say, 'Look, there is the fellow with ten million francs upon his back.' You like this idea, Monsieur? It pleases you?"

Drioli looked up at the tall man in the canary gloves, still wondering whether this was some sort of a joke. "It is a comical idea," he said slowly. "But do you really mean it?"

"Of course I mean it."

"Wait." the dealer interrupted. "See here, old one. Here is the answer to our problem. I will buy the picture, and I will arrange with a surgeon to remove the skin from your back, and then you will be able to go off on your own and enjoy the great sum of money I shall give you for it."

"With no skin on my back?"

"No, no, please! You misunderstand. This surgeon will put a new piece of skin in the place of the old one. It is simple."

"Could he do that?"

---

① Cannes: *Noun* a resort on the Mediterranean coast of France; pop. 69 360 (1990). An international film festival is held there annually 戛纳(法国地中海岸度假胜地,1990 年人口 69 360,每年在此举办国际电影节。)

② bathing trunks: swimsuit worn by men while swimming 游泳裤

"There is nothing to it."

"Impossible!" said the man with the canary gloves. "He's too old for such a major skin-grafting operation. It would kill him. It would kill you, my friend."

"It would kill me?"

"Naturally. You would never survive. Only the picture would come through."

"In the name of God!" Drioli cried. He looked around aghast at the faces of the people watching him, and in the silence that followed, another man's voice, speaking quietly from the back of the group, could be heard saying, "Perhaps, if one were to offer this old man enough money, he might consent to kill himself on the spot. Who knows?" A few people sniggered①. The dealer moved his feet uneasily on the carpet.

Then the hand in the canary glove was tapping Drioli again upon the shoulder. "Come on," the man was saying, smiling his broad white smile. "You and I will go and have a good dinner and we can talk about it some more while we eat. How's that? Are you hungry?"

Drioli watched him, frowning. He didn't like the man's long flexible neck, or the way he craned it forward at you when he spoke, like a snake.

"Roast duck and Chambertin②," the man was saying. He put a rich succulent③ accent on the words, splashing them out with his tongue.

---

① snigger: *Verb* laugh quietly 暗笑;窃笑

② Chambertin: *Noun* [mass noun] a dry red burgundy wine of high quality from Gevrey Chambertin in eastern France 香贝丹红葡萄酒

③ succulent: *Adjective* (of food) tender, juicy, and tasty(食物)鲜嫩多汁的

"And perhaps a soufflé① aux marrons②, light and frothy③."

Drioli's eyes turned up towards the ceiling, his lips became loose and wet. One could see the poor old fellow beginning literally to drool④ at the mouth.

"How do you like your duck?" the man went on. "Do you like it very brown and crisp outside, or shall it be..."

"I am coming," Drioli said quickly. Already he had picked up his shirt and was pulling it frantically over his head. "Wait for me, Monsieur. I am coming." And within a minute he had disappeared out of the gallery with his new patron.

It wasn't more than a few weeks later that a picture by Soutine, of a woman's head, painted in an unusual manner, nicely framed and heavily varnished, turned up for sale in Buenos Aires⑤. That—and the fact that there is no hotel in Cannes called Bristol—causes one to wonder a little, and to pray for the old man's health, and to hope fervently that wherever he may be at this moment, there is a plump attractive girl to manicure the nails of his fingers, and a maid to bring him his breakfast in bed in the mornings.

---

① soufflé or soufflé: *Noun* light fluffy dish of egg yolks and stiffly beaten egg whites mixed with e. g. cheese or fish or fruit 奶油鸡蛋饼

② marron: *Noun* (Plants) a large edible sweet chestnut(植物)栗子

③ frothy: *Adjective* full of or covered with a mass of small bubbles 充满泡沫的;被泡沫覆盖的(e. g. steaming mugs of frothy coffee 几杯热气腾腾地冒着气泡的咖啡)

④ drool: *Verb* [no obj.] drop saliva uncontrollably from the mouth 淌口水;流涎(e. g. The baby begins to drool, then to cough. 婴儿开始淌口水,接着咳嗽。)

⑤ Buenos Aires: the capital city and chief port of Argentina, on the River Plate; pop. 2 961 000 (1991) 布宜诺斯艾利斯(阿根廷首都及主要港口城市,位于普拉特河畔;1991 年人口 2 961 000。)

三、翻译探索

本篇小说的翻译中,涉及一些绘画和刺青方面的知识和词汇,需要准确加以传达。个别地名和法语词汇翻译起来有些棘手,但是通过查找,容易突破。

人皮刺青

那一年的冬天,也就是1946年的冬天,很是漫长。尽管已经到了四月份,但冰冷刺骨的寒风还是呼啸着吹过这个城市的大街小巷。头顶上空,一片一片的雪成云漂移而过。

一个老人拖着沉重的脚步沿着丽弗里大街走着,老人的名字叫德廖利。他感到寒冷,一副可怜兮兮的模样,整个人就像一只刺猬蜷缩在他那件脏兮兮的黑色外套里。从竖起的衣领上,只能看到他那两只眼睛和脑袋顶。

一家咖啡馆的门打开了,里面隐隐飘来一股烤鸡的香气,这令他胃口大开,却又痛苦地走开。他边向前走,边心不在焉地看着橱窗里的东西:有香水,有套着丝绸领带的衬衫,有宝石,有瓷器,有古董家具,还有装订精美的书籍。接下来,他走到一家画馆前。他一直都是很喜欢画馆的,而这家画馆的橱窗里只陈列了一幅帆布画。他停下脚步,看了看那幅画,转身就要继续往前走。可是,他却一下子停住,回头又看了看。现在,突然之间,他感到有一点点的局促不安,记忆开始流动,想起了遥远时空里的某种似曾相识的东西。他又看了看,发现那是一幅风景画,画面上有一簇树木,枝条杂乱倾向一侧,就好像被一阵强烈的大风吹过似的;天空云卷云舒、扭曲变形。画框上附带一个小标牌,上面写着:"哈伊姆·苏蒂纳(1894—1943)"。

德廖利呆呆地盯着那幅画,凭着记忆,模糊地感觉到这幅画里似乎有什么地方自己很熟悉。他想,这画古里古怪的。虽说古里古怪,却奇特异常,但是,我喜欢……哈伊姆·苏蒂纳……苏蒂纳……"我的天啊,"他突然大叫起来,"我可爱的小卡尔梅克,就是他啊。我可爱的小卡尔梅克竟然有画陈列在巴黎顶级画馆里！真是难以想象！”

这个老人把脸更贴近橱窗一点。他想起这个男孩子啦——没错，是他。他现在仍然记忆犹新。但，具体什么时候呢？关于这个男孩的其余事情，回忆起来，却不是如此容易。那是很久、很久以前的事，多久以前呢？二十年前吗——不，更像是三十年前的事情，对不对呢？且慢。想起来了，是那场战争——第一次世界大战——之前那一年的事情，也就是1913年。对了，就是那一年。那样的话，这个苏蒂纳，就是那个模样难看的小卡尔梅克啦。他是一个闷闷不语、若有所思的男孩子。他喜欢这个男孩子，几乎父亲般地爱这个孩子。他根本想不出什么原因这么喜欢这个孩子，但有一个原因除外：这个男孩子会画画。

哇，他那画画得太棒啦！昔日的场景更加清晰地浮现出来——那条大街，那些沿街排列的垃圾箱，那腐烂的气味，那些轻手轻脚在垃圾上行走的棕色猫咪，还有那些妇女。那些妇女胖胖的，身上湿漉漉的，坐在门口台阶上，双脚搭在大街表面铺设的鹅卵石上。是哪一条大街来着？那个男孩子住的地方叫什么来着？

法吉埃尔市，对，就是这个地方。老人频频点头，为想起这个名字而感到沾沾自喜。那时候，那男孩子有一个画室，里面的椅子只有一把，还有那个长沙发椅，是那男孩子用来睡觉的。那里有醉醺醺的聚会，喝的是便宜廉价的白葡萄酒，还有面红耳赤的争吵。而且，无论何时，总少不了男孩那张苦涩的脸，对着画作闷闷不语、若有所思。

德廖利寻思着，这也太古里古怪、不可思议了——现在，这些往事怎么一股脑儿都跑回来了啊。而且，每一个微不足道的往事，只要想起来一个，另一个似乎也连带着想了起来。

比如说，冲动而且荒唐的刺青那件事吧。现在看来，那真是史无前例的疯狂之举。刺青那事儿是怎么引发的呢？啊，想起来了——是这样的：有一天，他突然有钱了，就买了很多葡萄酒。这个老人现在清晰地记得，当时他走进画室，胳膊底下夹着一个小包裹，里面包着酒，他（德廖利）的妻子坐在画室中央，摆出姿势要那男孩子画像，男孩子坐在画架前。

“今晚，我们要庆祝一下，”他说，“就我们三个人，要小小庆祝一下。”

“庆祝什么？”男孩问道，头并没有抬起来，“你决定跟你妻子离婚，她就能嫁给我，是庆祝这个吗？”

“不，”德廖利回答，“我们庆祝，是因为我今天工作赚了一大笔钱。”

“我们也顺便庆祝一下，我一分钱没有赚到。”

“要是你愿意，也可以庆祝的。”德廖利在桌子旁停下，打开那个小包裹。他感觉很累，想马上就喝酒。就今天这一天，一共九个顾客，都很不错的。可是，这笔生意做下来，对眼睛伤害就大了。以前从来没有这么多顾客，今天是九个当兵的，个个都喝得酩酊大醉。但是，再好不过的是，他们当中有不下七个人能够支付现金，这下他可发了。可问题是，这生意做下来，两眼可就惨了。由于极度疲乏，德廖利的眼睛半睁半闭，白眼仁布满了彼此相连的红线条。更有甚者，每一只眼球后方大约二十五毫米的地方，感觉有微小的点，很是疼痛。管它呢，现在到了晚上，他可以像猪一般享受了。小包裹里有三瓶酒：一瓶给他妻子，一瓶给他朋友，最后一瓶给他自己。他找出螺丝瓶起子，开始起瓶塞。每只瓶塞拔出来时，都发出“嘭”的一声。

男孩子放下画刷。“噢，天啊，”他说，“好吃好喝都摆出来，让人怎么继续工作啊？”

德廖利的妻子走过来，看了看画像。他也凑过来，一只手举着酒瓶子，另一只手拿着杯子。

“不，”男孩突然发起火来，喊道，“拜托，别看！”他从画架上一下子拽下画布，靠墙竖放起来。可是，德廖利已经看到了。

“我很喜欢。”

“画得很糟的。”

“画得太绝了。跟你的其他画一样，太绝了。我都喜欢。”

“可问题是，”男孩子眉头一皱，露出不悦之色，说道，“这些画本身没有什么营养，我没法都吃下去。”

“可是，它们仍然是很绝妙的。”德廖利递给他一个玻璃酒杯，没有把的那种杯子，里面倒满了葡萄酒。“喝酒吧，”他说，“酒会令你开心的。”

他想，他从来没有遇到过像这个男孩子那样不开心的人，也从来没有看到过比那更忧郁的脸孔。大约七个月前，他在一家咖啡馆看见这个男孩子一个人独饮。因为男孩子看起来像俄罗斯人，或者亚洲某个地方的人，所以德廖利就在他桌子旁边坐下，跟他攀谈起来。

“你是俄罗斯人吗？”

“是的。”

“哪个地方的？”

“明斯克的。”

德廖利一下子跳起来，抱住了他，大叫道，他也在那个城市出生的。

“实际上，不是正好在明斯克，”男孩子说，“但是，离明斯克很近。”

“哪里？”

“斯米洛维奇，离明斯克大约二十二公里远。”

“斯米洛维奇！”德廖利大喊起来，又抱住了他，“我年纪很小的时候，曾经好几次步行去过那里。”然后，他又坐了下来，充满爱意地盯着男孩子的脸。“要知道，”他说，“你看起来不像西俄罗斯人。你像鞑靼人，或卡尔梅克人。你看起来跟卡尔梅克人一模一样。”

现在，德廖利站在画室里，又打量一下这个男孩子。只见他接过酒杯，往嘴里一倒，酒顺着喉咙一口吞了下去。是的，看他那张脸，确实像卡尔梅克人——脸阔，脸颊隆起，鼻子很宽，鼻孔粗糙；他的两只耳朵直勾勾地从脑袋上伸出来，脸颊就显得更宽阔；他一头黑发，两只眼睛窄窄的；他长了典型的卡尔梅克的嘴巴，嘴唇厚厚，闷闷不语；然而，他的那双手——那双手嘛，总是令人吃惊不已——指头纤细、肤色白皙，就像女人的手。

“再给我倒点儿，”男孩子说，“我们既然要庆祝，就好好庆贺一番。”

德廖利把酒分给大家，然后自己坐到一把椅子上。男孩子和德廖利的妻子一起坐在那个破旧的长沙发椅上,三瓶酒放在他们之间的地板上。

“今晚,我们几个放开了喝,”德廖利说,“我可不是一般地有钱啊。我想,我或许现在就应该出去,再买几瓶酒。买几瓶合适呢?”

“再买六瓶,”男孩子说,“一人两瓶。”

“好的。我现在就去把酒买回来。”

“那么,我帮你。”

在最近一家咖啡馆,德廖利买了六瓶白葡萄酒。他俩就一起把酒拿回画室,摆成两排,放到地板上。德廖利取来瓶起子,把六瓶酒的塞子都拔了出来。然后,他们几个又坐了下来,继续喝。

“只有很富有的人,”德廖利说,“才能花得起钱用这种方式来庆祝。”

“那倒没错,”男孩子说,“乔西,难道那话说得有错吗?”

“千真万确。”

“感觉如何,乔西?”

“很好。”

“你会离开德廖利嫁给我吗?”

“不会。”

“好酒啊,”德廖利说,“喝这酒,如同享受殊荣。”

他们几个慢慢地、一步步把自己灌醉了。每次喝醉的过程都是一样的,但是要履行某些程序,要维持某种严肃性,还要说很多的事情,说一遍还不行。每次必不可少的是,要对酒夸赞一番。最重要的是,每个阶段要慢慢地进行,这样就有足够的时间来品味从清醒到沉醉的那三个美妙的阶段。特别是对德廖利来说,这个阶段再好不过:开始感觉轻飘飘的,双脚不是真正属于自己。最美妙的时刻就是,低头能看到自己的脚,但是那两只脚却离他很遥远,他甚至纳闷起来:长着这两只脚的人该是多么疯狂啊!这个人的两只脚怎么能像那样跑到地板上很远的地方啊!

过了一会儿,他站起来,打开灯。看到这两只脚也跟着他一起去开灯,他吃惊不小,很特别的一个原因就是,他感觉不到那两只脚跟地面是接触的。当时,他感觉开心无比,如同空中漫步。接着,他就开始绕屋子走来走去,不时地瞥一眼靠在墙边那堆帆布画,一副诡秘的样子。

“听着,”他终于开口说话了,“我有一个想法。”他穿过屋子,站到长沙发椅前,身体轻轻摇晃着。“听着,我可爱的小卡尔梅克。”

“你说什么?”

“我有一个绝妙的想法。你在听我说话吗?”

“我在听乔西说话呢。”

“拜托,听我说啊。你是我的朋友——我可爱的、模样难看的、来自明斯克的小卡尔梅克。但是,对我来说,你却是一个很棒的艺术家,我十分想跟你讨要一幅画,一幅美丽动人的画——”

“都拿去吧。找到多少,你就拿多少。可有一点啊,我正跟你妻子说话,不要打扰就行。”

“不,不是那意思。现在,你听着啊。我的意思是,我想要一幅总能带在身边的画……永远不离身——无论我走到哪里——不管发生什么事情……那画总能在我身边……是一幅你画的画。”他向前移了移,摇晃着男孩的膝盖,“现在,听我说,拜托。”

“还是听他说吧。”他妻子说道。

“是这样的。我要你在我的皮肤上画一幅画,就在我后背的皮肤上。然后,把你画的文到我身上,永远保留下来。”

“你这想法太疯狂。”

“我教你怎么样文身。很简单,连小孩子都会的。”

“可我不是小孩子。”

“拜托了……”

“你简直是疯了。你想干什么啊?”这位画画的男孩抬起头来,看着那个男人的眼睛,那眼睛移动缓慢、颜色黝黑,因为喝酒而明亮起来。“老天啊,你到底想干什么啊?”

“你能做到,很容易的!你做得到!你做得到!”

“你的意思是说文身?”

“对,就是文身!两分钟,我就能把你教会!”

“不可能!”

“你是说,我糊涂到了竟然不知道自己说了些什么吗?”

不,男孩子不可能那样说的,因为要是真有什么人懂得文身的话,那个人非德廖利莫属。就是在上个月,难道不是他把一个人整个腹部文上了极其精致、奇妙的图案吗?那图案完完全全由一朵朵鲜花构成。难道他没有给那个长满胸毛的顾客文身吗?他给那个顾客胸部文了一幅画,画的是一只棕熊,设计得很是精巧,胸毛变成了棕熊毛茸茸的外衣。还有一个男子的胳膊难道不是他文的吗?他在那个男子的胳膊上文了一幅女子的肖像,肖像的位置跟胳膊浑然一体、天衣无缝,甚至于胳膊肌肉弯曲时,那女子复活了,还做出某些弯曲的动作,令人惊叹不已。

“我所说的意思是,”男孩子对他说,“你喝醉了,你那是醉意。”

“我们可以拿乔西做模特。在我背上画一幅乔西的草图。难道我没有资格把我妻子画到我背上吗?”

“画乔西?”

“是啊,”德廖利知道,他只有提到他的妻子,那男孩厚厚的棕色嘴唇才会松动,并且开始抖动。

“不。”他妻子说。

“亲爱的乔西,拜托啦。拿起这瓶酒,喝干,你就有感觉,更能大大方方的啦。我的想法美妙绝伦。我的一生中,从来没有过这样的想法。”

“什么想法?”

“想法就是,他把你画到我的背上。难道我没有这个资格吗?”

“画我?”

“一幅裸体草图,”男孩子说,“这个想法,我同意。”

“不要裸体啊。”女子说。

“我的想法美妙绝伦。”德廖利说道。

“什么该死的破想法,疯了你。”她说。

“不管怎么说,也是个想法啊,”男孩子说,“冲这个想法,就可以庆祝一番。”

他们几个又喝干了一瓶。然后，男孩子说："这样可不好，文身我不可能做得了。我就画吧。画到你的背上，然后只要你不洗澡或故意洗掉，就可以随身携带。你从此再也不洗澡的话，你就永远带到身上，除非你死去。"

"不。"德廖利说。

"可以的。哪一天你决定要洗澡的话，我就知道你不再珍惜我的画。你钦佩不钦佩我的艺术，这是很好的验证方法。"

"我不喜欢这个想法，"她说，"他十分钦佩你的艺术，很多年过去也不会洗澡的。但，还是文身吧，但不是裸体的。"

"那就文头部吧。"德廖利说。

"我文不好的。"

"再简单不过了。我负责教你，两分钟就会。等等，我取工具，就是针、墨水什么的，去去就来。我用的墨水有很多种颜色，就像你用的颜料，但我的墨水要漂亮得多……"

"不可能的。"

"我有很多墨水。乔西，我是不是有很多颜色的墨水呢？"

"是的。"

"等等啊，"德廖利说，"我取一下，去去就来。"他站起来，走了出去。虽说走起路来摇摇晃晃，但却果断坚毅。

半小时后，德廖利回来了。"东西我都带来了，"他边喊，边挥了挥一个棕色的手提箱，"文身艺术家所必须的用具都在这个包里装着呢。"

他把包放到桌子上，随即打开，摆出电针，还有一小瓶一小瓶的各种颜色的墨水。他把电针插上电，拿到手里，按了一下开关，立刻发出"嗡嗡嗡"的声音。同时，安装在电针头部的那根足有六毫米长的针头开始快速地上下振动起来。他脱掉夹克，左手的袖子也卷了起来。"现在看着，好好看着我。我示范给你看看，文身到底有多容易。我先在自己胳膊上文一个图案，就在这儿。"

他的前臂已经布满了蓝色的标记，但他从中选了一块干净的皮肤，在那上面做演示。

"首先,选择墨水——就用普通的蓝色墨水吧——把针尖浸到墨水里……你看……针要笔直握紧,轻轻地在皮肤表面掠过……像这样……有了电和马达的驱动,针就上下跳跃,在皮肤上刺出小孔,墨水就跟着滴进去,你看……看看,多简单啊……看看,我是怎么样在我胳膊的这个地方文出一幅灰狗的图案的……"

男孩的兴趣被激发起来了。"现在,让我稍微练习一下——就在你的胳膊上练习。"

随着针"嗡嗡嗡"作响,他开始在德廖利的胳膊上文出一道道蓝色的线条。"是很简单啊,"他说,"这类似于用蘸墨水的钢笔绘画一样啊。两者差别不大,但这个速度慢多了。"

"文身没什么高深的。准备好了吗?我们可以开始了吗?"

"马上开始。"

"模特,上!"德廖利喊道,"快点啊,乔西!"他一时兴起,开始催促起来。他趔趔趄趄地满屋子忙活,搬搬这儿,动动那儿,活像一个准备玩某种游戏的孩子,兴奋异常。"你把她安排到哪儿?她应该站在什么地方?"

"就让她站在那儿,我那梳妆台旁边。让她梳理梳理头发。我要画她长发披肩的样子,梳理一下呀。"

"好极了。你真是个天才。"

女子很不情愿地走过去,站到梳妆台旁边,手里仍然举着她那杯酒。

德廖利脱掉衬衫,脱掉裤子,身上只留下一条内裤、一双袜子,还有两只鞋。他站在那里,身子轻微地左右摇晃着。他个子矮小,人却很结实,皮肤白白的,身上几乎没有什么毛发。"现在,"他说,"我就是画布。你要把画布放到什么位置呢?"

"按常规,放到画架上。"

"别发神经,画布是我啊。"

"好吧,你把自己放到画架上吧,那是你应该待的位置。"

"那可怎么放啊?"

"你到底是不是画布呢?"

“我是画布。我已经开始感觉到了,我就是一块画布。”

“那就把自己放到画架上。这不应该是什么难做的事情。”

“说的没错,但,不可能做到啊。”

“好吧,那坐到椅子上,后背朝前。那样,你可以把喝得醉醺醺的脑袋靠到椅子后背上。现在加紧啊,我可要开始了。”

“我准备好了,正等着呢。”

“首先呢,”男孩说,“我要常规性地画一幅画。然后,要是对画满意的话,我就开始文。”说完,他拿起一支扁画刷,开始在这个男子裸露的皮肤上画了起来。

“唉哟哟!唉哟哟!”德廖利叫了起来,“怎么有一只可怕的蜈蚣沿着我的脊椎骨往下爬啊!”

“老实待着,别动啊!”男孩子干得很麻利,只涂了薄薄的一层蓝色颜料,不会妨碍随后的文身的过程。从开始绘画那刻起,他就全身心投入进去了,看起来无论如何也不像是一个喝醉酒的人。画的时候,他胳膊运笔利落、快捷,笔画起落自如,手腕坚挺有力。半个小时还没到,他就画完了。

“好了,就这样吧,”他对姑娘说。她立马奔向长沙发椅,一头栽倒,睡着了。

德廖利没有呼呼睡着。他看着男孩拿起针,蘸了点墨水;接着,随着针尖跟后背皮肤不断接触,他感到明显的、痒痒的刺痛感。虽然疼痛不是那么厉害,却也感到不是很舒服,痛感一阵一阵的,也省得他睡着了。感觉着针移动的轨迹,看着男孩使用的不同颜色的墨水,德廖利自己颇感愉悦,尽量在眼前勾画出后背的进展情况。男孩做起活来,十分专心、非常投入。他看起来完完全全着迷于这个小工具,沉醉于这个小工具能够产生的非同凡响的效果。

午夜已经过了很长、很长的时间,电针还在“嗡嗡嗡”地响着。那男孩还在工作着。德廖利能够记得的是,这位男孩艺术家最终向后退了一步,说道:“弄完了。”那个时候,天已经放亮,可以听见大街上人们行走的声音。

“我想看一看。”德廖利说。男孩举起镜子,调整好角度,德廖利就伸长脖子看了起来。

“老天啊!”他喊道。眼前的情景让他惊呆了。他整个后背——从双肩顶上一直到脊椎底下——色彩炫目:有金色,有绿色,有蓝色,有黑色,还有猩红色。整幅刺青用色厚重,看起来活像一幅涂着厚厚颜料的绘画作品。男孩尽可能再现画刷所勾勒的原始笔划,滴入墨水而定型。奇妙的是,他巧妙地利用脊椎和双肩肩胛骨突起的部分,与他的作品融合得天衣无缝。更有甚者,在不知不觉中,他加进了某种即兴发挥的因素——尽管整个文身过程很是漫长。因此,这幅刺青肖像相当逼真,活灵活现,包含更多的扭曲变形、饱受折磨的艺术风格,这也是苏蒂纳其他作品的典型风格。这不是一幅逼真再现真人的画像,而是一种情绪的宣泄:模特的脸模糊不清、醉意迷蒙,背景用一大片深绿色卷曲的笔触勾勒,仿佛绕着她的头部旋转一般。

“太奇妙了!”

“我本人甚是喜欢。”男孩向后一退,挑剔地审视着。“要知道,”他补充说,“我认为,我要是把名字署上,就完美了。”他再次拿起电针,用红墨水把他的名字文到右手边的一个位置——正好在德廖利肾的上方。

这个叫德廖利的老人站在那里,眼睛盯着画商店铺橱窗里的那幅画,神情恍惚。文身是很久、很久以前的事情了,那时候的一切,好像从来不曾发生在他的生命里。

对了,那个男孩子呢?他怎么样了?现在,他记得,战后归来之际——那是第一次世界大战,他就没有了那个孩子的音讯,为此他还问过乔西。

“我可爱的小卡尔梅克在哪儿呢?”

“他走了,”她回答,“我不知道他去哪儿了,但是听说一个商人接纳了他,派他去塞雷,目的是要他在那儿多画一些画。”

“或许,他会回来的。”

“或许吧。谁知道呢?”

那是他俩最后一次提到那个男孩。那次过后不久,他俩搬到勒阿弗尔,那里水手更多,生意也就好多了。一想起勒阿弗尔,老人就露出了笑容。在勒阿弗尔度过的那些年正处于两次战争的间隙，生活惬意美好。他在靠近码头那儿开了一个小店，店内的房间令人感到非常舒适，总有生意可做。每天都有三个、四个，甚至五个水手进来，要求往胳膊上文图案。那段时光里，生活真是惬意美好。

接着，第二次世界大战爆发，乔西死于战争。德国人来了，他的生意也就完了。从那以后，没有谁愿意往胳膊上文图案。那个时候，他年事已高，无力再做其他生意。绝望之下，他就打道回府，回到了巴黎，心存一点点希望，希望在大城市做事会容易一些。但是，实际情况并非如此。

眼下，战争结束，可他既没有工具，也没有精力再去做他那小本生意。一个老年人要想知道自己能做些什么来糊口——特别是在不愿意沿街乞讨的情况下——不是一件很容易的事情。然而，他还能怎么做来维持生计呢？

他仍然盯着那幅画，心想：噢，那就是我可爱的小卡尔梅克啦。看到类似于这幅画这样的小小的物件，就能激发无尽的回忆，而且回忆的速度竟然如此之快！就在刚才，还没有过去多大功夫呢，他甚至忘记自己后背上有一幅刺青。他已经有很多年没有想到这幅画了。他把脸更近地贴向橱窗，向画馆里面探望。他看到馆内四周的墙壁上挂了很多其他画作，似乎都是出自同一个艺术家之手。里面有很多人走来走去。很明显，这是一次特别的展览。

突然，德廖利一闪念，转过身，推开画馆的门，走了进去。

画馆的房间很长，地上铺了一块厚厚的、深红色的地毯。天啊，里面这么漂亮、这么暖和啊！那些人走来走去，欣赏着画作。他们洗得干干净净，显得高贵而有尊严，每人手里握着一个编目册子。德廖利刚好站到门的内侧，紧张兮兮地向周围观瞧，不知道是否该继续往前走，融入参观的人群。可是，他还没来得及鼓足勇气、迈步向前，就听到旁边传来一个声音："你进来干什么？"

问这话的人穿了件男式大礼服。他个头矮小，人胖墩墩的，一张脸刷白刷白的。整张脸松松地垂下，由于肌肉过多，两个脸蛋子从嘴的两侧耷拉下来，形成两个肉质薄片，如同长毛垂耳狗的两片耳朵。

他走近德廖利，又问道："你进来干什么?"

德廖利一动不动地站着。

"拜托，请——"这个胖男子说道，"主动离开我的画馆。"

"不允许我看画吗?"

"我已经请你离开了。"

德廖利站稳脚跟。突然，他感到怒火中烧，不可遏制。

"你我都不要惹麻烦，"胖男子说，"现在赶快，走这边。"他一只白白的胖爪子抓住德廖利的一只胳膊，使劲往门口推去。

那可不得了。"拿开你该死的手!"德廖利喊了起来。他的声音在画馆长长的房间清澈地响起。所有的脑袋顿时齐刷刷扭转过来。不管距离多远，一张张惊愕的脸都伸出来，盯着喊叫的人。一个身穿制服的男仆一路跑来，帮胖男子的忙。这两个家伙合起伙来，推推搡搡把德廖利送出画馆的门。大家站着不动，看着这推推搡搡的场面，脸上露出无关痛痒又稍感兴趣的神情，似乎在说："那没什么，对我们没有任何威胁，有人正在处理呢。"

"我，也有!"德廖利喊道，"我，也有，有一幅这位画家的作品!他是我的朋友。我有一幅画，是他给我的。"

"他是个疯子。"

"疯了，简直是个语无伦次的疯子。"

"应该有人叫警察。"

德廖利把身体猛地一扭，突然间就挣脱了那两个家伙的束缚。谁都没有来得及上前把他拦住，他就在画馆里跑开，边跑边喊："我露给你们看看！我露给你们看看！我露给你们看看!"他一下子甩掉外套，接着，夹克上衣、衬衫内衣也分别脱掉，随即转身，裸露的后背对着众人。

"看呐!"他喊道，喘气很是急促，"你们看到了吗？就在这儿!"

屋子里顿时静悄悄一片，鸦雀无声。不管方才在做什么，每一个人都戛然而止，一动不动地站着，都感到惊愕诧异、惶恐不安、迷茫疑惑。大家都盯着那幅刺青。他后背上的刺青依然完好、鲜艳如初。可是，老人的后背目前瘦多了，而且双肩的肩胛骨突起得更厉害。整幅刺青的效果没有那么棒了,但画面却因此看起来有了皱褶感、挤压感。

有人说道:“我的天呐,的确不假!”

接下来,大家潮涌般向前,拥挤在老人周围,兴奋激动,吵吵闹闹。

“肯定没错的。”

“他早期的风格,是吧?”

“真是奇妙,太神奇了!”

“看呐,竟然还有署名!”

“我的朋友,把你的肩膀向前弯一弯,好把刺青画面抻得平整些。”

“是老作品。什么时候完成的呢?”

“1913 年,”德廖利说道,身体并没有转过来,“是 1913 年的秋天。”

“谁教会苏蒂纳文身的呢?”

“是我教的。”

“那个女子是谁?”

“是我的妻子。”

画馆的主人挤过人群,来到德廖利面前。他现在也心平气和了,一副郑重其事的模样,嘴上却露出微笑。“尊贵的先生,”他说,“我要买下这幅刺青。”他的嘴巴一张一合的时候,德廖利看到他脸部松垮的肥肉一颤一颤的。“尊贵的先生,我是说,我要买下这幅刺青。”

“你怎么买啊?”他轻声问道。

“我出二十万法郎买。”这个画商的两只眼睛又小又黑,鼻子宽阔,鼻子基部两侧的肌肉开始抖动。

“不能卖啊!”人群里有人嘟囔着,“这幅刺青值那价的二十倍。”

德廖利张开嘴巴说话,却没有说出话来,所以干脆闭上了嘴巴。接着,他又张开嘴,慢慢说道:“可是,我怎么卖啊?”他的声音饱含了世间所有的悲伤。

“是啊!”人群里有人说道,“他怎么卖啊? 那幅刺青是他身体的一部分啊！”

“听着，”画商说完，向前靠了靠，“我会帮你的。我会让你富有的。你我私下里就这幅画好好安排一番，行不行？”

德廖利的眼睛缓缓地移向他，焦虑不安地看着他。“可问题是，尊贵的先生，你怎么买啊？付钱买下后，这幅刺青你打算怎么办？存放到什么地方？今晚存放到什么地方？明天呢？”

“噢，我把这幅刺青存放到什么地方呢？是啊，我把它存放到什么地方呢？现在，我把它存放到什么地方呢？那么，现在……”这个画商用他那根胖胖的、白白的手指来回触摸着自己的鼻梁。“看起来似乎，”他说，“要是买下这幅刺青，我也要把你买下。可把你买下来却不是很方便。”他暂停一下，又触摸着自己的鼻梁。“只有你死去，这幅刺青才会有价值。我的朋友，你多大年纪了？”

“六十一。”

“但是，你或许不是那么强壮，充满活力，是吧？”这个画商把手从鼻子上往下放低一些，上下打量着德廖利——慢慢地、细细地打量，就像一个农夫评估一匹老马能否干活似的。

“我不喜欢这样，”德廖利边说边缓缓地退去，“说实在的，尊贵的先生，我不喜欢这样。”他径直退进了一个高个子男子的臂弯处，只见那个男子伸出双手，轻轻地抓住他的双肩。德廖利一边向四周观瞧，一边向他道歉。这个男子俯身微笑着，用一只手拍着老伙计的一个裸露的肩膀，让他觉得安全可靠，那只手套在一只鲜黄色的手套里。

“听着，我的朋友，”这个陌生人说，仍然微笑着，“你喜欢游泳，游完后，享受晒太阳的乐趣吗？”

德廖利抬头看了看他，更加吃惊。

“你喜欢吃着美味佳肴，喝着享有盛名的波尔多酒庄出产的红葡萄酒吗？”这个高个男子仍然微笑着，露出结实的白牙，白牙中间还闪着金光。他说起话来轻声细语，有点好言哄劝的样子，套在手套里的那只手仍然搭在德廖利的肩膀上。“如此好吃好喝的，你喜欢吗？”

“噢——是的，”德廖利回答，仍然十分的疑惑不解，“当然啦。”

“还有，喜欢漂亮女士陪伴左右吗？”

“怎么能不喜欢呢？”

“还有呢，还有一橱柜的制服和衬衫。都是为你量身定做的，喜欢吗？看起来，你有那么一点缺衣少穿的。”

德廖利看着这位能说会道、温文尔雅的男子，等着听他的下一步提议。

“你是否穿过一双专门为你的脚定做的鞋子？”

“没有啊。”

“喜欢穿那样的鞋吗？”

“那……”

“还有，喜欢每天早晨有人为你刮胡子、修理头发吗？”

德廖利只是站在那里，瞠目结舌地看着。

“还有，喜欢丰满、迷人的女孩为你修剪指甲吗？”

人群里有人咯咯笑了起来。

“还有，床边放一个铃，早晨你一摇铃，就会把女佣召唤过来，端来早饭，喜欢吗？这么多好待遇，你喜欢吗，我的朋友？对你有没有吸引力呢？”

德廖利静静地站着，看着他。

“你看啊，我是戛纳一家叫布里斯托尔旅馆的经理。我现在正式邀请你光临我的旅馆，你的余生就住在我的旅馆，尽享豪华、舒适的生活。”这个高个男子暂停一会，好让他有时间品味一下这个令人兴奋不已的美丽前景。

“你唯一的义务——我可以把这个词换成‘乐趣’吗——就是穿着泳裤到我的海滩来，到客人中间走走，晒晒太阳，游游泳，喝喝鸡尾酒，以此来打发时间。你喜欢吗？”

没有回答。

“难道你不明白？这样做，所有的客人都能看到苏蒂纳的这幅迷人的刺青画作，你也会因此声名远扬，就会有人说：‘看啊，这个伙计后面背了一千万法郎。’你喜欢这个想法吗，尊贵的先生？这令你开心吗？”

德廖利抬头看了看这个戴着鲜黄色手套的高个男子，如堕五里雾中，拿不准他是不是在开玩笑。“这个想法有点滑稽好笑，”他慢慢说道，“可是，你是当真的吗？”

“当然是当真的。”

“等等，”先前那个画商插话进来，“看看啊，老伙计。我们问题的答案是这样的：我要买下这幅刺青，我会安排一名外科医生来，从你的后背移走皮肤，然后你就走你的，拿着我付给你的大笔钱去享受人生。”

“后背没有皮肤，我走的时候？”

“不，不，听我说！你误会了。我的这位外科医生会用新皮替代旧皮，很容易做到的。”

“医生能做到吗？”

“这不算什么事的。”

“不可能的，”戴鲜黄色手套的男子说道，“他年纪太大了，承受不了这样的大型皮肤移植手术。那会要他的命，他就会没命，我的朋友。”

“会要我的命吗？”

“那是自然的事情。你不会活下来的，只有那幅刺青会幸免于难。”

“我的老天啊！”德廖利喊道。他吓得目瞪口呆。他向周围看了看，看到一张张脸看着他，随后一阵寂静。接着，又传来一个人的声音，那声音低低地从人群后面传来，但仍然听得见：“或许，要是有人为这位老人出足够的钱，他就可能当场自杀。谁说得准呢？”有人窃笑起来，而那位画商却在地毯上不安地踱着步。

接着，那只戴鲜黄色手套的手又拍了拍德廖利的肩膀。“随我来，”他说，露出一排宽宽的白牙，“我和你去好好吃一顿，边吃边谈这事儿，怎么样？你饿了吗？”

德廖利看着他，皱起了眉头。他不喜欢这家伙旋转灵活的长脖子。或者说，他不喜欢这家伙说话时脖子高高伸向你的样子，就像一条蛇。

“吃烤鸭，红酒就喝香贝丹的，”高个男子说。他每一个字的发音都包裹着唾液，然后再用舌头把每一个字喷溅出来。“或许还吃点奶油鸡蛋松糕，再辅以栗子，既清淡又酥软。”

德廖利抬起头，两只眼睛看着天花板。他的双唇松弛下来，而且开始湿润。看得出来，这个可怜的老伙计实际上已经开始流口水了。

“鸭子你喜欢怎么个吃法？”高个男子继续说，“你喜欢鸭子外表烤得焦黄、酥脆，还是……”

“我跟你走。”德廖利快速说道。他已经拿起衬衫，忙乱地往头上套。“等我一下，尊贵的先生。我跟你走。”还不到一分钟的功夫，他就奔出画馆，跟着他新认识的大恩人走了。

一两个星期之后，苏蒂纳的一幅画，是一位女子的头部肖像画，开始在布宜诺斯艾利斯销售。这幅画的绘画方式很是奇特，画框装帧精美，画的表面光亮夺目。那幅画——还有戛纳没有一家叫作布里斯托尔的旅馆那件事，着实让人有一点点浮想联翩。人们也为那个老人的健康祈祷，也热切地期望：不管他此刻在什么地方，会有一个丰满、迷人的女孩为他修剪指甲，也会有一个女佣在早晨把饭菜端到他的床边来。

第三章 如堕雾中

汉语中，如果要比喻一个人陷入一种迷离恍惚、莫名其妙、疑虑重重的状态，如同落进茫茫的大雾之中，常用的一个表达就是“如堕五里雾中”——你简直分不清出现了什么状况，也辨别不出发生了什么情况。这时，一切似乎如雾里看花，怎么看都看不清楚。

据《后汉书》卷三十六《郑范陈贾张列传·（子）张楷》记载，张楷“性好道术，能作五里雾。时关西人裴优亦能为三里雾，自以不如楷，从学之，楷避不肯见。”能作五里雾的张楷何等了得，而堕五里雾中，便蒙头转向，抓不住要领，摸不着头绪，这就可以想象了。正因为传说中的张楷有道术，能够制造出五里雾，所以后来就用“五里雾”“张楷雾”“张公雾”“公超雾”等词语来形容烟雾迷漫的境况，或泛指迷雾。这样，“雾术”就借指“道术”，“学雾”也就用来借称“学道”了。从这个意义上来说，英国作家罗尔德·达尔“学雾”有成，在其作品《怪异乔治》中制造出“五里雾”，令人读罢如堕雾中。

生性腼腆的乔治是一位不显山露水的助理牧师，对女性避之唯恐不及，却蹊跷地被罗奇小姐“吸入”而无法逃脱……还是让我们走进罗尔德·达尔的世界，走进迷雾重重的《怪异乔治》，去看看“怪异”的乔治的具体表现吧。

第一节　《怪异乔治》(上部)
Georgy Porgy（Part A）

罗尔德·达尔的《怪异乔治》(*Georgy Porgy*)被收录到《罗尔德·达尔小说精品集》(*The Best of Roald Dahl*)、《吻了又吻》(*Kiss Kiss*)、《更多出人意料故事集》(*More Tales of the Unexpected*)、《后续出人意料故事集》(*Further Tales of the Unexpected*)、《完全出人意料故事集》(*Completely Unexpected Tales*)、《罗尔德·达尔短篇故事集锦》(*The Collected Short Stories of Roald Dahl*)、《五部畅销书集》(*5 Best-sellers*)、《罗尔德·达尔选集》(*The Roald Dahl Omnibus*)以及《罗尔德·达尔二十九篇成人故事集》(*Twenty Nine Kisses from Roald Dahl*)等书中,可见其影响力之大。

另外,这篇小说也被改编成电视系列剧——1980 年 4 月 26 日播映的《出乎意料的故事集》(*Tales of the Unexpected*)第二部中的第 9 集(Episode 2. 9),也被制作成由爱德华·皮瑟布里奇(Edward Petherbridge)朗读的有声读物《吻了又吻》(*Kiss Kiss*)。

值得一提的是,关于这篇小说的"歧义性",克里斯廷·霍华德(Kristine Howard)有这样的评述:"要是有人问我怎么看待这篇小说,我的回答是:这篇小说实际上相当令人感到不安。推荐给孩子阅读前,我肯定会三思而后行,以免孩子受到影响。其中的一些段落,尽管描写生动而形象,却只能算是'弗洛伊德式梦魇'的现实版。可怜的乔治对女人有着重重障碍,也就不足为奇了。他对异性、性以及自己母亲的感觉混乱到了令他无法正常生活的程度"(This story is actually quite disturbing, if you ask me. I'd definitely think twice before letting an impressionable child read it. It has some very vivid passages that can only be described as a Freudian nightmare come to life. It's no wonder poor George had such difficulty towards women. His own feelings towards females and sex and his mother were so confused that he simply couldn't function normally)①。可以说,这也是一篇具有"意识流"色彩的小说,同时还有一丝"荒诞"的成分。

一、原作导读

这篇小说是以第一人称"我"(名叫"乔治")的视角展开的,但跟罗尔德·达尔其他很多作品中的"我"不同的是,本篇叙述者"我"不是"隐身"的,而是具有举足轻重的地位,其作用不仅仅是"纽带"或者"桥梁",而是整部小说的主体。

乔治是一位不起眼儿的助理牧师,供职于一个小小的乡村地区。但是,对于女性,乔治内心充满了矛盾:一方面,他对女子很是痴迷,只要看到女子穿着高跟鞋就足以令他兴奋得不得了;另一方面,他对女子又很畏惧,女子触摸他,或者跟他靠得太近,都会令他无法忍受。对于这一矛盾心理,乔治自己也百思不得其解。事实上,这一矛盾可能源自乔治对自己母亲的一些记忆。

很明显,乔治的母亲是一位思想开放的妇女,耐心地将生活中的种种"真实"教给自己的儿子,一点儿也不避讳什么。因此,乔治十分崇拜她,并引以为荣。她对乔治进行"性"方面教育,持续了一周时间。一周后的一个夜里,她领着乔治到车库去看自家的蓝毛兔约瑟芬分娩,作为性教育的实践。看着约瑟芬分娩的过程,乔治惊奇不已,眼界大开。就在此时,兔妈妈约瑟芬却将兔宝宝活生生整个吞了下去。乔治吓得大声喊叫起来,转身却看见母亲张开了大嘴,俯身于自己上方。乔治又一次尖叫起来,向着茫茫的黑夜逃去……母亲在后面紧追不舍。穿越马路时,一辆汽车开了过来,轧死了母亲。也许

---

① 这段叙述由本书著者译自"罗尔德·达尔粉丝网"(*Roald Dahl Fans*),具体可参见克里斯廷·霍华德(Kristine Howard)创建并维护的网站"Roald Dahl Fans. com",网址为:*http://www. roalddahlfans. com/*。

是母亲这件事深深触动小乔治,并深深影响了他,使他在潜意识里对女性既痴迷又反感吧。

长大成人的乔治想方设法避开教区老处女或者寡妇的"骚扰"。一开始,他的方法很奏效,没有哪个女子敢贸然行动,可是到了后来,情况变得无法收拾了。

大约一年以前连续三周的时间里,乔治在布道时,一个名叫比利·斯内林的小男孩每次都将一对小白鼠拿到教堂里玩耍,令乔治很烦恼。于是,乔治干脆将小白鼠没收,但出于人道主义的考虑,又将这对小白鼠养了起来。看着小白鼠一天天逐渐长大并开始繁殖,乔治产生了一个想法:

就在它们数量达到十二只的时候,我决定用它们来做科学研究了。公鼠和母鼠的数量正好相等,各为六只,所以实验条件很理想。

It was at this point that I decided to use them for research purposes. There were exactly equal numbers of males and females, six of each, so that conditions were ideal.

至此,故事的前一部分结束。

二、原作释读

在这篇小说中,作家罗尔德·达尔娴熟地运用了多种手段来表达主人公复杂的内心世界,语言诙谐幽默,角度切换频繁,意识的流动与现实的描述融为一体,阅读中要注意体会和把握。另外,一些专业性较强的词汇构成了阅读的障碍,特别是人体解剖学方面的一些词,阅读中要注意去突破。还有就是,阅读中要体会好最后部分的"荒诞主义"色彩。

Georgy Porgy(Part A)[1]

Without in any way wishing to blow my own trumpet[2], I think that I can claim to being in most respects a moderately well-matured and rounded individual. I have travelled a good deal. I am adequately read. I speak Greek and Latin. I dabble[3] in science. I can tolerate a mildly liberal attitude in the politics of others. I have compiled a volume of notes upon the evolution of the madrigal[4] in the fifteenth century. I have witnessed the death of a large number of persons in their beds; and in addition, I have influenced, at least I hope I have, the lives of quite a few others by the spoken word delivered from the pulpit[5].

Yet in spite of all this, I must confess that I have never in my life—well, how shall I put it? —I have never really had anything much to do with women.

---

① 本部小说原文出自"DAHL, R. *The Best of Roald Dahl* [M]. London: Penguin Books Ltd., 2006"。

② blow one's trumpet: talk openly and boastfully about one's achievements 自我吹嘘;自吹自擂(e. g. He refused to blow his own trumpet and blushingly declined to speak. 他拒绝自我吹嘘,羞红着脸不肯发言。)

③ dabble: *Verb* [no obj.](figurative) take part in an activity in a casual or superficial way(喻)涉猎(e. g. He dabbled in left-wing politics. 他参与左翼政治。)

④ madrigal: *Noun* a part-song for several voices, especially one of the Renaissance period, typically arranged in elaborate counterpoint and without instrumental accompaniment 牧歌;(尤指无伴奏的)合唱歌曲

⑤ pulpit: *Noun* (the pulpit) religious teaching as expressed in sermons; preachers collectively(总称)布道;传教士;牧师(e. g. The movies could rival the pulpit as an agency moulding the ideas of the mass public. 作为一种塑造大众思想的手段,电影可与布道抗衡。)

To be perfectly honest, up until three weeks ago I had never so much as laid a finger on one of them except perhaps to help her over a stile① or something like that when the occasion demanded. And even then I always tried to ensure that I touched only the shoulder or the waist or some other place where the skin was covered, because the one thing I never could stand was actual contact between my skin and theirs. Skin touching skin, my skin, that is, touching the skin of a female, whether it were leg, neck, face, hand, or merely finger, was so repugnant② to me that I invariably greeted a lady with my hands clasped firmly behind my back to avoid the inevitable handshake.

I could go further than that and say that any sort of physical contact with them, even when the skin wasn't bare, would disturb me considerably. If a woman stood close to me in a queue so that our bodies touched, or if she squeezed in beside me on a bus seat, hip to hip and thigh to thigh, my cheeks would begin burning like mad and little prickles of sweat would start coming out all over the crown of my head.

This condition is all very well in a schoolboy who has just reached the age of puberty. With him it is simply Dame③ Nature's way of putting on the brakes and holding the lad back until he is old enough to behave himself like a gentleman. I approve of that.

But there was no reason on God's earth why I, at the ripe old age of

---

① stile: *Noun* an arrangement of steps that allows people but not animals to climb over a fence or wall(篱或墙)两边的阶梯(供人越过用)

② repugnant: *Adjective* extremely distasteful; unacceptable 使人极度反感的;难以接受的(e. g. The thought of going back into the fog was repugnant to him. 一想到要重新进入雾中他就感到很不愉快。)

③ Dame: *Noun* (Dame) (in the UK) the title given to a woman with the rank of Knight Commander or holder of the Grand Cross in the Orders of Chivalry(英国用法)夫人;女爵士;女大十字勋章获得者

thirty-one, should continue to suffer a similar embarrassment. I was well trained to resist temptation, and I was certainly not given to vulgar passions.

Had I been even the slightest bit ashamed of my own personal appearance, then that might possibly have explained the whole thing. But I was not. On the contrary, and though I say it myself, the fates had been rather kind to me in that regard. I stood exactly five and a half feet tall in my stockinged feet, and my shoulders, though they sloped downward a little from the neck, were nicely in balance with my small neat frame. (Personally, I've always thought that a little slope on the shoulder lends a subtle and faintly aesthetic air to a man who is not overly tall, don't you agree?) My features were regular, my teeth were in excellent condition (protruding only a smallish amount from the upper jaw), and my hair, which was an unusually brilliant ginger-red, grew thickly all over my scalp. Good heavens above, I had seen men who were perfect shrimps in comparison with me displaying an astonishing aplomb① in their dealings with the fairer sex. And oh, how I envied them! How I longed to do likewise—to be able to share in a few of those pleasant little rituals of contact that I observed continually taking place between men and women—the touching of hands, the peck② on the cheek, the linking of arms, the pressure of knee against knee or foot against foot under the dining-table, and most of all, the full-blown③ violent embrace that comes

① aplomb: *Noun* [mass noun] self-confidence or assurance, especially when in a demanding situation(尤指在苛刻的情形中)泰然自若;沉着;处变不惊(e.g. Diana passed the test with aplomb. 戴安娜沉着地通过了考试。)

② peck: *Noun* a light or perfunctory kiss 轻轻的一吻;漫不经心的一吻;敷衍的一吻(e.g. a fatherly peck on the cheek 一个在脸颊上的父爱般的轻吻)

③ full-blown: *Adjective* fully developed 充分发展(或演化)的;已完全形成的;达于顶点的

when two of them join together on the floor—for a dance.

But such things were not for me. Alas, I had to spend my time avoiding them instead. And this, my friends, was easier said than done, even for a humble curate① in a small country region far from the fleshpots② of the metropolis③.

My flock④, you understand, contained an inordinate⑤ number of ladies. There were scores of them in the parish⑥ and the unfortunate thing about it was that at least sixty percent of them were spinsters⑦, completely untamed by the benevolent influence of holy matrimony⑧.

I tell you I was jumpy as a squirrel.

One would have thought that with all the careful training my mother

---

① curate: *Noun* (also as "assistant curate") a member of the clergy engaged as assistant to a vicar, rector, or parish priest 助理牧师

② fleshpots: *Plural Noun* places providing luxurious or hedonistic living 寻欢作乐场所(e. g. He had lived the life of a roué in the fleshpots of London and Paris. 他曾在伦敦和巴黎声色场所过浪荡生活。)

③ metropolis: *Noun* a very large and densely populated industrial and commercial city 大都会;大城市

④ flock: *Noun* a Christian congregation or body of believers, especially one under the charge of a particular minister(尤指属某牧师所管的)基督教会众(e. g. Thomas addressed his flock. 托马斯向他的教徒讲道。)

⑤ inordinate: *Adjective* unusually or disproportionately large; excessive 过多的;过大的;过分的(e. g. a case which had taken up an inordinate amount of time 占用了过多时间的事情)

⑥ parish: *Noun* (in the Christian Church) a small administrative district typically having its own church and a priest or pastor(基督教)(本)堂区;牧区

⑦ spinster: *Noun* an unmarried woman, typically an older woman beyond the usual age for marriage 老处女

⑧ matrimony: *Noun* [mass noun] the state or ceremony of being married; marriage 结婚;婚礼

had given me as a child, I should have been capable of taking this sort of thing well in my stride[①]; and no doubt I would have done if only she had lived long enough to complete my education. But alas, she was killed when I was still quite young.

She was a wonderful woman, my mother. She used to wear huge bracelets on her wrists, five or six of them at a time, with all sorts of things hanging from them and tinkling against each other as she moved. It didn't matter where she was, you could always find her by listening for the noise of those bracelets. It was better than a cowbell. And in the evenings she used to sit on the sofa in her black trousers with her feet tucked up underneath her, smoking endless cigarettes from a long black holder. And I'd be crouching on the floor, watching her.

"You want to taste my martini, George?" she used to ask.

"Now stop it, Clare," my father would say. "If you're not careful you'll stunt the boy's growth."

"Go on," she said. "Don't be frightened of it. Drink it."

I always did everything my mother told me.

"That's enough," my father said. "He only has to know what it tastes like."

"Please don't interfere, Boris. This is very important."

My mother had a theory that nothing in the world should be kept secret from a child. Show him everything. Make him experience it.

"I'm not going to have any boy of mine going around whispering dirty secrets with other children and having to guess about this thing and that simply because no one will tell him."

---

① take something in one's stride: deal with something difficult or unpleasant in a calm and accepting way 从容对付;轻易解决;从容处理(e.g. I told her what had happened and she took it all in her stride. 我告诉她发生的事,她丝毫不动声色。)

Tell him everything. Make him listen.

"Come over here, George, and I'll tell you what there is to know about God."

She never read stories to me at night before I went to bed; she just "told" me things instead. And every evening it was something different.

"Come over here, George, because now I'm going to tell you about Mohammed①."

She would be sitting on the sofa in her black trousers with her legs crossed and her feet tucked up underneath her, and she'd beckon to me in a queer languorous② manner with the hand that held the long black cigarette-holder, and the bangles③ would start jingling all the way up her arm.

"If you must have a religion I suppose Mohammedanism is as good as any of them. It's all based on keeping healthy. You have lots of wives, and you mustn't ever smoke or drink."

"Why mustn't you smoke or drink, Mummy?"

"Because if you've got lots of wives you have to keep healthy and virile④."

"What is virile?"

"I'll go into that tomorrow, my pet. Let's deal with one subject at a time. Another thing about the Mohammedan is that he never never gets

---

① Mohammed or Muhammad: *Noun* (c. 570—632), Arab prophet and founder of Islam 穆罕默德(约 570—632 年,阿拉伯先知,伊斯兰教创始人。)

② languorous: *Adjective* lacking spirit or liveliness 无精打采的;倦怠的

③ bangle: *Noun* a rigid ornamental band worn round the arm or occasionally the ankle 臂镯;脚镯

④ virile: *Adjective* (of a man) having strength, energy, and a strong sex drive(男子)威猛的;强壮的;阳刚的

constipated①."

"Now, Clare," my father would say, looking up from his book. "Stick to the facts."

"My dear Boris, you don't know anything about it. Now if only you would try bending forward and touching the ground with your forehead morning, noon, and night every day, facing Mecca②, you might have a bit less trouble in that direction yourself."

I used to love listening to her, even though I could only understand about half of what she was saying. She really was telling me secrets, and there wasn't anything more exciting than that.

"Come over here, George, and I'll tell you precisely how your father makes his money."

"Now, Clare, that's quite enough."

"Nonsense, darling. Why make a secret out of it with the child? He'll only imagine something much more worse."

I was exactly ten years old when she started giving me detailed lectures on the subject of sex. This was the biggest secret of them all, and therefore the most enthralling③.

"Come over here, George, because now I'm going to tell you how you came into this world, right from the very beginning."

---

① constipated: *Adjective* (of a person or animal) affected with constipation 患便秘的(e.g. The baby is constipated. 这婴儿患便秘。)

② Mecca: *Noun* a city in western Saudi Arabia, an oasis town in the Red Sea region of Hejaz, east of Jiddah, considered by Muslims to be the holiest city of Islam; pop. 618 000 (est. 1986). Arabic name Makkah. 麦加(沙特阿拉伯西部城市,是红海地区汉志省的绿洲城,位于吉达市东面,伊斯兰教徒心目中最神圣的城市;1986年估计人口618 000,阿拉伯语名"Makkah"。)

③ enthralling: *Adjective* capturing interest as if by a spell 迷人的;令人着迷的

I saw my father glance up quietly, and open his mouth wide the way he did when he was going to say something vital, but my mother was already fixing him with those brilliant shining eyes of hers, and he went slowly back to his book without uttering a sound.

"Your poor father is embarrassed," she said, and she gave me her private smile, the one that she gave nobody else, only to me—the one-sided smile where just one corner of her mouth lifted slowly upward until it made a lovely long wrinkle that stretched right up to the eye itself, and became a sort of wink-smile instead.

"Embarrassment, my pet, is the one thing that I want you never to feel. And don't think for a moment that your father is embarrassed only because of you."

My father started wriggling about in his chair.

"My God, he's even embarrassed about things like that when he's alone with me, his own wife."

"About things like what?" I asked.

At that point my father got up and quietly left the room.

I think it must have been about a week after this that my mother was killed. It may possibly have been a little later, ten days or a fortnight, I can't be sure. All I know is that we were getting near the end of this particular series of "talks" when it happened; and because I myself was personally involved in the brief chain of events that led up to her death, I can still remember every single detail of that curious night just as clearly as if it were yesterday. I can switch it on in my memory any time I like and run it through in front of my eyes exactly as though it were the reel of a cinema film; and it never varies. It always ends at precisely the same place, no more and no less, and it always begins in the same peculiarly sudden way, with the screen in darkness, and my mother's voice somewhere above me, calling my name:

"George! Wake up, George, wake up!"

And then there is a bright electric light dazzling in my eyes, and right from the very centre of it, but far away, the voice is still calling me:

"George, wake up and get out of bed and put your dressing-gown on! Quickly! You're coming downstairs. There's something I want you to see. Come on, child, come on! Hurry up! And put your slippers on. We're going outside."

"Outside?"

"Don't argue with me, George. Just do as you're told." I am so sleepy I can hardly see to walk, but my mother takes me firmly by the hand and leads me downstairs and out through the front door into the night where the cold air is like a sponge of water in my face, and I open my eyes wide and see the lawn all sparkling with frost and the cedar① tree with its tremendous arms standing black against a thin small moon. And overhead a great mass of stars is wheeling up into the sky.

We hurry across the lawn, my mother and I, her bracelets all jingling like mad and me having to trot to keep up with her. Each step I take I can feel the crisp frosty grass crunching② softly underfoot.

"Josephine has just started having her babies," my mother says. "It's a perfect opportunity. You shall watch the whole process."

There is a light burning in the garage when we get there, and we go inside. My father isn't there, nor is the car, and the place seems huge and bare, and the concrete floor is freezing cold through the soles of my bedroom slippers.

---

① cedar: *Noun* a large tree of the pine family (genus Cedrus, family Pinaceae) 雪松(雪松属)

② crunch: *Verb* [no obj.] make such a sound, especially when walking or driving over gravel or an icy surface(尤指碾过沙砾或冰面时)发出嘎吱嘎吱的响声

Josephine is reclining[1] on a heap of straw inside the low wire cage in one corner of the room large blue rabbit with small pink eyes that watch us suspiciously as we go towards her. The husband, whose name is Napoleon, is now in a separate cage in the opposite corner, and I notice that he is standing up on his hind legs scratching impatiently at the netting.

"Look!" my mother cries. "She's having the first one! It's almost out!"

We both creep closer to Josephine, and I squat down beside the cage with my face right up against the wire. I am fascinated. Here is one rabbit coming out of another. It is magical and rather splendid. It is also very quick.

"Look how it comes out all neatly wrapped up in its own little cellophane[2] bag!" my mother is saying.

"And just look how she's taking care of it now! The poor darling doesn't have a face-flannel[3], and even if she did she couldn't hold it in her paws, so she's washing it with her tongue instead."

The mother rabbit rolls her small pink eyes anxiously in our direction, and then I see her shifting position in the straw so that her body is between us and the young one.

"Come round the other side," my mother says. "The silly thing has moved. I do believe she's trying to hide her baby from us."

---

① recline: *Verb* [no obj.] lean or lie back in a relaxed position with the back supported 斜倚;靠;躺(e. g. She was reclining in a deckchair. 她正躺在折叠帆布躺椅上。)

② cellophane: *Noun* [mass noun] (trademark) a thin transparent wrapping material made from viscose(商标)赛璐玢(一种由纤维胶制成的薄型透明包装材料);玻璃纸(e. g. flowers wrapped in cellophane 用玻璃纸包的鲜花)

③ face-flannel or face flannel: *Noun* (Brit.) a facecloth(英国英语)面巾

We go round the other side of the cage. The rabbit follows us with her eyes. A couple of yards away the buck[①] is prancing madly up and down, clawing at the wire.

"Why is Napoleon so excited?" I ask.

"I don't know, dear. Don't you bother about him. Watch Josephine. I expect she'll be having another one soon. Look how carefully she's washing that little baby! She's treating it just like a human mother treats hers! Isn't it funny to think that I did almost exactly the same sort of thing to you once?"

The big blue doe[②] is still watching us, and now, again, she pushes the baby away with her nose and rolls slowly over to face the other way. Then she goes on with her licking and cleaning.

"Isn't it wonderful how a mother knows instinctively just what she has to do?" my mother says. "Now you just imagine, my pet, that the baby is you, and Josephine is me—wait a minute, come back over here again so you can get a better look."

We creep back around the cage to keep the baby in view.

"See how she's fondling it and kissing it all over! There! She's really kissing it now, isn't she! Exactly like me and you!"

I peer closer. It seems a queer way of kissing to me.

"Look!" I scream. "She's eating it!"

And sure enough, the head of the baby rabbit is now disappearing swiftly into the mother's mouth.

"Mummy! Quick!"

But almost before the sound of my scream has died away, the whole

---

① buck: *Noun* a male hare, rabbit, ferret, rat, or kangaroo 公兔;公白鼬;公鼠;公袋鼠

② doe: *Noun* a female hare, rabbit, rat, ferret, or kangaroo 雌兔;雌鼠;雌雪貂;雌袋鼠

of that tiny pink body has vanished down the mother's throat.

I swing quickly around, and the next thing I know I'm looking straight into my own mother's face, not six inches above me, and no doubt she is trying to say something or it may be that she is too astonished to say anything, but all I see is the mouth, the huge red mouth opening wider and wider until it is just a great big round gaping① hole with a black centre, and I scream again, and this time I can't stop. Then suddenly out come her hands, and I can feel her skin touching mine, the long cold fingers closing tightly over my fists, and I jump back and jerk myself free and rush blindly out into the night. I run down the drive and through the front gates, screaming all the way, and then, above the noise of my own voice I can hear the jingle of bracelets coming up behind me in the dark, getting louder and louder as she keeps gaining on me all the way down the long hill to the bottom of the lane and over the bridge on to the main road where the cars are streaming by at sixty miles an hour with headlights blazing.

Then somewhere behind me I hear a screech② of tyres skidding③ on the road surface, and then there is silence, and I notice suddenly that the bracelets aren't jingling behind me any more.

Poor Mother.

If only she could have lived a little longer.

---

① gaping: *Adjective* deep and wide open 口的;张口的;敞口的(e. g. The antelope could not escape the crocodile's gaping jaws. 那只羚羊无法从鳄鱼张开的大口中逃脱。)

② screech: *Noun* a loud, harsh, squealing sound 刺耳的吱吱声

③ skid: *Verb* [no obj.] (of a vehicle) slide, typically sideways or obliquely, on slippery ground or as a result of stopping or turning too quickly(尤指车辆因路滑、刹车或转弯过快而)侧滑;打滑;滑行(e. g. The taxi cab skidded to a halt. 出租车滑行了一段距离停了下来。)

I admit that she gave me a nasty fright with those rabbits, but it wasn't her fault, and anyway queer things like that were always happening between her and me. I had come to regard them as a sort of toughening process that did me more good than harm. But if only she could have lived long enough to complete my education, I'm sure I should never have had all that trouble I was telling you about a few minutes ago.

I want to get on with that now. I didn't mean to begin talking about my mother. She doesn't have anything to do with what I originally started out to say. I won't mention her again.

I was telling you about the spinsters in my parish. It's an ugly word, isn't it—spinster? It conjures① up the vision either of a stringy② old hen with a puckered mouth or of a huge ribald③ monster shouting around the house in riding-breeches. But these were not like that at all. They were a clean, healthy, well-built group of females, the majority of them highly bred and surprisingly wealthy, and I feel sure that the average unmarried man would have been gratified to have them around.

In the beginning, when I first came to the vicarage④, I didn't have too bad a time. I enjoyed a measure of protection, of course, by reason of my calling and my cloth. In addition, I myself adopted a cool dignified attitude that was calculated to discourage familiarity. For a few months,

---

① conjure: *Verb* (of a word, sound, smell, etc.) cause someone to feel or think of (something)(词、声音、气味等)使感到;使想起;使追忆(e. g. a special tune that conjures up a particular time and place 令人想起特别时刻及场合的特殊曲调)

② stringy: *Adjective* (especially of hair) resembling string; long, thin, and lustreless(尤指头发)长而又稀疏无光的;枯草般的

③ ribald: *Adjective* referring to sexual matters in an amusingly rude or irreverent way 开淫荡玩笑的;言谈淫俗的(e. g. a ribald comment 下流的评论)

④ vicarage: *Noun* the residence of a vicar 教区牧师住所

therefore, I was able to move freely among my parishioners[1], and no one took the liberty[2] of linking her arm in mine at a charity bazaar[3], or of touching my fingers with hers as she passed me the cruet[4] at suppertime. I was very happy. I was feeling better than I had in years. Even that little nervous habit I had of flicking my earlobe with my forefinger when I talked began to disappear.

This was what I call my first period, and it extended over approximately six months. Then came trouble.

I suppose I should have known that a healthy male like myself couldn't hope to evade[5] embroilment[6] indefinitely simply by keeping a fair distance between himself and the ladies. It just doesn't work. If anything it has the opposite effect.

I would see them eyeing me covertly across the room at a whist drive[7], whispering to one another, nodding, running their tongues over their lips, sucking at their cigarettes, plotting the best approach, but al-

---

① parishioner: *Noun* an inhabitant of a parish, especially one who belongs to or attends a particular church(尤指本堂区的或参加本堂区礼拜的)堂区居民

② take the liberty: venture to do something without first asking permission 擅自做某事(e. g. I have taken the liberty of submitting an idea to several of their research departments. 我已自作主张地向他们的几个研究部门提出了一个想法。)

③ bazaar: *Noun* a fund-raising sale of goods, typically for charity(尤指慈善)义卖

④ cruet: *Noun* (Brit.) a small container for salt, pepper, oil, or vinegar for use at a dining table(英国英语)(餐桌上的)调味品瓶

⑤ evade: *Verb* escape or avoid, especially by guile or trickery 规避;躲避

⑥ embroilment: *Noun* an intricate and confusing interpersonal or political situation复杂人际关系;混乱的局面;纠纷

⑦ whist drive: (Card Games) a social gathering where whist is played(纸牌游戏)惠斯特牌会

ways whispering, and sometimes I overheard snatches① of their talk—"What a shy person ... he's just a trifle nervous, isn't he ... he's much too tense ... he needs companionship ... he wants loosening up we must teach him how to relax." And then slowly as the weeks went by, they began to stalk② me. I knew they were doing it. I could feel it happening although at first they did nothing definite to give themselves away.

That was my second period. It lasted for the best part of a year and was very trying indeed. But it was paradise compared with the third and final phase.

For now, instead of sniping at me sporadically③ from far away, the attackers suddenly came charging out of the wood with bayonets④ fixed. It was terrible, frightening. Nothing is more calculated⑤ to unnerve a man than the swift unexpected assault. Yet I am not a coward. I will stand my ground against any single individual of my own size under any circumstances. But this onslaught⑥, I am now convinced, was conducted by vast numbers operating as one skilfully co-ordinated unit.

---

① snatch: *Noun* a fragment of song or talk(歌曲或谈话的)片段(e. g. I just picked up snatches of conversation. 我只听到了对话的只言片语。)

② stalk: *Verb* [with obj.] pursue or approach stealthily 悄悄地追踪(或靠近)(e. g. a cat stalking a bird 一只悄悄靠近鸟儿的猫)

③ sporadic: *Adjective* occurring at irregular intervals or only in a few places; scattered or isolated 散乱的;零星的(e. g. Sporadic fighting broke out. 战斗零星爆发。)

④ bayonet: *Noun* a sword-like stabbing blade which may be fixed to the muzzle of a rifle for use in hand-to-hand fighting(枪上的)刺刀

⑤ calculated: *Adjective* (of an action) done with full awareness of the likely consequences(行为)蓄意的;故意的(e. g. victims of vicious and calculated assaults 被恶意攻击的受害人)

⑥ onslaught: *Noun* a fierce or destructive attack 猛攻;破坏性的攻击(e. g. a series of onslaughts on the citadel 对大本营一系列的破坏性攻击)

The first offender was Miss Elphinstone, a large woman with moles. I had dropped in on her during the afternoon to solicit① a contribution towards a new set of bellows② for the organ, and after some pleasant conversation in the library she had graciously handed me a cheque for two guineas③. I told her not to bother to see me to the door and I went out into the hall to get my hat. I was about to reach for it when all at once—she must have come tip-toeing up behind me—all at once I felt a bare arm sliding through mine, and one second later her fingers were entwined④ in my own, and she was squeezing my hand hard, in out, in out, as though it were the bulb of a throat-spray.

"Are you really so Very Reverend as you're always pretending to be?" she whispered.

Well!

All I can tell you is that when that arm of hers came sliding in under mine, it felt exactly as though a cobra was coiling itself around my wrist. I leaped away, pulled open the front door, and fled down the drive with-

---

① solicit: *Verb* [with obj.] ask for or try to obtain (something) from someone 请求;乞求得到(某物);征求(e. g. He called a meeting to solicit their views. 他召集了一个会议来征求他们的意见。)

② bellows: *Plural Noun* a kind of device with an air bag that emits a stream of air when squeezed, which is used in a harmonium or small organ(簧风琴或小风琴的)皮腔;风箱

③ guinea: *Noun* (Brit.) the sum of £ 1.05 (21 shillings in pre-decimal currency), now used mainly for determining professional fees and auction prices(英国英语)几尼(1 几尼等于 1.05 英镑,在十进制币值前等于 21 先令,现多用于确定专业服务费用和拍卖价格);畿尼

④ entwine: *Verb* [with obj.] (often as "be entwined") wind or twist together; interweave 使缠绕;使交错(e. g. They lay entwined in each other's arms. 他们互相拥抱着躺着。)

out looking back.

The very next day we held a jumble sale[①] in the village hall (again to raise money for the new bellows), and towards the end of it I was standing in a corner quietly drinking a cup of tea and keeping an eye on the villagers crowding round the stalls when all of a sudden I heard a voice beside me saying, "Dear me, what a hungry look you have in those eyes of yours."

The next instant a long curvaceous body was leaning up against mine and a hand with red fingernails was trying to push a thick slice of coconut cake into my mouth.

"Miss Prattley," I cried. "Please!"

But she'd got me up against the wall, and with a teacup in one hand and a saucer in the other I was powerless to resist. I felt the sweat breaking out all over me and if my mouth hadn't quickly become full of the cake she was pushing into it, I honestly believe I would have started to scream.

A nasty incident, that one; but there was worse to come.

The next day it was Miss Unwin. Now Miss Unwin happened to be a close friend of Miss Elphinstone's and of Miss Prattley's, and this of course should have been enough to make me very cautious. Yet who would have thought that she of all people, Miss Unwin, that quiet gentle little mouse who only a few weeks before had presented me with a new

---

① jumble sale: (Brit.) a sale of miscellaneous second-hand articles, typically held in order to raise money for a charity or a special event(英国英语)(多为慈善或特别事项筹集资金而举办的各色各样)旧杂货廉价出售;(义卖时的)杂物拍卖

hassock① exquisitely worked in needlepoint② with her own hands, who would have thought that she would ever have taken a liberty with anyone? So when she asked me to accompany her down to the crypt③ to show her the Saxon murals④, it never entered my head that there was devilry⑤ afoot⑥. But there was.

I don't propose to describe that encounter; it was too painful. And the ones which followed were no less savage. Nearly every day from then on, some new outrageous incident would take place. I became a nervous wreck. At times I hardly knew what I was doing. I started reading the burial service at young Gladys Pitcher's wedding. I dropped Mrs. Harris's new baby into the font⑦ during the christening and gave it a nasty ducking. An uncomfortable rash that I hadn't had in over two years reappeared on the side of my neck, and that annoying business with my earlobe came back worse than ever before. Even my hair began coming out in my comb. The faster I retreated, the faster they came after

---

① hassock: *Noun* (chiefly Brit.) a cushion for kneeling on in church, while at prayer(主要为英国英语用法)(教堂里祈祷用的)跪垫

② needlepoint: *Noun* [mass noun] embroidery worked over canvas 帆布刺绣

③ crypt: *Noun* an underground room or vault beneath a church, used as a chapel or burial place(用作礼拜室或墓穴的)教堂地下室

④ mural: *Noun* a painting or other work of art executed directly on a wall 壁画;壁饰

⑤ devilry: *Noun* [mass noun] wicked activity 邪恶的行为

⑥ afoot: *Adverb & Adjective* in preparation or progress; happening or beginning to happen 准备地(的);进行地(的);发生地(的);开始发生地(的)(e.g. There's something afoot here, but I don't know what it is. 这里有什么东西不对劲,但我不知道到底是什么。)

⑦ font: *Noun* a receptacle in a church for the water used in baptism, typically a free-standing stone structure 洗礼盆;圣水器

me. Women are like that. Nothing stimulates them quite so much as a display of modesty or shyness in a man. And they become doubly persistent if underneath it all they happen to detect—and here I have a most difficult confession to make—if they happen to detect, as they did in me, a little secret gleam① of longing shining in the backs of the eyes.

You see, actually I was mad about women.

Yes, I know. You will find this hard to believe after all that I have said, but it was perfectly true. You must understand that it was only when they touched me with their fingers or pushed up against me with their bodies that I became alarmed. Providing they remained at a safe distance, I could watch them for hours on end with the same peculiar fascination that you yourself might experience in watching a creature you couldn't bear to touch—an octopus②, for example, or a long poisonous snake. I loved the smooth white look of a bare arm emerging from a sleeve, curiously naked like a peeled banana. I could get enormously excited just from watching a girl walk across the room in a tight dress; and I particularly enjoyed the back view of a pair of legs when the feet were in rather high heels—the wonderful braced-up look behind the knees, with the legs themselves very taut③ as though they were made of strong elastic stretched out almost to breaking-point, but not quite. Sometimes, in Lady Birdwell's drawing-room, sitting near the window on a summer's afternoon, I would glance over the rim of my teacup towards the swim-

---

① gleam: *Noun* a brightness in a person's eyes taken as a sign of a particular emotion(眼中代表着某种情绪的)光亮(e. g. She saw an unmistakable gleam of triumph in his eyes. 她明白无误地看到他眼中闪着胜利的光芒。)

② octopus: *Noun* a cephalopod mollusc with eight sucker-bearing arms, a soft sac-like body, strong beak-like jaws, and no internal shell 章鱼;八爪鱼

③ taut: *Adjective* stretched or pulled tight; not slack 拉紧的

ming pool and become agitated[1] beyond measure by the sight of a little patch of sunburned stomach bulging between the top and bottom of a two-piece bathing-suit.

There is nothing wrong in having thoughts like these. All men harbour them from time to time. But they did give me a terrible sense of guilt. Is it me, I kept asking myself, who is unwittingly[2] responsible for the shameless way in which these ladies are now behaving? Is it the gleam in my eye (which I cannot control) that is constantly rousing their passions and egging them on? Am I unconsciously giving them what is sometimes known as the come-hither[3] signal every time I glance their way? Am I?

Or is this brutal conduct of theirs inherent in the very nature of the female?

I had a pretty fair idea of the answer to this question, but that was not good enough for me. I happen to possess a conscience that can never be consoled by guesswork; it has to have proof. I simply had to find out who was really the guilty party in this case—me or them, and with this object in view, I now decided to perform a simple experiment of my own invention, using Snelling's rats.

---

① agitated: *Adjective* troubled emotionally and usually deeply (e. g. His answers were all mixed up, so agitated was he. 他是那样心神不定,回答全乱了套。)

② unwitting: *Adjective* not done on purpose; unintentional 非故意的;无心的 (e. g. We are anxious to rectify the unwitting mistakes made in the past. 我们迫切想纠正过去无心犯下的错误。)

③ come-hither: *Adjective* suggesting that one finds someone sexually attractive; flirtatious 诱惑的;吸引人的;调情的(e. g. nymphs with come-hither looks 有着诱人容貌的美丽少女们)

A year or so previously I had had some trouble with an objectionable[①] choirboy[②] named Billy Snelling. On three consecutive Sundays this youth had brought a pair of white rats into church and had let them loose on the floor during my sermon. In the end I had confiscated the animals and carried them home and placed them in a box in the shed at the bottom of the vicarage garden. Purely for humane reasons I had then proceeded to feed them, and as a result, but without any further encouragement from me, the creatures began to multiply very rapidly. The two became five, and five became twelve.

It was at this point that I decided to use them for research purposes. There were exactly equal numbers of males and females, six of each, so that conditions were ideal.

(To be continued ...)

三、翻译探索

本篇小说的翻译涉及多方面的知识——宗教、音乐、解剖学等，特别涉及了人体解剖学方面的诸多词汇，翻译中做到精确的把握并非易事。另外，这篇小说中意识的流动性很强，角度的切换也很频繁，翻译中也要注意这方面的问题。

---

① objectionable: *Adjective* arousing distaste or opposition; unpleasant or offensive 引起不快的；令人反感的；引起反对的；令人厌恶的(e.g. I find his theory objectionable in its racist undertones. 我觉得他理论中的种族主义含意令人厌恶。)

② choirboy: *Noun* a boy who sings in a church or cathedral choir 教堂唱诗班男童

怪异乔治(上部)

我想,在大多数方面我敢断言,我这个人行为适度、思想成熟、兴趣丰富。我这样说,不管以什么样的方式来看,都不是异想天开、自吹自擂。我游历过许多地方,阅读广泛,会说希腊语和拉丁语,还涉猎理科方面的知识。对于他人在政见方面所持有的那种适度带点自由主义的态度,我能容忍。我把笔记汇编成一册书,是关于15世纪无伴奏合唱歌曲的沿革。我目睹了很多人死在病榻之上。此外,我在布道过程中说过的话已经对相当多的人的生活产生了影响。至少是,我希望,已经产生了影响。

尽管如此,在我的一生中,我从来没有——唉,怎么说好呢?——从来没有在真正意义上跟女性有过什么牵连。

诚诚恳恳地说,直到三周前,我还从来没有碰过任何一位女性——哪怕是一根手指头,除非形势所迫,我或许会帮帮其中的一位越过阶梯,或者做些其他什么类似的事情。即便是这样,我也总是想方设法做到只接触肩膀、腰部等部位,也就是皮肤没有裸露出来的部位,因为我永远都无法容忍的一件事情就是,我的皮肤跟她们的皮肤之间发生实质性的接触。皮肤接触皮肤,也就是说,我的皮肤接触一位女性的皮肤,不管接触的部位是腿、脖子、脸、手,或者仅仅是手指头,都会令我极度反感。因此,每每与女士碰面打招呼时,我始终把双手紧紧地扣到身后,避开了握手这一千篇一律的动作。

更有甚者,我可以说,不管跟女性有什么类型的接触——哪怕是接触皮肤没有裸露出来的部位,都会令我心绪烦乱、坐卧不安。排队时,要是哪位女性站得离我很近,我们的身体接触上了,或者我坐在公共汽车的座位上,一位女性挤到我旁边坐下——屁股紧挨着屁股、大腿紧靠着大腿时,我的脸颊就会"呼呼"地燃烧,随即脑袋顶一滴滴如刺状的汗珠就会"滋滋"地冒出来。

对于一个刚刚到达青春发育期的男学生来说,出现这种状况是恰如其分的。这种状况伴随着他的成长,如影随形——只不过是自然之母的杰作,如同刹车一般起到了抑制作用,直到他长成一个男子汉能规矩行事为止。这样说,我是同意的。

但是,对于生活在这个由上帝统领的地球上、年龄高达三十一岁的我来说,没有任何理由继续面对类似的窘境啊。况且,对于抵制诱惑,我已经训练有素,当然也就不会屈从于任何一种粗俗下流的激情行为。

倘若我对自己的外表产生最微乎其微的,哪怕就那么一点点羞耻感的话,或许整个这件事情本身还情有可原。但是,我并没有这种羞耻之感。正相反,尽管我是自卖自夸,但是在外表方面,命运之神对我还是垂青有加的。脚穿长筒袜站立时,我的身高正好是一米六八。尽管我的双肩自脖子处起,向两侧的下方呈斜坡状延伸,但与我小巧、利索的体型搭配却相得益彰。(我个人总是认为,对于一名个子不是高耸入云的男子来说,肩膀稍微耷拉一点儿反而更能为其增添一丝无以言表的、稍具美感的气质。难道你不同意我的观点吗?)我长相端正,牙齿状况极佳(只是上颌牙齿稍微凸出那么一点点儿),头发呈姜黄色,长势好得不得了,沿着整个头皮部分稠密地生长开来。苍天在上,我不敢撒谎,我曾经见过跟我比起来,个头如虾米一般矮小的男子,但跟甚为娇美的女子打起交道来,竟然如鱼得水,真是令人吃惊。噢,我多么羡慕他们啊!我多么渴望跟他们一样去做啊!那样的话,我就能够品尝到一些随着身体的接触而散发出来的美妙滋味。身体的接触就是一个个小小的礼仪程式,我经常看到男女之间发生这样的接触仪式:手与手之间的触碰、脸颊上轻轻的一吻、手臂间的互挽;在餐桌底下,膝盖顶在一起,或者脚抵到一块儿;更为显眼的是,异性间那种如胶似漆的、喘不过气来的拥抱,那种拥抱始于两个人在地板上交融到一起之际——也就是跳舞的时候。

但是,这样的事情不会发生在我身上。唉,正相反,我的时间都是在躲避她们之中度过的。我的朋友啊,这种躲避说起来容易,做起来可难啦,即使是对于我这样一个不显山、不露水的助理牧师而言,也是如此——尽管我住的地方是一个小小的、远离大都市的喧嚣和奢靡生活的乡村地区。

我的众多信徒中,有相当数量的女士,这你是明白的。其中很多女士在教堂区,但不幸的是,她们中至少有百分之六十是老处女——都是一些完完全全没有受到圣洁的婚姻生活驯服和影响的老处女。

我对你说啊,我就像松鼠一样警觉和不安。

有人可能会想,既然孩提时代的我得到了母亲所有细心的教育和训练,这类事情我就有能力从容面对的。毫无疑问,要是她活得时间很长,能够完成对我的教育的话,事情就迎刃而解了。唉,问题是,她年纪轻轻地就丢掉了性命。

她是一位很棒的女性,我指的是我的母亲。那时,她两只手腕上经常戴着大大的手镯,一戴就是五六只,每只手镯都要挂上各种式样的物件,走起路来物件相互碰撞、叮当作响。不管她身在何处,只要听到叮当的响声,就能找到她,比牛脖子上挂的铃铛可要响多了。到了晚上,她经常穿着一条黑裤子坐到沙发上,盘起腿来,两脚垫在身体下方。然后,用一根长长的、黑黑的烟嘴,一根接一根抽着香烟。我就蹲伏在地板上,看着她。

"乔治,想喝一口我的马提尼酒吗?"她经常这样问。

"现在,克莱尔,不要这样做,"我父亲就会如此这般加以制止,"要是你不当心的话,会影响儿子的成长。"

"喝啊,"她说,"不要怕,喝下吧。"

对母亲的吩咐,我总是百依百顺。

"可以啦,"我父亲说,"他只要尝尝是什么味儿,就可以啦。"

"鲍里斯,不要插嘴。这事十分重要。"

我母亲的理论是,对于一个男孩子来说,世界上的事情没有一件是可以保密的,什么事情都不要对孩子隐瞒,什么事都要让孩子去经历。

"我可不想让我任何一个儿子出门后,跟别的孩子嘀咕一些见不得人的秘密,然后大家就猜来猜去,就是因为没有人告诉他们谜底。"

一切都告诉他,一切都讲给他听。

"乔治,到这儿来,我要给你讲你应该知道的、有关上帝的事情。"

每天晚上我入睡前,她从来不给我照本宣科地读故事,而是把这些故事给我"讲"出来,每晚讲的都没有重样的。

“乔治,到这儿来。现在,我要跟你讲的,是关于穆罕默德的事。”

于是,她就会穿着一条黑裤子坐到沙发上,盘起腿来,两脚垫在身体下方。然后,她就无精打采地用一只手招呼我过去坐下,那只手里擎着一支长长的、黑黑的烟嘴。招呼我的时候,她戴的那些手镯就开始叮叮当当作响,令人稍稍感到有些异样。

“如果你一定要有宗教信仰的话,我想,穆罕默德伊斯兰教是一个不错的选择,其根基就是要保持身体健康。你可以娶很多妻子,但是绝对不允许吸烟、喝酒。”

“妈咪,为什么绝对不允许吸烟、喝酒呢?”

“因为如果你拥有很多妻子,你就必须保持身体健康,以及男子的阳刚之气。”

“什么是男子的阳刚之气?”

“我的宝贝,这个嘛,明天我再给你讲,我们一次只能涉及一个主题。关于穆罕默德还有一件事,那就是,他从来都不会便秘。”

“现在,克莱尔,”正在看书的父亲就会抬起头说道,“要实事求是。”

“我亲爱的鲍里斯啊,这件事你是一无所知的。现在,倘若你自己朝着麦加圣地的方向,每天的早晨、中午、晚上都屈身向前、以额头触地的话,或许在那个方向你本人就会少些困扰和烦恼。”

那个时候,我特别喜欢听她讲,哪怕是只能理解其中一半的意思。她是真正给我揭秘的人,没有什么比这更令人兴奋的啦。

“乔治,到这儿来,我要一五一十跟你讲讲,你父亲是如何赚钱的。”

“现在,克莱尔,可以啦,别讲了。”

“瞎说啊,亲爱的。这为什么要跟孩子保密呢?不讲的话,他只能猜测、想象,越想越糟。”

她开始给我详细地讲性事这一话题的时候,我刚刚到十岁。这个话题是诸多秘密之首,因此极其具有吸引力、令人着迷。

“乔治,到这儿来。现在,我要给你讲讲你是如何来到这个世界的,从最开始的时候讲起。”

此时，我看见父亲一声不响地抬起了头，张大了嘴巴，那架势表明，他要说一个重大的事情。可是，母亲那双敏锐的、闪闪发亮的眼睛已经盯上他，他就一言不发，慢慢地恢复到看书的状态。

“你可怜的父亲感到难为情了，”她说道。说完就冲我隐秘一笑，这种笑她从不给别人，只是给我。这种笑容是从脸的一侧开始的，只有一侧的嘴角慢慢向上抬起，露出一条长长的、可爱的皱褶，那条皱褶一直向上延伸到一只眼睛那儿，最后演变成某种眨眼微笑了。

“我的宝贝，不要难为情，我永远也不希望你感到难为情。永远也不要认为，你父亲是因为‘你’，才感到难为情的。”

父亲开始在椅子上动弹了几下。

“他单独跟我——他的妻子——待在一起的时候，我的天啊，他甚至还感到难为情。”

“待在一起的时候，对什么事情感到难为情呢？”我问。

至此，父亲站起身，一声不响地离开了房间。

我想，一定是这事讲完约一周后，我母亲才遭遇不测的。或许是稍晚一些的时候，十天，或者是两周后吧，我不敢肯定。我所能记得的就是，就在母亲给我讲的这一系列特别的“讲座”行将结束之际，她就遭遇不测了。一系列短暂的事件导致了母亲的死亡，而我当时就在事故的现场，所以对于那个奇特的晚上所发生事情的每一个细枝末节，我至今仍然记忆犹新，仿佛就发生在昨天。不管什么时候，只要我愿意，这件事就能在我的记忆里燃亮，在我的眼前播放，恰如电影胶片里的影像，始终一成不变地展现：总是在同一个地方结束——准确无误、分毫不差，总是以同样的方式开始——独特异常、猝不及防。放映之际，屏幕黑黑，我母亲的声音在我头上某个地方响起，呼唤着我的名字：

“乔治！醒醒，乔治，醒醒！”

紧接着，一束明亮的电灯亮起，照得我目眩眼花。尽管那束光离得很远，但仍能听到其中心区域发出的声音，对我喊道：

“乔治，醒醒啊，起床，穿好晨衣！要快！到楼下来，我要你看点东西。快，孩子，快啊！抓紧时间！穿上拖鞋，我们要到外面去。”

“外面？”

“乔治，不要反问，照我说的做。”我困得眼睛都睁不开，很难看清路。母亲牢牢抓住我的手，领着我下楼，穿过正门走了出去。外面夜色正浓，冷空气就像浸满水的海绵一样拂过我的脸。我睁大双眼，看见草坪上凝结了一层亮晶晶的霜，枝杈丛生的雪松在微弱、稀薄的月光映照下，黑乎乎地伫立着。头顶上方，一大片星星在夜空中闪烁。

我们匆忙穿过草坪——我和我的母亲。母亲的那些手镯叮叮当当响个不停，而我不得不一溜儿小跑，跟上母亲的步调。每迈一步，就能感觉到脚下结霜的草是软软的、脆脆的。

“约瑟芬已经开始生小宝宝啦，”母亲说，“机会难得，你应该看看整个分娩过程。”

到达时，车库里一盏灯亮着，我们就走了进去。父亲不在那儿，车也不在，车库似乎空旷旷的、光秃秃的。我那双拖鞋的鞋底往水泥地面一踩，感觉冷飕飕的。车库的一角放着一只用金属丝编的低矮的笼子，约瑟芬——一只大个头的、粉红色小眼睛的蓝毛兔——就躺在笼子里的一堆干草上。我们走近时，她就用警觉、多疑的目光看着我们。她的配偶叫拿破仑，现在被单独圈在对面角落的一只笼子里。我注意到，他正借助两只后腿高高站起，急不可耐地抓挠笼子的网格。

“看啊！”母亲叫道，“她正在生第一只呢！就要出来啦！”

我们轻手轻脚地靠近约瑟芬。我在笼子旁边蹲下来，脸靠上了金属网，看得入了迷。就在我的眼前，一只小兔子正从另一只兔子身上往外钻，速度很快。那场面如魔术般，十分壮观。

“小家伙全身都包裹了一层薄膜，干净利落地出来。看啊！”母亲说道。

“现在，看，她多么细心地照顾小宝宝啊！可怜、可爱的母亲没有面巾纸。即使有，她用爪子也拿不起来。所以嘛，她就取而代之，用舌头清洗小宝宝了。”

兔子妈妈朝我们这边看来，显得焦虑不安，两只粉红色的小眼睛转来转去。然后，她把身体在干草上换了一个位置，挡在小宝宝和我们之间。

“来另一侧看吧,”母亲说,“这个蠢蛋挪地方了。我确信,她试图要把小宝宝藏起来,不让我们看见。”

我们就绕到了笼子的另一侧,兔子妈妈的眼睛也跟着我们转动起来。两三米以远的地方,公兔发疯一般在笼子里上蹿下跳,抓挠金属网。

“拿破仑为什么这样兴奋异常呢?”我问。

“我不知道啊,亲爱的。这事你用不着放在心上,看着约瑟芬就是啦。我预期,她很快就要生另一只的。看啊,她清洗小宝宝是多么细致入微啊!简直就像人类的母亲对待婴儿一样啊!以前,我对你做的,几乎跟眼前的情景同出一辙。这样想,是不是很有意思呢?”

现在,这只大块头的蓝毛雌兔仍然看着我们,又一次用鼻子把小宝宝推开,慢慢地转动身体背对着我们。接着,继续用舌头舔小宝宝,清洗起来。

“做母亲的都清楚地知道该做什么,这是本能。难道这不是很美妙的事情吗?”母亲说,“现在,我的宝贝,你就想象一下吧,想象那个兔宝宝就是你,而约瑟芬就是我……等等,再回到这儿来,好好看看。”

我们轻手轻脚地绕着笼子又转了回来,以便能看到这只兔宝宝。

“看看她是怎么爱抚宝宝的,又是如何把宝宝全身舔了个遍的啊!看看啊!简直就是在吻小宝宝呢,哇!就像你和我一样啊!”

我靠近一些看着。对我来说,那种吻似乎令人略感不适。

“看啊!”我喊道,“她在吃宝宝呢!”

显而易见,兔宝宝的头迅速进了母亲嘴里,逐渐看不见。

“妈咪,快啊!”

但是,我的喊声还没有消失,那个微小的、粉红色的身体也全部消失不见,顺着兔子妈妈的嗓子就下去了。

我飞速转过身来。我知道的是,接下来,我看到了自己母亲的脸,就悬在我头顶上方约有十五厘米的位置上。不容置疑,她想要说点什么,或者她惊讶得什么也说不出来。但是,我清清楚楚看到的就是她的嘴，张得大大的，颜色红红的。这嘴张得越来越大、越来越宽，越来越宽、越来越大，简直就变成一个大大的、圆圆的敞口洞，洞的中心部分黑乎乎的，看不到尽头。我又一次喊叫起来，而且一喊就无法停止。紧接着，她的手一下子伸出来，我感觉到她的皮肤触碰到我的皮肤，她那长长的、冷冷的手指紧紧地攥住我的拳头。我向后一个惊跳，挣脱开来，奔向茫茫的黑夜。我沿着家用车道跑了起来，穿过正面的大门，边跑边喊叫。紧接着，透过我自己喊叫的声音，在黑暗之中，我听到身后传来手镯碰撞时发出的叮叮当当的声音，那声音越来越响、越来越响。母亲一路追了过来。她沿着坡度缓缓的小山跑来，跑到了小路的尽头，又越过桥跑上了主干道，那里车来车往、川流不息。车速将近每小时一百公里，车头灯明亮耀眼。

紧接着，在我身后某个地方，我听到轮胎在路面打滑，发出长长的一声"吱"，声音刺耳异常，随后就静悄悄的。我突然间注意到，我身后那叮叮当当的声音消失了。

可怜的母亲。

哪怕她再多活一点点也好啊。

我承认，那些兔子的事儿着实让我感到烦恼、恐惧，但那不是她的错。不管怎样，类似的令人略感不适的事情总会在我和她之间发生，而我则把这些事情看成是某种锤炼我的过程，对我是利大于弊的。但是，要是她没有死、完成对我的教育的话，我敢肯定，我身上就绝不会出现几分钟前我给你说的那件麻烦棘手的事情。

现在，我要继续说那件麻烦棘手的事儿。我本来没打算谈我母亲的事，她与我原先开始说的事情毫无关系。往下就不提她了。

下面，我要跟你说的，是我教区里的那些老处女。老处女这个词有些难听，是吧？它在脑海里勾起的意象，或者是一个细如麻绳的老丫头，嘴上还生出了皱纹，或者是一个粗俗的、大块头的怪胎，穿着马裤在房子四周不停地喊叫。但是，我教区里的这些老处女根本不符合上述意象。她们都干干净净、健健康康、结结实实，其中的大多数修养颇高、收入甚好。我敢肯定，正常的未婚男子跟她们交往起来会很惬意愉快的。

我刚开始来到这个教区供职的时候,日子过得还不算糟糕。当然,我的职业和穿着对我起到了一定的保护作用。此外,我自己采取了一种冷淡沉着、尊严十足的态度,那就等于阻止女性跟我套近乎。因此,几个月过去了,我得以在教区居民间自由穿梭:义卖市场上没有哪个女的擅自挽起我的胳膊,晚餐时递给我调料瓶的女子也没有哪一个擅自碰一下我的手指。对此,我很开心,感觉比以前那些年好多了。更为可喜的是,以前形成的那个小毛病——跟别人说话时一紧张,就用食指轻轻拨弄耳垂——也开始消失。

我把这段时间称为第一阶段,大约持续了六个月。那之后,麻烦就来了。

我认为,我应该了解的是,像我这样健全的男子,光靠在女士和自己之间保持一定的距离,是不可能永远避免卷入纠纷的。那样做根本不起作用,却更有可能取得相反的效果。

玩惠斯特纸牌游戏时,我就会注意到,她们的眼神穿过房间偷偷地抛了过来。与此同时,她们相互窃窃私语,频频点头,用舌头舔着嘴唇,吸着香烟,谋划着最佳的接近方法。但是,她们始终是在窃窃私语,甚至有时候我会无意中听到其中的只言片语:"多么腼腆的一个人……他有点紧张,是吧……神经绷得过紧……他需要交朋友……他得放轻松些……我们必须教教他如何去放松。"然后,随着时间一周一周地流逝,她们开始悄悄地靠近我,我就知道她们在向我靠近,我能感觉得到,尽管刚开始的时候她们没有那么明目张胆地暴露踪迹。

那就是我的第二阶段,整整持续了一年时间,的确煎熬。可是,跟我的第三阶段和最后阶段比较起来,那简直就是天堂。

到现在这个时候,她们不是小打小闹地从远处伏击我了,而是固定好枪杆上的刺刀,突然间从树林里冲出来进攻。那场面甚是吓人、令人恐惧。在挫伤一个男人的勇气方面,没有什么比出人意料的迅猛进攻更能出奇制胜。然而,我也并非胆小如鼠而甘做懦夫。任何情况之下,对于跟我体型相当的个体发起的单枪匹马的攻击,我还是会沉着应战、立稳脚跟。可是,现在令我信服的是,接下来这轮猛攻的发起者为数众多，却如同一个整体在协同作战，而且技术娴熟。

第一位进攻者是埃尔芬斯通小姐，她块头很大，一脸黑痣。当时，我正在募集一笔款项，用以购买一套新的管风琴的风箱。下午的时候，我就顺便拜访了她一下。在藏书室里跟她愉快地交谈了一番之后，她姿态优雅地递给我一张两畿尼的支票，这笔款项也就相当于两英镑多一点。告辞时，我对她说，不用麻麻烦烦出来送了，然后就走进门厅去拿帽子。刚要伸手够帽子，突然之间，我感到有一只赤裸的手臂冷不防滑过我的手臂。她当时一定是轻手轻脚地踮着脚尖跟上来的，所以弄得我猝不及防。一眨眼间，她的手指就开始使劲挤压我的手，一会儿向里挤、一会儿向外挤，一会儿向里挤、一会儿向外挤，我那只手就好像喷喉器的压力球似的。

“你总是摆出一副教长的尊贵模样，真的是这样吗？是不是装出来的呢？”她低声问道。

这个嘛！

我所能告诉你的就是，她那只手臂伸进来、从我的手臂下滑过时，感觉简直就像一只眼镜蛇盘卷着躯体，在我的手腕上缠绕。我一下子跳开，拉开正门，头也不回，沿着家用车道落荒而逃。

就在第二天，我们在村子里的集会厅举办了一次义卖拍售会，也是为买新风箱募集款项。快要结束的时候，我站在一个角落里，一声不响地喝着茶，留意着挤在货摊前的村民。突然之间，从我旁边冷不防传来一个声音：“天呐，看你那双眼睛就知道，你是饿得不行了吧。”顷刻之间，一个修长的、曲线优美的身体靠上前来，倚在我的身上。一只染了红指甲的手就要把一块厚厚的椰奶蛋糕往我嘴里塞。

“拜托，普拉特力小姐！”我喊道，“不要这样。”

但是，她步步紧逼，我身体都靠到墙上了。我一只手举着茶杯，另一只手端着碟子，根本无力反抗。我感觉汗水“唰”地一下涌遍了全身。我满嘴都是她迅猛塞进来的蛋糕，否则，说实话，我就会立马狂叫起来。

这又是一件令人作呕的事情，但更糟糕的还在后头。

第二天接着登场的，是昂温小姐。不凑巧的是，昂温小姐现在是埃尔芬斯通的密友,也是普拉特力的密友。这个事实当然应该引起我的重视,足以让我谨慎行事。然而,谁又会想到,茫茫人海之中,像昂温小姐这样一个娴静、温柔、小巧、羞怯的女子竟会擅自接触男子呢?就在几个星期之前,她还赠送给我一只新的、教堂里用的跪垫呢。那只垫子的花边是她亲手用针绣的。谁又会想到她这样一个人会那样呢?所以,当她要求我陪她到教堂的地下室、让我为她展示那里的撒克逊时期的壁画时,我做梦也不会想到,会有什么不对劲儿的恶行发生。但是,的确是有的。

这次遭遇令我痛苦不堪,我不想加以描述,但随后的那些遭遇就没有这次那么粗野、猛烈。从那时候开始,几乎每一天都会发生某个令人难以容忍的恶性事件,弄得我紧张兮兮、神经崩溃。有的时候,我神情恍惚,甚至都不知道自己在做些什么。在年纪轻轻的格拉迪斯·皮彻的婚礼上,我竟然念起了葬礼悼词。在洗礼仪式上,我把哈里斯太太的新生婴儿掉进洗礼盆中,结果让这个孩子浑身洗了个遍,很是令人不快。脖子旁边的那个令我颇感不舒服的疹子有两年多没有出现了,结果又冒了出来。还有,那个恼人的拨弄耳垂的毛病又犯了,犯得比以前更严重。更有甚者,一梳头,梳子上开始有了头发。我后撤得越快,她们追赶得也越快。女子都是那样的。男子越是矜持和腼腆,越能激发她们的兴趣。如果她们碰巧在这种矜持和腼腆里面探测到哪怕是一点点隐匿的、渴望得到什么的蛛丝马迹的话,她们就会加倍努力、穷追不舍。这种蛛丝马迹会在眼睛深处微弱地闪烁着光芒,会碰巧被她们探测到。这里,我要坦白交代一下——尽管坦白起来极其困难,她们在我身上探测到了。

你看看,实质上,我对女性也很着迷的。

是的,我知道你要说什么。我说了上面那么多之后,你却发现,我竟然会对女性着迷,这真令人难以置信,但是,这的的确确是真的。你必须了解的是,只是她们的手指触摸我,或者身体靠前贴上我时,我才会变得惊恐万状。要是她们站在一个安全的距离上,我会目不转睛地看上几个小时,为之着迷,但着迷的样子很是怪异。这跟你看到一个生物的感觉是一样的,比如一只章鱼,或者一条长长的毒蛇:

看着就感觉好，触摸一下却受不了。看着一只裸露的、光滑的、白色的胳膊从衣袖里伸出来，我喜爱，因为那裸露的样子很有意思，令人着迷，就像一根剥了皮的香蕉。只要看着一个女孩子穿着紧身衣走过屋子，就能令我激动不已、兴奋无比。女子的鞋跟要是相当高的话，我就特别喜欢从后面欣赏那两条美腿：膝盖后部紧紧绷起，完美无比；两条腿就好像是用结实的橡皮做的，被紧紧地拉直，拉伸得几乎到了要断裂的程度，但是离断裂还有一定的距离。有时候，在一个夏日的午后，坐在伯德韦尔夫人家客厅里靠近窗户的地方，透过茶杯的边沿向外面的游泳池瞥上那么一眼，顿时我就会变得激动不安、渴望无限，因为我看见女式分体泳装顶部和底部之间裸露的腹部，腹部的那小块区域已被太阳晒黑，凸显出来。

出现类似的想法并没有什么过错，任何一名男子时不时地都会怀有类似的想法，但却让我怕得要死，令我产生负罪感。尽管不是我故意所为，但我不断地问自己，这些女子现在这些不知羞耻的行为，责任是不是在我呢？难道是我眼里微弱闪烁的光芒（这，还真的无法控制住）燃起了她们的激情、怂恿她们继续向前吗？我每次瞥向她们的时候，难道有时候会产生所谓的勾引信号吗？是我无意中给她们发出了这种信号吗？

或者说，她们这种放肆的行为是所有女性与生俱来的吗？

我对这个问题的解答还是相当的公平合理，却不够完美。凑巧的是，仅仅凭猜测，我的良知是永远无法得到安慰的，必须得有证据才可以。在这种情况之下，负罪的一方究竟是她们，还是我？我必须查个水落石出。有了这样一个目标之后，我就决定用斯内林的老鼠做一个简单的实验，这个实验是我自己设计出来的。

大约一年以前，我跟教堂唱诗班的一个令人反感的男孩子有点纠葛，他名叫比利·斯内林。连续三个星期天，这个年轻人把一对白色的老鼠带进教堂。在我布道期间，还把它们放到地板上。最后，我把它们没收，带回家，放进棚屋里的一只盒子，棚屋在我住所花园的尽头。完全出于仁慈的原因，我就开始喂养它们，小家伙开始迅速繁殖起来，但我并不是有意鼓励它们繁殖。两只繁殖为五只，五只繁殖为十二只。

就在它们数量达到十二只的时候,我决定用它们来做科学研究了。公鼠和母鼠的数量正好相等,各为六只,所以实验条件很理想。

(待续)

第二节　《怪异乔治》(下部) *Georgy Porgy* (Part B)

如第一节所述,罗尔德·达尔的《怪异乔治》(*Georgy Porgy*)被收录到《罗尔德·达尔小说精品集》(*The Best of Roald Dahl*)、《吻了又吻》(*Kiss Kiss*)、《更多出人意料故事集》(*More Tales of the Unexpected*)、《后续出人意料故事集》(*Further Tales of the Unexpected*)、《完全出人意料故事集》(*Completely Unexpected Tales*)、《罗尔德·达尔短篇故事集锦》(*The Collected Short Stories of Roald Dahl*)、《五部畅销书集》(*5 Bestsellers*)、《罗尔德·达尔选集》(*The Roald Dahl Omnibus*)以及《罗尔德·达尔二十九篇成人故事集》(*Twenty Nine Kisses from Roald Dahl*)等书中,可见其影响力之大。

一、原作导读

乔治的实验进行得很顺利。他把不同的母白鼠看成他现实生活中教区里的一个个老处女或者寡妇。乔治认为,自己在实验中所产生的各种奇特想法很是荒谬可笑,但还是打算将其中一些想法应用到实际生活中,并带着这样的想法参加了伯德韦尔夫人举办的网球聚会。

在那次网球聚会上,罗奇小姐将乔治灌醉,并带着晕乎乎的乔治到花园散步。散步的时候,罗奇小姐将乔治紧紧搂住,乔治喝得晕乎乎的,无法抗拒。罗奇小姐随即吻了乔治,乔治看到罗奇小姐嘴巴大张,要将他整个吞下去,于是他大声喊叫起来……

被罗奇小姐"吞下"的乔治,对自己的新"处所"感到很好奇:

对于一个像我这样情趣保守的男子来说,这里的一切都有点儿怪异。就我个人而言,我更喜欢橡木家具和木条镶花地板。但是,无论怎么说,这里有一样东西还是令我身心得到极大的愉悦,那就是周围的墙壁。墙壁既惹人喜爱,又感觉柔软,就像是某种填充材料。其好处就是,我可以在上面尽情弹跳,而不会伤到自己。

It is all a trifle bizarre for a man of conservative tastes like myself. Personally I prefer oak furniture and parquet flooring. But there is anyway one thing here that pleases me greatly, and that is the walls. They are lovely and soft, like a sort of padding, and the advantage of this is that I can bounce up against them as much as I wish without hurting myself.

除了乔治之外,新处所里还有好几个男子,其中一个上了年纪的每天晚饭后都来看他。乔治每次问他来这里的原因,他都面露难色,不知如何回答。有一次,乔治干脆直截了当、直言不讳地对他说:

"我敢打赌,你跟罗奇小姐瞎搞来着,结果跟我一模一样,被活活吞下来。我敢打赌,实际情况就是那样,只是你羞愧难当、不肯张扬。"

听我说完后,突然之间,他看起来极其苍白、低头垂脸,我也感到歉疚不安。

"我给你唱首歌好吗?"我问。

但是,他却站起身来,没有作答,一声不响步入走廊。

"振作点儿,"我追着他喊,"不要垂头丧气。啥病都能治好,总能找到好药的。"

"I'll bet you were fooling around with Miss Roach and got yourself swallowed up just the same as I did. I'll bet that's exactly what happened, only you're ashamed to admit it."

He looked suddenly so wan and defeated when I said this that I felt sorry for him.

"Would you like me to sing you a song?" I asked.

But he got up without answering and went quietly out into the corridor.

"Cheer up," I called after him. "Don't be depressed. There is always some balm in Gilead."

阅读完整篇小说,你也许就会明白乔治的新"处所"实际上是一个什么样的所在了。

二、原作释读

在这篇小说中,作家罗尔德·达尔娴熟地运用了多种手段来表达主人公复杂的内心世界,语言诙谐幽默,角度切换频繁,意识的流动与现实的描述融为一体,阅读中要注意体会和把握。另外,一些专业性较强的词汇构成了阅读的障碍,特别是人体解剖学方面的一些词汇,阅读中要注意去突破。还有就是,阅读中要体会好最后部分的"荒诞主义"色彩。

Georgy Porgy (Part B)

(Continued from the above)

I first isolated the sexes, putting them into two separate cages, and I left them like that for three whole weeks. Now a rat is a very lascivious[①] animal, and any zoologist will tell you that for them this is an inordinately[②] long period of separation. At a guess I would say that one week of enforced celibacy[③] for a rat is equal to approximately one year of the same treatment for someone like Miss Elphinstone or Miss Prattley; so you can see that I was doing a pretty fair job in reproducing actual conditions.

When the three weeks were up, I took a large box that was divided across the centre by a little fence, and I placed the females on one side and the males on the other. The fence consisted of nothing more than three single strands of naked wire, one inch apart, but there was a powerful electric current running through the wires.

To add a touch of reality to the proceedings, I gave each female a name. The largest one, who also had the longest whiskers[④], was Miss Elphinstone. The one with a short thick tail was Miss Prattley. The smallest of them all was Miss Unwin, and so on. The males, all six of them, were ME.

I now pulled up a chair and sat back to watch the result.

All rats are suspicious by nature, and when I first put the two sexes

---

① lascivious: *Adjective* (of a person, manner, or gesture) feeling or revealing an overt and often offensive sexual desire(人、行为或姿势)好色的;淫荡的(e.g. He gave her a lascivious wink. 他朝她淫荡地眨了一眼。)

② inordinate: *Adjective* unusually or disproportionately large; excessive 过多的;过大的;过分的(e.g. a case which had taken up an inordinate amount of time 占用了过多时间的事情)

③ celibacy: *Noun* abstinence from sexual intercourse, especially by reason of religious vows 禁欲;贞洁

④ whisker: *Noun* a long projecting hair or bristle growing from the face or snout of many mammals(很多哺乳动物的)须

together in the box with only the wire between them, neither side made a move. The males stared hard at the females through the fence. The females stared back, waiting for the males to come forward. I could see that both sides were tense with yearning. Whiskers quivered and noses twitched① and occasionally a long tail would flick sharply against the wall of the box.

After a while, the first male detached himself from his group and advanced gingerly② towards the fence, his belly close to the ground. He touched a wire and was immediately electrocuted. The remaining eleven rats froze, motionless.

There followed a period of nine and a half minutes during which neither side moved; but I noticed that while all the males were now staring at the dead body of their colleague, the females had eyes only for the males.

Then suddenly Miss Prattley with the short tail could stand it no longer. She came bounding forward, hit the wire, and dropped dead.

The males pressed their bodies closer to the ground and gazed thoughtfully at the two corpses by the fence. The females also seemed to be quite shaken, and there was another wait, with neither side moving.

Now it was Miss Unwin who began to show signs of impatience. She snorted audibly and twitched a pink mobile nose-end from side to side, then suddenly she started jerking her body quickly up and down as

---

① twitch: *Verb* give or cause to give a short, sudden jerking or convulsive movement 抽动;使抽动(e.g. He saw her lips twitch and her eyelids flutter. 他看见她嘴唇抽搐,眼皮颤动。)

② gingerly: *Adverb* in a careful or cautious manner 小心谨慎地;战战兢兢地(e.g. She gingerly picked the flower. 她小心翼翼地摘下那朵花。)

though she were doing push-ups①. She glanced round at her remaining four companions, raised her tail high in the air as much as to say, "Here I go, girls," and with that she advanced briskly to the wire, pushed her head through it, and was killed.

Sixteen minutes later, Miss Foster made her first move. Miss Foster was a woman in the village who bred cats, and recently she had had the effrontery② to put up a large sign outside her house in the High Street, saying FOSTER'S CATTERY③. Through long association with the creatures she herself seemed to have acquired all their most noxious④ characteristics, and whenever she came near me in a room I could detect, even through the smoke of her Russian cigarette, a faint but pungent aroma⑤ of cat. She had never struck me as having much control over her baser⑥ instincts, and it was with some satisfaction, therefore, that I watched her flow as she foolishly took her own life in a last desperate plunge towards

---

① push-up or pushup: *Noun* an exercise in which a person lies facing the floor and, keeping their back straight, raises their body by pressing down on their hands 俯卧撑

② effrontery: *Noun* [mass noun] insolent or impertinent behaviour 厚颜无耻的行为;放肆(e. g. One juror had the effrontery to challenge the coroner's decision. 一位陪审员竟无礼地对验尸官的结论提出质疑。)

③ cattery: *Noun* a boarding or breeding establishment for cats 猫屋;猫窝;养猫

④ noxious: *Adjective* harmful, poisonous, or very unpleasant 有害的;有毒的;让人厌恶的(e. g. They were overcome by the noxious fumes. 他们被有毒烟气熏倒了。)

⑤ aroma: *Noun* a distinctive, typically pleasant smell 芳香;香味;香气(e. g. The tantalizing aroma of fresh coffee. 刚煮好的咖啡的诱人气味。)

⑥ base: *Adjective* (of a person or their actions or feelings) without moral principles; ignoble(人、行为或感情)卑鄙的;卑劣的(e. g. The electorate's baser instincts of greed and selfishness. 选民那贪婪自私的卑劣本性。)

the masculine sex.

A Miss Montgomery-Smith came next, a small determined woman who had once tried to make me believe that she had been engaged to a bishop. She died trying to creep on her belly under the lowest wire, and I must say I thought this a very fair reflection upon the way in which she lived her life.

And still the five remaining males stayed motionless, waiting.

The fifth female to go was Miss Plumley. She was a devious① one who was continually slipping little messages addressed to me into the collection bag. Only the Sunday before, I had been in the vestry② counting the money after morning service and had come across one of them tucked inside a folded ten-shilling note. "Your poor throat sounded hoarse today during the sermon," it said. "Let me bring you a bottle of my own cherry pectoral③ to soothe it down. Most affectionately, Eunice Plumley."

Miss Plumley ambled④ slowly up to the wire, sniffed the centre strand with the tip of her nose, came a fraction too close, and received two hundred and forty volts of alternating current through her body.

The five males stayed where they were, watching the slaughter.

---

① devious: *Adjective* showing a skilful use of underhand tactics to achieve goals 不光明正大的;狡诈的;阴险的(e.g. He's as devious as a politician needs to be. 他具有作为一个政治家必需的狡诈阴险。)

② vestry: *Noun* a room or building attached to a church, used as an office and for changing into ceremonial vestments(与教堂相连的)事务室;祭服室

③ pectoral: *Noun* (Medicine) a medicine or remedy for disorders of the chest or lungs(医学)治胸(肺)病的药;止咳药

④ amble: *Verb* [no obj., with adverbial of direction] walk or move at a slow, relaxed pace 漫步;悠闲散步(e.g. They ambled along the riverbank. 他们沿着河岸散步。)

And now only Miss Elphinstone remained on the feminine side.

For a full half-hour neither she nor any of the others made a move. Finally one of the males stirred himself slightly, took a step forward, hesitated, thought better of it, and slowly sank back into a crouch on the floor.

This must have frustrated Miss Elphinstone beyond measure, for suddenly, with eyes blazing, she rushed forward and took a flying leap at the wire. It was a spectacular jump and she nearly cleared it; but one of her hind legs grazed the top strand, and thus she also perished with the rest of her sex.

I cannot tell you how much good it did me to watch this simple and, though I say it myself, this rather ingenious experiment. In one stroke I had laid open the incredibly lascivious, stop-at-nothing nature of the female. My own sex was vindicated①; my own conscience was cleared. In a trice②, all those awkward little flashes of guilt from which I had continually been suffering flew out of the window. I felt suddenly very strong and serene③ in the knowledge of my own innocence.

For a few moments I toyed with the absurd idea of electrifying the black iron railings that ran around the vicarage garden; or perhaps just the gate would be enough. Then I would sit back comfortably in a chair in the library and watch through the window as the real Misses Elphin-

---

① vindicate: *Verb* [with obj.] clear (someone) of blame or suspicion 证明……是清白的,证明……是无辜的(e. g. Hospital staff were vindicated by the inquest verdict. 验尸结论证明医院职员没有责任。)

② trice: *Noun* (Used in the phrase "in a trice") in a moment; very quickly 瞬间;一刹那(e. g. He was gone in a trice. 一转眼他就不见了。)

③ serene: *Adjective* calm, peaceful, and untroubled; tranquil 安详的;宁静的(e. g. Her eyes were closed and she looked very serene. 她闭着眼看上去很平静。)

stone and Prattley and Unwin came forward one after the other and paid the final penalty for pestering① an innocent male.

Such foolish thoughts!

What I must actually do now, I told myself, was to weave around me a sort of invisible electric fence constructed entirely out of my own personal moral fibre. Behind this I would sit in perfect safety while the enemy, one after another, flung themselves against the wire.

I would begin by cultivating a brusque② manner. I would speak crisply③ to all women, and refrain from smiling at them. I would no longer step back a pace when one of them advanced upon me. I would stand my ground and glare at her, and if she said something that I considered suggestive④, I would make a sharp retort.

It was in this mood that I set off the very next day to attend Lady Birdwell's tennis party.

I was not a player myself, but her ladyship had graciously invited me to drop in and mingle with the guests when play was over at six o'clock. I believe she thought that it lent a certain tone to a gathering to have a clergyman present, and she was probably hoping to persuade me to repeat the performance I gave the last time I was there, when I sat at

① pester: *Verb* [with obj.] trouble or annoy (someone) with frequent or persistent requests or interruptions 不断打扰;纠缠(e.g. She constantly pestered him with telephone calls. 她老打电话纠缠他。)

② brusque: *Adjective* abrupt or offhand in speech or manner(言语或举止上)唐突的;无礼的(e.g. She could be brusque and impatient. 她可能会唐突无礼而且不耐烦。)

③ crisp: *Adjective* (of a way of speaking) briskly decisive and matter-of-fact, without hesitation or unnecessary detail(说话方式)干脆的;干净利落的;简明的

④ suggestive: *Adjective* making someone think of sex and sexual relationships 挑逗性的(e.g. a suggestive remark 一句挑逗的话)

the piano for a full hour and a quarter after supper and entertained the guests with a detailed description of the evolution of the madrigal through the centuries.

I arrived at the gates on my cycle promptly at six o'clock and pedalled up the long drive towards the house. This was the first week of June, and the rhododendrons① were massed in great banks of pink and purple all the way along on either side. I was feeling unusually blithe② and dauntless③. The previous day's experiment with rats had made it impossible now for anyone to take me by surprise. I knew exactly what to expect and I was armed accordingly. All around me the little fence was up.

"Ah, good evening, Vicar," Lady Birdwell cried, advancing upon me with both arms outstretched.

I stood my ground and looked her straight in the eye. "How's Birdwell?" I said. "Still up in the city?"

I doubt whether she had ever before in her life heard Lord Birdwell referred to thus by someone who had never even met him. It stopped her dead in her tracks. She looked at me queerly and didn't seem to know how to answer.

"I'll take a seat if I may," I said, and walked past her towards the

---

① rhododendron: *Noun* a shrub or small tree of the heather family, with large clusters of bell-shaped flowers and typically with large evergreen leaves, widely grown as an ornamental 杜鹃花属植物

② blithe: *Adjective* showing a casual and cheerful indifference considered to be callous or improper 漠视……的;把……不当一回事的;不顾他人利益的;随随便便的(e.g. a blithe disregard for the rules of the road 漠视道路交通规则、把它不当一回事的态度)

③ dauntless: *Adjective* showing fearlessness and determination 无所畏惧的;不屈不挠的

terrace where a group of nine or ten guests were settled comfortably in cane chairs, sipping their drinks. They were mostly women, the usual crowd, all of them dressed in white tennis clothes, and as I strode in among them my own sober black suiting seemed to give me, I thought, just the right amount of separateness for the occasion.

The ladies greeted me with smiles. I nodded to them and sat down in a vacant chair, but I didn't smile back.

"I think perhaps I'd better finish my story another time," Miss Elphinstone was saying. "I don't believe the vicar would approve." She giggled and gave me an arch① look. I knew she was waiting for me to come out with my usual little nervous laugh and to say my usual little sentence about how broadminded I was; but I did nothing of the sort. I simply raised one side of my upper lip until it shaped itself into a tiny curl of contempt (I had practised in the minor that morning), and then I said sharply, in a loud voice, "Mens sana in corpore sano②."

"What's that?" she cried. "Come again, Vicar."

"A clean mind in a healthy body," I answered.

"It's a family motto."

There was an odd kind of silence for quite a long time after this. I could see the women exchanging glances with one another, frowning, shaking their heads.

---

① arch: *Adjective* deliberately or affectedly playful and teasing 故意(或假装)调皮逗弄的(e. g. a somewhat arch tone of voice 带一点调皮的声调)

② Mens sana in corpore sano: It is a famous Latin quotation, often translated as, "A sound mind in a sound body."这是一句经常被引用的著名拉丁语,意思是"洁净的心灵寓于健康的身体"。

"The vicar's in the dumps[①]," Miss Foster announced. She was the one who bred cats. "I think the vicar needs a drink."

"Thank you," I said, "but I never imbibe[②]. You know that."

"Then do let me fetch you a nice cooling glass of fruit cup[③]?"

This last sentence came softly and rather suddenly from someone just behind me, to my right, and there was a note of such genuine concern in the speaker's voice that I turned round.

I saw a lady of singular beauty whom I had met only once before, about a month ago. Her name was Miss Roach, and I remembered that she had struck me then as being a person far out of the usual run. I had been particularly impressed by her gentle and reticent[④] nature; and the fact that I had felt comfortable in her presence proved beyond doubt that she was not the sort of person who would try to impinge herself upon me in any way.

"I'm sure you must be tired after cycling all that distance," she was saying now.

I swivelled right round in my chair and looked at her carefully. She was certainly a striking person—unusually muscular for a woman, with

---

① dumps: *Noun* (usu. in the phrase "in the dumps") a gloomy state of mind 忧郁;消沉(e.g. It's no use letting yourself fall into the dumps. 你听任自己的情绪消沉下去一点用也没有。)

② imbibe: *Verb* [with obj.] (formal, often humorous) drink (alcohol)(常含幽默之意的正式用法)饮(酒);喝(酒)(e.g. They were imbibing far too many pitchers of beer. 他们喝了太多罐啤酒。)

③ fruit cup: *Noun* (Brit.) a drink consisting of a mixture of fruit juices, typically with pieces of fruit in it(英国英语)什锦水果杯(有小块水果的果汁饮料)

④ reticent: *Adjective* not revealing one's thoughts or feelings readily 沉默寡言的;缄默的;保持沉默的(e.g. She was extremely reticent about her personal affairs. 她极不愿谈论私事。)

broad shoulders and powerful arms and a huge calf bulging on each leg. The flush of the afternoon's exertions was still upon her, and her face glowed with a healthy red sheen①.

"Thank you so much, Miss Roach," I said, "but I never touch alcohol in any form. Maybe a small glass of lemon squash ..."

"The fruit cup is only made of fruit, Padre②."

How I loved a person who called me "Padre". The word has a military ring about it that conjures up visions of stern discipline and officer rank.

"Fruit cup?" Miss Elphinstone said. "It's harmless."

"My dear man, it's nothing but vitamin C," Miss Foster said.

"Much better for you than fizzy③ lemonade," Lady Birdwell said. "Carbon dioxide attacks the lining of the stomach."

"I'll get you some," Miss Roach said, smiling at me pleasantly. It was a good open smile, and there wasn't a trace of guile④ or mischief from one corner of the mouth to the other.

She stood up and walked over to the drink table. I saw her slicing an orange, then an apple, then a cucumber, then a grape, and dropping the pieces into a glass. Then she poured in a large quantity of liquid from

---

① sheen: *Noun* [in sing.] a soft lustre on a surface 光泽;光辉(e. g. He seemed to shine with that unmistakable showbiz sheen. 他似乎浑身都散发出明显的娱乐业的光彩。)

② padre: *Noun* (informal) a chaplain in any of the armed services(非正式)随军牧师

③ fizzy: *Adjective* (of a drink) containing bubbles of gas; effervescent(饮料)有气泡的;冒泡的;充气的

④ guile: *Noun* [mass noun] sly or cunning intelligence 狡诈;奸猾(e. g. He used all his guile and guts to free himself from the muddle he was in. 他竭尽自己全部的狡诈和胆量来摆脱困境。)

a bottle whose label I couldn't quite read without my spectacles, but I fancied that I saw the name JIM on it, or TIM or PIM, or some such word.

"I hope there's enough left," Lady Birdwell called out. "Those greedy children of mine do love it so."

"Plenty," Miss Roach answered, and she brought the drink to me and set it on the table.

Even without tasting it I could easily understand why children adored it. The liquid itself was dark amber-red and there were great hunks of fruit floating around among the ice cubes; and on top of it all, Miss Roach had placed a sprig① of mint. I guessed that the mint had been put there specially for me, to take some of the sweetness away and to lend a touch of grown-upness to a concoction② that was otherwise so obviously for youngsters.

"Too sticky for you, Padre!"

"It's delectable③," I said, sipping it. "Quite perfect."

It seemed a pity to gulp it down quickly after all the trouble Miss Roach had taken to make it, but it was so refreshing I couldn't resist.

"Do let me make you another!"

I liked the way she waited until I had set the glass on the table, instead of trying to take it out of my hand.

"I wouldn't eat the mint if I were you," Miss Elphinstone said.

"I'd better get another bottle from the house," Lady Birdwell called out. "You're going to need it, Mildred."

---

① sprig: *Noun* a small stem bearing leaves or flowers, taken from a bush or plant(带叶或花的)小枝

② concoction: *Noun* a mixture of various ingredients or elements 调和物;调配物;调制品

③ delectable: *Adjective* (of food or drink) delicious(食物或饮料)美味的

"Do that," Miss Roach replied. "I drink gallons of the stuff myself," she went on, speaking to me. "And I don't think you'd say that I'm exactly what you might call emaciated①."

"No indeed," I answered fervently. I was watching her again as she mixed me another brew, noticing how the muscles rippled under the skin of the arm that raised the bottle. Her neck also was uncommonly fine when seen from behind; not thin and stringy like the necks of a lot of these so-called modern beauties, but thick and strong with a slight ridge running down either side where the sinews② bulged. It wasn't easy to guess the age of a person like this, but I doubted whether she could have been more than forty-eight or -nine.

I had just finished my second big glass of fruit cup when I began to experience a most peculiar sensation. I seemed to be floating up out of my chair, and hundreds of little warm waves came washing in under me, lifting me higher and higher. I felt as buoyant as a bubble, and everything around me seemed to be bobbing up and down and swirling gently from side to side. It was all very pleasant, and I was overcome by an almost irresistible desire to break into song.

"Feeling happy?" Miss Roach's voice sounded miles and miles away, and when I turned to look at her, I was astonished to see how near she really was. She, also, was bobbing up and down.

"Terrific," I answered. "I'm feeling absolutely terrific."

Her face was large and pink, and it was so close to me now that I

---

① emaciated: *Adjective* abnormally thin or weak, especially because of illness or a lack of food 消瘦的;皮包骨的;虚弱的(e. g. She was so emaciated she could hardly stand. 她身体虚弱得几乎无法站立。)

② sinew: *Noun* a piece of tough fibrous tissue uniting muscle to bone; a tendon or ligament 肌腱;筋

could see the pale carpet of fuzz① covering both her cheeks, and the way the sunlight caught each tiny separate hair and made it shine like gold. All of a sudden I found myself wanting to put out a hand and stroke those cheeks of hers with my fingers. To tell the truth I wouldn't have objected in the least if she had tried to do the same to me.

"Listen," she said softly. "How about the two of us taking a little stroll down the garden to see the lupins?"

"Fine," I answered. "Lovely. Anything you say."

There is a small Georgian summer-house alongside the croquet② lawn in Lady Birdwell's garden, and the very next thing I knew, I was sitting inside it on a kind of chaise-longue③ and Miss Roach was beside me. I was still bobbing up and down, and so was she, and so, for that matter, was the summer-house, but I was feeling wonderful. I asked Miss Roach if she would like me to give her a song.

"Not now," she said, encircling me with her arms and squeezing my chest against hers so hard that it hurt.

"Don't," I said, melting.

"That's better," she kept saying. "That's much better, isn't it?"

Had Miss Roach or any other female tried to do this sort of thing to me an hour before, I don't quite know what would have happened. I think I would probably have fainted. I might even have died. But here I was now, the same old me, actually relishing the contact of those enor-

① fuzz: *Noun* a fluffy or frizzy mass of hair or fibre 蓬松(或卷曲)的毛发(或纤维、绒毛、卷毛)

② croquet: *Noun* [mass noun] a game played on a lawn, in which wooden balls are driven through a series of square-topped hoops by means of mallets 槌球游戏(一种用长柄木槌击打木球使之穿过一系列球门的户外游戏)

③ chaise-longue or chaise longue: a sofa with a backrest at only one end 单背沙发;长靠椅

mous bare arms against my body! Also—and this was the most amazing thing of all—I was beginning to feel the urge to reciprocate①.

I took the lobe of her left ear between my thumb and forefinger, and tugged it playfully.

"Naughty boy," she said.

I tugged harder and squeezed it a bit at the same time. This roused her to such a pitch that she began to grunt and snort like a hog. Her breathing became loud and stertorous②.

"Kiss me," she ordered.

"What?" I said.

"Come on, kiss me."

At that moment, I saw her mouth. I saw this great mouth of hers coming slowly down on top of me, starting to open, and coming closer and closer, and opening wider and wider; and suddenly my whole stomach began to roll right over inside me and I went stiff with terror.

"No!" I shrieked. "Don't! Don't, Mummy, don't!"

I can only tell you that I had never in all my life seen anything more terrifying than that mouth. I simply could not stand it coming at me like that. Had it been a red-hot iron someone was pushing into my face I wouldn't have been nearly so petrified③, I swear I wouldn't. The strong arms were around me, pinning me down so that I couldn't move, and the mouth kept getting larger and larger, and then all at once it was right

---

① reciprocate: *Verb* experience the same (love, liking, or affection) for someone that has such feelings for oneself 回报;报答;酬答(爱、喜爱或感情)(e.g. Her passion for him was not reciprocated. 她对他的热情没有得到回报。)

② stertorous: *Adjective* (of breathing) noisy and laboured 打鼾的;打呼噜的

③ petrify: *Verb* [with obj.] make (someone) so frightened that they are unable to move or think 使惊呆;把……吓呆(e.g. His icy controlled quietness petrified her. 他克制住自己,那种冰冷的沉默把她吓呆了。)

on top of me, huge and wet and cavernous[①], and the next second—I was inside it.

I was right inside this enormous mouth, lying on my stomach along the length of the tongue, with my feet somewhere around the back of the throat; and I knew instinctively that unless I got myself out again at once I was going to be swallowed alive—just like that baby rabbit. I could feel my legs being drawn down the throat by some kind of suction, and quickly I threw up my arms and grabbed hold of the lower front teeth and held on for dear life. My head was near the mouth-entrance, and I could actually look right out between the lips and see a little patch of the world outside—sunlight shining on the polished wooden floor of the summer-house, and on the floor itself a gigantic foot in a white tennis shoe.

I had a good grip with my fingers on the edge of the teeth, and in spite of the suction, I was managing to haul myself up slowly towards the daylight when suddenly the upper teeth came down on my knuckles[②] and started chopping away at them so fiercely I had to let go. I went sliding back down the throat, feet first, clutching madly at this and that as I went, but everything was so smooth and slippery I couldn't get a grip. I glimpsed a bright flash of gold on the left as I slid past the last of the molars[③], and then three inches farther on I saw what must have been the

---

① cavernous: *Adjective* like a cavern in size, shape, or atmosphere(大小、形状或气氛)似大洞穴的(e. g. a dismal cavernous hall 一个如洞穴般阴沉的大厅)

② knuckle: *Noun* a part of a finger at a joint where the bone is near the surface, especially where the finger joins the hand 指关节;指节(e. g. Charlotte rapped on the window with her knuckles. 夏洛特用指节轻敲着窗户。)

③ molar: *Noun* (also as "molar tooth") a grinding tooth at the back of a mammal's mouth 臼齿;磨牙

uvula① above me, dangling like a thick red stalactite② from the roof of the throat. I grabbed at it with both hands but the thing slithered③ through my fingers and I went on down.

I remember screaming for help, but I could hardly hear the sound of my own voice above the noise of the wind that was caused by the throat-owner's breathing. There seemed to be a gale blowing all the time, a queer erratic④ gale that blew alternately very cold (as the air came in) and very hot (as it went out again).

I managed to get my elbows hooked over a sharp fleshy ridge—I presume the epiglottis⑤—and for a brief moment I hung there, defying the suction and scrabbling with my feet to find a foothold on the wall of the larynx⑥; but the throat gave a huge swallow that jerked me away, and down I went again.

From then on, there was nothing else for me to catch hold of, and down and down I went until soon my legs were dangling below me in the

---

① uvula: *Noun* (Anatomy) (also as "palatine uvula") a fleshy extension at the back of the soft palate which hangs above the throat(解剖学)悬雍垂;小舌

② stalactite: *Noun* a tapering structure hanging like an icicle from the roof of a cave, formed of calcium salts deposited by dripping water 钟乳石

③ slither: *Verb* slide or slip unsteadily on a loose or slippery surface(摇晃着)滑下;滑动(e. g. We slithered down a snowy mountain track. 我们顺着山上布满积雪的小道晃晃悠悠地滑了下去。)

④ erratic: *Adjective* not even or regular in pattern or movement; unpredictable 不稳定的;捉摸不定的;无规律的(e. g. He is a very erratic football player. 他是个技术非常不稳定的足球队员。)

⑤ epiglottis: *Noun* a flap of cartilage at the root of the tongue, which is depressed during swallowing to cover the opening of the windpipe 会厌

⑥ larynx: *Noun* (Anatomy) the hollow muscular organ forming an air passage to the lungs and holding the vocal cords in humans and other mammals; the voice box (解剖学)喉

upper reaches of the stomach, and I could feel the slow powerful pulsing of peristalsis① dragging away at my ankles, pulling me down and down and down ...

Far above me, outside in the open air, I could hear the distant babble of women's voices:

"It's not true ..."

"But my dear Mildred, how awful ..."

"The man must be mad ..."

"Your poor mouth, just look at it ..."

"A sex maniac② ..."

"A sadist③ ..."

"Someone ought to write to the bishop ..."

And then Miss Roach's voice, louder than the others, swearing and screeching like a parakeet④:

"He's damn lucky I didn't kill him, the little bastard! ... I said to him, listen, I said, if ever I happen to want any of my teeth extracted, I'll go to the dentist, not to a goddam vicar ... It isn't as though I'd given him any encouragement either! ..."

"Where is he now, Mildred?"

---

① peristalsis: *Noun* [mass noun] (Physiology) the involuntary constriction and relaxation of the muscles of the intestine or another canal, creating wave-like movements which push the contents of the canal forward(生理学)蠕动

② maniac: (Psychiatry, archaic) a person suffering from mania(精神病学方面的古旧用法)躁狂者;躁狂症患者

③ sadist: *Noun* a person who gets pleasure, sometimes sexual, by being cruel to or hurting another person(性)施虐狂者(e.g. He acted a sadist in that TV play. 他在那电视剧中演一个施虐狂。)

④ parakeet or parakeet: *Noun* a small parrot with predominantly green plumage and a long tail 长尾小鹦鹉;鹦鹉;鹦哥

"God knows. In the bloody summer-house, I suppose."

"Hey girls, let's go and root him out!"

Oh dear, oh dear. Looking back on it now, some three weeks later, I don't know how I ever came through the nightmare of that awful afternoon without taking leave of my senses①.

A gang of witches like that is a very dangerous thing to fool around with, and had they managed to catch me in the summer-house right then and there when their blood was up, they would as likely as not have torn me limb from limb on the spot.

Either that, or I should have been frog-marched down to the police station with Lady Birdwell and Miss Roach leading the procession through the main street of the village.

But of course they didn't catch me.

They didn't catch me then, and they haven't caught me yet, and if my luck continues to hold, I think I've got a fair chance of evading them altogether or anyway for a few months, until they forget about the whole affair.

As you might guess, I am having to keep entirely to myself and to take no part in public affairs or social life. I find that writing is a most salutary② occupation at a time like this, and I spend many hours each day playing with sentences. I regard each sentence as a little wheel, and my ambition lately has been to gather several hundred of them together at once and to fit them all end to end, with the cogs interlocking, like gears, but each wheel a different size, each turning at a different speed.

---

① take leave of one's senses: (in hyperbolic use) go mad(夸张用法)发疯

② salutary: *Adjective* (especially with reference to something unwelcome or unpleasant) producing good effects; beneficial(尤指不受欢迎的或使人不愉快的事)有益的;有利的(e.g. It failed to draw salutary lessons from Britain's loss of its colonies. 它没能从英国丧失殖民地这件事中吸取有益的教训。)

Now and again I try to put a really big one right next to a very small one in such a way that the big one, turning slowly, will make the small one spin so fast that it hums. Very tricky, that.

I also sing madrigals in the evenings, but I miss my own harpsichord① terribly.

All the same, this isn't such a bad place, and I have made myself as comfortable as I possibly can. It is a small chamber situated in what is almost certainly the primary section of the duodenal② loop, just before it begins to run vertically downward in front of the right kidney. The floor is quite level—indeed it was the first level place I came to during that horrible descent down Miss Roach's throat—and that's the only reason I managed to stop at all. Above me, I can see a pulpy sort of opening that I take to be the pylorus③, where the stomach enters the small intestine (I can still remember some of those diagrams my mother used to show me), and below me, there is a funny little hole in the wall where the pancreatic duct④ enters the lower section of the duodenum.

It is all a trifle bizarre for a man of conservative tastes like myself.

---

① harpsichord: *Noun* a keyboard instrument with horizontal strings which run perpendicular to the keyboard in a long tapering case, and are plucked by points of quill, leather, or plastic operated by depressing the keys. It is used chiefly in European classical music of the 16th to 18th centuries 羽管键琴;拨弦古钢琴

② duodenal: *Adjective* of or pertaining to the duodenum 十二指肠的

duodenum: *Noun* (Anatomy) the first part of the small intestine immediately beyond the stomach, leading to the jejunum(解剖学)十二指肠

③ pylorus: *Noun* (Anatomy) the opening from the stomach into the duodenum(解剖学)幽门(胃的远端开口,外包强大的环肌,胃内容经此开口排入十二指肠)

④ pancreatic duct or ductus pancreaticus (in Latin): the excretory duct of the pancreas, by which pancreatic juice is secreted into the duodenum 胰管

Personally I prefer oak furniture and parquet① flooring. But there is anyway one thing here that pleases me greatly, and that is the walls. They are lovely and soft, like a sort of padding, and the advantage of this is that I can bounce up against them as much as I wish without hurting myself.

There are several other people about, which is rather surprising, but thank God they are every one of them males. For some reason or other, they all wear white coats, and they bustle② around pretending to be very busy and important. In actual fact, they are an uncommonly ignorant bunch of fellows. They don't even seem to realize where they are. I try to tell them, but they refuse to listen. Sometimes I get so angry and frustrated with them that I lose my temper and start to shout; and then a sly mistrustful look comes over the faces and they begin backing slowly away, and saying, "Now then. Take it easy. Take it easy, Vicar, there's a good boy. Take it easy."

What sort of talk is that?

But there is one oldish man—he comes in to see me every morning after breakfast—who appears to live slightly closer to reality than the others. He is civil and dignified, and I imagine he is lonely because he likes nothing better than to sit quietly in my room and listen to me talk. The only trouble is that whenever we get on to the subject of our whereabouts, he starts telling me that he's going to help me to escape. He said it again this morning, and we had quite an argument about it.

"But can't you see," I said patiently, "I don't want to escape."

---

① parquet: *Noun* (also as "parquet flooring") [mass noun] flooring composed of wooden blocks arranged in a geometric pattern 镶木地板;拼花木地板

② bustle: *Verb* [no obj., with adverbial of direction] move in an energetic or noisy manner 匆匆忙忙地走;奔忙(e.g. People clutching clipboards bustled about. 手拿笔记板的人四处奔忙。)

"My dear Vicar, why ever not?"

"I keep telling you—because they're all searching for me outside."

"Who?"

"Miss Elphinstone and Miss Roach and Miss Prattley and all the rest of them."

"What nonsense."

"Oh yes they are! And I imagine they're after you as well, but you won't admit it."

"No, my friend, they are not after me."

"Then may I ask precisely what you are doing down here?"

A bit of a stumper① for him, that one. I could see he didn't know how to answer it.

"I'll bet you were fooling around with Miss Roach and got yourself swallowed up just the same as I did. I'll bet that's exactly what happened, only you're ashamed to admit it."

He looked suddenly so wan② and defeated when I said this that I felt sorry for him.

"Would you like me to sing you a song?" I asked.

But he got up without answering and went quietly out into the corridor.

"Cheer up," I called after him. "Don't be depressed. There is

---

① stumper: *Noun* (informal) a puzzling question(非正式)疑难问题

② wan: *Adjective* (of a person's complexion or appearance) pale and giving the impression of illness or exhaustion(人的脸色或外表)苍白的;病态的;疲倦的(e.g. She was looking wan and bleary-eyed. 她看上去脸色苍白,睡眼惺忪。)

always some balm① in Gilead②."

(The end)

三、翻译探索

本篇小说的翻译涉及多方面的知识——宗教、音乐、解剖学等,特别涉及了人体解剖学方面的诸多词汇,翻译中做到精确的把握并非易事。另外,这篇小说中意识的流动性很强,角度的切换也很频繁,翻译中也要注意这方面的问题。

怪异乔治(下部)

(接上)

我先把公的和母的分开,分放到两只笼子里,隔离了整整三周的时间。这样,老鼠就很好色了,而且任何一个动物学家都会对你说,这段时间是相当长久的一段分离时间。凭我的主观臆测,我敢说,强迫老鼠禁欲一周,大约等于强迫人禁欲一年,尤其像埃尔芬斯通小姐或者普拉特力小姐之类的人。所以嘛,对于实际场景的再现,我做得

---

① balm: *Noun* a tree which yields a fragrant resinous substance, especially one used in medicine(尤指产药用香树脂的)香脂树

② Gilead: *Noun* a mountainous region of ancient Palestine east of the Jordan River in what is now northwest Jordan 基列(古代巴勒斯坦的一个山区,位于约旦河东岸,也就是今天约旦的西北部。)

Gilead is a fictitious place in the old testament where there is no suffering 基列是《圣经》"旧约"篇中一个虚构的地方,那里没有任何痛苦的东西存在。

注:人们有时候会带有讽刺意味地引用《圣经》里的一句话:Is there no balm in Gilead? Is there no physician there? 翻译过来就是:难道基列没有止痛药?难道那里没有医生吗?据说,基列是死海边的一片山区,生长着许多药用植物。

十分出色。

三周时间结束的时候，我找来一只大盒子，盒子中间用一道小栅栏隔开，把公老鼠放到栅栏的一侧，母老鼠放到栅栏的另一侧。栅栏其实就是三股裸露的电线，上下相距两厘米半多一点，但是电线通上了强大的电流。

为了让实验过程更接近现实，我给每一只母鼠都起了名字。个头最大的一只，也是胡须最长的那只，是埃尔芬斯通小姐；尾巴短粗的那只是普拉特力小姐；最小的那只是昂温小姐，就不一一列举了。所有的六只公鼠都代表我。

现在，我抽出一把椅子一屁股坐下来，观看实验结果。

所有的老鼠都生性多疑。刚开始把它们一起放进盒子的时候，尽管中间只隔着电线，但是双方都不动地方。公鼠透过栅栏使劲盯着母鼠看，母鼠也盯着公鼠看，等着他们走上前。我看得出，由于渴望和冲动，双方都绷紧了神经：胡须抖动着，鼻子抽动着，有一只老鼠的长尾巴偶尔还抽打到盒壁上。

过了一会儿，第一只公鼠脱离了组织，肚子紧贴着盒子底部，小心翼翼地向栅栏爬去。他碰到电线，一下子就给电死了。余下的十一只老鼠僵住了，一动不动。

紧接着，有九分半的时间，双方都按兵不动。但是，我注意到，尽管所有的公鼠都盯着死去的同伴看，所有母鼠的眼睛却从没离开过公鼠。

接下来，短尾巴的普拉特力小姐再也忍受不住了。她一跳一跳地过来，碰到电线，倒地身亡。

公鼠都把肚子贴近盒底，盯着栅栏边两个同类的尸体，若有所思。母鼠也似乎都震惊不已。又是一阵等待，双方都按兵不动。

现在，昂温小姐开始耐不住性子了。听得见她喷鼻子的声音，也看得见她抽动着她那只粉红色的、好动的鼻头，并从一边歪向另一边。突然间，她快速地上下拉动自己的身体，好像是在做俯卧撑。她瞥了一眼剩下的四个同伴，把尾巴高高地举到空中，那样子不亚于在说："我去了，姐妹们。"随即，纵身一跃，敏捷地扑向电线，头穿过了栅栏,但还是被电死了。

十六分钟过后,福斯特小姐第一个开始动弹了。现实中的福斯特小姐是村子里的一位妇女,她饲养了很多猫。最近,她大胆放肆得很,竟在自家房前的海伊大街上竖起一个大大的牌子,上书“福斯特养猫场”。由于长时间与猫打交道,她身上似乎沾染了猫身上所有的令人厌恶的特性。在房间里,无论什么时候她靠近我,我都能微弱地嗅到猫身上那股刺鼻的气味,哪怕是她抽的俄罗斯香烟的味道很浓烈。她从来都没有能让我感觉到,她能控制住自己的更加卑劣的本能。因此嘛,现在看着她莽撞起来,要拼命地冲向对面的公鼠,我颇感得意和满足。

下一位是蒙特马利-史密斯小姐。现实中,她是一名个头矮小却意志坚定的妇女。有一段时间,她让我相信,她跟一位主教订了婚。只见她肚皮贴地,要轻轻地爬过最矮的那股电线,也不幸身亡。我必须说的是,我认为,这种行为恰好反映出她在现实中的生活方式。

剩下的那五只公鼠仍然一动不动地待在原地,等待着。

第五只冲刺的母鼠是普拉姆利小姐。她这个人不是很光明正大,一而再、再而三地把写给我的小纸条塞进募捐袋中。就在上一个星期天,上午的布道仪式结束后,我待在教堂边的小礼拜室里数钱,数着数着就在一张折叠起来的一先令钞票里碰到了一张此类的小纸条:“今天布道的时候,你那可怜的嗓子听起来很是沙哑。我拿一瓶樱桃味的止咳药给你治一下吧。”落款是:“最充满挚爱和深情的尤妮斯·普拉姆利。”

普拉姆利小姐从容地靠近电线,用鼻子尖嗅了嗅中间的那股,但是鼻子贴得太近了,导致全身遭到二百四十伏交流电的击打而死。

五只公鼠待在原地,看着这场杀戮。

现在,母鼠一方只剩下埃尔芬斯通小姐了。

在接下来的足足半个小时的时间里,双方剩下的成员都按兵不动。

最终,其中一只公鼠微微动了一下,向前迈出一步。犹豫再三、权衡利弊之后，就又蹲伏在地，不想动弹了。

这一举动一定是大大激怒了埃尔芬斯通小姐，因为就在突然之间，她两眼冒火，向前冲去，纵身一跃，飞向电线。这一跃真是壮观之极，几乎就要飞身而过。但是，一条后腿轻轻擦到了顶部的那股电线，因此她跟其余姐妹一样，也触电身亡。

我自己对自己说，这个实验很简单，但设计得却很不一般。看完这个简单的实验，我简直是无法描述，它给我带来多么大的好处。不费吹灰之力，我就揭示出女性好色淫荡、紧咬不放的本性，真是令人难以置信。这样，跟我一样的男性的罪过就得以澄清，而我自己的良知也得以洗刷清白。弹指一挥间，那些一直令我尴尬困惑、一闪而过的小小罪过，都飞到了窗外。知道自己是清白的之后，心里一下子就万里晴空，整个人也变得力量无穷。

接下来，有那么一会儿时间，我脑袋里产生了这样一个可笑而荒谬的想法，就是把围绕住所花园的黑色铁栅栏通上电，或者，只把大门通上电也就足矣。然后，我就舒舒服服地坐到藏书室的椅子上，透过窗户看着现实中真实的埃尔芬斯通小姐、普拉特力小姐以及昂温小姐接踵而至、扑上前来，最后因为骚扰一个无辜清白的男子而遭受惩罚。

多么愚蠢的想法啊！

我对自己说，现在我必须做的事情就是，在我自己的四周编织出一道看不见、通上电的栅栏。用我个人的道德规范做成纤维丝，栅栏就完完全全使用这种纤维丝制成。敌人接踵而至、纷纷扑向电网时，我就可以端坐栅栏之内，丝毫不受伤害。

那样的话，我的行为就可以开始唐突一点儿，对所有女性说话就可以干脆一点儿，也就可以不冲她们微笑了。她们其中的不管谁上前靠近我，我都可以不用再一步步后退，而是站稳脚跟，对她怒目而视。要是此时她说些挑逗性的话，我就会针锋相对，尖锐地加以反驳了。

接下来的那一天，我就是带着这种情绪去参加伯德韦尔夫人举办的网球聚会的。

我去是去,但并不打球。这位尊贵的女士好心好意邀请我光临,就是要我在六点钟打球结束的时候跟客人一起聚聚。我相信,她的想法是,聚会要是有牧师参加的话,会为之增添某种品味。或许,到时候她会说服我重复一下上一次聚会时,我当场所做的表演:晚饭后,在钢琴前坐了足足一个小时十五分钟,为客人详细讲述无伴奏合唱歌曲几个世纪以来的沿革。

六点钟的时候,我就骑着自行车到达她家大门口,然后沿着长长的家用车道向房子蹬去。现在是六月的第一个星期,车道两旁簇生着一大片、一大片的杜鹃花,有粉色的,有紫色的。当时,我可是今非昔比,感觉无拘无束、无所畏惧。就在刚刚过去的那一天,我用老鼠做了实验,出其不意的进攻是不可能让我惊恐万状的啦。我十分清楚会出现什么状况,我也相应地做了防备。在我的四周,小小的栅栏已经竖立起来。

"哦,晚上好,牧师。"伯德韦尔夫人一边大声问候,一边伸开双臂向我走来。

我站稳脚跟,径直看着她的眼睛。"伯德韦尔怎么样?"我问,"他还在城里忙吗?"

我想象不出,要是谁不曾与她的丈夫谋过面的话,不知道会不会当着她的面称其为"伯德韦尔先生"。我这一问令她一下子僵到那儿,用奇怪的目光看着我,不知道该如何回答。

"我就自己找个座位坐下吧。"我边说,边经过她,走向露台,那儿有九个或十个人,惬意地坐在藤椅上,小口喝着什么。这些人大多是女性,通常聚成一堆,都穿着白色的网球服。我在她们之间大步走过时,我想,在这种场合下我这一身朴素的黑色装束,似乎恰如其分地跟她们形成鲜明的对照。

女士们向我投以微笑,我并没有回敬以微笑,而是冲她们点点头,在一把空椅子上坐下来。

"我想,或许我最好另找个时间把这故事讲完吧,"埃尔芬斯通小姐说,"我相信,牧师不会同意我继续讲下去的。"她咯咯一笑,面带挑逗的神情看着我。我知道,她正等着我出现呢,等着看我那惯有的、略带紧张的笑容，等着听我以惯有的、轻描淡写的口吻，说我如何如何宽宏大量、不会去计较之类的话。但是，我什么都没有做，只是把上嘴唇一端翘起，让其微微卷曲，显示出一副不加理会的样子。这一动作，那天上午我对着镜子练习了好一阵子。然后，我清楚而大声地说道："Mens sana in corpore sano."

"那是什么意思呢？"她大声喊道，"牧师，再说一遍啊。"

"洁净的心灵寓于健康的身体，"我回答，"这是一则治家格言。"

接下来奇怪得很，有相当长的一段时间，大家鸦雀无声。我能看得出，那些女子你看看我、我看看你，紧皱眉头，还不时地摇头。

"牧师的情绪不高啊。"福斯特小姐说道。她就是养猫的那个女士。"我想，牧师需要喝一杯了。"

"谢谢你，"我说，"但，我从不碰酒。这，你是知道的。"

"那么，我就给你拿一杯好喝而凉爽的果粒饮料吧，好不好呢？"

这句话轻柔地飘来，是从我身体的右后方冷不防飘了过来。话语之中带有一种真心关怀的腔调，我忍不住转过身去。

我看见一个具有非凡之美的女士，以前只见过她一次，大概是一个月前吧。她就是罗奇小姐。我记得，她当时给我的印象就是，她这个人不落俗套、与众不同。她温文尔雅、沉默寡言，因此我对她印象特别深刻。事实上，跟她在一起，我感到舒畅、自在。无庸置疑的是，任何情况之下，她都不是那种变着法子要来冒犯我的人。

"我敢肯定，骑了那么长距离，你一定是累坏了。"她当着我的面说道。

我立刻从椅子上扭转身体，仔仔细细地看着她。当然啦，她容貌出众：对于一个女子来说，她肌肉过于强健、肩膀宽阔、手臂有力，而且每条腿都很粗壮，腿肚子凸出。下午打网球时体力的消耗令她脸色变红，还能看到她脸上红色的印记，整个人红光满面、旺盛康健。

"真是十分感谢，罗奇小姐，"我说，"可是，只要是含有酒精，我从不沾边。或许，来一小杯柠檬水吧。"

"牧师长，果粒饮料只含有水果。"

我太喜欢称呼我"牧师长"的这个人啦。这个称呼跟军队沾边，不禁让人想起严明的军纪和军衔的等级。

“果粒饮料吗?”埃尔芬斯通小姐问,“有益无害的。”

“亲爱的小伙子,它只不过是维生素C呀。”福斯特小姐说。

“比冒泡的柠檬水强多了,”伯德韦尔夫人说,“二氧化碳会侵蚀胃黏膜的。”

“我给你弄点来吧,”罗奇小姐边说边冲我微笑。她的笑容充满善意,也很坦率。笑容从嘴角的一侧延伸到另一侧,没有丝毫狡诈和顽皮的意味。

说完,她站起身,向饮料桌走去。我看着她先后切碎一个橘子、一个苹果、一根黄瓜、一粒葡萄,然后把碎粒装入一只玻璃杯,接着拿起一个瓶子,往杯子里倒了大量的液体。我没有戴眼镜,那瓶子的标签没有看清,但我想,我看到了上面标着“吉姆”“蒂姆”“皮姆”,或者类似朗姆酒中“姆”字样的名字。。

“我希望还有足够的剩余,”伯德韦尔夫人大声说,“我那几个贪吃的孩子太喜爱这种饮料啦。”

“多的是呢。”罗奇小姐回应。她把饮料拿到我这儿,放在桌子上。

即使不用亲自品尝,我也很容易理解为什么孩子们喜爱它。杯子里的液体本身呈暗琥珀色,还带有点红色,液体表面的冰块之间漂浮着一大块、一大块切碎的果肉。在冰块和果粒之上,罗奇小姐还放了一根带叶的薄荷枝。我猜测,那薄荷是特意为我放的,为的是中和一下甜度,在整体上为饮料增添一点成熟感。否则的话,就会明显看出来,那饮料是为年轻人准备的。

“牧师长,对你而言,是不是太黏稠了?”

“味道很好,”我边说,边喝下一小口,“相当可口。”

飞快地“咕噜”一声吞下去似乎有点可惜,毕竟,罗奇小姐费了好大的劲儿才弄好这么一杯。但是,这一杯也太凉爽、太提神了,令我无法抗拒。

“再给你弄一杯,好吗?”

我喜欢看她等待的样子——等着我喝完把杯子放到桌子上,而不是直接把杯子从我手里拿走。

“如果我是你,我就不会把薄荷吃掉。”埃尔芬斯通小姐说道。

“我最好再拿一瓶出来,”伯德韦尔夫人大声说,“你会用上的,米尔德里德。”

“那就再拿一瓶吧,”罗奇小姐回答。“我自己就能喝好几杯呢,”她接下来冲我继续说。“况且我想,你该不会说,我会体力不支、虚弱憔悴吧。”

“不会,真的不会的,”我热切地回答。我又一次看着她为我兑饮料了。我注意到,她那只胳膊举起瓶子时,胳膊皮肤下的肌肉如同泛起的涟漪一般,一褶一褶的;从后面看去,她的脖子也不是一般意义上的纤细——不像这些所谓的现代美人的脖子那样瘦瘦的、细细的,而是厚圆的、结实的,沿着脖子两侧各有一条不怎么明显的脊状棱线,也能看到一条条肉筋凸显出来。像这样一个人,其年龄是不容易猜出来的,但我肯定,她不会超过四十八九岁的。

刚刚把第二大杯果粒饮料喝完,我就产生了一种极为奇特的体验:我似乎从椅子上漂浮起来,阵阵温暖的小波浪从脚下成百上千地涌起,冲刷而来,将我越抬越高。我感觉自己就像一粒气泡一样轻轻地漂浮着,周围的一切似乎都不停地上下颠簸着,不停地左右摇晃着。一切都是那么的美妙,我也几乎抗拒不了,意欲引吭高歌。

“感觉开心吗?”罗奇小姐的声音从很远、很远的地方响起,但我转身看去时,却大吃一惊地发现她离我其实是很近、很近。当然,她也是在上下颠簸着。

“棒极了,”我回答,“我感觉简直是棒极了。”

她的脸大大的、粉粉的,现在离我太近了,几乎能看见遍布她脸颊上的那层颜色淡淡的绒毛。太阳照在每一根细小的绒毛上,令它们看起来如金子般闪闪发光。一闪念之间,我冲动起来,想伸出一只手,用手指抚摸她那两只脸颊。说真的,要是她当时也同样要抚摸我的脸颊的话,我丝毫不会拒绝和反对的。

“听着,”她轻柔地说,“我俩到花园里散一小会儿步,看看那里的羽扇豆,怎么样呢?”

“好的,”我回答,“很好的。都听你的。”

伯德韦尔夫人的花园里沿着槌球场的方向,有一座乔治王朝建筑风格的花园凉亭。我记得,接下来发生的事情就是,我坐在凉亭里的一个长靠椅之类的东西上,而罗奇小姐就坐在我的旁边。我仍然上下颠簸着,她也上下颠簸着,因而凉亭也上下颠簸着,但我感觉好极了。我问罗奇小姐,她是否喜欢听我给她唱一首歌。

“可以,但不是现在。”她说着,双臂把我搂住,胸部紧紧挤压着我的胸部,用劲儿很大,压得我的胸部疼痛起来。

“不要这样。”我说,感觉快被融化了。

“感觉更好了,”她一个劲儿地说,“感觉更好了,难道不是吗?”

一个小时之前,不管是罗奇小姐也好,还是任何别的女性也好,要是对我做此类事情的话,我还真不知道会发生什么事情呢。我想,我或许会晕倒,甚至会死掉。但是现在,在这儿,我还是原来的我,实际上却在尽情地享受那两只巨大的、裸露的手臂触碰我时所带来的快感。这真是奇闻中的奇闻啊!我也开始感觉有一种冲动:她投我以桃,我欲报之以李。

我用大拇指和食指夹住了她左耳的耳垂,像做游戏一样,猛地开始拽拉起来。

“淘气小子。”她说。

我开始越来越用劲儿地拽拉,同时还往一起挤压。这下可激发起她的快感,弄得她开始哼哼,如猪一般发出喷鼻的声音。她呼吸起来声音很响,甚至发出“呼噜呼噜”的声音。

“吻我。”她吩咐道。

“什么?”我没听清。

“快呀,吻我。”

就在那一刻,我看见了她的嘴。我看见,她这张大大的嘴,从我头顶上方慢慢往下;一边往下,一边开始张开;越往下,离我越近;离我越近,张开得就越大;越来越近,越张越大。突然之间,我整个胃部在身体里翻腾起来,吓得我浑身僵直。

“不!”我尖叫,“不要!”

我只能对你说，我整个一生中，从来没有看到过比那张嘴更为可怖的东西了。它那样靠近我，我简直是无法忍受。那张嘴要是换做一根赤红、炎热的铁棒，有人再用它捅到我脸上的话，我也不会如此这般被吓得浑身僵直。我发誓，我不会的。她两只强有力的手臂把我缠绕，按住我，让我动弹不得。这张嘴变得越来越大、越来越大，随即一下子罩在我头顶正上方，如同一个大大的、深深的、湿漉漉的洞穴。就一秒钟的功夫，我整个人都进去了。

我整个人都在这张巨嘴里面了。我趴在她整个舌头上，两只脚伸到了她喉咙后部的一个位置上。我本能地知道，我要是不立刻再一次努力把自己拉上来的话，我就会被活活吞下去，就像那只兔宝宝一样。我能感觉到，我的两条腿被某种吸力沿着喉咙往下吸去。于是，我飞速甩出双臂，抓住下门牙，使出吃奶的力气牢牢地抓紧不放。我的头部接近嘴的入口处，眼睛实际上正好能通过两唇间的空隙看出去，看见一小块外面的世界：阳光照射到凉亭抛光的木地板上，那儿有一只巨脚，穿着网球鞋。

我的手指正好能抓紧牙齿的边缘。不管吸力有多大，我仍然设法慢慢把自己往上拽，向有日光的地方爬，但突然间，她的上牙落下，要把我的指关节咬掉。看着它来势凶猛，我别无选择，只有松开。这样，由脚部开始，整个人沿着喉咙滑了回去。我一边往回滑，一边疯狂地抓来抓去，所有东西都是光溜溜、滑溜溜的，一个也抓不住。滑过最后一颗臼齿的时候，我瞥见左侧有一道明亮的金光忽闪一下。接着，就看到头顶上方约七厘米半处挂着一个东西，那一定就是小舌了，像一根粗粗的、红红的钟乳石从喉咙顶部悬垂下来。我用双手一下子抓了过去，但这东西不仅光滑，而且还摇晃，手指抓不住。于是，我继续滑落。

我没有忘记呼喊救命，但我几乎听不见自己的喊叫声，因为喉咙的主人呼吸时引发的风声过于强大，犹如狂风大作、永无停歇。奇怪得很，这种风飘忽不定、难以捉摸、忽冷忽热。估计情况是，吸入空气时，刮冷风，而呼出空气时，刮热风。

我设法弯起胳膊肘钩住了一个尖尖的肉质脊状突起物——我

想,这就是会厌部位吧。在那儿,我悬了一小会儿,与吸力抗争着,同时双脚胡乱踩踏,意欲在喉壁上找到一个立足点。但是,喉咙发出巨大的向下吞力,一下子把我甩开。于是,我继续下滑。

至此,我就再也没有什么东西可抓的啦。我就往下滑啊、滑啊,而且很快,我的双腿悬空,从胃的上部往下悬垂着。我能感觉得到缓慢而有力的蠕动所产生的脉冲力,那股力量扯动我的脚踝部位,将我往下拽,一点儿、一点儿、一点儿……往下拽。

在我头顶上方很远的地方,就在户外,我听到几个女子说话的声音,从遥远的地方传来,含混不清:

"这不是真的……"

"可是,我亲爱的米尔德里德啊,多么糟糕……"

"这小子一定是疯狂地……"

"你那张可怜的嘴啊,只要看它一眼就……"

"真是一个性躁狂……"

"真是一个性虐狂……"

"应该有人给主教写信,就说……"

接下来听到的,是罗奇小姐的声音,比其余人的声音都要大。她说起话来骂骂咧咧的,声音尖而刺耳,就像一只长尾巴的小鹦鹉:

"没要他的命,他真他妈的走运,这个小杂种!……当时我对他说:'听着,'我说,'就算我想拔哪颗牙的话,我会去找一名牙医的,也不会找该死的牧师……'好像当时我也没有暗示性地鼓励他去干什么啊!"

"米尔德里德,他现在在哪儿呢?"

"鬼才知道。我想,在该死的凉亭里吧。"

"嗨,姐妹们,我们一起去把他连根挖出来!"

噢,天呐,老天呐。现在,大约三周过去了,但回想起来,我根本不知道当时是怎么度过那个糟糕的、如同梦魇一般的下午。要是知道是怎么度过的,我不发疯才怪呢。

与那样一伙女巫厮混到一起,是一件很危险的事情。她们当时血脉贲张,要是千方百计到凉亭那儿逮住我的话,极有可能非要当场把我大卸八块不可。

要不当场把我拆卸,这伙人也会让我面朝下,提着我的四肢,走过村子的主大街,把我送到警察局,而伯德韦尔夫人和罗奇小姐会走在前面领队的。

当然,她们当时没有逮住我。

她们当时没有逮住我,现在仍然没有逮住我。要是我继续走运的话,我想我相当有可能完完全全避开她们的追捕。或者,无论如何,避开几个月,等她们忘得一干二净的时候,我再出来。

或许会如你所猜测的那样,我正完完全全与世隔绝,不参与任何的公共事务,也不参与任何的社交活动。在这样一个非常时期内,我发现,写作还算得上是一个极其有好处的职业。于是,我每天花掉数小时的时间玩弄文字。我把每一个句子当作一只小小的轮子,而近期我的目标就是,把成百只这样的轮子同时收集到一起,并把它们首尾排列,其间安装上轮齿,就像齿轮一样,但是,每只轮子大小不一、转速不同。我会不时地把大个头的轮子跟个头很小的轮子紧挨着放到一起。这样的话,转速缓慢的大轮子就会带动小轮子飞快地旋转,转得小轮子发出"嘎吱""嘎吱"的声响。很有意思的。

晚上,我也唱那些没有伴奏的合唱歌曲。我十分想念我自己的那个羽管键琴。

尽管如此,待在这样一个地方不算是件糟糕的事情,我也尽可能设法让自己待得舒适安逸。这是一间小小的腔室,现在几乎可以肯定的是,它位于十二指肠回路体系的初始位置。就在右肾的前面,这个体系开始向下延伸。这里的地面相当平坦。说实话,沿着罗奇小姐的喉咙下滑时,在可怖的下降途中,这里是我停留的第一个平坦的地方。我设法在这里停留下来的唯一原因,就是这里的平坦。头顶之上,我能看见有个多浆的开口,我认为那就是幽门口,胃里的东西经由那里排进小肠(我还能记得母亲过去经常拿给我看的那些示意图)。在我的脚下,胃壁上有一个很有意思的小洞,胰管经由那里通向十二指肠的底部。

对于一个像我这样情趣保守的男子来说,这里的一切都有点儿怪异。就我个人而言,我更喜欢橡木家具和木条镶花地板。但是,无论怎么说,这里有一样东西还是令我身心得到极大的愉悦,那就是周围的墙壁。墙壁既惹人喜爱,又感觉柔软,就像是某种填充材料。其好处就是,我可以在上面尽情弹跳,而不会伤到自己。

除我之外,周围还有好几个人,这倒令我大吃一惊。谢天谢地,好在这几个人都是清一色的男性。不管是出于何种原因,他们几个都穿着白色的外衣,四处奔走,假装出一副忙碌不堪、自命不凡的样子。实际上,他们只不过是一帮愚昧无知的家伙而已。他们似乎并不知道他们身在何处。我尽量告诉他们,他们身处何处,但是,他们拒绝倾听。有的时候,我对他们很生气、很恼火,忍无可忍之下就发了脾气,开始大声喊叫,而他们则个个脸上露出一副狡诈的、多疑的表情,一边开始慢慢后退,一边说:"听着,放轻松些。牧师,放轻松些,你可是一个好人啊。放轻松些。"

那说的算是哪门子话呢?

但是,这里有一位上了年纪的男子,每天早饭后他都过来看我。看起来,只有他活得比其他人更稍微接近点现实。他既有教养,又不失体面。我想象着,他之所以孤独,是因为他一无所好,除了喜欢静静地坐在我的房间、听我讲话之外。唯一棘手的就是,每每涉及我们的处境这一话题时,他总是一味地对我说,他要帮我逃出去。今天早晨,他又说了这样的话。对此,我俩还进行了好一番争辩。

"但是,难道你看不出来吗?"我耐心地说,"我不想逃啊。"

"我亲爱的牧师,为什么不想呢?"

"我不止一次对你说过的——外面,她们一直在搜捕我呢。"

"谁?"

"有埃尔芬斯通小姐,有罗奇小姐,有普拉特力小姐,还有其余很多女的呢。"

"简直是胡说八道。"

"噢,没错,就是她们!而且,我猜想,她们也在追捕你来着,可你就是不肯承认。"

"不,我的朋友,她们没有追捕我。"

“那么,我可以直言不讳地问你,你在这下面干什么呢?”

对他来说有点难——那个问题有点难。我看得出,他不知如何回答。

“我敢打赌,你跟罗奇小姐瞎搞来着,结果跟我一模一样,被活活吞下来。我敢打赌,实际情况就是那样,只是你羞愧难当、不肯张扬。”

听我说完后,突然之间,他看起来极其苍白、低头垂脸,我也感到歉疚不安。

“我给你唱首歌好吗?”我问。

但是,他却站起身来,没有作答,一声不响步入走廊。

“振作点儿,”我追着他喊,“不要垂头丧气。啥病都能治好,总能找到好药的。”

(终结)

参考文献

[1] DAHL R. The wonderful story of Henry Sugar and Six More [M]. London: Penguin Books Ltd., 2002.

[2] DAHL R. The best of Roald Dahl [M]. London: Penguin Books Ltd., 2006.

[3] DAHL R. The collected short stories of Roald Dahl [M]. London: Penguin Books Ltd., 1992.

[4] 陈钰. 畸形精神世界的工笔画家——谈罗尔德·达尔的小说创作特色[J]. 外国文学研究, 1985(4): 66-69.

[5] 商务印书馆辞书研究中心. 新华成语词典[M]. 北京: 商务印书馆, 2002.

[6] 新华社译名室. 世界人名翻译大辞典[M]. 北京: 中国对外翻译出版公司, 2007

[7] 周定国. 世界地名翻译大辞典[M]. 北京: 中国出版集团,中国对外翻译出版公司, 2008.

后　记

我们对罗尔德·达尔"非儿童类"短篇故事(小说)进行研究和翻译已经持续了四个年头了。其间,因教学和其他科研的缘由,有所间断,但多数时间是在研读和翻译达尔的这部分短篇小说中度过的。所研读、翻译的达尔这部分短篇作品共计六十篇。

在研究和翻译罗尔德·达尔这部分作品过程中,历尽了艰辛,特别是在翻译过程中,不时会遇到这样或那样的"坎坷"。达尔在写作过程中,时常会"卖弄"自己所掌握的某些专业方面的知识,如葡萄酒、收藏、音乐、医学等,这就逼着译者硬着头皮去熟悉相应的知识。另外,达尔还偶尔会"显摆"一下自己英语之外的词汇,如法语、拉丁语等,这对于译者来说,未免有些"捉襟见肘"了——有的词,任凭怎么查也不得结果。达尔原文中的某一段有时会罗列出若干的专有名词,本着一丝不苟的研究态度,翻译过程中译者对它们均一一查证——哪怕对其中某些表达已经相当熟悉了。对于这样的"坎坷",下笔前会来回踱步、反复思量、仔细斟酌,正如鲁迅先生在译完《死魂灵》谈到翻译时所言:"我向来总以为翻译比创作容易,因为至少是无须构想。但到真的一译,就会遇着难关,譬如一个名词或动词,写不出,创作时候可以回避,翻译上却不成,也还得想,一直弄到头昏眼花,好像在脑子里面摸一个急于要开箱子的钥匙,却没有。"(鲁迅《"题未定"草·且介亭杂文二集》)

在研究和翻译罗尔德·达尔的这部分作品过程中,还会遇到语言及文化差异方面的"绊脚石",处理起来颇费脑筋,正如严复在谈

《天演论》翻译的《译例言》中所言:“新理踵出,名目纷繁,索之中文,渺不可得,即有牵合,终嫌参差,译者遇此,独有自具衡量,即义定名。”另外,在翻译中对于查询无果的地方,也得认真加以思考,甚至经过了很长时间才“创造性”地下笔定论,可谓“一名之立,旬月踟蹰。我罪我知,是存明哲”(严复《译例言》)。由此可见,译事之难,不亚于李太白笔下的“蜀道之难,难于上青天”了!

幸运的是,在对罗尔德·达尔这些“非儿童类”短篇小说进行研究和翻译过程中,我们得到了许多朋友和同事热情的帮助和有力的支持,感激之情无以言表。

对罗尔德·达尔短篇小说的研究和翻译源于英国朋友马礼(他的英文原名叫“Jonathan Rackham”,时任渤海大学外籍英语教师)2009 年赠送给著者的一本书,书名叫《罗尔德·达尔小说精品集》(*The Best of Roald Dahl*)。在阅读这本书的过程中,得到了启发,萌生了要研究并翻译作家罗尔德·达尔“非儿童类”短篇小说的念头。我们于 2010 年 9 月开始动笔,从此一发而不可收。在对原文理解过程中所遇到的难题,得到了马礼耐心而细致的解答,甚至在他回到英国后,还继续通过电子邮件、越洋电话等方式给予我们热情的解答。在此,衷心感谢好友兼同行的马礼,感谢他的热情帮助!

译文从初稿到成稿,虽经数次校正和修改,仍然存在不少问题。此时,我们的学长兼兄长又兼同事和朋友的刘恩东先生及时伸出了援助之手,对最终的成稿在“忠实”的基础上进行了“通顺”方面的梳理。刘恩东先生虽身为渤海大学英语教师,但是,其汉语功力不可小觑,令吾等外语研究者难以望其项背,特别是他古汉语的功力,甚至超出很多古汉语的专业研究者。有了我们兄长的梳理和理顺,毛坯一样的成稿方焕发出光彩。兄长对书稿的修改,虽然有时只是增添一个字,或者是删除一个词,但却救译文于“水火”之中。可以说,没有兄长对书稿的理顺,名为“成稿”的译文只能如同一个咿呀学语、走路不稳的婴儿。在此,衷心感谢刘恩东先生,感谢他辛苦的付出!

研究伊始,一个偶然的机会,我们搜索到克里斯廷·霍华德(Kristine Howard)创建并维护的网站“罗尔德·达尔粉丝网”(*Roald*

Dahl Fans. com),并就罗尔德·达尔有关问题联系过霍华德女士,收到了她及时的回复。整个研究也因霍华德女士的网站而受益匪浅。在此,衷心感谢克里斯廷·霍华德女士,感谢她在网站里所提供的全面而翔实的资料!

同时,我们十分感谢渤海大学外国语学院领导和同事给予我们热情的帮助和有力的支持!十分感谢哈尔滨工业大学出版社田新华主任在出版方面提供的有力支持!同时感谢为本书的出版而忙碌的所有编辑人员和工作人员!同时,我们十分感谢为本研究提供帮助的所有朋友和同仁!

当然,由于时间和能力所限,错误在所难免,还望读者赐教、斧正,并多提宝贵意见。

对罗尔德·达尔"非儿童类"短篇故事(小说)研究、翻译所成之书,难免泛泛而论,甚至是流于平庸,但是,我们本着扎实做学问、做学问如做人的思想,从起点出发,稳扎稳打,力戒浮躁之风,勿求好高骛远。

记得《礼记·中庸》里有言:"君子之道,譬如行远,必自迩,譬如登高,必自卑。"愿以此语共勉。

陈　洁　王永胜

2015年深秋于渤海大学

请你来试一试.

$i^2=-1,(-i)^2=-1$,则 $x^2=-1$ 的根是____________.

$(2i)^2=-4,(-2i)^2=-4$,则 $x^2=-4$ 的根是____________.

结论　当 $a<0$ 时,$x^2=a$ 的根是____________;

当 $\Delta=b^2-4ac<0$ 时,你能给 $ax^2+bx+c=0(a\neq0,a,b,c\in\mathbf{R})$ 配方吗?

$$\left(x+\frac{b}{2a}\right)^2=\_\_\_\_\_\_\_\_\_\_.$$

$ax^2+bx+c=0(a\neq0,a,b,c\in\mathbf{R})$ 的根为

$$x_1=\_\_\_\_\_\_\_\_\_\_,\ x_2=\_\_\_\_\_\_\_\_\_\_.$$

任务二

探究实系数的一元二次方程 $ax^2+bx+c=0(a\neq0)$ 在复数集中解的情况,并填入表 9-3 中.

表 9-3　一元二次方程的解

判别式 $\Delta=b^2-4ac$	$\Delta>0$	$\Delta=0$	$\Delta<0$
一元二次方程 $ax^2+bx+c=0(a\neq0)$ 的解			

结论　实系数的一元二次方程的根与系数的关系为:

$$x_1+x_2=\_\_\_\_\_\_\_\_\_\_,x_1\cdot x_2=\_\_\_\_\_\_\_\_\_\_.$$

【典例解析】

例 1　已知复数 ω 满足 $\omega-4=(3-2\omega)i$.

(1) 求复数 ω;

(2) 若 ω 是实系数方程 $x^2+mx+n=0$ 的一个根,求 $m+n$.

解　(1) 设 $\omega=a+bi$,代入 $\omega-4=(3-2\omega)i$,整理,得

$$(a-4)+bi=3i-2i(a+bi)=2b+(3-2a)i,$$

根据复数相等的概念,有

$$a-4=2b,b=3-2a,$$

解得

$$a=2,b=-1,$$

所以
$$\omega=2-\mathrm{i}.$$

(2) 若 ω 是实系数方程 $x^2+mx+n=0$ 的一个根，则方程的另外一个根为 $2+\mathrm{i}$，根据一元二次方程根与系数的关系，得

$$m=-[(2-\mathrm{i})+(2+\mathrm{i})]=-4,$$

$$n=(2-\mathrm{i})(2+\mathrm{i})=5,$$

故
$$m+n=1.$$

例 2 若 $1+\sqrt{2}\mathrm{i}$ 是关于 x 的实系数方程 $x^2+bx+c=0$ 的一个复数根，求 b,c 的值.

解 因为 $1+\sqrt{2}\mathrm{i}$ 是关于 x 的实系数方程 $x^2+bx+c=0$ 的一个复数根，所以实系数方程 $x^2+bx+c=0$ 的另一个复数根是 $1-\sqrt{2}\mathrm{i}$，则

$$-b=(1+\sqrt{2}\mathrm{i})+(1-\sqrt{2}\mathrm{i})=2,$$

$$c=(1+\sqrt{2}\mathrm{i})(1-\sqrt{2}\mathrm{i})=1-(\sqrt{2}\mathrm{i})^2=1+2=3.$$

解得
$$b=-2,c=3.$$

备注 实系数方程若有虚根，则虚根成对出现且互为共轭复数，根与系数之间的关系在复数范围同样成立.

【课后练习】

1. 若关于 x 的实系数一元二次方程的两个根分别是 $x_1=1+\sqrt{3}\mathrm{i}$，$x_2=1-\sqrt{3}\mathrm{i}$，则这个一元二次方程可以是 ( )

A. $x^2-2x+2=0$　　B. $x^2-2x+4=0$

C. $x^2+3x+2=0$　　D. $x^2+2x+4=0$

2. 一元二次方程 $x^2-2x+5=0$ ( )

A. 有两个不相等的实数根　　B. 有一个实数根、一个虚数根

C. 有一对共轭虚根　　D. 有两个相等的实数根

3. 若 $1-2\mathrm{i}$ 是关于 x 的方程 $x^2-ax+b=0(a,b\in\mathbf{R})$ 的一个根，则 $|a+b\mathrm{i}|=$ ( )

A. 29　　B. $\sqrt{29}$

C. $\sqrt{21}$　　D. 21

4. 设 x_1, x_2 是方程 $4x^2-2x+3=0$ 的两个根，则 $x_1 \cdot x_2=$__________.

5. 在复数范围内分解因式：$x^2+4=$____________.

6. 已知实系数方程 $x^2+bx+c=0$ 的一个根是 $3-4\mathrm{i}$，求另一个根，并求 b, c 的值.

7. 能否将 6 分解成两数之和，使它们的积为 8?

8. 设 x_1, x_2 是方程 $x^2+2x+2=0$ 的两个根，求 $x_1^2+x_2^2$.

【数学文化】

方程发展史

人类对一元二次方程的研究经历了漫长的岁月. 早在公元前 2 000 年左右,居住在底格里斯河和幼发拉底河的古巴比伦人已经能解一些一元二次方程. 而在中国,《九章算术》"勾股"章中就有一题:"今有户高多于广六尺八寸,两隅相去适一丈,问户高、广各几何?"之后的古希腊数学家欧几里得、古希腊数学家丢番图、赵爽、张遂对一元二次方程都做出了很大贡献.

11 世纪,阿拉伯数学家阿尔-卡尔希第一次解出了二次方程的根. 阿拉伯数学家卡牙姆完成了一部系统研究三次方程的书《代数学》.

1545 年,意大利科学家卡尔达诺在《大法》中发表了求三次方程一般代数解的公式.

1572 年,意大利数学家邦贝利出版《代数学》,其中引入了虚数,完全解决了三次方程的代数解问题.

1591 年左右,德国数学家韦达在《美妙的代数》中首次使用字母表示数字系数的一般符号,推进了代数问题的一般讨论.

1669 年,英国科学家牛顿、雷夫逊发明解非线性方程的牛顿-雷夫逊方法.

1767 年,法国数学家拉格朗日发现分离代数方程实根的方法和求其近似值的方法. 在 1770—1771 年期间,拉格朗日把置换群用于代数方程式求解,这是群论的开始.

1779 年,法国数学家贝祖在论文《代数方程的一般理论》中,最早证明了齐次线性方程组有非零解的条件是系数行列式等于零. 他用消元法将只含一个未知数的 n 次方程问题与解联立方程组问题联系起来,提供了某些 n 次方程的解法. 他还用消元法解次数高于 1 的两个二元方程,并证明了关于方程次数的贝祖定理.

1799 年,德国数学家高斯证明了代数学的一个基本定理:实系数代数方程必有根.

【拓展应用】

复数是数学中的一个重要概念，它不仅在数学中有广泛的应用，同时也在物理学、工程学等领域中有着重要的实际意义.

一、复数在电路分析中的应用

1. 复数阻抗

在电路分析中，电感和电容都会产生相位差，而复数可以很好地描述相位差的存在. 因此，在电路分析中，我们常常使用复数阻抗来描述电路元件的特性.

2. 交流电源

交流电源是我们日常生活中经常使用的一种电源. 由于交流信号具有频率和振幅两个参数，因此需要使用复数来描述其特性.

二、复数在物理学中的应用

1. 波动方程

波动方程是物理学中非常重要的一个方程式. 在波动方程中，时间和空间都是变量，并且波函数也具有幅度和相位两个参数. 因此，在求解波动方程时需要使用复数来描述波函数.

2. 量子力学

量子力学是一门研究微观世界的科学，其中涉及很多复数运算. 例如，薛定谔方程就是一个复数方程式，它描述了粒子的波函数随时间演化的规律.

三、复数在工程学中的应用

1. 控制系统

控制系统是工程学中非常重要的一个领域. 在控制系统中，我们需要对信号进行处理和分析，并且需要使用复数来描述信号的特性. 例如，在控制系统中我们常常使用拉普拉斯变换和傅里叶变换来分析信号.

2. 通讯系统

通讯系统是工程学中非常重要的一个领域. 在通讯系统中，我们需要对信号进行处理和传输，并且需要使用复数来描述信号的特性. 例如，在调制过程中我们需要将模拟信号转换为数字信号,并且需要使用傅里叶变换将数字信号转换为频域信号.

复数在物理学和工程学等领域都有着广泛的应用和实际意义. 通过对复数理论的深入研究和应用,不仅可以提高我们对这些领域的理解和认识,同时也可以为我们解决实际问题提供更加有效的方法和手段.

自我检测

一、选择题

1. 下列命题中是真命题的为　（　　）

A. $-i$ 是负数　B. $3+i$ 是无理数

C. $\frac{i}{5}$是分数　D. 6 是复数

2. $(1-i)i=$　（　　）

A. $-1-i$　B. $1-i$　C. $-1+i$　D. $1+i$

3. 已知复数 $z=2-3i$,则 z 的模为　（　　）

A. $\sqrt{13}$　B. 2　C. 3　D. 1

4. 复平面内表示 $4+5i$ 与 $4-5i$ 的点的位置关系为　（　　）

A. 关于实轴对称　B. 关于虚轴对称

C. 关于原点对称　D. 重合

5. 已知复数 $a^2+a-6+(a^2-a-2)i(a\in\mathbf{R})$是纯虚数,则 $a=$　（　　）

A. -1　B. 2　C. -3　D. 2 或-3

6. 若$(x-2)+yi(x,y\in\mathbf{R})$和 $3-i$ 是共轭复数,则　（　　）

A. $x=5$ 且 $y=1$　B. $x=5$ 且 $y=-1$

C. $x=-5$ 且 $y=-1$　D. $x=-5$ 且 $y=1$

7. $(5+\sqrt{3}i)(5-\sqrt{3}i)=$　（　　）

A. -28　B. 28　C. -22　D. 22

8. 复数 $z=-2-3i$ 在复平面内对应的点位于　（　　）

A. 第一象限　B. 第二象限　C. 第三象限　D. 第四象限

9. 方程 $x^2=-9$ 的解为　（　　）

A. ±3　B. $\pm3i$　C. $-3i$　D. -3

10. 已知 $z_1=2-4i$,$z_2=1+i$,则 z_1+z_2在复平面内对应的点位于（　　）

A. 第一象限　B. 第二象限　C. 第三象限　D. 第四象限

11. 已知复数 $z=1+i$,则 $\frac{2}{z}=$ ( )

A. $2i$ B. $-2i$ C. $1+i$ D. $1-i$

12. 复数 $z=1+\sqrt{3}i$ 的三角形式为 ( )

A. $2\left(\cos\frac{\pi}{6}+i\sin\frac{\pi}{6}\right)$ B. $2\left(\cos\frac{\pi}{3}+i\sin\frac{\pi}{3}\right)$

C. $2\left(\cos\frac{2\pi}{3}+i\sin\frac{2\pi}{3}\right)$ D. $2\left[\cos\left(-\frac{\pi}{3}\right)+i\sin\left(-\frac{\pi}{3}\right)\right]$

13. 复数 $5i$ 的辐角为 ( )

A. $30°$ B. $45°$ C. $60°$ D. $90°$

14. 复数 $e^{\frac{\pi}{2}i}$的代数形式为 ( )

A. i B. $-i$ C. 0 D. $1+i$

15. 已知复数 $z=\sqrt{2}\left[\cos\left(-\frac{\pi}{4}\right)+i\sin\left(-\frac{\pi}{4}\right)\right]$,则其代数形式为 ( )

A. $-1+i$ B. $1-i$ C. $-1-i$ D. $1+i$

二、填空题

1. 复数 $3i^2$ 的虚部是________.

2. 复数 $a+(a+2)i$ 是实数,则 $a=$________.

3. 复数 $z=2+2i$ 的模为________,$\arg z=$________.

4. 已知复数 $z=1+\sqrt{3}i$,则 $z^2=$________.

5. 下列各数 $i,-i,1+\sqrt{3}i,(1+\sqrt{3})i,(1+\sqrt{3})^2i,10$,其中是纯虚数的是________.

6. 若等式 $a+3i=-1-bi$ $(a,b\in \mathbf{R})$成立,则 $a=$________,$b=$________.

7. 复数 $z=1+i$ 的三角形式为________.

8. 已知复数 $z=3-4i$,则 $z\cdot\overline{z}=$________.

9. 复数 $z=2(\cos 60°+i\sin 60°)$的代数形式为________.

10. 已知复数 $z=\cos 60°+i\sin 60°$,则 $z^6=$________.

三、解答题

1. 已知复数 $z=(1+i)m+(5-2)m+(6-5i)$,当实数 m 分别取什么值

时，复数 z 是实数、虚数、纯虚数？

2. 求下列等式中实数 a,b 的值.

(1) $\frac{a}{2}+b\mathrm{i}=1-\sqrt{5}\mathrm{i}$；

(2) $a+b\mathrm{i}=2$；

(3) $(a+b)+(b-1)\mathrm{i}=(2a+3b)+(2b+1)\mathrm{i}$.

3. 计算：

(1) $(1-4\mathrm{i})-(2+2\mathrm{i})+\overline{4+3\mathrm{i}}$；　(2) $(3+5\mathrm{i})\div(12-5\mathrm{i})$；

(3) $(2-3\mathrm{i})(3-2\mathrm{i})$；　(4) $(2-\mathrm{i})^2(2+\mathrm{i})^2$.

4. (1) 已知复数 $z=2-\sqrt{3}\mathrm{i}$，求 $z+\overline{z}$，$z-\overline{z}$；

(2) 已知复数 $z_1=2+\mathrm{i}$，$z_2=1+3\mathrm{i}$，求 $\frac{z_1}{z_2}$.

5. 解下列一元二次方程.

(1) $x^2+16=0$；

(2) $x^2-6x+10=0$.

6. 将下列复数的三角形式化为代数形式.

(1) $z_1=2\left(\cos\frac{\pi}{2}+i\sin\frac{\pi}{2}\right)$；

(2) $z_2=4\left[\cos\left(-\frac{\pi}{6}\right)+i\sin\left(-\frac{\pi}{6}\right)\right]$.

7. 计算：

(1) $\sqrt{3}\left(\cos\frac{\pi}{6}+i\sin\frac{\pi}{6}\right)\cdot 4\left(\cos\frac{\pi}{12}+i\sin\frac{\pi}{12}\right)$；

(2) $\dfrac{\sqrt{6}\left(\cos\frac{3\pi}{5}+i\sin\frac{3\pi}{5}\right)}{\sqrt{3}\left[\cos\left(-\frac{4\pi}{5}\right)+i\sin\left(-\frac{4\pi}{5}\right)\right]}\cdot\sqrt{2}\left[\cos\left(-\frac{2\pi}{5}\right)+i\sin\left(-\frac{2\pi}{5}\right)\right]$.

第10章　简单几何体

10.1　三视图

【学习目标】

1. 理解中心投影和平行投影的概念,会画简单图形的正投影.

2. 会画柱、锥、球及其简单组合体的三视图,能根据三视图描述简单几何体的形状.

【重点难点】

重点:画简单几何体的三视图和由三视图描述简单几何体.

难点:三视图中虚实线的处理,棱柱及几何组合体的三视图的绘制.

【微课导学】

扫下面的二维码,学习微课"投影""三视图""简单组合体的三视图".

投影　　三视图　　简单组合体的三视图

【自主学习】

1. 一个立体图形的三视图如图 10-1 所示,则该立体图形是 (　　)

A. 圆柱　　B. 三棱柱

C. 长方体　　D. 四棱锥

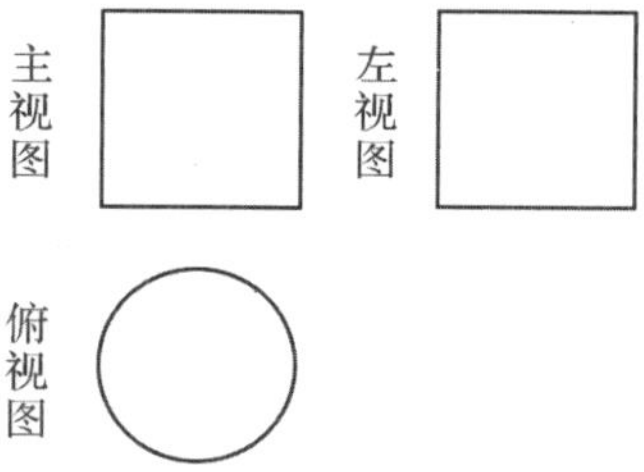

图 10-1

2. 平行投影中的光线是 (　　)

A. 平行的　　B. 聚成一点的

C. 不平行的　　D. 向四面八方发散的

3. 图 10-2 中的三视图所对应的几何体是 (　　)

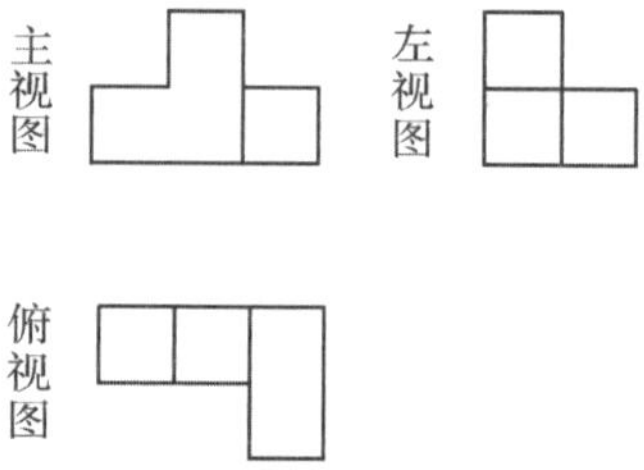

图 10-2

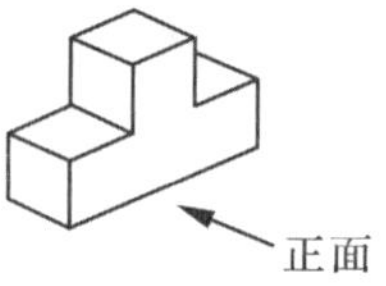

A.

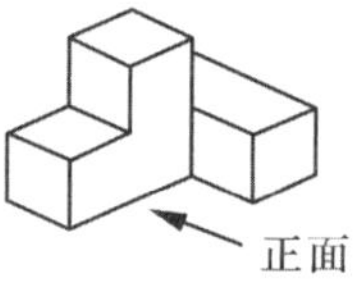

B.

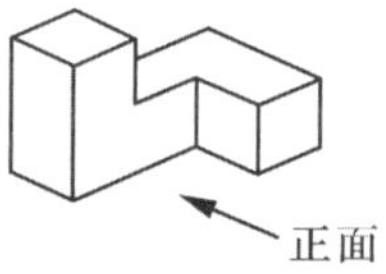

C.

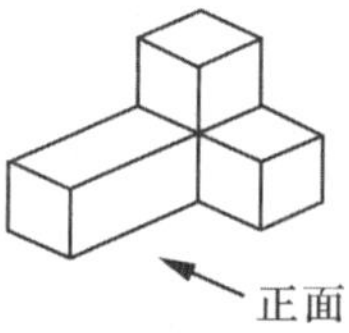

D.

4. ____________、____________、____________合称三视图. 在生活和生产实践中,我们经常要运用三视图来描述物体的大小和形状.

5. 如图 10-3 所示,该物体的正视图是________,左视图是__________,俯视图是__________.

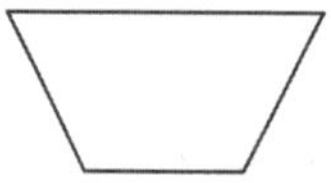

A.

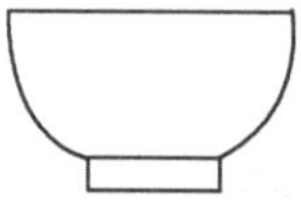

B.

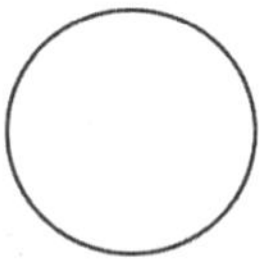

C.

图 10-3

6. 一张桌子上摆放若干碟子,从三个方向上看,三种视图如图 10-4 所示,则这张桌子上的碟子共有__________个.

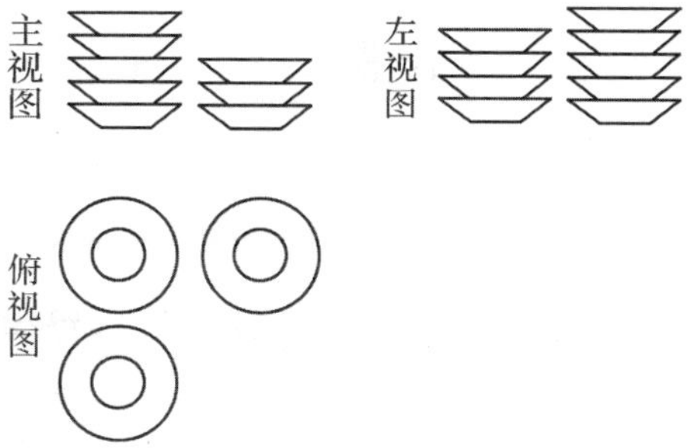

图 10-4

7. 画出如图 10-5 所示的三棱柱、半球和圆锥的三视图.

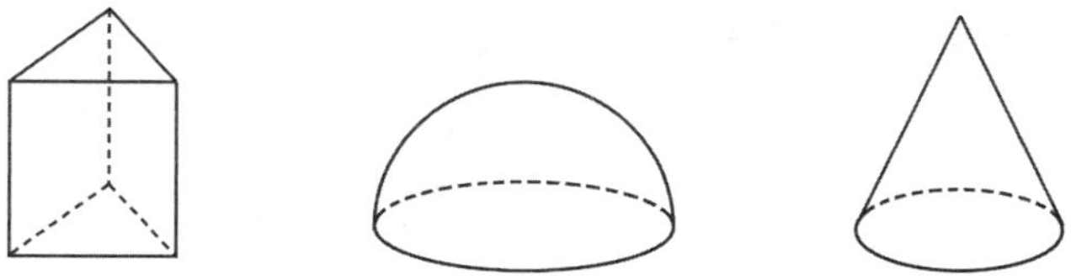

图 10-5

【探究任务】

任务一

材料 1　横看成岭侧成峰，远近高低各不同. 不识庐山真面目，只缘身在此山中. ——宋 · 苏轼《题西林壁》

材料 2　飞来山上千寻塔，闻说鸡鸣见日升，不畏浮云遮望眼，自缘身在最高层. ——宋 · 王安石《登飞来峰》

问题　阅读材料，尝试从数学的角度进行解读.

任务二

阅读材料,回答问题.

材料 运-20(图 10-6)是中国自主研发的新一代大型军用运输机,采用常规布局,悬臂式上单翼,吊挂四台发动机,高 T 型尾翼. 该飞机是中国目前研制的起飞重量最大的飞机(截至 2013 年),估计起飞重量在 200 t 左右,载重量 50 t 左右. 运-20 全面投入研制到首飞成功,历经 5 年.

图 10-6

问题 1 请你指出图 10-7 中的这些图形分别从哪个角度观察得到.

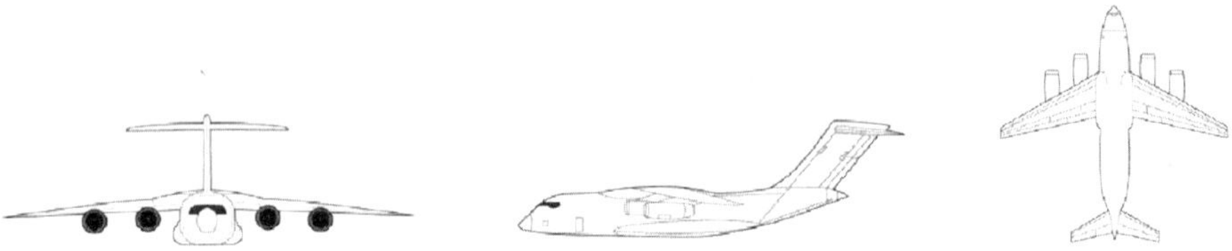

(a) (b) (c)

图 10-7

问题 2 如何从投影的角度来认识三视图?

任务三

小组合作,动手画一画.

问题 1 画出如图 10-8 所示的基本几何体的三视图.

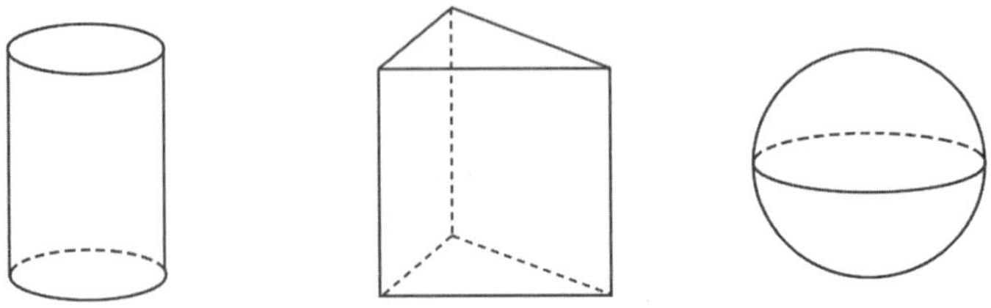

图 10-8

问题 2　组合体按其形成方式通常分为叠加型、切割型. 画出如图 10-9 所示的简单组合体的三视图.

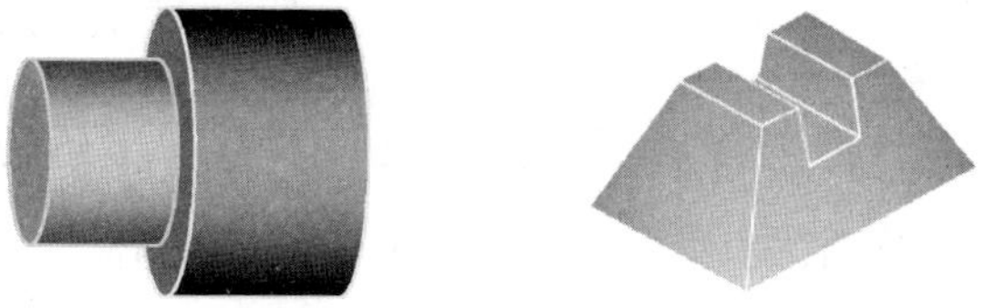

叠加型　　切割型

图 10-9

问题 3　尝试总结简单组合体的三视图的具体画法.

(1) 确定主视图的位置，画出________；

(2) 在主视图正下方画出俯视图，注意与主视图________；

(3) 在主视图正右方画出左视图. 注意与主视图________，与俯视图________.

【典例解析】

例 1　小王同学想利用树影测量校园内的树高. 他在某一时刻测得高为 1.5 m 的小树的影长为 1.2 m. 如图 10-10 所示，当他测量教学楼旁的一棵大树的影长时，因大树靠近教学楼，有一部分影子在墙上. 经测量，地面部分影长为 6.4 m，墙上影长为 1.4 m，那么这棵大树高约为多少？

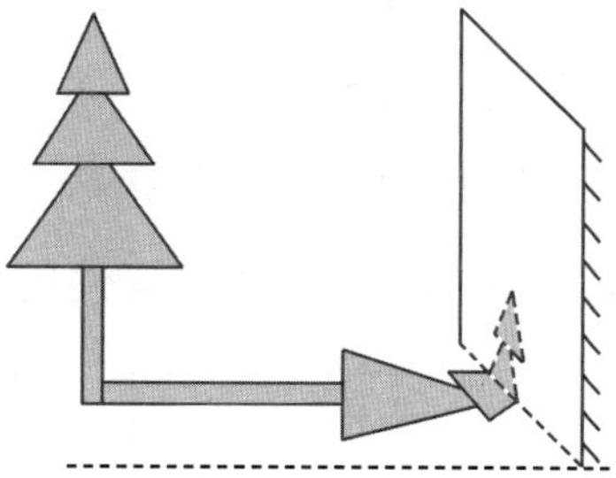

图 10-10

解　设这棵大树高为 x，根据平行投影特点：在同一时刻，不同物体的物高和影长成比例. 可得树高比影长为

$$\frac{1.5}{1.2}=1.25.$$

则有$\frac{6.4}{x-1.4}=\frac{1}{1.25}=0.8$,解得 $x=9.4$ m,故这棵大树高约为 9.4 m.

备注 本题考查平行投影特点:在同一时刻,不同物体的物高和影长成比例.

例 2 如图 10-11 所示是一根钢管的直观图,画出它的三视图.

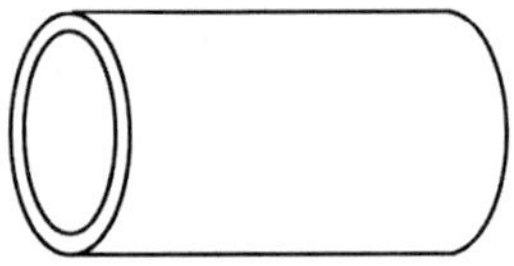

图 10-11

解 图 10-12 是钢管的三视图,其中的虚线表示钢管的内壁.

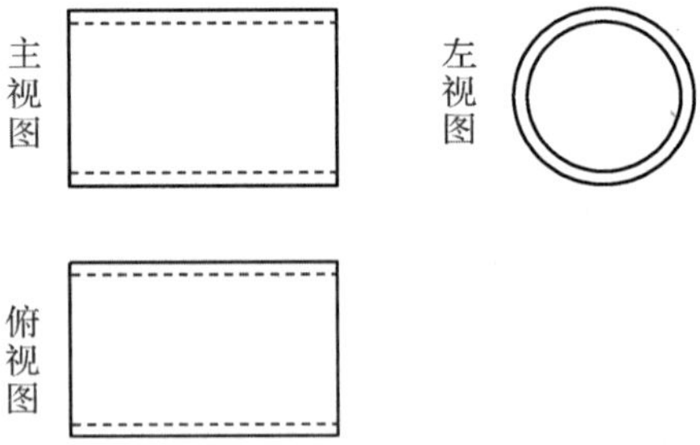

图 10-12

备注 钢管有内外壁,为全面地反映立体图形的形状,画图时规定:看得见部分的轮廓线画成实线;被遮挡而看不见部分的轮廓线画成虚线.

【课后练习】

1. 中国古建筑借助榫卯将木构件连接起来,构件的凸出部分叫榫头,凹进部分叫卯眼,图 10-13 中木构件右边的小长方体是榫头. 若如图 10-13 摆放的木构件与某一带卯眼的木构件咬合成长方体,则咬合时带卯眼的木构件的俯视图可以是 ( )

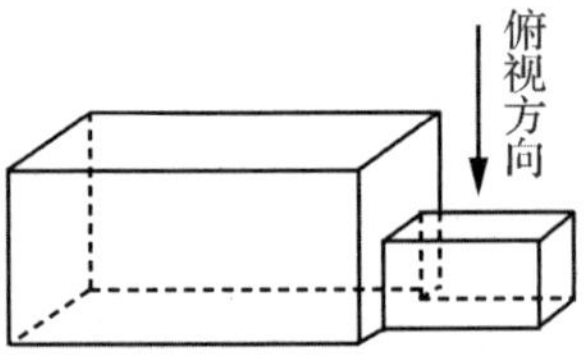

图 10-13

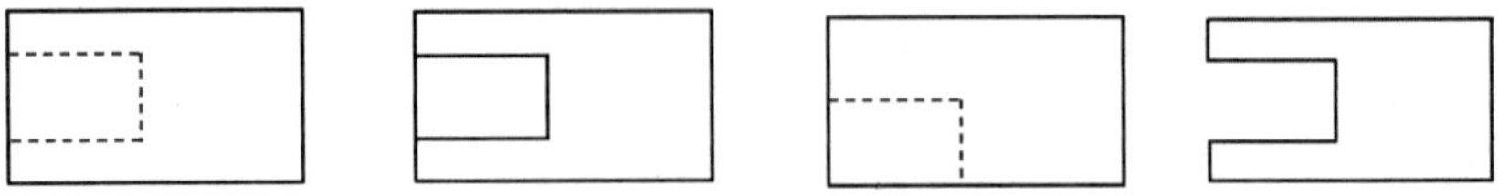

A. B. C. D.

2. 一天，小明的爸爸送给小明一件礼物，小明打开包装后画出了它的主视图和俯视图，如图 10-14 所示. 根据小明画的视图，你猜小明的爸爸送给小明的礼物是　　　　　　　　　　　　　　　　　　　　　　　　(　　)

A. 钢笔　　B. 生日蛋糕　　C. 光盘　　D. 一套衣服

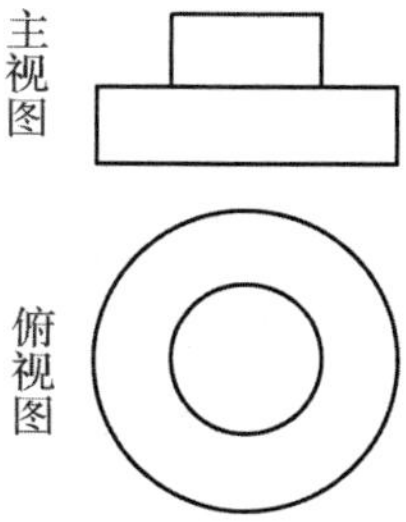

图 10-14

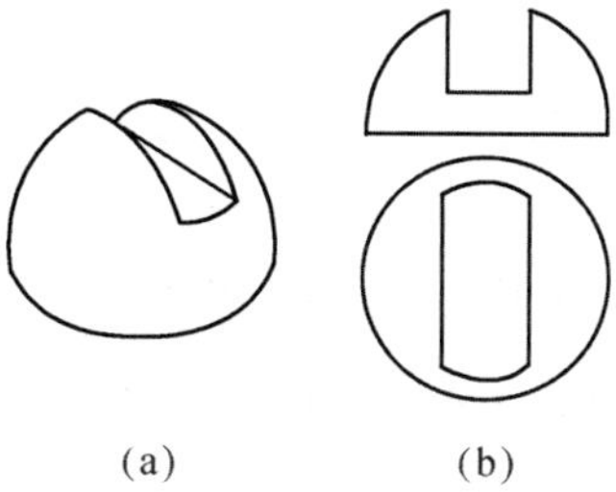

图 10-15

3. 图 10-15(a)是某零件的立体图，其主视图与俯视图如图 10-15(b)所示. 与之对应的左视图是　　　　　　　　　　　　　　　　　　(　　)

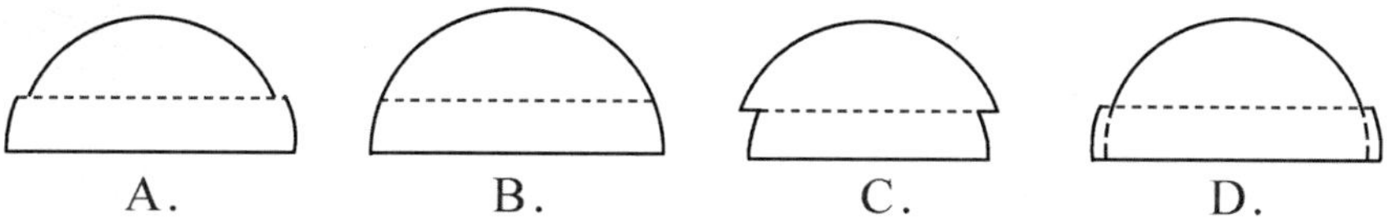

4. 小华拿一个矩形木框在阳光下玩，矩形木框在地面上形成的投影可能是图 10-16 中的____________. (填写序号)

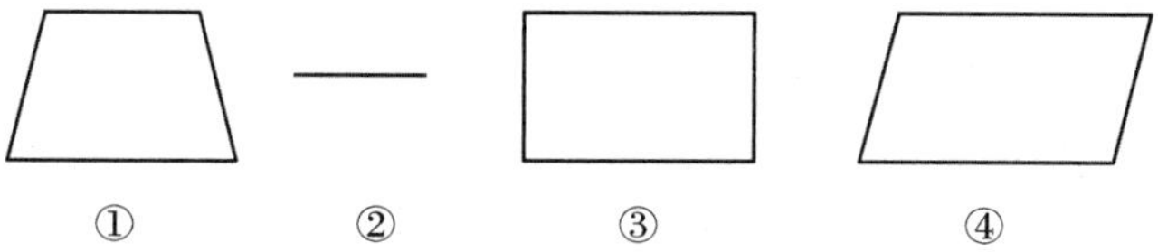

图 10-16

5. 圆桌面(桌面中间有一个直径为 0.4 m 的圆洞)正上方的灯泡(看作一个点)发出的光线照射平行于地面的桌面后，在地面上形成如图 10-17 所示的圆环形阴影. 已知桌面直径为 1.2 m，桌面离地面 1 m，若灯泡离地面 3 m，则地面圆环形阴影的面积是____________m^2.

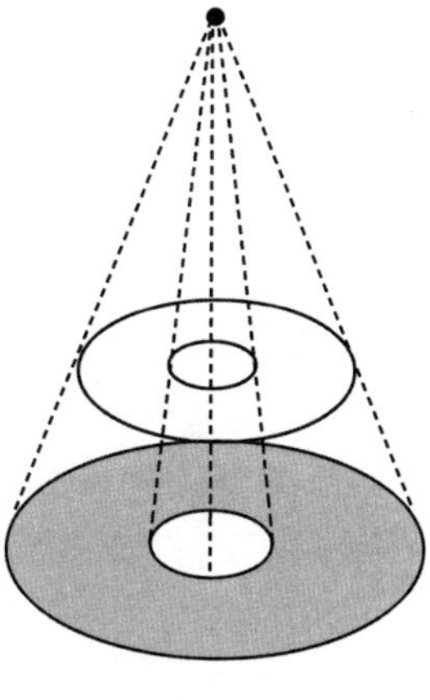

图 10-17

6. 画出如图 10-18 所示的简单组合体的三视图.

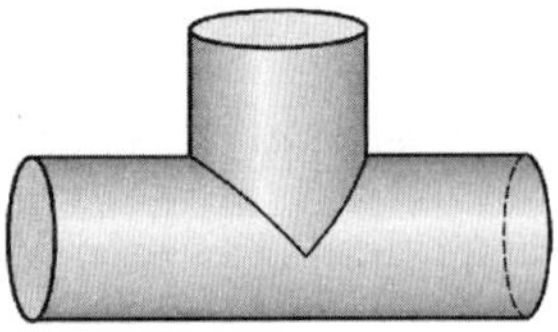

图 10-18

7. 一个高强度六角螺母如图 10-19 所示，底面正六边形的边长为 250 mm，高为 200 mm，内孔直径为 200 mm. 请画出该六角螺帽的三视图.

图 10-19

8. 如图 10-20 所示，某居民小区内甲、乙两幢楼之间的距离 $MN=30$ m，两楼的高都是 20 m，甲楼在乙楼正南，乙楼窗户朝南. 乙楼内一楼住户的窗台离小区地面的距离 $DN=2$ m，窗户高 $CD=1.8$ m. 当正午时刻太阳光线与地面成 30°角时，甲楼的影子是否影响乙楼的一楼住户采光？若影响，挡住该住户窗户多高？若不影响，请说明理由.

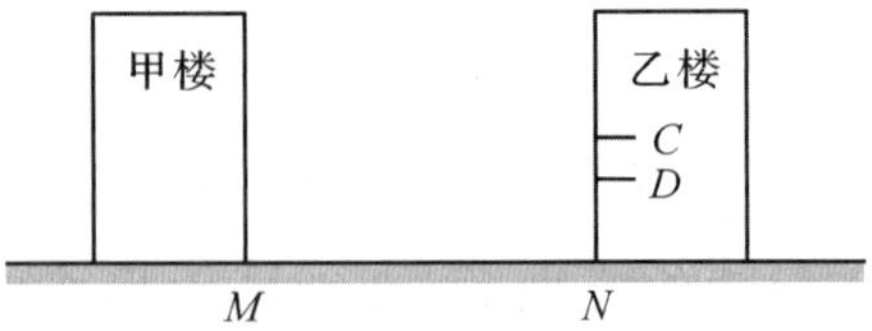

图 10-20

【信息手段】

简单几何体的三视图

案例　绘制点 $A=(2,0,0)$，$B=(2,2,0)$，$C=(0,1,0)$，$D=(0,0,2)$，利用多面体工具绘制多面体 $D\text{-}ABC$，如图 10-21 所示.

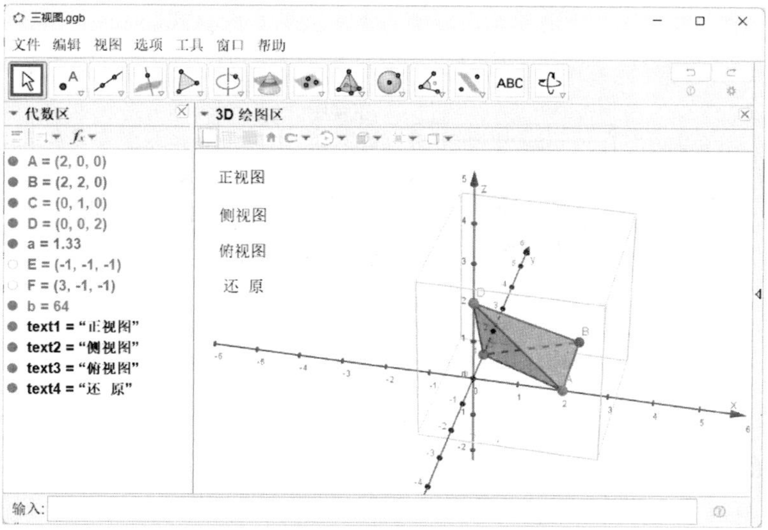

图 10-21

具体作图过程见表 10-1。

表 10-1　绘制多面体过程

步骤	名称	描述	数值
1	点 A	x 轴上的点	$A=(2,0,0)$
2	点 B		$B=(2,2,0)$
3	点 C	y 轴上的点	$C=(0,1,0)$
4	点 D	z 轴上的点	$D=(0,0,2)$
5	棱锥 a	棱锥(D,A,B,C)	$a=1.33$
6	点 E		$E=(-1,-1,-1)$
7	点 F		$F=(3,-1,-1)$
8	正六面体 b	圆周$(F$,距离(E,F),线段(E,F)上的$)$	$b=64$
9	文本 text1	设置视图方向[向量(0,1,0)]	"正视图"
10	文本 text2	设置视图方向[向量(1,0,0)]	"侧视图"
11	文本 text3	设置视图方向[向量(0,0,−1)]	"俯视图"
12	文本 text4	设置视图方向[向量(0,0,−1)]	"还原"

单击“正视图”“侧视图”“俯视图”“还原”,即可得到相应视图(图 10-22).

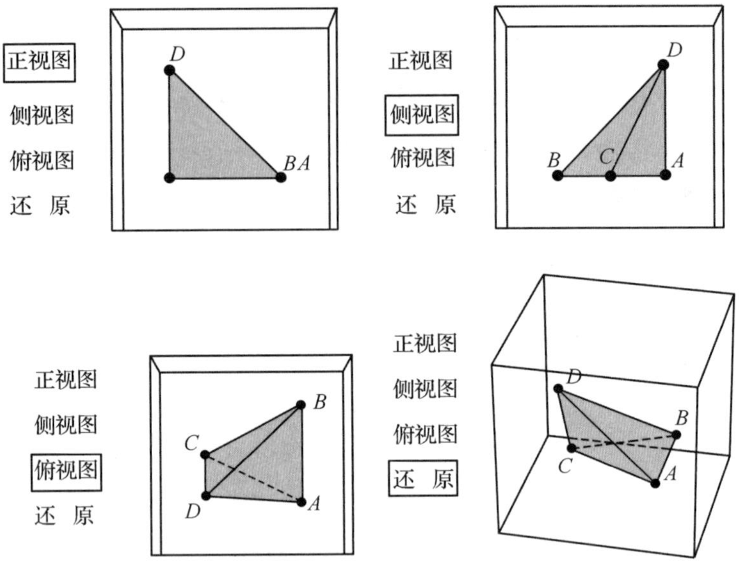

图 10-22

【数学文化】

蒙日(图 10-23),法国数学家、化学家和物理学家. 生于博恩的平民人家. 少年时在家乡一所天主教开设的学校学习,后转学里昂,留校任物理学教师,接着被推荐到梅齐埃尔皇家工程学院学习,后任该校教师,并被巴黎科学院选为通讯研究员,任皇家工程学院“皇家数学和物理学教授”,72 岁在巴黎逝世.

图 10-23

蒙日是 19 世纪著名的几何学家,他创立了画法几何学,推动了空间解析几何学的独立发展,奠定了空间微分几何学的宽厚基础,创立了偏微分方程的特征理论,引导了纯粹几何学在 19 世纪的复兴. 此外,他在物理学、化学、冶金学、机械学方面也取得了卓越的成就,他的《大炮制造工艺》在机械制造界影响颇大. 主要著作有:《曲面的解析式》(1755)、《静力学引论》(1788)、《画法几何学》(1798)、《代数在几何学中的应用》(1802)、《分析在几何学上的应用》(1805)等.

蒙日首次从理论上对多面正投影法加以系统地阐述,因此这种方法也称为“蒙日法”，但这种绘图法并非蒙日首创．欧洲文艺复兴时期的 1525 年，德国的丢勒已应用互相垂直的三画面画过人脚、人头的正投影图和剖面图．17 世纪末意大利人波茨措所著《透视图与建筑》中介绍了先画物体的二正投影图，然后根据正投影图画透视图的方法．可是，这些方法的表述不是系统的，而是零散的．蒙日的最大贡献在于用“投影”（或“射影”）的观点对这些方法进行了几何的分析，从中找出规律，形成体系，使经验上升为理论．同时使作图方法也形成了体系，利用这种体系，不仅所绘图形精确了，难画的部位容易被画出了，而且可以用来图解立体的空间几何性质，由“已知通向未知”，寻求“真相”．

在蒙日看来，画法几何学是每一个设计人员和技术工人必须具备的一种通用语言．按照这种语言，设计人员可以把自己头脑中设想的机器部件用一张图纸上的两幅平面图形表示出来，图纸到了工厂，熟练的技术工人根据这两幅平面图形立即想象出该部件的实际形状应该是什么样子，并把它制造出来．因此，他在《画法几何学》的导言中指出，画法几何学既是使法国摆脱长期对外国工业的依赖、普及工业进步不可缺少的知识，也是利用机器减轻手工劳动、提高产品精确度的不可缺少的知识．正因为如此，《画法几何学》公开出版后便不胫而走，迅速传入各国，起初在军工学校，之后在普通理工院校相继开设了这一科目，出现了英、德、俄、日等语种的译本．画法几何学得到广泛的推广应用，对各国工业的发展起了重要的推动作用．一位数学家评论说，没有蒙日的画法几何学，19 世纪机器的大规模出现也许是不可能的，我们人类文明的相当大一部分要归功于数学家蒙日．

【拓展应用】

材料 青花瓷(图 10-24)又称白地青花瓷,常简称青花,是中国瓷器的主流品种之一,属釉下彩瓷. 青花瓷是用含氧化钴的钴矿为原料,在陶瓷坯体上描绘纹饰,再罩上一层透明釉,经高温还原焰一次烧成. 钴料烧成后呈蓝色,具有着色力强、发色鲜艳、烧成率高、呈色稳定的特点.

图 10-24

问题 如何确定包装盒的形状和尺寸,才能满足青花瓷的远程运输要求.

10.2　空间图形的画法

【学习目标】

1. 通过实物观察和直观感知简单几何体的直观图，理解斜二测画法规则.

2. 会用斜二测画法画水平放置的平面图形和简单几何体的直观图.

3. 进一步提高运用空间想象认识和描述事物的能力，提升直观想象素养.

【重点难点】

重点：会利用斜二测画法画水平放置的平面图形和简单几何体的直观图.

难点：斜二测画法基本规则的具体应用和画图过程中辅助线的使用.

【微课导学】

扫下面的二维码，学习微课"平面图形的斜二测画法""空间图形的斜二测画法".

平面图形的斜二测画法　　　　空间图形的斜二测画法

【自主学习】

1. 若把一个高为 10 cm 的圆柱的底面画在 $x'O'y'$ 平面上，则圆柱的高应画成　　　　（　　）

A. 平行于 z'轴且大小为 10 cm　　B. 平行于 z'轴且大小为 5 cm

C. 与 z'轴成 45°且大小为 10 cm　　D. 与 z'轴成 45°且大小为 5 cm

2. 利用斜二测画法画边长为 1 cm 的正方形的直观图，可能是下面的（　　）

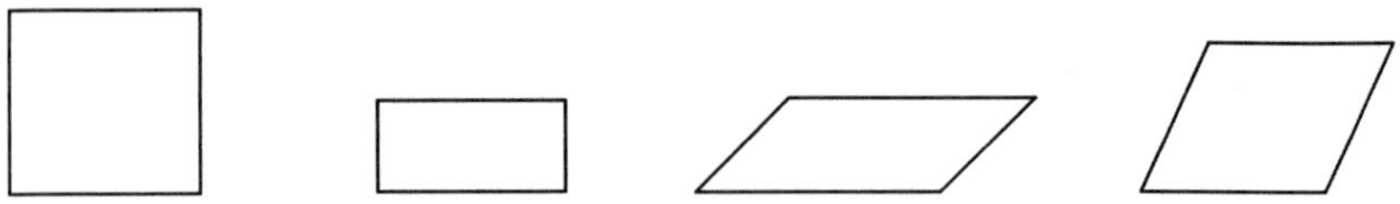

A.　　B.　　C.　　D.

3. 如图 10-25 所示的水平放置的三角形的直观图，D'是$\triangle A'B'C'$中 $B'C'$边的中点，且 $A'D'$边平行于 y'轴，那么 $A'B'$，$A'D'$，$A'C'$三条线段对应原图形中线段 AB，AD，AC 中（　　）

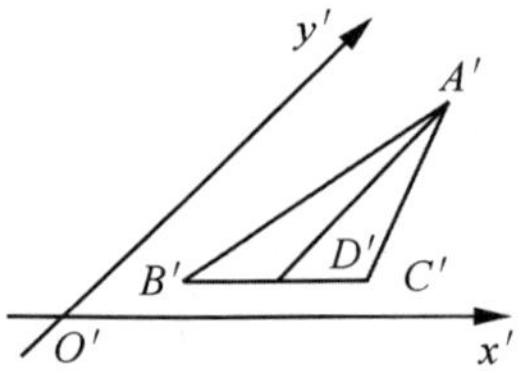

图 10-25

A. 最长的是 AB，最短的是 AC

B. 最长的是 AC，最短的是 AB

C. 最长的是 AB，最短的是 AD

D. 最长的是 AD，最短的是 AC

4. 水平放置的$\triangle ABC$，有一边在水平线上，用斜二测画法作出的直观图是正三角形 $A'B'C'$，则$\triangle ABC$ 是（　　）

A. 锐角三角形　B. 直角三角形　C. 钝角三角形　D. 任意三角形

5. 用斜二测画法画水平放置的平面图形的直观图，关于其中的线段，下列说法正确的是__________.（填序号）

① 原来相交的仍相交　　② 原来垂直的仍垂直

③ 原来平行的仍平行　　④ 原来共点的仍共点

6. 根据斜二测画法的规则画直观图时，把 Ox，Oy，Oz 轴画成对应的 $O'x'$，$O'y'$，$O'z'$，则$\angle x'O'y'$与$\angle x'O'z'$的度数分别为__________.

7. 水平放置的正方形 $ABCO$ 如图 10-26 所示，在平面直角坐标系 xOy 中，点 B 的坐标为(4,4)，用斜二测画法画出该正方形的直观图，并求顶点 B'到 x' 轴的距离.

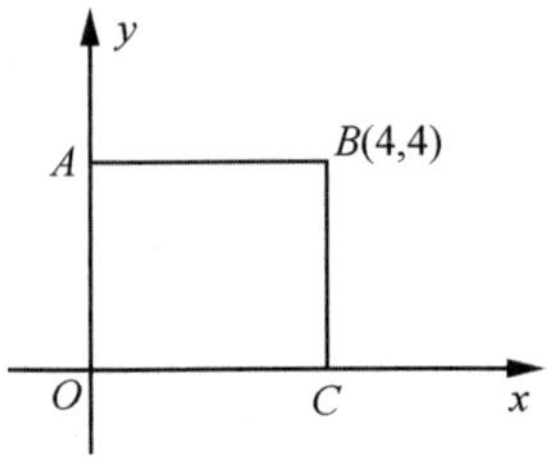

图 10-26

【探究任务】

任务一

阅读下列材料，回答相应问题.

材料 1　“一口叙说千古事，双手对舞百万兵”，非常生动形象地概括了皮影戏艺术的历史风貌. 皮影戏又称“影子戏”“灯影戏”“土影戏”，有的地区叫“皮猴戏”“纸影戏”等，是用灯光照射兽皮或纸版雕刻成的人物剪影以表演故事的戏剧. 它是广泛流传于中国民间的一种古老独特的民间戏曲艺术.

问题 1　皮影戏中有哪些科学原理？皮影戏运用的是哪种投影方式？

材料 2　3D 全息投影技术是在全息技术的基础上，利用特殊的光学元件和投影设备，将虚拟的三维影像投射到空间中. 这种技术通常需要一个透明的投影屏幕，如玻璃、亚克力等，以及一台高性能的投影仪和计算机. 通过精确的计算和校准，投影仪将虚拟影像投射到屏幕上，形成立体的、悬浮在空中的影像. 3D 全息投影技术作为一项创新的科技成果，不仅在科研领域取得了显著的进展，也在各行各业中得到了广泛的应用.

问题 2　3D 全息投影技术有哪些系统原理？3D 全息投影运用的是哪种投影方式？

任务二

小组合作,探究空间图形直观图的斜二测画法.

立体几何中常用平行投影(斜投影)来画空间图形的直观图,这种画法叫斜二测画法.观察图10-27,总结投影变化规律.

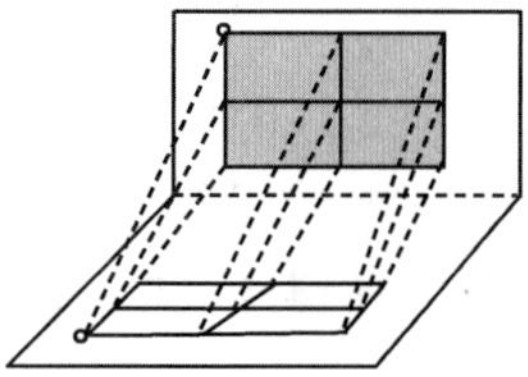

图 10-27

问题 1 从数量关系来看原图形与直观图,哪些数量关系发生了变化?哪些没有发生变化?

问题 2 从线的位置关系看原图形与直观图有什么变化?

问题 3 建立怎样的坐标系会使画图过程更简便?

问题 4 画水平放置的平面图形的关键是什么?

任务三

探究利用斜二测画法画水平放置的平面图形和简单几何体的直观图的方法.

问题 1 用斜二测画法画水平放置的正六边形(图10-28)的直观图.

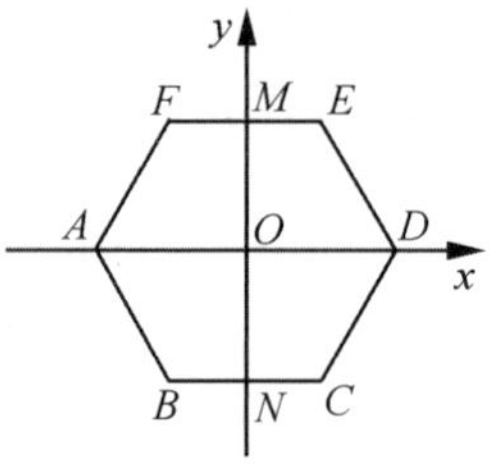

图 10-28

问题 2 尝试总结利用斜二测画法画水平放置的平面图形的方法步骤.

(1) 在已知图形中取互相垂直的 x 轴和 y 轴,两轴相交于点 O. 画直观图时,把它们画成对应的 x'轴和 y'轴,两轴相交于 O',且使 $\angle x'O'y'=$________,

它们确定的平面表示__________；

(2) 已知图形中平行于 x 轴、y 轴的线段，在直观图中分别画成__________于 x' 轴或 y' 轴的线段；

(3) 已知图形中平行于 x 轴的线段，在直观图中保持长度__________；平行于 y 轴的线段，长度为原来的__________.

问题 3　如何由画平面图形直观图过渡到画立体图形的直观图呢？

立体图形与平面图形相比多了一个 z 轴，其直观图中对应于 z 轴的是__________，平面 $x'O'y'$ 表示__________平面，平面 $y'O'z'$ 和 $x'O'z'$ 表示__________平面. 平行于 z 轴的线段，在直观图中__________和__________都不变.

【典例解析】

例 1　用斜二测画法画长、宽、高分别是 4 cm，3 cm，2 cm 的长方体 $ABCD\text{-}A'B'C'D'$ 的直观图.

解　(1) 画轴. 如图 10-29(a)所示，画 x 轴、y 轴、z 轴，三轴交于点 O，使 $\angle xOy=45°$.

(2) 画底面. 如图 10-29(b)所示，以 O 点为中心，在 x 轴上取线段 MN，使 $MN=4$ cm；在 y 轴上取线段 PQ，使 $PQ=1.5$ cm；分别过点 M 和 N 作 y 轴的平行线，过点 P 和 Q 作 x 轴的平行线，设它们的交点分别为 A,B,C,D，四边形 $ABCD$ 就是长方形的底面.

(3) 画侧棱. 如图 10-29(c)所示，过 A,B,C,D 各点分别作 z 轴的平行线，并在这些平行线上分别截取 2 cm 长的线段 AA',BB',CC',DD'.

(4) 成图. 如图 10-29(d)所示，顺次连接 A',B',C',D'，并加以整理(去掉辅助线，将被遮挡住的部分改为虚线)，就可得到长方体的直观图.

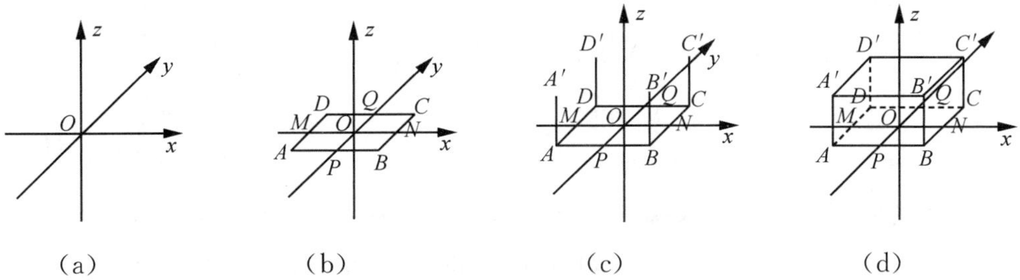

图 10-29

备注 解答本题时可先确定轴,再画下底面的直观图,最后画侧棱成图.

例 2 如图 10-30(a)所示,已知 T 型梁的两面投影,试徒手作出该 T 形梁的正面斜二测投影草图.

解 画法按如下步骤完成:

(1) 在视图上确定各坐标轴,如图 10-30(a)所示.

(2) 画特征面. 将 x、y、z 轴测轴的方向大概定出,然后从 O 开始画,先画出 T 形梁底面的特征形状,如图 10-30(b)所示.

(3) 画棱线和底面. 从特征面的各顶点沿着 X 轴方向画出这段梁的可见棱线,将另外一个底面上可见的轮廓线连接起来,如图 10-30(c)所示.

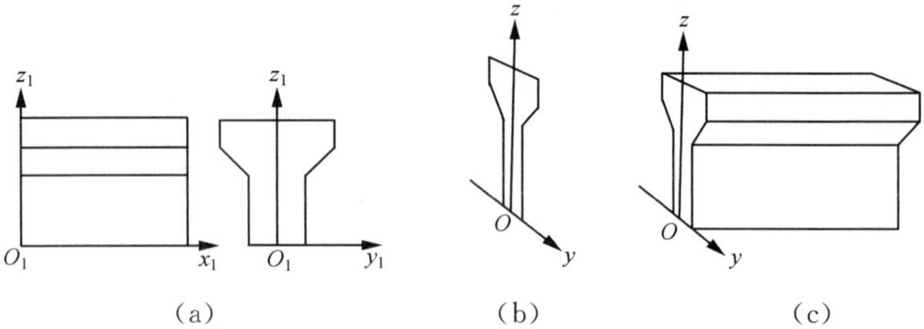

图 10-30

备注 该 T 形梁是一个柱体结构,特征面形状为一个八边形. 各尺寸画成近似尺寸,草图应近似满足斜二测投影图的基本参数.

【课后练习】

1. 如图 10-31 所示为某一平面图形的直观图,则此平面图形可能是 ( )

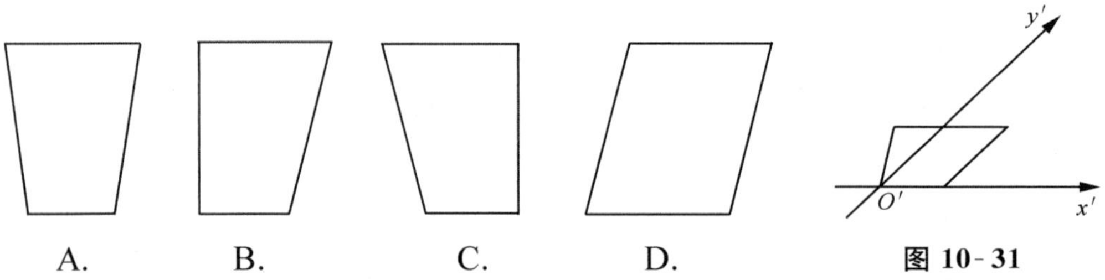

图 10-31

2. 已知一个建筑物上部为四棱锥,下部为长方体,且四棱锥的底面与长方体的上底面尺寸一样,长方体的长、宽、高分别为 20 m,5 m,10 m,四棱锥的高为 8 m. 如果按 1∶500 的比例画出它的直观图,那么在直观图中,长方体

的长、宽、高和棱锥的高应分别为　(　　)

A. 4 cm，1 cm，2 cm，1.6 cm　　B. 4 cm，0.5 cm，2 cm，0.8 cm

C. 4 cm，0.5 cm，2 cm，1.6 cm　　D. 4 cm，0.5 cm，1 cm，0.8 cm

3. 已知等边三角形 ABC 的边长为 a，那么等边三角形 ABC 的直观图 $\triangle A'B'C'$ 的面积为　(　　)

A. $\frac{\sqrt{3}}{4}a^2$　　B. $\frac{\sqrt{3}}{8}a^2$　　C. $\frac{\sqrt{6}}{8}a^2$　　D. $\frac{\sqrt{6}}{16}a^2$

4. 如图 10-32 所示，平行四边形 $O'P'Q'R'$ 是四边形 $OPQR$ 的直观图，若 $O'P'=3$，$O'R'=1$，则原四边形 $OPQR$ 的周长为__________.

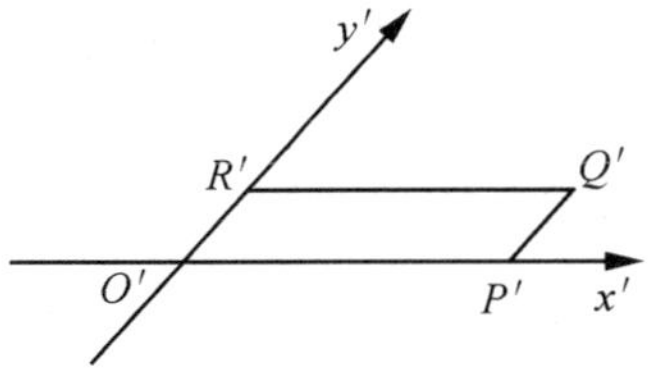

图 10-32

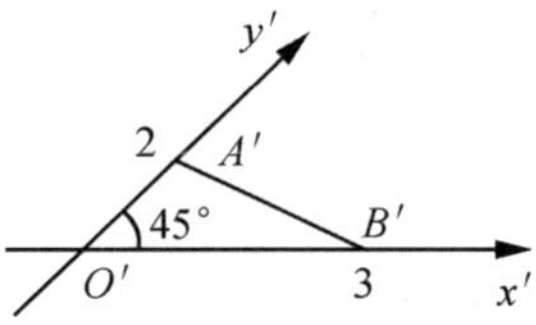

图 10-33

5. 已知如图 10-33 所示的直观图 $\triangle A'O'B'$，则其平面图形的面积为__________.

6. 画出底面是正方形，高与底面边长相等且侧棱均相等的四棱锥的直观图.

7. 如图 10-34 所示，$\triangle ABC$ 中，$AC=12$ cm，边 AC 上的高 $BD=12$ cm，作 $\triangle ABC$ 的直观图，并求其水平放置的直观图的面积.

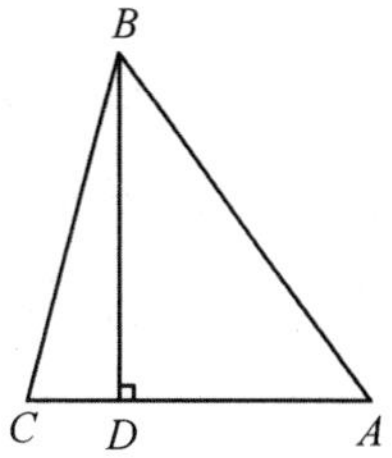

图 10-34

8. 已知几何体的三视图如图 10-35 所示,画出它的直观图.

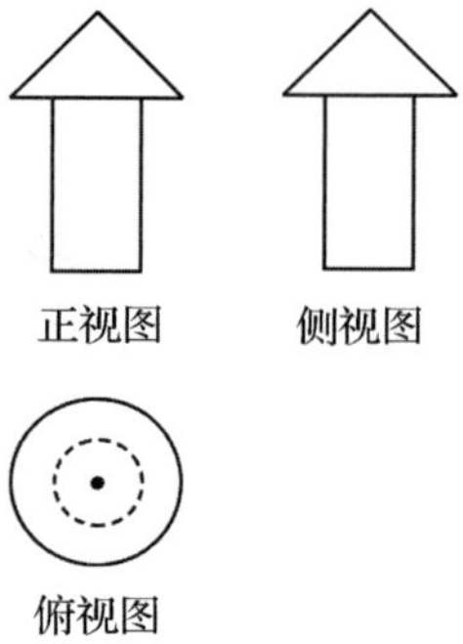

图 10-35

【信息手段】

简单几何体的画法

一、棱柱、棱锥

棱柱 先激活棱柱工具,然后用鼠标左键选择一个多边形 $ABCD$(多边形 1)作为棱柱的底面,再选择第一个最高点 E,即可绘制一个以 $ABCD$ 为底面、E 为第一个最高点的棱柱;也可先激活棱柱工具,直接绘制底面,再选择一个上底面顶点,可绘制棱柱,如图 10-36 所示.

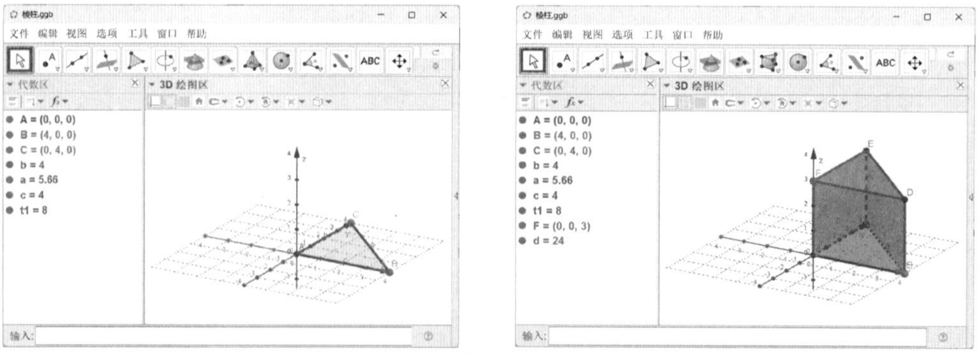

图 10-36

直棱柱 先激活直棱柱工具,然后在多边形 ABC(多边形 1)上按住鼠标左键不放向上或向下拖动适当的高度,释放左键后即可绘制以“多边形 1”为底面、高为所拖动高度的直棱柱,如图 10-37 所示.

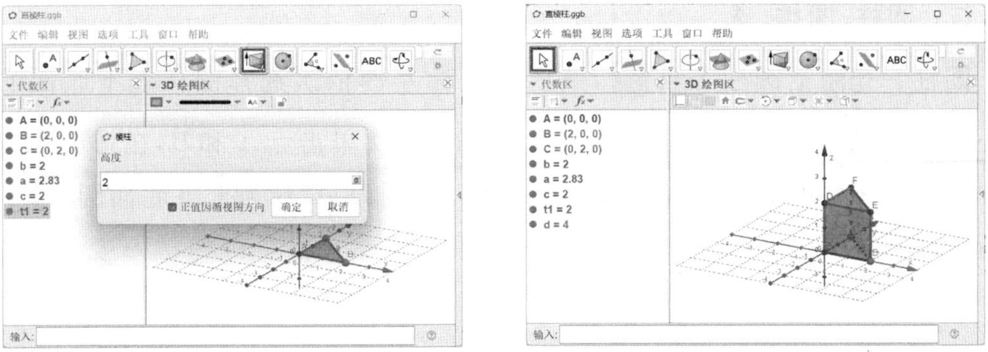

图 10-37

棱锥　先激活棱锥工具，然后用鼠标左键选择一个多边形 $ABCD$ 作为棱锥的底面，再选择一个顶点 E，即可绘制一个以 $ABCD$ 为底面、E 为顶点的棱锥；也可先激活棱锥工具，直接绘制底面，再选择一个顶点，同样可以绘制棱锥，如图 10-38 所示.

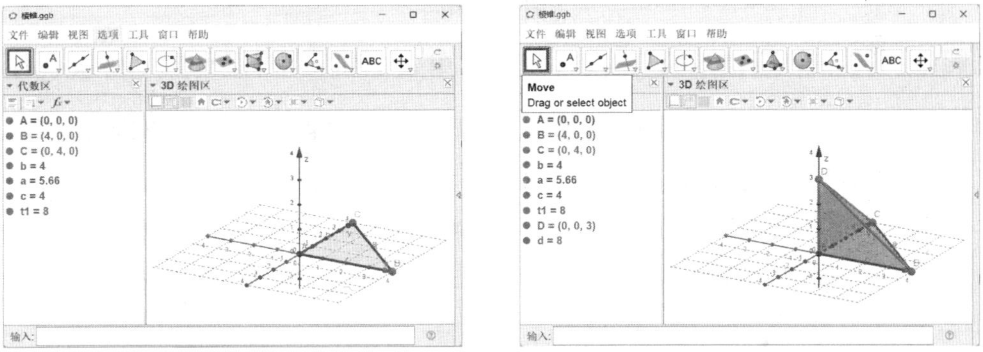

图 10-38

直棱锥　先激活直棱锥工具，然后在多边形 $ABCD$(多边形 1)上按住鼠标左键不放向上或向下拖动适当的高度，释放左键后即可绘制以“多边形 1”为底面、高为所拖动高度的棱锥，如图 10-39 所示.

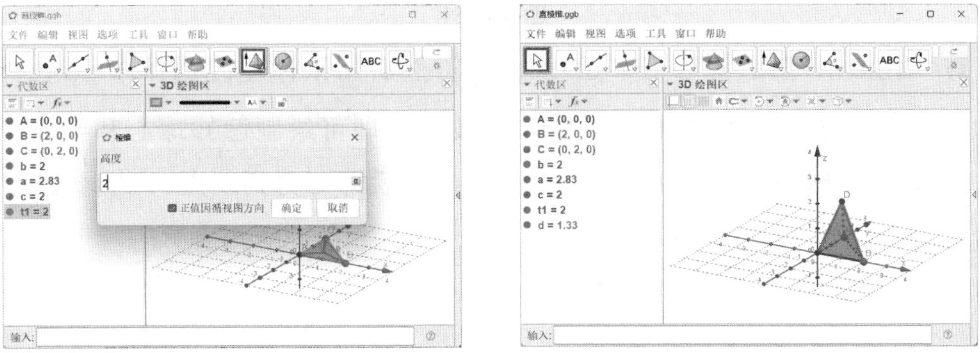

图 10-39

二、圆柱、圆锥、球

圆柱 先激活圆柱工具,然后用鼠标左键依次选择圆柱上下底面的圆心,再输入底面半径,即可绘制圆柱. 例如,依次单击点 A 和 B,在弹出的对话框中输入圆柱的底面半径,如输入 2,即可绘制以 A、B 为上下底面圆心,半径为 2 的圆柱,如图 10-40 所示.

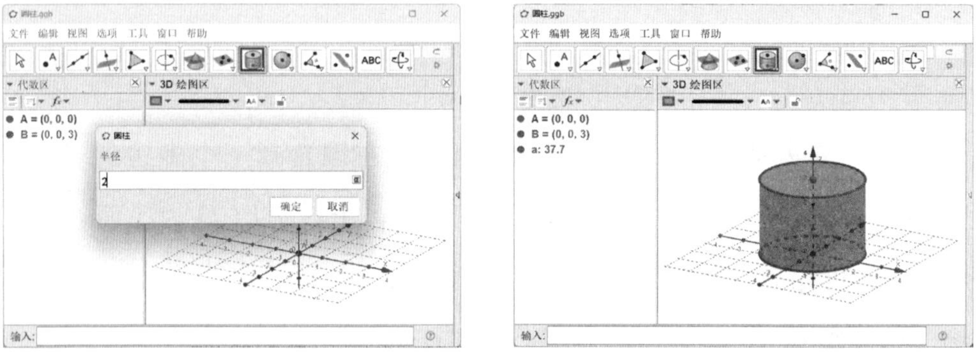

图 10-40

圆锥 先激活圆锥工具,然后依次单击圆锥的底面圆心 A 和顶点 B,在弹出的对话框中输入圆锥的底面半径,如输入 2,即可绘制底面圆心为 A、顶点为 B、半径为 2 的圆锥,如图 10-41 所示.

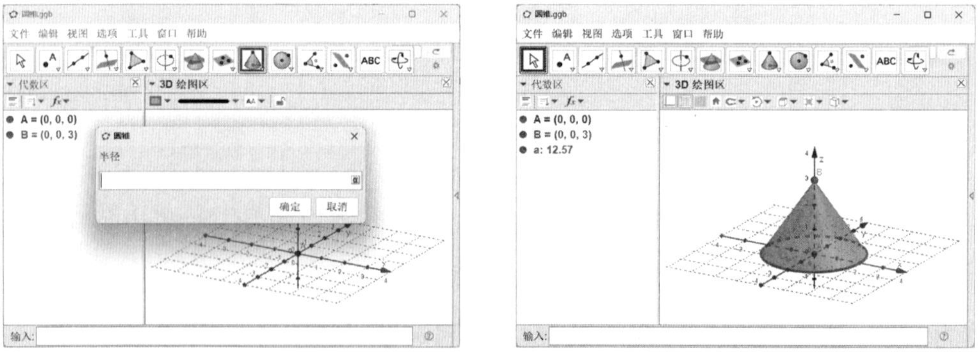

图 10-41

球 先激活球面(球心与半径)工具,然后用鼠标左键选择球心,在弹出的对话框中输入半径的值,单击"确定"按钮后即可绘制已知球心和半径的球. 例如,选择球心 A,然后输入半径值 2,确定后即可得到以点 A 为球心、半径为 2 的球,如图 10-42 所示.

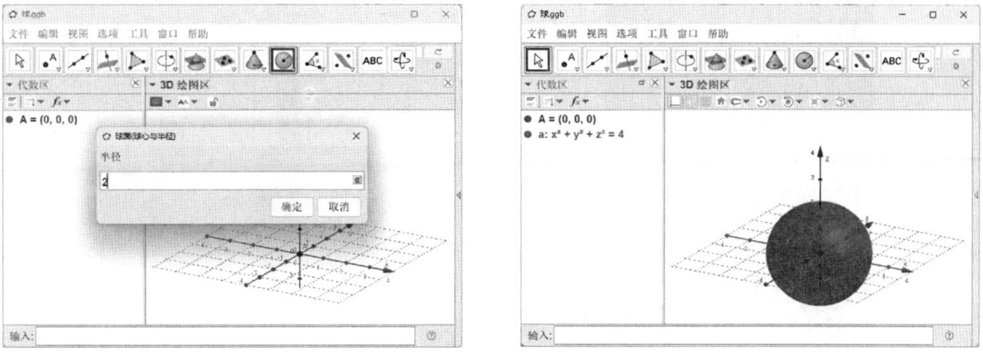

图 10-42

【数学文化】

斜二测画法是一种广泛应用于工程、建筑、地理信息系统等领域的绘图方法. 它是一种基于二维平面上的几何投影原理,使物体在平面上的表现更加直观和精确的绘图方法.

斜二测画法的历史起源可以追溯到法国. 在 18 世纪,法国数学家蒙日提出了用多面正投影图来表达空间形体. 这种方法主要用于绘制地形图、工程图纸等,为地理信息系统、建筑设计和工程领域提供了重要的技术支持.

斜二测画法的应用领域十分广泛. 在地理信息系统中,它是一种重要的地图投影方法,可以使地图上的地理要素保持较好的几何关系和面积比例;在建筑和工程设计中,斜二测画法可以帮助设计师更准确地表现建筑物的立面、平面和剖面,为施工提供重要依据.

在我国,斜二测画法的发展历程可以追溯到 20 世纪初. 随着科技的发展和现代化建设的需求,我国对斜二测画法的研究和应用逐渐深入. 目前,我国已经建立了完善的斜二测画法技术体系,广泛应用于各个领域.

【拓展应用】

材料　中银大厦(图 10-43)是中国银行香港总部大楼,位于中国香港中西区中环花园道 1 号,由美籍华裔建筑师贝聿铭(1917—2019)设计,原址为美利楼,地处中区经济和金融核心地带.

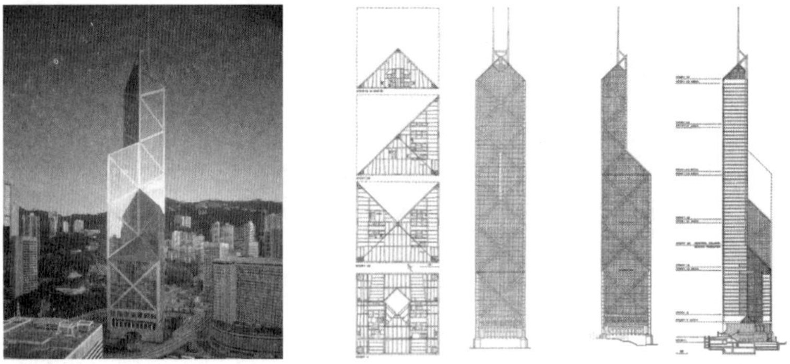

图 10-43

中银大厦基地面积约 8 400 m^2，总建筑面积 12.9 万 m^2. 楼高 70 层，另地库停车场 4 层，楼高 315 m，加顶上两杆的高度(约 53 m)共有 367.4 m.

中银大厦主体结构可简化地看成由四个不同高度的三角柱体构成，层层叠起，节节高耸. 最下面的 1～17 层大致是由四个三角柱体组成的立方体；从平面图上看来，即为正方形，每条周边长 52 m，由两条对角线分割成四个三角形. 再往上，则仿如分段切掉了一些三角柱：首先是在第 17 层，对角线北面的那个三角形被截去了，再往上是西面和东面两个三角柱切掉了，从而造成不同高度的三角柱体参差不齐的形状. 到第 52 层，就只截剩南面那个三角柱体，一直达到顶部第 70 层，其尖角即为大厦最高点. 从不同侧面看去，中银大厦犹如一支巨大的新篁，下大上小，节节升高，象征着力量、生机、茁壮和锐意进取的精神，基座的麻石外墙代表长城，象征中国.

问题 阅读材料，尝试描述三视图和直观图在建筑设计中的作用.

10.3　直棱柱、正棱锥的表面积

【学习目标】

1. 了解多面体和棱柱、棱锥的有关概念及其结构特征，理解直棱柱、正棱锥的侧面展开图.

2. 了解直棱柱、正棱锥的侧面积公式的推导过程，掌握直棱柱、正棱锥的侧面积公式，会计算直棱柱、正棱锥的表面积.

3. 发展数学运算能力，能有效借助运算解决简单实际问题.

【重点难点】

重点：直棱柱、正棱锥的有关概念，直棱柱、正棱锥的侧面积和表面积的计算.

难点：直棱柱、正棱锥的侧面展开图，推导直棱柱、正棱锥的侧面积公式.

【微课导学】

扫下面的二维码，学习微课“直棱柱的表面积”“正棱锥的表面积”.

直棱柱的表面积　　　　正棱锥的表面积

【自主学习】

1. 一般地，有两个面是全等的多边形，其余各面均为矩形的空间图形称为__________. 两个全等的多边形面称为直棱柱的__________，其余矩形面称为直棱柱的________,相邻两个侧面的公共边称为直棱柱的________,底边多边形的顶点也称为直棱柱的________.直棱柱的侧棱长就是直棱柱的高.特别地,底面为正多边形的直棱柱称为________.

2. 一般地,有一个面是多边形,其余各面是有一个公共顶点的三角形,这样的多面体称为________.多边形面称为棱锥的底面,三角形面称为棱锥的侧面,相邻两个侧面的公共边称为棱锥的________,公共顶点称为棱锥的________,连接顶点与它在底面内正投影线段的长称为棱锥的高.底面是正多边形,并且顶点在底面内的正投影是底面的中心的棱锥称为________.

3. 完成表 10-2 中直棱柱、正棱锥的侧面积和表面积公式.

表 10-2 直棱柱和正棱锥的表面积

名称	直棱柱	正棱锥
侧面积	$S_{直棱柱侧}=$	$S_{正棱锥侧}=$
表面积	$S_{直棱柱表}=$	$S_{正棱锥表}=$
注	c 为底面周长,h 为高	c 为底面周长,h 为高,h' 为正棱锥的斜高

4. 判断下列命题是否正确.

(1) 有一个面是多边形,其余各面是三角形的几何体是棱锥; (　　)

(2) 各侧面都是正方形的棱柱一定是正棱柱; (　　)

(3) 侧棱与底面所成的角相等的棱锥是正棱锥; (　　)

(4) 相邻侧面与底面垂直的棱柱是直棱柱. (　　)

5. 已知一个正四棱柱的底面边长为 2 cm,高为 3 cm,则这个正四棱柱的表面积为________.

6. 一个棱锥至少有________个面,面数最少的棱锥有________条棱.

7. 下列说法正确的是 (　　)

A. 正四棱柱是正方体

B. 直棱柱的底面一定是矩形

C. 正棱柱的所有棱长一定相等

D. 直棱柱的两个底面平行且全等

8. 棱长都为 1 的正三棱锥的表面积为 (　　)

A. 2　　B. 3　　C. $\sqrt{3}$　　D. $\frac{3\sqrt{3}}{4}$

【探究任务】

任务一

阅读材料，回答问题.

材料　“江山无限景，都取一亭中”. 亭是中国“园林之眼”. 六角凉亭是中国传统建筑的杰出代表，中华千年造园工艺的精髓，六角亭凭借其六角形独特造型和精湛雕刻，成为园林和文化遗产中的建筑文化印记[图 10-44(a)]. 自古以来，文人墨客偏爱独坐于亭中，相望于山湖之景，对景于树川之间，看轻舟，赏莲花，微风拂面.

(a)

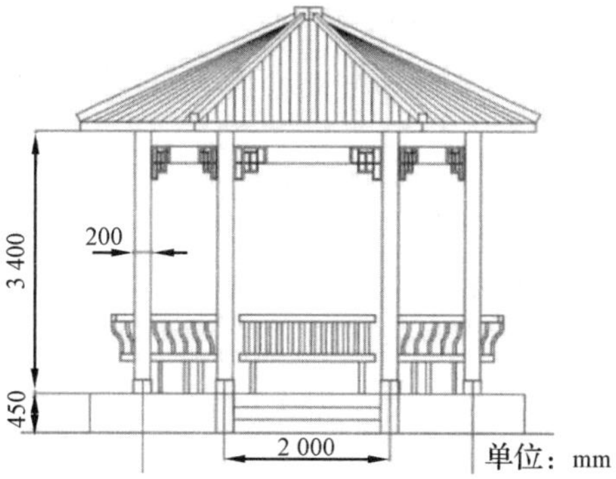

(b)

图 10-44

问题　小组讨论，如图 10-44(b)所示，六角凉亭的瓦檐的面积是多少？

任务二

阅读材料,回答问题.

材料 胡夫金字塔(图 10-45)的底部周长如果除以其高度的两倍,得到的商为3.141 59,这就是圆周率,它的精确度远远超过希腊人算出的圆周率3.142 8,与中国的祖冲之算出的圆周率在 3.141 592 6—3.141 592 7 之间相比,几乎是完全一致的. 同时,胡夫金字塔内部的直角三角形厅室,各边之比为3∶4∶5,体现了勾股定理的数值.

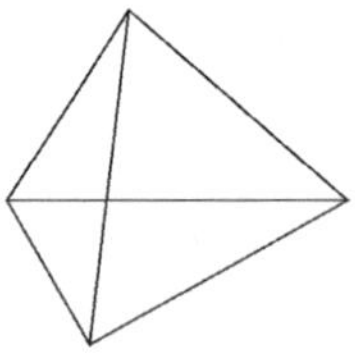

图 10-45

问题 小组讨论,已知正三棱锥的底面边长为 3 cm,高为 2 cm,求该正三棱锥的表面积.

【典例解析】

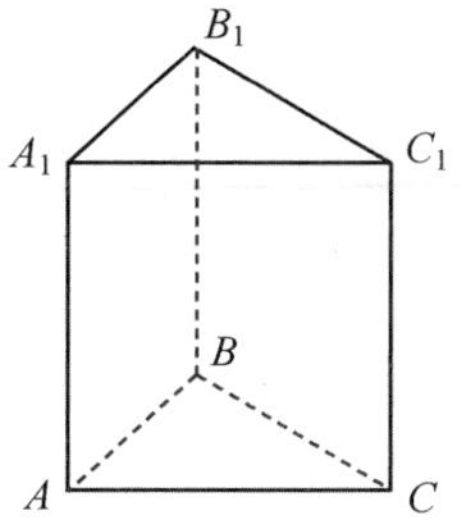

图 10-46

例 1　如图 10-46 所示，已知正三棱柱的底面边长为6 cm，高为 9 cm，求它的侧面积、表面积.

解　如图 10-47 所示，底面$\triangle ABC$是正三角形，边长 $AB=AC=BC=6$ cm，高 $CD=\sqrt{AC^2-AD^2}=\sqrt{6^2-3^2}=3\sqrt{3}$ (cm).

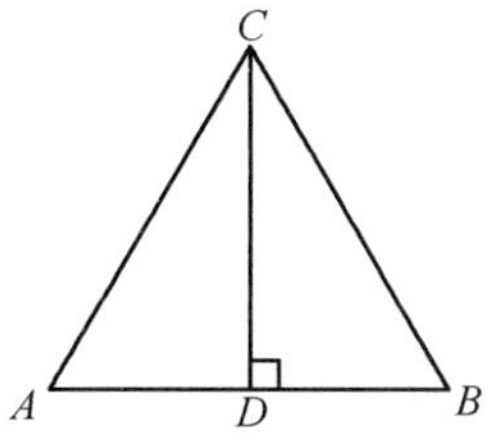

图 10-47

正三棱柱的底面积

$$S_{底}=\frac{1}{2}AB\cdot CD=\frac{1}{2}\times 6\times 3\sqrt{3}=9\sqrt{3}\ (\text{cm}^2),$$

正三棱柱的底面周长 $c=3\times 6=18$ (cm)，棱柱高 $h=9$ cm，则

$$S_{侧}=ch=18\times 9=162\ (\text{cm}^2),$$

该正三棱柱的表面积为

$$S_{表}=S_{侧}+2S_{底}=162+2\times 9\sqrt{3}=(162+18\sqrt{3})\ (\text{cm}^2).$$

即该正三棱柱的侧面积为 162 cm²，表面积为 $(162+18\sqrt{3})$ cm².

备注　正三棱柱的底面是正三角形，侧面是矩形，熟练掌握正三棱柱的几何特征是解题关键.

例 2　如图 10-48 所示，正四棱锥 S-$ABCD$ 的底面边长是 4，棱锥高 $SO=4$，求该正四棱锥的侧面积和表面积.

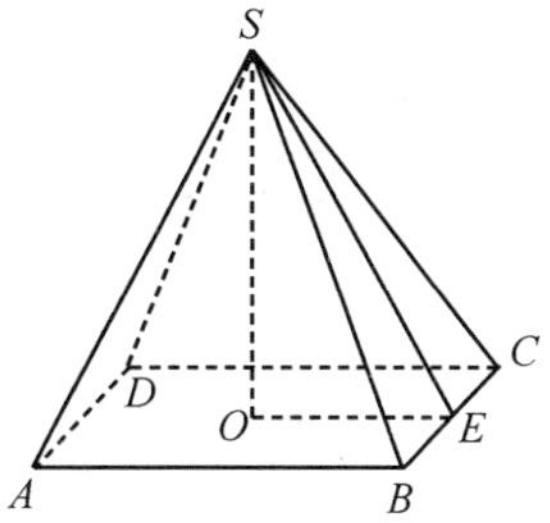

图 10-48

解　因为正四棱锥 S-$ABCD$ 的底面边长是 4，所以底面周长 $c=4\times 4=16$，作 SO 垂直于底面 $ABCD$，取 BC 的中点 E，连接 OE，在 $\text{Rt}\triangle SOE$ 中，$SE^2=SO^2+OE^2=4^2+2^2=20$，$SE=2\sqrt{5}$，即斜高 $h'=2\sqrt{5}$，所以侧面积

$$S_{侧}=\frac{1}{2}ch'=\frac{1}{2}\times 16\times 2\sqrt{5}=16\sqrt{5};$$

$$S_{底}=4\times4=16,$$

$$S_{表}=S_{侧}+S_{底}=16\sqrt{5}+16.$$

即该正四棱锥的侧面积为 $16\sqrt{5}$,表面积为 $16\sqrt{5}+16$.

备注 正四棱锥中,侧棱、高、对角线的一半组成直角三角形,斜高、底面边长的一半、侧棱组成直角三角形,熟练掌握正四棱锥的几何特征是解题关键.

例 3 如图 10-49 所示,某组合体的上半部分是正四棱锥 P-$EFGH$,下半部分是长方体 $ABCD$-$EFGH$.已知 $PE=EF=2$,$AE=1$,求这个组合体的表面积.

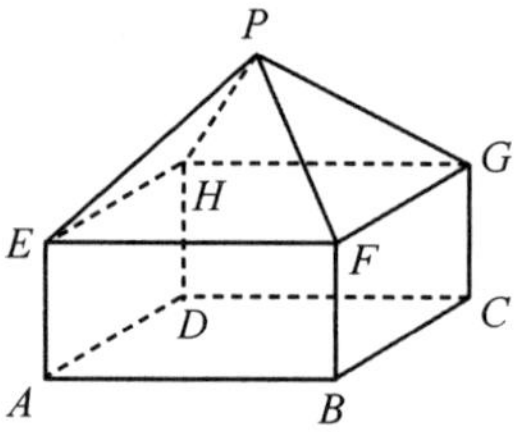

图 10-49

解 因为正四棱锥 P-$ABCD$ 的底面边长是 2,所以底面周长 $c=4\times2=8$.

正四棱锥的斜高 $h'=\sqrt{2^2-1^2}=\sqrt{3}$,其侧面积

$$S_{正四棱锥侧}=\frac{1}{2}ch'=\frac{1}{2}\times8\times\sqrt{3}=4\sqrt{3},$$

长方体的侧面积 $S_{长方体侧}=4\times2\times1=8$,

长方体的底面积 $S_{长方体底}=2\times2=4$.

该组合体的表面积

$$S_{组合体表}=S_{正四棱锥侧}+S_{长方体侧}+S_{长方体底}$$

$$=4\sqrt{3}+8+4=4\sqrt{3}+12.$$

即这个组合体的表面积为 $4\sqrt{3}+12$.

备注 该组合体的表面积为正四棱锥的侧面积,加上长方体的侧面积,再加上长方体的一个底面积.

【课后练习】

1. 已知某长方体同一顶点上的三条棱长分别为 1,2,3,则此长方体的表面积为 ( )

A. 22　　B. 20　　C. 11　　D. 10

2. 正六棱锥的底面周长为 12,高为 $\sqrt{13}$,则这个正六棱锥的侧面积为 ( )

A. 6　　B. 15　　C. $15\sqrt{3}$　　D. 24

3. 若正方体的表面积为 54，则它的棱长为　　　　(　　)

A. 6　　　　B. 5　　　　C. 4　　　　D. 3

4. 已知一个正三棱柱的底面边长为 6 cm，高为 9 cm，这个三棱柱的侧面积为__________，表面积为__________.

5. 如图 10-50 所示，已知正三棱锥 $S\text{-}ABC$ 的底面边长为 6，高为 3，则此正三棱锥的侧面积为__________.

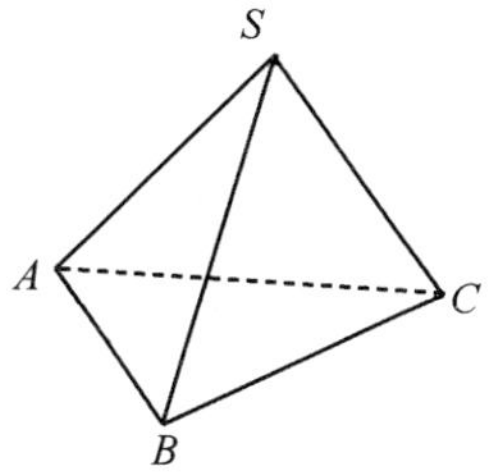

图 10-50

6. 已知一个正四棱柱的底面边长为 3，侧面的对角线长是 $3\sqrt{5}$，求这个正四棱柱的高和侧面积.

7. 已知一个正四棱锥的底面边长为 2，侧棱长是 $\sqrt{5}$，求这个正四棱锥的高和斜高.

8. 如图 10-51 所示,正四棱锥 $S\text{-}ABCD$ 的底面边长是 4,斜高 $SE=2\sqrt{5}$,求该正四棱锥侧面积和表面积.

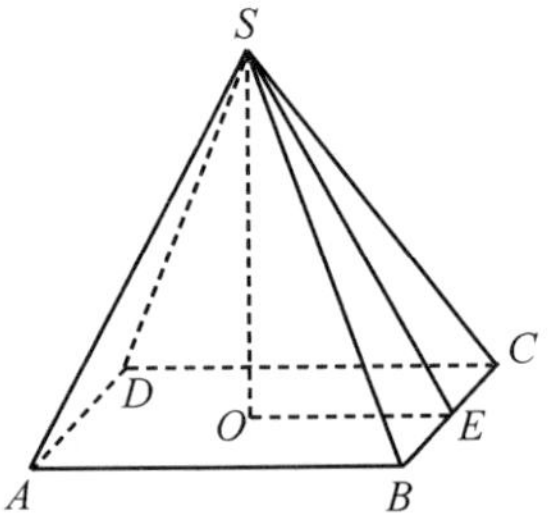

图 10-51

【数学文化】

父子数学家

祖冲之(图 10-52),字文远,南北朝时宋朝人,汉族,出生地今南京,我国杰出的数学家、科学家.

图 10-52

祖冲之对于自然科学和文学、哲学都有广泛的兴趣,特别是对天文、数学和机械制造有强烈的爱好.青年时期,他就有了博学多才的名声,被政府派到当时的一个学术研究机关——华林学省做研究工作.后来他又担任过地方官职.公元 461 年,他任南徐州(今江苏镇江)刺史府里的从事.464 年,宋朝政府派他到娄县(今江苏昆山市东北)做县令,宋朝末年,祖冲之回到建康(今南京)担任谒者仆射的官职.

祖冲之写的《缀术》一书,被收入著名的《算经十书》中,作为唐代国子篇算学课本,后失传.祖冲之算出 π 的值在 3.141 592 6 和 3.141 592 7 之间,相当于精确到小数点后第 7 位,简化成 3.141 592 6,是当时世界上最先进的成果.祖冲之入选世界纪录协会世界第一位将圆周率值计算到小数点后第 7 位的科学家. 这一纪录直到 15 世纪才由阿拉伯数学家卡西打破.

祖冲之设计制造过水碓磨、铜制机件传动的指南车，车中装有机械，车上装有木人，车子开行之前，先把木人的手指向南方，不论车子怎样转弯，木人的手始终指向南方不变，这种车子结构已经失传；利用轮子激水前进的原理制成一天能行一百多里的千里船等. 此外，他在音律、文学、考据方面也造诣颇深，他精通音律，擅长下棋，写有小说《述异记》，是历史上少有的博学多才的人物.

图 10-53

祖冲之死后，他的儿子祖暅(图 10-53)继承了他的事业，继续进行着他没有完成的工作.

祖暅和祖冲之小的时候一样，深受家庭的影响. 祖暅不但继承了祖冲之的科学事业，更重要的是继承了祖冲之献身科学的精神. 史书上记载了这么一个故事：有一回，祖暅一边走路一边思考问题，他不但没有注意到路边的景物，就连路上来来往往的行人也不曾注意到. 突然，祖暅撞到了一个叫徐勉的大官身上，把徐勉撞得倒退了一步，但祖暅并没感觉到，继续向前走，又撞到了徐勉身上. 徐勉正要发火，一看是祖暅，就哈哈大笑起来，连叫几声祖暅的名字，才把祖暅从沉思中叫醒. 祖暅在进行科学工作的时候，和他的父亲一样，也同样注重实践. 他为了更准确地观测天象，不怕艰难困苦，特地在嵩山立八尺高的铜表，进行不懈的观测，终于得出了北极星并不在北极，而是偏离一度多的正确结论.

由于认真学习，刻苦钻研，祖暅和他的父亲一样，也做出了很多成就，最突出的是在数学上求出了球体体积的正确公式，这个公式一直到现在还在运用. 著名的“祖暅原理”是祖暅对世界的杰出贡献. 祖暅总结了刘徽的有关工作，提出“幂势既同则积不容异”，即等高的两立体，若其任意高处的水平截面积相等，则这两立体体积相等. 祖暅应用这个原理，解决了刘徽尚未解决的球体积公式. 该原理在西方直至 17 世纪才由意大利数学家卡瓦列利发现，比祖暅晚一千一百多年.

【拓展应用】

某乡政府为了有效利用水资源,改善水利设施,需要修筑一条横截面为等腰梯形的灌溉水渠,如图 10-54 所示,已知水渠长 400 m,深 1.5 m,渠底宽 1 m,渠面宽 2 m.若在水渠的底部和侧面铺设水泥板,则需要的水泥板面积是多少(保留整数)?

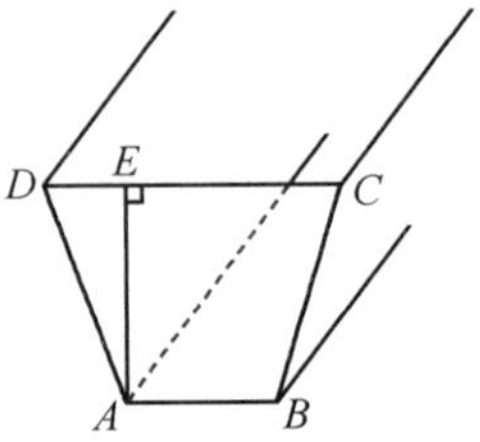

图 10-54

10.4　圆柱、圆锥、球的表面积

【学习目标】

1. 了解旋转体及圆柱、圆锥、球的有关概念.

2. 理解圆柱、圆锥的侧面展开图，掌握圆柱、圆锥的侧面积计算公式，会计算圆柱、圆锥的侧面积及表面积. 了解球的表面积公式，会计算球的表面积.

3. 进一步发展数学运算能力，能有效借助运算解决简单的实际问题.

【重点难点】

重点：圆柱、圆锥侧面积的计算，圆柱、圆锥和球表面积的计算.

难点：理解圆柱、圆锥的侧面展开图，了解球的表面不可以展开成平面图形.

【微课导学】

扫下面的二维码，学习微课“圆柱、圆锥和球”“圆柱、圆锥和球的表面积”.

圆柱、圆锥和球　　圆柱、圆锥和球的表面积

【自主学习】

1. 一般地，一条平面曲线绕着它所在平面内的一条定直线旋转所形成的曲面称为__________，封闭的旋转面围成的几何体称为__________，这条定

直线称为旋转体的__________，这条曲线称为旋转体的__________.

2. 以矩形的一条边所在直线为旋转轴，其余各边绕轴旋转所形成的封闭几何体称为__________，旋转轴称为圆柱的__________，垂直于轴的边旋转形成的圆面称为圆柱的__________，平行于轴的边称为圆柱的__________，母线旋转而成的曲面称为圆柱的__________，两个底面圆心之间的距离称为圆柱的__________.

3. 以直角三角形的一条直角边所在直线为旋转轴，其余各边绕轴旋转形成的封闭几何体称为__________.

4. 一个半圆绕着它的__________所在的直线旋转一周，半圆弧线形成的曲面称为球面，球面围成的几何体称为__________，简称__________.

5. 在旋转体中，通过轴的平面所得到的截面通常简称为轴截面，圆柱、圆锥、球的轴截面分别是__________、__________、__________.

6. 下列说法中不正确的个数为 (　　)

① 圆柱母线长与圆柱的高相等；② 圆柱的两个底面可以不平行；③ 圆柱的侧面展开图是一个圆.

A. 1　　B. 2　　C. 3　　D. 0

7. 下列说法中不正确的个数为 (　　)

① 圆锥的母线长等于圆锥的高；② 圆锥的侧面展开图可以是一个圆；③ 圆锥轴截面的高就是圆锥的高.

A. 1　　B. 2　　C. 3　　D. 0

8. 下列说法中不正确的个数为 (　　)

① 球的半径是球面上任意一点与球心所连线段的长；② 球的直径是球面上任意两点间所连线段的长；③ 用一个平面截一个球，得到的截面可以是一个正方形；④ 过球心的平面截球所得的圆是大圆.

A. 1　　B. 2　　C. 3　　D. 4

【探究任务】

任务一

阅读下面材料，回答问题.

图 10-55

材料 1　2023 年 10 月 26 日 11 时 14 分，搭载神舟十七号载人飞船的长征二号 F 遥十七运载火箭(图 10-55)在酒泉卫星发射中心点火发射. 约 10 分钟后，神舟十七号载人飞船与火箭成功分离，进入预定轨道，航天员乘组汤洪波、唐胜杰、江新林 3 名航天员状态良好，发射取得圆满成功.

图 10-56

材料 2　北京天坛(图 10-56)位于北京市东城区. 它始建于明永乐年间，初名“天地坛”，后更名为“天坛”，是明清两代皇帝“祭天”“祈谷”的场所. 天坛见证了中国封建社会的兴衰，也成了中国传统文化的重要载体. 天坛体现了中国古代的“天人合一”思想.

图 10-57

材料 3　中国科学院紫金山天文台(图 10-57)简称紫台，位于江苏省南京市玄武区紫金山上，毗邻钟山风景名胜区，是中国人自己建立的第一个现代天文学研究机构，被誉为“中国现代天文学的摇篮”. 紫台的建成标志着中国现代天文学研究的开始，中国现代天文学的许多分支学科和天文台站大多从这里诞生、组建和拓展. 2017 年 3 月 1 日，紫台新发现一颗彗星，命名为 Tsuchinshan. 2019 年 10 月 26 日，中国科学院紫金山天文台研究员常进荣获首届中国空间科学学会科学奖.

问题 1　观察以上图片，这些几何体抽象出来的空间图形显然不是多面体，这些空间图形有什么共同特征呢?

问题 2 这些几何体都有一个面是曲面，它们在水平面内的正投影是一个圆，这些曲面是怎样形成的？

任务二

探究圆柱、圆锥和球的侧面积、表面积.

小组合作，动手做一做，填写表格(表 10-3).

表 10-3 圆柱、圆锥和球的侧面积、表面积

几何体名称	图形及侧面展开图	侧面积	表面积
圆柱	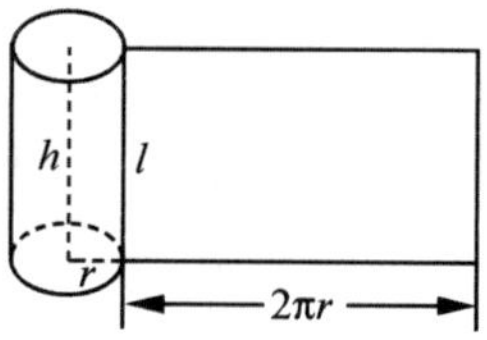		
圆锥	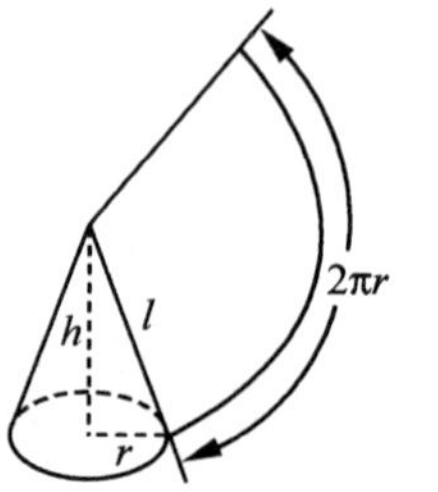		
球	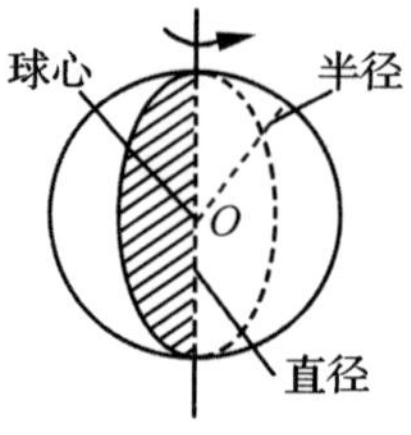		

【典例解析】

例 1　圆柱的一个底面的面积为 4π，侧面展开图是一个正方形，求这个圆柱的侧面积与全面积.

解　设圆柱的高为 h，底面圆半径为 r，由题意知，底面积

$$S_{底}=\pi r^2=4\pi,$$

得 $r=2$，$h=2\pi r=4\pi$. 圆柱的侧面积

$$S_{侧}=2\pi rh=16\pi^2,$$

圆柱的全面积

$$S_{表}=2S_{底}+S_{侧}=16\pi^2+8\pi.$$

例 2　将圆心角为 120°、面积为 3π 的扇形作为圆锥的侧面，求圆锥的高.

解　设扇形的半径即圆锥的母线长为 l，圆锥底面半径为 r，由于

$$\frac{120\pi}{360}\cdot l^2=3\pi,$$

所以 $l=3$.

由于

$$\frac{120\cdot 2\pi}{360}\cdot l=2\pi r,$$

得 $r=1$.

圆锥的高

$$h=\sqrt{3^2-1^2}=2\sqrt{2}.$$

例 3　已知两球的表面积之比为 25∶9，求这两球的半径之比.

解　设两球的半径分别为 r_1 和 r_2，则

$$\frac{S_{球1}}{S_{球2}}=\frac{4\pi {r_1}^2}{4\pi {r_2}^2}=\frac{25}{9},$$

则两球的半径之比为 5∶3.

【课后练习】

1. 圆锥的母线有　　　　（　　）

A. 1 条　　B. 2 条　　C. 3 条　　D. 无数条

2. 圆柱的侧面展开图是 (   )

A. 三角形　　B. 等腰三角形　　C. 矩形　　D. 扇形

3. 用一个平面截一个几何体,所得各截面都是圆面,则这个几何体一定是 (   )

A. 圆柱　　B. 球　　C. 圆锥　　D. 以上几何体均可能

4. 圆锥的顶点与底面圆心的连线__________于底面.

5. 已知圆柱的母线长为 5 cm,底面圆的半径为 2 cm,则圆柱的表面积为________ cm^2.

6. 已知圆柱的轴截面是边长为 8 cm 的正方形.求圆柱的侧面积.

7. 已知圆锥的母线长为 3 cm,高为 2 cm,求该圆锥的表面积.

8. 已知球的半径为 5 cm,它的一个球截面的圆心与球心之间的距离为 3 cm,求球截面的半径.

【信息手段】

圆柱、圆锥、圆台的侧面积和表面积

利用 GeoGebra 可以直接求平面图形的面积，对于立体空间中的曲面面积没有现成的指令和工具. 因而我们要借助公式文本求圆柱、圆锥、圆台的侧面积和表面积.

第一步，确定下底面半径 AD、上底面半径 BC 和母线 AB，选用曲面指令 Surface(<Curve>,<Angle>,<Line>)，绘制可以改变上下底面半径和高的圆台，从而作出圆柱、圆锥、圆台(图 10-58)，作图过程见表 10-4.

表 10-4　作图过程

步骤	名称	描述	数值
1	滑杆 h	范围[0,10]	$h=6$
2	滑杆 $r1$	范围[0,10]	$r1=6$
3	滑杆 $r2$	范围[0,10]	$r2=3$
4	输入框 InputBox1	输入框($r1$)	输入下底面半径 $r1=$
5	输入框 InputBox2	输入框($r2$)	输入上底面半径 $r2=$
6	输入框 InputBox3	输入框(h)	输入高 $h=$
7	点 A	$(r1,0,0)$	$A=(6,0,0)$
8	点 B	$(0,0,h)$	$B=(0,0,6)$
9	点 C	$(r2,0,h)$	$C=(3,0,6)$
10	点 D	x 轴与 Z 轴的交点	$D=(0,0,0)$
11	线段 f	线段 AD	$f=6$
12	线段 g	线段 AC	$g=6.71$
13	线段 i	线段 BC	$i=3$
14	曲面 a	曲面(f,360°,z 轴)	$a(u,v)=(6u\cos(v)+Ou(-\sin(v)),6u\sin(v)+Ou\cos(v),Ou)$
15	曲面 b	曲面(g,360°,z 轴)	$b(u,v)=((3+3u)\cos(v)+Ou(-\sin(v)),(3+3u)\sin(v)+Ou\cos(v),6-6u)$
16	曲面 c	曲面(I,360°,z 轴)	$c(u,v)=(3u\cos(v)+Ou(-\sin(v)),3u\sin(v)+Ou\cos(v),6+Ou)$

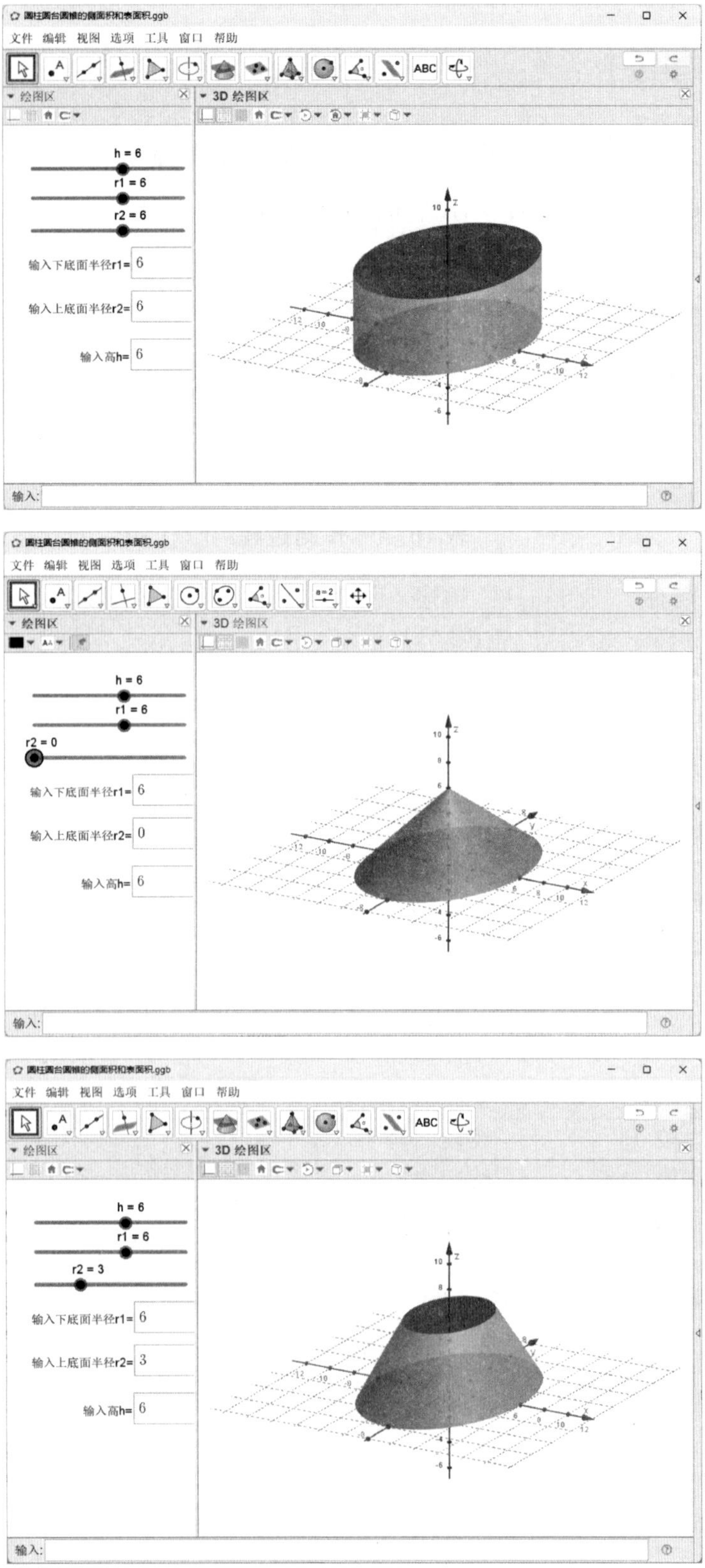
圆柱圆台圆锥的侧面积和表面积.ggb
文件 编辑 视图 选项 工具 窗口 帮助
绘图区
3D 绘图区
h = 6
r1 = 6
r2 = 6
输入下底面半径r1= 6
输入上底面半径r2= 6
输入高h= 6
输入:
圆柱圆台圆锥的侧面积和表面积.ggb
文件 编辑 视图 选项 工具 窗口 帮助
绘图区
3D 绘图区
h = 6
r1 = 6
r2 = 0
输入下底面半径r1= 6
输入上底面半径r2= 0
输入高h= 6
输入:
圆柱圆台圆锥的侧面积和表面积.ggb
文件 编辑 视图 选项 工具 窗口 帮助
绘图区
3D 绘图区
h = 6
r1 = 6
r2 = 3
输入下底面半径r1= 6
输入上底面半径r2= 3
输入高h= 6
输入:

图 10-58

第二步，借助文本框和公式文本指令公式文本(<对象>，<是否替换变量？true|false>，<是否显示名称？true|false>)，求可以改变上下底面半径和高的圆的侧面积和表面积，作图过程和求得的结果(图 10-59)见表 10-5.

表 10-5　作图过程

步骤	名称	描述	数值
17	文本 text1	公式文本(($2\pi r1+2\pi r2$)$f/2$，true，true)	“169.65”
18	文本 text1		“侧面积＝”
19	文本 text2	公式文本(($2\pi r1+2\pi r2$)$f/2+\pi r1^2+\pi r2^2$，true，true)	“311.02”
20	文本 text2		“表面积＝”

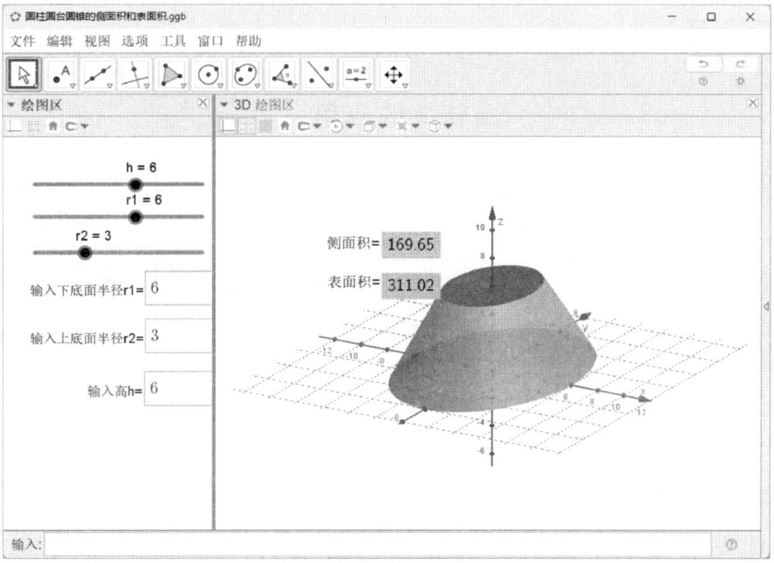

图 10-59

【数学文化】

图 10-60

阿基米德(图 10-60)是古希腊一位百科全书式的科学家，他是哲学家、数学家、力学家、静态力学和流体静力学的奠基人，享有“力学之父”的美称. 阿基米德和高斯、牛顿并列为世界三大数学家.

阿基米德把球体积推算视为他一生最得意的成果，曾留下遗嘱把球及其外切圆柱的图形刻在他的墓碑上. 阿基米德最后死于战争,关于他的死有多种说法. 其中一种说法是,当罗马军士冲到阿基米德身边时,这位正在思考数学问题的老人喊出的最后一句话是,不要踩坏我的图! 阿基米德死后,罗马军队的主帅马塞吕斯下令为阿基米德隆重建坟墓,并遵照阿基米德的遗愿,在他墓前竖了一块石碑(图 10-61),墓碑上刻着的正是那不朽的图形——球及其外切圆柱. 1906 年,记载着阿基米德球体积计算的羊皮书手稿,历经千年尘封后终于重见天日,被誉为 20 世纪最重大的考古发现.

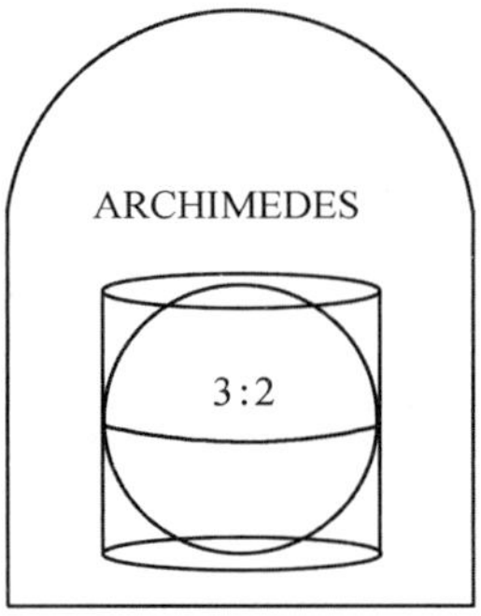

图 10-61

【拓展应用】

旋转体的应用

旋转体在我们的生活中有广泛的应用.

在机械工程、结构设计和流体力学等领域,旋转体被用于机械零部件设计、桥梁设计以及热力学的应用中. 例如,活塞和气缸可以看作是旋转体,其热特性直接影响到发动机的性能和燃烧效率.

在通信技术中,滑环旋转体连通技术是一种利用滑环和旋转体实现信号传输的技术,它在无人机通信、工业自动化、智能交通系统和医疗设备等方面都有应用. 这种技术可以实现高速、稳定且安全的通信传输,为多个领域的自动化和智能化发展提供了支持.

在智能制造中,滑环旋转体连通技术可以用于机器人控制、智能设备连接和数据采集与监测. 它的应用有助于提高生产效率、降低成本和风险,并实现设备的智能化管理和监控.

旋转体在现代社会中扮演着重要角色,无论是从工程学的角度还是从通信技术和智能制造的角度来看,它们都为我们带来了前所未有的便捷和高效.

10.5　柱、锥、球的体积

【学习目标】

1. 了解柱、锥及球的结构特征.

2. 掌握柱、锥、球的体积计算公式.

3. 培养学生的观察能力,进一步发展学生的数学运算能力,能有效借助运算解决简单实际问题.

【重点难点】

重点:会求棱柱、棱锥、圆柱、圆锥及球的体积.

难点:理解锥体的体积是等底等高的柱体体积的三分之一.

【微课导学】

扫右面的二维码,学习微课"棱柱、棱锥的体积""圆柱、圆锥、球的体积".

棱柱、棱锥的体积　　圆柱、圆锥、球的体积

【自主学习】

1. 填写棱柱、棱锥、圆柱、圆锥及球的体积公式.

表 10-6　柱、锥、球的体积

几何体名称	体积
直棱柱	$V_{直棱柱}=$____________
正棱锥	$V_{正棱锥}=$____________
圆柱	$V_{圆柱}=$____________
圆锥	$V_{圆锥}=$____________
球	$V_{球}=$____________

2. 若圆柱的侧面展开图是边长为 4 的正方形,则它的体积为________.

3. 各条棱长都为 2 的正四棱锥的体积为__________.

4. 已知圆锥的底面积是 5,高是 6,则其体积为 ( )

A. 30　B. 10　C. 15　D. 25

5. 已知球的半径为 3,则其体积为 ( )

A. 36π　B. 18π　C. 15π　D. 25π

6. 已知轴截面为正方形的圆柱的侧面积是 4π,那么圆柱的体积为 ( )

A. 2π　B. 3π　C. 4π　D. 5π

7. 已知正三棱柱的底面边长为 6,高为 10,求正三棱柱的体积.

【探究任务】

任务一

阅读材料,回答问题.

材料 1　如图 10-62 所示,大雁塔是中国古代建筑的代表之一,它建于唐朝时期,是楼阁式砖塔,塔通高 64.1 m,塔身为七层,塔体呈方形锥体,由仿木结构形成开间,由下而上按比例递减,塔内有木梯可盘登而上. 整个建筑气魄宏大,造型简洁稳重,比例协调适度,格调庄严古朴,是保存比较完好的楼阁式塔.

图 10-62

材料 2　如图 10-63 所示，东方明珠塔位于上海黄浦江畔、浦东陆家嘴嘴尖上．设计者富于幻想地将 11 个大小不一的球体组合在一起，创造了唐代诗人白居易诗中“大珠小珠落玉盘”的意境．东方明珠塔选用了东方民族喜爱的圆曲线体作为基本建筑线条，主体由三个斜筒体、三个直筒体和 11 个球组成，形成巨大的空间框架结构，总高 468 m，总建筑面积达 10 万 m^2，做到了现代科技与东方文化的完美统一．截至 2019 年，东方明珠塔为亚洲第六高塔、世界第九高塔．

图 10-63

材料 3　如图 10-64 所示，蒙古包是蒙古族牧民居住的一种房子．建造和搬迁都很方便，适于牧业生产和游牧生活．蒙古包呈圆形尖顶，顶上和四周以一至两层厚毡覆盖．普通蒙古包，顶高 10—15 尺，围墙高约 5 尺，包门朝南或东南开．蒙古包看起来外形虽小，但非常适合于经常转场的放牧民族居住和使用．

图 10-64

问题 1　观察以上图片，这些建筑物分别由哪些几何体组成？尝试描述这些几何体的特征．

问题 2　如何计算这些简单组合体的体积呢？

任务二

探究圆柱和圆锥体积之间的关系.

实验材料:等底等高的圆柱和圆锥容器各一个,足够的水,如图 10-65 所示.

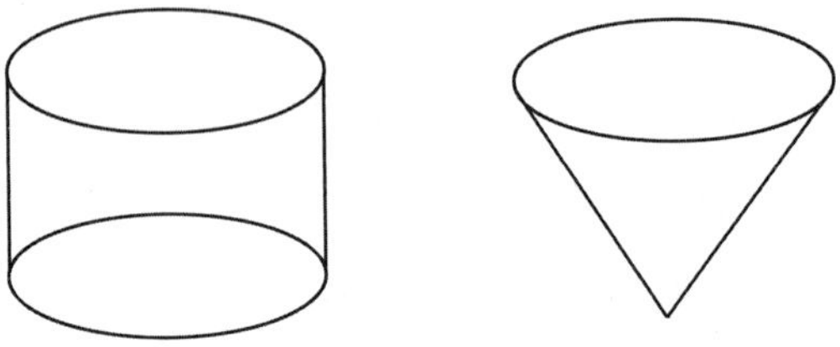

图 10-65

实验过程:

(1) 在圆锥容器中装满水;

(2) 将圆锥容器中的水全部倒入圆柱容器中;

(3) 重复步骤(1)(2)两次.

实验结果:____________________.

实验结论:____________________.

类比上述实验结果,________________棱柱和棱锥也适用.

【典例解析】

例 1 已知等边圆柱(轴截面是正方形的圆柱)的全面积为 S,求其内接正四棱柱的体积.

解 如图 10-66 所示,设等边圆柱的底面半径为 r,则高 $h=2r$.

因为

$$S=2\pi rh+2\pi r^2=6\pi r^2,$$

所以

$$r=\sqrt{\frac{S}{6\pi}},$$

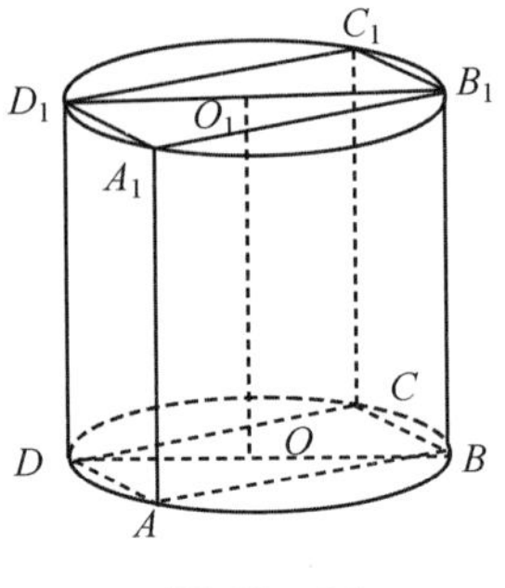

图 10-66

内接正四棱柱的底面边长 $a=2r\sin45^\circ=\sqrt{2}r$,则

$$V=(\sqrt{2}r)^2\cdot 2r=4r^3=4\left(\sqrt{\frac{S}{6\pi}}\right)^3=\frac{\sqrt{6\pi S}}{9\pi^2}S.$$

即圆柱的内接正四棱柱的体积为$\frac{\sqrt{6\pi S}}{9\pi^2}S$.

备注　求出等边圆柱的底面圆半径 r 是解题的关键.

例 2　如图 10-67(a)所示，一竖立在地面上的圆锥形物体的母线长为 4，一只小虫从圆锥的底面圆上的点 P 出发，绕圆锥侧面爬行一周后回到点 P 处，若该小虫爬行的最短路程为 $4\sqrt{3}$，求这个圆锥的体积.

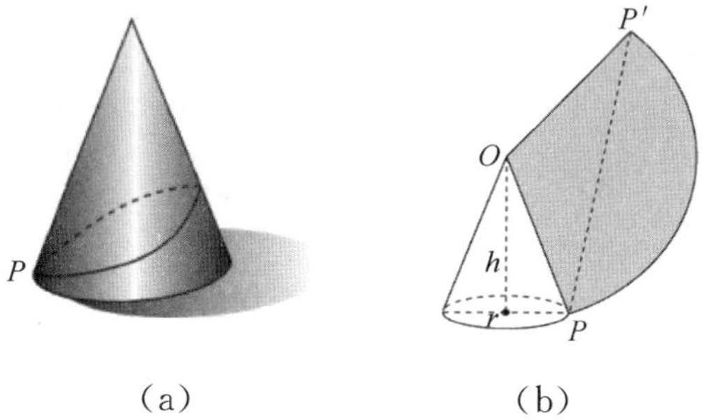

图 10-67

解　作出该圆锥的侧面展开图，如图 10-67(b)中阴影部分所示，该小虫爬行的最短路径为 PP'，因为 $OP=OP'=4$，$PP'=4\sqrt{3}$，由余弦定理可得

$$\cos\angle P'OP=\frac{OP^2+OP'^2-PP'^2}{2OP\cdot OP'}=-\frac{1}{2},$$

所以$\angle P'OP=\frac{2\pi}{3}$. 再设底面圆的半径为 r，圆锥的高为 h，则

$$2\pi r=\frac{2\pi}{3}\times 4,$$

解得

$$r=\frac{4}{3},$$

所以

$$h=\sqrt{4^2-r^2}=\frac{8\sqrt{2}}{3}.$$

圆锥的体积

$$V=\frac{1}{3}\pi r^2h=\frac{128\sqrt{2}\pi}{81}.$$

备注 掌握圆锥体积公式 $V_{圆锥}=\frac{1}{3}\pi r^2 h$ 是解题的关键.

【课后练习】

1. 若两个球的表面积之比是 1∶16,则这两个球的体积之比为 ( )

A. 1∶32　　B. 1∶24　　C. 1∶64　　D. 1∶256

2. 如图 10-68 所示,已知三棱柱 $ABC\text{-}A_1B_1C_1$ 的所有棱长均为 1,且 $AA_1 \perp$ 底面 ABC,则三棱锥 $B_1\text{-}ABC_1$ 的体积为 ( )

A. $\frac{\sqrt{3}}{12}$　　B. $\frac{\sqrt{3}}{4}$

C. $\frac{\sqrt{6}}{12}$　　D. $\frac{\sqrt{6}}{4}$

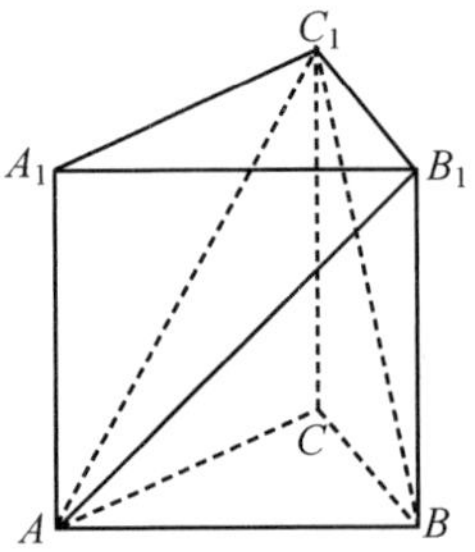

图 10-68

3. 如图 10-69 是一个圆台的侧面展开图,若两个半圆的半径分别是 1 和 2,则该圆台的体积是 ( )

A. $\frac{7\sqrt{2}\pi}{24}$　　B. $\frac{7\sqrt{3}\pi}{24}$

C. $\frac{7\sqrt{2}\pi}{12}$　　D. $\frac{7\sqrt{3}\pi}{12}$

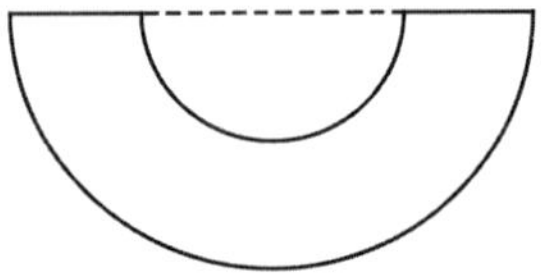
图 10-69

4. 学生到工厂劳动实践,利用 3D 打印技术制作模型.如图 10-70 所示,该模型为长方体 $ABCD\text{-}A_1B_1C_1D_1$ 挖去四棱锥 $O\text{-}EFGH$ 后得到的几何体,其中 O 为长方体的中心,E, F, G, H 分别为所在棱的中点,$AB=BC=6$ cm, $AA_1=4$ cm. 3D 打印所用原料密度为 0.9 g/cm^3.不考虑打印损耗,制作该模型所需原料的质量为__________g.

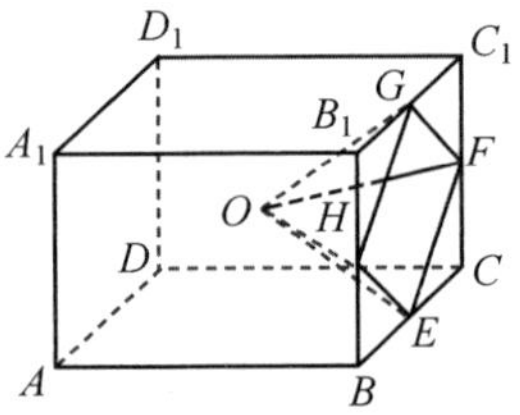

图 10-70

5. 如图 10-71(a)是一个正三棱柱容器,底面边长为 a,高为 $2a$,内装水若干,将容器放倒,把一个侧面作为底面,如图 10-75(b),这时水面恰好为中截面,则图 10-71(a)中容器内水面的高度是__________.

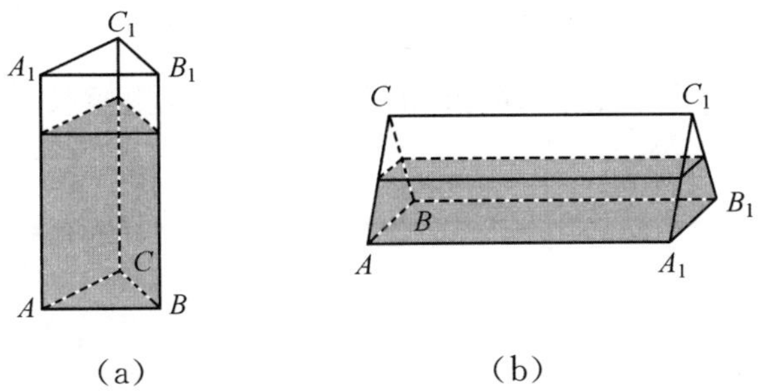

图 10-71

6. 已知圆柱的底面半径为 3 cm，高为 10 cm，求圆柱的侧面积和体积.

7. 在正方体 $ABCD\text{-}A_1B_1C_1D_1$ 中，M 为棱 BB_1 的中点，平面 A_1DM 将该正方体分成两部分，其体积分别为 V_1，V_2（$V_1<V_2$），求$\frac{V_1}{V_2}$.

8. 如图 10-72 所示，直棱柱 $ABC\text{-}A_1B_1C_1$ 的底面 ABC 是等腰直角三角形，$AB=BC$，$\angle ABC=90°$，$\triangle ABC$ 的面积是 8 cm^2，侧棱长为 4 cm，求棱柱的侧面积 S 和体积 V.

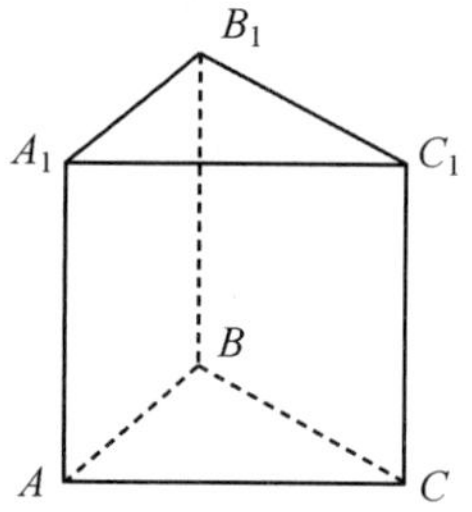

图 10-72

【数学文化】

“阳马”和“鳖臑”

《九章算术》中记载了两种特殊的三棱锥——“阳马”和“鳖臑”. 书中，将底面为长方形且有一条侧棱与底面垂直的四棱锥称为阳马，将四个面都为直角三角形的四面体称为鳖臑.

关于“阳马”和“鳖臑”是怎么来的，《九章算术 · 商功》写道：“斜解立方，得两壍堵. 斜解壍堵，其一为阳马，一为鳖臑. 阳马居二，鳖臑居一，不易之率也. 合两鳖臑成一阳马，合三阳马而成一立方，故三而一，验之以棋，其形露矣.”

“阳马”亦称角梁. 中国古代建筑的一种构件. 用于四阿(庑殿)屋顶、厦两头(歇山)屋顶转角 45°线上，安在各架椽正侧两面交点上.

【拓展应用】

如图 10-73 所示，一个圆锥形的空杯子上面放着一个半球形的冰淇淋，如果冰淇淋融化了，会溢出杯子吗？请用你的计算数据说明理由.

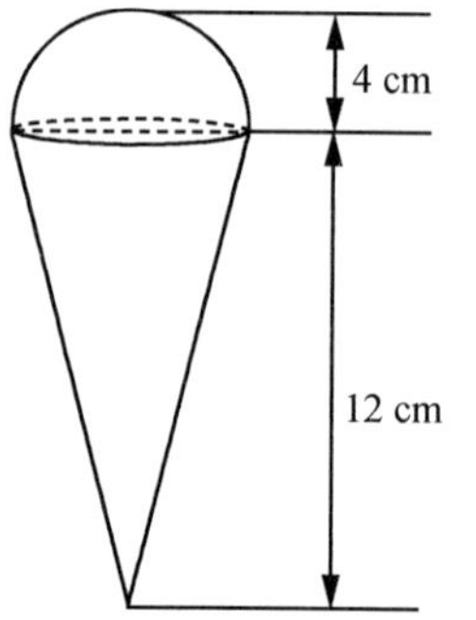

图 10-73

自我检测

一、选择题

1. 在太阳光的照射下，正方形在地面上的投影不可能是　（　　）

A. 正方形　　B. 菱形　　C. 线段　　D. 梯形

2. 已知正方形的直观图是平行四边形，若平行四边形某一边的边长为 4 cm，则正方形的边长是　（　　）

A. 4 cm　　B. 8 cm

C. 4 cm 或 8 cm　　D. 12 cm

3. 已知球的半径为 3，则其体积为　（　　）

A. 36π　　B. 18π　　C. 15π　　D. 25π

4. 已知正六棱锥的底面周长是 12 cm，高是 $\sqrt{13}$ cm，则它的侧面积是　（　　）

A. $15\sqrt{3}\ \text{cm}^2$　　B. $6\ \text{cm}^2$　　C. $24\ \text{cm}^2$　　D. $15\ \text{cm}^2$

5. 一物体的三视图如图 10-74 所示，该物体所对应的直观图是　（　　）

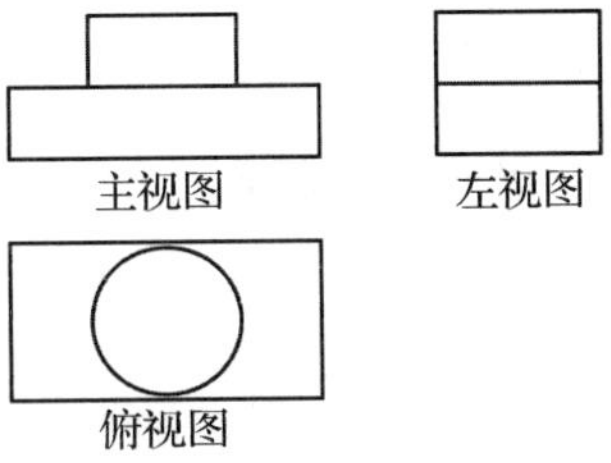

图 10-74

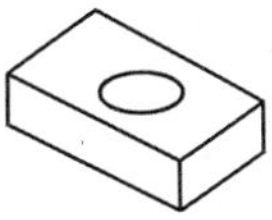

A.

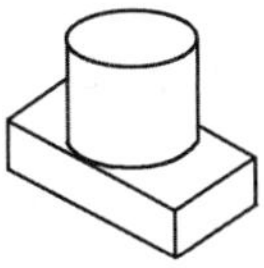

B.

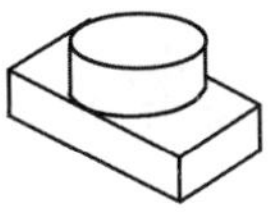

C.

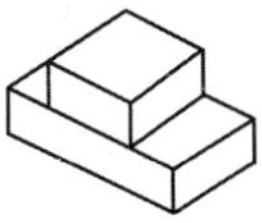

D.

6. 如图 10-75 所示的物体的左视图是　（　　）

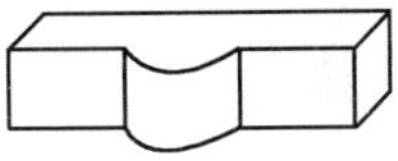

图 10-75

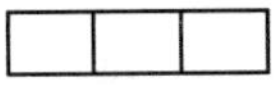

A.

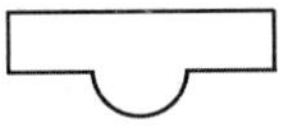

B.

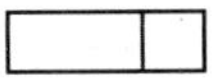

C.

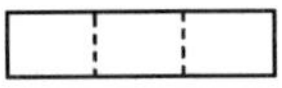

D.

7. 已知圆锥的底面积为 5，高为 6，则其体积为　（　　）

A. 30　　B. 10　　C. 15　　D. 25

8. 已知圆锥的母线长为 8,底面周长为 6,则它的体积为 ( )

A. $9\sqrt{55}\pi$　　B. $9\sqrt{55}$　　C. $3\sqrt{55}$　　D. $3\sqrt{55}\pi$

9. 五棱柱的面数为 ( )

A. 5　　B. 6　　C. 7　　D. 8

10. 长方体属于 ( )

A. 棱锥　　B. 圆柱　　C. 斜棱柱　　D. 直棱柱

11. 利用斜二测画法画水平放置的平面图形的直观图,下列说法正确的是 ( )

A. 等腰三角形的直观图还是等腰三角形

B. 直角三角形的直观图还是直角三角形

C. 三角形的直观图还是三角形

D. 菱形的直观图还是菱形

12. 已知正六棱柱的底面边长为 4,高为 3,则它的体积为 ( )

A. $72\sqrt{3}$　　B. 72　　C. $36\sqrt{3}$　　D. $12\sqrt{3}$

13. 已知圆柱的底面直径为 4,高为 6,则它的体积为 ( )

A. 36π　　B. 24π　　C. 72π　　D. 96π

14. 已知正三棱柱的底面边长为 3,高为 4,则其侧面积为 ( )

A. 12　　B. 24　　C. 36　　D. 48

15. 矩形纸板的正投影 ( )

A. 一定是矩形　　B. 可能是三角形

C. 可能是平行四边形　　D. 不可能是线段

二、填空题

1. 已知正方体的棱长为 1,则其表面积为________,体积为________.

2. 已知球的直径为 4,则其体积为________,其表面积为________.

3. 已知正方体的表面积是 54,则其棱长为________,体积为________.

4. 已知正四棱锥的底面边长为 3 cm,高为 4 cm,则其表面积为________,体积为________.

5. 圆锥的底面半径为 1,母线长为 2,则其体积为________.

6. 用斜二测画法画水平放置的平面图形时,平行于 x 轴的线段在直观图中保持长度__________.

7. 直棱柱的侧棱与底面的位置关系为__________.

8. 已知正四面体棱长为 4,则其体积为__________.

9. 已知球的直径为 6,则球的表面积为__________.

10. 用斜二测画法画水平放置的平面图形时,平行于 y 轴的线段在直观图中长度__________.

三、解答题

1. 如图 10-76 所示,已知 $S\text{-}ABC$ 为正三棱锥,$AB=2$,$SA=\sqrt{2}$,求棱锥的高和棱锥的体积.

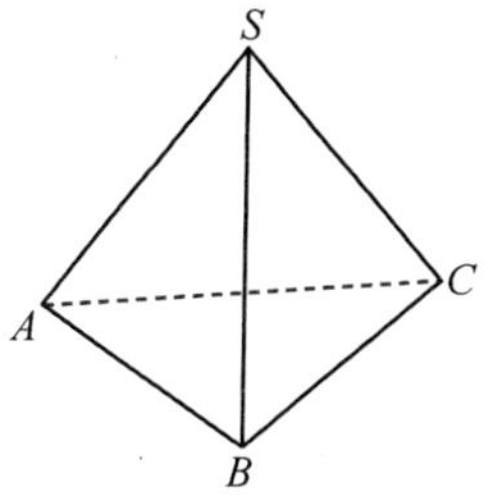

图 10-76

2. 如图 10-77 所示,一个铸铁零件,是由半个圆柱与一个正四棱柱组合成的几何体,圆柱的底面直径与高均为 2 cm,正四棱柱底面边长为 2 cm、侧棱为 3 cm.求该零件的质量(该铸铁的密度约 7.4 g/cm^3).(精确到 0.1 g)

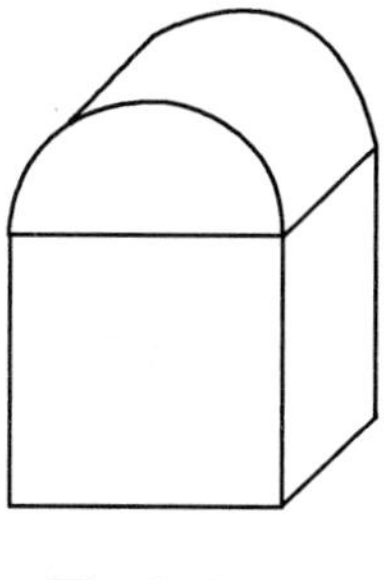

图 10-77

3. 用斜二测画法画出底面正方形边长为 2、高为 3 的长方体的直观图.

4. 根据如图 10-78 所示的三视图,画出物体的直观图.

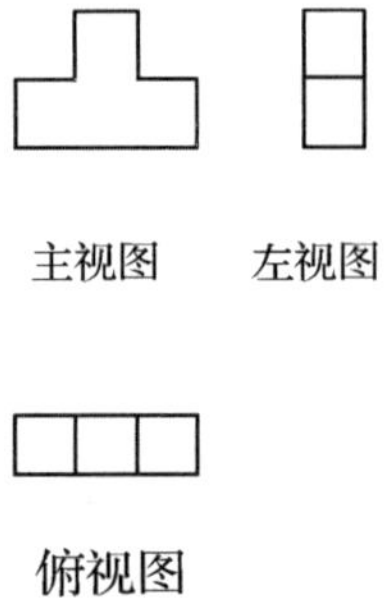

图 10-78

5. 已知圆柱的一个底面的面积为 9π，侧面展开图为正方形，求圆柱的侧面积、全面积和体积.

6. 已知圆锥的轴截面是等边三角形且面积为 $\sqrt{3}$，求圆锥的表面积和体积.

7. 已知球的半径为 10 cm,它的一个球截面的圆心与球心距离为 6 cm,求球截面的半径.

第 11 章　概率与统计初步

11.1　随机事件

【学习目标】

1. 理解随机试验的概念及特点，理解必然事件、随机事件、不可能事件的概念，并会判断.

2. 理解概率的统计定义，掌握频率与概率的区别.

【重点难点】

重点：随机试验、随机事件、概率的统计定义.

难点：概率的统计定义，频率与概率的区别.

【微课导学】

扫下面的二维码，学习微课“随机事件”“概率的统计定义”.

随机事件　　概率的统计定义

【自主学习】

1. 下列事件:

① 如果 $a>b$,那么 $a-b>0$;② 任取一实数 a($a>0$ 且 $a\neq0$),函数 $y=\log_a x$ 是增函数;③ 某人射击一次,命中靶心;④ 从盛有一红、二白共三个球的袋子中,摸出一球观察,结果是黄球.

其中是随机事件的是 ( )

A. ①② B. ③④ C. ①④ D. ②③

2. 下列说法一定正确的是 ( )

A. 一名篮球运动员,号称"百发百中",若罚球三次,不会出现三投都不中的情况

B. 一个骰子掷一次得到 2 的概率是 16%,则掷 6 次一定会出现一次 2

C. 若买彩票中奖的概率为万分之一,则买一万元的彩票一定会中奖一元

D. 随机事件发生的概率与试验次数无关

3. 对于给定的一个随机事件 A,在相同条件下,随着试验次数 n 的增大,事件 A 发生的频率会在某个常数附近摆动并趋于稳定,这个常数称为随机事件 A 的__________,记为__________,我们称频率的这个性质为__________.

在实际应用中,常将试验次数最多的频率值的最后一个有效数字四舍五入,作为____________.

4. 当 x 取任一实数时,"总有 $x^2<0$"是__________事件;"总有 $x^2\geqslant0$"是__________事件.

5. 判断正误.

(1) 设有一批产品,其次品率为 0.05,则从中任取 200 件,必有 10 件是次品. ( )

(2) 做 100 次抛硬币的试验,结果 51 次出现正面朝上,因此,出现正面朝上的概率是 51%. ( )

(3) 某事件发生的概率随着试验次数的变化而变化. ( )

(4) 小概率事件就是不可能发生的事件. ( )

6. 抛掷一颗骰子,观察出现的点数,下列事件中哪些是随机事件?哪些是必然事件?哪些是不可能事件?

A_1={点数是 1},A_2={点数是 2},A_3={点数是 3},…,A_6={点数是 6},B={点数不超过 3},C={点数不超过 6},D={点数是 7}.

【探究任务】

任务一

下面这些事件中哪些是随机事件?哪些是必然事件?哪些是不可能事件?

① 水满则溢;② 绳锯木断,水滴石穿;③ 铁杵成针;④ 守株待兔;⑤ 水中捞月;⑥ 瓮中捉鳖.

任务二

小组合作,完成抛硬币试验,并将试验结果填入表 11-1 中.

(1) 两人合作,一人抛硬币 10 次,一人负责记录,然后互换角色;

(2) 组长负责统计组内每个数据的总数量.

表 11-1　抛硬币

组别	一组	二组	三组	四组	合计
正面朝上次数					
反面朝上次数					
试验总次数					
$\dfrac{\text{正面朝上次数}}{\text{试验总次数}}$					

问题 1 根据表中数据,分别计算 4 组试验中正面朝上的频率.

问题 2 本场抛硬币试验正面朝上的概率估计值是多少?

问题 3 尝试总结频率与概率估计值的关系.

【典例解析】

例 1 同时转动如图 11-1 所示的两个转盘,记转盘①得到的数为 x,转盘②得到的数为 y,结果为 (x,y).

(1) 写出这个试验的样本空间;

(2) 求这个试验的基本事件的总数;

(3) "$x+y=5$"这一事件包含哪几个基本事件?"$x<3$ 且 $y>1$"呢?

(4) "$xy=4$"这一事件包含哪几个基本事件?"$x=y$"呢?

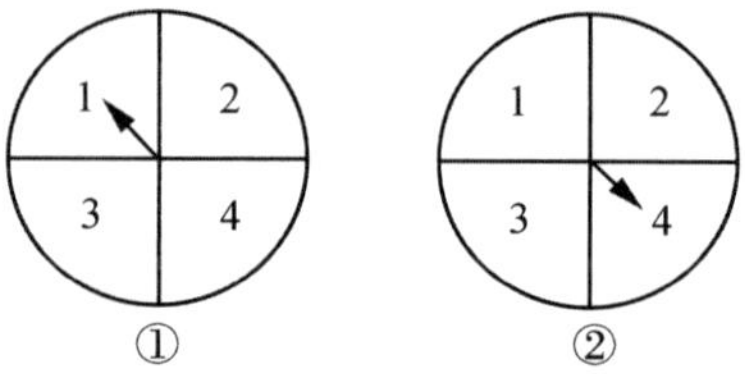

图 11-1

解 (1) $\Omega=\{(1,1),(1,2),(1,3),(1,4),(2,1),(2,2),(2,3)(2,4),(3,1),(3,2),(3,3),(3,4),(4,1),(4,2),(4,3),(4,4)\}$.

(2) 基本事件的总数为 16.

(3) "$x+y=5$"包含以下 4 个基本事件:$(1,4),(2,3),(3,2),(4,1)$;

"$x<3$ 且 $y>1$"包含以下 6 个基本事件:$(1,2),(1,3),(1,4),(2,2),(2,3),(2,4)$.

(4) "$xy=4$"包含以下 3 个基本事件:$(1,4),(2,2),(4,1)$;

"$x=y$"包含以下 4 个基本事件:$(1,1),(2,2),(3,3),(4,4)$.

例 2 某水果公司以 2 元/kg 的成本新进了 10 000 kg 柑橘,如果公司希望这种柑橘能够获得利润 5 000 元,那么在出售柑橘(已经去掉损坏的柑橘)时,每 kg 大约定价为多少元比较合适?

销售人员从所有的柑橘中随机地抽取若干柑橘，对损坏柑橘进行了统计，并把获得的数据记录在下表中，请你帮忙完成下表 11-2.

表 11-2　柑橘损坏的频率计算

柑橘总质量 m/kg	损坏柑橘质量 n/kg	柑橘损坏的频率$\frac{m}{n}$
50	5.50	0.110
100	10.50	0.105
150	15.50	
200	19.42	
250	24.25	
300	30.93	
350	35.32	
400	39.24	
450	44.57	
500	51.54	

解　填完表格，我们可得，柑橘损坏的概率为 0.1，则柑橘完好的概率为 0.9.

因此，在 10 000 kg 柑橘中完好柑橘的质量为 10 000×0.9=9 000(kg). 完好柑橘的实际成本为

$$\frac{2\times 10\ 000}{9\ 000}=\frac{2}{0.9}\approx 2.22(\text{元/kg}).$$

设每 kg 柑橘的销价为 x 元，则

$$9\ 000(x-2.22)=5\ 000,$$

解得，$x\approx 2.78$.

因此，出售柑橘时每 kg 大约定价为 2.78 元可获利润 5 000 元.

备注　(1) 频率是概率的近似值，随着试验次数的增加，频率会越来越接近概率.

(2) 频率本身是随机的，在试验前不能确定.

(3) 概率是一个确定的常数，是客观存在的，在试验前已经确定，与试验次数无关.

【课后练习】

1. “某彩票的中奖概率为 0.1%”意味着　　(　　)

A. 买 1 000 张彩票就一定能中奖

B. 买 1 000 张彩票中一次奖

C. 买 1 000 张彩票一次奖也不中

D. 购买彩票中奖的可能性是 0.1%

2. 设 Φ 是不可能事件,Ω 是必然事件,则下列结论正确的是　　(　　)

A. $P(\Phi)=0, P(\Omega)=0$　　B. $P(\Phi)=0, P(\Omega)=1$

C. $P(\Phi)=1, P(\Omega)=0$　　D. $P(\Phi)=1, P(\Omega)=1$

3. (多选)下列说法正确的有　　(　　)

A. 做 9 次抛掷一枚质地均匀的硬币的试验,结果有 5 次出现正面,所以出现正面的概率是 $\frac{5}{9}$

B. 盒子中装有大小和形状相同的 3 个红球、3 个黑球、2 个白球,每种颜色的球被摸到的可能性相同

C. 从 $-4,-3,-2,-1,0,1,2$ 中任取一个数,取得的数小于 0 和不小于 0 的可能性不相同

D. 设有一大批产品,已知其次品率为 0.1,则从中任取 100 件,次品的件数可能不是 10 件

4. 已知随机事件 A 发生的频率是 0.02,如果事件 A 出现了 10 次,那么共进行了__________次试验.

5. 在一次掷硬币试验中,掷 100 次,其中有 48 次正面朝上,设反面朝上为事件 A,则事件 A 出现的频率为____________.

6. 指出下列事件是必然事件、不可能事件还是随机事件.

(1) 中国体操运动员将在下届奥运会上获得全能冠军.

(2) 出租车司机小李驾车通过几个十字路口都将遇到绿灯.

(3) 若 $x\in\mathbf{R}$,则 $x+1\geqslant 1$.

(4) 抛一枚骰子两次,朝上面的数字之和小于 2.

7. 某学校有书法、街舞和茶艺 3 个社团，小明要选报其中的至少 1 个社团，观察选报结果.

(1) 写出这个试验的所有基本事件.

(2) "至少选报 2 个社团"这一复合事件包含哪几个基本事件？

8. 一名篮球运动员在罚球线上进行投篮练习，结果见表 11-3.

表 11-3　投篮投中频率

投篮次数 n	100	150	200	250	300	350	400
投中次数 m	55	83	111	138	165	194	221
投中频率 $\frac{m}{n}$							

(1) 计算这名篮球运动员投中的频率，并填入表格(保留到小数点后第 3 位)；

(2) 求篮球运动员投中的概率估计值.

【数学文化】

智猪博弈

设想猪圈中有两头猪：大猪和小猪. 在猪圈的一侧设置了食槽，而在另一侧安装了控制猪食供应的按钮. 每次按下按钮，就会有 10 个单位的猪食进入食槽，但同时，按下按钮也会消耗 2 个单位的猪食，作为"成本".

这一大一小两头猪展开博弈,一共有以下四种情况:

情况 1 两头猪同时按下按钮,再一起跑过去吃,大猪能够吃到 7 个单位的猪食,小猪能够吃到 3 个单位的猪食,减去每头猪按按钮消耗的 2 个单位的猪食,大猪净收益 5 个单位的猪食,小猪净收益 1 个单位的猪食.

情况 2 大猪去按按钮,小猪在食槽边等着先吃,大猪再赶过去吃,大猪吃到 6 个单位的猪食,小猪吃到 4 个单位的猪食,大猪去掉按按钮消耗的 2 个单位的猪食,大小猪都将净得 4 个单位的猪食.

情况 3 小猪按按钮,大猪在食槽边等着先吃,大猪吃到 9 个单位的猪食,小猪吃到 1 个单位的猪食,再减去小猪按按钮消耗的 2 个单位的猪食,小猪净亏损 1 个单位的猪食.

情况 4 两头猪都选择等待,结果是谁都吃不到猪食.

博弈的结果是大猪按、小猪等,这就是智猪博弈,又称为搭便车博弈.

【拓展应用】

儿童节期间,某公园游戏场举行了一场活动,活动中有一种游戏的规则是:从一个装有 8 个红球和若干个白球的袋中随机摸 1 个球,摸到 1 个红球就得到一个吉祥物海宝玩具. 已参加这种游戏的儿童达到 40 000 人次,公园游戏场发放海宝玩具 8 000 个.

(1) 求参加此次活动得到海宝玩具的概率;

(2) 估计袋中白球的数量.

11.2　古典概型

【学习目标】

1. 理解等可能事件的概念，能判断一个试验是否为等可能事件.
2. 理解古典概型的基本特点，能够准确计算等可能事件的概率.

【重点难点】

重点：古典概型概念的理解及古典概型概率公式的简单应用.

难点：将实际问题抽象为数学模型.

【微课导学】

扫下面的二维码，学习微课“等可能事件的概率”“古典概型的典型例题”.

等可能事件的概率　　古典概型的典型例题

【自主学习】

1. 有一副去掉了大小王的扑克牌(每副扑克牌有 4 种花色，每种花色 13 张牌)，充分洗牌后，从中随机抽取一张，则抽到的牌为“红桃”的概率为　(　　)

A. $\frac{1}{52}$　　B. $\frac{1}{4}$　　C. $\frac{1}{13}$　　D. $\frac{1}{26}$

2. 有 3 个兴趣小组，甲、乙两位同学各自参加其中一个小组，每位同学参加各个小组的可能性相同，则这两位同学参加同一个兴趣小组的概率为(　　)

A. $\frac{1}{3}$　　B. $\frac{1}{2}$　　C. $\frac{2}{3}$　　D. $\frac{3}{4}$

3. 从 1,2,3,4 中任取 2 个不同的数,则取出的 2 个数之差的绝对值为 2 的概率是 ( )

A. $\frac{1}{2}$　　B. $\frac{1}{3}$　　C. $\frac{1}{4}$　　D. $\frac{1}{6}$

4. 一个袋中装有 5 个红球、4 个白球和 3 个黄球,每个球除颜色外都相同,从中任意摸出一球,则摸到红球的概率是________,摸到白球的概率是________,摸到黄球的概率是________.

5. 在平面直角坐标系中,从下列五个点:$A(0,0)$,$B(2,0)$,$C(1,1)$,$D(0,2)$,$E(2,2)$中任取三个,这三点能构成三角形的概率是________.

6. 三张卡片上分别写上字母 E,E,B,将三张卡片随机地排成一行,恰好排成英文单词 BEE 的概率为________.

7. 甲、乙、丙三人是某商场的安保人员,根据值班需要甲连续工作 2 天后休息一天,乙连续工作 3 天后休息一天,丙连续工作 4 天后休息一天,已知 3 月 31 日这一天三人均休息,求 4 月份三人在同一天工作的概率.

【探究任务】

任务一

试验 1　掷一枚均匀硬币.

问题 1　可能出现的结果有几种?这些结果的可能性相同吗?试猜想:它们的可能性各是多少?

试验 2　掷一枚质地均匀的骰子.

问题 2　正面向上的数字可能有几种？这些结果的可能性相同吗？试猜想:它们的可能性各是多少？

问题 3　上述两个试验有什么共同点呢？

① 试验结果数是________________的；

② 每种结果出现的可能性____________________.

问题 4　在试验 2 中，设事件 $A=\{$正面向上的数字是 3 的倍数$\}$，事件 $B=\{$正面向上的数字是偶数$\}$，则事件 A,B 分别包含几种基本事件？事件 A,B 的概率分别为多少呢？以上两种问题怎么得到概率的值的？

任务二

材料　“蒙提霍尔问题”，又叫“三门问题”，出自美国一个电视游戏节目，问题的名字取自节目的主持人蒙提霍尔. 参赛者面前有三扇关闭着的门，其中一扇的后面是一辆汽车，选中后面有车的那扇门就可以赢得汽车. 而另外两扇门后面各有一只山羊. 当参赛者选定了一扇门,但未去开启它的时候,主持人会开启剩下两扇门中的一扇,露出其中一只山羊,并问参赛者要不要改变选择,去选另一扇仍然关着的门. 比赛节目一经播出就引起了热烈的讨论,大部分人都凭借直觉认为不应该换. 主持人给出的答案是应该换,并阐明了理由. 最后,这个问题通过计算机程序反复验证,结果是“应该换”.“蒙提霍尔问题”告诉我们,逻辑上没有问题的直觉很可能是错误的.

问题 尝试通过计算三扇门选定前和选定后的概率,判断参赛者应该维持原来的选择,还是转而选择另一扇没有开启的门?

【典例解析】

例 1 5 张奖券中有 2 张是中奖的,首先由甲抽一张,然后由乙抽一张,求

(1) 甲中奖的概率 $P(A)$;

(2) 甲、乙都中奖的概率 $P(B)$;

(3) 只有乙中奖的概率 $P(C)$;

(4) 乙中奖的概率 $P(D)$.

解 甲、乙两人按顺序各抽一张,5 张奖券分别为 A_1,A_2,B_1,B_2,B_3,其中 A_1,A_2 为中奖券,则基本事件为 (A_1,A_2), (A_1,B_1), (A_1,B_2), (A_1,B_3), (A_2,A_1), (A_2,B_1), (A_2,B_2), (A_2,B_3), (B_1,A_1), (B_1,A_2), (B_1,B_2), (B_1,B_3), (B_2,A_1), (B_2,A_2), (B_2,B_1), (B_2,B_3), (B_3,A_1), (B_3,A_2), (B_3,B_1), (B_3,B_2),共 20 种.

(1) 若“甲中奖”,则有 (A_1,A_2), (A_1,B_1), (A_1,B_2), (A_1,B_3), (A_2,A_1), (A_2,B_1), (A_2,B_2), (A_2,B_3), 共 8 种,故

$$P(A)=\frac{8}{20}=\frac{2}{5}.$$

(2) "甲、乙都中奖"含有的基本事件有(A_1,A_2),(A_2,A_1),共 2 种,所以 $P(B)=\frac{2}{20}=\frac{1}{10}$.

(3) "只有乙中奖"的基本事件有(B_1,A_1),(B_2,A_1),(B_3,A_1),(B_1,A_2),(B_2,A_2),(B_3,A_2),共 6 种,故 $P(C)=\frac{6}{20}=\frac{3}{10}$.

(4) "乙中奖"的基本事件有(A_2,A_1),(B_1,A_1),(B_2,A_1),(B_3,A_1),(A_1,A_2),(B_1,A_2),(B_2,A_2),(B_3,A_2),共 8 种,故 $P(D)=\frac{8}{20}=\frac{2}{5}$.

备注　利用古典概型的计算公式时应注意两点:(1)所有的基本事件必须是互斥的;(2) 求事件所包含的基本事件数时,要不重不漏.

例 2　设连续掷两次骰子得到的点数分别为 m, n, 令平面向量 $\boldsymbol{a}=(m,n)$, $\boldsymbol{b}=(1,-3)$.

(1) 求使得事件"$\boldsymbol{a}\perp\boldsymbol{b}$"发生的概率;

(2) 求使得事件"$|\boldsymbol{a}|\leqslant|\boldsymbol{b}|$"发生的概率.

解　(1) 由题意知,$m\in\{1,2,3,4,5,6\}$,$n\in\{1,2,3,4,5,6\}$,故(m,n)所有可能的结果共 36 种.

因为$\boldsymbol{a}\perp\boldsymbol{b}$,所以 $m-3n=0$,即 $m=3n$,共有$(3,1)$,$(6,2)$2 种结果,所以事件$\boldsymbol{a}\perp\boldsymbol{b}$的概率为$\frac{2}{36}=\frac{1}{18}$.

(2) $|\boldsymbol{a}|\leqslant|\boldsymbol{b}|$,即 $m^2+n^2\leqslant10$,有$(1,1)$,$(1,2)$,$(1,3)$,$(2,1)$,$(2,2)$,$(3,1)$,共 6 种结果,使得$|\boldsymbol{a}|\leqslant|\boldsymbol{b}|$,其概率为$\frac{6}{36}=\frac{1}{6}$.

【课后练习】

1. 任意抛掷三枚硬币,至少两枚正面向上的概率是(　　)

A. $\frac{1}{2}$　　B. $\frac{1}{3}$　　C. $\frac{1}{6}$　　D. $\frac{1}{8}$

2. 从由 1,2,3,4,5 这 5 个数字组成的没有重复数字的三位数中,任意取出的一个三位数,这个三位数是偶数的概率是(　　)

A. $\frac{2}{5}$　　B. $\frac{3}{5}$　　C. $\frac{24}{125}$　　D. $\frac{1}{30}$

3. 某导演先从 2 个获得金鸡奖的演员和 3 个获得百花奖的演员中挑选 2 名演员演主角,后又从剩下的演员中挑选 1 名演员演配角.这位导演挑选出 2 个获得金鸡奖的演员和 1 个获得百花奖的演员的概率为　　(　　)

A. $\frac{1}{3}$　　B. $\frac{1}{10}$　　C. $\frac{2}{5}$　　D. $\frac{3}{10}$

4. 从正方体的 8 个顶点中任选 4 个,这 4 个点在同一个平面的概率为__________.

5. 若分配甲、乙、丙、丁四个人到三个不同的社区做志愿者,每个社区至少分配一人,每人只能去一个社区.若甲分配的社区已经确定,则乙与甲分配到不同社区的概率是__________.

6. 小明有 4 枚完全相同的硬币,每个硬币都分正反两面. 他把 4 个硬币摆成一摞,相邻两枚硬币的正面与正面不相对的概率为__________.

7. 一个口袋内装有形状、大小完全相同的 5 个球,其中 3 个白球、2 个黑球,从中一次摸出两个球.

(1) 共有多少个基本事件?

(2) 摸出的两个球是白球的概率是多少?

8. 甲、乙两校各有 3 名教师报名支教,其中甲校 2 男 1 女,乙校 1 男 2 女.

(1) 若从甲校和乙校报名的教师中各任选 1 名,写出所有可能的结果,并求选出的 2 名教师性别相同的概率;

(2) 若从报名的 6 名教师中任选 2 名,写出所有可能的结果,并求选出的 2 名教师来自同一学校的概率.

【数学文化】

古典概型是一种数学概率模型，其由来与历史发展密切相关. 古典概型起源于赌博游戏和骰子游戏.

图 11-2

在 16 世纪，意大利数学家卡尔达诺（图 11-2）开始研究赌博中的概率问题. 他意识到，在某些情况下，即使一个事件发生的可能性很小，但只要试验次数足够多，这个事件最终还是有可能发生的，这个发现被视为古典概型的萌芽.

图 11-3

17 世纪中叶，法国数学家费马（图 11-3）在研究骰子游戏时，提出了古典概型的两个基本概念：样本空间和样本点. 他认为，在骰子游戏中，出现的每一个结果都是一个样本点，而所有可能的样本点组成了样本空间. 费马的贡献在于，他明确了古典概型中的基本概念，并为后续的发展奠定了基础.

图 11-4

18 世纪末，法国数学家拉普拉斯（图 11-4）在研究概率论时，进一步发展了古典概型，他引入了概率函数的概念，并给出了古典概型的定义. 拉普拉斯的贡献在于，他明确了古典概型的数学定义，并为其在理论和应用方面的发展奠定了基础.

古典概型的发展也受到了实际应用领域的推动. 在保险业、医学、经济学等领域中，人们经常需要预测某个事件发生的可能性，古典概型提供了一种有效的工具来估计这些概率. 此外，在统计学和数据分析中，古典概型也发挥了重要作用，它可以帮助人们理解和解释数据分布的特征，从而为决策提供依据.

【拓展应用】

套圈中的概率学

公园和集市一般都有各种套圈的游戏,通常是用一定数量的圆圈去套场子里面的礼物,还有很多的翻版,如用乒乓球往杯子里面投放等. 这些游戏展示的供玩家套圈的东西很多,但游戏结果一般都是玩家乘兴而来,败兴而归.

从概率的角度分析,如图 11-5 所示,只有当圆圈在礼物所形成的圆的外部时,圆圈才能套中礼物,中间的小圆点是圆圈套中礼物时其圆心可以移动的范围.

图 11-5

如图 11-6 所示,假设中间的小圆的半径为 1 cm,在长为 3 m、宽为 2 m 的场子中摆放 27 个礼物,在不考虑其他因素的情况下,随机抛一个圆环,计算套中礼物的概率,并谈谈你的感想.

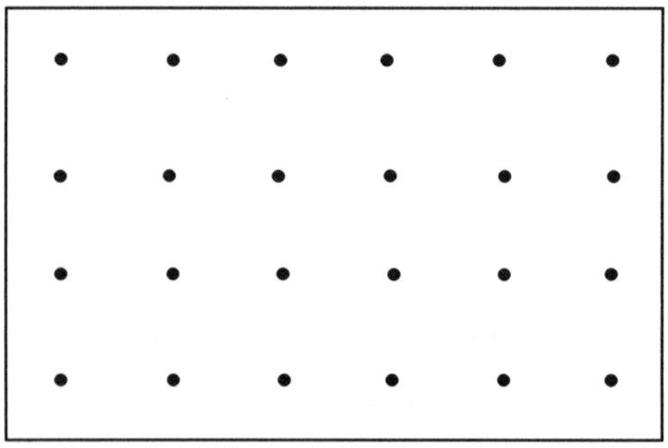

图 11-6

11.3　概率的简单性质

【学习目标】

1. 理解随机事件的概率取值范围.

2. 理解互斥事件及对立事件的概念,能判断某两个事件是否是互斥事件,进而判断他们是否是对立事件.

【重点难点】

重点:互斥事件和对立事件的概念、互斥事件和对立事件的概率计算公式.

难点:理解互斥事件与对立事件的联系与区别.

【微课导学】

扫下面的二维码,学习微课"互斥事件""对立事件".

互斥事件　　对立事件

【自主学习】

1. 根据概率的定义,可得到事件的概率具有如下基本性质:

性质 1:$P(\Omega)=$__________, $P(\varnothing)=$__________.

性质 2:对于任一事件 A,__________$\leqslant P(A)\leqslant$__________.

2. 我们把在一次试验中不可能同时发生的两个事件叫作____________.若 A,B 是互斥事件,则 $P(A\cup B)=$____________.

3. 我们把在一次试验中,其中必有一个发生的两个互斥事件叫作__________.一个事件 A 的对立事件通常记为$\overline{A}$.

4. 根据对立事件的意义,$A\cup\overline{A}$是一个必然事件,它的概率等于_________,又由于 A 与$\overline{A}$互斥,则 $P(A)=$__________.

5. 口袋内有一些大小和形状都相同的红球、黄球和白球,从中任意摸出一球,摸出的球是红球或黄球的概率为 0.4,摸出的球是红球或白球的概率为 0.9,那么摸出的球是黄球或白球的概率为 ( )

A. 0.7　　B. 0.5　　C. 0.3　　D. 0.6

6. 若某群体中的成员只用现金支付的概率为 0.45,既用现金支付也用非现金支付的概率为 0.15,则不用现金支付的概率为 ( )

A. 0.3　　B. 0.4　　C. 0.6　　D. 0.7

7. 从一箱分为四个等级的产品中随机地抽取一件,设事件 $A=\{$抽到一等品$\}$,事件 $B=\{$抽到二等品$\}$,事件 $C=\{$抽到三等品$\}$,且已知 $P(A)=0.65$,$P(B)=0.2$,$P(C)=0.1$,求抽到次品(一等品、二等品、三等品都属于合格品)的概率.

【探究任务】

任务一

阅读材料,回答问题.

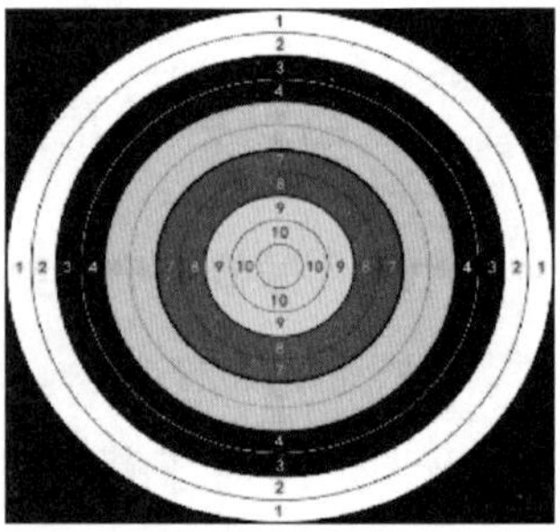

图 11-7

材料 1　如图 11-7 为气枪比赛靶纸.在 2023 年射击世锦赛男子 10 m 气手枪决赛中,中国选手张博文发挥稳健,打出了 10.4 环、10.3 环、10.1 环、10 环等优异成绩,最终以 244.3 环的总成绩获得冠军,并顺利拿到巴黎奥运会入场券.

问题　若将“打出 10.4 环”记为事件 A,“打出

10.3 环”记为事件 B,“打出 10.1 环”记为事件 C,“打出 10 环”记为事件 D,“打出超过 10 环”记为事件 E,则在一次射击中事件 A 与事件 B 能否同时发生? 事件 E 与事件 A,B,C 有什么关系?

材料 2　某地区年降水量(单位:mm)在下列范围内的概率见表 11-4.

表 11-4　年降水量概率

年降水量	[600,800)	[800,1 000)	[1 000,1 200)	[1 200,1 400)	[1 400,1 600)
概率	0.12	0.26	0.38	0.16	0.08

问题 1　如果降水量在 800～1 200 mm,被认为是雨水适宜,有利于农作物生长,那么该地区雨水适宜的概率是多少?

问题 2　如果降水量不小于 1 200 mm 就可能发生洪涝灾害,这时需要采取防洪措施,那么需要采取防洪措施的概率是多少?

问题 3　尝试总结互斥事件的含义及性质.

任务二

材料 1　在阿联酋富查伊拉举办的 2024 巴黎奥运会亚洲大洋洲落选赛上,中国选手沈晨鹏勇夺男子佩剑个人冠军,并取得巴黎奥运会个人参赛资格.

材料 2　社会保险是国家建立的社会保险制度,目的是保障公民在年老、疾病、工伤、失业、生育等情况下依法从国家和社会获得物质帮助的权利. 若被保险人有保险损失,依据保险合同进行赔偿;若没有损失,就不需要赔偿.

由此可见,在保险领域中,有两个互斥的状态"发生损失和不发生损失".

材料3 三国时期的赤壁之战中,曹操和诸葛亮处于对立状态,每一方都希望自己能够获胜,但只能一方最终获胜.

问题1 上述材料中提到了比赛赢与输、发生损失与不发生损失、战争的胜与负.请同学们结合实例,尝试描述对立事件的含义及性质.

问题2 尝试总结互斥事件和对立事件的区别与联系.

任务三

小组合作,完成表11-5.

表11-5 互斥事件与对立事件

事件的关系	定义	图形表示	符号表示
互斥事件	若 $A\cap B$ 为 ________,那么称事件 A 与事件 B 互斥.		$A\cap B=$ ________
对立事件	若 $A\cap B$ 为 ________, 且 $A\cup B$ 为 ________, 那么称事件 A 与事件 B 互为对立事件.		$A\cap B=$ ________ 且 $A\cup B=$ ________

【典例解析】

例1 袋中有9个大小相同、颜色不全相同的小球,分别为黑球、黄球、绿球,从中任意取一球,得到黑球或黄球的概率是$\frac{5}{9}$,得到黄球或绿球的概率是$\frac{2}{3}$.试求袋中黑球、黄球、绿球的个数分别是多少?

解 从中任取一球,分别记取到黑球、黄球、绿球为事件 A,B,C.由于 A,

B,C 为互斥事件，由题意知，

$$\begin{cases}P(A\cup B)=P(A)+P(B)=\dfrac{5}{9},\\ P(B\cup C)=P(B)+P(C)=\dfrac{2}{3},\\ P(A\cup B\cup C)=P(A)+P(B)+P(C)=1.\end{cases}$$

解得

$$\begin{cases}P(A)=\dfrac{1}{3},\\ P(B)=\dfrac{2}{9},\\ P(C)=\dfrac{4}{9}.\end{cases}$$

任取一球，得到黑球、黄球、绿球的概率分别是 $\frac{1}{3},\frac{2}{9},\frac{4}{9}$. 所以黑球的个数为 $9\times\frac{1}{3}=3$，黄球的个数为 $9\times\frac{2}{9}=2$，绿球的个数为 $9\times\frac{4}{9}=4$. 即袋中黑球、黄球、绿球的个数分别是 3，2，4.

备注　掌握互斥事件和对立事件的概率性质是解题的关键.

例 2　历史上有这样一个著名的概率问题：甲，乙两人做游戏，掷一枚钱币，若正面出现则甲得 1 分，反面出现则乙得 1 分，先得 10 分者胜，胜者获得全部赌金. 现在甲已得 8 分，乙已得 7 分，而游戏因故中断，问赌金应如何分配才合理？

解　不妨考虑甲胜的情形.

情形 1　掷两次甲胜，则概率

$$P_1=\frac{1}{2}\times\frac{1}{2}=\frac{1}{4};$$

情形 2　掷三次甲胜，则前两次必是一胜一负，最后一次甲胜，则概率

$$P_2=2\times\frac{1}{2}\times\frac{1}{2}\times\frac{1}{2}=\frac{1}{4};$$

情形 3　四次甲胜，则前三次中甲只胜了一次，最后一次甲胜，则概率

$$P_3=3\times\left(\frac{1}{2}\right)^4=\frac{3}{16}.$$

因为以上事件两两互斥，所以甲胜的概率为$\frac{1}{4}+\frac{1}{4}+\frac{3}{16}=\frac{11}{16}$.

又因为甲胜与乙胜的事件互为对立，所以乙胜的概率为 $1-\frac{11}{16}=\frac{5}{16}$.

故赌金的分配应是 11∶5(甲∶乙)比较合理.

备注 熟练掌握互斥事件和对立事件的含义及性质.

【课后练习】

1. 一个均匀的正方体玩具的各个面上分别标有数字 1,2,3,4,5,6. 将这个玩具向上抛掷 1 次，设事件 A 表示向上的一面出现奇数点，事件 B 表示向上的一面出现的点数不超过 3，事件 C 表示向上的一面出现的点数不小于 4，则 (　　)

A. A 与 B 是互斥而非对立事件　　B. A 与 B 是对立事件

C. B 与 C 是互斥而非对立事件　　D. B 与 C 是对立事件

2. 甲、乙两人下棋，两人下成和棋的概率是$\frac{1}{2}$，乙获胜的概率是$\frac{1}{3}$，则$\frac{5}{6}$是 (　　)

A. 乙获胜的概率　　B. 乙不输的概率

C. 甲获胜的概率　　D. 甲不输的概率

3. 投掷一枚质地均匀的骰子，记事件 A 为“出现奇数点”，事件 B“向上的点数不超过 3”，则 $P(A\cup B)=$ (　　)

A. $\frac{1}{3}$　　B. $\frac{2}{3}$　　C. $\frac{1}{6}$　　D. $\frac{5}{6}$

4. 中国乒乓球队甲，乙两名队员参加奥运会乒乓球女子单打比赛，甲夺得冠军的概率为$\frac{3}{7}$，乙夺得冠军的概率为$\frac{1}{4}$，那么中国队夺得女子乒乓球单打冠军的概率为__________.

5. 一只袋子中装有 7 个红玻璃球、3 个绿玻璃球，从中不放回地任意抽取两次，每次只取一个，取得两个红玻璃球的概率为$\frac{7}{15}$，取得两个绿玻璃球的概率为$\frac{1}{15}$，则取得两个同色玻璃球的概率为__________，至少取得一个红玻璃球的概率为__________.

6. 把一颗骰子投掷 2 次，观察出现的点数，并记第一次出现的点数为 a，第二次出现的点数为 b，试就方程组 $\begin{cases} ax+by=3, \\ x+2y=2. \end{cases}$ 解答下列问题.

(1) 求方程组只有一个解的概率；

(2) 求方程组只有正整数解的概率.

7. 现有 8 名奥运会志愿者，其中志愿者 A_1，A_2，A_3 通晓英语，B_1，B_2，B_3 通晓俄语，C_1，C_2 通晓德语. 从中选出一名通晓英语、俄语、德语的志愿者各 1 名，组成一个小组.

(1) 求 A_1 被选中的概率；

(2) 求 B_1，C_1 被选中的概率；

(3) 求 B_1，C_1 不全被选中的概率；

(4) 求 B_1，C_1 全不被选中的概率.

8. 八名学生中有两名班委，现从中任选三名学生参加学生代表大会，求下列事件的概率.

(1) 选出的学生中没有班委；

(2) 选出的学生中恰有一名班委；

(3) 选出的学生中至多有一名班委；

(4) 选出的学生中至少有一名班委.

【数学文化】

伯努利概型是一个非常重要的概型,涉及概率中两个重要的原理——小概率事件发生原理和小概率事件不发生原理. 若在每次试验中,事件 A 发生的概率为 $p(0<p<1)$,且 p 很小,则称这种事件为小概率事件. 我们在实际中认为,小概率事件在一次试验中是不发生的,称为小概率事件不发生原理. 但是在多次试验中事件是会发生的,又称为小概率事件发生原理.

下面用数学方法证明小概率实际发生原理.

设 B="在 n 次试验中事件 A 发生", A_i="在第 i 次试验中事件 A 发生" $P(A_i)=p, i=1,2,\cdots,n$,可看作是相互独立的,从而 $P(B)=1-(1-p)^n$. 当 $n\to\infty$ 时,$1-(1-p)^n\to 1$.

原理的解释,如:高速行驶在高速公路上的汽车,我们认为在一次行驶中不发生事故,但是在一个时间段必然发生事故,那降低事故的办法就是降低 p 的值. 就是说,我们规范行驶,以减少在交通中的事故数. 这两个原理也解释了我们常说的偶然与必然. 小概率事件发生的概率非常小,一次发生的概率几乎是 0,可以看作是偶然事情,但是在众多中必然会发生. 偶然中有必然,必然中伴随着偶然.

【拓展应用】

在商场付款处排队等候付款的人数及概率见表 11-6.

表 11-6 排队人数及概率

排队人数	0 人	1 人	2 人	3 人	4 人	5 人及以上
概率	0.1	0.16	0.3	0.3	0.1	0.04

求至少有 2 人排队的概率.

11.4　抽样方法

【学习目标】

1. 了解随机抽样的必要性和重要性，理解总体、个体及样本的意义，能举例说明普查和抽查的优缺点.

2. 掌握用抽签法、随机数表法进行抽样的步骤，会用简单随机抽样方法从总体中抽取样本.

3. 了解分层抽样和系统抽样方法. 了解各种抽样方法的适用范围，能根据具体情况选择适当的抽样方法.

【重点难点】

重点：简单随机抽样的理解.

难点：在三种随机抽样中，每个个体被抽到的可能性相等的理解.

【微课导学】

扫下面的二维码，学习微课“简单随机抽样”“系统抽样”“分层抽样”.

简单随机抽样　　　系统抽样　　　分层抽样

【自主学习】

1. 总体：把所考察对象的________________全体作为总体，构成总体的________________作为个体.

2. 样本:从总体中抽出__________叫作样本,样本中包含的__________叫作样本容量.

3. 从元素个数为 N 的总体中不放回地抽取容量为 n 的样本,如果每一次抽取时,每个个体被抽到的机会是均等而概率是相等的,这种抽样方法称为__________.

4. 当总体所含的个体较多时,可将总体分成均衡的几个部分,然后按照预先制定的规则,从每个部分中抽取一个个体,得到所需的样本,这种抽样方法称为____________.

5. 当总体由差别明显的几个部分组成时,为了使抽样更客观地反映总体情况,可先将总体中各个个体按差别特征,分成层次分明且互不重叠的几部分,然后按各部分在总体中所占比例进行简单随机抽样,这种抽样方法叫作分层抽样,其中所分成的各个部分称为"__________".

分层抽样的基本步骤:

(1) 分层:____;

(2) 计算:____;

(3) 确定各层应抽取的个体数:____________________________;

(4) 取样:____.

6. 已知某手机制造企业八月份生产智能手机 30 000 台,从中抽取1 000 台进行质量检测,其中被抽取的 1 000 台智能手机是____________,样本容量是____________.

7. 为客观了解某地区市民家庭存书量,该地区有关部门开展专项调查,访问了 3 000 位市民家庭. 在这项调查中,总体是___________________,个体是______________.

8. 某有奖明信片以 100 万张为一个开奖组,抽出号码后四位数是 2 569 为三等奖,这种抽样方法是__________.

9. 一个年级共有 20 个班,每个班学生的学号都是 1—50,为交流学习经验,要求每个班学号为 25 的学生参加座谈会,这里采用的抽样方法是______________.

10. 某学校教师共有 215 人,其中中年教师人数是老年教师人数的 2 倍,青年教师有 80 人,为了解教师的身体健康情况,现采用分层抽样的方法进行调查,在抽取的样本中有青年教师 16 人,则该样本中中年教师的人数为__________.

11. 某学校要抽查 1 200 名新生的体检结果，已知该校共有 20 个新生班级，若抽取一个样本容量为 80 的样本，应选择的抽样方法是　(　　)

A. 简单随机抽样　　B. 分层抽样

C. 系统抽样　　D. 以上答案都不对

12. 某公司有高层管理人员 5 人、中层管理人员 19 人、一般员工 253 人. 调查该公司员工的收入情况，从中抽取一个容量为 30 的样本，记这项调查为(1)；在中层管理人员中，抽取 8 人调查其收入和工作业绩情况，记这项调查为(2). 完成这两项调查应该采取的抽样方法依次为　(　　)

A. 分层抽样、系统抽样

B. 分层抽样、简单随机抽样

C. 系统抽样、分层抽样

D. 简单随机抽样、分层抽样

【探究任务】

任务一

阅读材料，回答问题.

材料　根据《中华人民共和国统计法》《全国人口普查条例》规定和《国务院关于开展第七次全国人口普查的通知》(国发〔2019〕24 号)要求，我国进行了第七次全国人口普查. 一年多以来，在以习近平同志为核心的党中央坚强领导下，在各地区各有关部门的大力支持下，在全国各级普查机构和普查人员的共同努力下，在广大普查对象的积极配合下，第七次全国人口普查圆满完成普查现场登记和普查主要数据的汇总评估工作，取得重大成果和显著成效.

问题　人口普查和人口抽样调查之间有何异同？抽样调查有几种方法？

任务二

材料 “大国工匠”是指有5年以上一线生产现场工作经历，长期践行执着专注、精益求精、一丝不苟、追求卓越的工匠精神，具有突出技术技能素质等基本条件，在引领力、实践力、创新力、攻关力、传承力方面显现明显发展潜力的工匠.

2024年1月4日，中华全国总工会印发《大国工匠人才培育工程实施办法(试行)》，提出计划每年培育200名左右大国工匠，示范引导各地、各行业每年积极支持培养1 000名左右省部级工匠、5 000名左右市级工匠.

问题 某职业院校调查学生观看《大国工匠》的比例.

(1) 某班级有40名学生，现在要从中抽出10名学生调查观看《大国工匠》的比例情况，每名学生被抽到的机会均等，怎样设计方案抽取这10名学生呢?

(2) 某年级1 200学生，从中抽取100名学生进行调查，如何在1 200名学生中合理抽取这100名学生呢?

任务三

为了解某城市居民的环保意识情况，调查机构从某社区的 120 名青年人、80 名中年人和 60 名老年人中，抽取 13 个人进行调查，怎样抽取才最合理呢？

任务四

小组合作，尝试总结三种抽样方法的相同点、不同点及适用范围，并填入表 11-7.

表 11-7　抽样方法的异同

抽样方法	相同点	不同点	适用范围
简单随机抽样	个体被抽到的可能性都一样		
系统抽样			
分层抽样			

【典例解析】

例 1　为办好职教周活动，用抽签法从某班级 50 名学生中抽取 6 人参加职教周活动，如何设计抽样方案？

解　用抽签法设计抽样方案：

（1）编号：将 50 名学生编号 01，02，03，…，50.

（2）做签：将号码分别写在 50 张大小、形状相同的纸条上，揉成团，做成签.

（3）抽签：将签放入同一个箱里，搅匀；每次从箱中不放回地抽取一个签，连续抽取 6 次.

（4）取样：取出与签号相应的学生，组成样本.

备注 理解抽签法，掌握抽签法的步骤.

例 2 某职业院校有一年级学生 1 000 人、二年级学生 900 人、三年级学生 600 人. 为了解该校数学课教学质量情况，从中抽取 100 名学生进行质量检测，如何设计抽样方案?

解 抽样方案如下:

(1) 分层:按一年级学生、二年级学生、三年级学生将总体分为三层.

(2) 计算:样本 100 人，总体 2 500 人，样本容量与总体个数的比值为

$$\frac{100}{2\,500}=\frac{1}{25};$$

(3) 确定各层应抽取的个体数:一年级学生 1 000 人，从中抽取 $1\,000\times\frac{1}{25}$人$=40$ 人;二年级学生 900 人，从中抽取 $900\times\frac{1}{25}$人$=36$ 人;三年级学生 600 人，从中抽取 $600\times\frac{1}{25}$人$=24$ 人.

(4) 取样:对三个年级学生采用简单随机抽样或系统抽样的方法，从不同年级中抽取一年级学生 40 人、二年级学生 36 人、三年级学生 24 人，合并，即得到 100 名学生组成的样本.

备注 当总体由差别明显的几个部分组成时，宜采用分层抽样方法进行抽样，而抽样后每一层的内部可采用简单随机抽样或系统抽样的方法抽取个体.

例 3 某公司生产甲、乙、丙三种产品 900 件，其中丙产品 300 件，丙产品的数量是乙产品的数量的 3 倍，检测员采用分层抽样的方法抽取部分商品进行质量检测，若在抽取的样本中甲产品有 10 件，则抽取的样本中乙产品有多少件?

解 因为丙产品有 300 件，丙产品的数量是乙产品的数量的 3 倍，所以乙产品的数量为 100 件，甲、乙、丙三种产品共 900 件，所以甲产品的数量为 500 件.

从 500 件甲产品中抽取了 10 件，故抽取比例为$\frac{10}{500}=\frac{1}{50}$，因此乙产品抽取了 $100\times\frac{1}{50}$件$=2$ 件，抽取的样本中乙产品有 2 件.

备注 确定样本容量与总体个数的比值即抽取比例是解题的关键.

【课后练习】

1. 为了了解某职业学校全体学生的身高情况，从该校学生中抽测了 100 人的身高，在这个问题中，总体是指　　　　（　　）

A. 100 人的身高　　　　B. 每个人的身高

C. 全体学生　　　　D. 职业学校全体学生的身高

2. 小李和小张是某职业学校同班的学生，现在学校要在该班随机抽取一人参加一项比赛，以下描述正确的是　　　　（　　）

A. 小李被抽到的可能性等于小张被抽到的可能性

B. 小李被抽到的可能性小于小张被抽到的可能性

C. 小李被抽到的可能性大于小张被抽到的可能性

D. 不确定

3. 某果汁生产企业一个月生产了 1 000 箱橙汁和 400 箱苹果汁，质检员要对这批产品进行抽样检查，准备抽样 70 瓶，下列选项对这次抽样描述正确的是　　　　（　　）

A. 应采用简单随机抽样的方法，在橙汁中抽样 20 瓶，在苹果汁中抽样 50 瓶

B. 应采用分层抽样的方法，在橙汁中抽样 40 瓶，在苹果汁中抽样 30 瓶

C. 应采用分层抽样的方法，在橙汁中抽样 50 瓶，在苹果汁中抽样 20 瓶

D. 采用简单随机抽样、系统抽样、分层抽样的方法均可

4. 已知三种型号冰箱的产量分别为 1 200 台、1 800 台、2 400 台. 用分层抽样法抽取 45 台进行检验，应分别抽取________台、________台和________台.

5. 某公司生产葡萄、香蕉、草莓三种不同口味的口香糖，葡萄、香蕉、草莓口味的口香糖生产量之比为 1∶3∶6，现在用分层抽样的方法抽出容量为 n 的样本，样本中葡萄口味的口香糖有 50 袋，那么样本容量 n 为____________.

6. 已知某学校有 1 682 名学生，用系统抽样的方法，从中抽取 84 人进行体能测试. 若随机剔除 2 名学生后，将剩余的 1 680 名学生随机编号，则在抽取的 84 人中，编号落在[61,160]内的人数有多少？

7. 某工厂有甲、乙、丙三个车间共生产 2 000 个机器零件，其中甲车间生产零件的数量与乙车间生产零件的数量之比是 4:3，丙车间生产 600 个零件，采用分层抽样的方法，从这 2 000 个零件中抽取 50 个零件进行检测，求从甲、乙、丙车间分别抽取多少个零件?

8. 某企业有 500 名员工，其中不到 35 岁的有 125 人，35～49 岁的有 280 人，50 岁以上的有 95 人. 为了解该单位职工年龄与身体状况的有关指标，从中抽取 100 名员工作为样本. 如果采用分层抽样的方法进行抽样，请简单描述抽样过程.

【数学文化】

中国概率统计事业的奠基人——许宝騄

许宝騄(图 11-8)，数学家，开创了概率论、数理统计的教学与研究工作. 在内曼-皮尔逊理论、参数估计理论、多元分析、极限理论等方面取得卓越成就，是多元统计分析学科的开拓者之一. 其研究成果推动了概率论与数理统计的发展. 至今“许方法”(多元分析统计学家谢菲称之为“数学严密性的范本”)仍被认为是解决检验问题的最实用方法.

图 11-8

《中国大百科全书 数学》称赞说：“许宝騄是中国早期从事数理统计学和概率论研究并达到世界先进水平的一位杰出学者.” 1983 年，德国斯普林格出版社(Springer-Verlag)刊印了《许宝騄全集》(Pao-Lu Hsu Collected Papers)，全集是由钟开莱主编的，共收集了已发表的、未被发表的论文 40 篇. 书评中有这样一句话：

许宝騄被公认为在数理统计和概率论方面第一个具有国际声望的中国数学家. 许宝騄的相片悬挂在斯坦福大学统计系的走廊上，与世界著名的统计学家并列.

【拓展应用】

党的十八大以来，以习近平同志为核心的党中央把脱贫攻坚作为全面建成小康社会的底线任务，纳入“五位一体”总体布局和“四个全面”战略布局，组织实施了人类历史上规模空前、力度最大、惠及人口最多的脱贫攻坚战. 2021 年，我国脱贫攻坚战取得了全面胜利，全国各地的调研人员用科学的方法为全国脱贫攻坚战的

图 11-9

全面胜利提供了重要保障,在具体的评估调研中,扬长避短,采用分层抽样与系统抽样相结合的抽样设计,提高了抽样效率以及样本的代表性. 查找相关资料,了解其中用到的抽样方法.

11.5　统计图表

【学习目标】

1. 掌握列频率分布表的方法，初步感受用样本频率分布估计总体频率分布规律的思想.

2. 学会用频率分布表作分布直方图的方法，学会用频率分布直方图对总体分布规律进行估计.

【重点难点】

重点：通过频率分布表、频率分布直方图对总体进行估计.

难点：频率分布直方图中以频率/组距为纵轴的理解.

【微课导学】

扫下面的二维码，学习微课“频率分布表”“频率分布直方图”.

频率分布表　　　频率分布直方图

【自主学习】

1. 列频率分布表的步骤.

第一步：计算极差，极差是指________________.

第二步：决定组距和组数，组距是指________________.

第三步：确定各组分点，确定各组分点的原则是________________.

第四步:列频率分布表.

2. 组距、极差、组数之间的关系是________________.

3. 绘制频率分布直方图的步骤.

(1) 先制作频率分布表,然后作直角坐标系,纵轴表示____________.

(2) 在横轴上标出频率分布表的各分点.

(3) 在坐标系中,分别将横轴上标出的点以相邻两点的线段为底作____________,高等于该组的____________.

4. 把横轴分成若干段,每一线段对应一个组的组距,然后以此线段为底作一矩形,它的高等于该组的____________,这样得出一系列的矩形,每个矩形的面积恰好是该组上的_____________,这些矩形就构成了频率分布直方图.

5. 一个容量为 20 的样本,数据的分组及各组的频数如下:

$[10,20)$,2;$[20,30)$,3;$[30,40)$,x;$[40,50)$,5;$[50,60)$,4;$[60,70)$,2;

则 $x=$____________;根据样本的频率分布估计,数据落在$[10,50)$的概率约为____________.

6. 某中学为了解学生数学课程的学习情况,在 3 000 名学生中随机抽取 200 名,并统计这 200 名学生的某次数学考试成绩,得到了样本的频率分布直方图(图 11-10).根据频率分布直方图推测,这 3 000 名学生在该次数学考试中成绩小于 60 分的人数是____________.

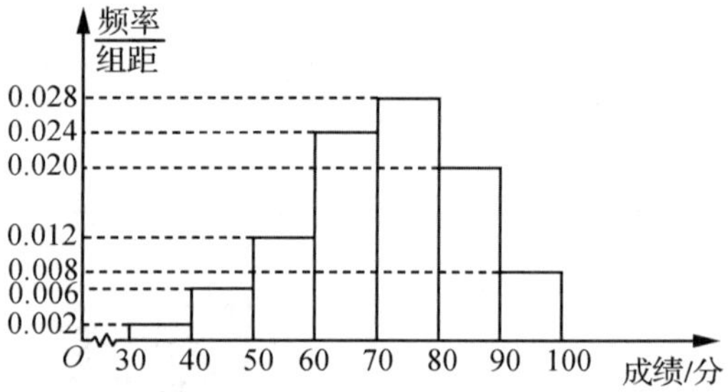

图 11-10

【探究任务】

任务一

阅读材料,回答问题.

材料 江苏省是位于长三角地区的沿海强省,因下辖的 13 座城市均为全国 GDP 百强市,且苏州和南京同时位列前 10,故有“十三太保”之称. 江苏省连续数十年 GDP 稳居全国第 2，2023 年实现 GDP 128 222.16 亿元．江苏省以制造业立省，2023 年制造业增加值高达 4.66 亿元，位居全国前列．如图 11-11 所示，2023 年全省公布的 13 市 GDP 依次为：苏州、南京、无锡、南通、常州、徐州、扬州、盐城、泰州、镇江、淮安、宿迁、连云港．其中，江苏已有 5 座城市达到万亿，均位于江苏南部．从增速来看，苏北地区高于苏南．苏州市 2023 年 GDP 已接近 25 000 亿，几乎等于南京与扬州的总和．

图 11-11

问题　用什么方法呈现能更直观地反映以上信息？

任务二

小组合作,调查你所在班级同学的身高,做好记录,并完成以下任务.

(1) 样本数据的极差是多少?

(2) 如果分为 6 组,组距是多少?

(3) 完成表 11-8.

表 11-8　身高调查

分组	频数	频率	$\frac{频率}{组距}$
合计			

(4) 绘制身高频率分布直方图(图 11-12).

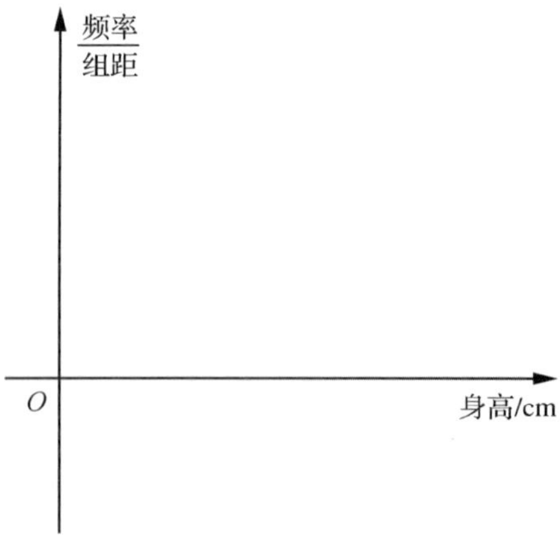

图 11-12

【典例解析】

例 1　某校 100 名学生期中考试语文成绩的频率分布直方图如图 11-13 所示，其中成绩分组区间是[50,60)，[60,70)，[70,80)，[80,90)，[90,100].

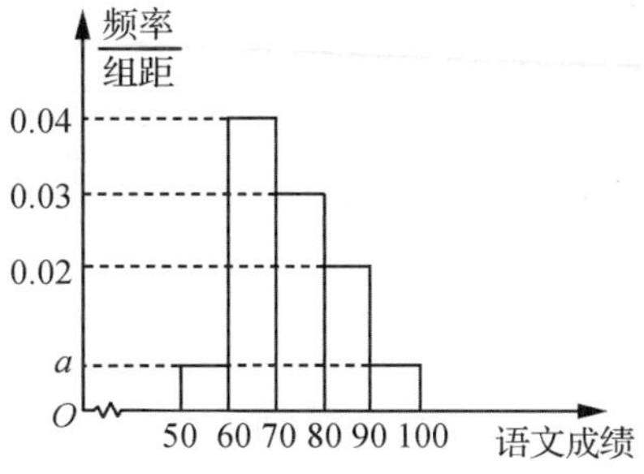

图 11-13

（1）求图中 a 的值；

（2）若这 100 名学生语文成绩某些分数段的人数（x）与数学成绩相应分数段的人数（y）之比见表 11-9，求数学成绩在[50,90)之外的人数.

表 11-9　数学成绩分布

分数段	[50,60)	[60,70)	[70,80)	[80,90)
$x:y$	1:1	2:1	3:4	4:5

解　（1）由频率分布直方图知

$$(2a+0.02+0.03+0.04)\times 10=1,$$

解得

$$a=0.005.$$

（2）由频率分布直方图知语文成绩在[50,60)，[60,70)，[70,80)，[80,90)各分数段的人数依次为

$$0.005\times 10\times 100=5,$$

$$0.04\times 10\times 100=40,$$

$$0.03\times 10\times 100=30,$$

$$0.02\times 10\times 100=20.$$

由题中给出的比例关系知，数学成绩在上述各分数段的人数依次为

$$5\times 1=5,$$

$$40\times \frac{1}{2}=20,$$

$$30\times \frac{4}{3}=40,$$

$$20\times \frac{5}{4}=25.$$

故数学成绩在[50,90)之外的人数为

$$100-(5+20+40+25)=10.$$

例 2 某校高一年级有 800 名学生,为了了解他们的数学期末考试情况,从中抽取一个容量为 60 的样本,数据的分组及各组的频数见表 11-10.

表 11-10 数学成绩分布

分组	人数	分组	人数
[0,30)	2	[30,40)	2
[40,50)	4	[50,60)	6
[60,70)	10	[70,80)	17
[80,90)	11	[90,100)	8

(1) 列出样本的频率分布表.

(2) 画出频率分布直方图.

(3) 试估计在什么分数段人数最多.

(4) 试估计不低于 80 分的人的百分比.

(5) 根据样本的频率分布表,估计该校高一年级学生数学期末考试的平均成绩.

解 (1) 频率分布表见表 11-11.

表 11-11 数学成绩频率分布表

分组	频数	频率	$\frac{频率}{组距}$
[0,30)	2	0.033	0.003 3
[30,40)	2	0.033	0.003 3
[40,50)	4	0.067	0.006 7
[50,60)	6	0.100	0.010 0
[60,70)	10	0.167	0.016 7
[70,80)	17	0.283	0.028 3
[80,90)	11	0.183	0.018 3
[90,100)	8	0.134	0.013 4
合计	60	1	

(2) 频率直方图如图 11-14 所示.

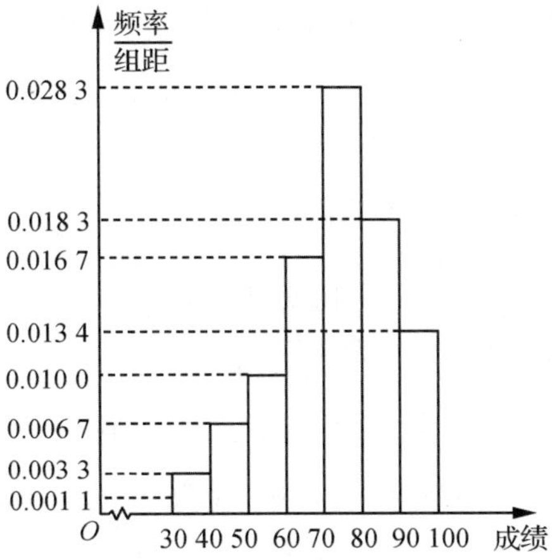

图 11-14

（3）从频率分布表可以看出在 70～80 分数段人最多.

（4）不低于 80 分的频率为

$$0.183+0.134=0.317,$$

所以可估计不低于 80 分的人约占 31.7%.

（5）期末考试数学年级平均成绩为

$$(15\times2+35\times2+45\times4+55\times6+65\times10$$
$$+75\times17+85\times11+95\times8)\div60=70.5.$$

备注　用样本的频率分布表和频率分布直方图估计总体均值及相应范围的百分比是频率分布表及频率分布直方图的重要应用.

【课后练习】

1. 一个容量为 80 的样本，最大值是 141，最小值是 50，组距为 10，则该样本可分为（　　）

A. 10 组　　B. 9 组　　C. 8 组　　D. 7 组

2. 在对 60 个数据进行整理的频率分布表中，各组的频率之和与频数之和分别是（　　）

A. 60，1　　B. 60，60　　C. 1，60　　D. 1，1

3. 数据 110，90，85，80，90，100，105，90 的极差为（　　）

A. 30　　B. 20　　C. 25　　D. 15

4. 在 2 000 个数据中,用适当的方法抽取 50 个作为样本进行统计. 在频数频率表中,67～69 这一组的频率为 0.20,则估计总体数据中落在 67～69 的个数约为__________.

5. 将 50 个数据分成 3 组,其中第一组与第三组的频率之和为 0.7,则第二组的频率为__________,第二组的频数为__________.

6. 某雷达测速区规定:凡车速大于或等于 70 km/h的汽车视为“超速”,并将受到处罚,如图 11-15 所示是某路段的一个检测点对 200 辆汽车的车速进行检测所得结果的频率分布直方图,则从图中可以看出被处罚的汽车大约有多少辆?

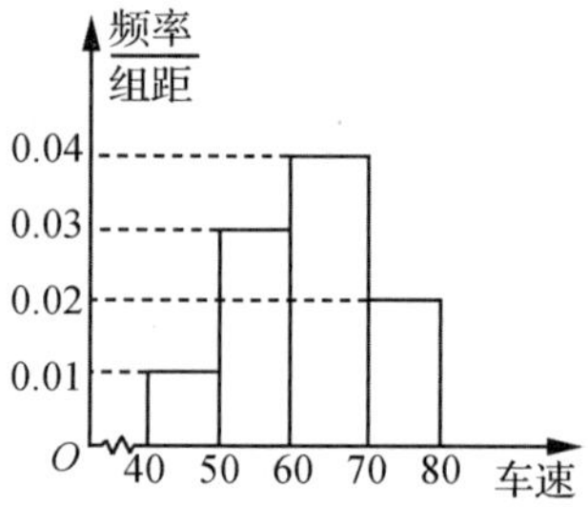

图 11-15

7. 有一个容量为 20 的样本,其数据如下.

45,45,29,42,58,37,53,52,49,34,27,32,42,55,40,38,50,26,54,26.

填写表 11-12 的频数、频率,并绘制频率分布直方图.

表 11-12　样本分组频率

分组	频数	频率
[20.5,29.5)		
[29.5,39.5)		
[39.5,49.5)		
[39.5,59.5)		
合计		

8. 对某种电子元件进行使用寿命追踪调查，情况见表 11-13.

表 11-13　电子元件寿命统计

寿命/h	100～200	200～300	300～400	400～500	500～600
个数	20	30	80	40	30

(1) 列出频率分布表.

(2) 画出频率分布直方图.

(3) 估计元件寿命在 100～400 h 以内的百分比.

【数学文化】

皮尔逊(图 11-16)，英国数学家、生物统计学家，数理统计学的创立者、自由思想者，对生物统计学、气象学等做出了重大贡献. 他被公认是旧派理学派和描述统计学派的代表人物，并被誉为现代统计科学的创立者. 皮尔逊是 20 世纪科学革命和哲学革命的先驱，“批判学派”代表人物之一. 直方图是数值数据分布的精确图形表示，被皮尔逊首先引入统计学中.

图 11-16

【拓展应用】

某班从甲、乙、丙三名候选人中选举一名学生代表，每张选票上只能选一人或不选，否则视为无效票. 得票超过半数者当选，无人超过半数时，得票前两位者再进行第二轮选举. 全班同学参加了投票，得票情况统计表和饼图如表 11-14 和图 11-17 所示.

表 11-14　得票数量统计表

项目	甲	乙	丙	其他
票数	20	x	3	1

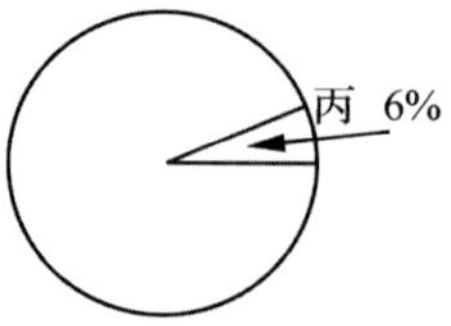

图 11-17

该班的总人数为__________，通过计算可知，__________当选学生代表.

11.6　样本均值与标准差

【学习目标】

1. 理解样本均值、方差及标准差的意义.
2. 会根据公式求一个样本的均值、方差及标准差.
3. 会用样本均值、方差及标准差估计总体数据的集中趋势和离散程度.

【重点难点】

重点:用样本平均数描述总体水平,用样本方差、标准差比较数据稳定性水平.

难点:理解平均数是刻画数据集中趋势的特征值,会用方差刻画数据离散程度.

【微课导学】

扫下面的二维码,学习微课“样本平均数”与“样本方差”.

样本平均数　　　　样本方差

【自主学习】

1. 在方差计算公式 $s^2=\frac{1}{10}[(x_1-20)^2+(x_2-20)^2+\cdots+(x_{10}-20)^2]$ 中,数字 10 和 20 分别表示 (　　)

A. 数据的个数和方差　　　　B. 平均数和数据的个数

C. 数据的个数和平均数　　　　D. 数据组的方差和平均数

2. 为促进精准扶贫,某县计划引进一批免费提供给贫困户种植的果树树苗. 为了解果树树苗的生长情况,现从甲、乙两个品种中各随机抽取了100株,进行高度测量,并将高度数据制作成了如图11-18所示的频率分布直方图. 由频率分布直方图求得甲、乙两个品种高度的平均值都是66.5,用样本估计总体,则下列描述正确的是 ( )

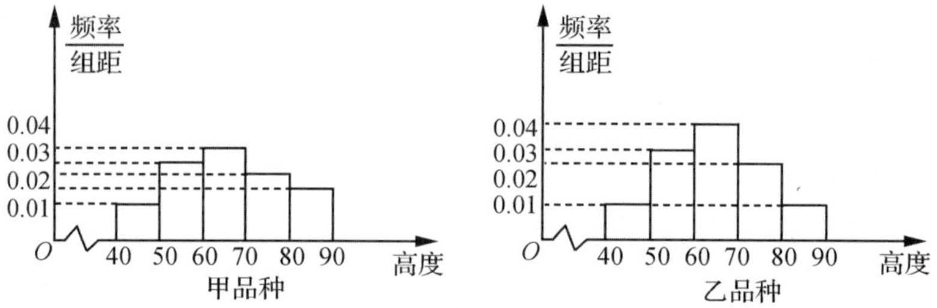

图 11-18

A. 甲品种的平均高度高于乙品种的平均高度,且乙品种比甲品种长得整齐

B. 乙品种的平均高度高于甲品种的平均高度,且甲品种比乙品种长得整齐

C. 甲、乙两品种的平均高度差不多,但甲品种比乙品种长得整齐

D. 甲、乙两品种的平均高度差不多,但乙品种比甲品种长得整齐

3. 甲、乙、丙三人投掷飞镖,他们的成绩环数如图11-19所示. 则甲、乙、丙三人训练成绩方差 $s_{甲}^2$、$s_{乙}^2$、$s_{丙}^2$ 的大小关系是 ( )

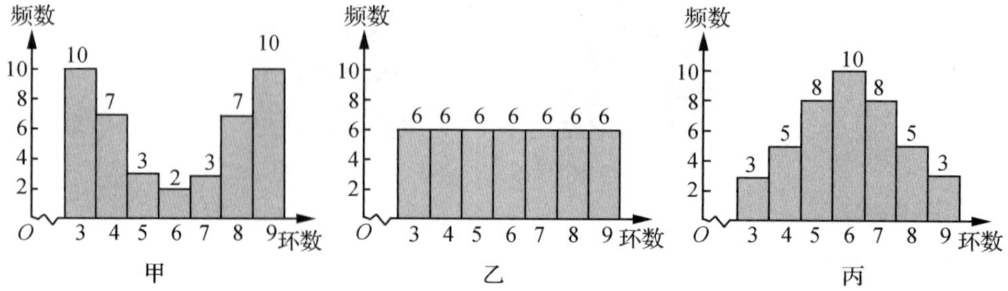

图 11-19

A. $s_{丙}^2<s_{乙}^2<s_{甲}^2$　　B. $s_{丙}^2<s_{甲}^2<s_{乙}^2$

C. $s_{乙}^2<s_{丙}^2<s_{甲}^2$　　D. $s_{乙}^2<s_{甲}^2<s_{丙}^2$

4. 方差越大,说明数据的波动越________,越不________.

5. 某校初三年级甲、乙两班举行电脑汉字输入速度比赛，两个班参加比赛的学生每分钟输入汉字的个数，经统计和计算后结果见表 11-15.

表 11-15　输入速度统计

班级	参加人数	平均字数	中位数	方差
甲	55	135	147	191
乙	55	135	151	110

有一位同学根据表 11-15 得出如下结论：

① 甲、乙两班学生的平均水平相同；

② 乙班优秀的人数比甲班优秀的人数多(每分钟输入汉字达 150 个以上为优秀)；

③ 甲班学生比赛成绩的波动比乙班学生比赛成绩的波动大.

上述结论正确的是____________.(填序号)

6. 某瓜农采用大棚栽培技术种植了一亩地良种西瓜，这亩地西瓜约 600 个. 在西瓜上市时随机摘了 10 个成熟的西瓜，称重见表 11-16.

表 11-16　西瓜质量

西瓜质量/kg	5.5	5.4	5.0	4.9	4.6	4.3
西瓜数量/个	1	2	3	2	1	1

则这 10 个西瓜的平均质量是____________kg，这亩地西瓜产量约是____________kg.

7. 已知一组数据 $x_1, x_2, \cdots, x_{10}$ 的方差是 2，且 $(x_1-3)^2+(x_2-3)^2+\cdots+(x_{10}-3)^2=380$，求 $\bar{x}$.

【探究任务】

任务一

阅读材料,回答下列问题.

材料1 市场监管总局发布2023年消费者投诉举报六大突出问题:售后服务、直播带货、智能设备、新能源汽车、合同签订及履行和虚假宣传. 其中售后服务连续两年居投诉问题首位.

材料2 为了对几个行业的服务质量进行评价,消费者协会在四个行业分别抽取了不同的企业作为样本. 最近一年中消费者对总共23家企业投诉的次数见表11-17.

表11-17 消费者对四个行业的投诉次数

观测值	行业			
	零售业	旅游业	航空公司	家电制造业
1	57	68	31	44
2	66	39	49	51
3	49	29	21	65
4	40	45	34	77
5	34	56	40	58
6	53	51		
7	44			

相应条形图如图11-20所示.

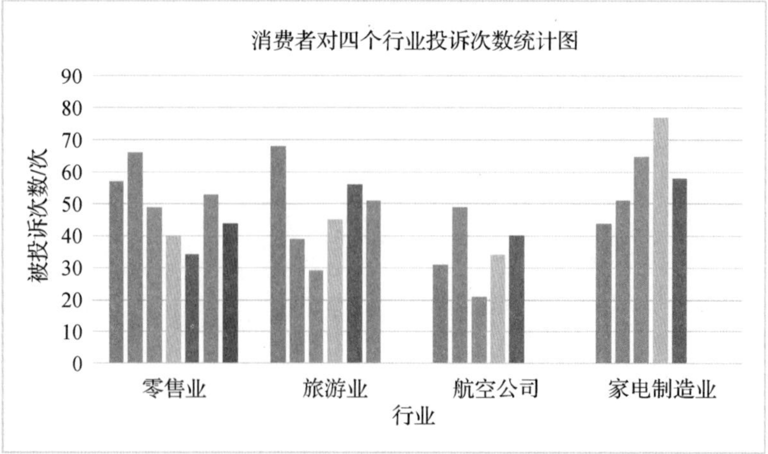

图11-20

问题　通过计算四个行业投诉次数的均值，分析四个行业之间的服务质量是否有显著差异，判断“行业”对“投诉次数”是否有显著影响？

任务二

阅读材料，回答下列问题.

材料　港珠澳大桥(图 11-21)是世界上最长的钢结构桥梁，仅主体工程的主梁钢板用量就达 42 万 t，相当于 10 座“鸟巢”体育场或 60 座埃菲尔铁塔的重量. 港珠澳大桥主桥的三座通航孔桥全部采用斜拉索桥，由多条 8 t～23 t、1 860MPa 的超高强度平行钢丝斜拉缆索从约 3 000 t 自重主塔处张拉承受约 7 000 t 重的梁面，保障了整座大桥具有跨径大、桥塔高、结构稳定性强等特点.

图 11-21

为了检测钢丝的抗拉强度，桥梁建设方从两家生产钢丝的厂方各随机抽取一个样本，检测它们的抗拉强度见表 11-18(单位：kg/mm^2).

表 11-18　钢丝的抗拉强度

甲	110	120	130	125	120	125	135	125	135	125
乙	115	100	125	130	115	125	125	145	125	145

问题 1　通过计算两厂家钢丝抗拉强度的均值，能否检测出哪家生产钢丝的抗拉强度高？

问题 2　表 11-18 中数据相应的折线图如图 11-22 所示，能否由图中观测出哪家生产钢丝的抗拉强度更稳定？

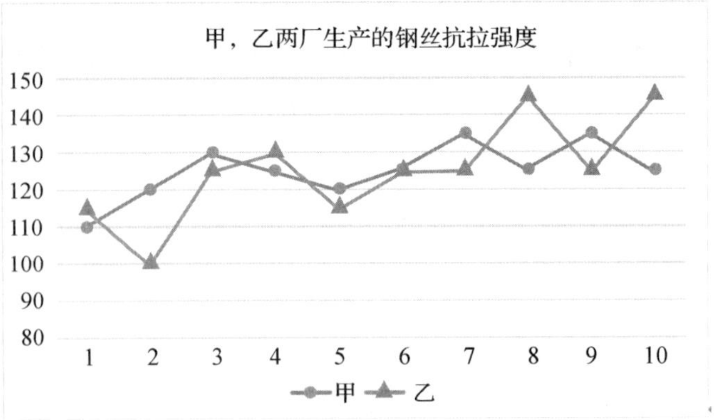

图 11-22

问题 3 先用各个数据减去它们的平均数,得到各个数据的偏差,再将各偏差相加得到一个数值.这个数值能否判断数据的波动大小?如果不能,该怎样改进?

【典例解析】

例 1 为了缓解道路交通高峰的压力,某市政府采取了错时上下班的措施.表 11-19 是新华路在采取措施前后每 30 min 通过的汽车量.

表 11-19 采取措施前后交通流量对比

时间段	6:30—7:00	7:00—7:30	7:30—8:00	8:00—8:30	8:30—9:00	9:00—9:30
采取措施前交通流量/辆	2 000	2 500	3 000	1 800	1 700	1 600
采取措施后交通流量/辆	1 800	2 200	2 500	2 300	2 000	1 800

(1) 从 6:30 到 9:30 这个时间段内,采取错时上下班前后,汽车的平均流

量有变化吗？

（2）分别计算两组数据的方差．你认为采取的措施是否有效果？

解 （1）采取措施前汽车的平均流量为

$$\overline{x}_1=\frac{1}{6}(2\ 000+2\ 500+\cdots+1\ 600)=2\ 100(\text{辆}),$$

采取措施后汽车的平均流量为

$$\overline{x}_2=\frac{1}{6}(1\ 800+2\ 200+\cdots+1\ 800)=2\ 100(\text{辆}),$$

所以，汽车的平均流量没有变化．

（2）采取措施前的方差为

$$s_1{}^2=\frac{1}{6}[(2\ 000-2\ 100)^2+(2\ 500-2\ 100)^2+\cdots+(1\ 600-2\ 100)^2]$$

$$\approx 246\ 667.$$

采取措施后的方差为

$$s_2{}^2=\frac{1}{6}[(1\ 800-2\ 100)^2+(2\ 200-2\ 100)^2+\cdots+(1\ 800-2\ 100)^2]$$

$$\approx 66\ 666.$$

因为 $s_1{}^2>s_2{}^2$，所以采取措施前后，汽车的平均流量没有变化，但采取措施后的方差小了，流量相对稳定，所以采取的措施有效．

备注 掌握平均数和方差的求法是解题的关键．

例 2 为了科学地比较考试成绩，有些选拔性考试常常将考试分数转化为标准分 Z，转化关系式为 $Z=\frac{x-\overline{x}}{s}$，其中 x 是某位学生的考试分数，$\overline{x}$是这次考试的平均分，s 是这次考试的标准差，Z 为这位学生的标准分．转化后的分数可能出现小数或负数，因此，又常将 Z 分数作线性变换转化为其他分数．例如，某次学业选拔性考试采用的是 T 分数，线性变换公式为 $T=42Z+58$．

已知一组学号为 1—10 的学生的某次考试成绩，见表 11-20．

表 11-20 某次考试成绩

学号 i	1	2	3	4	5	6	7	8	9	10
成绩 x_i	70	80	69	75	68	68	79	87	70	74

求学号为 2 的学生的 T 分数．

解 根据题意，平均成绩为

$$\overline{x}=\frac{1}{10}(70+80+69+75+68+68+79+87+70+74)=74,$$

则方差为

$$s^2=\frac{1}{9}[(70-74)^2+(80-74)^2+\cdots+(74-74)^2]=40,$$

标准差为

$$s\approx 6.325.$$

于是,学号为 2 的学生的标准分 $Z=\frac{80-74}{6.325}=0.9486$. 故该学生的 T 分数为 $T=0.9486\times 42+58\approx 98$.

备注 掌握平均数、方差 s^2 和标准差 s 的求法是解题的关键.

【课后练习】

1. 某地 2004 年第一季度应聘和招聘人数排行榜前 5 个行业的情况见表 11-21.

表 11-21 某地 2004 第一季度招聘情况

行业名称	计算机	机械	营销	物流	贸易
应聘人数	215 830	200 250	154 676	74 570	65 280
招聘人数	124 620	102 935	89 115	76 516	70 436

若用同一行业中应聘人数与招聘人数比值的大小来衡量该行业的就业情况,则根据表中的数据,就业形势一定是 ( )

A. 计算机行业好于化工行业　　B. 建筑行业好于物流行业

C. 机械行业最紧张　　D. 营销行业比贸易行业紧张

2. 从鱼塘捕得同时放养的草鱼 240 尾,从中任选 9 尾,称得每尾鱼的质量分别是 1.5,1.6,1.4,1.6,1.3,1.4,1.2,1.7,1.8(单位:kg). 依此估计这 240 尾鱼的总质量大约是 ( )

A. 300 kg　　B. 360 kg　　C. 36 kg　　D. 30 kg

3. 从观测所得的数据中取出 m 个 x_1、n 个 x_2、p 个 x_3 组成一个样本,那么这个样本的平均数是 ( )

A. $\frac{x_1+x_2+x_3}{3}$　　B. $\frac{x_1+x_2+x_3}{m+n+p}$

C. $\dfrac{mx_1+nx_2+px_3}{3}$　　D. $\dfrac{mx_1+nx_2+px_3}{m+n+p}$

4. 期末考试后班长算出全班 40 个人的数学成绩的平均分为 M，如果把 M 当成一个同学的分数，与原来的 40 个分数一起，算出这 41 个分数的平均值 N，那么 $M:N$ 为________.

5. 有一组数据：$x_1, x_2, x_3, \cdots, x_n$ $(x_1 \leqslant x_2 \leqslant x_3 \leqslant \cdots \leqslant x_n)$，它们的算术平均值为 10，若去掉其中最大的 x_n，余下数据的算术平均值为 9；若去掉其中最小的 x_1，余下数据的算术平均值为 11，则 x_1 关于 n 的表达式为________，x_n 关于 n 的表达式为________.

6. 将某班的 30 名学生分成 3 个小组，每个小组 10 个同学. 在一次考试中，第一小组的平均成绩是 80 分，第二小组的平均成绩是 77 分，第三小组的 10 个同学的考试分数分别为 76,85,86,92,83,81,89,73,78,87. 则该班这次考试的平均分为________.

7. 不通过计算，比较图 11-23 中(a)和(b)两组数据的平均值和标准差.(其中黑点 • 表示数据)

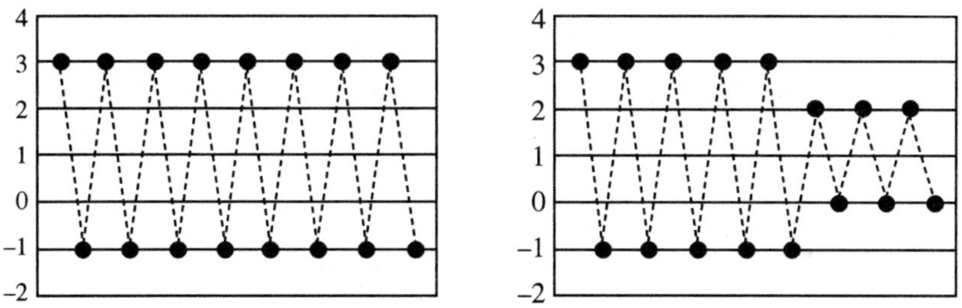

(a)　　(b)

图 11-23

8. 甲、乙两人同时加工一种零件,在 10 天中两人每天出现的次品数见表 11-22.

表 11-22　甲、乙两人产出的次品数(单位:个)

甲	0	1	0	2	0	3	1	2	4	2
乙	2	3	1	0	2	1	1	0	1	1

分别计算他们加工零件出现次品数的均值和标准差. 从计算结果来看,甲、乙两人哪一位操作更稳定一些?

9. 将某班 40 人随机平均分成两组,两组学生在一次考试的成绩情况见表 11-23.

表 11-23　考试成绩统计

组别	统计量	
	平均值	标准差
第一组	90	6
第二组	80	4

求全班的平均成绩与标准差.

【数学文化】

方差

方差是统计学中的一个重要概念，它用于描述数据的离散程度. 方差的发展史可以追溯到 19 世纪，当时欧洲的数学家和统计学家们开始研究如何更好地描述和理解数据的变化.

方差分析起源于对农业田间实验数据的分析研究，它是由著名统计学家费希尔于 20 世纪 20 年代创立和发展起来的. 方差分析现在已经成为统计学中的一个重要分支. 目前，方差分析不仅在农业科学实验和农业生产中有着广泛应用，而且在工业产品的试制与配方，以及物理与化学实验乃至生物学和医学等自然科学领域中发挥重要作用. 即使在人们对研究对象的影响因素难以控制的社会科学领域和经济管理活动中，如在社会学的研究和市场研究等方面，方差分析的应用也日益广泛.

【拓展应用】

材料 1　2024 年春运，是指中国在 2024 年农历春节前后出现的大规模的高交通运输压力的现象，也是一年中铁路、航运、公路客货流量最集中、人员流动最频繁的时期. 从 2024 年 1 月 26 日开始到 3 月 5 日结束，共计 40 天.

材料 2　有顾客反映某地高铁站售票处售票的速度太慢. 为此，某地高铁站收集了 100 位顾客购票时所花费时间的样本数据(单位：min)，结果如下：

2.3	1.0	3.5	0.7	1.0	1.3	0.8	1.0	2.4	0.9
1.1	1.5	0.2	8.2	1.7	5.2	1.6	3.9	5.4	2.3
6.1	2.6	2.8	2.4	3.9	3.8	1.6	0.3	1.1	1.1
3.1	1.1	4.3	1.4	0.2	0.3	2.7	2.7	4.1	4.0
3.1	5.5	0.9	3.3	4.2	21.7	2.2	1.0	3.3	3.4
4.6	3.6	4.5	0.5	1.2	0.7	3.5	4.8	2.6	0.9
7.4	6.9	1.6	4.1	2.1	5.8	5.0	1.7	3.8	6.3
3.2	0.6	2.1	3.7	7.8	1.9	0.8	1.3	1.4	3.5
11	8.6	7.5	2.0	2.0	2.0	1.2	2.9	6.5	1.0
4.6	2.0	1.2	5.8	2.9	2.0	2.9	6.6	0.7	1.5

某地高铁站认为,为一位顾客办理一次售票业务所需的时间在 5 min 之内就是合理的.

问题 1 根据原始数据计算中位数、均值和标准差,并进行分析.

问题 2 对数据进行适当的分组,分析数据分布的特点.

问题 3 你认为应该用哪一个统计量来分析上述问题?

自我检测

一、选择题

1. 下列事件属于必然事件的是　　（　　）

A. 抛掷一颗骰子,落地后朝上的点数是 6

B. 抛掷一颗骰子,落地后朝上的点数是奇数

C. 抛掷一颗骰子,落地后朝上的点数不是奇数就是偶数

D. 抛掷一颗骰子,落地后朝上的点数不是奇数也不是偶数

2. 小明连续投篮 3 次,给出下列各组事件:

① 事件 A:至少有一次命中,事件 B:都命中. ② 事件 A:至少有一次命中,事件 B:至多有一次命中. ③ 事件 A:恰有一次命中,事件 B:恰有两次命中. ④ 事件 A:至少有一次命中,事件 B:都没命中. 其中事件互斥但不对立的组数为　　（　　）

A. 0　　B. 1　　C. 2　　D. 3

3. 下列说法不正确的是　　（　　）

A. 必然事件的概率为 1,不可能事件的概率为 0

B. 在一次试验中,不可能同时发生的两个事件称为互斥事件

C. 事件 $E=\{a \mid a^2+1\geqslant 1\}$ 为必然事件

D. 4 件产品中有 3 件正品、1 件次品,从中随机抽取 2 件抽到的都是次品是随机事件

4. 若从 1,2,3,4,5 这五个数中任取两个数字构成一个两位数,则这个两位数大于 40 的概率为　　（　　）

A. $\frac{1}{5}$　　B. $\frac{2}{5}$　　C. $\frac{3}{5}$　　D. $\frac{4}{5}$

5. 从甲、乙、丙三人中任选两名代表,甲被选中的概率为　　（　　）

A. $\frac{1}{2}$　　B. $\frac{1}{3}$　　C. $\frac{2}{3}$　　D. 1

6. 先后抛掷两枚硬币,出现“一正一反”的概率是 ( )

A. $\frac{1}{4}$　　B. $\frac{1}{3}$　　C. $\frac{1}{2}$　　D. $\frac{3}{4}$

7. 一颗骰子连续投两次,前后两次点数的和为 3 的概率是 ( )

A. $\frac{1}{6}$　　B. $\frac{1}{9}$　　C. $\frac{1}{12}$　　D. $\frac{1}{18}$

8. 小明射击打中 9 环的概率是$\frac{1}{3}$,打中 10 环的概率是$\frac{1}{6}$,则小明至少打中 9 环的概率是 ( )

A. $\frac{1}{4}$　　B. $\frac{1}{2}$　　C. $\frac{1}{3}$　　D. $\frac{3}{4}$

9. 某职业学校为了解新生的身体发育情况,从 900 名学生中抽取一个容量为 90 的样本. 应选择的抽样方法是 ( )

A. 简单随机抽样　　B. 系统抽样

C. 分层抽样　　D. 以上选项都不对

10. 下列选项错误的是 ( )

A. 简单随机抽样的方式是对全部样本进行随机抽取,每个样本被抽到的概率一样

B. 系统抽样是将样本按事先确定的规则抽取

C. 分层抽样是将全部样本分成一定比例的样本,进行抽取

D. 以上选项都不对

11. 某草莓采摘园区种植了 10 亩 A 品种草莓和 50 亩 B 品种草莓,农业技术员要对两个品种的草莓施用某种肥料后的效果进行调查,准备抽样 60 颗草莓,对这次抽样的描述,下列选项正确的是 ( )

A. 应采用简单随机抽样的方法,在 A 品种草莓中抽样 30 颗,在 B 品种草莓中抽样 30 颗

B. 应采用分层抽样的方法,在 A 品种草莓中抽样 10 颗,在 B 品种草莓中抽样 50 颗

C. 应采用分层抽样的方法,在 A 品种草莓中抽样 30 颗,在 B 品种草莓中抽样 30 颗

D. 采用简单随机抽样、系统抽样、分层抽样的方法均可

12. 某水果商店现有苹果、香蕉、橘子三种水果，苹果、香蕉、橘子三种水果的数量之比为 5∶8∶13，现在用分层抽样的方法抽出样本，样本中苹果有 10 箱，那么样本容量为　(　　)

A. 48　　B. 49　　C. 50　　D. 52

13. 数据 6,7,7,8,10,10 的均值为　(　　)

A. 7　　B. 8　　C. 9　　D. 10

14. 一组数据的方差 $s^2=\frac{1}{9}[(x_1-2)^2+(x_2-2)^2+\cdots+(x_{10}-2)^2]$，则这组数据的平均数为　(　　)

A. $\frac{1}{10}$　　B. $\frac{1}{9}$　　C. 2　　D. 10

15. 一组数据的样本方差为 16，则样本标准差为　(　　)

A. 2　　B. 4　　C. 8　　D. 32

二、填空题

1. “抛掷一枚骰子，出现的点数小于 7”是____________事件.

2. 口袋中装有 100 个大小相同的红球、白球和黑球，其中红球 45 个，从口袋中摸出一个球，摸出白球的概率为 0.23，则摸出黑球的概率为________.

3. 小明的身高将会达到 5 m，这个事件的概率为____________.

4. 三人独立破译密码，他们译出密码的概率分别是 $\frac{1}{5}$，$\frac{1}{3}$，$\frac{1}{4}$，则能够将密码译出的概率为____________.

5. 抛掷两颗均匀的骰子，则点数之和为 8 的概率为____________.

6. 某社区医院在一周内为 4 000 人接种了疫苗，相关研究人员针对每个接种者在接种前和接种后分别做了各项监测，并记录在“留观监测表”上，现准备从中抽取 400 份做临床研究. 此案例中的样本为__________，样本容量为____________.

7. 为了解社区居民的垃圾分类意识，调查机构从某社区的 80 名青年人、100 名中年人和 60 名老年人中，采用分层抽样的方法进行调查，若从中抽取了 3 名老年人，则总共抽取样本容量 n 为____________.

8. 在某次跳远比赛前，体育老师为两名同学做了 10 次跳远成绩测试，发现两人的平均成绩相同，为在两人中选择一个人参赛，应分别计算两人成绩的________________.

9. 全班学生分为三组,三组分别有 12 人、13 人、15 人,数学考试的平均成绩分别为 87 分、81 分、83 分,这个班总体的平均成绩是______________.

10. 若一组数据 $-2,-1,0,x,1$ 平均数是 0,则 $x=$________________,方差为______________.

三、解答题

1. 对一批乒乓球进行检查,结果见表 11-24.

表 11-24 乒乓球检查结果

抽取球数 n	50	100	200	500	1 000	2 000
优等品 m	45	92	194	470	954	1 902
优等品频率 $\frac{m}{n}$						

(1) 将表格补充完整;

(2) 抽取一只乒乓球,求它为优等品的概率的估计值.

2. 从 0,1,2,3,4,5 这 6 个数字中随机抽取 2 个不同的数字,求:

(1) 这两个数字都是奇数的概率;

(2) 这两个数字之和是奇数的概率.

3. 一个罐子里有 20 个玻璃球，其中 6 个红色球、4 个黑色球、10 个白色球. 如果从罐子里随机抽取一个球，求：

(1) 取到红色球的概率；

(2) 取到白色球的概率；

(3) 取不到红色球的概率.

4. 某职业学校选拔 10 名学生作为参加省技能比赛的候选人，这 10 名学生中有 7 名男生、3 名女生，现从中选出 2 名作为最后的参赛选手，求：

(1) 选出的参赛选手全是男生的概率；

(2) 选出的参赛选手中至少有 1 名女生的概率.

5. 某学校想在甲、乙两名学生中选拔一人参加一项技能比赛，在相同的条件下，对他们进行了 10 次测试，成绩见表 11-25.

表 11-25　甲、乙成绩(单位:分)

甲成绩	76	84	90	86	81	87	86	82	85	83
乙成绩	79	73	89	90	80	79	89	85	84	82

(1) 分别求甲、乙的平均成绩；

(2) 应该选拔哪位学生参加技能比赛？

6. 为了弘扬传统文化，某校举办了诗词大赛. 现将抽取的 200 名学生的成绩从低到高依次分成六组：[40,50)，[50,60)，[60,70)，[70,80)，[80,90)，[90,100)，得到如图 11-24 所示的频率分布直方图. 解答下列问题：

(1) 求 a 的值；

(2) 若采用分层抽样的方法从 6 个小组中随机抽取 40 人，则应从第 1 组和第 2 组各抽取多少人？

(3) 从成绩不低于 80 分的学生中随机抽取 2 人，求所抽取的 2 名学生至少有 1 人来自第 5 组的概率.

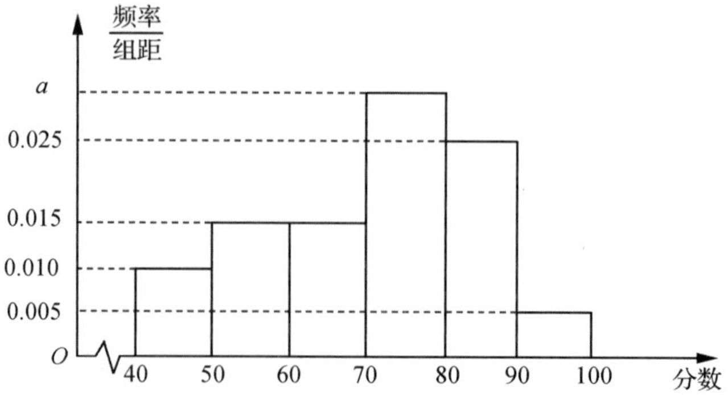

图 11-24

第12章　排列组合与二项式定理

12.1　分类、分步计数原理

【学习目标】

1. 掌握分类计数原理和分步计数原理.
2. 能运用计数原理分析和解决一些简单的应用问题.
3. 培养和提升学生的数据分析、直观想象和数学建模等核心素养.

【重点难点】

重点:对两个计数原理的理解.

难点:运用计数原理分析和解决一些简单的应用问题.

【微课导学】

扫下面的二维码,学习微课“分类计数原理”“分步计数原理”.

分类计数原理　　　　分步计数原理

【自主学习】

1. 分类计数原理:做一件事情,完成它可以有 n 类办法,在第一类办法中有 m_1 种方法,在第二类办法中有 m_2 种方法……在第 n 类办法中有 m_n 种方法,无论通过哪类办法的哪种方法,都可以独立完成这件事,那么完成这件事共有__________种不同的方法.

2. 分步计数原理:做一件事情,完成它分成 n 个步骤,做第一步有 m_1 种不同的方法,做第二步有 m_2 种不同的方法……做第 n 步有 m_n 种方法,必须经过每一步步骤才能完成这件事,那么完成这件事共有__________种不同的方法.

3. 一个三层书架每层依次有书 30,25,28 本,现要取出 1 本书,共有__________种不同的取法.

4. 某班有男生 25 人、女生 20 人,要在男、女生中各选 1 人参加演讲比赛,共有__________种不同的选法.

5. 书架上有按次序放置的空抽屉 4 个,现要存放 4 本不同的书,每个抽屉只能存放 1 本书,共有__________不同的放法.

6. 用 1,2,3,4,5 可以组成__________个不同的三位数.

7. 已知从 A 地到 B 地有 2 条路,从 B 地到 C 地有 3 条路,从 A 地到 D 地有 4 条路,从 D 地到 C 地有 2 条路,则从 A 地到 C 地共有__________种不同的走法.

8. 从 5 名男生和 5 名女生中各选 1 人参加校合唱队,不同的选法有 ( )

A. 1 种　　B. 5 种　　C. 10 种　　D. 25 种

9. 从数字 0,1,2 中任取 2 个数,可组成无重复数字的两位数共有( )

A. 2 个　　B. 4 个　　C. 6 个　　D. 8 个

【探究任务】

任务一

阅读材料,回答问题.

材料　2023 年,我国通信业全面贯彻落实党的二十大精神,认真落实党中央国务院各项决策部署，坚持稳中求进工作总基调，全力推进网络强国和数字中国建设，促进数字经济与实体经济深度融合，全行业主要运行指标平稳增长，5G、千兆光网等网络基础设施日益完备，各项应用普及全面加速，行业高质量发展稳步推进.

问题 1　手机在生活中的角色发生了巨大改变，它记录着光阴，分享着情感，珍藏着每个人的似水流年. 毕业 10 年后，作为班长的李某打算通过手机联系同学们，在徐州举行同学聚会.

李某用手机联系老同学的方式，有两类，第一类方式为通话，第二类方式为留言. 在第一类方式里有拨号通话、视频通话 2 种方法，在第二类方式里有短信留言、微信留言、QQ 留言 3 种方法. 那么李某一共有多少种可以联系老同学的方法？

问题 2　家在南京的张同学接到通知后，开始准备从南京到徐州的行程. 比较经济和舒适的交通工具有火车、飞机还有自驾. 其中火车有 3 种选择：快速列车、特快列车、高铁. 不考虑其他因素，张同学一共有多少种不同的选择呢？

图 12-1

任务二

阅读材料,回答问题.

材料 快递业繁荣发展彰显中国经济强劲动力. 近年来,随着市场需求的快速提升以及快递行业的高速发展,快递业务量也在高速增长. 2016—2021年,我国快递业务量迅速增长,保持在20%以上的增长速度. 2021年,全国快递业务量累计完成1 083.0亿件,较2020年增长29.9%.

问题1 李某为了参加聚会,打算网购衣服,假设包裹从上海经徐州中转站到其居住小区菜鸟驿站,由上海到徐州中转站有飞机、高铁、汽车3种方法,由徐州中转站到其居住小区菜鸟驿站有面包车、电动三轮车2种方法,共有多少种不同的送达包裹的方法?

问题2 若包裹中有4件不同的上衣、3件不同的裤子.

(1) 将上衣和裤子搭配起来,共有多少种装扮?

(2) 如果再搭配上两双不同的鞋子,共有多少种装扮?

任务三

小组合作,归纳分类计数原理和分步计数原理的联系与区别,完成表12-1.

表12-1 分类计数与分步计数的异同

	分类计数原理(加法原理)	分步计数原理(乘法原理)
共同点		
不同点		

【典例解析】

例 1　金坛刻纸是我国国家级非物质文化遗产扩展项目之一，现有《八仙过海》《孔雀开屏》《洛神》3 幅传统刻纸作品，以及《万马奔腾》《东方歌舞》《报晓图》《香飘四季》4 幅现代刻纸作品.

(1) 从两种不同类型的作品中任选 1 幅，共有多少种不同的选法？

(2) 从两种不同类型的作品中各选 1 幅，共有多少种不同的选法？

解　(1) 根据分类计数原理，不同的选法共有

$$3+4=7(\text{种}).$$

(2) 根据分步计数原理，不同的选法共有

$$3\times4=12(\text{种}).$$

备注　两种不同类型的作品中任选 1 幅，有两类方式，用分类计数原理计算；从两种不同类型的作品中各选 1 幅，分为两个步骤来完成，用分步计数原理计算.

例 2　现有甲、乙、丙三个品牌的新能源电动汽车，其中，甲品牌有 5 种型号，每种型号有 3 种颜色；乙品牌有 3 种型号，每种型号有 4 种颜色；丙品牌有 4 种型号，每种型号有 4 种颜色. 若要从中选购一款，共有多少种不同的选择？

解　第 1 类：从甲品牌的新能源电动汽车中选择，分两步：第 1 步选择汽车型号，有 5 种；第 2 步选择汽车颜色，有 3 种. 共有 $m_1=5\times3=15$(种)款式.

第 2 类：从乙品牌的新能源电动汽车中选择，分两步：第 1 步选择汽车型号，有 3 种；第 2 步选择汽车颜色，有 4 种. 共有 $m_2=3\times4=12$(种)款式.

第 3 类：从丙品牌的新能源电动汽车中选择，分两步：第 1 步选择汽车型号，有 4 种；第 2 步选择汽车颜色，有 4 种. 共有 $m_3=4\times4=16$(种)款式.

根据分类计数原理和分步计数原理，不同的选择方法共有

$$5\times3+3\times4+4\times4=43(\text{种}).$$

备注　解决这个问题需要综合运用分类计数原理和分步计数原理.

例 3　(1) 有 4 名同学选报跑步、跳高、跳远三个项目，每人可选报一项，共有多少种报名方法？

(2) 有 4 名同学争夺跑步、跳高、跳远三项冠军，共有多少种可能的结果？

解 (1) 每一名同学共有 3 种报名方法,故共有 $3\times3\times3\times3=3^4=81$(种)报名方法.

(2) 每一项冠军都有 4 种可能,故共有 $4\times4\times4=4^3=64$(种)可能的结果.

备注 (1) 每人可选报一项,项目可以没有同学选,但是同学必须选报一个项目,且缺一不可,所以是学生选择项目,即把同学作为分步标准.(2) 冠军花落谁家,同学可以得不到冠军,但每项冠军必有同学获得,且缺一不可,所以是冠军选择同学,即把冠军作为分步标准.

【课后练习】

1. 在一次读书活动中,一人要从 5 本不同的科技书、7 本不同的文艺书里任取一本书,那么不同的选法有 ( )

A. 5 种 B. 7 种 C. 12 种 D. 35 种

2. 小明同学去某乐园游玩,发现其喜欢的项目有 4 项,则小明至少玩其中 2 个项目的选择有 ( )

A. 11 种 B. 8 种 C. 6 种 D. 4 种

3. 邮政局门前有 3 个邮筒,现将 5 封信逐一投入邮筒,不同的投法共有 ( )

A. 5^3种 B. 3^5种 C. 8 种 D. 15 种

4. 连续抛掷同一枚质地均匀的硬币 3 次,一共可以出现__________种不同的情况.

5. 由 0,1,2,3,4 可以组成__________个没有重复数字的三位数.

6. 在一次读书活动中,有 5 本不同的政治书、10 本不同的科技书、20 本不同的小说可供学生选择.

(1) 从这三类书中任选一本,有多少种不同的选法?

(2) 从这三类书中各选一本,有多少种不同的选法?

(3) 从这三类书中选不属于同一类的两本书,有多少种不同的选法?

7. 有 9 个互不相同的小球，其中 4 个红球、3 个绿球和 2 个黄球. 现从中取 2 个颜色相同的球，分别放入两个不同的杯子，一共有多少种放法？

8. 已知 7 名学生会下围棋和象棋，其中有 4 名学生会下围棋，5 名学生会下象棋. 现从这 7 名学生中选出 2 名学生分别参加围棋和象棋比赛，共有多少种不同的选法？

【数学文化】

计数原理的起源

在古代，人们开始尝试理解并解决各种与数量相关的问题. 例如，如何计算物体的数量，如何分配物品，等等. 随着时间的推移，数学家们开始总结和归纳这些计数方法，形成了最初的计数原理.

在中国，计数原理的起源可以追溯到《九章算术》等古代数学著作. 这些著作中包含了许多计数原理的应用和解释,如“隔板法”等计数方法. 我国古代《易经》一书中记载,远古时期,人们通过在绳子上打结来记录数量,即“结绳记数”. 一位妇女在从右到左依次排列的绳子上打结,满六进一,用来记录采集到的野果数量.

在欧洲,计数原理的发展与数学、物理学等学科的发展密切相关. 例如,欧几里得在其著作《几何原本》中提出了组合数学的基础原理,为计数原理的发展奠定了基础.

随着时间的推移和数学家们的不断探索和总结,计数原理逐渐形成并发展至今.

【拓展应用】

我们在为网络账号设置密码时(图 12-2),会看到“输入长度为 8～16 个字符,至少含数字/字母/符号 2 种组合”这样的要求,运用分类计数原理和分步计数原理,可以求出能设置的不同密码的个数,这个数字是极其庞大的,因此这样设置的密码被破解的概率更小,能更大限度地保障用户的信息安全. 请同学们思考下列问题:

图 12-2

1. 手机的数字锁屏有四位,那么

(1) 可以设置多少种密码?

(2) 如果四个数字不重复,可以设置多少种密码?

2. 一张银行卡的密码由 6 个数字组成,每一个数字都是 0～9 中的任意一个,可以设置多少种不同的密码?

12.2　排列与排列数公式

【学习目标】

1. 理解排列的概念和特点，会计算排列数.
2. 能运用排列数公式解决简单的实际计数问题.

【重点难点】

重点：排列数的计算，运用排列数公式解决简单的实际计数问题.

难点：运用排列数公式解决简单的实际计数问题.

【微课导学】

扫右面的二维码，学习微课"排列""排列数公式".

排列　　排列数公式

【自主学习】

1. 一般地，从 n 个不同的元素中，任取 $m(m\leqslant n)$ 个元素，按照一定的顺序排成一列，叫作从 n 个不同元素中取出 m 个元素的一个________，所有不同排列的个数叫作________，记作 A_n^m.

2. 从 n 个不同的元素中任取 $m(m\leqslant n)$ 个元素的排列数为

$A_n^m=$________________.

由 1 到 n 的正整数的连乘积，称为 n 的阶乘，记作________，即 $A_n^n=$________.

3. (1) $\dfrac{A_{16}^3}{2A_8^4}=$________　(2) $7A_6^6-A_7^6=$________.

4. (1) 若 $A_n^2=72$，则 $n=$________.

(2) 若 $A_n^2=7A_{n-4}^2$,则 $n=$__________.

5. 现有 10 位学生,任意两位同学都互相通信一次,共通信__________次.

6. 用 1,2,3,4,5 可以组成__________个没有重复数字的五位数.

7. 有 5 本不同的书,从中选 3 本送给 3 名同学,每人各 1 本,共有__________种不同的送法.

8. 5 个人站成一排照相,甲不站在排头(左)的排法有 ( )

A. 24 种 B. 72 种 C. 96 种 D. 120 种

9. 将 6 张同排连号的电影票分给三名教师与三名学生.若要求师生相间而坐,则不同的分法有 ( )

A. 24 种 B. 36 种 C. 60 种 D. 72 种

10. 为增强学生的社会责任感,某职校组织学生参加志愿服务活动,现计划从甲、乙、丙、丁 4 名学生中选 2 名分别担任服务小组的正、副组长,共有多少种不同的选法?

【探究任务】

任务一

阅读材料,回答问题.

图 12-3

材料 近十年来,中国新能源汽车(图 12-3)产业发展取得了显著成效,并且正在引领全球汽车工业的电动化转型.我国锚定发展目标不动摇,坚定不移、坚持不懈、坚决有力推进新能源汽车产业的发展,取得了显著成效,建成了高效协同的产业体系,培育了全球最大的新能源汽车消费市场.

问题　在某一次汽车展销会上,主办方在入口处给某新能源汽车经销商提供了 3 个不同风格的展台. 该经销商有 a、b、c、d 共 4 种车型,需要从中选出 3 种车型放在 3 个不同的展台上展出,请写出所有不同的展出方案. 试给出选定 b、c、d 这 3 种车型后的展出方案.

任务二

小组合作探究排列数公式.

研究从 n 个不同的元素中任取 $m(m\leqslant n)$ 个元素的排列数 A_n^m 的计算方法. 假定有顺序排列的 m 个空位(图 12-4),从 n 个不同的元素 $a_1,a_2,a_3,\cdots,a_n$ 中任取 m 个元素去填空位,每个空位填 1 个元素. 由每 1 种填法得到 1 个排列;反之,每 1 个排列确定 1 种填法. 因此,所有不同的填法总数就是排列数 A_n^m. 小组合作,进行选取和填空,并推出排列数公式.

第 1 位	第 2 位	第 3 位	…	第 m 位

图 12-4

根据分步计数原理,不同的填法总数为

____.

因此,从 n 个不同的元素中任取 $m(m\leqslant n)$ 个元素的排列数为

$\mathrm{A}_n^m=$____________________________________.

当 $m=n$ 时,

$\mathrm{A}_n^n=$____________________________________.

任务三

阅读材料,回答问题.

材料 保障国家粮食安全是一个永恒课题,粮食安全这根弦任何时候都不能放松. 党的十八大以来,以习近平同志为核心的党中央始终把解决好十几亿人口的吃饭问题,作为治国理政的头等大事,实施国家粮食安全战略,不断提高我国粮食综合生产能力,使谷物总产量稳居世界首位,让十四亿多人的粮食安全得到有效保障. 粮食安全是“国之大者”.

图 12-5

问题 截至 2022 年,我国的谷物总产量稳居世界首位,谷物优良品种的培育是实现谷物增产增收的重要支撑(图 12-6). 谷物在我国可大体分为禾谷类、豆菽类和薯谷类. 某农业科研所准备对 3 种禾谷类、2 种豆菽类和 1 种薯谷类谷物进行培育试验,分别种植在 6 块不同的试验田中,共有多少种不同的种植方法?

【典例解析】

例 1 某职业技能大赛颁奖典礼结束后,3 名老师与 4 名获得一等奖的学生站成一排拍照合影留念.

(1) 共有多少种不同的排法?

(2) 站成两排,前排 3 人,后排 4 人,共有多少种不同的排法?

(3) 4 名学生必须站在一起,共有多少种不同的排法?

(4) 3 名老师必须互不相邻,共有多少种不同的排法?

解　(1)3 名老师与 4 名获得一等奖的学生站成一排的不同排法有

$$A_7^7=7\times6\times5\times4\times3\times2\times1=5\ 040(\text{种}).$$

(2) 根据分步计数原理,分两步完成:第一步,从 7 人中选出 3 人排在前排,有 A_7^3种排法;第二步,余下的 4 人排在后排,有 A_4^4种排法. 所以前排 3 人,后排 4 人,不同的排法共有

$$A_7^3\cdot A_4^4=7\times6\times5\times4\times3\times2\times1=5\ 040(\text{种}).$$

(3) 根据分步计数原理,分两步完成:第一步,将 4 名学生视为一个整体,将其与 3 名老师进行排列,有 A_4^4种排法;第二步,对 4 名学生进行排列,有 A_4^4种排法. 所以 4 名学生必须站在一起,不同的排法共有

$$A_4^4\cdot A_4^4=4\times3\times2\times1\times4\times3\times2\times1=576(\text{种}).$$

(4) 根据分步计数原理,分两步完成:第一步,将 4 名学生排列好,有 A_4^4种排法;第二步,因 4 名学生之间和两端共有 5 个空位,将 3 名老师进行安排到这些空位中去,有 A_5^3种排法. 所以 3 名老师必须互不相邻的不同排法共有

$$A_4^4\cdot A_5^3=4\times3\times2\times1\times5\times4\times3=1\ 440(\text{种}).$$

备注　对于有限制条件的排列问题,要优先考虑限制条件(或者说优先安排有特殊要求的元素),解决相邻问题用捆绑法,解决不相邻问题用插空法.

例 2　从数字 1,2,3,4,5 中任取 3 个,组成三位数.

(1) 可以组成多少个没有重复数字的三位数?

(2) 可以组成多少个没有重复数字且是 5 的倍数的三位数?

(3) 可以组成多少个没有重复数字的三位奇数?

解　(1) 要组成没有重复数字的三位数,只需从 5 个数字中选出 3 个并排列,有

$$A_5^3=5\times4\times3=60(\text{个}),$$

即可以组成 60 个没有重复数字的三位数.

(2) 要组成没有重复数字且是 5 的倍数的三位数,必须将数字 5 排在个位,即个位只有 1 种排法,然后再从剩下的 4 个数字中选出 2 个作为百位数字和十位数字,有 A_4^2种排法. 所以,可以组成的没有重复数字且是 5 的倍数的三位数一共有

$$1\cdot A_4^2=1\times4\times3=12(\text{个}).$$

(3) 先排有限制条件的个位,可排 1,3,5,有 A_3^1种排法,再排无限制条件

的十位和百位,有A_4^2种排法,根据分步计数原理可得,可以组成没有重复数字的三位奇数有

$$A_3^1 \cdot A_4^2 = 3\times4\times3 = 36(\text{个}).$$

备注 先考虑特殊元素或特殊位置,再考虑一般元素或一般位置.采用分步计数原理,先计算特殊位置上元素的排法,再计算没有限制条件的位置的元素的排法.

【课后练习】

1. 某班级举行文艺晚会,现准备安排9个节目的出场顺序,已知小品节目必须安排在中间,则不同的排法有 ( )

A. A_7^7种　B. A_8^8种　C. A_9^9种　D. $A_8^8A_2^1$种

2. 记者要为5名志愿者和他们帮助的2位老人拍照,要求排成一排,2位老人相邻但不排在两端,不同的排法共有 ( )

A. 480种　B. 720种　C. 960种　D. 1 440种

3. 用1,2,3,4,5这5个数字组成没有重复数字的四位数,其中偶数的个数为 ( )

A. 24　B. 36　C. 48　D. 60

4. 某校举办校园文化节文艺汇演活动,在安排5名歌手的演出顺序时,要求某歌手不是第一个出场,也不是最后一个出场,则有________种不同的排法.

5. 用0,1,2,3这4个数字可以组成________个没有重复数字且是5的倍数的三位数.

6. 某市小学开展“红色研学之旅”活动,供选择的基地共有6个.

(1) 若某小学计划从6个基地中选取3个基地参观,共有多少种不同的参观路线?

(2) 若3所小学分别从6个基地选取一个去参观,共有多少种不同的选择方法?

7. 某班联欢晚会的节目有 4 个舞蹈、1 个相声、3 个独唱，要求独唱节目不能连续出场，则节目的出场顺序共有多少种不同的排法？

8. 甲、乙、丙、丁、戊 5 个人排成一行照相.

(1) 甲在乙的左侧且相邻，有多少种不同的排法？

(2) 甲和乙相邻，有多少种不同的排法？

(3) 甲和乙不相邻，有多少种不同的排法？

【数学文化】

数学家杨辉的故事

杨辉，字谦光，与秦九韶、李冶、朱世杰并称“宋元数学四大家”.

民间相传杨辉对幻方的研究源于一个小故事. 当时杨辉是台州的地方官，一次外出巡游，碰到一孩童挡道，杨辉问明原因方知是一孩童在地上做一道数学算题，杨辉一听来了兴趣，下轿来到孩童旁问是什么算题. 原来，这个孩童在算一位老先生出的一道趣题：把数字 1—9 分行排列，不论竖着加、横着加,还是斜着加,结果都等于 15. 杨辉看到这个算题时,想起来他在西汉学者戴德编纂的《大戴礼》一书中也见过. 杨辉想到这儿,和孩童一起算了起来,直到午后,两人终于将算式摆出来了.

后来,杨辉随孩童来到老先生家里,与老先生论起数学问题来. 老先生说:“北周的甄鸾注《数术记遗》一书中写过‘九宫者,二四为肩,六八为足,左三右七,戴九履一,五居中央’.”杨辉听了,这与自己与孩童摆出来的完全一样. 便问老先生:“你可知这个九宫图是如何造出来的?”老先生说不知道. 杨辉回到家中,反复琢磨. 一天,他终于发现一条规律,并总结成四句话:“九子斜排,上下对易,左右相更,四维挺出.”就是说:先把数字 1—9 依次斜排,再把上 1 下 9 两数对调,左 7 右 3 两数对调,最后把四面的 2,4,6,8 向外面挺出,这样三阶幻方就填好了. 杨辉研究出三阶幻方(也叫络书或九宫图)的构造方法后,又系统地研究了四阶幻方至十阶幻方. 在这几种幻方中,杨辉只给出了三阶、四阶幻方构造方法的说明,四阶以上幻方,杨辉只画出图形而未留下作法. 但他所画的五阶、六阶乃至十阶幻方全都准确无误,可见他已经掌握了高阶幻方的构成规律.

【拓展应用】

某职业学校某一天的课程表有 7 节课,包括语文、数学、英语、体育与健康、思想政治、会计基础、经济法 7 门课程. 且每门课只安排 1 节,在下列不同条件下,求不同的排列方法的总数.

(1) 7 节课编排为上午 4 节、下午 3 节;

(2) 第一节课不排体育与健康;

(3) 语文课排在第 3 节,数学课不排在第 7 节.

12.3　组合与组合数公式

【学习目标】

1. 理解组合的概念和特点,能区分排列与组合问题.

2. 了解组合数的性质,会计算组合数,并能运用排列数公式和组合数公式解决一般实际问题.

【重点难点】

重点:组合数的计算,组合数的性质,用组合数解决具体的计数问题.

难点:组合数的性质,用组合数解决具体的计数问题.

【微课导学】

扫下面的二维码,学习微课“组合的概念”“组合数公式”“组合数性质”.

组合的概念　　组合数公式　　组合数性质

【自主学习】

1. 组合的概念:____.

组合的特点:

(1) ____________________元素;

(2) “只取不排”——____________________;

(3) 相同组合:____________________.

2. 组合数的概念:______________________,用符号______________表示.

3. 组合数的公式：________________________________.

4. 组合数的性质：

$$C_n^m = \underline{\qquad\qquad},$$

$$C_{n+1}^m = \underline{\qquad\qquad}(m \leqslant n).$$

5. 判断下列问题是排列问题,还是组合问题.

(1) 从 4 个景点中选出 2 个安排游览,有多少种不同的方法?

(2) 从 4 个景点中选出 2 个,并确定这 2 个景点的游览顺序,有多少种不同的方法?

6. 计算：

(1) C_7^4;

(2) C_{10}^7.

7. 从 3,5,7,11 这 4 个质数中任取 2 个相乘,可以得到多少个不相等的积?

【探究任务】

任务一

小组合作,探究组合的概念.

材料　为提升教育质量,拓展学生的学习领域,提高学生的综合素质,促进学生的全面发展,某职业学校决定在新学期开设 33 门选修课,其中有的课程拓展或深化必修课的内容,如英语基础语法、网店营销推广等;有的课程拓宽学生的知识视野,提高学生的文化素养,如《红楼梦》人物赏析、英美文学及影视赏析等;有的课程发展学生的兴趣特长,促进学生潜在能力和个性特长的充分发展,如排球、羽毛球、超轻黏土手作趣玩等.

问题 1　如果每位学生从 33 门选修课中任选 2 门课程学习,那么每位学生有多少种不同的选择方法?

问题 2　上述问题和排列问题有什么区别?

任务二

小组合作,探究组合数公式.

某职业学校开展"红色研学之旅"活动,供选择的基地共有 4 个. 若学校计划从 4 个基地中选取 3 个基地参观,有多少种不同的选择方法? 有多少种不同的参观路线? 如果基地记为 a,b,c,d,试完成下面的任务.

任务　从 4 个不同元素中取出 3 个元素的组合有哪些? 试列举每个组合的排列. 尝试填写表 12-2.

表 12-2　各组合的排列

组合	排列
abc	abc,bac,acb,bca,cab,cba

问题 1　求从 4 个不同元素中取出 3 个元素的排列数 A_4^3,可以分为两步:

(1) 考虑从 4 个不同元素中取出 3 个元素的组合,共有 C_4^3 个;

(2) 对每一个组合的 3 个不同元素进行全排列,共有 A_3^3 种方法. 由分步计数原理,得

$$A_4^3=C_4^3\cdot A_3^3,$$

所以

$$C_4^3=\frac{A_4^3}{A_3^3}.$$

问题 2　尝试总结"从 n 个不同元素中取出 m 个元素的排列数"的问题的步骤.

一般地,求从 n 个不同元素中取出 m 个元素的排列数 A_n^m,可以分两步解决:

(1) 选:____________________________.

(2) 排:____________________________.

根据分步计数原理,得

$$A_n^m=\_\_\_\_\_\_\_\_\_\_\_\_\_\_\_\_\_\_\_\_.$$

所以,

$$C_n^m=\_\_\_\_\_\_\_\_\_\_\_\_\_\_\_\_\_\_\_\_,$$

或

$$C_n^m=\_\_\_\_\_\_\_\_\_\_\_\_\_\_\_\_\_\_\_\_.\ (n,m\in\mathbf{N}^*,且\ m\leqslant n)$$

规定 $C_n^0=$____________________.

任务三

小组合作，探究组合数性质.

填写表 12-3，你有什么发现？

表 12-3　组合数的值

求值		结论
$C_3^1=$______	$C_3^2=$______	
$C_6^2=$______	$C_6^4=$______	
$C_4^2+C_4^3=$______	$C_5^3=$______	
$C_7^3+C_7^4=$______	$C_8^4=$______	

【典例解析】

例 1　(1) 平面内有 10 个点，以其中 2 个点为端点的线段共有多少条？

(2) 平面内有 10 个点，以其中 2 个点为端点的有向线段共有多少条？

解　(1) 以平面内 10 个点中的 2 个点为端点的线段的条数，就是从 10 个不同的元素中取出 2 个元素的组合数，即线段共有

$$C_{10}^2=\frac{10\times 9}{1\times 2}=45(\text{条}).$$

(2) 由于有向线段的两个端点中一个是起点、另一个是终点，以平面内 10 个点中的 2 个点为端点的有向线段的条数，就是从 10 个不同元素中取出 2 个元素的排列数，即有向线段共有

$$A_{10}^2=10\times 9=90(\text{条}).$$

例 2　在 100 件产品中有 98 件合格品、2 件次品. 从这 100 件产品中任意抽出 3 件.

(1) 有多少种不同的抽法？

(2) 抽出的 3 件中恰好有 1 件是次品的抽法有多少种？

(3) 抽出的 3 件中至少有 1 件是次品的抽法有多少种？

解　(1) 所求的不同抽法的种数，就是从 100 件产品中取出 3 件的组合数，所以共有

$$C_{100}^{3}=\frac{100\times 99\times 98}{1\times 2\times 3}=161\ 700(种).$$

(2) 从 2 件次品中抽出 1 件次品的抽法有 C_{2}^{1} 种,从 98 件合格品中抽出 2 件合格品的抽法有 C_{98}^{2} 种,因此抽出的 3 件中恰好有 1 件次品的抽法有

$$C_{2}^{1}\cdot C_{98}^{2}=9\ 506\ (种).$$

(3) 解法 1　从 100 件产品抽出的 3 件中至少有 1 件是次品,包括有 1 件次品和有 2 件次品两种情况. 在第(2)小题中已求得其中 1 件是次品的抽法有 $C_{2}^{1}C_{98}^{2}$ 种,因此根据分类加法计数原理,抽出的 3 件中至少有一件是次品的抽法有

$$C_{2}^{1}\cdot C_{98}^{2}+C_{2}^{2}\cdot C_{98}^{1}=9\ 604(种).$$

解法 2　抽出的 3 件产品中至少有 1 件是次品的抽法的种数,也就是从 100 件中抽出 3 件的抽法种数减去 3 件都是合格品的抽法的种数,即

$$C_{100}^{3}-C_{98}^{3}=161\ 700-152\ 096=9\ 604(种).$$

备注　"至少""至多"的问题,通常用分类法或间接法求解.

【课后练习】

1. 从 6 位候选人中选出 2 人分别担任班长和团支部书记,不同的选法有 (　　)

A. 30 种　　B. 15 种　　C. 20 种　　D. 10 种

2. 从 6 位同学中选出 2 人去参加座谈会,不同的选法有 (　　)

A. 30 种　　B. 15 种　　C. 20 种　　D. 10 种

3. 圆上有 10 个点,过每 2 个点画一条弦,过每 3 个点画一个圆内接三角形,一共可画弦和圆内接三角形的个数分别为 (　　)

A. A_{10}^{2}, C_{10}^{3}　　B. C_{10}^{2}, C_{10}^{3}

C. A_{10}^{2}, A_{10}^{3}　　D. C_{10}^{2}, A_{10}^{3}

4. 凸五边形有________条对角线;凸 n 边形有________条对角线.

5. 已知 $C_{n+2}^{n}=C_{n+1}^{5}+C_{n+1}^{6}$,则 $n=$________.

6. 计算：

(1) C_{15}^{3}；

(2) $C_{6}^{3} \div C_{8}^{4}$.

7. A,B,C,D,E 个足球队进行单循环比赛.

(1) 共需比赛多少场？

(2) 若各队的得分互不相同，则冠、亚军的可能情况共有多少种？

8. 空间中有 10 个点，其中任何 4 点不共面.

(1) 过 3 个点作平面，一共可作多少个平面？

(2) 以 4 个点为顶点作四面体，一共可作多少个四面体？

【数学文化】

抽屉原理

图 12-6

日常生活中,人们只要稍加留意,就不难发现某些带有规律性的事物. 如图 12-6 所示,将 5 个苹果放进 4 个抽屉,那么肯定有一个抽屉里放进了两个或更多的苹果. 该道理即被称为抽屉原理或鸽笼原理(把鸽子比作苹果,把笼子比作抽屉). 抽屉原理的一般形式为:将 $n+1$ 个苹果放进 n 个抽屉里,则至少有一个抽屉里放进了两个或两个以上的苹果.

千万别小看这个既平常又简单的原理,许多有趣的问题,都可以用抽屉原理来解决. 比如,任意 13 个人中,必然有 2 个人是在同一个月份出生的. 只需要将 13 个人看成苹果,12 个月份看成抽屉,于是由抽屉原理就得到了结论. 再比如,在边长为 1 的正方形内,任意取 5 个点,则其中必有 2 个点,它们之间的距离不会大于$\frac{\sqrt{2}}{2}$. 证明这个问题只需要将正方形分为面积相等的 4 等份,则 4 个小正方形的边长都是$\frac{1}{2}$,每个小正方形内任意两点之间的距离均不会大于小正方形的对角线长$\frac{\sqrt{2}}{2}$. 将 5 个点看成苹果,4 个小正方形看成抽屉,由抽屉原理,必然有一个小正方形中有 2 个点,于是这两个点之间的距离不大于$\frac{\sqrt{2}}{2}$.

【拓展应用】

有 10 把不同的锁,开这 10 把锁的 10 把钥匙混在一起了,最多要试多少次,才能把这 10 把锁和钥匙全部配对?

12.4　排列组合的应用

【学习目标】

1. 进一步加深对排列组合意义的理解，熟练判断所研究问题是排列问题还是组合问题.

2. 掌握有关排列组合综合题的基本解法，提高分析问题、解决问题的能力.

【重点难点】

重点：掌握排列数公式和组合数公式，体会排列与组合的数学思想.

难点：掌握有关排列组合综合题的捆绑法、插空法等基本解法.

【微课导学】

扫下面的二维码，学习微课“排列组合的应用”.

排列组合的应用

【自主学习】

1. 某记者要去 4 个地方采访，不同的采访顺序有　　（　　）

A. 4 种　　B. 12 种　　C. 18 种　　D. 24 种

2. 某班优秀学习小组有甲、乙、丙、丁、戊共 5 人，他们排成一排照相，则甲、乙相邻的排法有　　（　　）

A. 24 种　　B. 36 种　　C. 48 种　　D. 60 种

3. 现“学习强国”平台设有“阅读文章”“视听学习”等多个栏目. 在某时

段内,平台更新了 2 篇文章和 4 个视频,一位学习者准备学习这 2 篇文章和其中 2 个视频,则这 2 篇文章学习顺序不相邻的学法有 ( )

A. 24 种　　B. 36 种　　C. 72 种　　D. 144 种

4. 某旅游公司为推出新的旅游项目,特派出 5 名工作人员前往某地 3 个景点进行团队游的可行性调研. 若每名工作人员只去 1 个景点且每个景点至少有 1 名工作人员前往,则不同的人员分配方案有________种.

5. 从 1,3,5,7,9 中任取 3 个数字,与 0,2,4 组成没有重复数字的六位数,其中偶数有________个.

6. 如图 12-7 所示,$\angle MON$ 的 OM 边上有四点 A_1、A_2、A_3、A_4,ON 上有三点 B_1、B_2、B_3,求以 O、A_1、A_2、A_3、A_4、B_1、B_2、B_3 中的三点为顶点的三角形的个数.

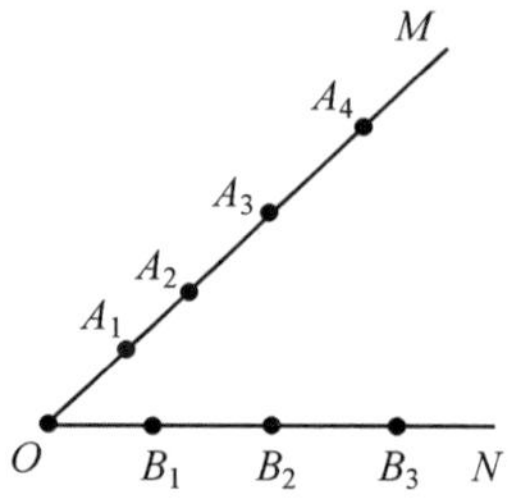

图 12-7

7. 用 4 种不同的颜色对图 12-8 中的 5 个区域涂色(4 种颜色全部使用),要求每个区域涂 1 种颜色,相邻的区域不能涂相同的颜色,则不同的涂色方法有多少种?

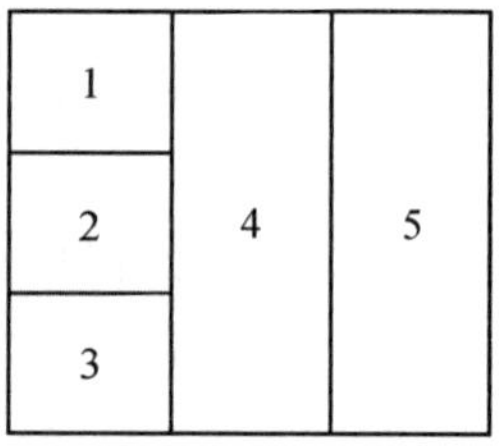

图 12-8

【探究任务】

任务一

阅读材料，回答下列问题.

材料　中老昆万铁路(图 12-9)即“中老国际铁路通道”，简称“中老铁路”是一条连接中国云南省昆明市与老挝万象市的电气化铁路，由中国按国铁Ⅰ级标准建设，是第一个以中方为主投资建设、共同运营并与中国铁路网直接连通的跨国铁路.

2024 年 4 月 13 日，中国西双版纳至老挝琅勃拉邦两大著名旅游城市间增开国际旅客列车 1 对，车次为 D85 次和 D86 次，旅客乘火车可实现两地间当日往返.

西双版纳至琅勃拉邦，全程停靠西双版纳站、勐腊站、磨憨站、磨丁站、孟赛站、琅勃拉邦站等站点.

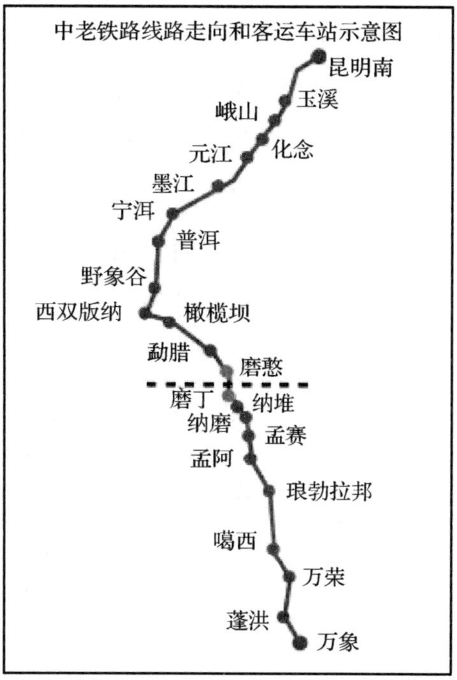

图 12-9

问题 1　西双版纳至琅勃拉邦全程有 6 个站点，需准备多少种不同的普通客车票？

问题 2　若往返票价相同，有多少种不同票价的普通客车票？

问题 3　问题 1,2 中，哪一个是排列问题？哪一个是组合问题？

任务二

阅读材料,回答下列问题.

材料 1 朱载堉(图 12-10),字伯勤,河南省怀庆府河内县(今河南沁阳)人,明代著名的律学家(有“律圣”之称)、历学家、音乐家. 他对文艺的最大贡献是他创建了“十二平均律”,此理论被广泛应用在世界各国的键盘乐器上,包括钢琴,故朱载堉被誉为“钢琴理论的鼻祖”.

图 12-10

材料 2 如图 12-11 所示,钢琴通常有 88 个键,其中包含 52 个白键和 36 个黑键. 钢琴上 52 个白键循环重复地使用 7 个基本音级名称. 因此,在音列中便产生了许多同名的音,为了区分音名相同而音高不同的各音,我们将音列分成许多组. 每组中包含 7 个白键和 5 个黑键,7 个白键表达 7 个基本音级名称,5 个黑键填充白键之间的半音. 每组的 12 个键中,每相邻的二键之间音程距离相等,都是半音,这也就是所谓的“十二平均律”.

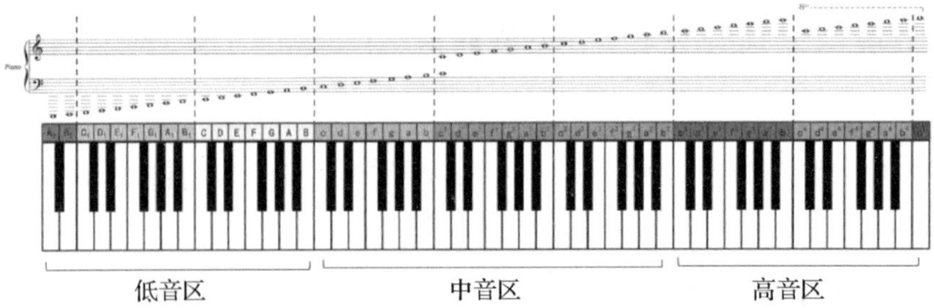

图 12-11

问题 1 若编制一个 10 字音符串,可编制多少种音符串?

问题 2 若编制一个 10 字音符串,其中 7 字音符来自白键,3 字音符来自黑键,共可编制多少种音符串?

【典例解析】

例 1　某县非遗运动项目“吹枪”队伍有 3 名男运动员和 3 名女运动员．6 名竞技运动员排成一行拍照留念．

（1）女运动员都排在一起，有多少种排法？

（2）女运动员与男运动员相间，有多少种排法？

（3）任何 2 名男运动员都不相邻，有多少种排法？

（4）3 名男运动员不排在一起，有多少种排法？

（5）男运动员甲与男运动员乙中间必须排而且只能排 2 名女运动员，且女运动员不能排在队伍的两端，有几种排法？

解　（1）将 3 名女运动员看作一个元素，就是 4 个元素的全排列，有 A_4^4 种排法．又 3 名女运动员内部有 A_3^3 种排法，所以共有 $A_4^4 \cdot A_3^3=144$（种）排法．

（2）男运动员自己排，女运动员也自己排，然后相间插入（此时有 2 种插法），所以女运动员与男运动员相间共有 $2A_3^3 \cdot A_3^3=72$（种）排法．

（3）女运动员先排，女运动员之间及首尾共有 4 个空隙，任取其中 3 个空隙安插男运动员即可，因而任何 2 名男运动员都不相邻的排法共有 $A_3^3 \cdot A_4^3=144$（种）．

（4）直接分类较复杂，可用间接法．即从 6 名运动员的排列总数中，减去 3 名男运动员排在一起的排法种数，得 3 名男运动员不排在一起的排法种数为 $A_6^6-A_3^3 \cdot A_4^4=576$（种）．

（5）先将 2 名女运动员排在男运动员甲、乙之间，有 A_3^2 种排法．又甲、乙之间还有 A_2^2 种排法，这样就有 $A_3^2 \cdot A_2^2$ 种排法．然后把他们 4 人看成一个元素（相当于一个男运动员），这一元素及另 1 名男运动员排在首尾，有 A_2^2 种排法．最后将余下的女运动员排在其间，有 1 种排法．故总排法有 $A_3^2 \cdot A_2^2 \cdot A_2^2=24$（种）．

备注　对于这类排列问题，主要按照“优先”原则，即优先安排特殊元素或优先满足特殊位置，对于“相邻”问题可用“捆绑法”，对于“不相邻”问题可用“插空法”，对于直接考虑较困难的问题可用间接法．

例 2　春风催新绿，植树正当时．2024 年 4 月 22 日，恰逢第 55 个世界地球日，某分公司要从 12 人中选出 5 人去参加总公司开展的义务植树活动．

(1) A,B,C 三人必须入选,有多少种不同选法?

(2) A,B,C 三人都不能入选,有多少种不同选法?

(3) A,B,C 三人只有一人入选,有多少种不同选法?

(4) A,B,C 三人至少一人入选,有多少种不同选法?

(5) A,B,C 三人至多二人入选,有多少种不同选法?

解 (1) 只需从 A,B,C 之外的 9 人中选择 2 人,有 $C_9^2=36$(种)选法.

(2) 由 A,B,C 三人都不能入选,只需从余下 9 人中选择 5 人,即有 $C_9^5=C_9^4=126$(种)选法.

(3) 可分两步,先从 A,B,C 三人中选出 1 人,有 C_3^1种选法,再从余下的 9 人中选 4 人,有 C_9^4种选法,所以共有 $C_3^1\cdot C_9^4=378$(种)选法.

(4) 可考虑间接法,从 12 人中选 5 人,共有 C_{12}^5种选法,再减去 A,B,C 三人都不入选的情况,有 C_9^5种,所以共有 $C_{12}^5-C_9^5=666$(种)选法.

(5) 可考虑间接法,从 12 人中选 5 人,共有 C_{12}^5种,再减去 A,B,C 三人都入选的情况,有 C_9^2种,所以共有 $C_{12}^5-C_9^2=756$(种)选法.

备注 遇到至多、至少的有关计数问题,可以用间接法求解. 对于有限制条件的问题,一般要根据特殊元素分类.

【课后练习】

1. 6 月,也称毕业月,高三的同学们都要与相处了三年的同窗进行合影留念. 现有 4 名男生、2 名女生照相合影,若女生必须相邻,则不同的排法有 ( )

A. 24 种　　B. 120 种　　C. 240 种　　D. 140 种

2. 某职业学校为预防春季流感暴发,计划安排学生在校内进行常规体检,共有 3 个检查项目,需要安排在 3 间空教室进行检查. 学校现有一排 6 间的空教室供选择使用,但是为了避免学生拥挤,要求作为检查项目的教室不能相邻,则不同的安排方式有 ( )

A. 12 种　　B. 24 种　　C. 36 种　　D. 48 种

3. 特岗教师是中央实施的一项对中西部地区农村义务教育的特殊政策. 某教育行政部门为本地两所农村小学招聘了 6 名特岗教师,其中体育教师 2

名、数学教师 4 名. 按每所学校 1 名体育教师、2 名数学教师进行分配,则不同的分配方案有　　　　(　　)

A. 24 种　　B. 14 种　　C. 12 种　　D. 8 种

4. 据《孙子算经》记载,中国古代诸侯的等级从低到高分为:男、子、伯、侯、公,共五级,若给获得巨大贡献的 7 人进行封爵,要求每个等级至少有一人,至多有两人,则恰有两人被封为伯爵的概率为____________.

5. 如图 12-12 所示,在圆上有 6 个不同的点,将这 6 个点两两连接成弦,这些弦将圆分割成的区域数最多为________个.

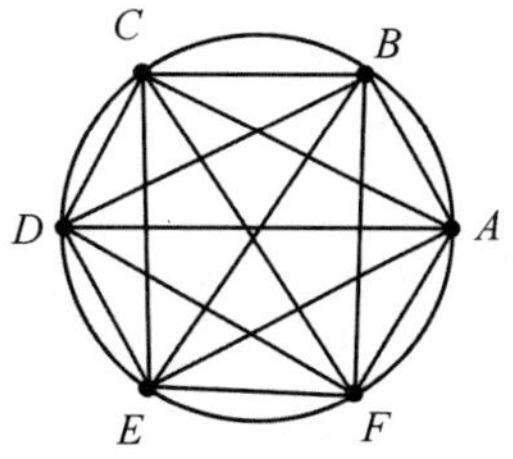

图 12-12

6. 用一颗骰子连掷三次,投掷出的数字顺次排成一个三位数,此时:

(1) 各位数字互不相同的三位数有多少个?

(2) 可以排出多少个不同的数?

(3) 恰好有两个相同数字的三位数共有多少个?

7. 有 4 名老师和 4 名学生站成一排照相.

(1) 4 名学生必须排在一起,共有多少种不同的排法?

(2) 任何两名学生都不能相邻,共有多少种不同的排法?

(3) 老师和学生相间排列,共有多少种不同的排法?(要求用数字作答)

8. 设集合 $A=\{0,2,4,6\}$, $B=\{1,3,5,7\}$,从集合 A, B 中各取 2 个元素组成没有重复数字的四位数.

(1) 可组成多少个这样的四位数?

(2) 有多少个是 2 的倍数或是 5 的倍数?

【数学文化】

排列组合问题最早见于我国的《易经》一书. 在汉代数学家徐岳的《数术记遗》中也曾记载与占卜有关的“八卦算”,即把卦按不同的方法在八个方位中排列起来(图 12-13). 它与“八个人围一张圆桌而坐,问有多少种不同坐法”这一典型的排列问题类似. 唐代张遂曾计算过棋局数,即围棋盘上所有可能的不同布局的总数,这相当于从事物(黑子、白子、空位)中每次取出 361 个(围棋盘的格点数)的排列数. 北宋时期的沈括在《梦溪笔谈》中,进一步讨论了围棋布局总数问题. 沈括指出,当 361 个棋子全用上时,棋局总数要连写 43 个“万”.

八卦图

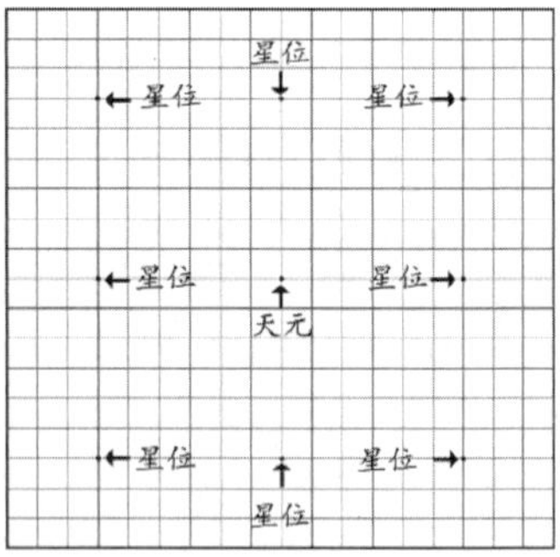

围棋布局

图 12-13

中世纪,欧洲许多学者得到过特殊的组合问题的结果.

18 世纪初,瑞士数学家伯努利(图 12-14)的巨著《猜度术》是一部系统论述概率论的科学著作，作为古典概型基础的排列组合知识几乎在书中囊括无遗，“排列”这个词也是伯努利首先使用的.在此之后，排列组合的知识几乎与今日中学教材所学到的内容大致无二，只是在一些解题的技巧上有所发展而已.

图 12-14

中国数学史上，首先对组合问题展开正面讨论的是汪莱（图 12-15）.他在《衡斋算学》第四册中称组合理论为“递兼数理”，并得出 $C_n^r=\dfrac{n(n-1)(n-2)\cdots(n-r+1)}{r!}$，$C_n^r=C_n^{n-r}$，$\sum\limits_{i=1}^{n}C_n^r=2^n-1$ 等重要关系.这些研究虽然迟于西方，但却由汪莱独立钻研所得，具有鲜明的中国特色.清末刘彝程作《简易庵算稿》，内中组合习题还要求用堆垛术来解.

图 12-15

排列组合源远流长，虽然它早在 17 至 18 世纪已具大观，但在科学高度发展的今日，仍是不可缺少的数学基础知识，概率论、数理统计、组合论、图论、规划论、对策论等数学分支都离不开排列组合，它是一门既古老又富有生命力的学问.

【拓展应用】

材料 上海崇明三岛包括崇明岛、长兴岛、横沙岛,陆地总面积达到了 1 411 km^2,其中崇明岛的面积最大. 崇明三岛除崇明岛小部分属于江苏之外,其他地区全部属于上海管辖. 崇明三岛位于长江入海口,多年来的泥沙沉积正是它们的形成原因,所以它们是中国典型的冲积岛.

问题 如果要建三座桥将崇明岛、长兴岛、横沙岛与陆地连接起来,不同建桥方案共有多少种?

12.5　二项式定理

【学习目标】

1. 能通过多项式乘法展开，归纳概括出二项式定理内容，并会用计数原理证明二项式定理.

2. 能从数列的角度认识二项式的展开式及其通项的规律，并能通过特例体会二项式定理的简单应用.

【重点难点】

重点：二项式定理的通项公式.

难点：用两个计数原理推导二项式定理的展开式、证明二项式定理.

【微课导学】

扫下面的二维码，学习微课“二项展开式”“二项式系数的性质”.

二项展开式　　　　二项式系数的性质

【自主学习】

1. $(x-y)^n$的二项展开式中，第 m 项的系数是　　(　　)

A. C_n^m　　B. C_n^{m+1}　　C. C_n^{m-1}　　D. $(-1)^{m-1}C_n^{m-1}$

2. 设 i 为虚数单位，则$(x+\mathrm{i})^6$ 的展开式中含 x^4 的项为　　(　　)

A. $-15x^4$　　B. $15x^4$　　C. $-20\mathrm{i}x^4$　　D. $20\mathrm{i}x^4$

3. 已知 $n=6$,那么 $\left(x-\dfrac{3}{x}\right)^n$ 展开式中含 x^2 项的系数为 ( )

A. 130 B. 135 C. 121 D. 139

4. 二项式系数具有对称性,首末两端"等距离"的两个二项式系数相等,即 $C_n^m=$__________.

5. 每行两端都是1,而且除1以外的每个数都等于它"肩上"的两个数的和,即 $C_n^m+C_n^{m-1}=$ __________.

6. 下列结论正确的是____________________.

① $a^{n-k}b^k$ 是二项展开式的第 k 项;

② 二项展开式中,系数最大的项为中间一项或中间两项;

③ $(a+b)^n$ 的展开式中,某一项的二项式系数与 a,b 无关;

④ $(1-x)^9$ 的展开式中,系数最大的项是第五、第六两项;

⑤ 若 $(3x-1)^7=a_7x^7+a_6x^6+\cdots+a_1x+a_0$,则 $a_7+a_6+\cdots+a_1$ 的值为128.

7. 已知 $(x-m)^7=a_0+a_1x+a_2x^2+\cdots+a_7x^7$ 的展开式中,含 x^4 项的系数是 -35,则 $a_1+a_2+\cdots+a_7$ 是多少?

【探究任务】

任务一

小组合作,根据组合数公式,探究二项式定理.

问题1 如图12-16所示,五个箱子均装着标有 a,b 字母的两个大小、形状一样的球,从每个箱子摸出一个球,共摸出5个球,有可能出现哪些结果?每一种结果有多少种情况?请填写表12-4.

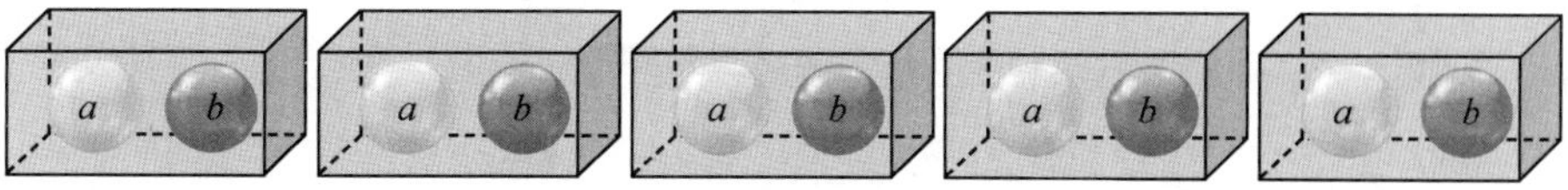

图 12-16

表 12-4　摸球结果及频数

结果	5 个 a 0 个 b	4 个 a 1 个 b	3 个 a 2 个 b	2 个 a 3 个 b	1 个 a 4 个 b	0 个 a 5 个 b
频数						

问题 2　根据多项式乘法法则，二项式 $(a+b)^5$ 的展开式有多少项？每一项的系数分别是多少？按照这个方法能否快速求出 $(a+b)^{10}$ 展开式的每一项及其系数？

二项式 $(a+b)^5$ 可写成 5 个 $(a+b)$ 相乘，即

$$(a+b)^5=(a+b)(a+b)(a+b)(a+b)(a+b).$$

问题 3　结合问题 1 和问题 2，猜想 $(a+b)^n$ 的展开式是怎样的？进一步研究二项式定理，同学们可以发现二项展开式有哪些特征吗？

1. $(a+b)^n=$________________________________.

2. 项数：共有________________项.

3. 次数：各项字母 a，b 指数和都等于________________.

字母 a 按降幂排列，次数由________________到 0；

字母 b 按升幂排列，次数由________________递增到 n.

4. 二项展开式的通项：式中的________________叫作二项展开式的通项，用 T_{k+1} 表示. 即通项为展开式的第 $k+1$ 项，$T_{k+1}=$________________.

5. 二项式系数：二项展开式的系数依次为____，这里 $C_n^k(k=0,1,2,3,\cdots,n)$ 称为二项式系数.

任务二

阅读材料，回答下列问题.

材料　杨辉三角是二项式系数在三角形中的一种几何排列（图 12-17）.

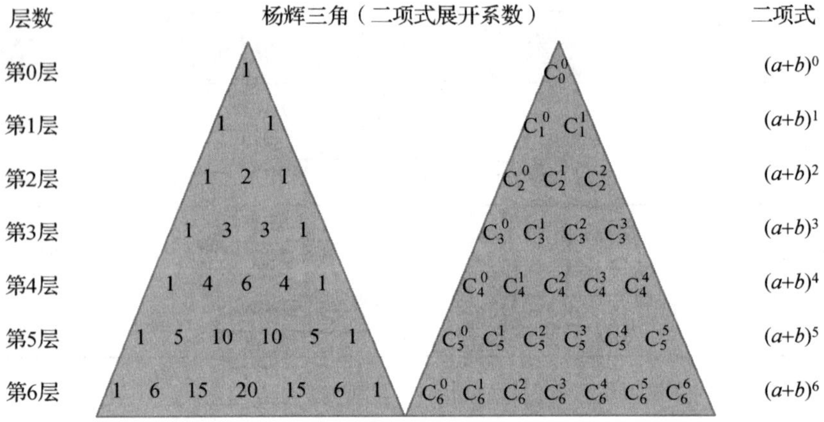

图 12-17

问题 由上图,总结归纳二项式系数的性质.

(1) 每一行的两端都是 1,其余的每一个数都等于它"肩上"两个数的和,事实上,假设图中任一不为 1 的数为 C_{n+1}^r,那么它"肩上"的两个数分别为________和________,可知 $C_{n+1}^r=$________.

(2) 二项式系数的对称性:距首末两端等距离的两项的二项式系数相等,即

$$C_n^r=\_\_\_\_\_\_\_\_.$$

(3) 增减性与最大值:对二项式系数 C_n^k,当 $k<\frac{n+1}{2}$ 时,二项式系数是________,当 $k>\frac{n+1}{2}$ 时,二项式系数是________.(填"递增的"或"递减的")

当 n 是偶数时,中间一项________取得最大值;当 n 是奇数时,中间两项________和________相等且取得最大值.

(4) 展开式系数总和:$C_n^0+C_n^1+C_n^2+\cdots+C_n^n=$________,其中奇数项系数的和等于偶数项系数的和,即

$$C_n^0+C_n^2+C_n^4+\cdots=C_n^1+C_n^3+C_n^5+\cdots=\_\_\_\_\_\_\_\_.$$

【典例解析】

例 1　已知在二项式 $\left(\sqrt[4]{\frac{1}{x}}+\sqrt[3]{x^2}\right)^n$ 的展开式中倒数第 3 项的系数为 45，求含 x^3 的项的系数.

解　由条件知 $C_n^{n-2}=45$，即 $C_n^2=45$，所以，$n^2-n-90=0$，解得 $n=-9$（舍去）或 $n=10$，由

$$T_{r+1}=C_{10}^r(x^{-\frac{1}{4}})^{10-r}(x^{\frac{2}{3}})^r=C_{10}^r x^{\frac{-10+r}{4}+\frac{2}{3}r},$$

由题意，知

$$\frac{-10+r}{4}+\frac{2}{3}r=3,$$

解得

$$r=6.$$

则含 x^3 的项是第 7 项，即

$$T_{6+1}=C_{10}^6x^3=210x^3,$$

系数为 210.

例 2　求 $(x^2+3x+2)^5$ 的展开式中 x 的一次项的系数.

解　解法 1　移项，得 $(x^2+3x+2)^5=[(x^2+2)+3x]^5$，

$$T_{r+1}=C_5^r(x^2+2)^{5-r}(3x)^r.$$

当且仅当 $r=1$ 时，T_{r+1} 的展开式中才有 x 的一次项，此时，

$$T_{r+1}=T_2=C_5^1(x^2+2)^4(3x)^1.$$

所以，x 的一次项为 $C_5^1\cdot C_4^4\times2^4\times3x=240x$，它的系数为 240.

解法 2　将 x^2+3x+2 因式分解，得

$$\begin{aligned}(x^2+3x+2)^5&=(x+1)^5(x+2)^5\\&=(C_5^0x^5+C_5^1x^4+\cdots+C_5^5x^0)(C_5^0x^52^0+C_5^1x^42^1+\cdots+C_5^5x^02^5)\end{aligned}$$

故展开式中含 x 的项为 $C_5^4x\cdot C_5^52^5+C_5^5\cdot C_5^4x2^4=240x$，故展开式中 x 的系数为 240.

备注　求解三项式的展开式问题的方法有：

(1) 因式分解法：通过因式分解将三项式变成两个二项式，然后用二项式定理分别展开.

(2) 逐层展开法:将三项式分成两组,用二项式定理展开,再把其中含两项的一组展开.

【课后练习】

1. $(1-x)^{13}$的展开式中系数最小的项是 ( )

A. 第 6 项　B. 第 7 项　C. 第 8 项　D. 第 9 项

2. 已知 $a+b>0,b=4a$,多项式 $(a+b)^n$的展开式按 a 的降幂排列,其中第 n 项与第 $n+1$ 项相等,那么正整数 $n=$ ( )

A. 4　B. 9　C. 10　D. 11

3. 若 C_{17}^n与 C_n^m同时有最大值,则 $m=$ ( )

A. 4 或 5　B. 5 或 6　C. 3 或 4　D. 5

4. 二项式系数从第一项起至中间项,二项式系数逐渐________,随后又逐渐________.(填"增大"或"减小")

5. $(2x+\sqrt{x})^5$的展开式中,含 x^3项的系数是________.(用数字填写答案)

6. 若将函数 $f(x)=x^5$表示为 $f(x)=a_0+a_1(1+x)+a_2(1+x)^2+\cdots+a_5(1+x)^5$,其中 $a_0,a_1,a_2,\cdots,a_5$为实数,则 $a_3=$________.

7. 已知二项式$(a+b)^{15}$.

(1) 求二项展开式中的中间项;

(2) 比较 T_3,T_7,T_{12},T_{13}各项系数的大小,并说明理由.

8. 求值：

(1) $C_6^0+C_6^1+C_6^2+\cdots+C_6^6$；

(2) $C_7^1+C_7^2+C_7^3+\cdots+C_7^7$.

9. 已知$(1-2x)^7=a_0+a_1x+a_2x^2+\cdots+a_7x^7$. 求：

(1) $a_1+a_3+a_5+a_7$；

(2) $a_0+a_2+a_4+a_6$；

(3) $|a_0|+|a_1|+|a_2|+\cdots+|a_7|$.

【信息手段】

在 MATLAB 中，可以使用嵌套循环来打印一个杨辉(Pascal)三角. 以下是一个简单的函数，用于打印给定阶数的杨辉三角.

杨辉三角

```
function printyh(n) % 一般格式输出参量=函数名(输入参量)
yh=1;
disp(yh)
if n==1
```

```
    return;
end
yh=[1,1];
disp(yh)
for k=3:n
    yh_old=yh;
    k2=ceil(k/2);
    for l=2:k2
        yh(l)=yh_old(l-1)+yh_old(l);
    end
    yh(k2+1:k)=yh(k-k2:-1:1);
    disp(yh)
end
```

调用语句:

```
>> printyh(9)
    1
    1    1
    1    2    1
    1    3    3    1
    1    4    6    4    1
    1    5    10   10   5    1
    1    6    15   20   15   6    1
    1    7    21   35   35   21   7    1
    1    8    28   56   70   56   28   8    1
>>
```

函数 printyh(n)接收一个参数 n,表示要打印的杨辉三角的阶数,然后使用嵌套循环来计算每一行的数值,并打印出来.

【数学文化】

二项式定理,又称牛顿二项式定理,最初的形式可以追溯到古巴比伦时期,他们在泥板上记录了相关的公式. 随后,古希腊数学家欧几里得在《几何原本》中对此进行了证明. 在中国,北宋数学家贾宪在《释锁算书》中提出了直到 6 次幂的二项式系数表,这被称为开方作法本源图(图 12-18),后来被称为贾宪三角. 元代数学家朱世杰在《四元玉鉴》中进一步扩展了这一概念. 在西方,13 世纪的欧洲数学家约丹努斯提出了这一数字三角形的概念. 1544 年,德国数学家斯蒂菲尔在《整数算术》中给出了直到 17 次的数字三角形,并引入了"二项式系数"这一术语.

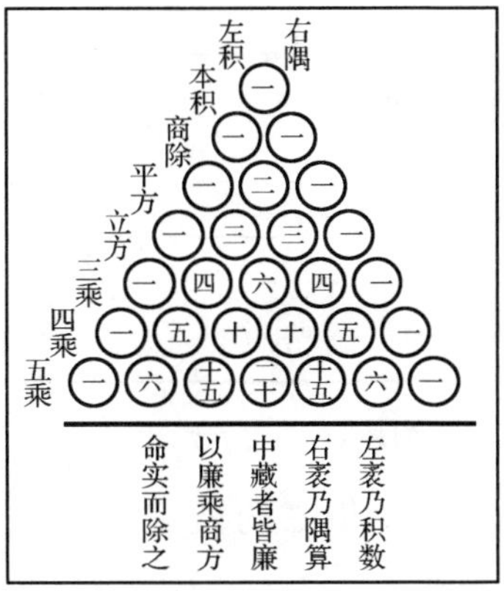

图 12-18

17 世纪时,法国数学家帕斯卡(图 12-19)在研究过程中发现了二项式系数与数字三角形的关系,并将其命名为帕斯卡三角. 他深入研究了二项式系数的一些性质,为后来的数学家提供了重要的基础. 同时期,伯努利等人也对二项式定理进行了研究.

图 12-19

到了 17 世纪末,牛顿(图 12-20)在 1664 年至 1665 年间提出了现代的二项式定理,他不仅将指数的范围扩展到有理数和负数,还首次提出了广义二项式定理. 他利用数学归纳法进行了严格的证明,为二项式定理的最终形式奠定了基础.

图 12-20

此后,多位数学家如欧拉、卡斯蒂隆等进一步证明了二项式定理的不同方面. 二项式定理在组合数学、概率论、微积分、统计学和工程学等多个领域都有着广泛的应用.

【拓展应用】

一般地,如果在一次试验中某事件 A 发生的概率是 p,随机变量 ξ 是在 n 次独立试验中事件 A 发生的次数,那么随机变量 ξ 的概率分布见表 12-5.

表 12-5　随机变量的概率分布

ξ	0	1	…	k	…	n
P	$C_n^0p^0(1-p)^n$	$C_n^1p^1(1-p)^{n-1}$	…	$C_n^kp^k(1-p)^{n-k}$	…	$C_n^np^n(1-p)$

其中 $0<p<1, k\in 0,1,2,\cdots,n$.

变量 ξ 的概率分布叫作**二项分布**. 称随机变量 ξ 服从**参数为 n 和 p 的二项分布**,记 $\xi\sim B(n,p)$.

二项分布中的各个概率值,依次是二项式 $[(1-p)+p]^n$ 的展开式中的各项. 第 $k+1$ 项 T_{k+1} 为 $P_n(k)=C_n^kp^k(1-p)^{n-k}$. 二项分布是以伯努利概型为背景的重要分布,有广泛的应用.

问题　气象站天气预报的准确率为 80%,计算(结果保留到小数点后第 2 位):

(1) 5 次预报中恰有 2 次准确的概率;

(2) 5 次预报中至少有 2 次准确的概率;

(3) 5 次预报中恰有 2 次准确,且第 3 次预报准确的概率.

自我检测

一、选择题

1. 由 1,2,3,4,5 这 5 个数字构成无重复数字的四位数,其中偶数有　(　　)

A. 24 种　　B. 36 种　　C. 48 种　　D. 60 种

2. 从 6 名志愿者中选出 4 人分别从事翻译、导游、导购、保洁 4 项不同的工作,若甲、乙 2 人不同时从事翻译工作,则选派方案共有　(　　)

A. 280 种　　B. 240 种　　C. 180 种　　D. 96 种

3. 有 7 名男生、3 名女生,从中选举 3 名代表,至少有 1 名女生的选法有　(　　)

A. 120 种　　B. 108 种　　C. 100 种　　D. 85 种

4. 在$(x-\sqrt{3})^{10}$展开式中,含 x^6项的系数是　(　　)

A. $-27C_{10}^{6}$　　B. $27C_{10}^{4}$　　C. $-C_{10}^{6}$　　D. $9C_{10}^{4}$

5. $\left(x^2+\frac{1}{2x}\right)^6$的展开式中,常数项是　(　　)

A. $\frac{3}{8}$　　B. $\frac{15}{16}$　　C. $\frac{5}{2}$　　D. $\frac{15}{32}$

6. $(x-1)^8$ 的展开式中,含 x^5项的系数是　(　　)

A. 56　　B. -56　　C. 28　　D. 224

7. 二项式$(2a+b)^8$ 展开式中,二项式系数最大的项是　(　　)

A. 第 3 项　　B. 第 4 项　　C. 第 5 项　　D. 第 6 项

8. $C_{12}^{5}+C_{12}^{6}=$　(　　)

A. C_{13}^{5}　　B. C_{13}^{6}　　C. C_{13}^{11}　　D. C_{12}^{7}

9. 书架上层有 5 本不同的文学书,中层放着 3 本不同的工具书,下层放有 6 本不同的数学参考书. 从中任取一本书的不同取法数有　(　　)

A. 14 种　　B. 90 种　　C. 1 种　　D. 3 种

10. 乘积$(a+b+c)(m+n)(x+y+z)$ 展开后,共有　(　　)

A. 8 项　　B. 9 项　　C. 11 项　　D. 18 项

11. 若从 n 个不同元素中取出 2 个元素的排列数是 56,则 $n=$ ( )

A. 8 或 -7　　B. 7 或 8　　C. 8　　D. 7

12. 满足方程 $C_{16}^{x^2-x}=C_{16}^{5x-5}$ 的 x 值为 ( )

A. 1,3,5,7　　B. 1,3　　C. 1,3,5　　D. 3,5

13. 从 0,1,2,3,4 中每次取出 3 个数,组成不同的三位数,不同的取法共有 ( )

A. A_5^3 种　　B. $A_4^1A_4^2$ 种　　C. $A_5^3-A_4^3$ 种　　D. $A_4^1A_5^2$ 种

14. 一个集合由 5 个不同的元素组成,则它的所有非空子集有 ( )

A. 30 个　　B. 31 个　　C. 32 个　　D. 25 个

15. 200 件产品中有 3 件次品,任意抽取 5 件,其中有 2 件次品的抽法有 ( )

A. $C_3^2\cdot C_{197}^3$ 种　　B. $A_6^2\cdot A_4^2$ 种

C. $C_6^3\cdot C_4^2\cdot A_5^5$ 种　　D. $(C_6^3+C_4^2)\cdot A_5^5$ 种

二、填空题

1. $(2x-3)^5$ 的展开式中,所有项的二项式系数之和等于________.

2. $(x-y)^7$ 的展开式中,系数最大的项是第________项.

3. 若 $(1-2x)^9=a_0+a_1x+a_2x^2+\cdots+a_9x^9$,则 $a_0+a_1+a_2+\cdots+a_9=$________.

4. $\dfrac{A_6^3-C_5^3+C_{100}^{99}}{4!-3!}=$________.

5. 要安排 6 个歌唱节目和 4 个舞蹈节目的演出顺序,任何两个舞蹈节目不得相邻,那么不同排法共有________种.

6. 若 $A_m^3=6C_m^4$,则 $m=$________.

7. 分配 5 人担任 5 种不同的职位,甲不担任第一种职位,那么分配方法共有________种.

8. 计算:$C_5^0+C_5^1+C_5^2+C_5^3+C_5^4+C_5^5=$________.

9. 从 5 种蔬菜品种选出 3 种,分别种植在不同土质的 3 块土地上进行试验,有________种不同的种植方法.

10. 从 5 个元素 a,b,c,d,e 中任取 2 个元素的组合数为________.

三、解答题

1. 4 个男同学和 3 个女同学站成一排.

(1) 不同的排法有多少种?

(2) 4 个男同学必须排在一起,有多少种不同的排法?

(3) 3 个女同学彼此不相邻,有多少种不同的排法?

2. 一个口袋内有大小相同的 7 个白球和 3 个黑球.

(1) 从口袋内取出 3 个球,共有多少种取法?

(2) 从口袋内取出 3 个球,其中至多含有 1 个黑球,有多少种取法?

3. 从 1 到 9 这 9 个数字中取出 3 个偶数、4 个奇数,求:

(1) 能组成多少个没有重复数字的七位数?

(2) 上述七位数中 3 个偶数排在一起的有几个?

4. 在二项式$\left(\sqrt{x}-\frac{2}{x^2}\right)^8$展开式中,求:

(1) 第 3 项的系数;

(2) 二项式系数最大的项.

5. 学校开设了 6 门任意选修课，要求每个学生从中选学 3 门，共有多少种不同的选法？

6. 4 名男生和 6 名女生组成至少有 1 个男生参加的三人社会实践活动小组，组成方法共有多少种？

7. 从 5 名男生和 4 名女生中选出 4 人去参加辩论比赛.

(1) 如果 4 人中男生和女生各选 2 人,有多少种选法?

(2) 如果男生中的甲与女生中的乙必须在内,有多少种选法?

第13章　坐标轴平移与参数方程

13.1　坐标轴平移

【学习目标】

1. 理解坐标轴平移的概念,会用坐标变换公式进行新旧坐标间的转换.
2. 会利用坐标轴平移化简曲线方程.

【重点难点】

重点:坐标轴平移,点的新旧坐标间的转换,利用坐标轴平移化简曲线方程.

难点:坐标变换公式的运用.

【微课导学】

扫下面的二维码,学习微课"坐标轴平移""坐标轴平移化简曲线方程".

坐标轴平移　　坐标轴平移化简曲线方程

【自主学习】

1. 坐标轴平移后,使点 $P(1,1)$ 的坐标变为 $(2,-1)$,则原坐标系的原点的新坐标是 ( )

A. $(3,0)$　　B. $(1,-2)$　　C. $(-1,2)$　　D. $(0,3)$

2. 平移坐标轴,把原点移到 $O'(2,-3)$,使 $M(x,y)$ 变成 $M(-3,1)$,则 M 点在原坐标系中的坐标为 ( )

A. $(-1,-2)$　　B. $(1,2)$　　C. $(-5,4)$　　D. $(5,-4)$

3. 平移坐标轴,把原点移到 $O'(-3,-2)$,则 $P(2,-3)$ 的新坐标是 ( )

A. $(-5,1)$　　B. $(5,1)$

C. $(4,0)$　　D. $(5,-1)$

4. 一般地,只改变原点的位置,而不改变________和________的坐标系变换,叫作坐标轴平移.

5. 一般地,若坐标系 xOy 平移后得新坐标系 $x'O'y'$,O' 在原坐标系 xOy 的坐标是 (x_0,y_0),则有以下关系

$$\begin{cases}x=\_\_\_\_\_\_\_\_,\\ y=\_\_\_\_\_\_\_\_\end{cases} \text{或} \begin{cases}x'=\_\_\_\_\_\_\_\_,\\ y'=\_\_\_\_\_\_\_\_.\end{cases}$$

其中 (x,y) 为点在坐标系 xOy 中的坐标,(x',y') 为点在坐标系 $x'O'y'$ 中的坐标,以上公式叫作坐标轴平移的坐标变换公式.

6. 下列说法正确的是__________.(填编号)

① 不改变原点位置,只改变坐标轴方向和单位长度的变换叫作坐标轴的平移.

② 将坐标原点平移至 $O'(1,2)$,点 $B(1,2)$ 在新坐标系中的坐标为 $(0,0)$.

③ 平移坐标轴,将坐标原点移至 $O'(1,1)$,则点 $(3,2)$ 在新坐标系中的坐标为 $(4,2)$.

7. 圆心在 $O'(2,2)$，半径为 1 的圆的方程为 $(x-2)^2+(y-2)^2=1$. 对应图形如图 13-1 所示. 如果不改变坐标轴的方向和单位长度，将坐标原点移至点 O' 处，那么，对于新坐标系 $x'O'y'$，求圆的方程.

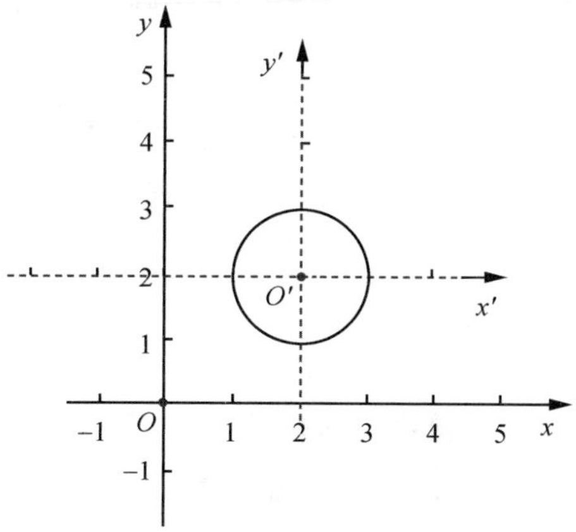

图 13-1

【探究任务】

任务一

阅读材料，回答下列问题.

材料 1　天门中断楚江开，碧水东流至此回. 两岸青山相对出，孤帆一片日边来. ——唐・李白《望天门山》

材料 2　在一个机器人系统中，每个测量元件测量同一物体得出的信息是不一样的，原因就在于“每个测量元件所测量的数据是基于不同坐标系所测量的”. 例如，在如图 13-2 所示的车中有激光雷达 M 和激光雷达 W，这两个雷达测量的数据截然不同，但是这辆汽车相对于测量物体的位置是唯一的，这就说明由不同位置雷达测量的数据代表的物理含义（即都表示汽车与被测物体的相对位置）是相同的. 那既然被测物体在不同坐标系中的坐标不同但物理含义相同，这就涉及不同坐标系中坐标的相互转化.

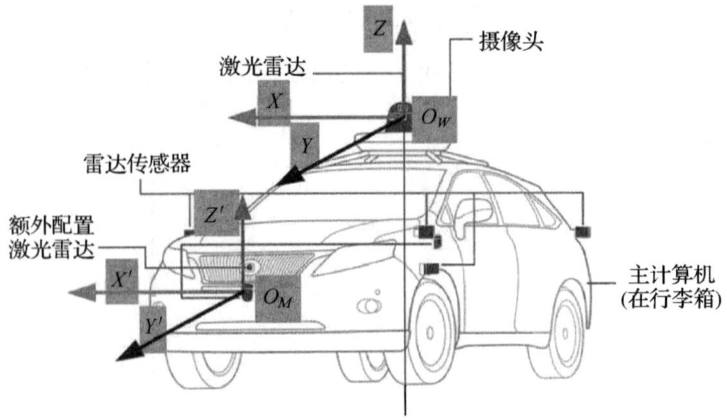

图 13-2

问题 1　李白在《望天门山》中写道:“两岸青山相对出,孤帆一片日边来.”这两句诗中描写青山与孤帆运动选择的参照系分别是什么?

问题 2　激光雷达 M 和激光雷达 W 观测的两个坐标系坐标轴的方向和长度单位有没有改变?所测量的被测物体在不同坐标系中的坐标与激光雷达 M 和激光雷达 W 的位置有没有关系?

任务二

小组合作,探索点的坐标变化与坐标轴平移间的关系.

问题 1　如图 13-3 所示,在实数轴上以 O 为原点,A 点的坐标是什么?以 O' 为原点,A 点的坐标又是什么?

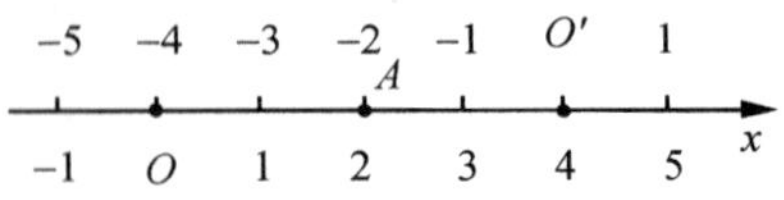

图 13-3

问题 2　如图 13-4 所示，设 O'是直角坐标系 xOy 中的一点，若将坐标原点 $O(0,0)$平移到 $O'(4,2)$，建立新坐标系 $x'O'y'$，且保持新坐标系的各坐标轴与原坐标系的各坐标轴方向不变，单位长度不变. 分别写出点 A,B,C,D 在新旧坐标系下的坐标，填入表 13-1. 观察点 A,B,C,D 在新旧坐标系下的坐标与 O'在坐标系 xOy 中的坐标之间有什么关系？

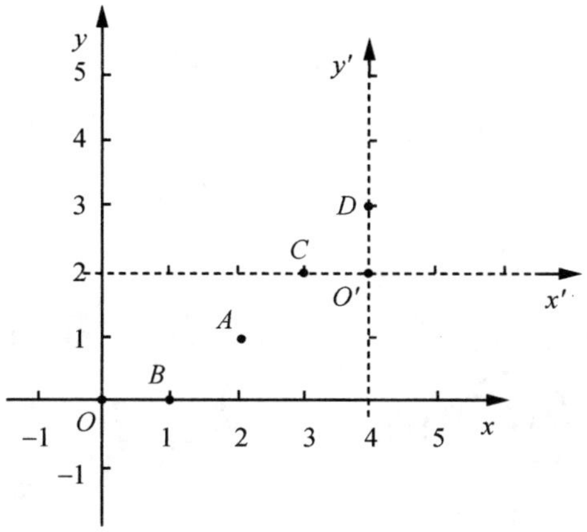

图 13-4

表 13-1　新旧坐标系中点的坐标

点	A	B	C	D
xOy 中的坐标				
$x'O'y'$中的坐标				

问题 3　如图 13-5 所示，设 O'在旧坐标系 xOy 中的坐标是(x_0,y_0)，点 A 在旧坐标系 xOy 中的坐标是(x,y)，在新坐标系 $x'O'y'$的坐标是(x',y')，这三者之间有什么关系？

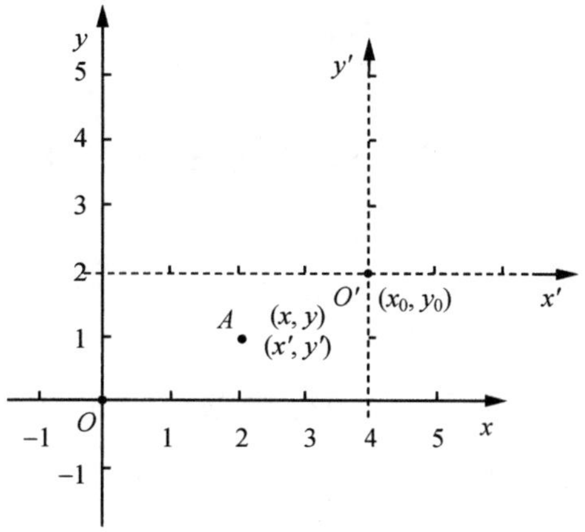

图 13-5

【典例解析】

例 1 数控车床设定坐标系的主要目的是确保机床可以准确地加工出预定位置、形状和尺寸的工件. 调整坐标系可以提高加工精度,降低加工误差,提高加工效率.

如图 13-6 所示,某零件在加工过程中,需要调整坐标系来提高精度. 观察点 A,B,C,D 在旧坐标系下的坐标,若将坐标原点 O 平移到 O',建立新坐标系 $x'O'y'$,求点 A,B,C,D 在新坐标系下的坐标.

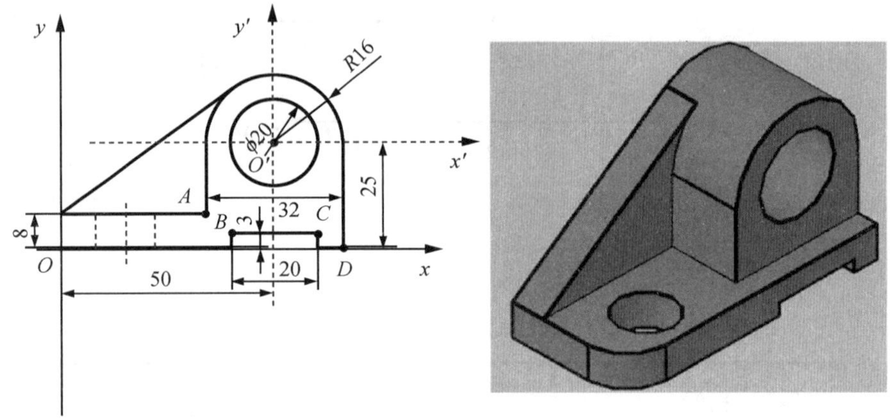

图 13-6

解 由图 13-6 可知,点 A,B,C,D 在旧坐标系下的坐标分别是(34,8),(40,3),(60,3),(66,0). O'在旧坐标系 xOy 中的坐标是 $O'(50,25)$.

由公式 $\begin{cases} x'=x-x_0, \\ y'=y-y_0 \end{cases}$ 得,点 A,B,C,D 在新坐标系下的坐标分别是(−16,−17),(−10,−22),(10,−22),(16,−25).

备注 掌握坐标轴平移的坐标变换公式 $\begin{cases} x'=x-x_0, \\ y'=y-y_0 \end{cases}$ 及其变形 $\begin{cases} x=x'+x_0, \\ y=y'+y_0 \end{cases}$ 是解题的关键.

例 2 将坐标原点 O 点平移至 $O'(2,-3)$,求以下各项在新坐标系中的坐标或方程.

(1) 点 $A(4,6)$;

(2) 直线 $x+3y=2$；

(3) 曲线 $9x^2+4y^2-36x+24y+36=0$.

解　根据平移公式,平移前后的坐标有以下关系：

$$\begin{cases}x=x'+2,\\ y=y'-3,\end{cases} ① \text{ 或 } \begin{cases}x'=x-2,\\ y'=y'+3.\end{cases} ②$$

(1) 由②式,得

$$\begin{cases}x'=x-2=2,\\ y'=y'+3=9,\end{cases}$$

故点 A 在新坐标系中的坐标为(2,9).

(2) 由①式,得

$$(x'+2)+3(y'-3)=2,$$

整理得,在新坐标系中的直线方程为

$$x'+3y'=9.$$

(3) 由①式,得

$$9(x'+2)^2+4(y'-3)^2-36(x'+2)+24(y'-3)+36=0.$$

整理得,在新坐标系中的曲线方程为

$$9x'^2+4y'^2-36=0.$$

即

$$\frac{x'^2}{4}+\frac{y'^2}{9}=1.$$

备注　坐标变换是化简曲线方程,以便于讨论曲线的性质和画出曲线的一种重要方法. 坐标轴平移的坐标变换公式是解决问题的关键.

【课后练习】

1. 平移坐标轴,将坐标原点移至 $O'(-1,3)$,则直线 $y=4x-5$ 在新坐标系中的方程为　　(　　)

A. $y'=4x'-8$　　B. $y'=4x'-10$

C. $y'=4x'-12$　　D. $y'=4x'-14$

2. 如果坐标平面内的点 $M(0,m)(m\neq0)$ 经坐标系平移后的坐标是 $(m,0)$,则新坐标系的原点 O' 在原坐标系中的坐标是　　(　　)

A. (m,m) B. $(m,-m)$

C. $(-m,m)$ D. $(-m,-m)$

3. 平移坐标轴,将坐标原点移至 $O'(2,-1)$,则直线 $y=-1$ 在新坐标系中的方程为 ( )

A. $x'=0$ B. $y'=x'+1$

C. $y'=0$ D. $y'=2x'+1$

4. 平移坐标轴,点$(-4,3)$在新坐标系中的坐标为$(2,-1)$,则原坐标原点移至了________.

5. 平移坐标系,将原点移到 $O'(-1,3)$,则曲线$(y-3)^2=2(x+5)$在新坐标系中的方程是________.

6. 如图 13-7 所示,已知点 A,B,C 在机床坐标系中的坐标分别为$(40,30)$,$(15,45)$,$(65,15)$,现在以点 A 作为工件坐标系的原点,求 B,C 在工件坐标系的坐标.

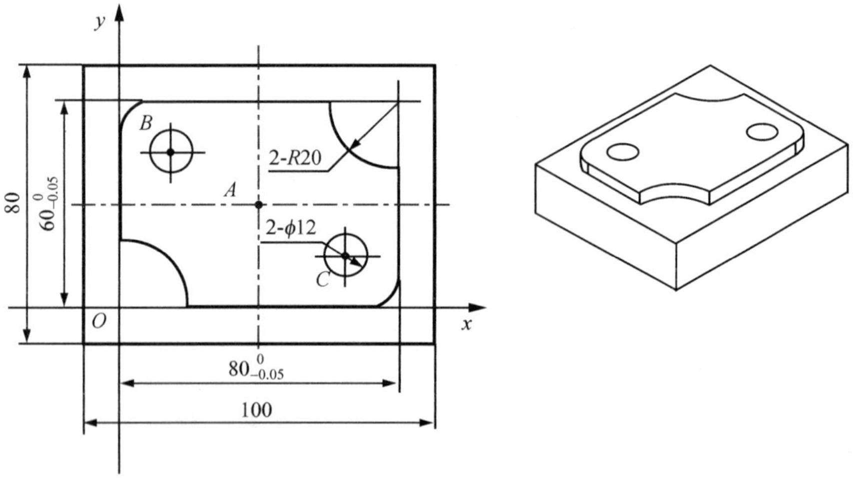

图 13-7

7. 利用平移坐标轴，化简下列曲线方程，并指出新坐标系原点的坐标.

(1) $x^2+y^2-16x+10y+32=0$;

(2) $\dfrac{(x-2)^2}{4}-\dfrac{(y+1)^2}{9}=1$.

8. 如图 13-8 所示，经过怎样的平移变换，可把抛物线方程 $(y+2)=(x-2)^2$ 化为最简形式?

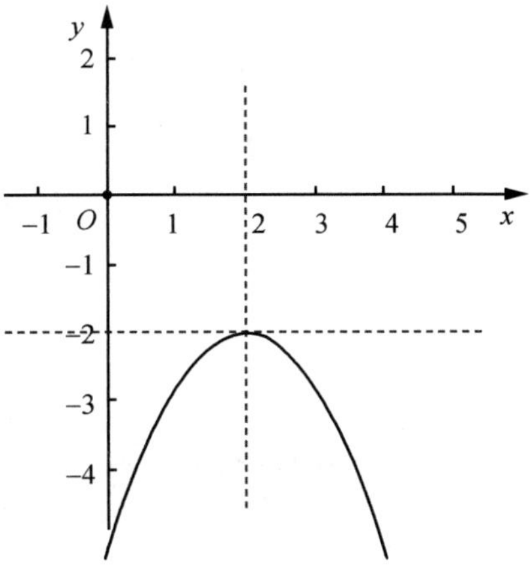

图 13-8

【信息手段】

函数图像平移变换

案例 1 上下平移变换作图过程见表 13-2.

表 13-2 上下平移变换作图过程

顺序	步骤	输入内容	备注
1	文本框	“上下平移变换”	
2	文本框	“$y=f(x)\Rightarrow y=f(x)+a$”	
3	函数	$f(x)=x^2$	
4	输入框	$f(x)=$	关联函数 $f(x)$
5	数值滑杆	a	范围$[-5,5]$
6	函数	$g(x)=f(x)+a$	
7	公式文本	公式文本[g,ture,ture]	

如图 13-9 所示,在绘图区的输入框中可以输入函数,滑杆 a 可以移动更改上下平移的数值,相应的 $g(x)$ 函数解析式及其图象随着平移而改变(图 13-10).

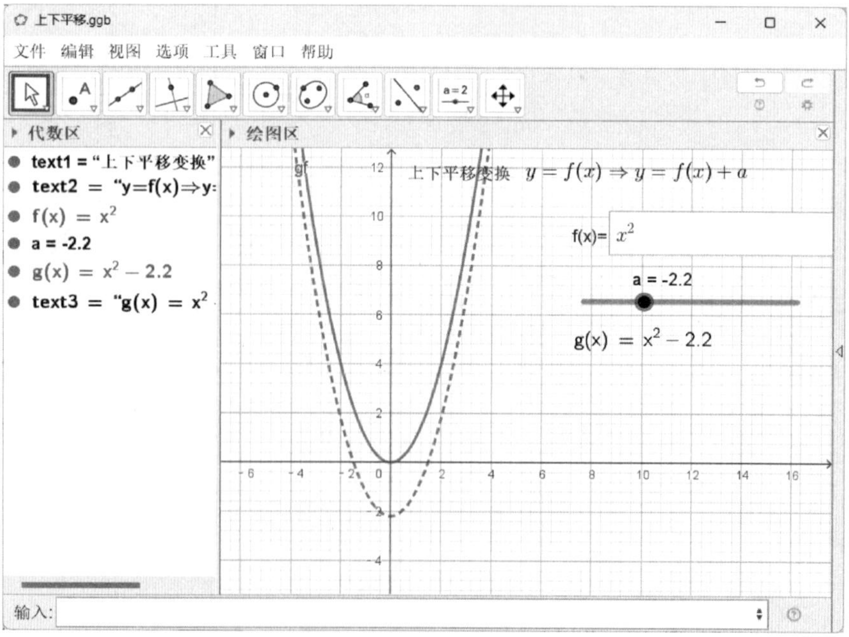

图 13-9

案例 2　左右平移变换作图过程见表 13-3.

表 13-3　左右平移变换作图过程

顺序	步骤	输入内容	备注
1	文本框	“左右平移变换”	
2	文本框	“$y=f(x)\Rightarrow y=f(x+a)$”	
3	函数	$f(x)=x^2$	
4	输入框	$f(x)=$	关联函数 $f(x)$
5	数值滑杆	a	范围[-5,5]
6	函数	$g(x)=f(x+a)$	
7	公式文本	公式文本[g,ture,ture]	

如图 13-11 所示,在绘图区的输入框中可以输入函数,滑杆 a 可以移动更改左右平移的数值,相应的 $g(x)$ 函数解析式及其图象随着平移而改变(图 13-10).

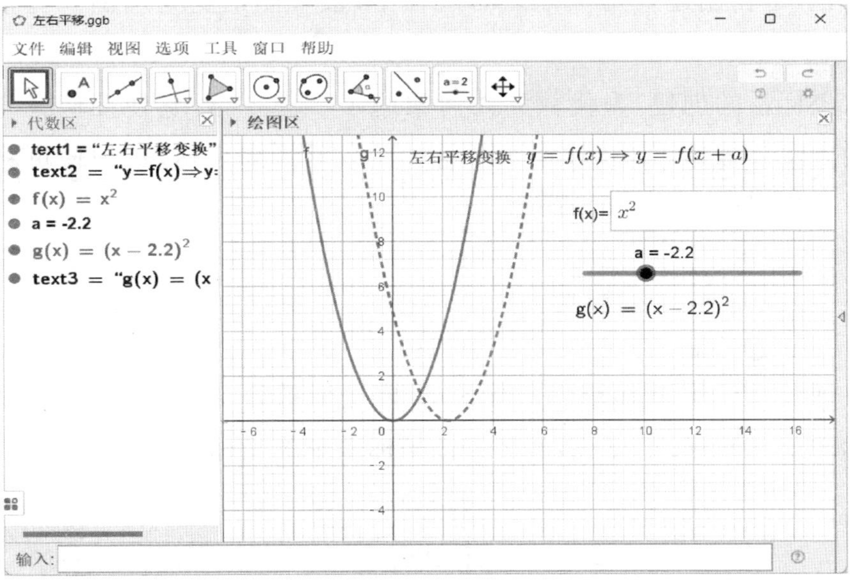

图 13-10

【数学文化】

笛卡尔是法国哲学家、数学家、物理学家. 有一天,他生病卧床,但他头脑一直没有休息,在反复思考一个问题:几何图形是直观的,而代数方程则比较抽象,能不能用几何图形来表示方程呢? 这里,关键是如何把组成几何图形的点和满足方程的每一组“数”挂上钩. 他拼命琢磨,通过什么样的办法,才能把“点”和“数”联系起来. 突然,他看见屋顶角上的一只蜘蛛,拉着丝垂了下来,一会儿,蜘蛛又顺着丝爬上去,在上边左右拉丝. 蜘蛛的“表演”,使笛卡尔思路豁然开朗. 他想,可以把蜘蛛看作一个点,它在屋子里可以上、下、左、右运动,能不能把蜘蛛的每个位置用一组数确定下来呢? 他又想,屋子里相邻的两面墙与地面交出了三条线,如果把地面上的墙角作为起点,把与之相交的三条线作为三根数轴,那么空间中任意一点的位置,不是都可以用这三根数轴上找到的有顺序的三个数来表示吗? 反过来,任意给一组三个有顺序的数,如 3,2,1,也可以用空间中的一个点 P 来表示. 同样,用一组数 (a,b) 可以表示平面上的一个点,平面上的一个点也可以用一组两个有顺序的数来表示. 于是在蜘蛛的启示下,笛卡尔创建了直角坐标系.

无论这个传说的可靠性如何,有一点是可以肯定的,笛卡尔是个勤于思考的人. 这个有趣的传说,就像瓦特看到蒸汽冲起开水壶盖发明了蒸汽机一样,说明笛卡尔在创建直角坐标系的过程中,很可能是受到周围一些事物的启发,产生了灵感.

直角坐标系的创建,为代数和几何架起了一座桥梁. 它使几何概念得以用代数的方法来描述,几何图形可以通过代数形式来表达,这样便可将先进的代数方法应用于几何学的研究.

【拓展应用】

某零件尺寸标注如图 13-11 所示,机床坐标系为 xOy,现将点 C 设置为工件坐标的坐标原点,求点 A,B 在工件坐标系中的坐标.

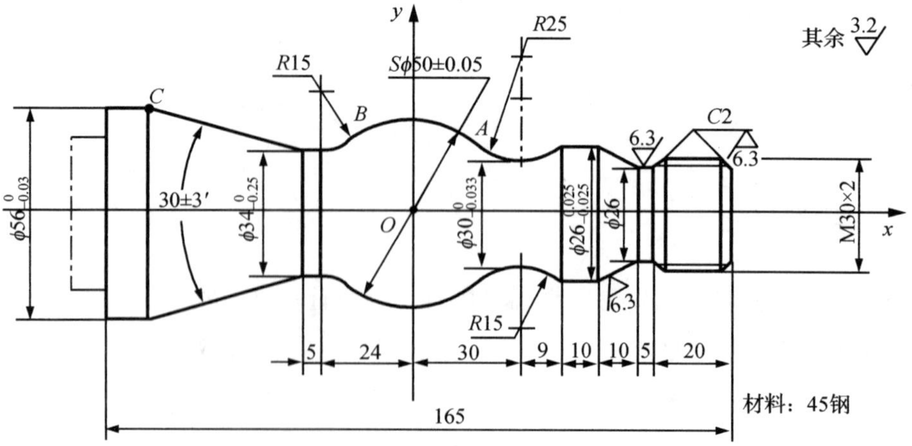

图 13-11

13.2　参数方程

【学习目标】

1. 了解参数方程的概念,会在给定参数的条件下求简单的参数方程.
2. 掌握直线和圆的参数方程,能把曲线的参数方程化为普通方程.

【重点难点】

重点:在给定条件下求简单的参数方程和把曲线的参数方程化为普通方程.

难点:参数方程和普通方程的互相转化.

【微课导学】

扫下面的二维码,学习微课“参数方程”“直线的参数方程”“圆的参数方程”.

参数方程　　直线的参数方程　　圆的参数方程

【自主学习】

1. 将参数方程 $\begin{cases} x=2+t, \\ y=t \end{cases}$ (t 为参数)化为普通方程为　　(　　)

A. $y=x-2$　　B. $y=x+2$

C. $y=-x-2$　　D. $y=-x+2$

2. 参数方程$\begin{cases}x=3\cos\theta,\\ y=3\sin\theta\end{cases}$($\theta$为参数)所表示的曲线是 ( )

A. 一条射线　　B. 两条射线

C. 半径为3的圆　　D. 半径为$\sqrt{3}$的圆

3. 直线l的参数方程为$\begin{cases}x=a+t,\\ y=b+t\end{cases}$($t$为参数),$l$上的点$P_1$对应的参数是$t_1$,则点$P_1$与$P(a,b)$之间的距离是 ( )

A. $|t_1|$　　B. $2|t_1|$　　C. $\sqrt{2}|t_1|$　　D. $\frac{\sqrt{2}}{2}|t_1|$

4. 已知直线的普通方程为$x-2y=1$,若选取参数$t=2y$,则直线的参数方程为____________.

5. 若圆的参数方程为$\begin{cases}x=1+5\cos\theta,\\ y=5\sin\theta,\end{cases}$则圆的半径为____________.

6. 若直线的参数方程为$\begin{cases}x=1+2t,\\ y=2-2t\end{cases}$($t$为参数),则直线的斜率为________.

7. 在平面直角坐标系xOy中,直线l的参数方程为$\begin{cases}x=t,\\ y=t+1\end{cases}$(参数$t\in\mathbf{R}$),圆$C$的参数方程为$\begin{cases}x=\cos\theta+1,\\ y=\sin\theta\end{cases}$(参数$\theta\in[0,2\pi)$),求圆心$C$到直线$l$的距离.

【探究任务】

任务一

材料　2023 年 5 月 16 日，“应急使命 · 2023”高山峡谷地区地震灾害空地一体化联合救援演习在滇举行，本次演习投放了直升机 11 架，其中包括 6 架直 8 系列直升机，中国飞龙执飞的米-171、卡-32、米-26 等多个型号. 在演习场内装备展览展示区，AR500C、“翼龙”无人机和运 5 改装无人机等数十架国产航空装备在本次演习中凸显航空力量，空中力量和地面力量衔接，形成立体救援、精准救援、高效救援.

问题　如图 13-12 所示，一架救援飞机在离灾区地面 500 m 高处以 100 m/s的速度沿水平直线飞行. 为使投放救援物资准确落于灾区指定的地面(不计空气阻力)，飞行员应如何确定投放时机呢？

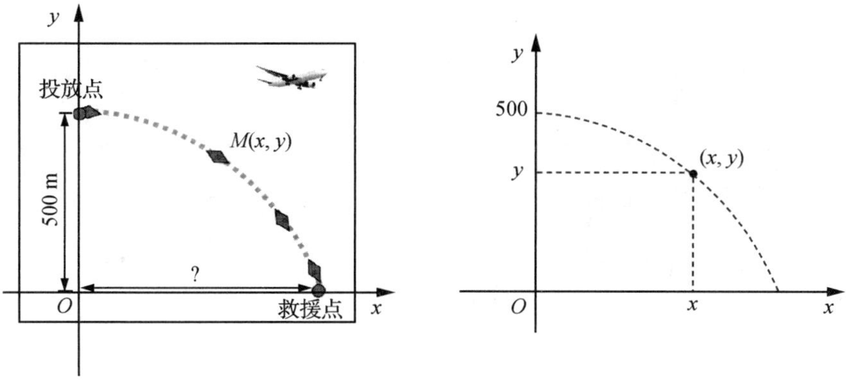

图 13-12

物资出舱后，在不考虑阻力的情况下，水平方向以 100 m/s 的速度匀速运动，垂直方向做自由落体运动(重力加速度 $g=9.8\ \text{m/s}^2$). 设在时刻 t，物资的水平位移为 x，垂直高度为 y，则

$$x=\underline{\qquad\qquad\qquad\qquad},$$

$$y=\underline{\qquad\qquad\qquad\qquad}.$$

令 $y=0$，得 $t=$__________ s. 代入 $x=100t$，得 $x=$__________ m.

所以，飞行员在离救援点的水平距离约为____________m 时投放物资，可以使其准确落在指定位置.

任务二

材料 一些景区为了提供更好的观光体验,已经开始修建室外步行电梯(图 13-13).这项工程可谓一个充分展示现代科技与传统文化相结合的杰作,而其中最引人注目的项目之一,便是位于三省交界的湖北恩施大峡谷,那里拥有世界上最长的手扶电梯.

图 13-13

问题 1 如图 13-14 所示,旅客由 $A(x_0,y_0)$点上电梯,到达 $B(x,y)$点下电梯,电梯总长度为 t,电梯的倾斜角为$\frac{\pi}{6}$,到达 B 点时,该旅客的水平位移是多少?垂直上升的高度是多少?当电梯长度发生变化时,如何用表达式描述 $B(x,y)$点的坐标.

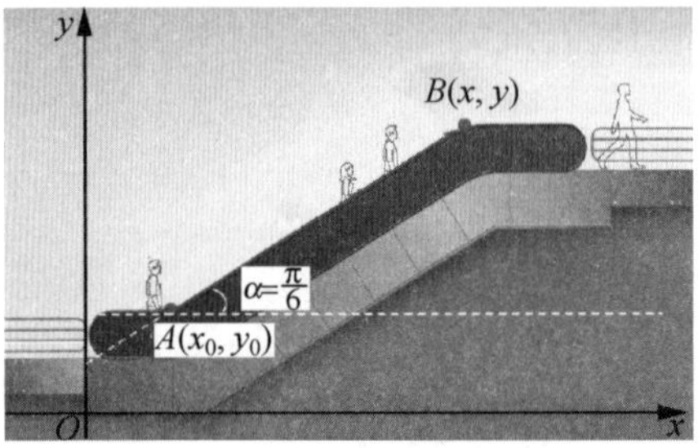

图 13-14

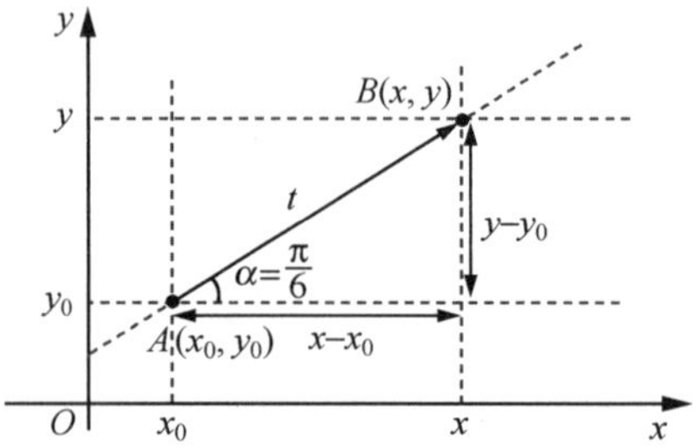

图 13-15

由图 13-15 可知,水平方向的位移为

$$x-x_0=\underline{\qquad\qquad\qquad\qquad},$$

垂直上升的高度为

$$y-y_0=\underline{\qquad\qquad\qquad\qquad}.$$

当电梯长度发生变化时,$B(x,y)$点的坐标

$$x=x_0+\underline{\qquad\qquad\qquad\qquad},$$

$$y=y_0+\underline{\qquad\qquad\qquad\qquad}.$$

问题 2 如图 13-16 所示,已知直线过点 $A(x_0,y_0)$,且倾斜角为 α.设 $P(x,y)$为直线上任意一点,选取有向线段 AP 的数量 t 为参数(当点 P 在 A 点上方时 $t>0$,当点 P 在 A 点下方时 $t<0$,当点 P 与点 A 重合时 $t=0$),求直线上任意一点 $P(x,y)$的横坐标、纵坐标与 t 的关系.

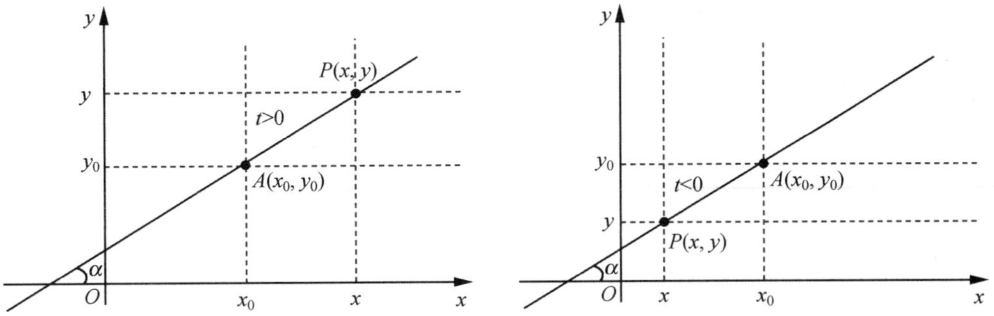

图 13-16

任务三

材料　渤海之眼位于我国山东省潍坊市滨海技术开发区，是我国在营业的第二高摩天轮，也是世界上最高的无轴摩天轮. 乘坐渤海之眼摩天轮，可近观白浪河、远眺渤海湾，俯瞰滨海中央城区城市美景，饱览海河风光.

问题 1　已知该摩天轮的直径约为 125 m，逆时针匀速旋转一周需 30 min. 如图 13-17 所示，某游客现在 A 点(其中 A 点和摩天轮中心的连线与水平面平行). 经过 t s，逆时针旋转的角度为 θ. 此时，该游客的位置在何处(x，y 与角 θ 的关系式)?

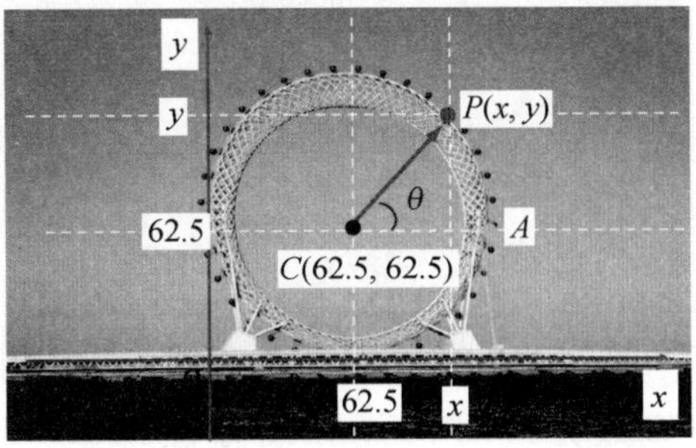

图 13-17

如图 13-18 所示,建立直角坐标系,此时,圆心的坐标为 $C(62.5,62.5)$,圆的半径为 62.5 m,A 点的坐标为 $A(125,62.5)$,经过 t s,逆时针旋转角度 θ,设该游客的位置在 $P(x,y)$,则在 Rt$\triangle PCB$ 中

$|CB|=$____________,

$|PB|=$____________.

所以

$x=62.5+$____________,

$y=62.5+$____________.

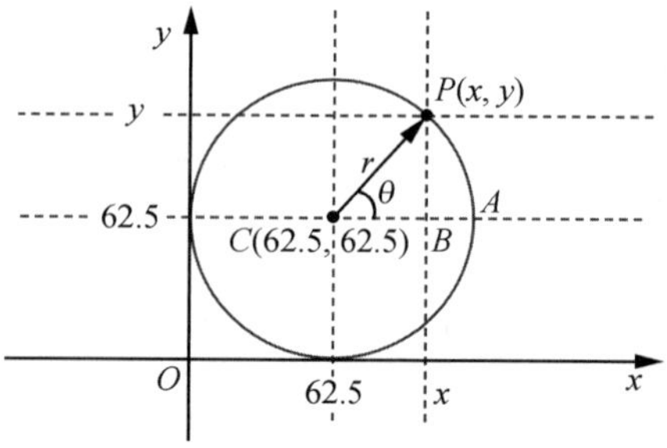

图 13-18

问题 2 如图 13-19 所示,已知圆的圆心的坐标为 $C(a,b)$,半径是 r,$P(x,y)$是圆上的任意一点,A 点在圆上,OA 所在直线与 x 轴平行,以 OA 为始边绕着点 O 按逆时针方向旋转,转角为 θ. 现取 θ 为参数,试写出该圆的参数方程.

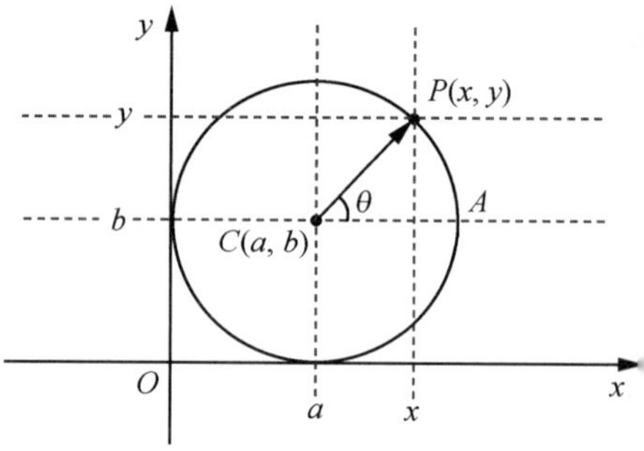

图 13-19

【典例解析】

例 1 在平面直角坐标系 xOy 中,圆 C 的参数方程为$\begin{cases}x=4\cos\theta,\\ y=4\sin\theta\end{cases}$($\theta$ 为参数),直线 l 经过点 $P(2,2)$,倾斜角 $\alpha=\dfrac{\pi}{3}$.

(1) 求圆的标准方程和直线 l 的参数方程;

(2) 设 l 与圆 C 相交于 A,B 两点,求$|PA|\cdot|PB|$的值.

解 (1) 由圆 C 的参数方程可得其标准方程为 $x^2+y^2=16$.

因为直线 l 过点 $P(2,2)$,倾斜角 $\alpha=\dfrac{\pi}{3}$,所以直线 l 的参数方程为

$$\begin{cases}x=2+t\cos\dfrac{\pi}{3},\\ y=2+t\sin\dfrac{\pi}{3},\end{cases}$$

即

$$\begin{cases}x=2+\dfrac{1}{2}t,\\ y=2+\dfrac{\sqrt{3}}{2}t\end{cases}(t\text{ 为参数}).$$

（2）把直线 l 的参数方程 $\begin{cases}x=2+\dfrac{1}{2}t,\\ y=2+\dfrac{\sqrt{3}}{2}t\end{cases}$（$t$ 为参数）代入圆 C：$x^2+y^2=16$ 中，得

$$\left(2+\frac{1}{2}t\right)^2+\left(2+\frac{\sqrt{3}}{2}t\right)^2=16,$$

$$t^2+2(\sqrt{3}+1)t-8=0.$$

设 A,B 两点对应的参数分别为 t_1,t_2，则

$$t_1t_2=-8,$$

即

$$|PA|\cdot|PB|=8.$$

图 13-20

例 2　当前台风（图 13-20）中心 P 在某海滨城市 O 向东 300 km 处生成，并以40 km/h的速度向西偏北 45°方向移动. 已知距台风中心 250 km 以内的地方都属于台风侵袭的范围，那么经过多长时间后该城市开始受到台风侵袭？

解　取 O 为原点，OP 所在直线为 x 轴，建立直角坐标系（图 13-21），则点 P 的坐标是 (300,0).

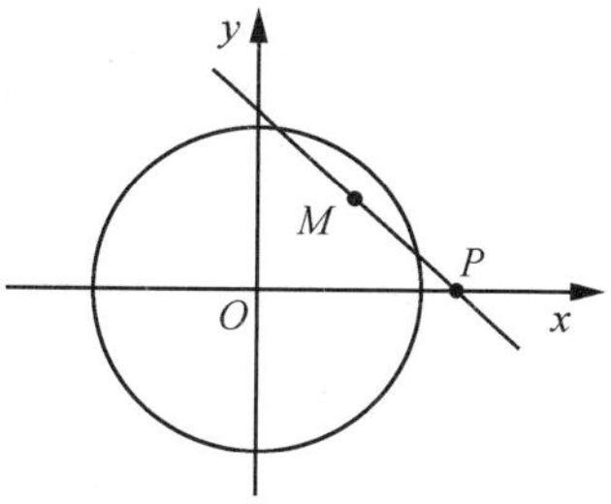

图 13-21

以 O 为圆心，250 km 为半径作圆 O，当台风中心移动后的位置 M 在圆 O 内或圆 O 上时，城

市 O 将受到台风侵袭.

圆 O 的方程为

$$x^2+y^2=250^2.$$

设经过时间 t 后,台风中心 M 的坐标为 (x,y),根据条件知台风中心 M 移动形成的直线 l 的方程为

$$\begin{cases}x=300+40t\cdot\cos135^\circ,\\ y=40t\cdot\sin135^\circ\end{cases}(t\text{ 为参数},t\geqslant0),$$

即

$$\begin{cases}x=300-20\sqrt{2}t,\\ y=20\sqrt{2}t.\end{cases}(t\text{ 为参数},t\geqslant0)$$

当点 $M(300-20\sqrt{2}t,20\sqrt{2}t)$ 在圆 O 内或圆 O 上时,有

$$(300-20\sqrt{2}t)^2+(20\sqrt{2}t)^2\leqslant250^2,$$

即

$$16t^2-120\sqrt{2}t+275\leqslant0.$$

解得

$$\frac{15\sqrt{2}-5\sqrt{7}}{4}\leqslant t\leqslant\frac{15\sqrt{2}+5\sqrt{7}}{4},$$

由计算器计算可得

$$2.0\leqslant t\leqslant8.6.$$

所以,大约在 2 h 后该城市开始受到台风侵袭.

【课后练习】

1. 已知圆的圆心在(0,1),半径是$\sqrt{3}$,则圆的参数方程为 ( )

A. $\begin{cases}x=\sqrt{3}\cos\theta,\\ y=1+\sqrt{3}\sin\theta\end{cases}$($\theta$ 为参数)

B. $\begin{cases}x=\sqrt{3}t,\\ y=1+\sqrt{3}t\end{cases}$($t$ 为参数)

C. $\begin{cases}x=1+\sqrt{3}\cos\theta,\\ y=\sqrt{3}\sin\theta\end{cases}$($\theta$ 为参数)

D. $x^2+(y-1)^2=3$

2. 下列各点中,在曲线$\begin{cases}x=\sin2\theta,\\ y=\cos\theta+\sin\theta\end{cases}$($\theta$ 为参数)上的为 ( )

A. $\left(\frac{1}{2},-\sqrt{2}\right)$　　B. $\left(-\frac{3}{4},\frac{1}{2}\right)$　　C. $(2,\sqrt{3})$　　D. $(1,\sqrt{3})$

3. 曲线$\begin{cases}x=1+t^2,\\y=4t-3\end{cases}$（$t$ 为参数，$t\in\mathbf{R}$）与 x 轴的交点坐标是　　（　　）

A. $(1,4)$　　B. $\left(\frac{25}{16},0\right)$　　C. $(1,-3)$　　D. $\left(\pm\frac{25}{16},0\right)$

4. 直线 l_1：$\begin{cases}x=1-t,\\y=-5-\sqrt{3}t\end{cases}$和直线 $x-y-23=0$ 的交点 P 的坐标是________.

5. 动点 M 做等速直线运动，它在 x 轴和 y 轴方向的速度分别为 5 和 12，运动开始时位于点 $P(1,2)$，则点 M 的轨迹参数方程为________.

6. 将下列参数方程化为普通方程.

(1)$\begin{cases}x=\dfrac{3k}{1+k^2},\\y=\dfrac{6k^2}{1+k^2};\end{cases}$　　(2)$\begin{cases}x=1-\sin2\theta,\\y=\sin\theta+\cos\theta.\end{cases}$

7. 选择适当的参数，将下列方程转化为参数方程.

(1) $(x-a)^2+(y-b)^2=r^2$；　　(2) $\frac{x^2}{9}+\frac{y^2}{4}=1$.

8. 已知直线 l：$\begin{cases}x=1+t\cos\alpha,\\ y=t\sin\alpha\end{cases}$ (t 为参数)，C：$\begin{cases}x=\cos\theta,\\ y=\sin\theta\end{cases}$ (θ 为参数).

(1) 当 $\alpha=\frac{\pi}{3}$ 时，求直线 l 与圆 C 的交点坐标；

(2) 过坐标原点 O 作 l 的垂线，垂足为 A，P 为 OA 的中点. 当 α 变化时，求 P 点轨迹的参数方程，并指出它是什么曲线.

【信息手段】

在 GeoGebra 中，参数方程都是由曲线指令来绘制的，通过一些具体的例题，让我们来看看那些美丽的参数方程曲线.

案例 1 椭圆：$\begin{cases}x=a\cos\theta,\\ y=b\sin\theta.\end{cases}$

在 GeoGebra 中，先设定两个滑动条 a、b 作为可变系数，其范围根据需要确定，然后输入表 13-4 中的曲线指令绘制椭圆，移动滑杆 a、b，就可以得到如图 13-22不同大小的椭圆曲线.

表 13-4 椭圆曲线绘制

步骤	名称	指令
1	数字 a	滑动条(0,10)
2	数字 b	滑动条(0,10)
3	曲线 d	曲线($a\cos(\theta)$,$b\sin(\theta)$,θ,0,2π)

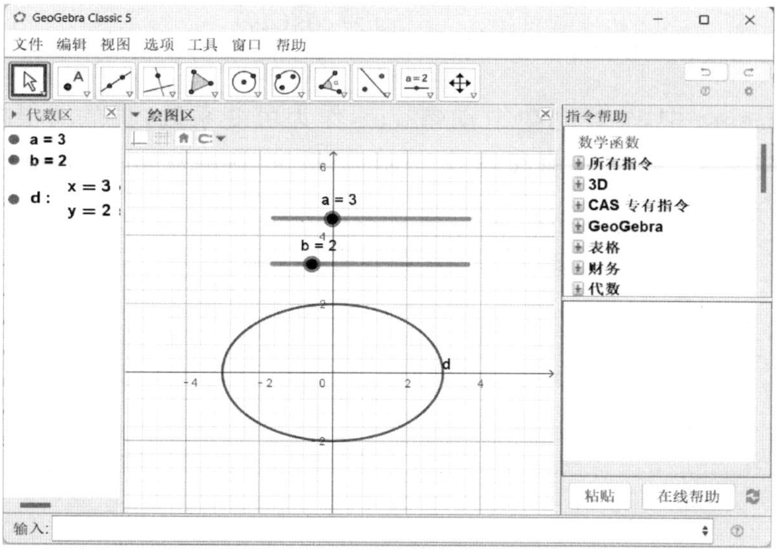

图 13-22

案例 2　参数方程为$\begin{cases} x=\sin^3\theta, \\ y=\dfrac{1}{16}(13\cos\theta-5\cos2\theta-2\cos3\theta-4\cos4\theta) \end{cases}$的曲线.

在 GeoGebra 中,输入表 13-5 中的曲线指令绘制参数方程,得到如图 13-23 所示的心形曲线.

表 13-5　心形曲线绘制

步骤	名称	描述
1	曲线 a	曲线$(\sin^3(\theta),1/16(13\cos(\theta)-5\cos(2\theta)-2\cos(3\theta)-\cos(4\theta)),\theta,0,2\pi)$

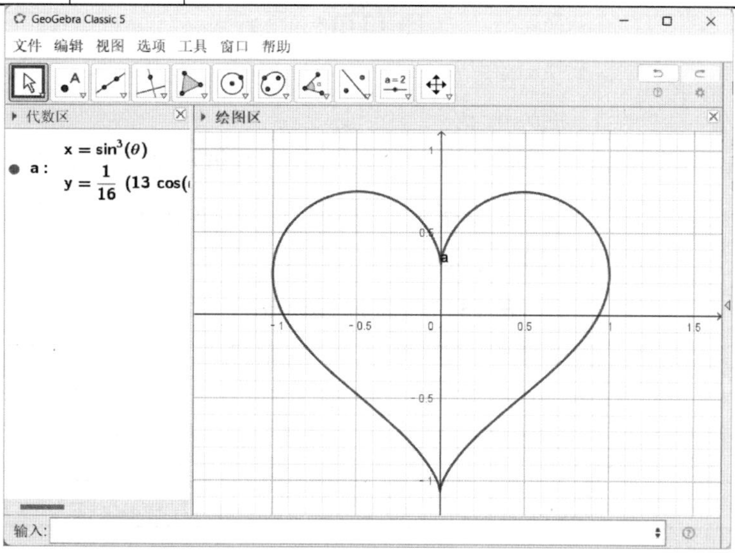

图 13-23

案例 3 千变万化的李萨如曲线：$\begin{cases}x=\cos(a\theta),\\ y=\sin(b\theta).\end{cases}$

在 GeoGebra 中，先设两个滑动条 a、b，作为可变系数，其范围根据需要确定，然后输入表 13-6 中的曲线指令绘制曲线，移动滑杆 a、b，就可以得到如图 13-24 所示的李萨如曲线.

表 13-6 李萨如曲线绘制

步骤	名称	指令
1	数字 a	滑动条(−10,10)
2	数字 b	滑动条(−10,10)
3	曲线 c	曲线($\cos(a\theta)$,$\sin(b\theta)$,θ,0,2π)

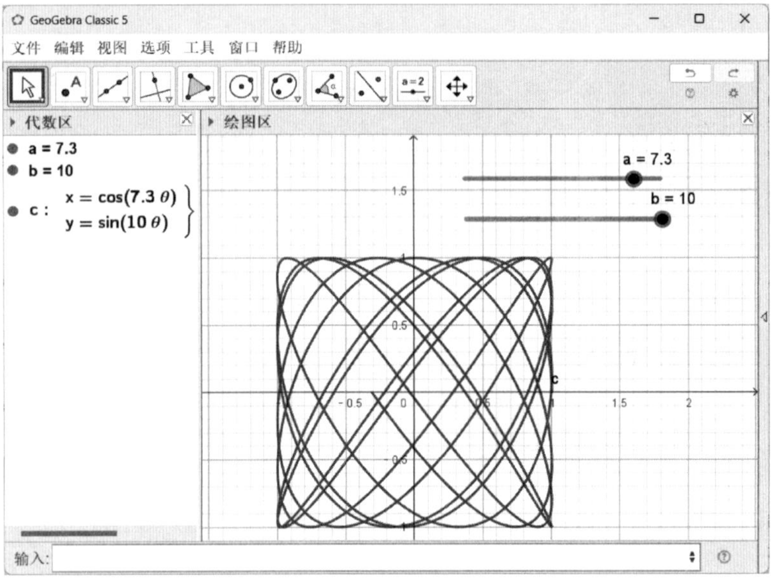

图 13-24

案例 4 星形线：$\begin{cases}x=a\cos^3\theta,\\ y=b\sin^3\theta.\end{cases}$

在 GeoGebra 中，先设定两个滑动条 a、b，作为可变系数，其范围根据需要而定，然后输入表 13-7 中的曲线指令绘制曲线，移动滑杆 a、b，就可以得到如图 13-25所示的不同大小的星形线.

表 13-7 星形线绘制

步骤	名称	指令
1	数字 a	滑动条(−1,1)
2	数字 b	滑动条(−1,1)
3	曲线 c	曲线($a\cos^3(\theta)$,$b\sin^3(\theta)$,θ,0,2π)

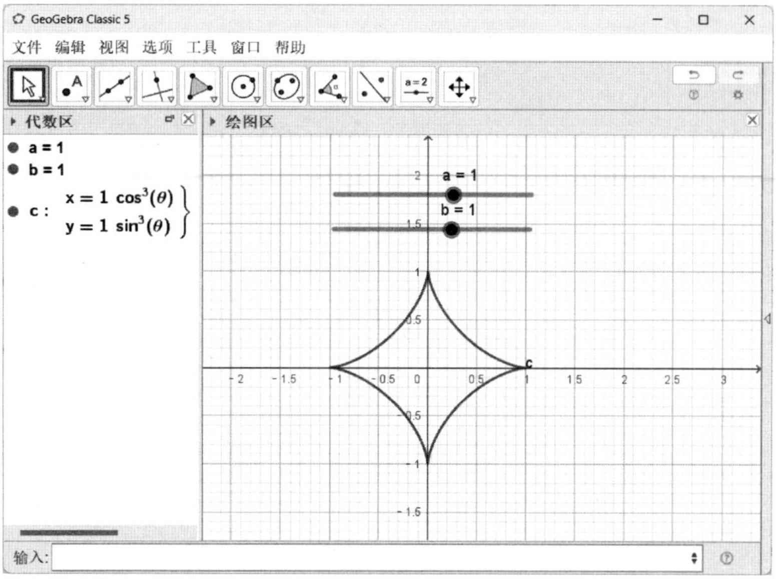

图 13-25

案例 5　千变万化的外摆线：$\begin{cases} x=(a+b)\cos\theta-b\cos\dfrac{a+b}{b}\theta, \\ y=(a+b)\sin\theta-b\sin\dfrac{a+b}{b}\theta. \end{cases}$

GeoGebra 中，先设定两个滑动条 a、b，作为可变系数，其范围根据需要而定，然后输入表 13-8 中的曲线指令绘制曲线、移动滑杆 a、b，就可以得到如图 13-26 所示的不同形状的外摆线.

表 13-8　外摆线绘制

步骤	名称	指令
1	数字 a	滑动条(−10,10)
2	数字 b	滑动条(−10,10)
3	曲线 c	曲线($(a+b)\cos(\theta)-b\cos((a+b)/b\theta)$,$(a+b)\sin(\theta)-b\sin((a+b)/b\theta)$,$\theta$,0,$2\pi$)

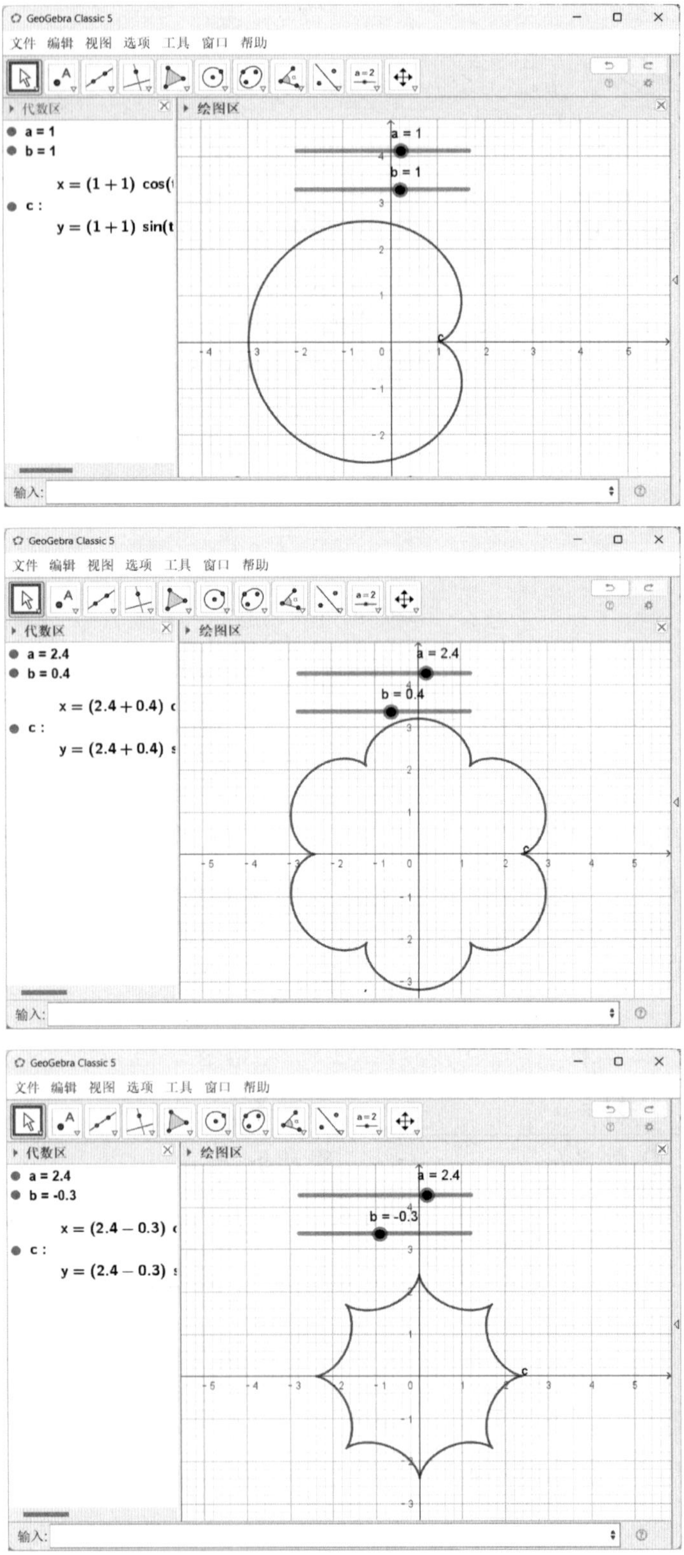
GeoGebra Classic 5
文件 编辑 视图 选项 工具 窗口 帮助
代数区
绘图区
a = 1
b = 1
x = (1 + 1) cos(
c :
y = (1 + 1) sin(t
输入:
GeoGebra Classic 5
文件 编辑 视图 选项 工具 窗口 帮助
代数区
绘图区
a = 2.4
b = 0.4
x = (2.4 + 0.4)
c :
y = (2.4 + 0.4)
输入:
GeoGebra Classic 5
文件 编辑 视图 选项 工具 窗口 帮助
代数区
绘图区
a = 2.4
b = -0.3
x = (2.4 − 0.3)
c :
y = (2.4 − 0.3)
输入:

图 13-26

【数学文化】

参数方程的概念最初是为了解决物理学和工程学中的问题而提出的，后来逐渐发展成为数学领域的一个重要分支.

17 世纪，牛顿和莱布尼茨(图 13-27)试图解决一些关于物体运动和曲线形状的问题时，发现使用传统的代数方程表示非常复杂. 为了简化问题，他们引入了参数方程的概念，将曲线上的点的坐标表示为与某个变量(参数)相关的函数. 这种新的表示方法不仅简化了问题的处理，还可以更好地描述一些复杂的曲线和曲面.

图 13-27

18 世纪，法国数学家欧拉开始使用参数表示极坐标系中的函数关系.

19 世纪，法国数学家傅里叶(图 13-28)提出了三角函数形式的参数方程，为解决热传导等物理问题提供了有力的工具.

20 世纪以来，参数方程在数学领域的应用越来越广泛，涉及微分几何、微分方程、统计学等多个领域.

图 13-28

参数方程为数学建模提供了重要的工具，使得数学问题能够更加直观和形象地被描述和解决. 参数方程在物理、工程、计算机科学等领域也有着广泛的应用，为解决实际问题提供了有效的途径. 参数方程的概念和方法不仅对数学和自然科学的研究有着重要的意义，也对社会科学、经济学等领域的研究有着深远的影响.

【拓展应用】

渐开线是任意曲线，只有取点描线的方法，作图过程如图 13-29 所示，其步骤为：

① 画出基圆，并将基圆分为适当的等份，图中为 8 等份.

② 过等分点作圆的同一方向的切线.

③ 在圆周上截取同样的等份,依次在各切线上量取基圆周展开长度 $C=2\pi r$ 的同样等份长度,即长度分别等于 $\frac{1}{8}C$,$\frac{2}{8}C$,…,$\frac{8}{8}C$ 等,即为渐开线上的点;依次光滑连接各点,即完成圆的渐开线作图.

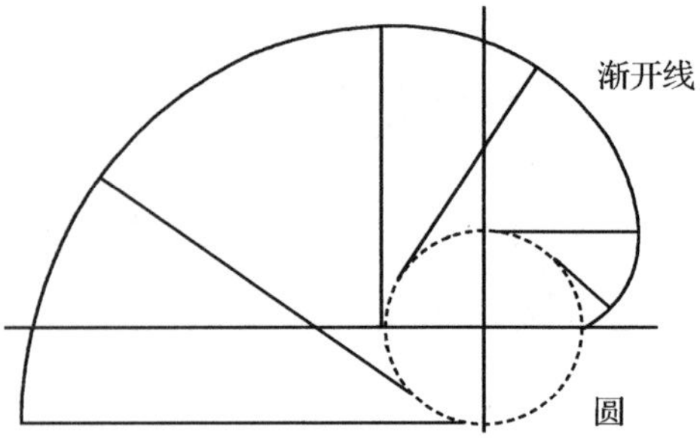

图 13-29

以基圆心 O 为原点,直线 OA 为 x 轴,建立平面直角坐标系(图 13-30).

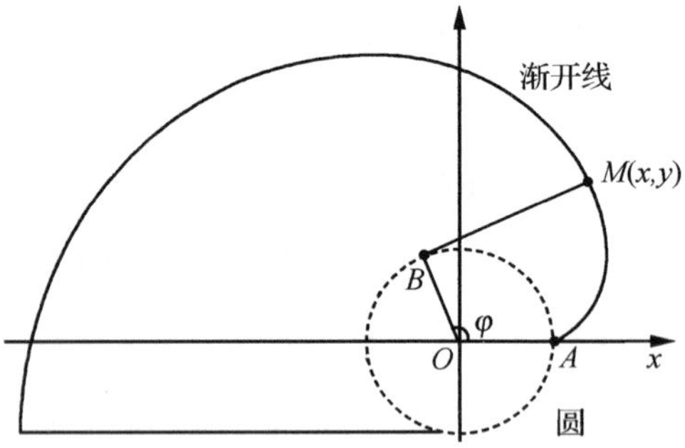

图 13-30

设基圆的半径为 r,渐开线上任意一点 M 的坐标为 (x,y). 显然,点 M 由角 φ 唯一确定.

取 φ 为参数,则点 B 的坐标为 $(r\cos\varphi,r\sin\varphi)$,从而,

$$\overrightarrow{BM}=(x-r\cos\varphi,y-r\sin\varphi),\ |\overrightarrow{BM}|=\overset{\frown}{AB}=r\varphi.$$

由于向量 $\boldsymbol{e}_1=(\cos\varphi,\sin\varphi)$,是与 $\overrightarrow{OB}$ 同方向的单位向量,因而向量 $\boldsymbol{e}_2=(\sin\varphi,-\cos\varphi)$ 是与向量 $\overrightarrow{BM}$ 同方向的单位向量,所以 $\overrightarrow{BM}=r\varphi\boldsymbol{e}_2$,即 $\overrightarrow{BM}=(x-r\cos\varphi,y-r\sin\varphi)=r\varphi(\sin\varphi,-\cos\varphi)$.

解得 $\begin{cases}x=r(\cos\varphi+\varphi\sin\varphi),\\ y=r(\sin\varphi-\varphi\cos\varphi)\end{cases}$($\varphi$ 是参数).

这就是圆的渐开线的参数方程.

在机械工业中,广泛地使用齿轮传递动力. 由于渐开线齿形的齿轮磨损少,传动平稳,制造安装较为方便,因此大多数齿轮采用这种齿形. 设计加工这种齿轮,需要借助圆的渐开线方程.

自我检测

一、选择题

1. 将坐标原点平移至 $O'(1,2)$，则点 $A(0,8)$ 在新坐标系中的坐标是　（　　）

A. $(-1,8)$　　B. $(-1,6)$　　C. $(-2,8)$　　D. $(-2,6)$

2. 已知点 A 在坐标系 xOy 中的坐标是 $(-3,1)$，在新坐标系 $x'O'y'$ 中的坐标是 $(4,2)$，则原点 O 移到了点　（　　）

A. $(1,3)$　　B. $(-7,3)$　　C. $(7,1)$　　D. $(-7,-1)$

3. 平移坐标轴，将坐标原点移到 $O'(-1,2)$，已知点 A 在新坐标系 $x'O'y'$ 中的坐标是 $(-4,6)$，则点 A 在原坐标系 xOy 中的坐标是　（　　）

A. $(3,-4)$　　B. $(3,4)$　　C. $(-5,8)$　　D. $(5,-8)$

4. 平移坐标轴，把原点移到 $O'(2,1)$，则曲线 $x=2$ 在新坐标系中的方程是　（　　）

A. $x'=0$　　B. $x'=-2$　　C. $y'=0$　　D. $y'=-2$

5. 已知平移坐标轴时的移轴公式是 $\begin{cases}x=x'-1,\\y=y'-1,\end{cases}$ 点 A 在新坐标系下的坐标为 $(2,3)$，则其在原坐标系中的坐标为　（　　）

A. $(3,1)$　　B. $(-3,-1)$　　C. $(1,5)$　　D. $(-1,-5)$

6. 平移坐标轴，新坐标原点是 O'，化简曲线方程 $x^2+y^2+2x-4y+1=0$ 为 $x'^2+y'^2=4$，则新坐标原点 O' 在原坐标系中的坐标是　（　　）

A. $(1,2)$　　B. $(-1,2)$　　C. $(1,-2)$　　D. $(-1,-2)$

7. 直线：$3x-4y-9=0$ 与圆：$\begin{cases}x=2\cos\theta,\\y=2\sin\theta\end{cases}$ （θ 为参数）的位置关系是　（　　）

A. 相切　　B. 相离

C. 直线过圆心　　D. 相交但直线不过圆心

8. 参数方程$\begin{cases}x=t+\dfrac{1}{t},\\ y=-2\end{cases}$($t$ 为参数)所表示的曲线是 ( )

A. 一条射线　B. 两条射线　C. 一条直线　D. 两条直线

9. 已知 $r>0$,则直线 $x\cos\theta+y\sin\theta=r$($\theta$ 是常数)与圆$\begin{cases}x=r\cos\varphi,\\ y=r\sin\varphi\end{cases}$($\varphi$ 为参数)的位置关系是 ( )

A. 相交　B. 相切

C. 相离　D. 视 r 的大小而定

10. 若直线的参数方程为$\begin{cases}x=1+2t,\\ y=2-3t\end{cases}$($t$ 为参数),则直线的斜率为 ( )

A. $\dfrac{2}{3}$　B. $-\dfrac{2}{3}$　C. $\dfrac{3}{2}$　D. $-\dfrac{3}{2}$

11. 下列点在曲线$\begin{cases}x=\sin2\theta,\\ y=\cos\theta+\sin\theta\end{cases}$($\theta$ 为参数)上的是 ( )

A. $\left(\dfrac{1}{2},-\sqrt{2}\right)$　B. $\left(-\dfrac{3}{4},\dfrac{1}{2}\right)$　C. $(2,\sqrt{3})$　D. $(1,\sqrt{3})$

12. 将参数方程$\begin{cases}x=2+\sin^2\theta,\\ y=\sin^2\theta\end{cases}$($\theta$ 为参数)化为普通方程为 ( )

A. $y=x-2$　B. $y=x+2$

C. $y=x-2(2\leqslant x\leqslant 3)$　D. $y=x+2(0\leqslant y\leqslant 1)$

13. 已知圆的参数方程为$\begin{cases}x=2\cos\theta,\\ y=2\sin\theta\end{cases}$($\theta$ 为参数),则此圆的圆心为 ( )

A. $(2,0)$　B. $(0,2)$　C. $(0,0)$　D. $(2,2)$

14. 曲线$\begin{cases}x=-2+5t,\\ y=1-2t\end{cases}$($t$ 为参数)与坐标轴的交点是 ( )

A. $\left(0,\dfrac{2}{5}\right),\left(\dfrac{1}{2},0\right)$　B. $\left(0,\dfrac{1}{5}\right),\left(\dfrac{1}{2},0\right)$

C. $(0,-4),(8,0)$　D. $\left(0,\dfrac{5}{9}\right),(8,0)$

15. 直线$\begin{cases}x=t+3,\\y=-3-t\end{cases}$与圆$\begin{cases}x=2\cos\theta,\\y=2+2\sin\theta\end{cases}$的位置关系是　　(　　)

A. 相交　　B. 相离　　C. 相切　　D. 无法判断

二、填空题

1. 平移坐标轴，把原点移到点 $O'(3,-2)$，则点 $(4,5)$ 在新坐标系中的坐标是____________.

2. 平移坐标轴，把原点移到 $O'(-2,-3)$，则曲线 $y=x+1$ 在新坐标系中的方程是____________.

3. 平移坐标轴，新坐标原点是 $O'(-3,2)$，曲线方程 $x^2+y^2+6x-2y-6=0$ 可化简为____________.

4. 曲线$\begin{cases}x=3t-2,\\y=t^2-1\end{cases}$与 x 轴的交点坐标是____________.

5. 一条直线的普通方程是 $x+2y=0$，若选取参数 $t=x$，则直线的参数方程是____________.

6. 将曲线$\begin{cases}x=-2t,\\y=3t-1\end{cases}$($t$ 为参数)化成普通方程为________________.

7. 直线$\begin{cases}x=1+t\cos35^\circ,\\y=-t\sin35^\circ\end{cases}$($t$ 为参数)的倾斜角为____________.

8. 曲线$\begin{cases}x=t^2,\\y=-t\end{cases}$($t$ 为参数)的普通方程为____________.

9. 已知实数 x,y 满足 $x^2+(y-1)^2=1$，则代数式$\dfrac{y-1}{x+2}$的取值范围是________________.

10. 若点 $P(x,y)$ 在圆 $(x+2)^2+(y+2)^2=4$ 上，则 $x+y$ 的最小值为__________________.

三、解答题

1. 平移坐标轴,使曲线方程 $4x^2-y^2-8x+10y-22=0$ 不含有一次项,并指出原点应平移的位置.

2. 利用坐标轴平移,化简下列曲线方程.

(1) $x^2+y^2+4x+4y+1=0$;

(2) $x^2+6x-2y+11=0$.

3. 已知直线 $l_1:\begin{cases}x=1+3t,\\y=2-4t\end{cases}$ (t 为参数)与直线 $l_2:2x-4y=5$ 相交于点 B 与点 $A(1,2)$,求 A,B 两点间的距离.

4. 求直线$\begin{cases} x=2-\dfrac{1}{2}t, \\ y=-1+\dfrac{1}{2}t \end{cases}$（$t$ 为参数）被圆 $x^2+y^2=4$ 所截得的弦长.

5. 求直线$\begin{cases} x=-2-\sqrt{2}t, \\ y=3+\sqrt{2}t \end{cases}$（$t$ 为参数）上与点 $A(-2,3)$ 的距离等于$\sqrt{2}$的点的坐标.

6. 若 $x^2+y^2=16$,试求 $x+y-1$ 的最大值.

7. 已知直线 l 经过点 $P(1,1)$,倾斜角 $\alpha=\frac{\pi}{6}$.

(1) 写出直线 l 的参数方程;

(2) 设 l 与圆 $x^2+y^2=4$ 相交于两点 A,B,求点 P 到 A,B 两点的距离之积.